Praise for

Matthew Ward and the Legacy Trilogy

"Hugely entertaining."

—John Gwynne

"As intricate as a precision-engineered watch."

—Gareth Hanrahan

"Epic fantasy as it should be: big, bold and very addictive."

—*Starburst* magazine

"Ward has created a novel with such intention and craftsmanship that it brings back that feeling of excitement fantasy readers felt when discovering masters like J. R. R. Tolkien and C. S. Lewis."

—*Shelf Awareness*

"Packed with big battles, shadowy intrigue, and a large cast of characters, *Legacy of Ash* is an absorbing debut." —James Islington

"This is the first epic fantasy book I've enjoyed getting immersed in for *ages*....A great fat romp in a brilliantly realised setting....I have lost sleep, forgotten food...and made this the thing I pick up every moment I can get." —*SFFWorld*

"A perfect blend of Martin's A Song of Ice and Fire and Bernard Cornwell's The Last Kingdom." —*FanFiAddict*

"An incredibly impressive piece of fantasy fiction."   —*Fantasy Inn*

"Outstanding.... Ward presses all the right, well-worn buttons with enough vigor to make them feel fresh. The result is a ripping yarn that more than earns its length."

—*Publishers Weekly* (starred review)

THE FIRE WITHIN THEM

By Matthew Ward

THE LEGACY TRILOGY

Legacy of Ash

Legacy of Steel

Legacy of Light

THE SOULFIRE SAGA

The Darkness Before Them

The Fire Within Them

THE FIRE WITHIN THEM

Book Two of the Soulfire Saga

MATTHEW WARD

orbitbooks.net

Copyright © 2024 by Matthew Ward
Excerpt from *Between Dragons and Their Wrath* copyright © 2024 by Devin Madson

Cover design by Charlotte Stroomer
Cover illustration by Joe Wilson
Author photograph by Photo Nottingham

Orbit
Hachette Book Group
1290 Avenue of the Americas
New York, NY 10104
orbitbooks.net

First Edition: June 2024
Simultaneously published in Great Britain by Orbit

Orbit is an imprint of Hachette Book Group.
The Orbit name and logo are registered trademarks of
Little, Brown Book Group Limited.

The publisher is not responsible for websites (or their content)
that are not owned by the publisher.

The Hachette Speakers Bureau provides a wide range of authors for speaking events. To find out more, go to hachettespeakersbureau.com or email HachetteSpeakers@hbgusa.com.

Orbit books may be purchased in bulk for business, educational, or promotional use. For information, please contact your local bookseller or the Hachette Book Group Special Markets Department at special.markets@hbgusa.com.

Library of Congress Control Number: 2024932515

ISBNs: 9780316476805 (trade paperback), 9780316476904 (ebook)

Printed in the United States of America

LSC-C

Printing 1, 2024

For my sister Emma.

No cats in this one, sorry. Maybe next time.

Dramatis Personae

Enna	A woman of secrets and shadows
Serrîq	Contemplative advisor
Esram	A student of history

UPSTANDING CITIZENS

Hargo Rashace	Furibund husband
Fadiya Rashace	Disgraced countess
Zaran Ossed	Hierarch of the Alabastran temple
Sumaramadîq	Royal advisor
Terrion Arvish	Artist and scholar (deceased)

THE REGAL AND THE DIVINE

Caradan Diar	The Eternity King
Isdihar Diar	The Voice of the Eternity King
Amakala	Forgotten Queen
Eskamarîand	Forgotten King
Nyssa Benevolas	The Goddess of Benevolence
Nyssa Iudexas	The Goddess of Judgement
Tzal	Ancient enemy of the Issnaîm

Notes on language and place can be found in the Glossary on page 551

THE FIRE
WITHIN
THEM

One

Being reborn hurt more than dying.

White-cold flame seared extremities for which she'd no name. That weren't even her. Not yet. She wasn't anything to which they could belong. Not yet. But somehow the instinct that she had been – and could yet be again – held her together in the darkness.

Little by little the pain receded. Icy fire thawed beneath a warm, heavy pulse.

Blind endurance yielded to the first stirrings of awareness. Of echoing screams – *her* screams – fading into a pervasive, distant shudder more heard than felt, and cracked tiles beneath hip and shoulder. Half-lidded eyes creaked open on a circle of gloom-edged starlight. Decades-old dust and jasmine incense ash choked her first conscious breath to a ragged cough. Only touch remained distant, defiant, offering no sensation of the air moving across her naked body.

Limbs remained truculent, yielding only to supreme effort of will. Rotted carpet bunched and tore beneath her fingers as she dragged herself into a sitting position. Starlight streaming through the broken roof shaped rows of fluted columns marching into the darkness. The statue of a figure in lamellar armour lay on its side just beyond reach, severed head and shattered sword arm forlorn in the dust. Just visible beyond, the yawning, ragged arch of a stained-glass window rose above a bare altar.

1

Another hacking, jasmine-scented cough set her chest heaving. She sank onto splayed fingers, head hanging, and froze.

Trembling, she raised her left hand full into the starlight. Though self and memory remained disarrayed, both recalled smooth, lily-pale skin – not the charred, blackened limbs of a pyre-burned corpse. Hurried, horrified examination confirmed it was not her hands alone, but every inch of her.

"No ..." Her cracked, raw whisper echoed back from the darkness.

Gagging, she formed a fist to ward off rising panic. Black ash crackled from her crusted knuckles. Indigo flame sparked from the fissures. Barely a glimmer and then gone. Just enough to awaken a stirring. A name. Her name.

Tanith.

Glimpses of memory hardened to certainty. Tanith flexed her fingers, perversely offended by the lack of pain. She pressed fingertips to her cheek and her scalp. They offered no sensation, only pressure and a grinding whisper as black ash trickled away.

Perhaps it was for the best she'd no way of seeing her face. A life that had given her little had at least granted her a simple, delicate beauty – winsome, beguiling or threatening as her mood dictated. She'd revelled in the power it offered, a way of touching the world and its people that made her feel ... like she belonged. The prospect of its loss hurt more than the memory of rebirth, for the latter pain at least lay in the past. Only her left forearm retained any semblance of who she'd been. The ebony spider-work lines of her aetherios tattoo had survived where her creamy skin and golden hair had not; embossed dark and sullen in her scorched flesh. Her father's gift.

The curse that had bound a daemon in her blood, and had turned that blood to flame.

Of course it had survived.

Tanith set her jaw. It didn't matter. She was alive. Or at least as close to alive as she'd ever been. The rest ... ? She'd been hurt before, but never like this. There was an eternity of difference between reknitting sword wounds and recoalescing a body torn apart by the Deadwinds. How she'd done so, she couldn't imagine. But then, so much of what she did was instinct.

She gazed up through the splintered rafters and shattered tiles. The night sky offered no glimpse of the distant Deadwinds, swirling far away atop the roof of the world, and no clue as to how she'd arrived here ... wherever here was. Memory remained evasive, indigo vapour concerning everything after the Deadwinds had consumed her.

Before was a different matter, offering dim recollection of a standoff above the clouds, the deck of the tiny skyship bucking and heaving beneath her feet. Starving, she'd feasted on the Deadwinds, and the Deadwinds had feasted on her in exchange. All as her sister had looked on, eyes blazing with triumph.

The recollection provoked a flash of anger. Kat. Always their father's favourite. She should have helped. But instead, she'd tricked her.

Weariness turned Tanith's anger ashen. She'd been half mad with hunger by then, raving as the daemon within had asserted itself. And perhaps Kat *had* tried to help and the Deadwinds had consumed her in turn? Or perhaps the stricken ship had finally surrendered to the seething air currents and plunged from the skies, killing Kat and her pathetic friends?

She shook the past away. Only the present mattered. The present, and the empty, sly slither in the hollows of her heart that presaged rising hunger.

But Kat's final, triumphant sneer refused to leave the darkness behind Tanith's eyes.

Shaking with exertion, she collapsed against the altar. Impact jarred every bone and woke brief tongues of indigo fire from her creaking, cracking skin. A walnut-sized chunk of her left arm fell away. It struck tile in an explosion of black ash, prompting a rat to skitter from one shadow to another in terror. She stared dully at the remains. There'd been no sensation to mark its departure, no pain. With numb fascination, she entertained the notion that her rebirth might not be so permanent as she'd assumed.

Hunger pangs took hold, gnawing inside out.

Cold fear seeped in their wake. She was running out of time.

Back braced against the altar, Tanith closed her eyes and sought meaning in the distant sounds. Beneath the hoots of owls and the rasping trill of nightjars, she heard the rumble of wagon wheels and the clop of hooves. What might have been a railrunner's steam whistle. And behind it all, the deep, breathy growl of mill and forge.

A city then, but which? It didn't matter. Better a city than some abandoned wayshrine out in the wilds. Cities meant people, and people meant ... everything she needed to survive. Cities also meant ifrîti – the fragments of mortal souls pressed into service as watchdogs to messengers, or to cast light and govern mechanisms. She stared down at her aetherios tattoo, cold and dark against her forearm, spent of the Deadwinds' soulfire. Had it been otherwise, she might have been able to reach out to those nearby, learn something of her surroundings – maybe even draw sustenance from their thin scraps. But its flame – her flame – was all but spent, and fading further at every moment.

Her left hand spasmed, its fingers drawing inwards like claws. She clasped them with her right and willed herself to stillness. Panic only fuelled the hunger, scratched away the veneer of civilisation she worked so hard to cultivate. She couldn't afford that.

She had to move. While she was still capable of making decisions.

Pushing away from the altar, she lurched to her feet.

The hollow boom of a door slamming back echoed through the darkness.

"Still nae sure about this, Rathiq." A man's voice, leavened with a hint of northland burr, the speaker lost in the gloom. "Alabastra disnae like folk picking o'er its bones."

"Stop squalling," Rathiq replied, his gruff tone re-treading a well-worn path. "The temple gave up on Qosm years ago. Just us and the darkness. Maybe a shîm-head lurking ..."

"Or reavers."

Rathiq snorted. "Reavers got out before the wall went up. Got more

4

sense than to hang around waiting for the lethargia to take them. Not like you, Gifra."

Tanith slunk behind the nearest column. Even that small effort set her shaking, her fingers twitching where she pressed them up against the discoloured marble.

A hooded lantern flared into existence, the lumani ifrît within spurred to radiance at the wielder's command. The cold spill of whitish-indigo light revealed three figures. The lantern-holder was a heavyset, stubbled fellow of late middle years whose bronzed features bore the scars of lost brawls. A cadaverous man with a scavenger's twitching body language threaded the columns to his left. The third mirrored him on the right, watchful, but unconcerned. All three had short scimitars buckled at their waists and a practical mix of travel-stained silks and leathers.

Tanith rested her charred brow against the column. Street skelders: petty criminals scratching whatever living they could while staying one step ahead of custodium law. Bad news for her.

"We just need to find the starfall," said Rathiq, now revealed as the lantern-wielder. "Looked like a bright one. Meteoric iron. Astoricum. Maybe something shinier. Enough to bribe the custodians on the watch gates, even after Faraqan takes his cut."

"If it landed here," said Gifra, his craggy face done no favours by the lumani-cast shadows.

The third, watchful man pointed up at the hole in the roof. "They don't build temples like that. See? The tiles are smouldering."

Gifra scowled. "Then where did it land? Tell me that. Starfall leaves a crater."

"Then *find* it," replied Rathiq, with thinning patience. "And make it fast. We weren't the only ones saw it come down."

Footsteps tracked closer, the concealing darkness blurring to grey twilight.

The hollow in Tanith's heart grew deeper as the hunger gained ground. She couldn't fight them, but she didn't need to. Just leave them to their precious starfall meteor and escape into the night. Find some clothes. A friendlier face . . . or at least an unwary one. It had to be *now*, while the choice was hers to make – while the skelders were distracted by their search for plunder.

She gave it another five-count and scrambled for the next column along. Nearer to Gifra, but out of the lantern's immediate path.

"Reckon this is the spot." Rathiq's fingers traced the broken tiles where Tanith had awoken. His gaze tracked through the dust towards the fallen statue. "Hello? Footprints. Guess we *weren't* the first ones here."

Tanith stifled a curse and flattened herself again the column. Rathiq was smarter than he looked. Not a difficult proposition, but ruinous now.

Gifra twitched, accusation in his voice. "I told ye. Reavers."

Rathiq rounded on him. "Reavers run barefoot, do they?"

"Maybe."

Tanith broke for the next column. A chunk of rubble scuffed away from her foot and skittered into the darkness.

"Who's there?" Rising to his feet, Rathiq swept the hooded lantern around, bringing its light to bear on the column she'd left. He dropped his free hand to his belt. Steel glinted as he eased the first couple of inches of his scimitar free of its scabbard. "Come out. Nothing to be worried about."

His companions drew their swords and sidestepped out of the light and into the shadows.

Tanith shrank completely behind her column. *Nothing to worry about.* Even if she hadn't been a walking horror show, trusting to that sentiment was a guarantee of being left dead . . . or worse. Folk with hooded lanterns weren't generally counted among the upstanding.

The lantern swung left. She stumbled right, making for the safety of the next column.

She all but collided with Gifra, who flung her away with a startled yelp. She missed her footing, crunching against a column. Gasping, she clutched at the fluted stone to steady herself.

Gifra levelled his trembling sword, its point level with her breastbone.

Rathiq brought his lantern to bear. "Stars Below," he breathed, lip curling in revulsion. "A skrelling grave crawler. Used to be a woman ... I think."

Used to be? He *thought*?

The nerve of the man.

"Maybe the hierarch's right." The watchful man moved to stand at Rathiq's shoulder. "Maybe Qosm is cursed."

Gifra stepped closer, his twitching eyes never leaving Tanith's. His scent was all sweat and spices, wrapped in leathers long overdue a cleaning. But beneath it the sweet, peppery aroma of his soul, as thin and unremarkable as his appearance. A muscle leapt in Tanith's gut. He daemon-half sighed. She was in no position to be choosy. Even a threadbare skelder could be a saviour.

"Ye reckon that thing stole the skyfall?" asked Gifra.

Rathiq gave a heavy-shouldered shrug. "Nah. Look at it, poor trallock. Just a wisp of soul that doesn't know it's dead. Put it down. Make it quick." He jerked his head back past the altar. "Attar? We'll check the other side."

Tanith braced her palms against the column as Rathiq and Attar withdrew. Three paces. Four. Enough time and distance to offer hope.

"Please ..." she breathed. "Help me."

Gifra blinked. His sword point dipped. "What the—?"

With her last strength, Tanith flung herself at him and bore him to the ground, her knees straddling his waist, her crackling, crumbling hands planted in the dust either side of his neck and her nose an inch from his. She dimly registered Rathiq's alarmed bellow from somewhere ahead ... and ignored it, taking Gifra's head in her hands.

"Thank you," she whispered, and pressed her cracked, blistered lips against his.

Her pulse blossomed to a sonorous roar as the fire in her blood embraced him.

Gifra struggled for a heartbeat before the cold outer flame of his

7

being peeled away and hissed to nothing. Last breath, the shriversmen called it when they tended the dying – the first part of the soul to flee upon death and possessed of healing properties more valuable than gold if stoppered. Tanith took everything Gifra had to offer. Heard his sword clang onto tile. His wail at a pain that went deeper than muscle and bone.

She shuddered with delight as strength returned. Charred skin sloughed away and wasted muscle reknitted. Sensation blazed in fire-deadened flesh, the cold of the night air sweet after the numbness of awakening. The spiderweb of her aetherios tattoo crackled to life, her fires rushing along its lines.

And that was just the first course in a banquet. Even as Gifra went limp, Tanith closed her eyes and plunged deeper, stripping away his soul's fire to replenish her own.

There was joy in the feeding. There always was. Ecstasy and revulsion. The fulfilment of what her father had made of her: an amashti, a soul-drinking daemon that knew nothing of righteousness and everything of appetite. Part of her – the innocent she'd been before her father had first inked her forearm – cared about that. *Hated* it. But she'd learned to live with it, for food and drink had long ago lost the power to ease her cravings.

The other part lived for this. Loved it.

Rathiq's desperate shout penetrated the flame-lit darkness. "Kill it! Kill it!"

A hot red flash set Tanith's skull ringing. She slewed sideways into the dust, the joy of the feast dispelled by stinging pain. Rolling to hands and knees – for the first, glorious time since awakening, her limbs responding as they should – she pressed a hand to her scalp. Indigo flame rippled out from the wound and twisted to vapour about pale, perfect fingers. Pain ebbed as the lingering backwash of last breath closed the wound as if it had never been.

Gifra lay motionless, his corpse spattered with the black ash she'd shorn in rejuvenation, his desiccated body already crumbling in on

8

itself as the last, pitiful sliver of his soul hissed invisibly skyward to join the swirling Deadwinds.

Rathiq's scimitar shook in his hand, the lantern rattling in its chain loop. "Wh-what are you?" he stuttered.

Smiling softly at the itch of fresh stubble under her fingertips, Tanith dropped her hand from her scalp and rose to her feet. How to answer? Even a man like Rathiq deserved some truth before he died. She settled on the words her father had used when he'd first set the needle to her flesh.

"I'm glorious."

She sprang. Her right hand found the grips of Gifra's sword. The blade gleamed, scything out in a vicious arc.

Rathiq's lantern shattered against the tiles before his gurgling, terrified scream faded, the lumani ifrît preceding the skelder's grubby soul to the Deadwinds.

Tanith stood alone in the starlight as the adrenaline rush receded. She stared down at her handiwork, as ever proud and appalled. Every food chain had its apex. She couldn't help that. But killing was a choice.

She shook away the tendril of guilt. They were all in the gutter together. Some floated. Some drowned. Better a murderer than a corpse.

She froze, remembrance piercing the tangle of remorse and elation. The third man. Attar. If he made it to the streets, raised a hue and cry . . .

She started at the *thud* of a falling body. She spun around. Attar lay face down in the dust.

"Very impressive." The sincere, basso tone turned wry. "But I'm afraid you missed one."

The speaker – a tanned man of middle years, bulky without yet having run to fat – stood on the edge of the starlit circle behind Attar's corpse, black robes blurring into the surrounding gloom. Silver glinted at the temples of a brushed-back receding hairline and where his full beard touched the corners of his lips. His expression was as avuncular as his voice, all save in his unblinking hazel eyes. He seemed almost not to be aware of the bloodied dagger dangling from his hand.

Tanith turned side-on and shifted her grip on her borrowed sword. How long had he been lurking in the darkness? Watching. *Waiting*. She flexed the fingers of her left hand, softly rejoicing in the feel of muscles behaving as they should. At the indigo flames rippling along her tattoo. "Who are you?"

He held up a placatory hand. "I mean you no harm, I assure you." Melodic vowels and gently rolling Rs imbued the words with benevolence she dared not trust. A smile tugged at the corner of his mouth. "Not that I imagine I could offer you any. Not from what I just witnessed."

He remained on the far side of the starlit circle, out of easy reach. A very different proposition to Rathiq's band. Maybe even a dangerous one. Revived, Tanith knew herself to be faster and stronger than most, but she was hardly impervious. Silver burned like the hottest fire. Blackthorn blossom sapped her strength and disoriented her senses. The list went on, and was nowhere near as short as she might have liked.

"And yet you're not afraid of me?" she asked.

"No. As a matter of fact, I've waited a long time to meet you."

She snorted, doubting he'd have offered the sentiment freely to the charred thing she'd been minutes before. "Am I supposed to blush?" She rolled her eyes. "You're a scavenger, just like them."

"Not so. They came looking for starfall metal, whereas I sought something infinitely more precious – the one prophesied to restore Nyssa's third face and usher in a new age for this poor kingdom of Khalad. But I'm getting ahead of myself. Where are my manners?" He stepped fully into the starlit circle and offered a low, generous bow. "My name is Ardoc . . . and you and I are going to change this world."

10

Two

Tanith favoured Ardoc with a long, slow look. "Of *course* we are."

What had she gotten herself into now? The man was either having a joke at her expense or entirely mad. His reasonable, melodic words might have concealed either. In her experience, insanity cloaked itself in affability as often as malice.

A breeze stirred the dusty flagstones. She shivered and folded her arms, gooseflesh raising beneath her fingertips. She glanced down at Rathiq's corpse. In life and death he was a good bit larger than her, and his skelder's garb was hardly something she'd have chosen, but she wasn't in any position to be picky.

She set to work with her fingers, pleased to discover that Rathiq's black silk robes were a rather better fit than she'd expected, at least when cinched tight at the waist with his studded belt. The sleeves reached down past her wrists, long enough to shield the tattoo's cold flames from idle observers. The leather overtunic and vambraces were as oversized as she'd feared, so she abandoned them. So too were the boots, and a glance at Gifra and Attar's corpses revealed no help to be had there. A half-step forward at best, but given that she'd awoken as a crisped and disintegrating corpse, even half-steps counted.

Smoothing the last errant fold of silk into place, Tanith retrieved Rathiq's scimitar. She breathed mist onto the blade and buffed it away with a sleeve to catch her reflection in the starlight.

Even with cheeks and brow smudged with ash from the charred corpse she'd been, there was enough to recognise. Sapphire eyes stared back from a pale, smooth-skinned face. Better. So much better. Everything was as it should have been, except her golden hair, but that would grow in. Another notch of tension bled away. She was truly herself again.

Maybe – *maybe* – Nyssa did love her, just a little.

She laughed bitterly under her breath. What she'd taken from Gifra would sustain her for a while, but the hunger would return. She'd again be forced to sacrifice a piece of herself to retain anything at all. Be the daemon – the amashti – just long enough, and no more.

Nyssa didn't love her. No one loved her.

Ardoc gave a soft grunt of approval. "Feeling more composed?"

"What do you care?"

A weighty shrug. A glint of teeth revealed the half-smile beneath his beard. "Ah. You're watching me closely. Maybe wondering if I'm a violent lunatic as well as a deluded one?"

"Maybe."

His smile broadened. "You needn't trouble yourself. I'm well accustomed to sceptics."

"Good for you." She made to turn. "Goodbye."

"You're really not going to make this easy, are you?"

She halted, mid-step, curious despite herself. "Why should I?"

He prodded Attar's body with his foot. "I *was* of some small assistance. That should at least buy me a hearing."

Tanith strained her ears, searching for a breath, a scuff of sole on stone ... anything that would betray Ardoc's accomplices. She found nothing. That made those accomplices very good indeed, or Ardoc as alone as he appeared. "I could have handled him."

"And if he'd had a fistful of blackthorn? Perhaps a silver pendant?"

She stifled a wince. He knew – or had guessed – entirely too much. "You're very bold, old man." Bold or not, he'd made no attempt to move towards her. Wisdom born of fear, certainly. But whose fear? His, or hers?

"The goddess makes me so."

"Then she did better by you than she ever has by me."

He spread his arms. "Those she loves above all others, she tests above all others. And she loves you deeply . . ." For the first time, he scowled. "I'm starting to feel ridiculous. Won't you tell me your name?"

"You came here looking for me, and you don't even know that?"

"Why ask otherwise?"

Tanith hesitated. As far as the world was concerned, she was dead, burned away aboard the deck of the felucca and blown to ashes on the Deadwinds. Offering her name would begin the process of undoing all that. On the other hand, her name was her only remaining possession. Better to stake the claim before Ardoc bestowed another. He looked the type. "Tanith."

The family name would keep. Besides, she'd had so many, and none of them felt as though they belonged to her. She'd worn both her mother's married and maiden names in her time, the former to claim authority she didn't wield and the latter in hopes of snaring an inheritance. Both had opened doors as only a fireblood's noble blood-line could. Her father's, she never used. A cinderblood commoner's name got you nowhere in Khalad, even if Terrion Arvish had been a celebrated artist.

Besides, prudence dictated not telling Ardoc more than she had to. Which begged the question why she'd given him her real name at all. She could have told him anything. The answer was as obvious as it was infuriating. Part of her *liked* Ardoc – or was at least sufficiently intrigued by him as made no difference. More accurately, part of her wanted Ardoc to like *her*. He'd seen what she was capable of and had neither run away screaming, declaimed her as an abomination, nor tried to kill her. In all her twenty years clinging to Khalad's shadows, only one person other than her parents had ever reacted thus.

Of course, she'd saved Yennika on that occasion, painting the night with the screams of fireblood twins whose drunken braggadocio had turned darker once away from the bright lights and potential witnesses of their uncle's palace, so the circumstances were hardly the same. She'd wanted Yennika to like her too. She'd thought they were friends, but that had slipped away as soon as Kat had come onto the scene, Tanith banished to the shadows as Yennika trailed around besotted after her elder sister. Maybe it wasn't surprising that Kat had betrayed her to the Deadwinds. Their whole lives, she'd stolen everything. People couldn't be trusted – those who claimed to care most of all.

And still she wanted Ardoc to like her.

How pathetic was that?

Ardoc nodded slowly to himself and pursed his lips. "I am honoured to meet you, Tanith."

"Because you think I'm the herald from your prophecy?"

"I know you are. After all, you fell from the Deadwinds, wreathed in flame."

"Don't be ridiculous ..." She stared past the fallen statue to the scorched and cracked patch of tile where she'd awoken. Directly beneath the roof's gaping hole. Rathiq had come searching for starfall – a meteorite from the firmament, laden with rare metals. The Deadwinds had consumed her and ... what? Spat her out? Had she broken free? Had someone – or some*thing* – helped her escape? Helped her re-form from dissipating spirit to some semblance of mortal flesh? She'd no recollection of that, but then everything was so jumbled.

Maybe the goddess *had* freed her from the Deadwinds.

And if she had, who was to say that she wasn't this herald Ardoc expected?

She stared up through the hole in the scorched timbers into the midnight sky. One thing was for certain: the Deadwinds had carried her a long way from Athenoch. "Where am I? What city?"

"Zariqaz," Ardoc replied. "The Qosm district, if you need something more precise."

Tanith snorted. Of course she was in Zariqaz, Khalad's gloried capital and the one place she never wanted to be. No matter how she tried, it always drew her back. But then it wasn't called the City of Lost

14

Souls for nothing. In life, death and rebirth, the past kept her anchored there. "And this place?"

Ardoc spread his arms, his voice filling with passion as his words gathered pace. "Long ago, the faithful worshipped Nyssa within these walls. The *true* Nyssa, not the simplistic concepts of judgement and benevolence the Alabastran Church impose upon Khalad. They all died, of course. The archons who led the ceremonies were rounded up and beheaded on the Golden Stair for refusing the Eternity King's orthodoxy. Centuries passed and their great temple became merely another forgotten ruin." He offered another smile, this one with a touch of darkness beneath, and pressed on in quiet, reverent tones. "But some of us keep the faith."

Zariqaz – like all of Khalad's cities – crawled steadily skyward. The buildings of yesteryear were repurposed as foundations for those of tomorrow, raising a great spire above the sprawl of Undertown slums and the sprawl of Gutterfield shanties beyond the outer walls. Zariqaz's spire was an amalgam of abandoned mansions and bricked-up warehouses, the thoroughfares of the past become tunnelling, skyless streets, only winding into the open air across viaducts and bridges when they served the palaces and gardens of the fireblood nobility. Altitude was the highest status.

At last, the pieces fell into place. "You're part of the Obsidium Cult."

He raised an admonishing finger. "Ah. The Obsidium Cult does not exist. Alabastra are quite firm on the matter, and have expended considerable effort in the hopes of making their words truth." The humour returned to his voice. "But if the cult did exist, I might concede that I do, in some small way, contribute to its efforts."

"Would it have killed you to just say 'yes'?"

"Or you to tolerate an old man's eccentricities?"

Tanith rolled her eyes. "You're not afraid that I'll tell someone?"

Ardoc gathered the skirts of his robe and sat on the toppled statue's plinth. "Whom would you tell? Alabastra? The custodians? The Eternity King's redcloaks?" He waved dismissively at the darkness. "Let them search these old bones. They're long since picked clean. Besides . . ."

"I'm Nyssa's herald, so I won't betray her cause?"

"Precisely."

"You're very certain of yourself."

"No, but I am very certain of her. Change is coming to Khalad. An Age of Fire that will see the world reborn."

"*I* was reborn less than an hour ago. It was unpleasant."

"The necessary often is. There's nothing natural about the order of things in Khalad. Nyssa has been stolen and subverted. They've sealed pieces of her away and used what remains to prop up the Eternity King's throne. If it is to change – if Khalad is to be truly reborn in Nyssa's image – we all have our part to play."

There it was. "So you want to use me?"

"We're all of us used, Tanith. It's merely a question of whom we permit to do the using."

"Oh, that's deep," she said, not caring to conceal her bitterness.

"It's a simple truth. They can't all be palatable."

Yennika had always said that you found your place in Khalad, or one was found for you. Submit. Conform. Do as we say, or you'll have nothing but ash. The mantra of Alabastra and the Eternity King and of Tanith's own stepfather.

"Thanks, but I'll find my way alone. I'm used to that."

"It's no easy thing to get out of Qosm these days. Not since they raised walls to contain the lethargia. Even if you get over the walls, there are patrols of trigger-happy custodians everywhere."

Tanith narrowed her eyes. "The lethargia?"

Ardoc offered a slight, one-shouldered shrug. "The King's Council claim it started here, and perhaps it did, but it's bound to be all over the city by now. The Enlightened Lodge of Physicians deem it some form of infection. Alabastra's archons claim it's a blight upon the soul." He shook his head, a man at a loss for having witnessed such stupidity.

"And you?"

"I think it's a sign from Nyssa. A portent for the next Age of Fire."

"Of *course* you do."

16

He sighed and clasped his hands in his lap. "Listen to me. Forget Nyssa. Forget prophecy. Forget everything beyond what's in front of you." He spoke softly, imploring with every word, a perfect echo of what Tanith recalled of her father. "You are alone in a city that tolerates loneliness poorly. You need somewhere safe to sleep. People around you that you can trust. I'm offering you that, and in exchange . . . ?"

"Yes?"

"A simple trade. Service for shelter. You don't have to believe as we do."

"How can I be this herald of yours if I *don't* believe?"

"Say yes and we'll find out together."

Part of Tanith, the part that yearned for family, to be loved – the part that always got her into trouble and set her up for disappointment – urged her to accept. There was a solidity to Ardoc, a confidence you could cling to while the waters rose. She needed that. Her sister Kat might have provided it, had fate – and their father's favouritism – not brought them together as enemies.

But she'd only to let her guard down for a moment to risk finding herself dead, or else handed over to Alabastra for a very public exorcism. Worse, there were plenty of Undertown hawkers ready to sell amashti blood, teeth and bone to the gullible – the former as an aphrodisiac, and the rest as folk charms to ward off other daemons. Tanith resolutely did *not* want to pass her last moments on a shriver-man's slab, a saw chewing her flesh and her final thought regret at having let down her guard.

But then there was pride. She'd never had a dearth of it, even when she'd had nothing else.

Especially when she'd had nothing else.

"I'm not interested in being part of someone's holy cause," she said at last. "Find your herald elsewhere."

Ardoc rose heavily to his feet, brow furrowed. "If that's what you want."

Tanith tilted her head. "It's as easy as that?"

"I should rant and rail? Clap my hands and summon an army to drag you away?"

"Maybe."

He smiled without mirth. "More than ever, I wish you'd choose otherwise, but I won't stop you. However, I will have a watch kept on this place for as long as I am able. I'll be around, should you make it back. Nyssa isn't done with you, Tanith. She brought you here for a reason."

In that moment, Tanith almost relented. Almost let acceptance overwhelm hard-won suspicion. Before it could do so, she turned on her heel and left Ardoc alone in his circle of starlight.

Three

The gateway's motley frontage – hewn stone to the second-storey level and weather-worn adobe brick for the three above – had once belonged to a long-vanished warehouse, of which only the double-arched facade and its paired cast-iron gates survived. The adjoining mud-brick wall was as sun-bleached as the gateway itself, while its crowning wooden palisade bore all the crooked hallmarks and misaligned logs of a structure assembled out of haste more than artistry.

Even in dawn's amber embrace, the shadows of the spire not yet lapping at Qosm's time-worn streets, it looked sad and tired. If walls could sigh, these wouldn't have found the energy even for that.

Tanith watched from amid the tangle of brightly awninged stalls at the edge of the adjoining souk as a handful of folk in scuffed work garb broke off from the crowds to join the dozen or so already bellowing discontent. Six custodians looked on from beyond the bars of their impassive silver *vahla* masks, cast in the androgynous likeness of spirits who led the deceased to Nyssa's judgement, offering no clue to their thoughts.

Were they bored? Angry? Possibly. Maybe even a little afraid, despite the gates keeping the crowd at bay and a disparity in weaponry. Even at that distance, with protesters milling about in between, Tanith noted that the gate wardens had stocky brass-barrelled

19

shriekers holstered at their hips as well as scimitars sheathed at their shoulders. Heavy armament for a simple blockade. Most would have made do with crossbows.

A tall, foreboding figure in layered black lamellar armour joined the custodians, the eye sockets of its gilded skull blazing with magenta flame. Even at that distance, with the comfort of iron bars between them, the sight of it turned Tanith's blood to ice. A koilos: a criminal pressed to serve the Alabastran temple as an indentured, mummified guardian until its body disintegrated, the ifrît that was the bleak remnant of its soul screaming for death all the while.

She hated koilos more than anything – no small feat in a world that had offered up so much worthy of loathing – not least for the primal, instinctive fear they awoke in her. They were everything she sometimes feared she was: a mortal shell urged to malice by something deemed alive only by the most generous definition. She thought back to the blackened, stumbling thing she'd been on first awakening in the ancient temple, barely aware, and desperate. The division between them seemed thinner than ever.

One thing was for sure: she wasn't getting out that way.

Shivering away the koilos' lingering malice, Tanith tracked back through the souk, alert for anyone showing her too much interest. She wasn't worried about reprisals on behalf of the late, unlamented Rathiq, but Ardoc seemed the type to have her followed.

Air abuzz with rich spices and the sea tang of fresh fish suggested that the blockade of Qosm wasn't as complete as first appearances suggested. Trade carts apparently still came and went, their passage doubtless eased by permits and bribes. Firebloods loved bureaucracy almost as much as they loved the clink of dinars and tetrams. Few would readily abandon either over the mere *rumour* of contagion.

Or perhaps supplies were winched down from skyships? Even at that early hour, Tanith marked three tacking the winds above, sails billowing as captains directed motic ifrîti to lay out yard and canvas to catch the wind. All too far skyward to dock at Qosm's modest altitude,

20

instead auguring for the well-to-do quays of the Golden Citadel at the spire's pinnacle.

Eyes still on the crowds – if Ardoc had set a tail on her, they were at least very discreet – she plucked a waxy red apple from out under a stallholder's inattentive gaze.

A custodian's indecipherable command barked out from the gateway.

She felt the shrieker's discharge before she heard it, the wrathful fizz of its captive ifrît like the scrape of metal down her spine.

Fire gouted through the gate, the weapon's telltale scream melding with that of its victim as it set a nest of rooks to panicked flight. Protesters scattered, shoving and jostling, their once-strident voices stuttering to panicked babble as they fled for shelter in the marketplace crowd. All save one, who lay where she'd fallen, sightless eyes skyward and her unbound greying hair fanned out on the dust-choked cobblestones. Flames flared briefly about the charred wound high on the corpse's chest, and then went out.

Tanith slipped into the side streets as renewed commotion shook the souk, following the unbroken run of palisaded wall. She found what she was looking for in what had once been a broad courtyard, an over-lapping section of palisade barely a foot higher than the rooftop twenty feet opposite.

She buffed her apple on her sleeve, took a bite ... and scowled. What should have been sweet and moist tasted like ash. It had been thus ever since her father had inked the tattoo. Sweetness – indeed, all manner of flavours – belonged to a girlhood memory she could no longer be sure was anything more than fantasy.

She choked it down all the same. Mortal food might not have satis-fied – all save hard liquor, and that offered an entirely different kind of fulfilment – but it kept her daemon-half quiet for a time. On the fourth bite she gagged, unable to any longer fight the wilfulness of a body desperately rejecting the poison she insisted on consuming. Spluttering, she hurled the remains across the road. The apple splattered against the palisade, the pulp clinging briefly to the wall before dripping down into the gutter.

Ignoring several pointed looks, Tanith ghosted across the cobbles to a building whose ornate, fluted window frames evoked more prosperous times. The lower floor was boarded up, but washing lines stretching across the flanking alleyway suggested that those above were at least partly inhabited. Through a cast-iron gate surround long since robbed of its gate, a steep, narrow stone stairway served doors let into the alley wall.

At the top of the stairs, she reached an uppermost landing being entirely bereft of a guardrail and barely wide enough for her to stand comfortably. From there, tenuous handholds on door lintel, creaking washing-line brackets and missing bricks permitted an undignified vertical scramble that ended with her fingers hooked over a gutter's rim and her body dangling out over the alleyway. One last pull on creaking elbows and she was standing on the tiles. Further along the ridgeline, a crow regarded her with impassive disdain, then returned to pecking at a clump of reddish-green moss.

So far, so good.

Tanith edged back towards the ridge. The downward slope lay in her favour, but she'd barely four paces to pick up speed before launching out over the street.

It'd be fine.

It would, wouldn't it? The cobbles seemed an awfully long way away.

Tiles clattered under her feet once, twice, three times. She launched up and forwards.

The distance between rooftop and palisade vanished in a heartbeat, the murmurs and shouts of alarm from the street below drowned out by a peal of triumphant laughter she couldn't have controlled if she'd wanted to. The only thing finer than accomplishing what others couldn't was doing so before an audience.

Just as she'd planned, her bare right foot landed squarely on the sawn-off top of the palisade.

What *hadn't* been in the plan was for momentum to completely overcome what little balance her frantically windmilling arms provided.

Her legs and hips came to a precarious halt, but her head and body kept moving, pitching her head-first over the palisade into the courtyard's forbidden side. She twisted as she fell so that her shoulder – not her skull – took the bone-jarring impact against the cobbles. Sky spinning, she rolled twice and slammed into a verdigrised fountain.

Bruised and shaking, she made it to hands and knees before a voice rang out.

"You there! Stay where you are!"

Clutching at the fountain's basin for support as certainty oozed back to jangling limbs, Tanith clambered to her feet. A silver-masked custodian – the courtyard's sole inhabitant – came running from the derelict buildings opposite the palisade, shrieker drawn.

Wonderful.

Turning her back to the approaching footsteps, she dabbled her fingertips in the fountain, wetting her lower eyelids and dribbling trails across her cheeks. The chill, filthy water stung her eyes, threatening real tears alongside.

Behind her, the footsteps halted. "I said don't move!"

The hollow timbre granted by the silver *vahla* mask couldn't disguise the uncertainty of the voice beneath. A young man, judging by his tone.

Tanith shrank inwards, shoulders hunched, and faced him, trembling hands upraised to ward off a blow. Five paces away. Good. Shrieker already levelled. Not so good. His black robes were shot through with the telltale shimmer of House Ozdîr's golden thread. Smaller cities might surrender to the rule of a single fireblood house, but Zariqaz's sprawling streets were an ever-shifting tangle of vying dominions.

"I'm sorry, I'm sorry, I'm sorry," she babbled. "I didn't want to. But they were going to ..."

Hiding her face in her hands – but leaving a crack between her fingers to see through – she sank against the fountain and stuttered out her best pitiable whine. The old game. Keep them focused on what she wanted them to see. A seductive smile, a daring neckline, a whispered promise – or in this case, the shuddering trauma of a waif in need of protection. Arouse interest, desire, tug the heartstrings. Anything to discourage the custodian from wondering how such a girl could have climbed the palisade . . . and why she'd a scimitar sheathed at her back.

He stepped closer. "You know the penalty if you don't go back."

There. The note of doubt. Any halfway decent actress could have pulled off the trick, but even the best couldn't hold a candle to an amashti. Her soul being too big for her body, Yennika had called it. A strong will could resist the glamour, as could one who'd already witnessed her do something horrific. Awash in desire to possess or protect, most couldn't help themselves.

Judging by his tone, the custodian fell into the latter category.

Tanith hated herself in that moment. More precisely, she hated the illusion of it all. No matter how lustful or empathic the response, it always faded, leaving her alone with the cold reality that folk only cared for her – only loved her – for as long as she willed it. It wasn't real. It was just a weapon. The more she wielded it, the emptier the future grew.

She sank deeper onto her haunches, careful to brace a foot against the base of the fountain. "I can't go back," she sobbed. "You don't know what they'll do to me . . ."

The custodian hesitated. "I don't make the rules." The barrel of his shrieker dipped. "I can take you back to the gate, talk to my overseer. She'll—"

Brushing his shrieker aside with her left hand, Tanith hooked the fingers of her right around the back of his neck and slammed his head down on the fountain basin's rim. He went limp, the dull chime of metal meeting metal swallowing his pained grunt.

Letting him fall, she cast about for sign of potential witnesses, and found none.

Stooping, she rifled through his pockets, gaining a handful of copper dinars for her trouble. As she withdrew, her aetherios tattoo flared coldly about her wrist, the first slithering hunger pangs worming through her heart.

Her daemon-half wanted to feed. *She* wanted to feed. Didn't she? To

24

smooth away the bruises from her ungainly descent. To feel better. To feel whole. And he was just *lying* there. She didn't have to drain his fires dry, just take a little. As long as she was careful, he might live another five, ten, even twenty years before his soul dissipated, unable to sustain itself any longer because of what she'd taken. No one would ever know.

She swallowed hard. *She'd* know.

Her glamour had no purchase on stony hearts. On some level, the custodian had wanted to help, just as Amsin had wanted to help, years before. And Josco, back in Tyzanta. And all of the corpses she'd left at the roadside since. Entries in the ledger of sins by which cruel Nyssa Iudexas doomed her to a loveless existence.

She couldn't change what she was, but she *could* choose what she did.

Willing the hunger to subside, Tanith pressed on into the city.

Four

"I'm sorry, Mistress Floranz, I can't let you pass."

Tanith looked from one sentry to the other, and then to the distant lights of the palace beyond the gilded railings and swaying cypress trees. With fraying patience strained by the insistent, piercing yap of a dog somewhere in the grounds, she offered her most winning, fragile smile. "Count Aroth assured me I'd always be welcome."

The custodians shared a brief glance, though as ever the masks denied any clue as to their thoughts. The leftmost shrugged. "Not for me to speak to the count's reasons, miss."

A neat conversation-closer, wielded by an old hand well accustomed to deflecting fireblood frustrations. Not that Tanith entirely resembled a fireblood heiress at that moment. She'd taken the time to scrub her face, straighten her clothes and steal a pair of almost-fitting boots, but there was only so much to be done with the erstwhile Rathiq's skelder's garb.

Careful not to lose the mask of the timid, diffident young thing she'd worn during her earlier sojourns at the Aroth Palace, she weighed her options.

Her glamour couldn't help her, in the first case because it never worked as well on groups as individuals – a reality shared readily asserted itself over the illusions her daemon-half wove – and in the second because winning over a pair of custodians wouldn't help convince their master. Violence was out of the question for much the same reason, especially now that she'd given her name.

She offered the nearer custodian a winsome smile and the slightest flutter of eyelashes. "I'm sure there must be some mistake. Tell Julan I'm here. He'll vouch for me."

The custodian twitched. "Lord Julan's dead," he said, his tone that of a man uncertain as to whether or not a jest was in the offing. "Killed by Vallant's lot."

Tanith blinked. "What?"

She'd not much liked Julan Aroth. Not that it would have mattered if she had, as Yennika had twisted the man so tightly around her little finger that he'd practically been a figure of eight. However, he'd been alive – and unctuous – enough the last time she'd set eyes on him. Then again, that *had* been in the middle of a battle against Vallant's rebels, hundreds of miles away. Word couldn't possibly . . .

Kiasta. Just how long had she been in the Deadwinds, anyway?

"Do you think I might speak to Castellan Annaj?"

After another brief, silent communion, the rightmost custodian shrugged. "I can ask. You'll wait here with Custodian Barja."

He passed through the gate and began the long walk up the land-scaped path to the palace proper, crossbow clattering against his back. A full three acres of gardens separated the double-winged residence from its outer wall. With space ever at a premium in Zariqaz, and the streets of both Overspire and Undertown crammed side-by-side and top-to-bottom, richer firebloods flaunted their wealth through emptiness. The only other structure in sight was the estate's torch house, indigo flames blazing from its summit to burn away the all-consuming mists of the Veil. The smoke from its blesswood pyre sweetened every breath with notes of juniper and jasmine.

Behind the palace, the spire continued its skyward climb, windows dotting the gilded stone and balconies jutting out at all angles. Almost everything above the Aroth mansion belonged to Caradan Diar, the Eternity King: mazes of temples, staterooms and storehouses; barracks for the red-cloaked Royal Guard, and the quaysides where royal sky-ships docked. And then higher still, the gleaming walls of the Golden Citadel, a city within a city.

The first raindrops spotted the path. Tanith shot the remaining sentry an imploring glance and nodded at the squat gatehouse lodge, tucked almost out of sight behind the cypress trees. "I'm not really dressed for this."

No longer able to resist her glamour now he was alone, Barja grunted and swept out his hand towards the lodge. "No harm in it, I guess."

As Tanith crossed the gateway threshold, she felt the attention of the hestic ifrît imprisoned in the gatepost's prism as a brief pressure in her thoughts. Not the angry fizz of a discharging shrieker, but a calm, vigilant presence – proof that the custodian had commanded it to let her pass. Had he done otherwise, the hestic would have set her aflame, little caring that doing so would have also been its own demise – the last of its soulfire spent in defence of the Aroth estate.

To command an ifrît, a mortal therefore had to possess a suitable soul-glyph tattooed somewhere on his or her body. Each glyph was unique – to command a different ifrît, the wielder needed another tattoo, or to at least have an existing design modified. Tanith's aetherios tattoo was different. Its inks were part of her, and with sufficient force of will she could reshape its design into anything she pleased, in theory matching the soul-glyph of any given ifrît. In practice, she'd learned time and again that she lacked the artistry for anything more involved than goading ifrîti to self-destruction. On those rare occasions where she'd attempted something more complicated, it had drained her thin patience down to the dregs.

Kat was different, of course. She'd inherited their father's artistic instincts, and had proven herself capable of adjusting her aetherios tattoo on the fly, cajoling an ifrît as one might soothe a panicked child.

One more advantage life had given her and denied her younger sister. Tanith waited in silence under the lodge's porch while the rain pattered across the tiles and hissed away down the drainpipes. Probably Barja was wondering why he'd allowed her into the estate. The glamour took them that way, sometimes. Unable to understand *why* they'd done something at odds with their own interests, the subconscious patched over inconsistencies with whatever shaky logic filled the void. During her involuntary exile in Kaldos, more than a few men had unconsciously invented indiscretions committed by their lovers to justify how readily they themselves had awoken in the wrong bed.

Those who awoke at all, of course.

One – a minor and distant son of House Hythaka, consumed with jealousy for events that had existed entirely in his own mind – had even murdered his supposedly unfaithful wife so that he might be free to pursue the alluring golden-haired young woman with whom he'd crossed paths one summer afternoon. Bayrad Hythaka had never once guessed that seduction's course had run entirely counter to his belief. Tanith, fifteen years his junior and little more than a girl at the time, had considered the murder the ultimate romantic gesture. She'd fallen hopelessly, giddily in love ... for all of five days, until Bayrad's psyche had fractured, torn between the reality he shared with the rest of Khalad and the one that existed only in his head. It marked the first time Tanith had truly understood the gulf between genuine love and whatever stirred into being in those around her.

As far as she knew, he was still locked away in that Kaldosi asylum, asking for her one day and his wife the next, unable to comprehend why neither visited.

Thankfully, she'd outgrown her romantic phase before returning home to Zariqaz. Kaldos was a such long way off, with the notoriety that only distant places readily attained. Very little of what transpired there was taken as fact in more civilised climes.

Unfortunately, the brooding figure stalking closer through the rain was a spark flung from an altogether hotter flame than poor Bayrad. Amashti or not, one had as much chance of charming a stone as the famously cheerless Prenthi Annaj.

Nonetheless, Tanith hardened herself to the attempt. "Castellan, thank you for—"

Annaj glared at Barja. "What is *she* doing on the grounds? The count left clear instructions."

"I know, Castellan, but ..." Cause and effect failed to connect behind his eyes. "I ..."

She waved an impatient hand. "Get out of my sight."

Barja hastily fell into step with his erstwhile companion, who had returned alongside Annaj, greeted by a disbelieving tilt of the head.

Annaj looked Tanith up and down, a slight curl to her lip. "What happened to your hair?"

Tanith scowled a perfect blend of embarrassment and anger. "The rooms I took at Osios weren't as lice-free as the proprietor claimed. I could still feel them scritching around even after three treatments of kazini water." She ran a hand across her scalp and dribbled a little self-pity into her voice. No acting required. For all that her hair was as eager to rejuvenate itself as the rest of her – after only a few hours it had grown long enough to cover her fingertips – she wouldn't feel complete until it was much longer. "I don't think it suits me."

Annaj folded her arms. "You've a deal of nerve, showing up here."

An icy fingertip brushed Tanith's back. During her time at the Aroth palace, she'd been careful to always present herself as diffident and nervous. Those rumours she hadn't left behind in Kaldos had readily been dismissed. It was a rare fireblood who didn't attract gossip of some kind. "I ... I don't understand."

"Where's that trallock Yennika Bascari?"

The fingertip became a full hand, its digits scuttling up and down Tanith's spine. "We ... Well, we parted ways some time ago." She shook her head and let her lower lip tremble. "Please ... What's this about? What happened to Julan?"

"The younger Lord Aroth permitted himself to get caught up in some scheme of Yennika Bascari's," Annaj replied stiffly. "Something about ending Vallant's rebellion. He was killed in the attempt, his army obliterated. Why do you think Tyzanta declared for the rebels?"

Tanith gaped, buying time to make sense of Annaj's words. Tyzanta had been Yennika's inheritance, one she'd schemed long and hard to claim. "I didn't know . . . Yennika and I, we quarrelled. I've been travelling ever since." If Julan was dead, likely so too was anyone who could have told Annaj the truth. "It feels like an age ago."

"You were fortunate to reach Zariqaz at all. The East's been a mess with Qersal rising and so many cities throwing in with Vallant. The Eternity King should have set his redcloaks marching weeks ago." Annaj pursed her lips. There were some things even a castellan should hesitate to say. "So you don't know where Yennika can be found?"

"I was hoping you could tell me."

Her expression, never friendly, went flat and cold. "If I knew where to find her, she'd already be dead. Those are the count's standing orders to anyone who wants a hundred thousand dinars in their pocket."

Tanith blinked. Even for the heir of a fireblood house, that was quite the bloodgild bounty. "That's . . . a lot."

"The count loved his son." Annaj's tone offered no clue as to her own opinion. "Keep it in mind, should you find Yennika. But don't think about it too long."

She'd never have dared say as much to a true fireblood, of course. But etiquette scarcely applied to the half-blood and penniless Tanith Floranz, about whom not *all* rumours could be discounted. After all, those of proper breeding didn't deal in lowly dinars, but the higher-denomination tetrams that were as much a mark of societal standing as actual wealth.

"I couldn't betray her."

"The count's friendship opens doors," Annaj glanced towards the lights of the main palace, "and the streets of Zariqaz are not kind to those of delicate disposition."

Tanith almost laughed. The streets of Zariqaz may have been home to cut-throats and predators of all stripes, but they remained a distant peril to someone whom the Deadwinds had burned to a crisp and spat out whole. And yet . . . there was living and there was survival. Annaj was offering her a chance at the former. In that moment, Tanith was glad she didn't know what had become of Yennika. It meant she didn't have to choose. Yes, they'd been allies – maybe even friends – but it had been a transactional friendship even before Kat had come on the scene.

"It's a shame I don't know where she is," she murmured, and wondered if it was true.

Annaj stared pointedly at the estate's ornate gateway. "Then those doors remain closed."

Tanith bit her tongue to stifle an angry retort. "Goodbye, I suppose."

She squelched back down along the path, sodden before she'd even reached the gate.

The Aroth palace had been her best chance of shelter, but Yennika – wherever she was – had managed to sabotage that. Now what? Crawl into Undertown and find someone susceptible enough – willing enough – to offer shelter? Trawl the Overspire taverns for a mark unconcerned with *what* he welcomed over his threshold so long as she followed him in? Either could take hours, without guarantee of success, and the mix of anger and weariness swirling in her heart only lengthened the odds. Glamour wasn't a cure-all. It amplified what was already there. It couldn't weave a smile over a scowl, nor hide the contempt in her voice.

Then what? Robbery might garner enough dinars to pay for a room somewhere, but violence brought her daemon-half closer to the surface, and she badly wanted it to remain quiet.

That left precisely one option. The longest of long shots.

At the end of the palace drive, the road branched. The left plunged into the dense mismatched streets of the Overspire's middling districts – well-to-do on the surface, but beneath the veneer a seething mass of braggarts, marks and private pleasures for a weary amashti to exploit. To the right, much the same. But a quarter-mile down that road, beyond the cloistered temple of Nyssa Benevolas and past the wall of engraved Etranta marble and the row of crooked yews?

The House of Broken Promises.

Tanith dropped from the branches of the ancient carob, landing neatly within the crumbling boundary wall. Clammy from the climb and her sodden clothes, she steadied herself and strove to remind herself why this had been a good idea.

Skirting the stone garden and its ornamental pond, she arrived at the grand double-helical stairway serving the southern terrace and the House of Broken Promises' atrium. In that grey, rainy afternoon it looked every bit as imposing as she remembered. Thirty-one steps in each flight, the pair winding around one another like snakes. At the summit, a statue of Nyssa Benevolas – who forgave all as readily as her judgemental aspect offered punishment – held her arms spread wide in welcome. The statue hadn't been present on her last visit. A costly acquisition judging by its size – easily twice Tanith's own height – and the gold trim on its white marble robes.

Again she hesitated, staring up through the rain at Nyssa's beatific face. The welcome was a lie, as everything in this house had always been a lie. She'd been a fool to come.

She nurtured the spark of anger, fanned it to purpose, and took the stairs two at a time. Breathless, she squelched past Nyssa Benevolas and crossed the terrace. A familiar figure filled the atrium doorway, his arms folded and his bronzed features hewn to an implacable scowl.

He shouldn't have been here, not now. Count Hargo Rashace was a man of strict habit and scant trust in those who ran his mills and factories. Once he left the estate he seldom returned before nightfall. The sound of his thunderous voice at the gate had always been her cue to scurry to the arms of her foster mother, lest his ire find her.

The intervening years hadn't been kind. Her stepfather had once been a great bull of a man who'd indulged prize-brawling as his hobby – though naturally only against respectable opponents. Now he seemed shrunken beyond the physical decline of latter years, his once bristled black hair grey, almost white. Yet his will remained. Even at a distance, its pressure stifled.

Fighting the urge to shy from an upraised hand that existed only in memory – Hargo's arms were still tightly folded – Tanith stepped closer. "I want to see my mother."

"You've no family here."

Now she flinched, the words as much a physical blow as those she'd borne when he'd learned she wasn't a servant's brat, but living proof of his wife's betrayal. "Let me see her!"

"I don't take demands from trespassers, nor bastard half-bloods," he snarled. "Go back to whatever nest you oozed your way out of and leave my wife in peace."

Tanith's throat thickened with a bitter brew of emotion. She'd not even tried to see her mother the last time she'd been in Zariqaz. She'd been too afraid of what might be said. Ten years, at least, since they'd properly spoken. Too long. "It just kills you, doesn't it, that a penniless cinderblood gave her the child you never could?"

"You were never a child, daemon. Kinder on us all if I'd drowned you in the lake. But she loved you, and I was weak."

The rush of anger that had carried Tanith up the stairs blossomed anew, drowning out old fears. She sprang, closing the distance in a single pounce. He roared and swung, the right hook that had made him the terror of the prize-ring arcing at her face. Even old, he was fast.

But not fast enough to challenge an amashti.

With his bunched fist and its collection of heavy gold rings still inches from her face, Tanith stepped lightly aside and grabbed his throat. Hargo howled as her fingers dug into his jowls.

Tanith heaved him up against the fluted stone of the atrium, the aghast expression on his paling face at being manhandled by a woman half his size every inch as satisfying as the deed itself. Above the frame, the doorway's hestic stirred in its glossy black prism, and subsided when it realised she'd no intention of trespass.

"You were weak then. You're weaker now," she hissed, nose inches from his. Her stepfather scrabbled at her hand, trying to break her grip. She closed her other about his and forced it back, his sharp gasp of pain the sweetest music. "You think you can stop me going anywhere?"

Her daemon-half slithered awake, roused by anger, fear and proximity. It would be so easy to set it loose. Settle the debts from the beatings and bellowed malice, from her eventual banishment to distant Kaldos, where she'd been fostered by a family that had loved only the retainer her stepfather had paid.

So easy.

Her lips brushed his. No one would miss Hargo Rashace for long. Not the servants whose lives he made miserable, nor the custodians he bullied. Maybe not even his wife.

And he would taste *so* good.

"Do it," he breathed, tremor and defiance fighting for dominance. "And at last she'll see you for what you are."

Tanith's breath caught in her throat, flitterwings in her stomach. She'd never had much use for right and wrong, only for getting away with things or getting caught. Her mother might not mourn her husband, but nor would she easily forgive his killer – especially if she witnessed the death. "She's here?"

Hand still locked around her stepfather's throat, she peered through the atrium window. A shape moved in the gloom within. It could have been anyone. But it could have been *her*.

"She wanted to see you," Hargo croaked. "It was the first thing she said as soon as we were told you were coming. She still thinks you can be saved."

Tanith tore her attention from the dark shape beyond the glass. "You knew I was coming?"

"The runner arrived a little before you did."

Annaj. Firebloods always stuck together, which by extension meant so did their castellans. The Rashaces and Aroths weren't exactly allies, but they weren't enemies either.

Warned by the crunch of boot and stone, she glanced behind. A semicircle of eight custodians tightened around her, shriekers levelled. Hidden among the cypress trees at the terrace edge most likely, and she too lost in the past to notice.

"Go on." Hargo's breath brushed her cheek. "Kill me. I earned it long ago, I know that."

For the first time she marked the sweet notes of arask brandy. Bottled courage. Disappointing somehow. Through the anger, through the yearning of her daemon-half, Tanith struggled to make sense of unfolding events. Did her stepfather *want* her to kill him? Or was that merely what he wanted her to believe?

"Just go," murmured Hargo. "If she means anything to you at all, just go. No one will stop you. Go, and don't come back."

Tanith growled through her teeth – a sharp, frustrated exclamation that at least offered the satisfaction of making the nearest custodian flinch. Hargo's motives no longer mattered. What slim chance she'd had of finding shelter in her family home had depended on speaking privately with her mother and the mercy of strained affection. Now her choices were simple. Murder her stepfather, maybe dying in a hail of shrieker fire soon after . . . or go, leaving Hargo with victory.

Let him win or lose with him.

Pride demanded the latter.

Snarling, she slammed Hargo against the wall and let him drop. She whirled about. One of the custodians stumbled a half-step back. Another's gloves creaked as she gripped her shrieker for dear life. The silver masks could hide their faces, but not their fear. Even through the rain, they stank of it.

There was some satisfaction in that, but not enough.

She glanced back at her stepfather, still lying in the puddled rain-water, his back against the wall. "I was leaving anyway."

The rain had stopped by the time Tanith returned to Qosm, the sun restored to dominion of a cerulean sky, but the old temple was as dark as before. Dark, and empty. Even the corpses had gone.

"Ardoc?" Echoes rebounded beneath the vaulted ceiling. "Ardoc, are you here?"

Her shout returned to her full force, a trick of the acoustics amplifying her weariness, her loss, her frustration twofold.

Throat thick with self-pity, she collapsed against the altar. Yennika was gone, maybe dead already. Julan *was* dead, and Tanith tainted by association. She couldn't go home, because she'd never really had one. And now, despite his promises, Ardoc too had reneged.

So much for fine talk of her being a herald of prophecy. All the goddess had ever wanted was for her to be alone, unloved, to let the daemon loose and be all the terrible things anyone had ever thought of her – the corrupt, unfeeling predator that was all appetite and no morals, and was yet the only part of her anyone had ever valued.

She brushed away tears. How long had she been crying? Somewhere along the line, she'd blanked out the humiliating, snivelling noises that could only have been hers. How long had she sat alone in the dark, for that matter?

At least the dark was welcoming. It didn't expect anything.

It didn't judge her failures.

She could just sit there, couldn't she? Sit there until she grew so hungry she was no longer truly herself. That way she wouldn't be responsible for what came next.

It would just be Nyssa's will.

Maybe she was a herald of the goddess after all.

Maybe the goddess was angry.

The darkness stirred. Ardoc emerged from the gloom, a reassuring, warming presence in a world gone cold. "So you changed your mind?"

She stared up at him through bleary eyes. "I don't have anywhere else to go."

Stars Below, but she sounded pathetic.

Moving with the same deliberate, measured pace that infused his every word, Ardoc approached the altar. He took Tanith's hands in

37

his and raised her to her feet, then dried her cheeks with the hem of his sleeve. "No tears, Qori Arvish. You're home now."

Drawing down a shuddering breath that was part sorrow's aftermath and part disbelief, Tanith clung tight to him, and wished the world away.

Five

Kat glanced out from the shadows gathered beneath the hostelry's awning, past the cracked, stuttering fountain and across a street seared by the bright midday sun. "Come on, come on . . . you were supposed to be here by now."

But he wasn't there, which could unfortunately not be said for the pair of custodians standing sentry outside the crooked townhouse's simple red door. A small house by the standards of those who held sway over Zariqaz's districts, just one in a tightly packed row of similar dwellings, so surely they had better things to do than to stand guard over it?

Apparently not.

The Hazarid district wasn't part of Undertown but not quite part of the Overspire either. Sufficiently downmarket that factory workers, skelders and labourers rubbed shoulders with guildsmen, Alabastran archons, slumming firebloods and occasional redcloaks – all fending off the sweltering sun with headwraps, broad-brimmed hats and shawls. Not that anyone *actually* rubbed shoulders with redcloaks. They gladly stepped into the gutter to avoid confrontation with the Eternity King's famously intemperate soldiery.

Kat and her companion fitted right in, their silk gowns suitably behind prevailing fashion to pass for cinderblood merchantry rather than firebloods. Kat always felt out of place in a dress, but her companion had insisted.

She turned her attention back to the mug of feldir tea. It had long since ceased steaming, the best of the apple and honey flavour vanishing into the rising bitterness. There was nothing quite so maddening as a plan gone wrong.

Across the table, Yali brushed a wayward strand of chestnut hair back from her eyes and shot Kat a long-suffering look. ||Will you relax?|| Her lithe tawny-brown fingers blurred through the shapes of the Simah sign language. ||It happens when it happens, honest and true.||

Kat scowled, annoyed at being caught out. Too easy to forget that Yali's lipreading allowed her to "overhear" things in the right circumstances, despite her deafness. But annoyance seldom lasted around Yali. She smiled readily and always with mirth rather than bitterness, and her mischievous green eyes were as apt to wonder as empathy. Seven or so years Kat's junior, her gangling frame still awkward as girlhood fell away, she made her feel old.

But that was the way of things with friends, or so Kat supposed. Friendship was a relatively new concept.

||I'll relax when he gets here.|| Her signs were serviceable, but nowhere near as crisp as Yali's.

Six months since her railrunner had steamed into Zariqaz. Six months of obstacles, dead ends and teeth-grinding frustration. Her arm was itching again, warning of cramps soon to follow. She clutched her mug with both hands as the spasm hit, elbow creaking as the muscles locked. Shadows danced behind her eyes.

Yali's expression darkened. ||Your wrist again?||

"It's fine." The tremors faded. Just a mild attack this time. Good. The last one had left her gasping with pain and she could hardly hide *that* from Yali. "I'm getting used to it."

It wasn't and she wasn't. Careful application of last breath and apothecary's salves had mended the burnt and blistered flesh but hadn't restored what the burns had stolen – not the aetherios tattoo and not . . . Kat shook the thought away. You moved forward and did what you could to set things right.

So far as her friends knew, the fearsome itch was the beginning and the end of it. It had certainly begun that way, easily missed and soon forgotten. She'd only realised something was wrong when the attacks of nausea started. Badly wrong. The same omen rot that had killed her mother. Not as debilitating – not yet. That it had manifested only after she'd lost her tattoo left little room for doubt that the two were related – the damage done by the Deadwinds had been more than skin deep.

And Tanith . . . The Deadwinds fires that had scarred Kat had burned her sister to ash, and just in the moment where Kat had *maybe* glimpsed something worth saving in the murderous little trallock. Tanith still lived, or so Nyssa had claimed when she'd come to Kat in a vision. Kat had assumed she'd find her in Zariqaz, for where else to seek a wayward sibling but in the City of Lost Souls? But six months of searching had turned up nothing.

Quite likely, she'd never even seen Nyssa at all, the "goddess" just a pain-woven hallucination. But . . . if Nyssa had been an illusion of her own making, why had she beheld the goddess in chains? And what of the jealous, smothering presence that had been the goddess' captor? Could pain and loss and terror really have woven that? Scripture held no explanations, and no amount of pleading prayer had exhorted the goddess to send another vision.

A server flitted expertly between the tables. Kat beckoned to her, tossed a coin onto the table and patted the mug. The server – whose ink-black hair was a perfect match for Kat's own, and her bronze skin perhaps a shade lighter – pocketed the coin and whisked the mug away, her eyes meeting Kat's for just long to enough to maybe – *maybe* – offer a deeper interest than patronage.

Kat smiled politely and glanced away. Another wound that hadn't quite healed. Worse, she wasn't sure she wanted it to, despite everything Yennika had done.

Yali rapped lightly on the tabletop and jerked her head towards the crooked house. ||What did I tell you?||

A House Yesabi overseer, identified by the inverted green triangle

41

on the brow of his *vahla* mask and the starched, precise pace practised by a certain self-satisfied sort, stalked towards the red door. He didn't so much thread his way through the crowd as will it to part, the twin threats of fireblood authority and a holstered shrieker – the sentries only had scimitars sheathed at their shoulders – clearing a path as readily as any redcloak's reputation.

The custodians stiffened to attention. The overseer jabbed a gloved finger at each, then hooked a thumb over his shoulder, down the street to the seven-arched bridge leading clear over the Hazarid reservoir. The intervening crowd stole away his words, but his slight lean forward and a second, more insistent jerk of the thumb told a story all their own.

Yali leaned across the table, the better to shield her signing from other patrons. Simah was widespread enough that it was better to take no chances. ||Doesn't look like they want to go.||

But go they did, following the overseer back along the street. The crowd swallowed them almost at once.

Kat made a silent ten-count. Another to avoid tempting unhappy fate. She pushed back her chair. ||Time to go.||

She slipped out into the jostling crowd, the sun already prickling at her bare shoulders and making her regret she'd not thought to bring a shawl. Yali was three steps ahead, stepping into newly opened spaces with the experience of the perennially unnoticed. A burly, bearded docker collided with Kat and offered a terse growl in place of an apology. By way of reply, she levelled a glare capable of cracking stone. He flinched and changed course, almost trampling a red-sashed courier in the process.

Well satisfied, Kat darted past an oncoming clatter wagon. The motic ifrîti driving the vehicle's four brass-shod wheels burbled with satisfaction as she passed, while the helmic responsible for maintaining the wagon's heading murmured darkly at the challenge of doing so in so heavy a crowd. Most folk couldn't hear ifrîti, but then most folk didn't have an aetherios tattoo. Even with hers cold and dark – as it had been ever since the Deadwinds had all but seared it from her flesh – Kat still caught snatches. Enough to remind her of what she'd lost.

She slipped gratefully into the cool shadows beneath the crooked house's steps. A golden seal sat stark against the door's flaking red paint, its outspread wings the simple circlet of the Eternity King's crown and the tail of its accompanying parchment far too ornate for so mundane a purpose.

Yali's eyes widened. ||You really think he ordered this place sealed?||

||I doubt it.|| In theory, every decree issued in Khalad was backed by Caradan Diar's authority – at least, north and west of Tyzanta, away from Bashar Vallant's alliance of breakaway cities. Nevertheless, what occurred in the Eternity King's name was seldom the result of his will. Only those commands issued by his descendant and Voice, Isdihar Diar, truly issued from the throne immortal, as she was the only one who could hear his words. Everything else sprang from firebloods scurrying to do his bidding, real or imagined. The heads of the fireblood houses, Alabastra's archons, the ministers of the King's Council, all of them acting with an authority they may or may not have possessed. But still Kat's fingers stumbled a little as she signed. Defying custodians was one thing. Defying the Eternity King was something else. ||Why would he know about Yarvid, much less care?||

||Might be your father moved in grander circles than you ever knew.||

||Not that grand.|| Though he'd certainly done well enough for a cinderblood, his services ever in demand by Zariqaz's great and good. That status had earned him a position as the household artist for the Rashace family, alongside whose children Kat had been raised, not quite a cinder but certainly not flame, for all that Countess Fadiya Rashace had been kind to her. Youthful innocence had blinded her to the true depth of Terrion Arvish's relationship with the countess. In fact, it wasn't until coming face to face with Tanith, long after his death, that she'd truly understood it. ||Can you handle the lock?||

Yali sniffed derision and eased her lock charmer's tools – nothing more complicated than a pair of carefully shaped needles with

43

notches and bars set at the end – from her capacious sleeve. ||What a thing to say.||

Though the door frame was as worn and weathered as any in Zariqaz – between the Mistrali rainy season and the hot winds that raked the city from the arid plains, nothing remained pristine for long – the sculpted crest of Nyssa Benevolas, wreathed in flame-like hair, appeared suspiciously new. So too did the black prism set behind the goddess' eyes. Whoever had ordered the house sealed hadn't been one to rely on locks alone.

Six months before, Kat could have immersed herself in the spirit world, tailored her aetherios tattoo to mimic the hestic's soul-glyph and set it sleeping. Now . . . ? She slipped her left hand into her pocket – she'd relented to Yali's insistence that she wear a dress on the condition that it was at least a *practical* dress – and patted the aether bomb's comforting, egg-sized metal sphere.

Yali set to work, her hands cupped to help sell the illusion that she was wrestling with a stiff key. The lock *clicked* inside a three-count.

She palmed her tools and offered a pained faux-scowl. ||Can I handle the lock. Honestly.||

Still in her pocket, Kat's left thumb briefly caressed the aether bomb's activator, then stabbed down. The tiny plunger met the slight resistance of the thin glass plate set to prevent accidental activation. But only for a moment. The complex balance of internal pressures compromised, the sphere quietly imploded, setting free the ravati ifrît within.

Most ifrîti shriven from the dead and dying were defined by purpose, rather than character. The shriversmen cared nothing for the soul's nature in life so long as it retained power and purpose in death. Ravati were different, harvested from the condemned at the moment of execution, wisps of black, choking malice thick with the bleak rage shared by the guilty and innocent alike.

Kat, with the tiniest part of her being touching the spirit world, shivered as the black wisp of soul washed over her and soared towards the Deadwinds. The hestic ifrît, rooted in the same plane as the ravati and unnerved by its presence, fled as far and deep as it was able, folding the spirit world's blind nothingness over itself like a tortoise retreating into its shell. It was too vibrant a spirit to remain there long – maybe minutes, maybe an hour – but that was more than long enough.

She tapped Yali twice on the shoulder. "Go," she murmured, the spoken word instinct.

Yali eased open the door. Kat drew up short at a screech of gears as the clatter wagon came to a tortured and complete halt.

"*Kiasta,*" she breathed, repeating her father's favourite curse. The ravati had been more powerful than the trafficker had claimed, spooking not just the crooked house's hestic, but also the ifrîti of the clatter wagon – and Nyssa only knew how many others nearby as well.

||That's going to be trouble,|| said Yali, her expression deadpan.

Kat let the obvious go unanswered and passed inside, pulling the door closed behind her.

Six

Kat had seen many such houses in the preceding weeks. A handful of high-ceilinged rooms split across three storeys – the better to accommodate the steep slope as the spire slunk away into the streets of Qosm far below – and a shabby decor that spoke to the owner having long ago abandoned the battle against the passing years.

Even in that street-facing room, which served as both dining room and kitchen, there was a pride on display in the stern portrait of a middle-aged man and a handful of statuettes whittled from a pale timber. Kat turned one over in her hands – a stylised rendition of an ilfri daemon, with long, thieving fingers and a shifty expression. Others bore the likeness of curvy, seductive palkas, starving, pot-bellied gavalras and peremptory, scrawny pikari. All of them sculpted by the house's owner, no doubt. Yarvid's fascinations coming to the fore.

||Let's make this quick,|| she told Yali. ||You start downstairs, I'll take the upper floor.||

A ramshackle study dominated the upper storey. A low desk overlooked a broad, half-leaded window set in a varnished timber casement – a sort fallen out of favour due to metal shortages caused by the troubles in the east. Close-packed bookshelves spoke to an ordered and inquisitive mind. Emptiness – save for a few scraps of abandoned paper – confirmed that Kat hadn't been the first to come calling.

The room stank of death. Quite why, Kat couldn't say. Certainly the shriversmen had long since removed Yarvid's body – there wasn't even a bloodstain, just that cold, crystalline feeling of the mortal and spirit worlds being out of alignment. It felt like an absence. A hole.

Realising that her right hand was absently scratching at her left wrist, Kat clutched it to her chest and began what she already knew would be a pointless search.

Playbills from the bawdy-stage six streets away on the Undertown border. Receipts for books no longer present on the shelves. A pamphlet proclaiming the glory of Alabastra, with a woodcut of Nyssa Iudexas in full panoply of armour and helm, her sword held to rally the reader to support Khalad's less-than-perfect justice. On and on, and nothing worthy of the risk, let alone the one hundred and fifty dinars the aether bomb had cost.

The obvious discarded, she turned to the possibility of concealment, rapping on floorboards, desk timbers and the underside of drawers in hopes of *something*.

Nothing.

Another dead end. The eleventh, to be precise. Someone was killing her father's old associates as fast as she could hunt them down.

When Kat had been a girl, her father had spoken readily of the *what* of his interests, but never the *why*, save for when it touched on the subject of her tattoo – a secret he'd shared with no one else except her half-sister, Tanith. He'd devoured abstruse theological texts, accounts of Khalad's sprawling histories, fragments of the past so strange and brittle that serious scholars derided them. He'd become obsessed by the secretive Issnaîm – whom the ignorant named "veilkin", if they were aware of them at all.

A bribe to the Great Library's records clerk had revealed a list of like-minded men who'd made study of similar topics – often arriving at and departing from the deep archives at the same time, day after day. She'd hoped one of them might have understood his work enough to help her cure Tanith of what she'd become . . . if, of course, she ever found her. Or she was even still alive. And if Nyssa was really with her,

47

maybe she'd even learn how to repair the damage to her own tattoo – and to the rest of her – before it killed her. That the two were linked she didn't doubt. Though the spasms spread with each attack, they'd begun in her ravaged left wrist.

Half of those she'd sought had passed away since her father's own death. The others had scattered, burying themselves as deep in Zariqaz's sprawling streets as could be managed.

Eli Yarvid had been the last. The trail was cold.

Growling, she stared out across mist-shrouded Qosm. She thought back six months, to the skies above Athenoch. The ecstasy and agony as she'd channelled the Deadwinds to unmake Yennika's army of unliving koilos soldiers to save the city. Would she have done so if she'd known the consequences of her audacity?

Yes. Of course she would. But that didn't mean the cost hurt any less.

A footstep on the creaking stairs presaged Yali's arrival. ||Any luck?||

Kat shook her head. ||You?||

||Whoever did the taking took everything.||

Kat's heart sank another notch. ||Looks like.||

Though Vallant had done what he could to muddy the rumours coming out of Athenoch, someone had clearly pieced together enough to understand at least part of what she'd achieved. The only question was *who*? Who was killing her father's associates and spiriting away anything that might have contained a clue to their work? Not the custodians, whose fireblood masters could have arranged any number of excuses for jailing Yarvid and seizing his possessions. The same was true of the Eternity King and his court, to whom the law was the most trivial of concerns.

And underneath it all, the deeper question: what had her father *really* been up to?

Yali joined her at the desk and stared out across Qosm's greenish-white mists. ||I still can't get used to that. The Veil being inside the city, I mean.||

Kat suppressed a shudder. ||Nor me.||

48

One of Khalad's great truths was that the Veil was to be held at bay. It was the Eternity King's highest law and his greatest purpose, for the whole of his ancient being was dedicated to holding back the mists from the kingdom's boundary. But even his deathless will couldn't accomplish the task alone, especially on nights when the Aurora Eternis shimmered across the skies. Thus did the torch houses burn day and night, their blesswood fires holding the Veil at bay. Except in Qosm, where one night they had fallen dark, damning half the district.

‖I don't understand why they don't relight the torch houses,‖ said Yali.

‖I heard an archon preaching that it was Nyssa's punishment for letting the lethargia take hold. My old friend Hierarch Ossed, in fact.‖

Yali offered a wry smile. ‖And I thought the lethargia was Nyssa's punishment for loose morals and impiety.‖

Kat shrugged. ‖Alabastra preaches whatever suits Alabastra. It's not the punishment that matters, but who's being punished. The King's Council is probably hoping that the Veil will eradicate the lethargia.‖ Nothing survived within the Veil. Those caught within, ifrît or mortal, just . . . faded away, body and soul. ‖The rest is just theatre.‖

‖But it's everywhere,‖ protested Yali. ‖There's a street up on the Haymain where every door bears the mark.‖

Kat shrugged. ‖Like I said, theatre. Keep the mills turning, the factories productive, and hope the sickness burns itself out.‖

‖I still think that skyfall's to blame,‖ Yali replied, deadly serious.

‖For the mists, or the lethargia?‖

‖Maybe both. Three months since it landed in the heart of Qosm and—‖ She broke off and tilted her head. ‖You did check the window, didn't you?‖

Kat scowled. ‖Checked the window? Do you mean outside?‖

Yali sighed. ‖Never send a society upstart to do a thief's job.‖

‖What did you call me?‖

‖Oh, I'm sorry, m'lady. Do my words offend?‖

Bracing her palms on the desk, Yali hopped up to sit facing Kat, her

49

back to the window. ||I saw one of these back in Tyzanta. The warden's office in Spildra Factory. Used it for stashing the jewellery he took as bribes ... you know, from women desperate to keep their posts. Lots of dead space around a window, if you know what you're doing.||

She shuffled backwards until she sat inside the casement, her feet kicking idly where they overhung the desk, her fingertips tracing the beading around the moulded edge. She prised a section of beading away, revealing an oiled lock. Letting the beading drop, she brought her lock charmer's tools to bear, tongue protruding slightly from between her teeth as she worked.

With a grin, she pulled down the wood panel that concealed the window's underhang. A frayed leather-bound book and a small purse dropped into her lap. She tossed the book to Kat and hefted the clinking purse. ||All donations gracefully accepted. What about that? Any use?||

Kat riffled the pages, revealing a bewildering array of scratchy black symbols hanging from a horizontal line like carcasses from a butcher's rail. Not Daric, which she spoke as fluently as only someone educated at a fireblood's expense could be. Nor Qersi, which she knew by sight but of which she was otherwise wholly ignorant. Not any language with which she was familiar, in fact. ||It's in code.||

||Sounds like something for Tatterlain.||

||Probably,|| Kat replied. Maybe it wasn't a dead end after all. ||At the very least—||

The metallic scrape of a key in a lock sounded from the floor below.

Kat thrust the journal into her pocket and darted to the small, round window overlooking the street. Two custodians, likely the same pair from before. As she watched, the nearer one pocketed the useless key – with the door bolted from the inside, it could hardly have done him much good – and rammed his shoulder against the door.

A hollow thud echoed up the stairs.

Kat glanced at Yali. || Is there a back way out?||

||Just a window—||

Already taking the stairs three at a time, Kat lost the rest of Yali's frantic sign.

The basement room was half the size of those above, and of plainly rougher construction – an upper chamber of old become a cellar as Zariqaz climbed haphazardly skyward. A single saggy-springed bed rested against one wall, a ransacked brass-bound travel chest opposite. The window opposite the stairway stared out across a tight, sloping alleyway. That part, Kat didn't mind. In fact, it was far easier to lose pursuers in the tangleways than the main street. The twelve-foot drop she liked rather less.

At least it wasn't enough – not quite enough – to set her vertigo screaming.

She beckoned to Yali. ||After you.||

Yali shot her a sour look. ||Thanks.||

She clambered up onto the cracked sill. A heartbeat later, she was just a row of fingertips, clinging to the lower frame. Then she was gone.

The *crunch* of the front door breaking open sent Kat scrambling after her.

Impact with the cobbles pitched her forward. Yali shot out a hand to steady her. ||You all right?||

Kat nodded, trying not to think about the fresh twinge in her lower back. ||I will be.||

A custodian's masked head appeared at the window. "Halt in the name of the Eternity King!"

Yali flashed him a Simah sign that questioned his parentage, hitched her skirts and hurtled into the alleyway. Kat followed. Halfway to the next turning, a thump of boots and a muffled curse warned that at least one custodian had risked the drop.

"Halt, skelders!"

Skidding on a patch of gutter filth, Yali rounded the corner. Kat hesitated only long enough to confirm that not one but both custodians were pursuing, then followed as fast as her legs would carry.

She hurtled down the narrowing alleyway, running perpendicular to the prevailing slope of the spire. A brewyard passed away to the left, its low wall more cast-iron bracing than brick. She hung a right and crossed a sagging bridge over what had once been a stream but was now no more than an open sewer, shoved clear of the left-hand wall to avoid colliding with a bemused onlooker, then followed Yali's breakneck turn at the time-worn statue of Nyssa Benevolas and plunged, half running, half skidding, down the sheer cobbled slope.

She flung up a hand to ward off sunlight strobing through washing lines and wooden struts that kept the alleyway's buildings from collapsing in on one another. Her shoulder scraped against crumbling brick. By the time she'd righted herself, Yali had vanished around the next turning.

The wrong turning.

Kiasta.

"Yali!" The useless shout dying on her lips, Kat stumbled to a halt at the crossway, the thunder of custodian feet crowding ever closer.

It was a mistake easily made – the tangleways never looked more the same than when running for your life. Their contingency had called for them to go one way, but they'd gone another. That left a simple, stark choice: follow Yali into possible disaster, or save herself.

She ran after Yali.

The alley curved right, then left, and ended in an uneven mud-brick wall topped with rusting spikes and packed with tangled refuse at its base.

Yali stared at it aghast. ||I might have taken a wrong turn.||

Breathless, Kat peered up at the alley's side walls. Not a door or window in sight – or at least in reach. Those at street level – or in several cases partly *below* street level – had been bricked up years ago.

"This way!" The custodian's shout echoed around the corner. "We have them!"

Yali scowled, crestfallen. ||I'm sorry.||

Kat pointed at the mud-brick wall. It offered all manner of suitable crannies and projections for handholds. ||Can you climb it?||

52

||Not fast enough.||

She shot a glance at the pursuing custodians. Realising that their quarry had nowhere to run, they slowed to a cautious advance. She fished the journal from her pocket and held it out. ||Let me worry about that.||

Yali took the journal, her face falling even further. ||Kat . . . ||

||Go. They'll take me to the custodium. You can't get me out if they take you too.||

She dug in the refuse at the wall's base, looking for something – anything – to use as a weapon. She'd a dagger buckled beneath her knee, but without the benefit of surprise it wasn't going to be much use against two scimitars. She looked up to see Yali standing frozen at the wall's foot.

||Go!||

Yali grimaced and began to climb.

Kat's hand closed around a bent metal pipe a little longer than her forearm. Better than nothing. With a last glance at Yali, she stalked towards the custodians.

She brandished the pipe as menacingly as appearances allowed. "Stay back!"

The custodians advanced, shoulder to shoulder.

"Why don't you just come quietly?" said the tallest.

"Why don't you make me?" Kat filled the words with bravado.

The two exchanged a glance.

"You want her?" asked the tallest.

His companion shrugged. "You're always telling me how good you are with a sword, Marah. She's all yours."

"Fine." Marah reached up and drew his scimitar. "Last chance, skelder."

He moved with entirely too much confidence for Kat's liking, a man well used to picking fights and winning them. Beneath the uniform, very little separated custodians from the leg-breakers employed by Undertown's gang leaders. Had she a sword, she might have given him

53

a challenge – six months of on-and-off lessons had transformed her from a mediocre swordstress to a half-respectable one. But the broken pipe suddenly felt useless.

More useless was her hand, suddenly overcome by a knuckle-wrenching spasm of a kind experienced too often in recent weeks.

She stifled a gasp and clutched at her wrist. The pipe clanged to the ground.

Marah kicked it away. "Smart little skirl." He raised his voice. "Here, Vosri, how much resistance do you reckon she put up?"

Vosri chuckled. "At least two minutes' worth. As long as she can answer questions when we get her back, no one's going to care. Want me to hold her?"

Her muscles at last regaining a semblance of normality, Kat clung tight to her rising anger. Better to make it last. Fear would come soon enough. She glared at the pair. "Really?" She squeezed every last drop of contempt into the word.

Marah shrugged. "Shouldn't have run, should you?"

Again as close to fighting fit as she'd ever be, Kat aimed a kick at his groin. With a beating in the offing, it made sense to get her reprisals in while she could.

Marah deflected her kick with his knee and slammed the basket hilt of his scimitar into her face. Kat twisted aside and the full-force punch became a raking blow. Red stars burst behind her eyes. She let herself drop, hands and knees jarring on the cobbles.

"Looks like she's still got some fight after all," said Vosri.

"Looks like," Marah agreed. He stared up at Yali, who'd halted with one foot either side of the ridge spikes. "If you come down, we'll go easy on her."

Kat blinked away the last of the stars. Yali couldn't hear him, of course, and nor could she read lips hidden behind the *vahla* mask. But she'd take his meaning. Either that, or she'd make a doomed attempt to help. Guilt and loyalty were a toxic brew.

Making the most of the custodians' divided attention, Kat slipped a hand under her skirts and closed her fingers around the dagger's grips. The blade slipped free with barely a whisper.

She pushed up off the cobbles, steel glinting.

"Watch it!" roared Vosri.

Lunging, he grabbed her wrist and yanked it up behind her back. Kat yelped as fire shot along her arm, the dagger slipping from nerveless fingers. Vosri thrust her against the wall, his weight against her. Her cheek scraped against brick.

"I don't think a two-minute beating's going to cover it, do you, Vosri?" said Marah, his words all the more chilling for their thoughtful tone.

"No," murmured Vosri. "Calls for something lasting."

Kat blinked back tears as he twisted her arm higher.

Shadows shifted at the open end of the alleyway. Rose-water scent danced through the bitter reek. A husky voice issued forth. "Are you sure you wish to go through with this?"

Kat's fear bled away into a ragged chuckle.

Vosri released his grip and stepped back to draw his scimitar.

Kat hit the cobbles. Through watery eyes, she glimpsed the broad-brimmed hat, the tails of the long, time-worn coat. The spill of white hair framing a straight, slender sword resting lazily across the woman's shoulders. A black scarf tied across nose and mouth offered nothing of her expression, but her eyes promised death.

"You can't help her," growled Marah. "Put it down, unless you want the same."

Rîma sighed. "Well, I tried."

Shrugging the sword off her shoulders, she started forward.

Vosri died in a wet gurgle, the tip of the slender sword taking his throat before he'd chance to raise his scimitar. A brief scrape of vying steel and Marah followed him to Nyssa's judgement, Rîma's sword buried hilt-deep in his chest. If he made a sound as his soul fled into the Deadwinds, the thump of his falling body smothered it.

Rîma planted a boot on his corpse and wiped her sword clean on his robes.

"Even a child should know to run when something terrible walks his way," she murmured.

Yali scrambled down to Kat's side and pulled her upright. ||Are you all right?||

||"I will be."|| Kat signed as she spoke, wincing at the pain in her wrist and shoulder.

Rîma straightened, her sword back across her shoulders. She brushed at a blood speck on her coat's lapel. "You're in the wrong place."

"I know."

"And you're a mess."

Kat traced her brow, wincing at the bruise already forming. "I know that too."

"Did you get what you were looking for?"

She glanced at the journal clasped in Yali's hand. "Let's find out."

Seven

K at emerged from the bath a new woman, grime banished, tensions eased by chamomile oil and the worst of her injuries speeded to recovery by a vial of last breath. The washroom mirror confirmed that the livid gash inflicted by the strike of Marah's hilt had faded to little more than a dark line.

But even as she brushed the scar, her fingers spasmed. The room swam. She held her breath and clung to the washbasin until the attack faded.

No doubt about it, they were getting more frequent. And worse.

A package awaited her on the bureau, arrived while she'd been in the bath. Postmarked from Tyzanta and still sealed, thank Nyssa. Kat trusted her friends, but some things were too personal to share. She couldn't bear the humiliation of their sympathy, the prospect of being coddled, even confined. They'd trap her for the best of reasons.

After a brief hesitation – until breached, the box held the prospect of good news as well as bad – she ripped it open. Inside lay a vial of glutinous, tawny fluid and a letter penned by an elegant hand, perfume clinging to it despite the long, dusty miles.

Katija,

I trust your search has borne fruit. Mine, alas, has offered little. The only physicians who've displayed enthusiasm for

57

studying your condition are those to whom I'd not readily entrust a potted plant, let alone a friend. I have enclosed a vial of ashanaiq. The Qersali claim it more potent than last breath. I hope it will prove more effective than the last elixir I sent. It was not without cost.

Nyssa walk with you,
Marida

Kat held the vial to catch the light. Despite the letter's tone, they were allies more than friends, and distant allies at that. Marida was a qalimîri – a deathless soul who survived by possessing living hosts, suppressing the rightful inhabitant. Just meeting her black, glimmerless stare was like standing on the edge of a hungry grave. But she was a businesswoman first and foremost. Omen rot claimed thousands each year, some of them wealthy and very, very desperate for the same cure Kat sought.

Careful to first burn the letter in the votive bowl of her tiny shrine to Nyssa Benevolas and thus preserve its secrets, Kat uncorked the vial and set it to her lips. The ashanaiq didn't taste of much of anything, but it chased away the lingering nausea and left her feeling ready to face the rest of the day.

Dressing swiftly in practical skelder's garb, Yali's tastes be damned, she descended the spiralling staircase to the ground floor of the abandoned theatre. It was a building of modest but labyrinthine qualities, complete with dressing rooms, a stage, a pair of boxes where fireblood patrons could partake of the entertainment without chancing exposure to the cinderblood masses, and a dizzying array of lumani prisms that in the building's heyday would have bathed the players in all manner of soft, flattering hues.

That heyday lay long in the past, when what had passed for the Maraji district's cultural centre had retreated up-spire and away from the ever-expanding docks fronting the Silent Sea. The gilding was dull and peeling, the carpets faded, and the light filtering in through the boarded-up windows could hardly have been said to be flattering. But it was weatherproof, and the warren of rooms provided any number of dark, quiet spaces to which Kat could retreat in those not infrequent times when she wanted nothing to do with the world – or even her closest friends.

She found those friends waiting in the informal conclave circle Tatterlain had fashioned in the centre of the stage. He'd dragged the mismatched chairs from all corners of the building, insisting that "standards should be met, even in adversity".

He'd even crafted a makeshift representation of Nyssa Iudexas out of a trio of rope-lashed broom handles, some battered costume armour he'd found in the spider-infested storeroom beneath the stage, and a stolen *vahla* mask. It would never have passed muster in the formalised conclave circles where firebloods, guild masters and the like discussed weighty matters before the goddess' stone likeness. Not least because despite Tatterlain's best efforts – and to his great annoyance – no amount of rebalancing and retying could make Nyssa stand up entirely straight. Nyssa Collapses, Yali had named her, provoking a rare spark of ire from the unfortunate idol's creator.

Kat hoped the real Nyssa took no offence. Nyssa Benevolas – her gracious and forgiving aspect – would almost certainly have forgiven the impiety, but the stern Nyssa Iudexas, who judged the souls of the deceased and guided them to penance or rebirth as warranted . . . ? Little in scripture suggested she'd a sense of humour.

Tatterlain, still wearing overseer's uniform – sans mask – and sprawled across the chaise immediately to the right of Nyssa Collapses, hitched himself up onto one elbow and ran a hand through his tousled black hair. "Look who's still with us. And here I was wondering if you'd gone straight down the drain and out into the Silent Sea." He grinned, a man accustomed to harvesting smiles from the stoniest field.

Yali, legs tucked beneath her in an overstuffed and threadbare arm-chair opposite, rolled her eyes. ||You're lucky she's here at all.||

Though her words were directed at Tatterlain, Kat judged that Yali meant them just as much for herself. She bore mistakes badly, always trying to measure up – as she saw it – to Kat, who she'd long since adopted as her older sister. Kat knew the feeling all too well. She hoped that Yali grew out of it before it led her into trouble.

||"Well, if she's going to pick fights with custodians . . ."|| He signed as he spoke, as was polite around Yali, his speed nearer to hers than Kat's, though a series of unnecessary flourishes made them challenging to read. ||"I thought you'd taught her how to handle herself, Rîma?"||

Rîma alone spurned the use of a chair – she always did – and sat cross-legged on the floor, equidistant to the others on the circle's circumference. Hat and scarf were in abeyance, her long white hair a cold spill across her shoulders, but even in the humidity of the late afternoon she wore her duster coat, its tails draped across her knees and black linen wrappings showing beneath. Her scabbarded sword lay on the floorboards beside her, belt wrapped over and over around its length.

Kat had never really worked out why Rîma had accompanied her to Zariqaz – her manner didn't exactly encourage interrogation – she was simply grateful she had. Certainly, she admired Rîma – even envied her quiet certainty – but she'd never quite understood what the other woman took from her in return. Rîma had once spoken of the bonds between soulmates taking as many forms as the love that forged them. Perhaps it was that. Family wasn't blood alone.

||"And she's an apt pupil,"|| Rîma replied evenly, her workmanlike signing slow and precise – a perfect match for the calm, almost priestly tone with which she framed her thoughts. Most learned Simah at a young, malleable age, but Rîma's education had come much later in life – she was far older than the language. ||"Far better than some I might mention."||

Kat wasn't so certain. After six long months of tutelage, the gulf between her skills and Rîma's felt wider than ever. At the same time, she took pride in the knowledge that the swordstress was no longer going *quite* so easy on her.

Stepping into the circle, she claimed her own seat – a beaten-up rocking chair chosen because it reminded her of the one in which her father had passed long evenings reading by lumani light. "The real trick to winning a sword fight is having a sword to start with ... And *someone* assured me that he could keep the custodians distracted, didn't he?"

Tatterlain had the decency to look at least a little shamefaced. "I did my best. Unfortunately, fear of the Eternity King's unhappiness overcame the inimitable authority of Overseer Tuzen Karza."

Kat groaned. Tuzen Karza was the closest thing Tatterlain had to a real name, for he insisted on using it no matter what face he wore. And he wore a *lot* of faces, employing clay prosthetics, wigs and make-up with the accomplished flair of the most dedicated theatrical performer – even if his distinctive lantern jaw made such disguises challenging. Hiding behind an overseer's mask was the least of it. He was a chameleon in mood and manner.

Yali leaned forward. So the house *was* sealed at the Eternity King's order?

Tatterlain shrugged. "Who can say? For lowly custodians – and no overseer worth his pointy triangle would have trusted those two with anything more complicated than sentry duty – the mere possibility would be enough. Not a forgiving fellow, our good Caradan Diar. I take it you found your parcel, by the way?"

"I did," said Kat, readying the rehearsed lie. "I asked Maxin to pick over what was left of the Bascari library. Nothing worth the trouble. He sent me a fainting romance novel by way of a joke and apology. Any joy with the other book?"

"Ah." Sitting upright, Tatterlain produced Yarvid's battered book from beneath his robes and set it in his lap with the reverence of the bereaved siting a memorial pinwheel on a grave. "I did make something of a study. I think it's written in some kind of language."

The corner of Rîma's mouth twitched in what was for her an expressive smile. Yali covered her eyes with her hands.

Kat shook her head. "An expert speaks."

Tatterlain concealed his offence with all the massive dignity at his command. ||"Much as I admire your deep and abiding respect for my talents, I have my limits. The characters could be an obscure language, or even a purpose-crafted cipher. You should have seen the ones House Bascari used ten years back. Stare at them long enough and you'd get dizzy."||

Having made a brief study of the book herself while the boiler's jolly pyrasti ifrît had set about heating the bathwater, Kat sympathised. Aside from a few scribbled studies of Alabastran architecture, there'd been nothing to make sense of, just line after line of those jagged, line-hung letters.

||"May I see?"|| asked Rîma.

||"Whatever the lady wants."|| Tatterlain tossed the book.

Rîma caught it with the same fluid grace with which she accomplished everything. Removing the string noose that kept the book closed, she flicked through a handful of pages with a gloved finger.

||"It's Adumaric,"|| she said at last. ||"The characters, anyway."||

||"Adumaric. Of course it is."|| Tatterlain waved a triumphant finger, the picture of an absent-minded man seizing on a misplaced memory. With a rueful smile, he dropped his hands to his lap. ||"What's Adumaric?"||

"The priestly language of my people." Rîma turned the book over and over, her thoughtful frown as much a sign of her consternation as the fact that she'd forgotten to sign the reply. "I haven't heard it uttered aloud in centuries."

Kat's pulse quickened. Her eyes still on Rîma, she offered a Simah translation for Yali. All too easy to forget that Rîma was far older than anyone else in the room. Indeed, she wasn't even mortal – not in the ordinary way. ||"You can read it?"||

Khalad wasn't the first civilisation to have grown up around the shores of the Silent Sea. Though few historians admitted the fact – and the archons of Alabastra actively suppressed it – other realms had come and gone across the millennia. Most had vanished into history as mortal bodies dissipated in the Veil, but a handful endured – Hidden Cities, buried deep. One such place had exiled Rîma long ago. She had since walked the sunlit world for a hundred thousand years, her withered, deathless body increasingly held together by steel and splints beneath her linen grave clothes. While her flesh didn't falter, nor did it readily heal. Only her face retained an echo of youth, its striking, angular features kept ageless through the imbibement of last breath that was her only vice. A piece of self she preserved to remind herself who she was, where so many of her kin had forgotten everything they'd once been.

||"The characters, but not the words,"|| said Rîma. ||"It's incomprehensible."||

||So we're back to it being a code?|| asked Yali.

||" I can undertake a proper study. That may reveal something."|| Rîma glanced at Tatterlain. ||"Especially if other talents are loaned."||

He sniffed. ||"It's Saint Pennan's Masquerade tonight. I'd a mind to wander up-spire and relieve a fireblood darling of—"||

Kat rolled her eyes. ||"Spare us the details."||

He conjured a wounded expression. ||"I was going to say 'a few tetrams'. Or perhaps a valuable ring or two. The young and flighty are always desperate to help a fellow down on his luck, and there are few more down at heel than Count Tuzen Karza."||

||Or more handsome?|| put in Yali.

||"Alas, modesty forbids."|| He sighed. ||"But I suppose if my intellect's in demand . . ."||

Rîma shook her head. ||"It's unlikely that one evening of debauchery . . ."||

||"Hey!"||

||". . . will matter more or less. I'm offering only a possibility. It will take time to explore."||

Kat scowled, the familiar sense of doors slamming shut dissipating her good mood. ||"So the trail's cold? Perfect."||

||"Maybe not,"|| said Tatterlain, all business again. ||"We're not without contacts, or without *contacts* without contacts. I can copy one of the

pages and take a railrunner back to Tyzanta. Even if Marida can't make sense of it herself, she might know someone who can."||

Marida, like Rîma, belonged to an earlier age of the world, though Rîma at least had the decency to linger in her own flesh, however withered. Kat shook her head. ||"The more people who know we have it, the more likely that word will get back to whoever killed Yarvid. Whoever killed my father."|| There, she'd said it. She'd no way to be certain that it was true, but when following a trail marked by a dozen corpses, it was naïve to insist that the thirteenth death was unconnected. ||"I don't want to drag anyone else into this."||

||"Uh-uh."|| Tatterlain's signing grew expansive with disbelief. ||"Very noble. And the real reason?"||

That was the problem with having friends. Lying to them just cheapened you. ||"I don't want to be in debt to anyone, much less a daemonic crime lord."|| She already was, of course, and Marida wouldn't have cared to be described thus, but Marida wasn't there. ||"I want to do this alone."||

Tatterlain stared pointedly at Yali, then at Rîma. ||"You don't appear to be alone."||

True. And at moments like this, Kat hated it as much as she loved it. Hated even more that she couldn't bring herself to be honest with them. ||" I didn't ask for you to help. You offered."||

He gave a mournful shake of the head. ||"Such a beautifully broken soul. You'd make a fantastic muse for the right kind of fatalistic poet. What about Vallant?"||

||"What about him?"||

||"He has contacts all across the east. With the Qersali, the Kaldosi – even the veilkin. Or don't you trust him?"||

Kat was the first to admit that her relationship with Bashar Vallant was complicated. A hero to the masses though he undoubtedly was – and well earned, for he'd fought for their freedom across two decades against horrific odds – ten minutes spent in his company and she invariably wanted to slap that earnest, empathic expression off his face.

||"He has more important things to deal with."||

Her deflection held truth. Ever since the Battle of Athenoch six months before, Vallant's dream of freeing the cinderblood masses from the tyranny of venal firebloods – and maybe even the Eternity King – lay closer than ever. The city of Tyzanta, once the easternmost jewel in Caradan Diar's crown, now answered to a citizen triad of Vallant, Marida and the qalimîri's fellow crime lord, Ardin Javar.

Neighbouring cities had initially remained studiously neutral – their masters not wishing the bleak fate of Tyzanta's ruling House Bascari to become theirs. However, Vallant's daring capture of the shipyards at Azran had convinced Naxos, Sumarand and Azzarin to throw their enthusiastic support behind him, gambling that they'd more to gain by siding with the infamous rebel than from backing the throne immortal. Though the zol'tayah of conquered Qersal remained loyal to the Eternity King, her people were less sanguine, and rumours abounded that Kaldos – which hadn't been a separate realm for centuries – now scented opportunity in the winds. For the first time in millennia, Khalad was truly a realm divided. Not bad given that six months earlier Vallant had been little more than a carefully managed nuisance.

And against all expectation, the Eternity King's legions . . . had done nothing. But reprisals were coming. They had to be. If Vallant had any hope of riding out the storm, he'd need to be ready.

Rîma cocked her head, precursor to a polite lecture. ||"Vallant knows what he owes you."|| Victory at Athenoch, for one thing. The short, sharp kick to the head that had snapped him out of his own legend and into reality for another. ||"He stands by his friends."||

||"Until he gets them killed,"|| Kat replied stiffly.

The circle fell silent, the atmosphere suddenly taut. Proof positive that Vallant wasn't good for her, or she for him. Whenever he came up in conversation, she always wound herself so tight her bones creaked. Vallant's flame burned hottest in the bodies of those around him. They all knew it, especially Rîma, who'd known him longer than anyone.

Better to be his friend at a distance than close to.

65

||It's too nice a day to dwell on that,|| signed Yali, her expression shot through with the forced humour of someone desperate to lighten the mood. ||I'm picturing what will happen when Zephyr finds out Tatterlain's been using the word *veilkin*.||

Tatterlain sniffed. ||"Zephyr adores me."||

Veilkin wasn't a slur, not exactly, but over the centuries it had become a lazy shorthand for Zephyr's people, the Issnaîm.

||"She'll bat you around like a cat with a dead mouse,"|| said Rîma. ||"It is perhaps not overstating things to say that you will beg for death."||

||"What can I say? Love's complicated."||

Yali bobbed her head from side to side, teeth gleaming briefly as she chewed thoughtfully on her lower lip. When she at last began signing, she did so hesitantly. Her attention, normally divided between those to whom she was speaking, was given over entirely to an unremarkable patch of the stage's scuffed planking. ||I'll say it if no one else will ... We need to consider that your father might have been involved with the Obsidium Cult.||

Depending on who you asked, the Obsidium Cult were either a shadowy brotherhood ruling Khalad from the shadows, a cabal worshipping the heretical third face of Nyssa, or merely a paranoid dream. Officialdom made no acknowledgement of its existence even as it executed those suspected of involvement with it. Alabastra's archons occasionally flirted with the possibility, their long-winded sermons alluding to apostate subversives hiding amongst the goddess-fearing populace. Dead languages, ancient secrets, the heretical spirit-binding practices of which Kat herself was living proof ... Her father's interests, and the Obsidium Cult's as well. Hard to accept, but harder to deny.

||"It's possible,"|| she said slowly.

Tatterlain nodded, serious for the first time. ||"If it is the Obsidium Cult, we've treacherous sands underfoot. And after today's escapades ... well, we've probably drawn their attention."||

||"If we hadn't before."||

66

He nodded again, unhappily. ||"Perhaps you're right to not want anyone else involved. It's safer ... for us, and for them."||

The stage's oppressive shadows grew longer. For years, Kat had assumed that Count Hargo Rashace had ordered her father's murder in a fit of jealousy over his wife's infidelity, but everything she'd seen since returning to Zariqaz made it more and more likely that he'd died because of the Obsidium Cult – whether because he'd been a part of it, had refused to join, or had simply been in their way. They hadn't even left her a body to mourn – or rather, Alabastra hadn't. They'd spirited the corpse away to the shriversmen so that the lingering soul could be sliced into talent wisps even before sending word to Kat's small cottage on the Rashace estate.

Kat stared down at her left wrist. Though her sleeve covered the pale, burn-scarred lines of her aetherios tattoo, she felt it all the same – the itch that never really faded, the warning of a spasm to come. Giving up meant not only abandoning hope of helping Tanith – were she still alive – but of saving her own life.

||"I have to keep trying,"|| she said. ||"I'll understand if any of you feel differently."||

||I'm not going anywhere,|| said Yali. ||I just want us to do this eyes open, honest and true.||

Tatterlain nodded. ||"What she said."||

Rîma twitched an almost-smile. ||"You have your answer. Take it, and be content."||

Kat dipped her head, a hand covering an expression that couldn't decide if it was a grin or a frown. Stars Below, how she loved them at that moment. How she hated them for putting their lives in her hands. But that was the problem with life: you were either part of it – and people were part of it with you – or you were alone. And she had learned the hard way that she wasn't good on her own. But if she couldn't bring herself to share the truth, was she truly otherwise?

||"Thank you,"|| she murmured.

||"So, what of our next move?"|| asked Rîma.

What indeed? "I'll think about Vallant ... and the others. Just ... just see what you can get out of that book."

Rîma inclined her head. "And for you? Idleness doesn't suit you."

What indeed? Their funds were healthy enough, but that wasn't to say it would do any harm to replenish them with a little discreet burglary. However, open acknowledgement of the Obsidium Cult's involvement had left her yearning for progress more than ever.

One last possibility to explore. One she'd spent six months avoiding. But she'd never have a better opportunity than on the night of Saint Pennan's Masquerade.

She fixed a suspicious Tatterlain with her most disarming smile. "Actually, I was hoping that Count Karza might accompany me to a ball."

Eight

"You look lost," called a voice from the shadows.

Tanith quashed a flash of annoyance and drew up short. At least the words hadn't been tinged with mockery. They might even have held concern.

Fancy that.

And she *was* lost. At least a little. She was well used to navigating Underways – the catacombic tangle of buried streets, collapsed dwellings and spire-fall rubble that served as the ever-growing foundation of any city. However, the run of passageways and chambers that constituted this particular part of Ardoc's haven –*stronghold* would have been too grandiose a word – defied her sense of direction.

It wasn't that there weren't landmarks. A statue projecting from a spill of rubble here, an ornate lintel projecting crosswise from a gaping wall there. Graffiti etched into stone and mud-brick, the ancient letters still legible in the dull green lichen-light glow. Even the smells shifted, the dry dust of long-forgotten passageways yielding to the bitterness of stagnant water or seeping sewage. The individual components were readable enough; it was in the assembly that everything fell apart, a blurry mishmash of half-remembered images and growing doubts.

Forcing a neutral expression – though it was doubtful that nuance of brow and lip would carry in gloom that smothered the light from her lumani lantern – she turned about.

There he was, shoulder propped against a column into which some long-dead mason had graven images of dancing ilfri. An invitation to the thieving ifrîti, or a protective ward for a now-forsaken home? The past had never much interested Tanith.

He was a boyish, copper-skinned young man whose wavy dark brown hair brushed at the collar of his robes. Perhaps a year or two Tanith's junior, and short enough – he was no taller than she – to remain untroubled by the passageway's low, uneven ceiling. He wore a form of skelder's garb common among Ardoc's followers, the short tunic and scuffed jacket nondescript enough to draw little attention. He'd no lantern of his own, which meant he'd come all this way with only the lichen-light to guide him.

His posture was stiffer than it had appeared at first, suggesting he expended entirely too much effort on his effortless nonchalance. A boy desperately masquerading as a man. He'd respond better to vulnerability than to strength, and with her golden hair finally grown out to shoulder length – impossibly fast by ordinary standards, but it still felt as though it had taken an age – pretending innocence was simplicity itself.

Tanith drew inwards, her shoulders drooping. A lost lamb, stumbling towards a wolf's den and in need of rescue. "I am ... but only a little."

"It's the tsrûqi." He stared off over her shoulder. "They're everywhere down here. They play havoc with perception."

She stifled a shiver. "I didn't think I'd come so deep."

"This hasn't been ground level for thousands of years. Nothing here but stray wisps and lost souls."

Tsrûqi were among the first fragments of soul to escape the dying. While the buoyant, delicate last breath dissipated without a body to contain it, a tsrûqi – weighted down by the deceased's sins – sank deeper and deeper into the ground until at last it reached Nyssa's Obsidium Palace in the Stars Below. Some never even made it that far, becoming trapped in the city's foundations, their frustration boiling outwards to distort the perception of those who strayed close, jumbling sensory input until the victim staggered out of range, or collapsed in a drooling, broken-minded mess.

Just one of many reasons why a city's Underways were best avoided, and what made them the perfect hiding place for people who didn't want to be found.

"I'll be more careful next time." Tanith cast ruefully about. Three passages fed the crossway, and she was *almost* certain she knew by which she'd entered. "Assuming I can find my way out."

It would be a long journey back up at the best of times, scrambling over rubble spills and subsided stairways, even before reaching the pulley-drawn elevators that would bring her back to the heart of the haven.

He pushed away from the wall and offered her a smile. A nice smile, but that wasn't especially surprising. Men smiled at her all the time if she wanted them to. Still, this particular smile was refreshingly lacking in need, and warmed a part of Tanith that seldom felt the sun.

"It's that way." He nodded at a threshold thick with calcified stalactites.

Tanith transmuted a scowl of irritation into something prettier. "You're sure? You wouldn't be trying to lead me astray?"

He blushed, though she'd barely bothered to spice the words with suggestion. Not much. Barely enough to be visible, but enough to prompt her to recast the roles of lamb and wolf. Some folk shouldn't be let out alone.

"I've been coming down here for weeks. The tsrûqi don't bother me as much as they used to." He winced. "Not out here, anyway . . . I haven't seen you before, I don't think."

"That's fair, because I've not seen *you* before."

He blinked, his smooth cheeks taut. "I didn't mean to offend."

Tanith felt like she'd just kicked a puppy. He *really* wanted to be liked. The question was whether to relent or kick him again. But . . . in the three months since she'd plunged from the Deadwinds and

71

followed Ardoc into the Underways, the boy was the first of her new-found "family" who'd shown any interest in straying beyond the bright lights of the haven's halls. It was agreeable to find common cause. More agreeable still to find someone her own age.

And he *did* have a nice smile.

"You're forgiven," she replied mock-primly, and flashed a smile of her own. "I'm Tanith."

"Esram." He frowned. "Ardoc must have warned you … about the tsrûqi, I mean."

"He only told me that the depths were dangerous."

"But you came down here anyway?"

"I don't like being told what to do." Long experience had taught her that she was seldom warned off from things for her own good, but it seemed that Ardoc had genuinely sought to protect her from the tsrûqi. That was disappointing – she'd hoped for grand secrets waiting to be uncovered. But it was also reassuring, at least in part. In three months, Ardoc had never once strayed from his word. He'd provided shelter, coin and, more importantly – more insidiously – understanding. "But I *do* like exploring. Especially forgotten, abandoned places like this. They're full of mystery and romance, and I—"

She caught herself before she blurted out the rest. Kaldos was shot through with abandoned aqueducts, tunnels and roadways – enough to honeycomb the mountains. Wandering them, she'd imagined worlds beyond counting behind every turning, every collapsed passageway. Palaces and gardens buried deep. Great arched roadways winding down beneath the mountains and into the Stars Below. A wealth of adventure, just waiting for her.

But fantasies aside, abandoned places were safer. Solitude was sanctuary, but it would hardly be wise to say as much to Esram. If he hadn't known her name, he certainly didn't know *what* she was. It was nice to hold a conversation unframed by need. More than nice. In the darkness she could be anyone … any*thing*.

In any case, she was talking too much. "Why are *you* down here?"

"Maybe I don't like being told what to do either." The defiance in Esram's expression didn't suit him, but it soon passed, so Tanith forgave him. "I'm like you. I think it's wonderful down here. There's so much to learn."

She narrowed her eyes. "Learn?"

"Oh yes." He nodded energetically. Picking his way down a steep rubble crest, he beckoned for her to follow. "Take a look at this."

"I really should be getting back." Ardoc had spoken of wanting her at conclave that evening, and one of the many challenges of living largely underground was marking the passage of time.

And yet Tanith found herself following, swept up by Esram's enthusiasm. How long had it been since *that* had happened? She crouched shoulder-to-shoulder beside him as he ran his fingers across a stone panel, half buried by the detritus of centuries, prompting a swarm of dark, iridescent beetles to click with outrage and scurry from sight. Smooth grey-white stone rather than the adobe and sandstone that dominated the rest of the chamber. Bas-relief sculpture depicted an armoured woman with feathered wings standing beneath a starlit sky dominated by a single, perfect disc. The disc glimmered like silver as the light from Tanith's lantern touched it; the woman's armour was a dull red-gold.

"I found it a few days ago." Esram's voice gained confidence. "There are others scattered all through here. More of the stone as well. Imagine what we'd see if we could split the spire open – all of history laid out at a glance. Nyssa's truth is here. If only we could read it."

"It's just stone, Esram. It doesn't care about truth."

"No! Men and women shaped the stone. They gave it purpose and form. Everything that happens does so because Nyssa willed it. If we are faithful to the goddess, our every action *reveals* the goddess. On the surface, wind and rain wash those proofs away, but down here? Here, the past endures. Waiting to be understood."

His eyes shone. More than his eyes. A face Tanith had dismissed as unremarkable came alive, and in so doing was unremarkable no longer.

73

Esram would never be handsome, not even when he finally grew into his hooded eyes and patrician nose, but his new-found fervency set his soul soaring, the pressure of it – of a formidable will she'd never have guessed existed beneath his meek, unconfident exterior – stifling the giggle gathering on her lips.

For a fleeting moment, she wondered what it might take to have him regard her the same way he looked at the ancient, filthy stone. "You really believe that, don't you?"

"Touch it."

"I beg your pardon?"

"Trust me."

Too prideful to risk losing face, Tanith laid an experimental fingertip on the sculpted details, then the flat of her palm. Nothing. She glanced at him, her eyes briefly meeting his before he glanced guiltily away.

Her hand touched the silvered disc.

It was cold. Not cool as the Underways were cool, but cold as a river beneath the night sky. The shock of it shot up her arm and stole her breath. She snatched back her hand and glared at Esram. "Trust me, you said."

"Try again."

"Try again? You must think I'm—"

"Please." Again, that wonderful, warming smile did its wicked work. "It's easier the second time."

Tanith laid her hand on the disc once more.

It wasn't cold any longer. It wasn't *anything*. No, that wasn't quite right. She had the strangest of sensations, as though the piece of her that was mortal, or perhaps the piece that was amashti – though she seldom admitted it even in her own mind, Tanith could never be certain if she were a woman bound to a daemon or a daemon desperately hoping it was really the woman it had long ago devoured – was drifting away from the rest.

"Esram . . . ?" Was that really her voice? So small, so *scared*.

The lumani light flickered and grew dark. For the briefest of moments, Tanith was alone. A little girl once more, shuddering in the darkness beneath the roots of the world.

She felt a presence at her shoulder. A tall, magisterial woman of incandescent indigo fire, silver shackles gleaming around her wrists, and about whose brow swirled a thousand wisps of fading light. In the moment Tanith beheld the goddess, she beheld herself also through Nyssa's eyes. A spark only before the flame, but cherished. Loved. Wanted. Adored. She reached out her hand – Nyssa's hand – to comfort the shivering mote.

Cold metal dug into her wrist. The darkness abated, taking the goddess and her chorus of souls with it. Tanith, whole again, for better or worse, found herself in the cool darkness of the crossway, the lumani lantern flickering ever lower as its ifrît dissipated.

"You saw her, didn't you?" asked Esram breathlessly, his rapturous eyes inches from hers. "Everybody does. Everybody worthy."

Tanith blinked away the after-images. Already the vision was fading from memory, muddled light and darkness, undercut by a loss so profound that it hurt.

"She was in chains. I ..." She swallowed and gingerly touched the silver disc a third time. Nothing. "What *was* that?"

"Truth. Truth so perfect we can only contain it for a moment." He smiled with only a hint of I-told-you-so. "Truth sealed in stone."

She lifted her eyes to his. Though they were practically nose-to-nose, Esram felt impossibly far away. Everything did in the vision's aftermath. As if she were smaller or the world larger. Larger, and colder. As if the stone had stolen a piece of her ... or perhaps had revealed a void within her that she'd theretofore never known existed.

Tanith wasn't sure when she'd chosen to kiss him. Probably from that first endearing smile, but now it was more that she needed Esram's warmth to replace that which the stone had stolen. To feel like the part of her it had left in the cold, grey darkness was a part still alive.

Her daemon-half slithered awake and reminded her that it too had needs – that the old man in the Hazarid townhouse had been too faded

75

and dissolute to offer anything more than a brief respite. It scented the lavender aroma of Esram's young, vital soul, filled with vigour and garnished with sweet piety. A delectable feast, and no witnesses.

Tanith's pulse quickened, the daemon's hunger becoming her own. She gripped Esram's wrists as he tried to pull away. Her lips brushed his.

No shortage of hiding places in the Underways. His body would never be found.

No one would know.

She'd know. And she'd never see that wonderful smile again.

No. She wasn't going to do this. Not on her daemon-half's terms. Esram promised the possibility of being something more than a meal.

And if he wasn't, there was always tomorrow.

She drew back, the wispy scent of his soul tantalising in her nostrils. Her daemon-half hissed its unhappiness, but wasn't yet hungry enough to force the issue. A piece of her joined it in lamenting missed opportunity. The rest revelled in the small triumph of abstinence, and in that triumph found warmth to fill the emptiness the vision had provoked.

Tanith released Esram's wrists and clambered to her feet, leaving him confused but very much alive.

"I'm sorry," she whispered. "But I really *should* be getting back."

Nine

Tanith arrived in the haven's central square just as the chimes of the ornate brass guild master's clock struck six.

Barely on time, which meant she was late.

She winced away unaccustomed remorse. Disappointing Ardoc always left an unhappy brew burbling. She resented the feeling for the weakness it was. Ardoc had given her so much – not least a home and understanding – but it wouldn't last for ever.

Or maybe it would. The warmth of her recent vision still aglow in her mind, Tanith for the first time entertained the possibility that Ardoc's claims of a new Age of Fire and Khalad's rebirth might not be fantasy. That alone swayed her to a detour via her modest bedchamber, in truth little more than four bare walls and a tiled floor in the row of lopsided, overbuilt townhouses. There, she brushed out her hair and exchanged her cavern-stained skelder's garb in favour of the expensive silken gown she'd purchased in the Marajî azasouk. That would mollify him. He liked folk to look their best for conclave.

Even further behind than before, she broke into a semi-dignified run through the buried, lumani-lit streets, drawing curious glances from those she passed. People were always coming and going from the haven. Some had lives on Zariqaz's surface and journeyed below only to deliver reports or supplies. Most of the permanent residents came and went only under the strictest supervision, their access to the surface controlled by the array of ever-vigilant hestics who watched over the concealed doors leading from the Underways proper into the haven itself. Trust was a limited commodity. Its lack kept the haven safe.

In the unlikely event an intruder *did* find a way into the haven, there were still the blackmasked and white-robed kathari guards and slumbering koilos sentries to contend with. Koilos were supposed to be unique to Alabastra, but Ardoc had access to many things he should not.

Take the haven itself, its six uneven, canted streets buried by a spire-fall centuries before. Undertaking the engineering works to isolate the haven from the wider Underways and strengthen the struggling sandstone pillars holding the stalactite-forested roof at bay – in secret, no less – meant a long trail of influence, bribery and bodies.

A pair of kathari stood aside as she climbed the double-helix staircase to the lodge door. They knew her by reputation. Gowned and glittering in the lumani-light, she could hardly be mistaken. Golden hair was rare and, so far as Tanith knew, otherwise non-existent among Ardoc's followers. Not that a mere two kathari could have kept her out. Recruited and trained to serve as the haven's private army, and much like the custodians they mimicked, kathari were more impressive in appearance than ability. But they were loyal, and they *believed*.

She passed through the outer chambers and their weathered, soot-darkened finery – the spoils of what Ardoc was pleased to call *equitable liberation* from fireblood estates and Alabastran temples. A final set of doors – and another pair of kathari, this time with a silent, malevolent koilos slumbering, arms folded across its chest, in an alcove behind them – and she reached the conclave hall. Suppressing a shudder at the koilos' proximity – more for the bitter hollowness of its ifrît than the baleful stare emanating from its empty-eyed, scrimshawed skull – she pushed the doors open and passed inside.

Three men and one woman waited in the circle of light, all in variations of simple black robes. It was the only natural light in the haven's cavern, brought deep underground by an array of mirrors in inlets and tunnels high above. The remainder of the room lay in utter darkness, necessitating a measured advance across a floor some ten degrees off horizontal, and missing more than a handful of its oxblood tiles.

The conclave wasn't a council as such. Ardoc's voice held sole sway, but he valued the opinions of those around him ... or at least enjoyed playing court. Nor was there a statue of Nyssa in the circle. Such statues were Alabastran conceit, traditionally believed to carry words spoken at conclave to Caradan Diar's ears – something that would only have been counterproductive here.

Ardoc broke off from conversation with the cadaverous copper-skinned man to his right. "Ah, here she is, forever yearning to be the centre of attention through fashionable lateness." He shook his head. "But at least you've dressed for the occasion."

Tanith took a place opposite in the circle. "I'm sorry, Ardoc. I lost track of time."

"I still don't understand why she's even here." The cadaverous man's expression contrived disdain even in stillness. Though reasonably young – barely a hint of grey touched his neatly trimmed hair – he carried himself with the stiffness of age. His earthy, flat-vowelled speech held an accent that was pure Zariqaz Undertown. He'd resented Tanith from the first. Or rather, he'd resented Ardoc's fondness for her.

Ardoc sighed. "Please, Qolda, we've been over this. Tanith is essential to the goddess' designs."

"Easier to believe if you'd tell us why," said Enna, the only other woman in the circle. The white streak in otherwise pitch-black hair hinted at middle age, as did her damnable confidence, but her voice – in character similar to Tanith's own guttural Kaldosi accent – lacked that texture. She was willowy rather than slender, giving the impression that a simple gust might carry her off, never to be seen again. She was also pale of skin, but not as Tanith was pale, lacking even the slightest flush to her cheeks. Her blue eyes missed nothing, and Tanith had yet to find anyone in the haven who'd any affection for her.

Ardoc shrugged. "All will become clear in time."

That was pretty much the same phrase he used whenever Tanith broached the subject. Like Enna, she'd yet to receive an answer worthy of the name.

Serrîq, the final member of the circle, offered a thin smile. A tanned, white-haired fellow approaching dotage, and about whom the musky jasmine scent of Alabastran incense invariably clung, he had a ready smile, though it tended towards the cold and knowing. "Your delight in mystery will be your undoing. Perhaps it's you who yearns to forever be the centre of attention."

"Perhaps, so," Ardoc replied. "But what you mistake for theatricality is simple precaution. I survived Nazaric's purges by being careful. That care guides me now. Trust me a little longer."

"Of course, Ardoc," said Enna. "No one's questioning you."

He chuckled. "Yes, you are. You'd hardly be useful to the goddess if you weren't given to questions. You'd still be bowing and scraping to the Eternity King and mouthing Alabastra's simplistic devotions. But there is a time for questions and a time for action. With the conjunction almost upon us, questions will only prove distracting. And speaking of the conjunction . . . I assume the heavens continue to arrange themselves in a satisfactory manner?"

Enna's lips thinned to a bloodless slash. "You know they do. They will align on the Descension of Saint Marindra, mere weeks from now."

"Excellent. Most excellent." Ardoc paced counterclockwise around the circle's grey boundary of light and shadow, his bonhomie unable to disguise anticipation. "The goddess' cage weakens for the first time in a thousand years. We must be ready. We *will* be ready. *Abdon Nyssa ivohê.*"

"*Abdon Nyssa ivohê,*" Tanith murmured along with the others, for the first time imbuing the ancient Adumaric avowal of faith – literally "as Nyssa wills it" when translated into Daric – with genuine emotion. Difficult to resist the ritual and pomp of conclave when she'd beheld the shackled goddess.

Ardoc laid his hands upon her shoulders. Still lost in reverie, she

80

almost jumped out of her skin. "As to Tanith, do any of you truly question her aptness to the cause? She's remarkable."

The praise, its like so rarely received before the Obsidium Cult had embraced her, warmed the cockles of Tanith's heart. She already *knew* she was remarkable, of course, but it didn't hurt to hear someone else say so. Especially to hear Ardoc say so.

She'd killed for him so often since the night he'd embraced her in the old temple. Not just helpless old men and women who'd died with barely a struggle, but custodians, Undertown enforcers and onlookers who'd seen more than they should. She felt no guilt. Aptitude for murder was a Nyssa-given gift. Its practice – like any such skill – was therefore an act of worship. Yes, it was a sorrow for those she killed, but their souls would see reincarnation in time, according to the balance of their sins. If her victims had known that she had it within her gift to extinguish them entirely, removing them for ever from the cycle of death and rebirth, they might even have been grateful for her mercy.

"She has been an inspiration in tidying up loose ends," Ardoc continued, steel beneath his words. "*Your* loose ends, Serrîq."

Serrîq scowled, his eyes downcast.

"I offered to wipe those particular steps clean many times," said Qolda. "Or don't you think my kathari are up to the task of silencing a handful of scholars?"

Ardoc's hands slipped away. "Oh, I surrender to no one in my admiration for the work you've done training our little army, but they are perhaps too blunt an instrument for such things."

Qolda bristled, his finger stabbing at Ardoc across the circle. "That's unfair."

"Is it really?" The steel faded from Ardoc's voice until he was once again the amiable uncle, offering sage advice. "Need we again discuss your 'quiet removal' of dear Elnatha, a year ago almost to this very day?"

"She was going to tell the Voice everything. You were unavailable, I had to act."

"You turned half of the Hazarid district into a battleground!" Ardoc

81

snapped, his curtness a thunderbolt. "But for Enna's quick thinking, the redcloaks would have traced Elnatha's blood trail right to our door. That kind of subtlety we can well do without."

Qolda flinched. The corner of Enna's mouth curled in quiet satisfaction. Tanith listened with rapt attention. Almost from the first, she'd noted the rivalry crackling between Qolda and Enna, though she'd never known the cause – beyond the obvious fact that Ardoc wouldn't live for ever, and only one could inherit his mantle. Now she had part of an answer.

Ardoc sighed. "Alas, speaking of subtlety … Even the remarkable can disappoint."

Tanith's blood ran cold. "I don't understand."

Except she did. She'd simply hoped her transgression would go unnoticed.

Serrîq stirred, his smile now wintry. "When the shriversmen came for Yarvid, the lack of any trace of soul clinging to his corpse did not go unnoticed. It cuts into their profits if they can't harvest even a single wisp. Rumour is spreading. I understand that the street nymphs are *very* nervous." Courtesans were inevitable suspects when an amashti was on the prowl. "Last night, one almost came to Nyssa's judgement before her time. A drunken would-be customer tipped her into the reservoir to see if she was weighted down by a soul."

Tanith fidgeted, all eyes in the circle upon her. "I had no choice. I was starving, you know that!"

And it was all her own fault, for having gone too long without prowling the shanty slum of Zariqaz's Gutterfields for someone who wouldn't be missed. Worse, Yarvid's thin soul had offered almost nothing in the way of sustenance. A day or two, and she'd have to feed again. She'd only last that long by fighting her daemon-half every hour of the day, as her encounter with Esram had proven.

Ardoc's gaze bored into the base of her skull. "If you're hungry, I'll see that you're fed. But you must be disciplined, or all of this will be for nothing."

The Tanith of a year ago would never have submitted. The Tanith of three months prior, freshly reeling from her Deadwinds rebirth, would have stalked from the circle, safe in the knowledge that she'd only ever planned to stay in the haven long enough to catch her breath. But that evening, beneath the timeless, gilded ceiling of the forgotten guild master's hall, she bit her tongue. Not just because Ardoc's disappointment stung as no anger could, but because she knew her best chance of glimpsing the goddess again was to remain in the haven.

"I'm sorry," she said in a small voice, and begged him silently not to demand that she repeat it with greater conviction. "It won't happen again."

Ardoc squeezed her shoulder and stepped into the circle, his arms spread wide. "You see? She understands. She's humble before the goddess. As should be we all." His gaze touched on both Qolda and Enna. "We live in a time of wonder. The first portent came to pass when the Veil parted and returned Athenoch to the world. The second, when Nyssa sent Tanith to us. It's more vital than ever that we move as one."

He let the words hang on the air, inviting challenge. When none came, he looped his arms behind his back. "Now, to other business. How is our good friend Hierarch Ossed?"

"Anticipating his descension to the Qabirarchi Council," said Serrîq. "If Enna's calculations are correct, he'll have time to make a contribution to their . . . labours before the conjunction."

Ardoc echoed Serrîq's smile with one of his own. "He's been a useful ally over the years. I hope he finds his reward for ever singing Nyssa's praises everything he wished . . . And you, Qolda? How are things in the Golden Citadel?"

"Three redcloak *gansalar* commanders have seen Nyssa's true flame. A fourth demands tetrams to buttress his faith."

"Then pay him," said Enna.

"The man's a jackal. I doubt there's any sum that will bind him."

Ardoc grunted. "Now, that does change things. Are his juniors of a more spiritual bent?"

"One in particular," Qolda replied. "She's already one of us."

"Then Nyssa provides us with a solution. Tanith will attend to our avaricious friend. Hierarchy will do the rest."

Qolda scowled. "But—"

"I said Tanith will attend to him. Don't make me repeat myself." He turned to Tanith. "Tomorrow night, I think. Leave no trace, and you have my permission to indulge yourself."

Tanith's pulse quickened in that familiar, hated way. His doting smile had left no room for misunderstanding. "Thank you."

"Serrîq, what of the Voice's schedule?" asked Ardoc.

"Her principal scribe insists she'll return to Zariqaz within days," he replied. "A lengthy tour of the eastern cities that remain loyal, the better to keep Vallant at bay."

"Seeing which are prepared to throw their support behind a campaign?"

"Most likely."

"Do we know how that will play out?"

"I can make enquiries. The answers may be some time in arriving. Our initiates in the east have a tendency to die in unusual circumstances. I suspect the qalimîri is to blame."

"Ah, Marida. Ever the thorn in my side."

"You should let me eliminate her," growled Qolda.

"Better than you have tried. But by all means send your kathari. Someone is bound to learn a valuable lesson, but I'll wager it won't be Marida." Ardoc shrugged. "In any case, it's entirely of academic interest. A month from now, she'll come grovelling for Nyssa's forgiveness."

"Assuming these portents of yours are all you take them to be," said Enna.

The circle went silent with the frisson of a rule transgressed. Tanith shuddered despite herself. Serrîq and Qolda shared a wary glance. Enna's left eye twitched, as if she realised too late the consequences of her words.

Only Ardoc didn't seem to notice. "Assuming that, yes. But you're quite correct, of course, and practical as ever. We shouldn't let portentous times distract us. You may of course continue with your work with the downtrodden."

Enna inclined her head in acknowledgement. "Thank you."

The objection, inevitably, came from Qolda. "We're about to go to war with the Eternity King, and you waste our resources feeding beggars?"

"Nyssa Benevolas may be an Alabastran construct, but her nature remains a part of the true goddess," said Enna sweetly. "Charity is more than kindness. It is duty."

So it always went between Qolda and Enna, he brash and intemperate, she deflecting his aggression with a duellist's skill. And, as with the finest duellists, offering a smile to boot.

"And it makes for a fine method of recruitment," added Serrîq.

"Indeed it does," said Ardoc, shaking his head. "Now, if you're all quite done questioning my leadership, was there anything else?"

There was, but Tanith's attention – never generous when others were talking – proved insufficient to keep her anchored in the minutiae. Her thoughts, when they were not on the goddess, returned unbidden to Esram. Should she seek him out after the conclave ended? No. Better to wait for the day after tomorrow, after she'd feasted on the avaricious redcloak commander and would thus be as close to herself as she'd ever be. That seemed important, somehow.

Eventually the lodge's clock struck for eight. What anyone made of the tolling beyond the haven's bounds was anyone's guess. But as Tanith herself had lately discovered, there were stranger things in the Underways than phantom chimes, even if they could be sifted from the clocks striking in the spire above. There was always something under your feet in Zariqaz. Besides, the shim-heads, wisp addicts and cut-throats who laired in the Underways couldn't be rightly counted as reliable witnesses. Thus the chimes went as unnoticed as the smoke from the pyrasti hearth fires that crept upwards through fissures and vents.

Ardoc clapped his hands. "I think that concludes matters . . . Tanith, I wonder if you'd spare an old man the pleasure of your company?"

As the others departed, Tanith followed Ardoc up the misaligned steps to the simple chamber serving as his quarters. Save for a table groaning beneath a pile of books, and an empty circular window overlooking the conclave hall, the room had little to recommend it over her own.

Gesturing for her to take a seat, he took a slender-necked bottle and two worn wooden goblets from a shelf. "Calvasîr? I find it keeps out the chill. Tonight promises to be a cold one."

In point of fact, in the haven – as in the wider Underways – the temperature seldom changed, but Ardoc was a man full to the brim with foibles.

"A little." Liquor quieted her daemon-half, at least for a time. She readily took the proffered goblet and savoured the musky aroma, the bitterness of the akra leaves leavened by sweet apple.

"Enna has asked for your assistance."

Tanith frowned. "Enna hates me."

Ardoc chuckled. "Ah, but they all hate you."

"Because I'm a daemon."

"Daemon is a word to frame fear. Don't let it shape your self-perception." He shook his head. "No, they hate you because you're young."

He sank into a chair opposite. In the brief time Tanith had known him, he'd grown noticeably frailer, vigorous, melodic speech and bombastic manner concealing advancing age. "When the Age of Fire comes and the world turns, you'll stand tall in what follows. Qolda and the rest belong to this age." He shrugged ruefully. "Just like these old bones. Jealousy is a terrible thing. Especially when it is so misplaced. When the goddess is finally free, we'll look back upon these days and marvel that folk could be so selfish."

"What should I do?"

He waved a dismissive hand. "All that mumbo-jumbo about

86

prophecies and portents will keep them content, but it's going to go very hard with me if Nyssa's been playing me for a fool." He crooked an eyebrow. "You still don't believe that the goddess speaks to me, do you?"

"I ..." Tanith lowered her goblet. Pride made confessions hard at the best of times. With her daemon-half still restless, it was more challenging than ever.

Ardoc leaned forward, brow furrowed. "What is it?"

Kiasta, why was this so difficult? "I ... I've seen her myself."

She recounted her experience in the depths as best she could, which to her own ears wasn't very well at all, weaving a story full of stutters and gaps.

Ardoc waited until she'd petered out, then nodded. "Ah, Esram. I have great hopes for him, if only he can focus on the moment in which he stands and not the past. He has much to learn."

Was he warning her off pursuing ... whatever it was she was considering pursuing with Esram? Ardoc had a knack for using a great many words to say nothing at all and a mere handful to imply a great many things. "What are you saying?"

"Saying? I'm just thinking aloud, that's all." He brandished his goblet absent-mindedly. "I find words take firmer purchase when aired. But you've seen the goddess. I knew you would, if you opened yourself to her."

"I might have seen her before." Now the words came firmer and faster, the nervousness dispelled by his approval. "In the Deadwinds. When I ..."

When she what? Died? She couldn't bring herself to speak the word.

"When I was in the Deadwinds," she finished. "Why did you bring me here, Ardoc? If I'm her herald, shouldn't I know?"

He rubbed at his beard. "If I tell you, it needs to stay between us. Not a word to the others."

As if she'd tell them anything she didn't have to. "If that's what you want."

"It's what *Nyssa* wants. But where to start? Where to start?" He

87

shook his head slowly. "The vision, as is the nature of these things, is more metaphor than truth. Nyssa is chained, yes. Not by silver. She is chained with souls."

Tanith narrowed her eyes, uncertain if he was speaking truth, even now. "Souls?"

"Of course. The Eternity King siphons their power to his own purpose. But Nyssa's creation – this world and everything within it – knows it is misused. The world trembles with the pain of it. The outrage. The fabric of reality decays. The Veil is the result of that decay. The faster it spreads, the faster our world falls apart."

"But ... the Eternity King holds the Veil at bay ..."

"So he would have you believe. He's had millennia to distort the truth. It courses like poison through the bloodstream of our history." He leaned forward, his ordinarily laid-back voice insistent. "Your father made you a perfect conduit for the very soulfire that Caradan Diar plunders. When the stars align and the Deadwinds falter, you will break her chains and in so doing change everything."

Her father? Tanith drew back her sleeve and stared down at the spidery curse inked on her left wrist. Had he laboured for a higher calling all that time? "He was one of you, wasn't he?"

"Not in his heart," Ardoc replied softly. "He was a creature of obsession and selfish pleasures. But the goddess works with what tools she has."

He stared into his goblet. Tanith watched closely, as if she could somehow divine the truth from the curl of a lip or the twitch of a wrinkle. "Did you kill him?"

"No," he sighed. "He was a wretched man, with no shortage of creditors, detractors—"

"Jealous husbands."

"Indeed so."

Tanith sipped her calvasîr and let its fire burn away her questions. Her father belonged to the past, mourned and forgotten. "You want me to kill the Eternity King, don't you?"

Ardoc shot her an appraising look. "I don't imagine you can. He's glutted on a mass of soulfire beyond even your appetites. You will stand by my side when we free the goddess. She will do the rest. You need only open the way."

His answer was somehow disappointing. But even if she wasn't to *kill* the Eternity King, there would be challenge enough. He never left his palace. According to all rumour, he'd not even risen from his throne in a thousand years, and there were more guards in the Golden Citadel than in the rest of Zariqaz. "What of his redcloaks?"

"What else do you suppose Qolda's kathari are for? They are brutes, but even brutes can fight and die in a holy cause, if spurred to it. By their blood they will buy us time. The goddess will rise from the Stars Below in a torrent of cleansing flame, and a new age will begin." He set aside his goblet among the pile of books and levelled an earnest stare. "And you will be free of your burden. I promise."

The daemon. He could mean nothing else. A goal she'd long since given up on as impossible. "How can you know that?"

"Because the goddess told me so. Why else?" Eyes still on hers, he took her hand – her *left* hand – in both of his. "Can I rely on you?"

"Yes." To Tanith's surprise, she meant it. "*Abdon Nyssa ivohê.*"

Ten

Kat's hackles rose with a mix of soured memories and present contempt as she passed beneath the gilded gate of the Rashace estate.

Masquerades were invariably lavish, and the one held at the Rashace palace that night was no exception. Firebloods in stylised masks mimicking everything from animals to ifrîti gathered beneath the cold light of the stars. They mingled with Alabastran archons in high-collared black silks, redcloak officers and even a handful of those rarest of souls: cinderblood merchants whose influence and wealth had grown so great that societal snobbery bent just enough to admit them. Servants brandished trays of crystal goblets and delectable morsels. Undertown dancers swirled bright silks to the thump of drums and the lyres' breathy yearning.

The jasmine and juniper smoke wafting through the pleasure maze of age-bowed yews was a particularly audacious touch. Blesswood was too rare to waste as mere incense ... at least for a cinderblood's purse. The smoke was sharper than normal, bitter with some mystery ingredient.

Kat scowled the distraction away. She'd walked these gardens, her father's hand tight about her own. She'd played with the Rashace children and their friends. It hadn't been until she'd left – or rather, Castellan Krevîr had escorted her from the estate's bounds – that she'd realised how little she'd truly belonged.

"Easy, *easy*." Tatterlain's hand was a soft pressure in the small of her back. Smile unwavering, he nodded at a passing couple, lavish in silver-trimmed silks and grinning, feathered-crested ilfri masks the colour of an angry dawn. He smoothed his false goatee – the only part of his face visible beneath his own lion mask, complete with extravagant mane. "A good servant doesn't let her feelings show, remember?"

Kat didn't really care. "Maybe I'm not a good servant."

"I'm certain you will be absolutely the worst, but let's not get ahead of ourselves. This was your idea, remember?"

"Don't remind me."

He snatched a goblet from a passing tray and took a sip. "Ah, delightful. Hargo always did have such exquisite taste." He wiggled his shoulders, a man settling into his chosen character as if it were a favourite armchair, and snapped his fingers. "Let's be about our business."

Kat shot an envious glance at the goblet's ambrosial courage, not that she could have got the vessel between the cheeks of her cherubic half-mask. White at nose and brow, it darkened to indigo and then to black, melding seamlessly with the straight spill of her unbound, oiled hair. Alongside the diaphanous indigo skirt and a blouse that complemented her dark bronze skin perfectly – but would have left little to the imagination save for the black cotton shift dress belted beneath – the mask mimicked the aethereal, popular stylisation of a gloami ifrît.

By tradition, gloami were souls too humble to embrace the Deadwinds. Instead, their soft light dappled gravesides to ward off daemons. The perfect masquerade costume for a servant – or so a boorish master might think. Other gloami ushered back and forth through the maze, mostly young women and younger boys, their costumes shimmering in the blesswood smoke and all of them as barefoot as she.

"Yes, Count Karza," she replied.

Tatterlain rounded on her, wine spilling over the goblet's rim to stain his gloved fingers. "Then why aren't you in motion, dear Arica?" he snapped, his accent plump with Zariqaz vowels. "Hurry along!"

Kat flinched. Every face in sight was masked, whether it belonged to fireblood or custodian, dancer or servant. Still there were clues enough that they'd already drawn attention. The dips in conversation, the swishing gowns as women turned just enough that they could put their backs to the commotion. Even the momentary sympathetic grimace from a passing lyrist, shuffling along the broad flagstoned path towards the stone garden.

She bobbed her head. "Of course, Count Karza."

Tatterlain drained his goblet and let it go. Kat lunged, a sudden spasm in her fingers leading her to fumble an already difficult catch. Whatever the benefits of the ashanaiq, they were clearly spent. The expensive crystal shattered to fragments, speckling her toes – Tatterlain had insisted boots would have spoiled her costume – with the remnants of the wine.

"Oh dear, Arica," he sighed. "I do hope you're not going to be an embarrassment all night."

The muscles of her left arm knotted tight and trembling from shoulder to wrist, Kat hung her head and begged the spasm to recede. They had the full attention of everyone in sight, divided between disgust and empathy according to the onlooker's station. "No, Count Karza. Sorry, Count Karza." She gestured to a quartet gathered around a blesswood brazier. "Perhaps this way?"

She headed out with short, hesitant steps, her breathing returning to normal as her muscles unclenched. Tatterlain closed the distance with his longer, bombastic stride, fortunately too lost in his role to notice that hers wasn't performance alone.

"You're enjoying this," murmured Kat.

"The very idea," he replied softly, his voice briefly his own and thick with almost-credible hurt. In character once more, he raised it to full, plummy glory. "Ah, is that Hayathi Odessi I spy beneath that wonderful crow mask? It *has* been such a long time since we danced the night away atop Icorum's pinnacle, hasn't it?"

The aghast woman's companion interjected with introductions. A round of small talk followed, touching on the magnificence of the

92

grounds, the lamentable state of the Starji district and Zariqaz itself . . . and inevitably, Bashar Vallant. The quartet managed perhaps as many words between them as Tatterlain uttered alone. Once in full spate, he was as irresistible as a mill race.

Kat only caught snatches, for she spent much of that time scurrying in search of refreshments for her unquenchable count. Tatterlain's gestures ensured that little of the goblets' contents slaked his thirst. The greater balance ended up spilled across the flagstones, the yew maze's waxy needles . . . and Kat herself – which was, of course, loudly proclaimed to be her fault.

Somewhere along the line, she became invisible, her humiliations no longer remarkable but still sufficiently discomforting to encourage onlookers to turn away. Tatterlain's performance was just grotesque enough to catch the eye, but sufficiently credible that no one could have doubted it. By the time he'd granted two other circles the benefit of his company, the plight of Arica the browbeaten gloami had spread far and wide.

Azra would have approved.

Kat froze halfway towards a sumptuous buffet table. She'd not thought about Azra in months. Yennika, yes, but Yennika Bascari was the conniving trallock who'd manipulated her, used her, betrayed her. Azra had been different. At least, so Kat had thought. But Azra had proved to be nothing more than a mask Yennika had worn to gain her confidence . . . or so Kat repeated to herself night after night. Otherwise Azra – and Yennika – might have truly loved her, and she really wasn't sure how she'd cope with that.

Suddenly aware of the dampness from the spilled wine and the soreness of feet unused to bootless travel, she stalked over to Tatterlain and his audience of two giggling young women half his age. Her mood soured further at suspicion that the empty-headed little skirls were genuinely enthralled by his boorishness. They deserved to be taken for whatever he could get.

Offering an unsteady bow to his admirers, Tatterlain kissed the bunched fingers of one, the cheek of another, intercepted Kat beneath the stern statue of the long-dead Count Ebor Rashace and snatched yet another doomed goblet from her hand.

"Really, Arica! A man might die of thirst waiting for you to remember your duty!" Under cover of raising the goblet to his lips, he pressed on in softer tones. "Have you found her?"

"No," Kat replied, careful to move her lips no more than necessary. She'd seen a Rashace manservant signing at one of the other gloami maids, a timely reminder that Yali wasn't the only one in Zariqaz capable of overhearing. "Count Hargo's holding court by the fountain, but I can't see Fadiya anywhere."

Tatterlain grunted. "One of my new *friends* tells me that the good Countess Rashace has been ill for some time now. Rumour is that it's the lethargia. She may not be up to playing hostess."

Kat grimaced. It was a complication she didn't need. Especially if it *was* lethargia. Not that it would make a great deal of difference, given her own declining health. Let the two diseases battle for the privilege of killing her. "I'll have to get inside."

Tatterlain sank drunkenly against her, his arm about her shoulders and his mouth level with her ear. "Are you sure that's a good idea?"

"I don't have a choice. Besides, how often are rumours true?"

He sighed. "When I spread them, almost always." Planting one hand against her shoulder, he stumbled away. "Hit me. Nice and hard. And be careful."

Kat balled a fist and swung, filling the blow with all the sorrow and frustration of her ersatz homecoming. Tatterlain rode it out as best he could, but still her knuckles shattered the cheekpiece of his mask and snapped his head aside. Bellowing slurred aristocratic outrage, he clutched at his damaged mask and sank against the statue for support.

"I hate you!" shrieked Kat. "I never want to see you again!"

Head in hands, she ran sobbing into the maze.

For the first dozen strides, she felt eyes boring into her, heard the rough whispers of outrage. They faded readily. Sympathy couldn't sustain itself without intervention. No fireblood was prepared to lower themselves to it and no servant dared risk getting embroiled.

Still sobbing, Kat plunged deeper into the maze.

Within three turnings, she was alone. It wasn't yet late enough in the evening for guests to venture into the labyrinth in search of intimate moments. For Kat, it had been the site of countless childhood games of hunter and prey, each a cavalcade of small triumphs, scuffed knees and bitter tears. She knew every twist and turn, every sandstone grotesque peering from between the needles. She'd always been the quarry, of course, harried by the Rashace children. And she'd always lost, often through choice. Fireblood temperament was never more fickle than in competition, especially among children.

She reached the palace in under a minute, eyes red and puffy, cheeks tear-stained and the gloami mask dangling listlessly from one hand. The servants ferrying fresh trays about the maze's perimeter spared her no glance; nor did the custodians standing watch at the palace atrium. How fast Arica's legend had spread.

Not wanting to push her luck, she stalked dejectedly round a corner and down a short concealed stair. The gentle arch of the wine cellar door beckoned.

Her heart sank as she examined the door. No need to worry about hestics, not tonight. They'd be sleeping – no one wanted to spoil the party by having overzealous ifrît charbroil a wayward guest. But the lock? Kat knew herself to be an enthusiastic lock charmer at best. She could have buttressed her meagre skill by imbibing a talent wisp harvested from one of the greats, but she'd always loathed the idea of giving another soul – however faded – the run of her body. Far easier to have brought Yali, but she relied so much on body language and lipreading to navigate her interactions that a crowd of masked strangers would have been the worst torture.

She eased a pair of lock charmer's tools from beneath the gauzy fabric of her gloami costume.

"Oi! You're not one of ours. You can't be down here."

Heart leaping, Kat palmed the lock charmer's tools. A manservant stood at the head of the stairway she'd just descended, one who'd been permitted to keep his dignity and his black silk uniform both, rather than being forced into costume.

She cuffed at her eyes, cheeks dark with smeared make-up. "You don't know what Count Karza will do to me if I don't bring him a bottle of Tyzium Red. I can't go back without one . . . I just can't."

The manservant descended a step. "Oh, so it *is* you." He grunted empathically. So close to a weeping woman and his head filled with tales of the night's performances – servants gossiped like nothing else – he'd have been made of stone not to. "Having a night of it, aren't you?"

Kat nodded morosely. "You've no idea. He's not always like this, but when he starts drinking . . ."

"Yeah. They're all the same. Hold on, Tyzium Red? You're risking a hiding over that bitter muck? It's only good for cooking."

"The count's a man of . . . unusual tastes."

"I don't want to know." The manservant gave a belly-deep sigh and fished a key from his belt. "Get your bottle. Isn't like anyone will notice one more gone tonight."

Kat sagged with relief. "Thank you. I can't tell you what this means."

"Yeah, I know, I know. We've all been there." He turned the key in the lock. The door swung open. "Make it fast. The rack's on the left, just inside the door."

"Thank you," said Kat, awash with gratitude and regret. Azra wouldn't have hesitated, but then Azra had been Yennika, and therefore as close to a moral void as anyone Kat had ever known. "You're a life-saver."

She stepped into the cool darkness of the cellar, blinking as her eyes adjusted.

As promised, the floor-to-ceiling rack to the left of the door held a dozen bottles of Tyzium Red. Hundreds more bottles stretched away around the walls towards the short wooden stair leading up into the house proper. Empty, except for the dull lumani lantern fixed beside the inner door, its fading ifrît on the brink of dissipation.

Stepping out of sight, she eased a random bottle from the shelf. "I can't find it!"

The manservant gave the sigh of someone wishing he'd made different choices. "I told you, by the door."

"There's nothing here. The rack's empty."

Footfalls on the outer stairs presaged his arrival. "What? Let me—"

Kat swung the bottle. He collapsed with a dull moan, shoulders propped against the door jamb and feet inside.

She set the bottle – happily unbroken – back on the shelf. "Never mind. I found one."

Eleven

The tremors struck again as Kat trussed the manservant. Vision blurring, she sank against the cellar wall until they passed, her left arm a useless, clubbed weight and her lungs burning. That was new. Somewhere along the way the disease had crossed another threshold. They said that omen rot killed you slowly until it killed you all at once.

She clung to the wall with her good hand, begging Nyssa that no one would stumble upon her. For mercy, the goddess heard her pleas – the goddess alone, for no other graced the cellar until she was fit to move.

Leaving both the outer layers of her gloami costume and the now-trussed manservant behind a row of hogsheads, she wiped away her tears – both the fake from her play-acting and the real ones drawn forth by her attack – and slunk into the palace proper.

Everything was as she remembered. The sumptuous furnishings she'd always been scolded for touching. The portraits of Rashaces past. The polished ebony panels. The woven carpets, soft as down beneath her bare toes and their geometric ochres, browns and yellows dizzying. And of course the frescoed ceilings, alive with details of a Zariqaz that had never truly existed, gleaming gold and rich with promise. However much her father had fallen from favour, his work abided.

Careful not to be seen by toiling servants, she slipped out to the back staircase and padded upstairs.

While the first-floor landing's wood panelling and carpets were much the same as those of the floor below, dark oblongs on the walls betrayed the removal of paintings hung for many a long year. It was also oddly bereft of furniture, with not even a simple vase or table in sight.

As she drew closer to Fadiya's private chambers – husband and wife had shared little more than a married name in at least a decade – the passageway crowded with travellers' trunks and heavy wooden crates. The small library where Kat's father had taught her to read and write was so full of them she could barely see the empty shelves.

More convinced than ever that something was amiss, she crept to the heavy door of Fadiya's suite. Dull amber light flickered beneath. Heavy bolts held them closed at hip and shoulder.

Disappointment growled resentment at having wasted an evening. The countess hadn't shown her face because she'd never been there, had perhaps not dwelled in the palace for weeks.

But she'd come all this way. Even if Fadiya wasn't home, there was at least the *possibility* that she might have kept something of Terrion Arvish close.

The very slimmest of chances, but what else was there?

With a final glance over her shoulder, Kat tried the door. The handle met the resistance of a lock almost at once. Not entirely unexpected, especially as no hestic prism glinted above the ornate architrave.

A handful of soft tinyscrapes whispered as she knelt and probed the lock, awkwardly putting into practice all the things Azra, Yali and others had taught her. She imagined Yali crouching in the shadows of the passageway, shaking her head in despair at her inartful – and slow – efforts. She winced as her fingers briefly shook to a fresh spasm, but apparently even omen rot knew better than to interrupt her while at work.

Click. The mechanism yielded. Kat eased open the door and pulled it shut behind her.

Thick drapes left open to the night, a low chaise, a pair of side tables – a single, solitary bookcase – these were all that remained of a chamber that had once been the most luxuriously appointed Kat had ever seen.

The light, such as it was, came from a pyrasti crackling away in the hearth, gleefully devouring the timbers. The fireplace was an old childhood friend, the witness to games played with her collection of dolls, the companion by whose light she'd read her first books. The moulded rose petals of its facade remained precisely as she remembered. Nyssa, but it even smelled the same, offering safety and warmth. Bare feet soundless on the thick carpet, she drew close enough to touch the mantelpiece's stone. Did it remember her? Stone forgot slowly, and metal never at all. But Kat heard nothing – felt nothing – beyond the quiet burble of the ravenous pyrasti. All she had were memories, nothing more.

Memories, and the tingling feeling of something amiss.

She set the fireplace to her back. Memory recalled that Fadiya's bedchamber lay to the left, a modest dining room off to the right. Start with one, and make a methodical search.

She glanced back at the fire, unease coalescing into coherent concern.

Why keep a fire burning in a locked room no one used?

A patch of darkness detached itself from the shadow of the drapes. Not much, barely a sway to one side. A woman, a heavy shawl about her head and shoulders, standing at the window as witness to the strains of revelry in the grounds below.

Breath catching in the back of her throat, Kat rounded the chaise and approached from behind.

Five paces distant. Four. Three.

She halted. Coming closer would invite notice, and a scream she couldn't afford.

She recalled the rumours that the Countess Rashace was afflicted with lethargia, and discounted them. A woman confined with that sickness couldn't have stood unaided at a window. But how to proceed? She'd no weapon with which to threaten, no leverage of any kind. But maybe she didn't need any.

"Please don't cry out, *Mathami*," she murmured. "I'm not going to hurt you."

The woman stiffened. The shawl fell away. Golden hair gleamed in the darkness.

"*Mathami?*" Her voice crackled with emotion as she repeated the old-fashioned Daric name for a woman who was family, and yet was not – the name by which Kat had always addressed her.

Kat's heart ached in empathy. There'd been a time, and one not so long in the past, when she'd have given anything to hear that voice again – to see that wonderful, saintly smile – rather than have to conjure it from the rhythm of dry copperplate handwriting in letters that had expressed regret without real apology.

"Katija, is that you?"

The woman turned, her identity no longer a question. Fadiya Rashace's laughter lines were deeper than Kat remembered, her hair's lustre fading as she passed deeper into middle age. She was leaner and paler than ever, but remained as beautiful in life as in memory. A blue-gowned ghost in a darkened room. A foreshadowing of how Tanith would look thirty years hence.

That bitter realisation scattered the warmth of Kat's fond recollections. She'd been happy, yes, but that happiness – her childhood – had been built on lies.

"Katija …" Fadiya's disbelieving smile faded, her eyes wide. "You can't be here. If Hargo finds out—"

"I'll be gone soon," Kat replied stiffly.

Fadiya flinched, shocked by her coldness. Good.

The consternation didn't last. It couldn't. Before Fadiya had become a Rashace by marriage, she'd been a Floranz, and no woman of Floranz blood would be taken aback for long. A last glance back across the grounds and she stepped away from the window. "How have you been?"

"I'm surviving."

"I heard you settled your father's debts with Alabastra."

"After a fashion." Kat's throat tightened. She'd come so close to ending up as a koilos in service of those debts. In the end, they'd been annulled through Vallant's blackmail. The greatest gift anyone had ever

101

given her. She could never have walked openly in Zariqaz otherwise. Even with her name cleared of other crimes, bounty-hunters would have dogged her every step.

"I also heard you destroyed Tyzanta's xanathros."

"That's the story." The Alabastran high temple hadn't been destroyed. It had simply lost its upper floors to a devastating explosion. And Kat hadn't truly been responsible. Azra – and Tanith – had used her. "I suppose that's how it always goes with family, isn't it? The older sister getting the blame for what the younger did?"

Fadiya shrank inwards, ageing ten years in a few short moments. "So you know."

"She told me just before she broke my arm and tried to throw me off a building."

"You were fortunate that was all she did."

"It wasn't. I know what she is, *Mathami*."

"She's my daughter," Fadiya snapped. "I don't care about anything else. I never have."

"Or any*one* else?" Kat replied in a voice every inch as cold. "There was a time when I thought you loved *me* as a daughter. But it wasn't true, was it? It wasn't ..."

She pinched her eyes shut, partly to contain rising anger, partly to hold back tears. This was *precisely* why she'd tried never to come back.

A cool hand found hers. She shook it off and pulled away.

"I'm not here to argue." She kept her voice flat and level to keep old memories at bay. "I hoped you might have some of Father's old things. His books. His papers. You owe me that much."

Fadiya dipped her head. "I understand your anger."

"Anger?" Kat hissed, almost forgetting to keep her voice low. "Why would I be angry? Because you threw me out almost before Father's body was cold? Because you cut me off? Because you abandoned me to those impossible debts? At his graveside, you promised that I'd never be alone. That was the last time you ever spoke to me."

"I had no choice." No repentance in her tone. None. "My marriage hung by a thread."

"Your marriage? I was days from having Alabastra hollow me out and use me as a koilos!" If it hadn't been for Azra, they'd have succeeded. Whatever else Yennika had done – whatever her reasons – Kat owed her for that. She grimaced. She was getting them mixed up again. The Azra she'd loved, the Yennika she hated; the illusion and the reality. It wasn't healthy. "I needed you."

"I had a duty to my own family. Accusations of treachery had already destroyed my father. Another scandal would have broken the Floranz name." Pale cheeks flushed with colour. "When Hargo found out that I was sending you money . . . I thought he'd kill me. I wish he had, and saved us all the trouble."

Kat crushed a spark of sympathy for the woman who had and hadn't been her mother. "Do you have anything of Father's or not?"

Fadiya sighed. "A few of those cursed books of his, the margins full of his scribbles. They're long since packed away. There's a railrunner out at Kanzîr Station full of my possessions. The rest go tomorrow. I'm to join them in four days. There'll be no trace of me left here."

That explained the empty chambers. "Why are you leaving?"

"I'm not leaving, I'm being sent. To a hospice in Oracum." She offered a wan smile. "I'm ill, hadn't you heard?"

"Lethargia." Kat nodded towards the window. "That's what he's telling people."

"I don't have lethargia. But I *am* an embarrassment. Your father? Tanith? Hargo spent a fortune covering up the rumours, but after everything your sister did in Kaldos? All those little 'accidents' . . . ? He could have bankrupted us three times over and still the whispers would have spread." Fadiya met Kat's gaze, sapphire eyes shining in the reflected firelight "She's not wicked at heart, Katija. But she was born in shame, and shame festers. She always had the sweetest smile."

"She's a daemon."

"She's a girl struggling with a gift. That's what your father always said."

Her eyes grew distant. "I wanted us to leave Zariqaz, you know? Just the four of us. But he refused. He didn't want to destroy my reputation, for all the good that did. And now? Ever since your sister paid us a visit, Hargo can bear the stigma of me no longer. It's given him strength."

Kat grabbed her shoulder. "Tanith's alive? In Zariqaz?"

"She came calling three months ago. Hargo wouldn't let her see me, but I saw her."

Kat couldn't decide whether or not she was glad. Six months searching, and at last she had proof. Her sister was *alive*, just as Nyssa had promised. "Did she look ... normal?"

"Whatever do you mean, child?"

"She was ... injured." Fadiya could be spared the knowledge that the Deadwinds had burned Tanith to a crisp. "I imagine she's feeling better."

"It took the threat of a dozen shriekers to tear her from Hargo's throat, so I'd say so." Fadiya spoke the words with relish.

"And she's never been back?"

"If she has, she never got further than the outer walls. Why do you think Hargo has blackthorn burning alongside blesswood every night?"

So that was it, the scent she'd not quite recognised in the grounds. Kat had seen for herself how the merest breath of blackthorn had set Tanith reeling. If she collapsed in a cloud of the vapour, it might even kill her. "Do you know where she is?" Bitterness blossomed. "No, I imagine you've never troubled yourself to even look."

"Katija, I'm a prisoner here. They don't bolt the doors for my protection."

Kat scowled away embarrassment. Yet another thing she'd missed tonight, lost in her distraction. "What about your other children? Can't they stop this?"

Fadiya snorted. "Iskander sees only that it will place him a full decade closer to his inheritance. As for Etenah ... she disowned me when the truth came out. After all, what manner of decent woman would lower herself to loving a cinderblood?"

Raucous merriment rushed up from the grounds. Kat reflected that firebloods objected little to loving beneath their station so long as the arrangement remained transactional, rather than familial. Entire establishments catered to that singular truth.

Fadiya stared out of the window. "No, I am to go to Oracum and wither away. And then, when the stories of my infirmity are sufficiently widespread, Hargo will have me killed." She snorted. "Don't look so shocked. He's not sending me there to mend my health, but rather his reputation."

"You think I care?"

"I wouldn't in your place. I don't deserve your forgiveness. And I certainly won't ask for it. I'm still a Floranz." She stood straighter, weakness gone. "Why do you want your father's books? They won't bring you happiness. I don't know how much you remember, but he was less and less lucid towards the end. Almost like a man possessed. The books I kept, I stole from a bonfire in the cottage garden. He'd have been furious had he known."

Kat's left hand spasmed, the attack of cramp lasting barely long enough to set her teeth on edge. "I lost something. I'm trying to get it back. They might hold the key. And I want to help Tanith . . . if I can."

Fadiya faced her once more. "Good. Family is everything, Katija. Don't turn your back on it. Learn from my mistakes."

Kat didn't know what to say to that. The longer she remained in Fadiya Rashace's company, the harder it was to hate her. And she wasn't ready to let that hate go. She *needed* it. More than that, her *mathami* deserved it. "Kanzîr Station, you said?"

"Hargo's hired half the railrunner." Fadiya offered a wan smile. "I travel into banishment with style. Bolt the door behind you, if you would. I'd like my last days in Zariqaz to be free of shouting."

Kat picked her way across the room and opened the door a crack. The passageway beyond was just as empty as before.

"I hope you find what you're looking for," Fadiya called softly from behind.

Kat hesitated. But what could she say? Regrets were the cheapest currency going. They bought nothing that the purchaser didn't already possess.

So she said nothing, and left as quietly as she'd arrived.

The chill of night had fully descended by the time Kat had scrambled over the wall by the ancient carob and into the street, grateful for the cloak and shoes stolen from a partygoer more interested in amorous entanglements than the whereabouts of her possessions. Still aglow with anger after her confrontation with Fadiya Rashace, she doubted she'd have felt the cold in any case.

And so she did what the wise never dared do at that hour, and wandered wherever whim took her. She barely saw which streets passed away beneath the stars, her footsteps guided by the sonorous rumble of Undertown's factories and the beckoning cheer of hostelries that closed their doors only come the dawn. What opportunistic shadows lurked in the overhang of alley and rooftop let her be, sensing that whatever they sought from the encounter would in no way be worth the price.

As she walked, she picked over the details of a conversation badly mishandled. When else was she likely to get another chance to set the record straight? To get her dear *mathami* to understand the full extent of her betrayal? Reason insisted that Fadiya already understood that extent, and moreover had offered as much of an apology as she was likely to.

Reason could go hang.

Why couldn't Fadiya have just apologised? It *might* have thawed Kat's heart. Might even have let her offer comfort or forgiveness. That Fadiya yearned for such forgiveness, she didn't doubt. There was a world of difference between asking for and receiving. Pride might block one, but it would welcome the other.

But had the apology been necessary at all? Fadiya had passed years subject to the angry whims of a jealous, abusive husband, imprisoned in her own house. She hadn't scavenged the gutters for survival as Kat had, nor had she chanced execution or a koilos' existence, but she was a victim still. Of her pride, certainly. Of her own wayward heart, possibly. And of Hargo Rashace's weakness – the kind that always presented itself as strength in callow, unremarkable men – of course.

But what had truly been Fadiya Rashace's crime? Nothing more than yearning to be loved. Everything Kat had suffered had been willed into being not by Fadiya's actions, but by her husband's. And Kat had abandoned her to the mercy of the man who meant to exile her, then kill her, in order to save his own pride.

She couldn't have freed Fadiya. It would have taken a small army to sneak her from the palace, and contacts across Undertown to get her out of Zariqaz before Hargo's custodians tracked her down. Kat didn't have an army, and what contacts she had were in Tyzanta, half a kingdom away.

But she could have offered a kind word. She could have forgiven her.

Fadiya had spoken true. Family was everything. Kat had never known much of it. Her mother, Siette, had died young, bedridden and gasping until omen rot swept her away. Thereafter, Kat had just had her father. Now Yali, Tatterlain and Rîma were as close to kin as made no difference . . . maybe even Vallant too. But before them – years before – a fireblood countess had welcomed Kat into her home.

Kiasta.

Too late now to offer that kind word. The formal phase of the masquerade had been dying down even as Kat had skirted the shadows at its edge. Without a crowd to hide among, without Tatterlain to serve as cover – where he'd ended up, she shuddered to think – she stood little chance of getting back inside.

Nothing to do but let regret fester.

It was as she reached the open culvert marking the unofficial border of the Maraji district that she heard it: the stifled yelp of someone else with too much pride, determined to deny their tormentor some small pleasure from the beating. A dull growl echoed from where the culvert vanished into a tunnel, chased along by the even duller thump of flesh striking flesh and a gravelly cheer. A gutter-strutting nightjar, startled from its perch, peered beadily down at Kat.

"What?" She spread her hands to answer a question she was morbidly aware she'd heard only in her mind. "You think I've not pushed my luck enough tonight?"

Another yelp sounded from the tunnel. Unmistakably a woman's voice, just as the jeers belonged to men. Two men. Long odds to risk for a stranger, especially unarmed.

But with a toxic brew of anger, guilt and regret boiling in her veins, all Kat really, really wanted to do was hit someone.

She stabbed an accusing finger at the nightjar. "Fine. You win."

The bird didn't seem to care much either way.

Kat dropped down to a narrow stone walkway and ducked into the tunnel. Wary of the fast-flowing fluid in the culvert – no one would have described it as water – she stayed close to the curving wall and tried not to gag on the sweet, brackish stench.

Ahead, a heavy-shouldered man loomed against a lantern's light. The woman huddled at his feet, head tucked to her chest and one hand splayed to ward off the next blow. The lantern – oil, not lumani – sat beside her. A second man, too tall to stand upright in the tunnel, stood bow-backed on the far side, a palm pressed to his left eye.

"That's enough," growled the first man. "Fight's gone out of her now."

"Easy for you," said the second. "Wasn't your eye she clawed out, was it?"

Kat ducked under the jutting remnant of a pipe. The scuffed footfalls from her borrowed shoes sounded impossibly loud.

"Look," continued the first, "if Annaj can't recognise her, we won't get paid until the swelling goes down. And I want to get paid. I *like* getting paid."

"And *I* like being able to judge distance." The second rammed his foot into the woman's stomach. Her stuttered, racking moan stuttered along the tunnel.

"You'll heal," said the first, sounding bored.

"So will she."

Kat broke into a run. The first thug, his back to her, was casting about for the source of the racket when her shoulder slammed into his. His blind grab at her throat cost him the last of his balance. Eyes widening in premonition, he vanished in a fetid spray as the current took him.

The second man roared a challenge, his breath sickly sweet with illicit isshîm powder. Too late, Kat realised that the hand not clapped to his eye clutched a stubby leather blackjack. He swung, the weapon almost invisible in the heavy shadows cast by his body.

Fortunately, Rîma's lessons in swordcraft had covered more than the blade alone. Foremost had been one simple axiom: don't get hit. Kat doubted she'd ever read an attacker's body language as swiftly and cleanly as Rîma, but the thug's wild swing asked little of translation.

She ducked the blackjack with inches to spare, grabbed a handful each of jerkin and greasy hair, and slammed him into the tunnel wall. A hollow thud, the slight, musical *ping* of a broken tooth ricocheting off stone, and he collapsed, wits gone.

Kat, who'd earlier felt guilty for knocking a man cold, felt only a rush of satisfaction. Careful not to back-step into the rushing culvert, she moved towards the woman.

"It's all right. They won't give you any more trouble." She edged closer, her hand outstretched. "Let me get you somewhere safe."

The woman groaned, and uncurled just enough for Kat to realise – an age too late – that she'd made a terrible mistake.

She hadn't risked her life for a stranger. It was far worse than that. Though the woman's face was already red and puffy from the beating, the right side entirely masked in blood, Kat would have known it in the dark. She knew it better than her own.

"Hello, darling," croaked Yennika. "Fancy seeing you down here."

Twelve

The redcloak's arms flailed in a last, desperate effort. Tanith squeezed, her forearms crushing his cotton shirt against his chest, her lips drawing level with his ear.

"Oh, do stop fighting," she breathed playfully, as much to soothe her daemon-half as to torment her victim. "You're just embarrassing yourself."

The redcloak drove a heel back at her shin, the attempt so slow as to be disappointing.

"MMMMMmmmph!"

Her hands, clamped across his nose and mouth, smothered the attempted curse. That it *was* a curse, Tanith didn't doubt. Big strong men didn't like losing, much less to a waif . . . or more accurately, someone who *looked* like such. Prey always lost to the predator, and he *was* losing, his struggles fading fast.

"Sleep now," she murmured. "You did your best."

"mMMmm." The protest was barely a whisper, the struggle barely a twitch.

A ten-count more, and he sagged in her arms.

She kissed him on the cheek. No danger from her daemon-half in that. Unconscious prey didn't taste as good. "See? That's better, isn't it?"

He collapsed to the worn floorboards with a thud.

Sighing at the bother of it all, Tanith unwound the length of trusser's cord from about her waist and left him bound and gagged. Crossing to the other end of the watch house, she stepped over the body of the first sentry – this one disabled by the rather more effective means of a baulk of timber swung at the forehead – and tied her fast as well.

She hesitated in the doorway. A strange feeling, leaving living, breathing folk in her wake. It wasn't generally something she indulged. After all, the dead told no tales. But Enna had framed her instructions with enough challenge that Tanith hadn't had much choice other than to agree. Pride again, she supposed.

It wasn't as though tales would do the redcloaks any good. They'd remember the black eyeshadow and the tightly braided hair more readily than the rest of her. Folk always did, even before her glamour blurred memory further. The disguise, such as it was, might not even have been necessary, but Tanith indulged it anyway. Redcloaks, custodians, archons ... they all wore a costume and called it uniform, so why shouldn't she? She missed the gold-trimmed coachman's coat she'd worn in Tyzanta, presumably now claimed as plunder by one of Vallant's rebels. Black skelder's leathers cultivated the proper enticing menace, but they weren't the same.

She passed into the cool night air of the provisions yard and its neat tarpaulined rows of crates. Penned in as it was by the towering flank of a decaying boarded-up mansion and the buttressed rubble from a long-ago spirefall – Zariqaz might have been wealthier than Tyzanta, but acceptable maintenance had a similarly low ceiling – little in the way of starlight made it down to the uneven cobbles. That suited the night's work. Deeds inappropriate for sunlight were better accomplished in the darkness.

The front gate's hestic sent flickers of flame to test her as she approached, the invisible feathery caress searching for a soul-glyph tattoo. It hadn't bothered her on the way in, but then it was concerned only with the gate, and she'd come in over the wall.

When it didn't find what it sought, the hestic's vigilance turned dark and angry. The air crackled as its fire roused to a killing wrath. Most folk lacked the awareness even to notice a hestic, let alone its changing mood. Those who did had the good sense to scramble beyond its reach before the screaming started.

Tanith didn't even break stride.

With a snap of her fingers, she sent a sliver of flame from her aetherios tattoo coursing through the spirit world. The hestic uttered a thin wail as it perished, the backwash of the invisible detonation prickling her cheeks. No tears for the hestic. Ifrîti weren't people. She'd set it free. Back to find the rest of its whole down in the Stars Below.

Planting her feet against the cobbles, she heaved the heavy wooden gate wide and stared down the steep, townhouse-crowded street. Dark figures broke from an alleyway and began the knee-curling climb to the provisions yard. The ponderous silhouette of a clatter wagon climbed with them. The clank and rattle of its motic-driven wheels were irritatingly loud, no friend to the kind of cloak-and-dagger subtlety Tanith preferred. But clatter wagons made light work of heavy burdens, and she supposed they'd be gone long before the noise drew any trouble. Ordinary folk – which in this case included custodians – didn't readily involve themselves in redcloak business, even when that business went astray.

Predictably, Enna was the first to arrive. Her wine-dark cloak was her only concession to the temperature – save on the cloudiest of nights, the stifling heat of the day soon gave way to a bone-shivering chill. She was otherwise dressed as she always was, in practical – but not inelegant – silk coat, waistcoat and skirt, bereft of gold or silver detail, but with the merest hint of emerald green shot through the black. All told, the ensemble blurred the line between a high-status governess and a fireblood fallen on less than profitable times. Perfect for a woman who was rumoured to cross society's strata as easily as penitents climbing the Miser's Ascent to Zariqaz's Xanathros Alabastra.

"I suppose I should be impressed." Nothing of the climb's exertions showed in Enna's voice or her cheeks. Nothing of the implied compliment either, but that wasn't anything new. Tanith strove not to take offence. Everyone in the Obsidium Cult knew that Enna was, well . . . "distant" was the kindest way to put it. "And the guards?"

"They're alive. All four." The two on the walls had barely seen Tanith coming, much less offered any resistance. "I still don't see why that matters."

Enna shrugged. "We don't add to unkindness unless we must." She stepped aside as her companions flooded through the gateway, all anonymous beneath heavy hoods. Breathing hard from the climb, they fanned out and busied themselves with the crates. "As the years pass, you'll not resent the men and women you didn't kill, but you *will* regret those you didn't save."

Tanith bristled. "I don't have regrets."

Enna smiled, as ever with little in the way of warmth. "You will."

The arrival of the clatter wagon robbed Tanith of the chance to retort. Her every conversation with Enna ended with the older woman having the last word. If she *was* older. Despite the white streak in her raven hair, Enna was easily the most vital of Ardoc's followers. She and Tanith might even have been the same age, but for her obnoxious poise. Not the brittle confidence of a young fireblood, but a deeper, measured certainty. More concerningly, she set Tanith's daemon-half on edge. Not with hunger, but . . . Well, that was the problem. Tanith didn't have a name for the sensation. It certainly wasn't anything pleasant.

"I'm starting to think you don't like me," she said sweetly, once the clatter wagon was past.

"I haven't decided yet. That's part of the problem," Enna replied. "How's your hunger?"

Tanith scowled. After years of hiding her nature as an amashti, she was uncomfortable with how readily Ardoc had shared it with his inner circle – with half the wider cult, for all she knew. It wouldn't be the first time that someone had used her as some perverse status symbol. Which in truth she didn't mind . . . as long as it was on her terms. Fear provoked the same obsession as love. The one eased the absence of the other. "Not that it's your business, but I'm fine."

113

She wasn't fine – four redcloaks had presented four opportunities for temptation. The familiar refrain of *it won't matter, and you need this.* But the prospect of another humiliating admonition had given her the strength to bite it down. Besides, she'd feed well tomorrow night, and with Ardoc's blessing . . . even if a part of her railed at how easily he'd tamed her.

Enna offered a long, appraising stare. "Your appetites don't have to define you."

"You've no idea what you're talking about," Tanith replied sourly.

"I'm sure you know best." Enna glanced to where industrious loading of the clatter wagon had begun. "I suppose you're not going to help?"

"You suppose right. I've done my part."

"I thought you'd say that."

Enna withdrew towards the yard, her status as giver of the last word uncompromised.

Tanith kept to her post at the gate, attention split between the still-empty street and the loading of the clatter wagon. The latter passed with the efficiency underpinning any task Enna undertook. Tarpaulins were dragged clear and the crates checked so that the desired cargo could be hauled aboard the wagon's canvas-awninged truck bed. The provisions yard's block and tackle was pressed into service to lower crates from the upper stacks, but for the most part elbow grease and strong backs prevailed.

Tanith supposed that Ardoc wouldn't appreciate her refusal to get involved, but she didn't work for Enna. She didn't work for anyone. She *chose* to help Ardoc because he'd been kind and because he promised better days to come. Helping other people had never really worked out for her, had it?

At last, the final crate was aboard. Enna climbed up into the clatter wagon's windowed cab. Her band of helpers clambered to join the stolen cargo. Hauling hard on the guidance wheel, the driver sent the contraption rattling through the gate. Tanith jogged in pursuit. It took only the lightest and, she fancied, the most elegant of leaps to plant both feet on its timber tail board. Knocked off-centre by a sudden lurch, her grab at the canvas frame wasn't *quite* so refined.

She stayed on the tail board as the clatter wagon wound through the streets, ostensibly still standing watch, but mostly avoiding conversation. She caught hushed snatches from beneath the tarpaulin, only paying attention when her own name surfaced, and by then it was gone, vanished beneath the shifting sands of nervous gossip.

Definitely better to be feared if you couldn't have anything else.

The wagon juddered on through the streets, heading always downhill. The townhouses of Undertown gave way to the crowded warehouses of the seaward docks. A sharp turn at a crossways dominated by a weather-pitted bronze statue of a begowned Nyssa Benevolas – her arms outspread and her smile levelled in welcome to those approaching from the quayside – and they were running parallel to the sunken-roofed wharves along a street whose lumani lanterns had long since fallen dark with age. Off to Tanith's right, the Silent Sea glittered beneath the stars, the wind sour with the tang of spoiled fish.

A final turn beneath a cracked and silent lamp, and the clatter wagon shuddered to an imprecise halt.

Tanith jumped down into the overgrown rubble and stared up at vast, time-humbled statues framed by the rafters of a vaulted ceiling long since destroyed by fire. No, not statues ... not *just* statues. The cracked and blackened remnants of a casting crucible lay in the rubble at one's feet. Another held aloft a pole-like axle. It was easy to conjure the image of molten metal pouring from between the hands of those vast stone saints; to see the docking points for chainways and running tracks in the moss-encrusted brick walls. The ghost of a foundry, fashioned in the image of something grander than itself, now left to ruin.

Enna picked through the spoil and started out towards the foundry gate. "Looks like the kathari aren't here yet. Hazla? Sammar? Halfway down the street. Irthan?" She pointed at a crumbling stairway that, though it vanished entirely before it reached the remnants of the fourth

115

floor, was far better off than the adjoining walls. "You'll see half the district from up there."

"I'll go," said Tanith. The orphaned staircase was as good a way as any to avoid her peer.

Enna frowned rare surprise. "Thank you." She turned her attention to the remainder of the group. "That leaves the rest of us to get Qolda's crates unloaded. Weapons only, understand? We'll take the rest down to the Gutterfields when we're done. Lots of hungry bellies down there."

"Lots of hungry bellies back at the haven, too." The speaker froze as Enna's blue stare found him.

"We've enough to get by," she said, stern but without anger. A woman for whom this was an old, wearying argument. "The folk in the Gutterfields have nothing. Every soul among us has committed small evils in Nyssa's name. Every soul among us can afford some small good. Don't you want a balanced ledger when you reach the Stars Below?"

Ardoc would have made the instruction a sermon, a means to chastise and exhort. Enna spoke the words simply, as if they were nothing more than fact, and inevitable fact at that. Inspirational in a different way . . . at least until Tanith remembered how much she disliked her.

Thirteen

Sitting on a hunk of brickwork on the remains of the crumbling third-floor landing, Tanith stared out across the wharves to the distant waters of the Silent Sea. It struck her that in all her travels she'd never been aboard a seagoing vessel. The skyships of the Cloudsea, yes, but that was different. Fall into water and you could at least swim. Plunge from the deck of a skybound felucca and there was nothing.

Well, not until you hit the ground.

A footstep on the stairs dispelled the idle thought. She spun about, hand on one of the daggers sheathed at her waist. The interloper backed away, almost, but not quite, missing his footing.

One palm extended in apology, Esram pulled back his hood. "I didn't mean to intrude."

"You didn't." Tanith left the dagger where it was. She hadn't known Esram had been recruited to Enna's raid. Then again, she hadn't bothered to enquire. "What do you want?" The words came out harsher than she'd meant. It wasn't his fault she didn't do well with surprises.

"I brought you something." He proffered a fold of greasy paper and a glimpse of pastry. "I heard Enna ask if you were hungry. I thought—"

Tanith's heart skipped. What else had she said to Enna, or Enna to her? As far as she recalled, neither of them had spoken openly about her "challenges" – or the reason behind them – but memory was fickle,

117

especially when you weren't expecting to have to remember what you'd said. "What else did you hear?"

He blinked, a man in receipt of an unexpected reception. "I told you. That you were hungry."

"Nothing more?"

"No! I was just ... Look, I'm sorry. I thought ..." He was back to looking like a kicked puppy. "I didn't mean to offend you."

Tanith sighed. So he hadn't discovered that she was a monster. Only that she behaved like one. "You didn't."

"*Are* you hungry?" He held out his offering a second time. "It's not from the wagon. Enna won't mind."

"Ravenous," she replied, though it wasn't true – at least, not concerning anything that Esram would willingly offer or that she was in the mood to readily take. She accepted the pastry anyway and took a bite. Some kind of meat. Good quality from the texture. It didn't stop it turning to ash on her tongue, but that wasn't his fault. "Thanks. Just what I needed."

She focused on finishing the last of the snack without looking as though she were choking it down. It wasn't easy, but it was dark, and she'd had a lot of practice over the years.

"I'm surprised to see you out here," she said.

Esram's brow twitched. "You think I'm a coward, is that it?" His tone was playful more than offended.

"You strike me as being more comfortable in a library, that's all."

"You're not wrong. I'd much rather be curled up with a book. But Enna has ... interesting ideas. Qolda, Serrîq, even Ardoc ..." He glanced about. Seemingly content that he could speak freely, he pressed on, gaining confidence with every breath. "They talk about Nyssa setting the world to rights, but they're content to leave it all to her. Enna's the only one who cares about justice in the here and now. That's worth a little discomfort. If we don't help each other, we're not worthy of Nyssa's love."

Tanith nodded, not particularly convinced. Life had given her little save misery, and she was seldom inclined to match its indifference in anything other than kind. Not like Esram, whose passion for others surrendered little to his love for the past. Strength took many forms, and not for the first time she found herself wondering how deep his went.

Maybe he even had enough to share with her.

He sat beside her and stared out into the night. "Hazla and Merrîa wanted to go with you tonight. Enna said you didn't need them."

Tanith swallowed the last mouthful and wished he hadn't sat so close. Harder now to ignore the burnt lavender of his soul. "Enna was right."

"Enna's usually right. It's why Qolda hates her. That, and because she's risen so far, so fast."

Tanith's ears pricked up. Gossip bored her, but not where potential enemies were concerned. "She has?"

"So Merrîa told me, and she's lived in the haven for years." Esram hesitated. "I almost didn't recognise you tonight."

"That was the point." She winced, realising that the words could be taken more personally than intended. "For people not to recognise me, I mean. It's . . . freeing."

"You look older. Harder." He frowned. "Which one's really you?"

"I . . ." Tanith's turn to hesitate. Yennika had never asked that question. No one did. They just assumed the version of her they preferred was the "real" her. For the first time in a long time, she felt truly seen. Vulnerable. But vulnerability wasn't all bad . . . was it? "That's complicated. Most people prefer to keep things simple."

His brown eyes met hers. Wary, expressive, but above all, *understanding*. "I'm not most people." He looked as though he meant to develop the thought, but then his cheek twitched and he turned away, staring off across the quayside. "Tonight . . . four redcloaks – *redcloaks* – and none of them sounded the alarm. How did you manage it?"

So Ardoc *hadn't* told the entire cult what she was. Or if he had, Esram hadn't quite got the message. He increasingly seemed the type to miss

119

the obvious. The clever ones were always dumber than they knew. "I'm stronger than I look."

He narrowed his eyes. "No wonder I'm scared of you."

Something twinged in Tanith's chest. She didn't *want* Esram to be scared of her. She wasn't entirely sure what she wanted him to feel, but it wasn't that. Her glamour at work, instinctively pushing him away so she wouldn't hurt him? No. In the depths, she'd caught a glimpse of the passionate, determined soul at Esram's core. Her glamour would find only the slightest of purchases. Harder to make him leave, and harder to make him stay. Good and bad.

"Scared of me?" she asked slowly. "Why?"

He glanced away. "Back in the depths . . . that was a little scary."

Ah. The kiss that hadn't quite been a kiss. She'd certainly been . . . forceful. Certainly more forceful than was appropriate for a lost lamb. What was he thinking? Hard to tell. It wasn't fair. *She* was supposed to be the mysterious, unreadable one. "Good scary, or bad scary?"

"I don't know. I didn't get chance to form a lasting opinion."

He'd come closer than he knew to never forming another opinion ever again. Or maybe he *did* know, and didn't care. That would be flattering. Or maybe she just hoped that was the case, making excuses to absolve herself of what she – what her daemon-half, rather – might do to him. The worst glamour was the one woven about oneself.

"So you're an empiricist?" she said, striving for a joke of her own. "Don't look at me like that, I know words. I'm voracious. I once ate a *very* learned tutor."

She paused, horrified at the unbidden truth. It was too easy to talk around Esram. Too easy to say things she really, really shouldn't.

But he laughed. And without even a hint of nervousness.

He'd taken it as a joke. Quickly, distract him before he had chance to re-evaluate.

"Perhaps we should do something about that?" she heard herself saying.

"What?" He blinked. "Now?"

120

"Yes, now," she said firmly, more to convince herself than him. "Nothing's happening here."

"True, and it's nicer out here than down in the depths."

It was. In the dark, you could forget Undertown's squalor. The starlit expanse of the Silent Sea was far more attractive than the slime-smeared walls of the Underways. And so high up they had as much privacy as they were likely to get. "I thought you liked stones. And dirt."

"I like *history*." Esram ventured a smile. "It's not the same. And the past doesn't have a monopoly on beauty. Right now, I'd much rather be in the present."

It wasn't the most artful line, and the nervousness of his delivery didn't do it any favours. But Tanith couldn't fault the sentiment, nor deny the blush warming her cheeks. She leaned in, daring her daemon-half to stir as the burnt lavender of Esram's soul grew thicker. This time, at least, it knew better than to get involved. There was risk – of course there was risk – but Enna was right. Her appetites didn't have to define her.

She closed her eyes. "Well?"

An urgent hoot echoed up from the streets below and received another in answer. Not owl hoots, but close enough that the inattentive might mistake them for such. Tanith's heart sank. Was one kiss too much to ask? Nyssa really did hate her.

She sprang to her feet and stared out down the hill.

Esram frowned. "What is it?"

There. A tall figure moving through the starlit shadows, slinking towards the foundry. Another. A third. The first halted briefly, hands cupped to his mouth. Another pair of not-quite-hoots fluttered beneath the stars. "We've got guests."

Esram clambered to his feet, but hung back from the edge. "It'll be the kathari."

The kathari had a fine – and barely warranted – opinion of themselves. They wouldn't have come creeping up the street, but marched into the foundry ruins like heroes. And then there were those other details, barely visible in the starlit darkness. A motionless body lying in an alleyway mouth where Hazla and Sammar should have been keeping watch.

Kiasta.

"It's not the kathari."

And if they knew enough to be there, it wouldn't just be three of them.

Tanith glanced down at the foundry, at the figures toiling in the lamplight. Unawares of what was coming. Cupping her hands to her mouth, she trilled her best tongue-tingling impression of a nightjar – the warning Hazla and Sammar should have given. The one she'd have given before, if she'd not allowed Esram to distract her.

The foundry erupted into violence. Dark figures rushed in from the perimeter, naked steel shining. An initiate shrieked, impaled from behind. Another crashed into the rubble, borne down by an attacker twice her size. Even as the air thickened with screams and bellowed challenges, a second wave of attackers joined the first.

Esram blanched. "What do we do?"

Tanith bit back an unkind retort. Esram wasn't a fighter, otherwise Qolda would have poached him for the kathari long ago. He was just a man who loved history and believed in the goddess enough to try changing the world. An innocent.

Her eyes darted left and right, gauging the flow of the chaos. The attackers hadn't bothered with the stairway yet, but that would change soon enough. The majority of them had entered the ruins from the north, along the same street as the clatter wagon. No escape to the south – the cliff face of ancient subsided buildings made for a challenging climb at best. But to the west . . . ?

She pointed. "That way. The floor looks sturdy enough. Jump to the neighbouring rooftops. Get down into the streets and disappear."

He nodded fitfully, his eyes barely leaving the slaughter below. "What about you?"

"I won't be long."

Esram started away, then pulled up short and gazed back at her. "What does that mean?"

"Just *go*." Tanith pursed her lips, wrestling with what was to her an unfamiliar concept. "And be careful."

He turned and bolted across the sagging floor.

She watched him go. By rights, she should be hard on his heels. She didn't much like Enna. She didn't know the others. But they'd relied on her to keep watch. Was it pride? The sting of disappointing Ardoc? All she knew was that she couldn't leave without doing *something*.

She took the stairs at a run, her boots skidding on grit and withered weeds. Reaching the first-floor landing, she picked out a figure amid the carnage and marked him down for death. Two bounding steps took her to the edge of the crumbling landing. A third propelled her out into the night.

A breath. A brief, dizzying moment of freedom, the air stinging her cheeks.

She thumped into the attacker, her left knee in his face. They toppled together, his thin scream left behind as they crunched into the overgrown rubble of the foundry floor. Tanith rolled to her knees, her dagger stabbing down into his open mouth even as she found her balance. Her victim jackknifed, his scream dying as his soul fled.

Rising, Tanith stomped on his hand to free his scimitar. Her eyes fell on his parted cloak. Black without, scarlet within. A redcloak reversed. Had someone followed them from the provisions yard? She'd seen no one. Was she twice the failure?

Giving the scimitar an experimental twirl – well balanced, but then redcloaks had the best of everything – she stalked deeper into the fray.

Another disguised redcloak, witness to her bloody arrival, howled and whirled her sword. Tanith took her measure with a glance. A swordstress confident in her skill, and with good reason. She'd already killed at least one tonight: Irthan, his body at her feet and his empty eyes staring skyward. Probably she'd killed more over the years – in service to the Eternity King and out.

But to Tanith, she was moving in slow motion.

A parry. A riposte. A wet rip of flesh. Tanith left the redcloak rasping her last beside Irthan's corpse.

Her spark of pleasure didn't last. In the brief time since she'd descended the stairs, a battle in name only had become a massacre. The night was full of damp, breathy moans, the hurried scramble of desperate feet and the bellowed triumph of pursuers. Bodies lay scattered among upturned crates. A handful in the turned cloaks of the attackers. Most in the simple, unassuming skelder's garb of Enna's companions.

Tanith bit back a snarl of self-reproach. Too late with the warning. Too late with the intervention. Twice the failure. She *hated* failure. Better not to try at all than to fall short.

Nothing left to do but leave.

A new smell rose above the fish stink of the harbourside, the thick musk of sweat and the copper of spilt blood. Bitter, choking bone ash, stale and lifeless. Less a scent and more its absence, the dull emptiness of a space in the senses. The smell of death gone cold in a rotting soul.

Breath staling in her throat, Tanith gripped the scimitar tight and spun around, jaw set to conceal her sudden fear.

The koilos glowered back from the edge of the lanternlight, its death-rattle screech splitting the night air and magenta flame blazing in the cold, empty eye sockets of its skull. Golden robes and flame-etched crown gleaming, it lurched forward, the black lamellar of its armour whispering as it picked up speed, the rippling curve of its vast two-handed flamberge like a silver flame.

A piece of Tanith recognised that the koilos' presence meant they hadn't been followed. Ember-saints weren't awoken for trivia and off-chances, but for certainty. Someone had been ready, even if the guards at the provisions yard had not.

The rest screamed at her to run.

But try as she might, her legs wouldn't move, survival instinct smothered by the koilos' oily remnant of a soul. Everything had a predator. Even an amashti.

The koilos picked up speed, flamberge rising in a ritual execution-er's stance.

124

Her legs still frozen, Tanith beheld her death reflected in the flamberge's steel.

Kiasta.

A slight figure lunged from the darkness, bearing her to the ground. The koilos thundered past, the magenta flames of its eyes dancing in the dark.

Jolted from paralysis by the impact, Tanith struggled to rise. Her rescuer was still atop her, pinning her down.

"Let me go!" Tanith hissed. A hand closed across her mouth. "MMMmmph!"

Enna's eyes bored into hers. "Not a sound, do you hear me?" she said in an urgent whisper. "Not a sound, or it'll kill us both. Stay down."

Her knees either side of Tanith's, Enna drew her into what might have been called an embrace but for its dry dispassion. Left elbow braced against the ground, she looped her right forearm under Tanith's neck and drew her head – none too gently – against her own shoulder.

"Don't even breathe," she murmured.

Over the curve of Enna's shoulder, Tanith watched with increasing horror as the koilos lurched about towards them. She felt the cold magenta fires of its eyes freezing her inside-out. Heard the thin, shuddering screech of its breath.

Then, without warning, it lowered its flamberge and stalked off into the darkness.

After another ten-count, Enna took a shallow, silent breath. "You see?"

A whisper of movement and she was gone, running for the shelter of a vast, fallen crucible. One eye ever on the darkness of the koilos' wake, Tanith scrambled after her and collapsed against the crucible's cracked rim. A semblance of eerie quiet had fallen, the battle faded as soon as it had begun.

"What just happened?" she gasped. "It looked right at me. Why aren't we dead?"

Her hands braced against the crucible's flank, Enna risked a glance towards the clatter wagon. "Just be glad it did. Esram was with you?"

"He got out." Tanith hoped he had. Nothing was certain that night. "Hazla and Sammar are dead. Irthan too."

"They're in good company."

"I might have killed some redcloaks. I hope you don't mind." She'd meant to imbue the words with sarcasm, but the aftermath of panic and relief smoothed the edges away.

Enna stared across the ruins, bleak and implacable, winsome youth replaced by something older, harder and unused to defeat. The shadows around her lengthened, and for the briefest of moments Tanith had the impression that even unarmed, she meant to wade back into the redcloaks' midst . . . and stranger still, that she might actually *win*. But the moment passed as moments do. The shadows retreated and Enna sagged, overcome.

"There's nothing more we can do here," she said softly. "We'd better get back to the haven."

"If we can."

She nodded. "Yes, if we can."

Fourteen

Careful not to wake the occupant, Kat eased the bedroom door closed. Yali waited at the bottom of the stairs, chestnut hair tousled with sleep and arms folded, blocking the passageway to the woebegone theatre's auditorium.

||What you were thinking, bringing that trallock here?||

No need to guess at the trallock's identity, not when Kat had left Yennika sleeping off both her injuries and a heavy dose of last breath.

Kat halted two steps from the bottom, brought up as much by Yali's angry, jagged signing as the words themselves.

||What was I supposed to do?|| she replied wearily, stumbling fingers making heavy weather of the simple signs. It had been a long, draining night with the prospect of another to come. She was hungry, she stank, and the last thing she wanted to do was argue. ||Leave her there?||

||Yes!|| Yali slapped the wall for emphasis. ||That or finish her off.||

||Calm down. Please?|| Kat knew the words to be a mistake as soon as the signs had flown. Tact and tiredness made for poor bedfellows.

Yali's eyes blazed. ||Calm down? Calm *down*?|| Stiff fingers and a curled lip made the latter sign – a downward swipe from shoulder to hip – vicious, uncompromising. ||She sold you out in every possible way and left you in pieces. What are you thinking? *Are* you thinking?||

Kat's cheeks coloured, anger goading her to demand why Yali

127

considered it any of her business. But the advantage of communicating in a second language was that forming the words took a heartbeat longer. That heartbeat offered the chance not to say a stupid, hurtful thing just because your accuser had a damn good point.

||Look,|| she signed slowly, buying time for surging anger to bleed away. ||Do you mind if we talk about this elsewhere?||

Yali stalked into the auditorium, leaving Kat to follow. Rubbing at her tired eyes, she did so, though at a markedly slower pace – part weariness and part breathing room.

What had she been thinking, bringing Yennika to the theatre? Even now, she wasn't entirely sure. And it *was* Yennika, not Azra, she told herself firmly. Azra was gone, had never existed. Yennika Bascari was a selfish, manipulative daemon-in-mortal-form who'd cold-bloodedly conspired to the downfall of her own family. The first person Kat had truly loved, and it had all been a lie.

Or had it? Throughout, Yennika had insisted that their love had been the one verity amid the lies. It might even have been true. It had *felt* true enough for temptation. She'd offered to share the spoils of victory. She'd cleared Kat's name just as Vallant had cleared her debts.

But that wasn't why Kat had brought her home.

The truth was far, far worse, and damned her for a fool.

Yali hauled herself up onto the stage. But instead of making for Nyssa Collapses and the makeshift conclave circle, she sat on the platform's edge, her feet kicking at the air. ||Well? I'm listening.||

||"Listening to what?"|| Coat tails brushing at the uneven seating, Rîma emerged from the darkness beneath the stage-right box.

Kat sighed. Wonderful. A battle on two fronts.

||Kat found the Bascari harlot wandering the streets,|| said Yali. ||She's upstairs.||

Rîma folded her arms and cocked her head. ||"I see."||

Kat glanced from one to the other. ||"She'd been beaten to a pulp. I didn't even know who she was until after I'd gotten involved."|| She was babbling. She could *hear* that she was babbling. Stars Below, could she

128

sound more defensive? ||"I'd have done the same for anyone else, you know that. It wasn't about Az— *Yennika*. It was about me."||

Firmer ground here. When she'd first met Azra, on the run from Alabastra's debt collectors, self-pity had blinded her to the struggles of others. Compassion was something she'd learned much later, and a hard thing to set aside, even in the cause of self-interest. But even that wasn't the whole truth. In the end, she'd taken Yennika in not out of compassion, but because in the darkness of the culvert tunnel, just for a moment . . . she'd reminded her of Azra.

Rîma held up a finger. ||*Who* attacked her?"||

||"There wasn't time for introductions. Why?"||

||"Curious, isn't it, how the present echoes the past?"|| From Rîma's flat tone, she didn't find it curious at all. ||"A woman in the gutter, desperate for a helping hand, and then Nyssa provides? Some might call that overly convenient."||

Kat winced. It *was* an uncomfortable mirror to how she and Azra had first met, only then she'd taken the beating and Azra had offered the helping hand. The first manipulation among many. ||"She didn't plan this."||

Yali rolled her eyes. ||Of course not.||

||"She couldn't have known where I'd be. *I* didn't know where I'd be. As soon as she's fit to walk, she'll be on her way."||

||With all our secrets ready to trade.||

Kat flung her hands wide, suddenly tired of arguing. ||"What secrets? Last I checked, we don't have any."||

She had one, of course, but this was hardly the time.

||"There's your connection with Vallant,"|| said Rîma.

||"Which is no more or less provable now than it was yesterday,"|| Kat retorted.

The legend of Katija Arvish, apostate demolisher of Tyzanta's Xanathros Alabastra, had faded with the passing months, but she still caught folk giving her strange looks when she offered her name. Stars Below, even Fadiya Rashace had heard the rumours, and she

129

was a prisoner in her own home. But for every tale that claimed Kat a nefarious rebel, another insisted she'd been working for Zaran Ossed, formerly Tyzanta's hierarch, to prevent the same explosion she'd sort of caused. That Ossed had publicly forgiven her debt to the Alabastran temple lent rather more weight to the latter than the former … even if that forgiveness had arisen from Vallant's blackmail, rather than altruism.

Storm clouds receded from Yali's expression. ||You should have asked first.||

||"I did,"|| Kat replied. ||"Tatterlain didn't give me this much hassle."||

When countering suspicions about one serial liar, the blessing of another was priceless.

Yali frowned. ||Where is he?||

||"He wanted to make his rounds."|| Tatterlain's routine – no matter how late or drunken the night – was to prowl every nearby dive, tavern and shîm-joint. Firebloods, custodians and even redcloaks were prone to slips of the tongue while in the process of satiation. ||"Countess Rashace did have some of my father's books, but they're sealed away in Kanzîr Station."||

Kat quickly recounted events, sparing only her turbulent feelings for Fadiya Rashace. The morning was already complicated enough.

Yali's eyes shone. ||So we're hitting Kanzîr tonight?||

||"If Tatterlain can get us in."|| Kanzîr Station sat on the border of Starji district and the Golden Citadel, its railrunners shuttling passengers, cargo and redcloaks to Khalad's outer cities. ||"Does that mean I'm forgiven?"||

Yali dropped from the stage, her eyes appraising. ||I'm just looking out for my big sister.|| She embraced Kat, then pulled away to regard her with piercing, earnest eyes. ||If she hurts you, I'll kill her, honest and true.||

||"I told you,"|| said Kat, ||"once she's up and around, she's gone."||

Yali's level stare didn't falter. ||Yeah. Sure.||

Kat glanced at Rîma for support. In reply, she received the slightest of shrugs that conveyed concern, empathy and quiet support more completely than words ever could. ||"There is little more powerful than the yearning to remain true to oneself. But tread carefully."||

||"I intend to."|| Leaving the auditorium behind, Kat clomped wearily off to bed.

Tatterlain returned in the late morning. Habitual good cheer markedly absent, he called a meeting in the theatre's tiny kitchen – a small mercy that permitted Kat to take a light breakfast of spiced irka tea, buttered bread and komestri sausage while he laid out the bad news.

||"No two ways about it,"|| he said glumly, ||"there's just no way of getting into Kanzîr Station's depot at this notice. Even Lamilla can't provide us with access papers."||

Kat scowled, her breakfast losing its flavour mid chew. ||"I thought Lamilla could forge anything."|| She needed to if she was to keep her illicit talent-wisp trade running.

||"She says everything related to redcloak business has been harder of late."|| He shrugged and sank into a chair opposite. ||"It happens. Some officer gets his hands burnt and locks down. She says it'll clear in a week, maybe two."||

||"A week's too late!"|| snapped Kat. ||"If we don't get inside Kanzîr in the next three days, we'll be right back where we started."||

Rîma stirred from her post by the door. ||"Maybe it's no bad thing to let it leave. Oracum's a fraction of Zariqaz's size. Much harder to hide something."||

||"Assuming it reaches Oracum. Count Rashace wants his wife to disappear."|| Kat crushed a twinge of guilt. ||"It might be neither she nor her possessions will be getting off when the railrunner arrives."||

Yali rubbed at bleary eyes. According to Rîma, she'd kept watch at the foot of the stairs ever since Kat had gone to bed, vigilant for mischief from their unwelcome guest. ||You're sure it's worth the bother?||

||"I'm not sure of anything, but unless Rîma's made progress with that code ... ?"||

Rîma shook her head. "I warned you it might not even be possible."

"Then this might be my last chance."

Tatterlain nodded slowly. "We've three days. Maybe we'll catch a break."

Not long before, Kat wouldn't have worried, but with her attacks growing ever more severe, three days was a lifetime. Or the last of one.

"Perhaps we're looking at this the wrong way," said Rîma.

"You're questioning my judgement?" sniffed Tatterlain. "I'm shocked, I tell you."

"I simply wonder if it might not be better to let the railrunner leave, but make sure we're on it. Once it's out of the city, we'd have all the time in the world to ransack the cargo."

Except it'll be crawling with custodians, said Yali.

Rîma's small, quiet smile concisely expressed what she thought of *that*.

"Maybe she's right," said Kat.

"At the first sign of trouble, the driver will shoot off an emergency heraldic," said Tatterlain, referring to the swift ifrîti that bore messages between the cities. "Then we'll be trapped on the railrunner as a pair of vicious little dhows with vicious little captains come to see what all the trouble is about."

"So it's Kanzîr Station or it's nothing?" asked Kat.

"It's Kanzîr Station or a miracle. I don't suppose Nyssa owes anyone any favours?"

Kat thought back to the vision of the shackled goddess she'd seen in the skies above Athenoch. "Just . . . just keep trying to find us a way inside."

"Of course." He rose. "Oh . . . I nearly forgot: Rîma, someone's asking after you."

"Who?"

"I don't have a name. Tall. Thin. Bald. Dark brown skin – darker than Kat, I mean. Unremarkable, Lamilla said."

"Asking after me by name?"

||"By your sword, actually. A very detailed description, according to Davari."||

Kat found her gaze drawn to the hilt of that sword, just visible behind Rîma's left shoulder. Its smooth, straight lines were remarkable enough to draw notice in central Khalad, where a scimitar was the favoured weapon. More than that, its blade's flowing, gold-etched writing suggested value. Kat had never quizzed Rîma about it. The swordstress had never been one to welcome questions. So far as Kat knew, her true origins were known only to the three people in the kitchen, Vallant, and perhaps a handful of others.

Rîma's jaw tightened, the smooth skin around her eyes creasing in what was for her an outrageous gesture of concern. ||"Davari? You just said Lamilla."||

Tatterlain shrugged. ||"Davari mentioned him a few days back. Apparently he was personable enough. Davari assumed you'd found yourself an admirer. I completely forgot about it until Lamilla mentioned that this fellow had been asking her about your sword as well."||

Rîma's frown blossomed into a glower. She started towards the door. ||"I want to talk to Lamilla."||

||"You know she won't see anyone during the day. We can—"||

She'd already gone into the passageway. A single leaden word boomed back into the kitchen, thick with impatience. "Now."

Tatterlain pushed his chair away from the table. "All right, all right. Now it is," he muttered. On the threshold, he recovered his manners and offered a farewell bow. ||"Ladies."||

He ran to catch up. A door slammed.

Kat drummed her fingers on the tabletop, intrigue holding frustration at bay. ||I've never seen Rîma so worked up about something. Vallant excepted, of course.|| Vallant and Rîma went way back, and quarrelled as only old friends could. ||What do you suppose that's about?||

Yali shrugged, an odd glint in her eye. ||She loves that sword. And love makes us difficult.||

133

Ah. There it was. ||Will you leave it?||

||Yennika's a scorpion.||

||A scorpion can't sting you if you're watching it.||

Yali yawned and stumbled to her feet. ||It can if you're too close. But you're not in the mood to listen and I'm exhausted. Just remember that if she slits my throat while I'm sleeping, I'll never forgive you. I'm not against dying in bed, but I don't plan on doing so for a good long while.|| She grinned. ||And this particular bed's always too empty for my taste.||

Kat swirled the dregs of her tea, the shoal of leaves chasing one another around the mug. So easy to forget that the others also had desires. Tatterlain found companionship readily enough, or so she assumed, for he never brought his conquests back to the theatre. And Yali? Ungainly as she sometimes seemed, give her a drumbeat loud enough to shake the air so that even she could feel it, and she danced like a woman possessed, and that energy always drew admirers. Nothing had lasted, but Yali didn't seem to mind. Kat couldn't understand that. She found nothing more difficult than giving away even a piece of her heart.

Had that been part of the reason she'd taken pity on Yennika? Because some indefinable piece of her was with her still? Better that, perhaps, than for the reason to be the one Yali clearly preferred: that time and distance had eroded her ability to recognise a scorpion readying its sting.

She was still mulling on that unhappy possibility when Yennika appeared in the doorway.

She looked better than she had the previous night, last breath having done its soothing work. Nonetheless, the dark bruises on her brow and cheek – the crimson slash of a cut along her jaw – marked her as a woman back from the wars.

In Tyzanta, folk had taken them for sisters, bronzed, dark and elegant. Even now, the comparison held, despite the bruises, despite the fact that Yennika's black hair now barely brushed the nape of her neck while Kat's hung to her shoulders. For Kat, looking into those dark eyes was still like looking into a mirror. Her prouder, more courageous self, freer with laughter and feeling than she'd ever be; sharper-tongued and quicker-witted. The simple shirt and trousers hung loose on a gaunter frame than the one Kat recalled. A far cry from the fabulous silks and figure-hugging gowns of Yennika Bascari at her height.

She had never looked more like Azra than at that moment. Knowing that meant trouble, Kat stared into her tea and ran the lengthy roster of betrayals past.

"My gallant rescuer," said Yennika. "Good morning, darling."

She even sounded the same. The playful demureness that was nothing of the sort. The amusement behind even the most banal statement. Harder to hear it in the morning light. In the dark, you could convince yourself it hadn't been real. And that last flourish. The *darling*. It didn't mean anything – it was just a word Yennika used as punctuation – but still a knot formed in Kat's gut.

"How are you feeling?" she asked without looking up.

"Starving."

Eyes downcast, Kat heard the wicked smile. She pushed her plate across the table – having misjudged the extent of her own hunger, plenty remained. She glanced up as Yennika reached the table – the aftermath of injury lending her an uneven, raggle-taggle gait – and hurriedly dipped her eyes to her mug once more.

Somehow, she'd convinced herself she was ready for this. She wasn't.

Yali was right. She should never have brought Yennika back.

Yennika sat at the table and picked at the plate's contents with slender, bruise-mottled fingers. "The deaf girl glares at my door as if she wants it to burst into flames and me alongside."

"She's trying to protect me."

"From me?" Yennika paused, mid reach for a piece of bread. "Oh, I am flattered."

"Don't be. Pull yourself together and leave."

"Just like that?"

"Just like that."

135

Yennika shook her head. "And I thought you loved me."

"You don't get to make jokes like that!" For the first time, Kat met her eye to eye, straining for composure already blasted to hot red dust by equal parts anger and loss. This was *precisely* what she'd been afraid of. She'd never been good at just giving pieces of herself away. It was everything or nothing, and when it was everything, it wasn't her in control. "One more crack like that and I'll let Yali set you ablaze!"

Yennika's lips parted, a little colour gone from her cheeks. "Yes … Yes, of course, darling. A poor joke. I'm sorry. Would you believe this is awkward for me, too?"

Kat didn't, but accepted the concession with a brief nod, all the same.

Yennika set her hands on the table, fingers interlaced and eyes downcast. "I'll go. Of course I'll go, but can't we … talk for a while? I've been running so long I've almost forgotten what it's like to have a civil conversation."

Kat frowned. "Why are you running at all? Why aren't you in Kezedi?"

"I was, for a while. Only dear Julan's father got it into his head that I was in some way responsible for his death. Can you believe it?"

"This would be the Julan Aroth you seduced into raising an army? Who you murdered when it all went wrong?"

Yennika frowned. "Yes, but it wasn't *personal*, darling. And he was trying to kill you at the time."

"If you think I owe you anything—"

"Not at all," she replied hurriedly. "The past's the past. I'm just explaining why every bounty-hunter, sell-sword and opportunist in Khalad is looking to drag me off by the heels. Kezedi's such a tiny little place. Much easier to hide in Zariqaz."

"And how's that going?"

Yennika glanced down at her borrowed clothes. "I didn't thank you yet, did I?"

"No. You didn't say much at all."

"Honestly, I'm surprised I could even walk. I'll admit, I'm surprised you didn't finish the job. It's not like I haven't given you reason. If you change your mind, just walk me up to the Aroth estate and hand me over. Castellan Annaj will shower you in tetrams."

"You really think I'd do that?"

A sly smile tugged at Yennika's mouth. "You're being very coy. And to think I used to read you like a book." The smile bled into an introspective frown. "Or maybe not. I suppose if I'd been right about that, neither of us would be sitting here."

"I suppose not."

Yennika filled a mug from the teapot. She swirled the steaming liquid and gave it an experimental sniff. "Can I be honest with you, darling?"

"I don't know. Can you?"

A muscle twitched in her cheek. "All the time I was Azra, I wanted nothing more than to be Yennika again. Not the Yennika everyone thought they knew – the shîm-head embarrassment the family disowned – but the one I *knew* I could be. And for a while, I *was* her. Really her. I never realised how much I wanted dear Ihsan's respect until I had it."

Kat grunted. Ihsan Damant was – or rather, had been – castellan to the Bascari family. Straightforward, decent and uncompromising, he was a hard man to like – much like his one-time pupil, Bashar Vallant. "And?"

"I've spent a lot of time wondering what would have happened if I'd really been that woman. Really *tried* to be worthy of Ihsan's trust … and of yours." Yennika stared into her tea, face pinched and crestfallen. "But it wasn't to be. Yennika Bascari is a selfish little trallock. I don't think I like her very much."

Kat sifted the swirl of sympathy and resentment sloshing around her soul. "Then maybe you should put her behind you." Stars Below, what was she saying? More than that, for whose benefit was she saying it? But still the words came. "Maybe … maybe you should try being Azra again. Start over."

Yennika looked up from her tea. "You really think Azra was any different?"

Kat hesitated. "If I was ever anything more to her than an opportunity for Yennika, maybe she can be."

Yennika gave a small, thoughtful nod. "I hadn't considered that. Thank you, Katija."

They sat in silence, Yennika with her thoughts Nyssa only knew where and Kat desperately grateful that Yali hadn't wandered in. The words had just . . . been there. Saying them had been the most natural thing in the world. Perhaps it was because with her hair grown out, Yennika *looked* more like Azra than she had at their last parting. Yes. That was it.

Wasn't it?

"What is it you need from Kanzîr Station?" asked Yennika at last.

Kat bristled. "You've been listening that long?"

Yennika waved the accusation away. "Survival, darling. You think this is the first strange house I've woken up in?"

"I don't want to know."

A shadow passed behind her eyes. "You're right. You don't." She sipped from her mug, back on balance once more. "You were going to tell me about Kanzîr Station."

Yennika didn't need to know anything. She didn't *deserve* to know anything. But almost everything Kat knew about Tanith, she'd learned from Yennika. She couldn't dismiss the possibility that Yennika knew more about her father's work than she did.

Detail by detail, she recounted her frustrated search for answers, all the way from her arrival in Zariqaz to her confrontation with Fadiya Rashace.

Yennika planted her elbows on the table and her chin in her upturned hands. "I'm impressed, darling. I spent months searching out your father's associates and never found a trace."

Kat winced the praise away before it took root. "For all the good it's done. Have you seen her?"

"Who?"

"Tanith."

Yennika frowned. "Back in Tyzanta, you told me she was dead."

"I told you I *thought* she was dead. She's not. She's in Zariqaz."

"Oh."

Kat had expected *some* sort of reaction, but Yennika's words held only the idlest of idle interest. *Is it raining? Oh.* "Is that it? I thought you were friends."

"Can one be friends with a daemon?"

"You're practically a daemon yourself."

"Why, darling, is that a compliment?" Yennika fluttered her eyelashes, then glanced away. "Tanith and I . . . Our needs aligned, that's all. We were complicated."

"You and everyone is complicated," Kat replied sourly. Did Tanith know the limits of Yennika's attachment? Probably not. Julan Aroth hadn't perceived the shallowness of his relationship with Yennika, nor had Kat herself. All of them puppets dancing on affection's strings.

Yennika brushed the criticism away. "She was always so self-absorbed."

"And you're not?"

"No more than you, darling. Perhaps it's what the three of us have in common. Well, that and one other thing." Yennika sighed. "You want to help her, I suppose? But why the trouble getting into Kanzîr Station? I can't think a few hestics are any barrier to you."

Kat drew back her sleeve and extended her wrist. "This is why."

Yennika's eyes met hers. Kat closed and withdrew her hand. "Ah. Does it hurt?"

"Not any more," Kat replied. "It itches sometimes." She nearly blurted the rest then and there, and wondered why. To garner sympathy? To see if the woman she'd loved was even capable of that?

Yennika leaned closer, her dark eyes boring into Kat's. "It must be like losing a piece of yourself." She held her gaze a heartbeat longer, then grinned. "Aha! I knew it. There's the Kat I remember. This isn't just about Tanith, is it? It's about you."

"It's not like that." Was she so easily read, even now?

139

"If you say so." Yennika shrugged. "Look . . . I think I can get you into Kanzîr. The station overseer's an old . . . friend of mine."

"How close a friend?" Kat hated how hurt she sounded.

Yennika smiled, enjoying her discomfort. "Don't be like that. It was a long time before I met you, and it's not like any of it was particularly memorable." Her smile broadened. "Well, not for me at any rate. I doubt he'll have forgotten."

"I don't want your help."

"It's not help, darling. Call it an exchange. Honour among skelders. Azra or Yennika, that's what I am now, isn't it? I owe you. Let me clear the debt. Then we'll go our separate ways. If that's what you want."

Kat hesitated. Yennika – *Azra* – had said something similar just before the disaster at Xanathros Alabastra, when she'd faked her death and left Kat to pick up the pieces.

All she had to do was refuse.

Once she's up and around, she's gone, she'd told Yali. Well, Yennika *was* up and around. She could walk her to the door. Be rid of her. That was what she wanted, wasn't it?

Wasn't it?

Kiasta.

"Tell me what you have in mind," she said instead.

140

Fifteen

"What's keeping him?"

No one answered Enna's terse question. No one had answered it on the preceding three occasions. Ardoc was now a full half-hour overdue. More than long enough for tempers to fray.

Tanith, hands looped behind her back, clenched her fingers tight as another shiver racked her body. Headlong flight from the foundry had taken too much. She'd known even before the tremor had struck, warned by the lingering, intoxicated glances of Qolda's kathari. Her glamour was never stronger than when hunger was upon her. She'd bare hours before her sanity slipped. By rights, she'd have fed already. A redcloak. A lost, unloved stray. But she'd promised Ardoc. Now, every tick of the distant guildhall clock sliced pieces of her away. How long before even the cadaverous Qolda looked appetising?

Another shudder struck. She gripped her hands tight, grateful that, standing as she was on the threshold between the conclave circle's light and the shadows beyond, no one saw her fidget.

"Ardoc's comings and goings are his own," sneered Qolda. "He'll be here when he chooses."

"And what of your punctuality?" Enna spoke softly, but tension beneath the words revealed a woman holding back the tide. "If you'd been on time, Irthan and the others would still be alive."

A wise man might have held his tongue, rather than wasting his breath on circular arguments, but whatever wisdom Qolda possessed was slave to self-regard. "How many times? Some overseer took it upon himself to raid Lakia's Warren. It was either go the long way round or turn up with half the Ozdîr custodium at our backs. You think I wanted this? Four crates of shriekers, their glyphs uncured. Each worth more than an antique tetram to us. Now they're back in redcloak hands."

Shriekers were closely controlled by the shriversmen who created them, their glyphs – once cured – shared only with redcloaks, custodians and those firebloods of sufficient wealth or prestige to barter for them. Uncured weapons weren't supposed to leave the binding halls, much less find themselves crated up in a lightly defended provisions yard. But paperwork so often went astray where Ardoc's contacts were concerned.

Enna's tone grew colder still. "You lost weaponry. Irthan and the others lost their lives."

His face reddening, Qolda rapped the knuckles of his right hand against his breastbone in a muddy rendition of a Simah sign for grief. "You think I don't know that?" His words burned hotter, angrier. "I can't change the past."

"And isn't that convenient?"

"What's that supposed to mean?"

"I remember how hard you argued against me handling this."

"The kathari are soldiers. This operation should have been mine to run."

"Soldiers? They're thugs with all the subtlety of a railrunner collision. They'd have left a trail of bodies across three districts."

"Better that than what actually happened. Or shall we ask Irthan?"

Enna stepped into the circle. An unspeakable breach of protocol among firebloods, it was only slightly less so here. "If you wanted to teach me a lesson, Qolda, there were other ways. You want to fight me, have the decency to fight *me*."

He lurched towards her, shoulders squared and fists balled. "You sanctimonious, self-righteous little—"

Serrîq, thus far so quiet that Tanith had forgotten he was present, laid a hand on Qolda's shoulder. "This doesn't help anyone." A careful smile accompanied his mediator's tone. "Perhaps it would be better if we reconvened once Ardoc arrives."

Qolda pulled free. "She's accusing me of abandoning my friends!"

Enna snorted. "Friends? What a lot of new words you're learning today." She reached the centre of the circle, eyes locked on his. "Don't hold back, show me just how much of a soldier you are. But make it count. You might not get another chance."

He stepped closer, teeth bared. "I only *need* one chance."

"ENOUGH!" Ardoc marched into the circle. In place of his usual bonhomie he wore a flat, impassive mask that rivalled Enna's for its coldness. "One trial. Is that truly all it takes to divide us?"

Qolda, his scowl bitter, returned to the circle's edge. Enna hesitated, then withdrew. Neither uttered a word. The wind knew better than to howl at the mountain. Ardoc's expression remained impassive. Too impassive, perhaps, for someone newly come to the conflict. How long had he been lurking in the darkness, waiting for the storm to break so that he could blow it out?

"That's better." Tension slipped from his face. "There is no tragedy that disharmony cannot make worse. I thought all of you understood that. Clearly, I was wrong."

Serrîq cleared his throat. "Did our guest shed any light on what happened?"

The "guest" in question was a redcloak captive – the katharis' sole tangible contribution to the night's misadventure. They'd been none too gentle, pieces of his soul already wisping away to the Deadwinds before he'd been dragged, blindfolded and gagged, into the haven.

Ardoc rubbed his hands, the skin ruddier than it should have been, the colour richest of all about his cuticles. "Alas, very little. We prayed together before he left us." Among his other accomplishments, Ardoc was a master of the passive voice.

"I could have spoken with him." Tanith's pulse quickened at the

143

spoiled prospect of a feast even as her mind recoiled in disgust. "He'd have told me everything."

"My dear, even beauty as persuasive as yours pales before fading mortality." Ardoc shrugged. "In any case, soldiers are seldom entrusted with the motive, only the means. I believe such was the case here. I'm afraid we must consider the possibility that this was a trap."

Serrîq stiffened. "I have full confidence in my sources, as I hope you have in me."

Ardoc frowned. "Of course. I meant nothing so dramatic as betrayal..." And yet despite that, Tanith couldn't help but note how his gaze lingered on Qolda. "It may simply be that the shriekers we sought to claim were not sent by Nyssa's grace, but as bait."

Tension eased from Serrîq's shoulders. "And perhaps not even for us."

"Indeed. Uncured shriekers fetch a fine price in Undertown. We acted as swiftly as we did to get to these before Zerrican added his outrageous markup. I think it likely the noose was set for him, and we stumbled into it. You might make enquiries upon your return." Ardoc held up a cautioning hand. "But carefully, of course."

Serrîq nodded. "Of course."

Glad of the distraction from the rising emptiness of her hunger, Tanith mentally filed away the rare clue to Serrîq's true identity. Unlike Qolda and Enna, he seldom remained in the haven once conclave was concluded, implying responsibilities elsewhere. Those of a custodium overseer, perhaps? Or maybe even a redcloak, if one far beyond the age of front-line service.

"As to the rest," Ardoc addressed the full conclave once more, "how many did we lose?"

Barely a muscle flickered in Enna's face. "Esram and Ioni made it to the refuge on Asari Street. I brought them in this morning." Neither possessed the glyphs to enter the haven directly, and would instead have dispatched one of the cult's valuable concealed heraldics to request help. "It might be that there are others who slipped the redcloak net ... but it doesn't look good."

Tanith stifled a pang of empathy. Herself included, that made a mere four survivors. At least Esram had made it to safety. It mattered that she'd not steered him false.

"Was anyone taken alive?" asked Serrîq.

"If they were, we'll find out soon enough," Qolda replied.

Ardoc glanced down at his hands in distaste and folded his arms behind his back. "Let us hope it's not marching feet in the Underways that grant revelation. We do not have doctrine to control us as Alabastra does. We do not have the custodium's contracts of service or the threat of its law to keep us in line. Trust. That is what binds us. If we do not have trust? Now, when we are on the brink of attaining everything we have ever sought? Then we have nothing at all."

He stepped back from the circle and paced the darkness, his footfalls measured, his voice low and resonant. "Whether last night's trap was intended for us or we blundered into one meant for parties unknown scarcely matters. We received a warning. A reminder that vigilance *is* survival. The possibility remains that there are those among us in whom faith does not flow as strongly as they would have us believe. We must have vigilance, now and always, or we will burn like those who came before us ... and the goddess will remain for ever a prisoner."

He halted behind Tanith, the scent of his soul thickening the air. Tanith held her breath. But Ardoc was too near, the lavender of his immortal essence enticing for all that it had thinned with age. Intermingled yearning and horror tingled at the base of her spine.

Go away, she begged silently. *Please.*

When Ardoc spoke, it was in little more than a warm, rumbling whisper, so much so that she wasn't sure if the words were meant for anyone other than her, much less if they carried. "We are so close. So very close. They must not stop us now."

She clenched her fists to control a sudden tremor, pinched her lips to smother a whimper as her control threatened to slip.

Lost in a lavender nightmare, she barely heard Qolda clear his throat. "We need to focus our efforts. Charity's all well and good, but maybe we'd have avoided last night's tragedy if some of us hadn't been slowed by the prospect of feeding Gutterfield rats?"

Enna started forward, only to be brought up short by Ardoc's authoritative wave. Tanith drew down a relieved, stuttering gasp as he strode past her into the circle, his soul-scent going with him.

"You are in no position to criticise laggardliness, Qolda," he rumbled. "An army that does not march when it is needed makes a fine argument for its own dissolution."

"I already explained that. The Ozdîr—"

"Excuses do not endear themselves to me. You agreed to support Enna. You broke your promise. If it happens again, it will be more than your standing at risk. Am I understood?"

Qolda's brow flickered resentment, his shoulders shaking with barely contained anger, but he nodded. "Yes. You've been very clear."

Ardoc's expression smoothed. "Then I believe we can call the matter concluded for now. *Abdon Nyssa ivohê.*"

"*Abdon Nyssa ivohê.*" Tanith murmured the words with her eyes closed, the better to ravel herself back in. When she opened them again, she and Ardoc were alone in the circle.

"I understand you acquitted yourself well last night."

Her heart swelled at the compliment, but she couldn't keep a scowl from her lips. Concealing truth from Ardoc took more than she had. It was harder to deceive people you liked.

He hooked an eyebrow, his face crowding with concern. "What is it?"

"It was my fault. I was supposed to be keeping watch." The detail, at least, she could spare, if only because it might get Esram in trouble. "I failed."

"There is blame enough to go around, with Enna and Qolda most of all." He grunted with mirthless humour. "Along with this old fool for showing too much trust and not enough leadership, as I'm sure has occurred to them both by now. Have you learned your lesson?"

"I think so."

"Then you're doing better than the rest of us. How can I not forgive that?" He tapped a knuckle to his lips. "You're very pale. Abstinence is sitting poorly with you, I assume?"

She swallowed. How much had he noticed when standing at her shoulder? "It's not easy." An understatement vast enough to blot out the stars.

Ardoc nodded. "Nothing worthwhile ever is. But I promised that you'd be free to indulge yourself tonight, and you shall. Speak to Qolda. He'll give you all the details. *Abdon Nyssa ivohê.*"

"*Abdon Nyssa ivohê.*"

Her eyes open this time, Tanith missed nothing of Ardoc's fatherly smile.

The buried streets were as busy as Tanith had ever seen, and she avoided her fellow initiates as much as the narrowness of the thoroughfares permitted. Though her cravings had passed from their peak to an uneasy, gnawing valley, she was bitterly aware that they'd return. Better not to take chances. Especially as her sense of smell grew steadily sharper the longer she went unsated.

A pair of hands seized her by her lapels, dragging her out of the lumani-lit street and into a darkened alley. Before she'd chance to register what was happening, Esram's warm lips found hers.

Adrift on lavender clouds, she dragged him deeper into the alleyway, the outer flame of his soul irresistible.

He tasted so *good.*

"No!"

With her last ounce of self-control, she flung him across the alley, then collapsed, shuddering and gasping, to hands and knees. The dull *thock* of head striking stone and the sharp yelp of pain suggested he'd landed rather worse. Tanith focused on the grit beneath her palms, and the cool stone beneath that. The pain in her wrists from her awkward fall. The footfalls beyond the end of the alley. Anything to drown out the lavender and the wrong kind of desire.

But nothing could erase the knowledge of what she'd almost done.

147

Twisting awkwardly about, she planted her haunches on the cobbles, her shoulders against the uneven stone wall. "Never do that again! Never!" she shouted, voice raw and tears pricking at her eyes. "What were you thinking?"

Esram slumped opposite, one hand clasped to the back of his head and his cheeks tight. "I was thinking how glad I was that you're alive." He managed to sound apologetic and offended all at once. "I didn't expect ... Look, I'm sorry. I thought ... I wanted to surprise you. Apparently I did."

Tanith ground the heels of her hands into her eyes and fought the urge to scream. "I'm glad you're alive too." She wished she sounded like she meant it. "But you shouldn't have done that."

Esram blinked. "So it's all right if you kiss me, but not the other way round?"

"That's not how it is."

"Then how is it? I don't understand."

Of course he didn't understand, because she hadn't told him. But she owed him *something*. "People who get close to me die, Esram."

He frowned. "You're not responsible for what happened last night."

Clever enough to be stupid, that was him. But even with his head still ringing from chiming against the alley wall – from *her* chiming it against the alley wall – he was more concerned for her than for himself. "That's not what I meant."

The first frustration crowded his expression. "Then what *do* you mean?"

All of a sudden, Tanith realised she was tired of lying. "I kill them. I kill them, or they leave. All right?"

She glared, defying him to react, all the while wondering what form that reaction would take. Would he laugh? Flee? Pity would be the worst. The soft twist of the lip and the embarrassed downcast glance people reserved for things broken beyond mending. She'd seen it too often. She knew just how broken she was, and didn't need the reminder.

Better just to walk away.

Wincing at the pain in her jarred wrists, she pushed against the wall until she was on her feet once more, and started for the alley mouth.

Esram's hand closed about her wrist.

Not insistent. Not demanding. Just . . . there.

"You haven't killed me yet." He shrugged ruefully, his free hand again gingerly pressed against the bloodstain half hidden by his hair. "Maybe not for lack of trying, but you haven't. And I'm not going anywhere. I promise."

He thought she was simply the product of a shattered home, or a Gutterfield rat, traded over and over as a commodity, wounds buried deep beneath her smile. He wouldn't have been wrong on either count. But the rest? He couldn't know that. And she wouldn't tell him. Not today. Maybe tomorrow, when she wasn't trembling with hunger. When the burnt lavender of his soul wouldn't smell quite so good. When she could think straight.

Musky soul-scent swirling ever thicker about her, and with the uttermost ironclad self-control, she kissed him on the lips. Merely a moment of fleeting warmth in the haven's cool air – she didn't dare risk anything more – but even that moment was a triumph. More, it offered hope. If she could keep control now, with her daemon-half wailing for sustenance, then maybe she wasn't a monster after all, except for when she wanted to be.

"Next time, try leading with that," she murmured.

She left him standing there and, with a spring in her step, went to murder a stranger.

Sixteen

Kanzîr Station perched on the border of Starji district and the Golden Citadel, its three storeys of platforms and winding rails jutting out towards the duskward horizon. They rushed down-spire on a spiderweb scaffold of bowed timber and corroded iron until they vanished into the streets of Qosm, thence through the city walls, the outlying Gutterfield slums and across Khalad's arid red plains.

Kat descended to a station concourse already thick with passengers, porters, travellers' trunks and luggage of just about every shape and size. Khalad's panoply at its finest, with the bright colours and geometric jag-jag patterns of the western cities intermingling beneath the vaulted glass ceiling with the earthy, practical garb of migrating millworkers. Even Rîma blended in, her sword of little note in a crowd thick with escorts and bodyguards.

Kat plunged into the morass, a swimmer fighting against a current flowing to the curlicued archway where custodians processed entry visas and arrival tolls. She reached the relative shelter of the buttressed clock tower battered, bruised and trampled, her lungs thick with the bitter mingling of wood smoke, steam and straining bodies . . . but, she hoped, unremarked.

Things were already challenging enough. Her spasms had grown more in strength and frequency across the past three days than in the months before. She'd imbibed as much last breath as she'd dared before leaving the theatre. Taking too much risked hallucinations, even dependency. All her life, she'd resented her mother for slipping away on last breath rather than face the pain of omen rot. Now . . . Well, now she understood. Only folk with a future worried about addiction.

Rîma, serene as ever, reached her in a swish of coat tails. Yali joined them, a broad grin plastered across her face and a haversack on her thin shoulders.

The hestic above the clocktower doorway shifted restlessly behind the graven flame-haired likeness of Nyssa Benevolas. Kat cast a long and deceptively unconcerned glance along the concourse. It just so happened to take in the nearest of the five squat towers, festooned with cables and brightly coloured discs, that served as signal boxes and guard stations. A pair of custodians stood on the upper balcony, their attention on a growing commotion at the station's far end. Raised voices, a steadily clearing circle in the crowd and the spreading stain of black uniforms spoke to a confrontation well under way.

"I hope Tatterlain knows what he's doing," she muttered.

Rîma gave one of her almost-there shrugs. "He's already further from that than we are and cackling with delight."

True enough. Nothing easier than to start an argument in a crowd and then slip away. "And Yenni—" Kat scowled. "*Azra?*"

Rîma nodded past an elderly couple lost in an expressive Simah argument, oblivious to the frustration they were causing in those who had to navigate around them. "There."

Azra, glamorous in a stolen coat of emerald silks and with heavy eyeshadow and blush to hide lingering bruises, walked arm-in-arm with a tall, copper-skinned custodian with close-cropped hair and a fastidiously trimmed beard. The two looked to be as lost in conversation as the elderly couple . . . at least until Kat realised that Azra was doing all the talking. The custodian's expression, already the tight-lipped near scowl of an uneasy man, darkened further as Azra guided him into the clocktower's shadow. "Everyone, this is Overseer Jazal. He's kindly agreed to offer his assistance."

"This isn't what we discussed," he growled. "Just you, that's what you said."

The smallest hint of dismay touched Azra's brow. "Oh, darling, don't disappoint me." For all the lightness in her words, there was no mistaking the threat. "Ammar wouldn't like that at all."

Jazal went deathly still. "What does my son have to do with this?"

Azra's frown grew puzzled. "After his nursemaid met with a terrible accident about an hour ago, a friend of mine took it upon himself to keep the boy entertained. Only I have so *many* friends. I might forget which of them decided to be so selfless." She shrugged. "If *that* happened? Why, you might never see your son again."

For all that Rîma didn't move a muscle, her whole sense changed, her unspoken threat every bit as apparent as Azra's. Yali stiffened, her expression a good match for the one Kat, her stomach knotted tight, fought to keep from reaching her own face.

Jazal shot a glance at the nearest signal tower and its custodians, all too distant to help him, much less his son. "Damn you, Yennika. This afternoon—"

"This afternoon, I was the brightest star in your sky, and your family a distant, inconvenient memory." Azra's saccharine smile didn't touch her eyes. "I'd focus on that."

Jazal opened his mouth, then closed it without a word as something broke behind his eyes. Kat's heart ached in sympathy. She knew better than anyone what it was like for Azra to cut you off at the knees.

"You win," he muttered, his cheeks newly haggard.

Azra beamed. "Why *of course* I do, darling."

Moving like a man in a dream, Jazal crossed to the clocktower door and raised his left hand to the hestic's sentry prism.

The tower's confines were barely lit and musty with spreading damp. The maintenance tunnels at the foot of the narrow stairway were even worse, their crumbling walls dark with unknowable stains and furred mould. But so long as you knew where they led – as Azra apparently did and Jazal surely had to – you could go anywhere.

152

Ten paces in, Yali and Rîma exchanged a look with no need of Simah to grant it meaning. Rîma lengthened her stride and took Jazal by the elbow, leaving Azra behind.

"Now wait a—" Azra broke off as Yali shoved her hard against the tunnel wall. "Hey!"

Jazal glanced briefly back before Rîma's insistent tug drew him onwards.

Azra reached for the dagger hidden beneath her silk coat.

Yali's was already in her hand. ||Tell me about the child.||

Azra blinked. She'd never troubled herself to learn Simah.

"She wants to know what you've done with the boy." Kat moved to stand beside Yali. ||"So do I."||

Yali's grateful nod brought a welcome flicker of warmth to the cool tunnels. It had taken a full hour's argument to even get her to accept that Azra would be coming with them – an argument Kat hadn't so much won as outlasted. Now, she wished she'd listened.

"Can we talk about this later?" hissed Azra.

"No."

"Darling, are—"

"Don't call me that," snapped Kat.

Azra sagged against the tunnel wall and shot a furtive glance at Jazal, now a good twenty paces ahead. "I've done nothing," she breathed. "Not with the boy, and not with his nursemaid. Nor has anyone done so on my behalf."

Kat blinked. "But you said—"

"You know how it works, darl—" Azra pursed her lips. "Jazal only has to believe Ammar's in danger. It's almost a waste of effort for it to be true."

"What about these 'friends' of yours?"

"The only friend I have left is you, Katija."

"And even I'm not really your friend."

Her expression fell further. "I suppose not."

Kat swallowed the rush of remorse she *mostly* believed Azra had meant to provoke. But her words, at least, held true. Things didn't have to be real in Khalad, only real *enough*.

||What do you think?|| she asked Yali.

||You know what I think.|| Green eyes on Azra's, Yali offered a small sigh. ||But that looked like the truth.||

Kat jerked her head down the tunnel. With fragile dignity, Azra peeled herself off the wall.

They passed a handful of cracked, empty sentry crests and a pair where the hestics set the remains of Kat's tattoo itching until Jazal hushed them. Like the ifrît watching the clocktower door, their focus rested solely on who entered, not who left. Living souls, Kat saw only twice. Once when a stray maintenance worker ventured into a crossway up ahead and swiftly doubled back without glimpsing the five interlopers pressed flat against the darkened wall. Again when the tunnel briefly became a corroded, slatted bridge over a crow's nest of viaduct scaffolding, the lowermost of Kanzîr Station's platforms and its thin crowd just about visible a hundred yards below. The bridge's heyday lay long in the past. A section of its mesh wall was entirely absent, and the structure swayed alarmingly with every step.

Kat's vertigo loved every moment of it; Kat less so.

A short scramble up a ladder, another down a spiral stair, and they were out beneath the tangle of scaffolds and trackway trestles, the smoggy air thick with the heavy rattle and breathy rush of trains serving platforms high above. Beyond a low crumbling wall, the flames of the station's torch house danced heavenwards. Fluttering scarlet banners served as demarcation between the civilian station and the redcloak compound. A dozen warehouses and barracks, swarming with Royal Guard. Kat suppressed a shudder. A place only a madwoman would lightly tread.

Fortunately, the austere brick arches and high windows of Kanzîr Station's siding depot lay in the opposite direction. Gesturing for the others to follow, she struck out into the shadows.

*

Gezamîr Arloq, *gansalar* of the Royal Guard, Pacifier of Azamora and Templar of Holy Alabastra, tasted *good*. Good enough that Tanith no longer felt the torch house flames crackling behind her. So good, in fact, that even awash in the dizzying lavender warmth of a fading soul, she found the restraint to slow her feasting and savour the moment.

Trapped in her embrace, Arloq whimpered.

Cheek to cheek and lips at his ear, Tanith stroked his hair and inhaled another wisp of his inner soul. "Hush. Hush, hush, hush. You were a soldier, weren't you? Die well."

Another breath. Another moan. Another frisson of ... something Tanith had never really been able to name. It lurked on the edge of every feeding, a glimpse of the spirit world, or something *beyond*. Always tantalising. Always just out of reach. But somehow it was different this time. Her hunger sharper, the plundered soul sweeter. The shape that wasn't a shape clearer than ever. The fruits of self-denial? Some archons preached that the greatest abandon was to reject abandon entirely – to remove oneself from sensation and thus court divine ecstasy.

No amount of restraint would save Arloq now. Tanith was the only thing holding him upright against the balustrade. A big, strong man with appetites that her glamour had scarcely coaxed, he'd soon forgotten his need to know how she'd found her way past the hestic watch-spirits. He'd followed her like a lamb up the spiral stair to the flame platform, and then ... ?

Well, by then she'd been so hungry that all the strength in Khalad wouldn't have counted for anything.

But no tears for Gezamîr Arloq, who'd broken the mineworkers' strike at Azamora and left two hundred dead in the dust. Whose brutalities were forgiven only because of his uniform. She was *allowed* to enjoy this, and not just because Ardoc had said so.

Amashti weren't the only monsters in the world.

One last, stuttering breath. One last sweet wisp of soul, and then all Tanith held in her hands was a nerveless lump of meat wrapped in scarlet.

She giggled – she hadn't meant to, it was just *there* – and kissed him on the cheek. "Thank you."

The corpse offered no answer, as a good corpse should.

Tanith let the body drop and opened her eyes. For the first time in weeks, she felt like herself. The gnawing, ever-present edginess that she only noticed by its absence? Gone. The self-pity? Well, that was always a work in progress. A wicked man was dead, she was whole and Ardoc would be pleased. A fine night.

Leave no trace, Ardoc had said. Nothing by which the shriversmen could identify an amashti's work. Fortunately, Kanzîr's torch house was a modern design, the flames birthed by a pyrasti-driven furnace in the minaret's belly rather than from stacked timbers at its summit. Braids spilling over her shoulders, Tanith dragged the corpse across the fire platform by its ankle. Skin prickling from the magenta flames, she hoisted Arloq by the armpits and tipped him into the furnace shaft.

"Oops." She fought to stop another giggle fluttering free.

There. No shriversman would linger long examining a burned corpse.

Furtive movement beyond the compound wall drew her eye as she brushed her hands clean. Five figures, clinging to the shadows of rail-runner carriages as they crossed the interwoven tracks. She indulged a smile. There was more mischief than hers abroad that night.

Her smile faltered as the leading intruders strayed close enough to a lumani lantern to reveal their faces.

Kat? Kat *and* Yennika? Together?

Tanith's smile faded, the afterglow of feeding turning cold and bitter. "And what do we have here, dear sister?"

||What do you mean, you can't open it?|| Disappointment curdled at the back of Kat's throat. ||I thought you were the greatest lock charmer in Khalad.||

Yali set down her tools and leaned against the vault door. ||I didn't say I can't open it. I said I can't open it *quickly*.||

The Rashace train, one of a dozen waiting beneath the depot's sloped

156

roof, comprised six carriages waiting for the railrunner engine that would haul them to Oracum in three days' time. Three goods wagons for furniture, two first-class passenger coaches for Fadiya and whatever household accompanied her into exile, and a vault wagon for personal possessions. Yali had taken one look at the latter's outer lock, sniffed her derision, and opened it in less than a minute. The vault itself was proving to be another matter.

The vault occupied the entirety of its namesake wagon save for a narrow corridor running the carriage's length and the small lobby in which they crouched – itself otherwise empty but for a large tarpaulined picture frame set against one wall. Visible were no fewer than three key-driven locks, one governed by a combination dial. On top of those, Kat's itching tattoo suggested at least one more lock controlled by a stubborn motic ifrît and an unknown number of hestics buried on the threshold.

Yali rubbed her brow with the back of her hand. ||The regular locks? Maybe a quarter-hour, because I *am* the greatest lock charmer in Khalad. The combination? That's going to take longer. Quicker now than if this heap was moving. I need to feel the chambers catching, and railrunners aren't exactly a smooth ride.||

For all that Yali often spoke of locks talking to her, her deafness meant that tremor and touch were their shared language, rather than the telltale *click* for which others might yearn.

She patted her haversack. ||I can pipe in belcher's acid to eat away the motic bolts, but that's not fast. We could still be here come dawn, and that's before you even start picking over whatever's inside. Even assuming that hestic you say is in there doesn't immolate us both.|| She shook her head glumly. ||You wanted a blasting prism for this, not me.||

||We'd get a lot of friends, very fast.||

||I didn't say it was a perfect plan.||

No, a perfect plan would have relied on Kat twisting her aetherios tattoo into a shape the ifrîti would have recognised. Typical. They couldn't even use a ravati as they had at Yarvid's house. A terrified motic couldn't slip a bolt. ||So what do we do?||

157

Yali grinned. ||That's your problem. You're the brains, I'm just the fingers.||

||But?||

||But this isn't happening tonight.||

It probably wasn't happening *any* night. Jazal, currently hunkered down outside with Rîma and Azra, knew too much. Whatever they did from there he had to be kept from talking, which in turn meant that one of their number would have to serve as his jailer until they could make another – hopefully successful – attempt.

Yali patted the covered picture frame. ||We could cut this free and sell it? Make a small profit on the night.|| She peeled back the tarpaulin, revealing a tall, blonde woman in a flowing white gown, surrounded by children. ||Is that the countess?||

Kat, still lost in frustration, nodded absently. ||My father painted it. She was always smiling back then.||

And Fadiya Rashace *was* smiling in the portrait, her radiant joy, long since lost, captured by the careful brushwork of a man she'd loved, and who had loved her in return. Her children, Iskander and Etenah, dark-featured like their father and both in matched blue silks, stood to either side; adult relatives – the grim Hargo among them – a crowd at her shoulders. And standing at the very front, the countess's hands on her upper arms, a black-haired, bronze-skinned girl in a simple grey dress, whose delight at being included transcended mere pigment to become unanswerable truth.

Yali tilted her head. ||Kat . . . is that *you*?||

Kat swallowed, choked by emotion long since buried at seeing herself like that – as her father had seen her – so young, so innocent. ||It wasn't long after my mother's death. It was supposed to be family only, but *Mathami* insisted.|| She'd more than insisted. Kat had heard Fadiya arguing with Hargo from three rooms over, and there'd been no peace in the household for weeks afterwards. ||She told me . . . that I was family too.||

No wonder it wasn't in the vault proper. Hargo Rashace would be glad to be rid of it.

She pinched her eyes shut before the floodgates burst. Still tears pricked her cheeks. Family. Fadiya hadn't needed to name her thus, just as no one had forced her to give small presents on festival days, or arrange for Kat to study alongside her own children, with tutors no Arvish could ever have afforded. For the first time, Kat saw how the cynicism of adolescence had warped those memories, recasting kindness as collateral offered in the countess' affair with her father even though the one far pre-dated the other. So obvious now that after Nyssa had called Kat's mother to the Stars Below, the countess had helped raise the daughter she'd left behind, propriety be damned. Had risked what remained of her marriage and livelihood to help Kat after her father's death . . .

. . . and Kat, caught up in blaming Fadiya for things that weren't really her fault, had left her a prisoner in her own house, at the whim of an embittered husband.

"Nyssa forgive me," she breathed. "I'm a selfish little trallock."

Yali regarded her carefully, a woman venturing out onto uncertain ground. ||So, are we coming back tomorrow night?||

Kat wiped her cheeks dry, yesterday's sorrow reborn as tomorrow's purpose. ||No.||

Forewarned by creaking hinges, Tanith hopped up onto the goods wagon's running board and flattened her shoulders against the soot-smeared planks. One by one, her quarry filed into the sidings yard, taking cover behind a pile of disused rails while a custodian patrol – the same patrol Tanith had shadowed ever since leaving the redcloak compound – vanished deeper into the night.

From there, they retraced the route back to the station proper, track-side lanterns casting just enough illumination for Tanith to identify the others. Kat and Yennika. The deaf girl who'd tried to kill her in the skies above Athenoch; the white-haired woman who'd come damn close to finishing the job with a sword whose steel had seared Tanith's flesh like no fire ever had. Only the man was a complete stranger. An unwilling participant, if facial expressions and Yennika's proximity were anything to go by.

Tanith ducked back as they approached. With the aftermath of Arloq's soul still buzzing within her own, could she take all five? Kat she remembered as determined but unskilled. The deaf girl was barely an obstacle. Yennika would likely run – abandoning people was what Yennika did, wasn't it? The overseer was a potential ally if he was anything.

That left the white-haired woman. The woman, and that sword.

Tanith scowled. *Four* of them. Four of them she could take.

If only the white-haired woman were elsewhere.

Maybe they'd get split up. Maybe *she* should split them up.

And what then?

It had all seemed so clear from the top of the torch house. Things always did from up high. But the darkness of the sidings yard brought only questions. Or maybe it wasn't the darkness, but the fading euphoria of the feeding. She was never at her most rational while awash in someone else's soul. Maybe Kat didn't deserve to die. Just suffer a bit.

As for how much? Well, they'd figure that out as they went along.

Boots crunched on gravel. Two pairs passed away behind the wagon. Yennika and the overseer, their voices muttered and unfriendly; his with hatred, hers with quiet threat. A third set of footsteps, lighter than the others, belonging to the girl. Hushed voices accompanied the remaining pair.

"You're sure you wish to go through with this?"

Tanith's heart skipped at the soft, guttural words she'd last heard issued as a challenge, moments before the white-haired woman had opened her up like a side of meat. She had her hand to the sword at her back before she realised they weren't meant for her.

"I don't see any other way, not now," Kat replied. "When that rail-runner leaves, I need to be on it. We've three days to work out the rest."

The footsteps tracked away, the voices hushed by distance.

"What you're proposing will be dangerous."

"I have to try." Kat's voice became an indignant whisper. "Why are you looking at me like that?"

"For a moment – just a moment – you sounded like Vallant."

The steam whistle of a distant railrunner swallowed Kat's snort. Then they were gone from earshot.

But it didn't matter any longer. Not now Tanith knew where Kat would be in three days.

Thoughts abuzz with possibilities, she jumped down to the track.

And froze as she spotted a silent shadow atop the roof of a broken-down passenger carriage. The starlight barely touched him. What shape it offered hinted at long coat tails twitching in the breeze and paired sword hilts at his back. Of the shadow himself, Tanith made out little, save that his attention was on Kat's retreating party.

Even as the thought formed, it became a lie. The shadow's head dipped, his hidden stare boring into her. Confident. Appraising. For the second time in as many minutes, Tanith reached for her sword.

Teeth gleamed a smile. The shadow bowed as one among peers, then suddenly turned, staring off towards the torch house and a pair of *vahla*-masked custodians advancing along the track, their tread measured and bored.

When she looked back, the shadow was gone.

By the time Kat reached the corroded bridge, she had the makings of a plan. Jazal would have to be their unwilling guest for a few days, yes, but that was manageable. As for the rest? It was all in the timings. They could make it work.

So fixated was she on what was to come that she made it most of the way across the creaking bridge without her vertigo issuing even a flutter of protest. It helped to keep her eyes firmly on Yali and Rîma, waiting in the tunnel up ahead. Azra and Jazal had fallen to the rear at the former's unexpected suggestion that Kat would find passage of the bridge less traumatic if it wasn't bucking up and down under the weight of others.

As she reached the tunnel mouth, a thin wail split the air.

161

"Azra?"

Kat spun around, fearful instinct overriding good sense.

One glance at the body plunging towards the platform far below set the darkness spinning. Gorge thick with nausea, she remained upright only because Yali reached her and held her tight.

Panic rising, she clamped her eyes shut. The world steadied. "What happened? Is Azra . . . ?"

"I'm here."

She opened her eyes, fighting a rush of relief. She wasn't *supposed* to feel anything about Azra any longer, much less relief. Azra stood beside the gaping hole in the bridge's mesh wall, wearing the indulgent smile of a woman finding amusement in the most inappropriate of places.

"What happened to Jazal?" Kat asked tiredly. Some puzzles only ever had a single solution.

"Oh, I'm afraid he fell, darling," Azra replied, with lashings of almost-sincere innocence.

"You mean you killed him."

She shrugged. "He was an unfaithful husband and, I'm sure, a terrible father. Ammar's better off without him."

Seventeen

With a shrill blast of its steam whistle and a shudder of reluctant gears, the railrunner pulled away. The rising *chuff-chuff-chuff* of pistons quickened, the soot-stained buildings passing by the timber-framed window ever faster as the engine found its pace. Kat fidgeted against the slatted bench. Workers' carriages weren't supposed to be comfortable but *efficient*, cramming in as many bodies as possible.

At least this one – the third and final on this particular railrunner – was reasonably empty. Had the railrunner plied the labour route from Zariqaz to the shoreside mines, it would have been full to bursting, with two hundred overalled workers crammed tight as matchsticks. That afternoon, there were perhaps forty passengers, all fleeing Zariqaz's sprawl for the hope of better futures in the airier, smaller cities of Hezira, Osios and Oracum.

There were only three workers' wagons and two of the considerably more comfortable travellers' wagons immediately behind engine and tender. Hargo Rashace's six wagons brought up the rear: three goods wagons loaded with furniture, one carriage loaded with custodians to serve as his wife's protectors and jailers, Fadiya Rashace's private carriage, and then the vault wagon bringing up the rear.

Sitting opposite, beside Rîma, Azra scowled. "I don't know what you're smiling at."

Like Kat, she wore labourer's garb, the smock, coat and trousers patched many times over, their bright reds and yellows long since faded. Only the shimmering black and gold headscarf retained any vibrancy. Even in Undertown, standards remained – only a destitute worker wore a shabby scarf. It was typical of Azra that she infused even those rags with glamour. Beauty was more presentation than practicality, and she a mistress of presentation. Even silent, she screamed to be admired.

Kat stared down the carriage to the ochre-silked steward checking tickets. "I'm not smiling." She softened her cheeks to make truth of the lie.

Even with the future filled with trials, there was just *something* about travelling by railrunner. Perhaps it was the warming, brackish smell of the soot? Or perhaps the sense of a self-contained world, separate from the troubles and travails swirling about the real one. Or maybe – just maybe – the tremors shivering through the carriage's timber and steel frame made her feel as though the engine's power was somehow part of her. That she could reach out and claim it. Make it part of her, as she'd briefly made the Deadwinds part of her.

Throat thickening with loss, she clamped her eyes shut and fought the urge to scratch at her ruined aetherios tattoo.

Azra yawned and spread her arms along the bench's backrest. "The railrunner I took to Tyzanta made for the longest three days of my life."

"Perhaps you should have remained behind." Alone of the trio, Rîma wore her customary garb, her face all but hidden between hat and tightly wound scarf. Her only concession to a low profile had been to conceal her sword inside a thick bundle of the beribboned *streza* canes so popular with children at festival times, as much for the ear-splitting hum they made when whirled just *so* as for the bright, spiralling colours evoking Nyssa's flames. "Whatever debt you owed, you've paid."

Azra shrugged. "Perhaps I like being in profit?"

Rîma offered Kat an unhappy glance, but nodded all the same. She'd waged and lost that campaign – provoked by what could be charitably described as Azra's "practical" murder of Overseer Jazal – two days prior. Neither Rîma nor Yali had wanted her along. Only Tatterlain had agreed that they needed all the help they could get.

With a squeal of brakes, the railrunner slowed. Prala district. Just one station more and they'd be out onto the open plain. Hours of uninterrupted travel in which the railrunner was isolated. Vulnerable.

No more time for doubts.

Swallowing hers as best she could, Kat rose. "Let's get moving."

Kat hung back in the vestibule as Rîma and Azra made their way through to the first of the travellers' carriages, alert to suspicious eyes. None made themselves known. While it wasn't encouraged to travel between carriages, nor was it unheard of.

Passing through the door, she took the long step from one stoop to the next. The railrunner had barely departed the station, but already the timber sleepers – clearly visible through the gap between the heavy, clasped-hand steel couplers – were rattling past at disagreeable speed. Though the motics in the couplers couldn't disengage without a command from their twin in the railrunner's engine cab, Kat's fear remained that they'd snap open the moment she attempted to cross.

Doing her best to blot out the suddenly deafening rattle and clank of the juddering carriages, she half-lidded her eyes and stepped across. Clinging to the uprights of the roof access ladder, she passed through the travellers' carriage door and closed it behind her.

Unlike the workers' carriage – which other than the vestibules at either end was entirely open-plan – the travellers' carriage comprised eight separate compartments set along a single narrow corridor. More than that, the walls were of finished, polished timber, the compartment doors etched with Nyssa's spiralled flame. Too expensive for most folk; priceless to those who valued their privacy, especially on a multi-day railrunner haul.

Rîma and Azra had already reached the far end.

Kat was halfway along the corridor when a compartment door slid open and an impact with something large flung her against the wall.

Winded, she glanced back along the corridor, but Azra and Rîma were already gone.

She spun around as best she could, bringing her assailant into view even as she reached for the dagger concealed by her coat's folds. Her fingertips barely brushed the hilt as another spasm hit.

Not now! she screamed silently, frustration and panic clogging her throat.

Scarcely able to breathe, her vision dancing and her left knee as useless as her left arm, she clawed leadenly at the wall. All her efforts achieved were a slow, sliding descent rather than an outright collapse.

"Sorry ... sorry ..." The bald-headed man backed away, eyes wide in a lined face the colour of weather-worn yew as his gaze tracked from the corridor's far end back to Kat. "Here, let me ... let me help you up."

Her vision clearing, Kat stared blearily up. Not a custodian, thank Nyssa. He was dressed in layered robes of a type popular in Qersal, with bright colours made metallic by an overlay of meshwork silk. Gloved hand outstretched, he lurched forward, unsteady gait owing more to drunkenness than the motion of the carriage. The stink of liquor was palpable even above the bitter backwash of railrunner smoke.

"I can manage." Willing recalcitrant trembling limbs to motion, she knocked his hand aside and pushed upright against the wall. "Next time, watch where you're going."

The man nodded morosely and made a laborious effort to close his compartment, his frustrated mutters carrying clearly over the rattle and thump of the railrunner's motion. Still shaking, Kat left him be and fumbled with a stoppered vial of last breath. Ragged breathing shallowed as the wisp of soul stuff hit her lungs, the numbness fading from her fingers. Too close. Much too close.

She found the others in the next vestibule, Azra regarding her with aggrieved, hollow-cheeked impatience. "Where have you been?"

"A fireblood mistook me for a door."

Rîma tilted her head. "Is there a problem?"

Kat considered, but had read no danger in the man. "I don't think so."

"Then can we . . . ?" A muscle jerked in the underside of Azra's chin. She clamped her eyes shut, throat bobbing as she swallowed. "Can we get on with this?"

"What's wrong?"

She briefly touched a hand to her stomach and glared. "I told you. I hate railrunners."

The beginnings of a smile crept across Kat's face. In good times and bad, she'd never known anything throw Azra off her stride. But for all her faults, Azra had never once mocked her vertigo. *And* she'd insisted on coming aboard, even knowing what it would mean. Betrayal's scars faded a little more.

"We've still one stop before we leave the city," she said. "We can manage without you."

"Not a chance, darl—" Azra winced. "Not a chance. I *want* to be here."

Kat glanced at Rîma, who twitched a shrug. "If you're sure."

"I'm always sure."

Passing the final compartment and the small galley – firebloods not, of course, being expected to fend for themselves – they crossed into the vestibule of the first of the three Rashace goods wagons just as the railrunner pulled away from its final station.

Tatterlain and Yali were waiting. Tatterlain wore the ochre silks of a railrunner steward – complete with the tasselled short scimitar meant to discourage rowdiness – hair three shades paler than normal and sporting a ridiculous moustache. Yali, as ever when she had the choice, had arrayed herself in sumptuous silks. She'd taken the sole travellers' compartment Tatterlain had managed to acquire and had insisted on playing the part.

Tatterlain stiffened to attention. "Sorry, ladies, you can't be in here." He shouted to be heard over the noise of the railrunner – in the box-like goods wagon, the *rattle-thump* sound carried far clearer than in the passenger carriages.

Azra rolled her eyes. "Hilarious."

167

The wagon bucked at some unseen imperfection in the rails. Eyes wide, she lunged for the vestibule window, yanked it down and thrust head and shoulders out into the open air. The industry of the railrunner *almost* covered the wet splutter of her lost battle with motion sickness.

Yali grinned.

Azra was a shade paler when she pulled herself back in, a hair shakier, but her hazel eyes offered dire warning.

"It'll make for unusual wagon livery, I'll grant you that." Fishing in a pocket, Tatterlain produced a small cotton handkerchief and handed it to her. She took it with a facial expression frozen somewhere between fury and gratitude. "All … *that* … aside, are we good to go?"

Kat shot a warning glare at Yali, who mostly smothered her grin. ||"You tell me."||

Yali hefted her haversack. ||Locks are clear from here to the guards' carriage. I've everything I need for the vault, including belcher's acid and a couple of small blasting prisms for any hestics.|| A hestic prism was tough, but even a small crack in the glass would free the captive ifrît. In the confined space of the vault, the pressure from even a fist-sized prism would be more than sufficient. ||I just need someone to clear out the custodians.||

Rîma unwound her bundle of *streza* canes. ||"How many?"||

||"Three, maybe four,"|| said Tatterlain. ||"I tried to offer my services, but didn't get further than the door."||

||"Only four."|| Rîma sighed, a woman accustomed to doing terrible things in worthy causes, and swung her sword up onto her shoulder. ||"Shall we?"||

The first goods wagon was half empty, with double-stacked crates against one wall and very little else to get in the way. The next pair held an agglomeration of crate stacks, rope webbing and tarpaulined furniture that forced a zigzag journey. Before long, Kat stood on the stoop of the last goods wagon, breath stolen by the wind and squinting against the brilliance of the low afternoon sun. Zariqaz's high outer wall was already a dark shape at the railrunner's back, shrinking ever deeper into the arid red plains and stark black pine forests. Tatterlain and Yali were already on the stoop of the guards' carriage, Tatterlain with one elbow hooked over the ladder's rungs while he held Yali steady above the thundering track, the wind setting her hair and skirts streaming.

"Want any help in there?" asked Azra, still sheltered inside the cargo wagon's vestibule.

Kat shook her head. "Rîma will handle it."

"What? Four custodians, he said."

"Rîma will handle it."

Yali gave a thumbs-up and swung clear. Rîma crossed from wagon to carriage, not leaping the gap as Kat had learned to do, but walking along the shuddering coupling with the casual stride of a woman walking a meadow path. Pausing briefly on the opposite stoop, she pushed the door inward and ducked inside.

A man's voice bellowed out in challenge, the words lost beneath the hungry rumble of the railrunner's wheels.

Not so Rîma's reply, higher-pitched and more guttural. "Are you sure you wish to go through with this?"

Another bellow, this one broken by a wet, rasping scream. Others followed, interspersed by the brief musical slither of steel scraping against steel and punctuated by the thuds of falling bodies.

The carriage was half open-plan, with a short corridor at the far end hinting at sleeping compartments. Rîma stood three paces beyond the vestibule door, a shrieker at her feet, the bloody tip of her sword touching the planked floor and a lifeless custodian dangling from her free hand. A second body lay across the remains of a wooden table. A third sprawled on an upholstered bench seat. The last custodian lay at the mouth of the sleeping compartment corridor.

"My apologies," said Rîma. "I didn't expect him to draw so swiftly."

She brought her heel down on the shrieker's prism, shattering it to fragments.

"She apologises." Azra entered behind Kat and shook her head in wonder. "Four dead in about as many heartbeats, and she apologises."

Rîma let the body drop. "If the shot was noted further along the train, I'll have much for which to be sorry."

Kat peered up at the roof. A scorched ceiling, a tiny hole and – as luck would have it – no fire. "They won't have heard, not with the speed we're going."

Azra's lip twisted. "Someone might have seen. You get started here, and I'll check."

"Take Tatterlain with you," Kat replied. "A steward's uniform might calm restless souls."

Offering a wry smile tainted by a hint of queasiness, Azra retreated towards the vestibule. "If only I could take the uniform without *him*."

Kat picked her way through the dead. The rear door opened without a lock's resistance. Not so the one opposite, but Yali handled that.

||Give me a sixty-count before you come through,|| signed Kat, trying not to think about the rails rushing away beneath her feet.

Yali grinned. ||Never underestimate a countess, is that it?||

||Something like that.||

Kat had seen the inside of that carriage only three nights before at Kanzîr Station and knew it to contain a single large day room with richly upholstered chairs bolted to the floor, two sleeping compartments, a third for a galley and a fourth that served as a washroom. Darkness and dust sheets had done little justice to the gilded monstrosity, which was a subdued riot of artful pastels and darkly polished wood. But it wasn't quite the fireblood home from home. The walls were bare of portraiture and the metal hoops above the wall-fixed dresser and tables were bereft of statuary to secure. A sumptuous prison car it might have been, but a prison car it remained.

Fadiya Rashace stood in the centre of the day room, arms folded across her chest and her chin elevated in a portrait-perfect expression of defiance at odds with the bucking carriage. "Do whatever you intend, but if you think you'll earn the satisfaction of hearing me beg—" She blinked, hauteur falling away. "Katija? Katija, is that you?"

"It's me, *Mathami*."

Fadiya frowned. "I heard a shrieker. Screams. What's happening? What is this?"

"This?" Kat's reluctance bled into giddy relief. "Among other things, this is a rescue. The hospice will have to manage without you."

Fadiya shook her head sadly. "Bless you, child, but you can't be serious. Do you even know what that would entail? Hargo's custodians—"

"Are dead. The ones on this railrunner at least." Kat smiled. It wasn't often that she liked herself, but this was a moment to treasure. "We'll get off at Hezira and be far away before anyone's the wiser. You're free, *Mathami*."

"Free ..." Fadiya shook her head. "I'm not sure I know what that even means."

"You'll have plenty of time to work it out." Kat turned and beckoned to Yali. ||"Get started on the vault."||

Haversack bobbing against her shoulder, Yali scurried to the far door.

"Your father's books?" said Fadiya. "They're really why you came, aren't they?"

"That's how it started, only ..." Kat swallowed, the confession dry at the back of her throat. "I ... I finally remembered that my father wasn't the only one you loved. Forgive me, *Mathami*. I should never have said what I did."

Fadiya embraced her. "There's nothing to forgive, Katija. There never was." She drew back and laid her hands on Kat's upper arms. "I made myself a bystander in your life long before Hargo forced it upon me. But your friend will never get through that vault. Hargo bought the very best."

"My friend ... My *sister* is the finest lock charmer in Khalad." Kat twisted a wry smile, the tension she'd carried for the past three days finally bleeding away. There was quiet joy to be found introducing a sister who wasn't really her sister to a mother who wasn't quite her mother. "And we've blasting prisms too ... just in case she's having an off day."

"What interesting company you keep, Katija." If reproof lurked beneath Fadiya's words, it was exceedingly well hidden.

"You don't know the half—"

Brakes screeched. The carriage lurched, sending Kat stumbling towards the outer door. Thoughts reeling no less than her body, she grabbed at the upper frame. Still two hours out from Hezira. Why were they stopping?

"Rîma! What's going on?"

The swordstress appeared in the guards' carriage door. "We appear to be slowing." She shrugged in tacit admission at the answer's uselessness. "You'd better find Tatterlain."

Kat was halfway along the guards' carriage when it adopted the telltale camber of one rounding a corner. Beyond the right-hand windows, the main rail line shot off into the distance, arrow-straight through the black pines. Through those to the left, she glimpsed the wind-blasted timber platform and squat adobe buildings of a station siding, the bright pennants of a redcloak fortress and its attendant torch house fluttering behind. Two minutes, maybe three, and they'd be there.

Kiasta.

Stricken, she glanced at Rîma. There'd not yet been time to dispose of the custodians' bodies. Until moments prior, there'd not even been a need to give the matter consideration, save for the unpleasantness of leaving corpses underfoot. "Close the curtains. Make sure nothing happens to Fadiya and Yali."

Rîma nodded. "Of course."

With the family who weren't her family left in the safest hands she knew, Kat ran headlong in search of Tatterlain.

Eighteen

Kat twitched the curtains closed, blotting the redcloak-crowded platform from sight. It didn't help.

"All this for us," she murmured. "I should feel flattered."

At least with the curtains closed, the gloom in Yali's compartment hid her woebegone expression. Not that Azra, sitting on the edge of the fold-down cot and staring at her threaded fingers, was paying much attention.

The door slid open. Kat went for her dagger and relaxed at the sight of Tatterlain's ridiculous moustache. "Well?"

"I spoke to one of the other stewards," he replied, his voice barely carrying above the commotion in the corridor. "Nothing to do with us. Rumour has it that Osios is thinking about turning independent. These fine specimens are strengthening the garrison to serve as deterrent."

The pressure in Kat's chest eased. She sank against the wall. "So it's Vallant's fault?"

Tatterlain shrugged. "I seem to recall he had some help last time he was up this way."

She shot him a poisonous glare. "Fine, so it's my fault."

Azra looked up from her hands. "It doesn't matter whose fault it is. I take it they're cramming the redcloaks into the workers' carriages?"

"No," replied a woebegone Tatterlain. "They're coupling a pair of troop carriages to the rear."

173

Kat's heart, barely having broken the surface of despair, sank again. Two carriages. At least fifty redcloaks, probably nearer a hundred. All just the other side of the vault wagon. "We have to warn the others."

She pushed past Tatterlain, opened the door ... and was almost swept away by a grumbling tide of silken firebloods, flowing reluctantly from the second travellers' carriage and into the workers' carriages, luggage in tow. A pair of redcloaks stood guard at the door between Kat's carriage and the one by which the aggrieved travellers had entered.

"About that," said Tatterlain. "The officers aren't travelling with the troops."

"How many are we talking?"

"Five, I think."

"They cleared out a whole carriage for that?"

He shrugged. "They like their privacy."

With a distant whistle blast, the railrunner lurched into motion once more.

Kat gripped the door frame as the last of the firebloods filed past – the drunk in the shimmering robes among them. At least she didn't have to worry about Yali triggering the blasting prism and alerting the redcloaks in the carriages behind. She wouldn't have heard the commotion, but she'd have felt the shudder of the troop carriages being coupled up. Rîma would fill her in on the rest. But without the blasting prism, they couldn't get into the vault. They could all get off at Hezerin – Fadiya included – but they'd have to leave her father's books behind.

"We're done," she murmured. "That's it."

A heavy hand spun her about. "We are *not* done." Azra's hazel eyes bored into hers. "There's always a way."

"Then what is it?" snapped Kat. "Tell me that! You were always the audacious one. It's not as though I can just wave my hand and make them all disappear ..."

Azra grinned. "Keep talking."

The redcloak officers didn't matter, they were just in the way. The real problem lay with the small army coupled up at the vault wagon's rear.

But Kat and Azra were proof that even the most unbreakable of bonds didn't necessarily last. "We decouple the troop wagons."

"Can't be done," said Tatterlain. "There's a motic cut-out, remember? Last I checked, ifrîti don't find you as convincing as they used to."

"So someone's going to have to talk their way into the engine and attend to that. Sounds like a job for the great Tuzen Karza to me."

Azra bristled. "I can handle it."

"That engine's a forest of levers. Do you know which one you're looking for?"

"You know I don't."

Which meant she'd just pull anything that drew her eye, likely starting with the brake. "That's why Tatterlain's going."

Tatterlain offered as much of a florid, courtly bow as the compartment's confines allowed.

Azra folded her arms. "Where does that leave you and me?"

Kat glanced up at the ceiling. "We're going outside."

In the neighbouring compartment, Tanith pushed her ear away from the wall and swivelled around on the cot. Her booted feet kicking idly in the air, she ruffled the hair of the compartment's rightful occupant, now thoroughly bound, gagged and lashed – fully clothed – to the cot's upright.

"You see? I knew if I followed the deaf girl long enough she'd lead me to Kat."

Not that it had gone *entirely* to her satisfaction. She wasn't happy about engaging in skulduggery without the make-up and plaits that usually concealed her identity, much less in the expensive sapphire gown and elbow-length black gloves that had cost her every dinar she'd scrounged during her time with the Obsidium Cult. But then, the elderly stationmaster had practically fallen over himself to help the weeping innocent who'd begged till her heart ached.

"MMmmmm Mph," muttered her captive, his red-rimmed eyes brimming with murder. Fair.

Tanith patted his cheek. "Oh shush. This could be going a lot worse for you."

The dull thud of footsteps tracked away down the corridor. She kissed her captive on the cheek, stifling an involuntary tremor as she scented the cold, peppery aroma of his soul. She jerked back, throat tight. She'd fed well on Arloq three days before and taken care not to exert herself in the meantime. She shouldn't be hungry yet. She *wasn't* hungry. And yet the desire was there, quickening her breath and setting her pulse aflutter.

She turned away before temptation became unbearable. "Don't wait up."

Not for the first time in her life, Kat was a bundle of regrets.

Climbing the ladder had been bad enough. Her vertigo took abundant, dizzying delight in even that modest ascent – the rooftop of the carriage stood barely two and a half times her own height above the rails – and cackled with joy at the ground rushing away below.

That, she fought out of practised habit, by keeping her eyes dead level to the horizon, removing the troublesome concepts of "up" and "down" from the equation. But there was nothing to be done about the stinging swarm of wind-blown plains dust hissing crosswise over the rooftops – driven by the same wind whose every gust threatened to sweep her to a bone-crunching landing at the trackside. And then there was the second, artificial wind awoken by the railrunner's rattling advance, a heavy hand in her back ushering her ever faster to the carriage's rear.

Balancing the two would have been a nightmare at the best of times; with one arm bent across her face to protect against the dust and the other flailing for balance, these were hardly that. Thus it was with inexpressible relief that at last she ducked behind the sparse cover offered by the truncated steel minaret of the carriage's rearmost ventilation louvre.

A gasping, pale-cheeked Azra grabbed at the louvre's rounded metal hood. "I don't think I like your plan."

Kat swallowed, her throat tight, as another jolt shook the rooftop.

Her vertigo might have been enjoying the moment, but Azra's motion sickness was having the time of its life. Perhaps she should have sent Azra with Tatterlain, but that would have meant letting her out of her sight, and despite her protestations to the others, the trust wasn't quite there yet.

"Is it me, or is this railrunner going faster than most?" asked Azra.

Kat stared at the trailing carriages, the lattermost red-liveried troop wagons curving gracefully inward around a bend. "It's carrying less weight." Most railrunner engines hauled thirty to forty carriages at a time. She forced a smile. "Why? Want more rooftops to crawl across?"

Lips a thin, queasy slash, Azra shook her head. "You?"

"Two's my limit." More to the point, two would get them past the redcloak-commandeered travellers' carriage and onto the first cargo wagon. "Maybe we should rethink our career as railrunner reavers? We make a right pair."

"We always did." Azra scowled an apology. "Sorry, I don't know where that came from."

"Forget it." Kat wished she could banish her insidious flash of longing as easily. "Ready for another hike?"

"No." The accompanying smile lacked its customary arrogance. It might even have been charming, had the shadows of the past not clung so heavily to it. "But we can't stay here."

Azra glanced back the way they'd come, a frown touching her lips.

"What is it?" asked Kat.

"I don't know. I thought I saw someone."

One hand on the louvre's hood and a forearm crooked against the swirling dust, Kat twisted around. Rooftops stretched away towards the distant engine's billowing, bitter steam, their interplay weaving strange shadows even beneath the bright afternoon sun.

She coughed up a spray of grit. "Who'd be crazy enough to follow us up here?"

"Good point."

As they inched their way rearwards, dense black pines swallowed the plains first to the north, then to the south, the cover of the trees at last bringing relief from the wind. At the gap between the two travellers' carriages – a divide that seemed far larger at roof level than at the stoop – Azra crossed first, the light footfall of her landing lost in the cacophony of the rails. Kat followed, her eyes more closed than open.

The second carriage passed away faster, though Kat couldn't tell if that was because the wind was no longer an obstacle, or simply due to her growing confidence. Another leap, another landing, and they stood atop the first goods wagon. After the ordeal of the rooftop, shimmying down the ladder to the stoop was nothing.

"I am never doing that again," gasped Kat, crossing into the vestibule.

Azra snorted. "Always with the dangerous promises." She brushed herself down in a doomed attempt at regaining respectability – like Kat's, her already scruffy clothes were stained filthy red from the flying dust – and set off along the row of double-stacked crates. "Let's hope it was worth it."

"It will be." Kat followed her from the vestibule and eased the door shut.

In the moment before the catch caught, it crashed open, catapulting her against a crate. Winded, she dropped to the floor. Through blurred vision she made out a slender blonde figure in the now-open doorway, one hand reaching up to catch the rebounding door, the other twirling a short-bladed dagger by its pommel.

"Hello, dear sister." Her voice was guttural with the heavy syllables of the east, and rippled with vicious mirth. "Fancy meeting you here."

Tanith had fantasised about reuniting with Kat. How would it go? What would she say? Would she pretend magnanimity, or proceed straight to chastisement? A hundred plans, drawn up on the cusp of sleep, refined over and over until they sang sorrows and triumph in the sweetest voice.

This was better than any of them. Perhaps it was the sight of Kat gasping and retching on her knees. Perhaps it was Yennika's wide-eyed stare – Yennika, who ever beheld delight and disaster without a flicker.

Or perhaps it was simply that fantasy never matched reality.

"Tanith?" gasped Kat, struggling to rise. "Nyssa was right—"

Tanith rammed her toes into Kat's gut, the *whoomph* of expelled air provoking a fresh flash of satisfaction. "No thanks to you, dear sister." She rolled the dagger up and over the back of her hand and closed her fingers around its grips. "I owe you a death."

"No!" Yennika lunged, her own dagger gleaming in the wagon's wan lumani-light.

Tanith hesitated, dumbfounded. Yennika putting herself in danger for someone else? Alone of almost anyone else in Khalad, she knew *precisely* how overmatched she was.

Tanith sidestepped. The dagger flashed past her ribs. She grabbed a fistful of Yennika's hair and headscarf and slammed her into the door frame. Then she split a rope with a lazy slice of her blade, and with a lazy tug toppled a stack of crates. With a crash of unhappy porcelain, they buried Yennika in timber, packing straw and the remains of a priceless dinner service.

Tanith tutted. "Wait your turn."

Kat lurched to her feet, one hand tucked to her ribs and her expression that pathetic, pleading rictus she'd worn in the skies above Athenoch. She hadn't even drawn a weapon. "I don't want to fight you. I've been looking everywhere for you."

Tanith sprang and grabbed her by the throat. Dagger pressed up against the soft folds beneath her sister's chin, she drove her against a stack of crates with enough force to set them creaking.

"I was looking for you too," she breathed, craning her neck until her nose was barely an inch from Kat's. "Now we both get what we want."

But what *did* she want? Even a thirty-count before, she'd known. But now, with her sister – her blood – at her mercy, she found she was no longer certain.

She drew down a deep breath, as much a mistake here as it had been in her stolen compartment. The tantalising honeysuckle and jasmine of Kat's soul swamped her senses and lured her on. She dived deeper, pulsing black veins crackling across the umbral shadows of her sister's outer flame. Instinct jarred at something amiss.

She saw Kat's lips move, but the words drowned beneath the rising throb of her own yearning heartbeat. Little by little, even those sounds faded. Hunger without appetite. Desire without reserve. Kat sagged, all resistance gone, her eyes falling closed.

With rising terror, Tanith realised that somewhere along the line she'd lost control.

What was wrong with her?

"Tanith!" Somehow Yennika's shout pierced the indigo fog about her brain. "Stop! If you've a quarrel, it's with me."

Almost grateful for the distraction, Tanith turned her head just enough to bring Yennika, still struggling to free herself from the ruin of the crates, into sight. "Oh, that's special. Still choosing her over me? Why?"

"Because ..." Yennika pursed her lips, a flicker of disgust ... no, *embarrassment* ... chasing briefly across her face. "Because I love her."

"You don't love anyone!"

"Yennika Bascari didn't love anyone. She couldn't afford to. They always used her, or let her down. You know that. You saw plenty of it. Azra's different. *I'm* different. I'm trying to be." She pinched her eyes shut. "Trust me, you don't want to be like Yennika. Being alone wears you thin. It makes you into something awful."

"Maybe I don't care." Those words, always reflex, were never more so than at that moment. "I'm already something awful."

"You care," coughed Kat, her eyes fluttering. "Otherwise ... otherwise you wouldn't have tried to see your mother."

Tanith sagged. She'd sought to breach the estate twice more after her confrontation with Hargo, only to be forced into retreat by the enervating stench of blackthorn. On the second attempt, she'd passed out just inside the grounds. Only a change in the wind had saved her, otherwise her stepfather's custodians would have found her, and then ... Well, she tried not to think about that.

Unbidden, her fingers eased their grip on Kat's throat. Her dagger inched away, leaving a bright bead of blood behind. "How do you know that?"

"She told me." Kat drew down a shuddering breath. "She also told me you weren't wicked, not really. She, at least, still loves you."

Tanith swallowed to clear a lump from her throat. "You're lying."

"Ask her."

"How?" Tears pricked her eyes. "I can't even get near her."

"She's on this railrunner. Your stepfather's sending her away so that he can dispose of her. I couldn't live with that."

"I should have killed him when I had the chance."

"There's always tomorrow," said Yennika/Azra, earning a fierce glare from Kat.

What was it Enna had told her? *You'll not resent the men and women you didn't kill.* Proof that she'd never met Hargo Rashace. Had he been in her grip at that moment, she'd have gladly drained him dry, even if it meant losing a piece of herself in the process. But her sister? Perhaps she'd not regret sparing her. And if she did? As Yennika – *Azra* – had said, there was always tomorrow.

Fighting a tremor in her throat, Tanith backed up, pulling down her sleeve to conceal the fires of her tattoo. It made it easier to think like herself. "I want to see her."

Kat brushed a rivulet of blood from her throat and nodded. "Sure."

Azra frowned. "Kat . . ."

"It's not like we have a hope of stopping her."

Tanith almost laughed at that, mostly for Kat's world-weary tone. But she allowed that there might also have been the tiniest speck of relief. To ensure that neither Kat nor Azra noticed, she offered the latter her sweetest, toothiest smile. The one that few people saw twice that side of the Deadwinds.

To Kat's surprise, Rîma put up no argument, just a minimalist shrug.

Yali, predictably, was less sanguine.

181

||What is *she* doing here?|| she signed angrily. ||And why is there an army of redcloaks tied to our tail?||

Kat glanced at Tanith, clasped tight in Fadiya's embrace at the day room's far end. So hard to believe they shared anything, much less a father. It wasn't just the physical differences – golden hair and lily-pale skin against ink and bronze. Tanith had confidence fit to crack the kingdom, and a dubious moral core that might drive her to do so. But then Kat thought back to how she herself had been changed by a life on the run. She'd been a fugitive all of a year. Tanith had been running her whole life.

In her mother's arms, her eyes closed and her expression relaxed, for the first time in their brief and troubled history Tanith looked almost to be at peace, even contented. If Kat tried – *really* tried – she could almost forget that the young woman, still barely more than a girl in so many ways, was something more than a murderous little trallock with a daemon in her blood.

At least, she hoped so. Easier to keep the faith these past months without having set eyes on that malicious, swaggering smile . . . much less suffer another beating at her hands. Tanith in the flesh was a challenging prospect.

||In order?|| Kat replied. ||I'm not sure yet, and our usual rotten luck. What about your end?||

||I've charmed two of the outer locks, and the acid's working on the motic bolt. Once that's burned through, I can work on the combination.|| Yali's lip twisted, her usually carefree expression darkening. ||But unless the redcloaks are all as deaf as me, I can't use the blasting prisms. And if I can't use the blasting prisms to shatter the sentry stones, the hestics in the vault are going to scream out their imaginary lungs as soon as we cross the threshold.||

||Tatterlain's working on it.|| Kat raised her voice. "Azra? Is it done yet?"

Azra appeared in the rear doorway and shook her head. "Still locked down."

||Hezerin's getting closer all the time,|| said Yali. ||If we miss our stop, we're bound for Osios with everyone else.||

||I know.|| Kat threw up her hands in frustration, only to belatedly remember that the gesture took on accusatory connotations in Simah. ||Sorry, wasn't thinking.||

Yali flashed a small smile. ||It's fine, honest and true. So, what do we do?||

Kat picked up one of the blasting prisms. Smaller than those she'd used before, it fitted neatly in the palm of her hand. She heard the faint echoes of the desperate, nihilistic ifrîti squalling within as soon as the glass touched her bare flesh. ||Can we use one on the carriage coupling?||

Yali shook her head. ||There's nothing to direct the explosion. I bet you wished you'd let me send a heraldic to Vallant now.||

This *again*? Careful not to disturb the blasting prism's short, five-second fuse and snap-flint primer, Kat slipped it into her pocket. ||Not now, please.||

||I'm just saying.||

Kat scowled at Yali's perverse delight in raking old coals. A locked vault and a company of redcloaks. Explosives they couldn't use on the one without alerting the other. There was no way of knowing how long it would take Tatterlain to charm his way close enough to the cut-out. She could do without Yali playing "I told you so" about Vallant. Now, more than ever, they needed her aetherios tattoo.

Or at least *an* aetherios tattoo.

She glanced back at Tanith. ||Actually, there might be something we can try.||

Nineteen

Azra intercepted Kat in the vestibule doorway. "Are you sure this is a good idea?"

Kat stared past her into the vault chamber, where Tanith, arms looped behind her back, regarded the glass pipes and leather bladders of the belcher's acid dispenser with cold disdain. Yali, all unblinking suspicion, watched her in turn. Tanith hadn't wanted to cooperate at first, even with Fadiya's urging. A lifetime's resentment wasn't swept away by a single embrace, even when that resentment was born of a mix of real and imagined deeds . . . *especially* when that was true.

"It's our best chance if Tatterlain doesn't come through," she replied.

"You know how unstable she is," hissed Azra. "If this works, you'll be putting another weapon in her hand."

Kat dragged her back into the vestibule, out of Tanith and Yali's sight. "Maybe she's unstable because of people like you. People who've done to her *precisely* what your family did to you."

Azra stiffened. "And what's that, exactly?"

Kat hesitated. She wasn't entirely certain *what* horrors Azra's peers had forced upon her. "Encouraged all her worst instincts."

To her surprise, Azra's eyes shone with amusement. "Your claws are showing." She sighed, her smile fading. "So you trust her?"

"I want to. Just like I want to trust you, despite everyone screaming that I shouldn't."

184

Azra bristled. "I'm nothing like her."

"No. You had a choice. Tanith never did. If I can't offer one to her, why should I offer one to you?"

"Ah." Azra stared down at her feet. "So you heard that? I thought you were out of it."

Kat shivered, the memory of being lost on indigo clouds too strong to shake. *I love her.* Three simple words that had dragged her back to consciousness. "We should probably talk about that."

Azra's eyes met hers. Defiant. Hopeful ... and against all expectation, *vulnerable.* "We probably should. But not until we're out of here."

Slipping into the spirit world was simple enough. It always was, with the daemon-half of her soul already tethered there. That didn't mean it was pleasant. The deeper Tanith trod, the more she felt it calling, urging her mortal half to cast loose and simply ... drift into the darkness. Without meaning to, she squeezed Kat's hand tighter, and cursed herself for showing weakness. But the hand offered solace. It helped remind her she was still among the living, standing foursquare in front of a vault door that no longer existed save for the heavy shadow it cast across black aether.

What do you see? Kat was nothing but a faint flicker of magenta flame in the darkness.

Tanith gazed past the vault door's shadow to the sparks of flames within. *Three ... no, four. A motic and three hestics. They're watching me.*

They do that.

They're whispering. I can't understand them. I never can.

You're not meant to, Kat replied. *They don't really think. They're just appetite and awareness. You're looking for a weakness. Curiosity, anger, boredom ... something that it can't control. Let yours rise to meet it. Show it you're the same.*

Tanith focused on the nearest hestic: a bright wreath of indigo flame, seething with resentment.

Show it you're the same? She'd resentment to spare.

185

She uncoiled a fraction of her anger at Kat, Azra and the world entire. It wended along her forearm like a coiling snake, rushing along the spiderweb of her aetherios tattoo and out into the dark. The hestic shifted as the flames made contact, its own dim anger rising in kinship to the incandescent flame, then detonated in a blaze of rippling light. Its thin, dying moan echoed through the spirit world's cold void.

What did you do? snapped Kat.

What you told me, Tanith rejoined. Rather, she'd fallen back on what she always did when confronted by a recalcitrant ifrît – a recalcitrant anything. *It can't raise an alarm if it's dead, can it?*

That's fine for the hestics, Kat replied, her tone carrying the forced patience that Tanith had heard a lot over the course of her life. *But we need the motic to draw the bolt. It can't do that if it's soul-scraps on the Deadwinds.*

Easy for you. Tanith's tattoo-flames burned brighter as her temper failed. *Everything's always been easy for you.*

Kat's sigh rippled through the darkness. *You think any of this came naturally? It took me months to learn how to do what you just did.*

Months? Pride warmed Tanith's heart. Stifling ifrîti was as instinctive as breathing to her, because what was a mortal soul but an ifrît in the making, waiting to be smothered by its natural predator? She'd snuffed half of the lumani on the Rashace estate before she was five years old.

Maybe I'm better at this than you are.

Prove it.

Tanith reached for the second hestic, sullen and watchful in the darkness. This time, she tethered her wrath close, letting barely a fraction seep through her coiling flames. Just a caress, hot with pride but ragged at the edges where her control frayed.

Even that small pressure was enough to tear the hestic apart, its death wail drowned by Tanith's own choked, frustrated scream.

Are you even listening? asked Kat. *You can't force this.*

Tanith rounded on Kat's flickering, magenta presence, her physical body a pale after-image seen with the soul more than the eye.

You're no help! she snarled, her frustration as much at herself at her sister. If Kat could do it, *she* could do it. Leverage her father's rifted gift for something useful. *You're a terrible tutor.*

Probably, Kat replied, with more humour than the situation merited. *But I'm trying to be better. Are you? You have to persuade ifrîti, even if you show them something that isn't true.*

Tanith glared at Kat's naked soul, its magenta flame shot through with pulsing, spidery black veins. She didn't understand. How could she? For all that they were sisters, they weren't the same. She was amashti. Instinct urged her to dominate ifrîti just as it urged her to dominate mortals.

She stared again at Kat to tell her so . . . and hesitated.

The black veins. She'd seen them before, during their confrontation in the goods wagon, but had been too distracted to mark their significance.

Omen rot.

It shouldn't have mattered. Somehow it did.

Unsettled, she stared at the final hestic. New considerations arose from the corpses of the old. What power she held over the living seldom began with threats or force, but with empathy and seduction. The promise of something that wasn't true that had the power of something that was.

She reached out for the third hestic. Not with flame or anger, not with certainty, but with promises of kinship and company; of a bond that transcended the spirit world's darkness. She became a reflection of the hestic's desires, and in response its flames blossomed like spring petals, offering up the secret of its soul-glyph. She held the ifrît tight as the lines of her tattoo shifted to mimic the recursive, swirling design. As the last line flowed into place, she breathed a simple command.

Sleep.

The ifrît faded into darkness, not dispersed, but content.

Laughter rippled through the spirit world, heartachingly pure and disturbingly saccharine. It was therefore to Tanith's great surprise that

187

she learned the laughter didn't belong to Kat, but to *her*, a release for an unfamiliar buoyant feeling. She'd done it. Something she'd thought impossible.

Still laughing, she reached for the motic.

Kat opened her eyes at the dull *thunk* of the bolt snapping aside, and was greeted by the unfamiliar sight of a smiling Tanith. It wasn't the smile itself that was unusual but the motivating spirit, which to all appearances was neither malevolent nor braggartly. It was merely that of a young woman lost in joy at her own achievement.

"I did it," Tanith murmured, her hand slipping from Kat's. "I actually did it."

"You did," Kat replied, impressed despite herself . . . and a little bit jealous. She scratched at her aetherios tattoo, which had itched horribly while Tanith was in the spirit world but had stopped short of provoking fresh spasms, thank Nyssa. "Maybe you *are* better at this."

"I *definitely* am." Tanith thrust out her chin, daring Kat to disagree, only for her defiance to soften almost immediately. She held up her left forearm, examining flames duller than before. "It's harder than killing. Talking to them, I mean. I feel . . . not quite here."

"It'll pass. Tessence helps. You know, the dust that's left after an ifrît dissipates? Archons use it for incense. If you breathe it in, it'll restore your tattoo."

"I didn't know." She flashed a small, wicked smile. "I normally just eat people."

Kat shuddered. "Please don't. It would spoil this nice family moment we've got going on."

"I'll try. What's so important anyway? The contents of that vault must be priceless."

"Only to the right person," said Kat, not yet ready to trust her with the truth. "It might be that we've all been wasting our time."

Which meant she'd soon be dead, and Tanith would never be free of her curse.

Tanith's smile faded. She even had the decency to look abashed. "Thank you."

"Thank you? Not an hour ago, I had the distinct impression you wanted to kill me."

"I did. I do. I ... don't know. I ..." Tanith's brow softened. "I know you have omen rot."

Kat cursed softly. "You're not the only one who reached into the Deadwinds at Athenoch. You're not the only one they took from in return." She managed a wan smile. "The others don't know. Please don't tell them."

To her surprise, Tanith offered a solemn nod. "I suppose I owe you that much." She frowned. "Is there nothing that can be done to—"

The wagon lurched. Kat grabbed at the vestibule doorway for support. Tanith, slower to react, planted face first against the vault door, her splayed palms either side of the ornate combination lock.

"Ow."

Braced against vying forces, Kat staggered through the vestibule and onto the stoop. Track bed and flanking pine forests whipped past faster than before. She glanced down at the coupling. Though the steel hands remained linked, their thumbs no longer gripped the fingers of the opposing hand as they had before, but projected out to the side at an almost ninety-degree angle.

Azra and Yali appeared in the doorway to the countess' carriage.

"What just happened?" Azra shouted over the heightened wail of the railrunner's slipstream.

||"Tatterlain's thrown the cut-out."|| Kat shook her head. Typical of her luck – everything went right or wrong all at once, but at least it distracted Tanith from her discovery. ||"Just past the nick of time."||

Yali half-lidded a suspicious eye. ||Then why are we speeding up?||

A body shot past in the track bed's ruddy gravel. Yali and Azra stared after it with remarkably similar expressions from the opposite stoop.

"That wasn't him, was it?" asked Azra.

The body had worn filthy overalls. ||"I think that was the driver."||

189

||Oh, that's all right then,|| signed Yali, deadpan. ||We didn't need one of those.||

Kat winced, but there was no helping that detail right now. ||"Tanith's dealt with the hestics and the motic. That just leaves the combination lock."||

||Then why am I standing around here?||

Yali crossed the couplers in a swirl of wind-blown skirts and vanished into the vault room. Eyes dead ahead, Kat crossed in the other direction, gladly accepting Azra's helping hand to reach the opposite stoop. Grabbing at the door frame for support, she glanced back towards the rear of the railrunner. No need to use the blasting prisms now, but still . . .

"I'm thinking we'd all feel happier with those redcloaks gone," said Azra.

Kat nodded. So easy to forget how readily they'd once finished each other's thoughts. "Can you handle it?"

"If Tanith helps. I'll persuade her."

She leapt across to the opposite carriage, pausing in the doorway at Kat's call.

"Azra? . . . Be careful."

A rakish smile and Azra was gone.

Kat found Fadiya by one of the day room's gilt-framed windows, staring out through the blurring, strobing pines to the half-hidden magenta flames of a torch house in the middle distance. Rîma stood on guard in the far doorway, back straight and untroubled by the carriage's increasing turbulence.

"Do all your endeavours go this smoothly, Katija?" asked Fadiya wryly.

"Sorry, *Mathami*. Believe it or not, this one's going better than most."

She gave a bubbling, musical laugh. "Actually, I'm rather enjoying myself. It's a lot more interesting than my days have lately been . . . And I got to hold my daughter again. Wherever the day takes us, it was worth it for that alone."

190

"All part of the service." Kat strode quickly past to hide a blush. Graceless at the best of times, she'd none at all when accepting thanks or compliments. Lack of practice. "Rîma? We should look in on Tatterlain."

Rîma stared meaningfully up at the roof. "You don't need to come."

Kat stifled a wince. "I'll manage."

She'd reason to regret her words sooner than expected. On reaching the foremost of the three cargo wagons, they discovered that the tussle with Tanith and the subsequent lurch of the accelerating railrunner had left the door to the forward vestibule completely blocked by fallen crates, necessitating they double back and make their way to the roof an entire carriage earlier.

Propelled aloft by unhealthy pride as much as the ladder's rungs, Kat went first. As soon as her head was above roof level, the stinging backwash from the engine did its best to rip her from the ladder. Worse still, the trees, once six feet away to either side, were now close enough for their branches to *rat-tat-tat* against the carriages, adding shed needles to the raking dust.

Then she stared past the goods wagon's louvres to the billowing red silks ripping and snapping above the far ladder. Three of the five redcloak officers.

Kiasta.

"What are *they* doing up here?"

Rîma drew level. "Maybe they overheard your disagreement with Tanith? Maybe the falling crates? Does it matter?"

"No," Kat replied through gritted teeth. "It only matters that they're here."

"You're learning." Rîma tilted her head in approval. "Try not to fall off."

Kat clung to the nearest louvre as Rîma stalked along the carriage roof, head bowed, one hand planted on the crown of her hat and the tails of her battered coat streaming behind. At the midpoint, she drew up straight and swept her sword diagonally down, its back-curved point barely an inch from the rooftop.

"Are you sure you wish to go through with this?"

The windborne words whipped back past Kat. The redcloaks either didn't hear or more likely didn't care, secure in their status as the Eternity King's chosen guard. Somehow word about Rîma had never gotten around.

One redcloak came on faster than the others, but not through choice. An accident of posture set his cloak billowing like a sail against the stays of his outstretched arms. Boots skidding along the rooftop, he hurtled towards Rîma. Sword still point-down, she took the smallest of side-steps, a booted foot left plain in the redcloak's path, pitching him face first onto the roof. He skidded full stretch into the middle ventilation louvre, scimitar clattering over the side.

His companions tugged at the golden clasps at their throats. Unburdened by the weight of their erstwhile owners, the scarlet silks spiralled into the railrunner's slipstream, leaving the redcloaks in infinitely more practical skirted grey tunics and layered black lamellar at chest, wrist and shins.

Rîma met them between the front and middle louvres. Sword blurring and one hand still preserving her beloved hat from a wind-blown fate, she held them there, parrying when needed, but as often blunting a strike through a twist of the hips or a simple sidestep that made mockery of the treacherous footing.

The first redcloak stirred from his involuntary repose by the middle ventilation louvre and ripped his cloak free, sending it soaring and snapping past Kat's head. Drawing a curved knife from his boot, he struck out towards Rîma from behind.

Kat pushed away from the louvre. Elbow crooked across her face to shield her eyes from the flurry of grit and pine needles, heart skipping with every small slip of her soles on the rooftop's planks, she hurled herself at the redcloak.

Deafened by the wind, his first warning was her shoulder slamming into his spine. For the second time in as many minutes, he sprawled face down on the roof, his cheek scraping blood across the pitch-darkened timbers.

Kneeling atop him and half blinded by the wind, Kat reached for her dagger. With a throaty growl, the redcloak jackknifed, flinging her away and sliding backwards towards the roof edge.

She skidded to a halt just before the rim at the cost of the fabric of her sleeve and what felt like half the skin of her elbow besides. The redcloak rose up, a dagger wicked in his hand. He howled as Kat slammed a boot into his right kneecap. Fighting the wind all the way, she grabbed a handful of his tunic to haul herself up. Her rise became his downfall. Even as she reached her feet, he plunged over the side and vanished in a storm of crackling branches.

Unsteady with exertion as much as the wind, Kat twisted about in time to witness the end of Rîma's confrontation. A choked scream and a spray of arterial blood marked one redcloak's demise. Rîma spun away counterclockwise before he fell, ducking low beneath the survivor's vicious beheading sweep. At the close of the circle, she rose in a single fluid motion, her sword's point spearing up between the layered cured-leather straps of the redcloak's breastplate.

They stood there a moment, face to face, the hilt of Rîma's sword hidden by the press of bodies and its point protruding from his right shoulder. Then, with an almost kindly touch, she pushed him away over the side of the railrunner, her sword's bloody steel coming free.

By the time Kat stumbled to join her, Rîma was facing the railrunner's front, hand on her hat and sword across her shoulders as she stared into the low western sun, and smiling with joy her scarf hadn't a hope of concealing.

"What's so wonderful?" asked Kat, through a mouthful of grit and pine needles. The trees were thinning as Hezerin's low spire came into view, the dark stain of its low-lying districts spreading across the railrunner tracks and reaching north to the Silent Sea.

Rîma's smile faded, the accompanying twitch of her shoulder heralding a return to understatement. "I've walked this land for a thousand centuries, but I've never fought a duel atop a railrunner."

They'd become so close these past six months – though Kat still struggled to define a bond that transcended friendship or family – it was easy to forget the gulf of years yawning between them. "Whatever works for you. Can we go inside now?"

"As you wish." Shaking her head in mock dismay, Rîma started towards the front ladder.

And went rigid as a bald man with rich dark brown skin climbed onto the roof.

He wasn't a redcloak. It wasn't just his robes that gave it away, their metallic colours shimmering through the gauzy black silks. It was how he *moved*. Redcloaks carried themselves with arrogance born of borrowed authority, but the newcomer moved with confidence so steady that even the bucking carriage couldn't throw it off. The broad, easy-going smile was the grace note to the performance, the expression of a man who'd chosen to be in that time and that place. But there was nothing easy-going about his posture, which offered only finality. It made the howling wind of the open rooftop feel like a closed box. Only a handful of people possessed such presence. Marida, the deathless qalimîri who ruled half of Tyzanta's Undertown was one. Rîma another.

The transformation was so complete that Kat scarcely recognised the drunk from the travellers' carriage corridor. There was certainly nothing inebriated about him now.

He bowed low, framed to perfection by the low western sun. "Greetings, Principessa Eskamarîma."

It took Kat a moment to parse Rîma's name from among the formal-sounding syllables. The voice matched the man to perfection. Calm. Confident. Tutored. She glanced at Rîma, hoping for a clue, but the swordstress had eyes only for the newcomer, what was visible of her face between hat and scarf rigid with frustration. Frustration, and fear. No surprise. She'd been expecting this, or something like it.

Tatterlain. He'd spoken of a man scouring Undertown for Rîma.

"What do you want, Hadîm?" Rîma's voice was colder than the wind.

"Your grandfather asks that you return home peaceably."

"You've had a wasted journey. I will do no such thing."

194

Hadîm's smile broadened. Eyes on Rîma, he reached behind his back and drew a pair of short, viciously curved shamshir swords from their inverted scabbards. "I was hoping you'd say that."

Twenty

The platform shot by in a blur of startled faces and gesticulating custodians. Maids and manservants lunged to steady their fireblood employers' luggage. Unsecured headscarves twirled in the railrunner's slipstream, dancing higher and higher above buildings bright with yellow and blue paint. A ten-count more and those streets slipped away into a landscape of irrigated fields and lazy windmills. Only the pungent jasmine and juniper smoke of the city's torch houses remained, captured by the railrunner's wake.

Braced on the vault wagon's rear stoop, Tanith stared back along the rails. "Was that Hezerin?"

Azra didn't look up. "I guess we're not stopping there." She gave another fruitless heave on the decoupling bar and swore. "If you're done taking in the sights, maybe you'd consider helping?"

Tanith folded her arms. Perched as she was atop the stoop railing, the wind tugging at skirts, sleeves and hair, it felt *glorious*. "If you ask nicely . . . and if you stop looking at me like that."

Feet braced, Azra hauled on the lever again. "Like what?"

"Like I'm a monster." Stars Below, did she really sound so childish? "I don't like it."

"You *are* a monster."

"Kat doesn't think so."

196

"Kat doesn't know how many bodies you've left in your wake." Azra fixed her with a stare. "Do you even remember them all?"

"Of course I do," Tanith lied, and struck out for firmer ground. "You didn't seem to mind when I was killing for you. You're every inch the monster I am."

"I never said I wasn't. But even monsters are afraid of something."

Tanith flinched. She'd halfway convinced herself that maybe she and Azra had been friends after all – that time, distance and circumstance had simply heightened innate distrust that always steered her false. "You're using my sister, aren't you?"

"Oh, please," Azra replied scornfully. "Don't act like you're concerned."

"You really *are* a monster."

Rushing wind swallowed Azra's sigh. "Believe what you like. But please, Lady Tanith, prettiest and wisest in the land, would you be so good as to help me with THIS SKRELLING LEVER?"

Gathering her skirts as a fireblood should, Tanith dropped from the railing. "You didn't have to shout."

As she smiled sweetly at her former co-conspirator – maybe even her former friend – and hauled on the decoupler, she silently resolved herself to the truth that Kat couldn't be expected to tolerate *two* monsters. One would have to go.

The decoupler creaked a fraction of the way along its guide rail.

"That's it," gasped Azra, her cheeks tight. "Just a little more ..."

The troop wagon door crashed open. A grey-bearded redcloak stood on the threshold, his golden gorget and black sash marking him as a *sarhana* veteran – not quite an officer, but more than a simple trooper. His eyes flickered from Tanith to Azra. His hand went to his sword. "What is the meaning of this?"

"Oh, thank Nyssa you're here!" Lips parted in heartfelt relief, Tanith stepped lightly from one stoop to the other and threw her arms around him. "There's about to be a terrible accident."

She crushed her head against his chest, her small, stuttering sobs deadened by the press of his robes. His suspicion buckled, tension bleeding away beneath her glamour's onslaught. His soul smelled so *good*. Earthen and oaky, aged like the finest wine.

All it would take was a gentle tug . . . then something less gentle. Her pulse raced, urging her on.

She started in horror, her sobs no longer entirely counterfeit. It was happening again. What was wrong with her?

With a stifled cry, she shifted her weight. The redcloak, lost in protector's empathy, had no chance to do anything but scream as she heaved him over the stoop's thin railing.

"See?" she murmured. "I was right."

"Oh, very good," said Azra, still wrestling with the decoupler. "No one's going to have heard that."

"I don't care what they heard." Tanith slammed the outer door on the empty vestibule and wrenched the handle. It came away in her hand, the clatter of its counterpart on the far side more imagined than heard over the cacophony of the rails. "Let's get this over with."

Hadîm's shamshirs flashed, steel shining red in the fading sun. Rîma turned a pirouette, sparks flaring as she swept her sword to the parry. Her riposte bled seamlessly into a low lunge at Hadîm's guts. He stepped aside and tapped the flat of a sword against her overextended forearm.

"You've been fighting glints too long. It's made you slow."

Growling, Rîma ripped her sword away and brought it arcing back in a merciless three-cut, driving Hadîm back along the rooftop.

Kat watched from the middle ventilation louvre, buffeted by crosswinds and throat tight with uselessness. The preceding minutes had reinforced beyond doubt that she'd never match Rîma's skill with a blade. The sheer fluid efficiency of every thrust and parry; the precision of every footfall placed with the meticulousness of a formal dance.

Impossible that she could fight so, wreathed in steam and assailed by the wind.

More impossible still that Hadîm matched her move for move.

For all that they resembled instinct, Kat glimpsed echoes of forms she'd struggled to master, tapestries woven of chiming steel where she barely managed threads. She finally understood how much Rîma held back against opponents she considered to be little more than children, as if to fight with her full skill was somehow unsporting.

Rîma's long, straight sword gave her reach that Hadîm lacked, but he'd two blades to her one, making her every parry an opening. A meeting of equals so perfect as to be worthy of applause, or even tears. A contest in which Kat had no more place than a scurrying rat.

Blades clashed again. Rîma spun away in a whirl of coat tails towards the carriage's front.

Hadîm pursued, trailing sword tips scraping slender furrows in the roof. "You shouldn't have kept the sword. I might never have found you otherwise."

"This sword is my birthright!"

Rîma's back-cut was so vicious that Hadîm stumbled away, off balance for the first time. Rîma stepped into the gap, a feinting slash at his neck flowing effortlessly into a brutal downward cut that struck the shamshir from his left hand and sent it skittering along the roof.

Unfazed, he ducked low and slashed out at her shins. As she back-stepped, he twisted side-on, right arm and remaining sword levelled at her face.

"It belongs to the city. *You* belong to the city." He raised his voice over the howl of the wind, the words pulsing, hypnotic. "The bells are tolling for you. Tell me you don't hear them."

"I ..." Rîma's shoulders sagged. Her hat tumbled away into the slipstream. Her long white hair writhed in the wind like maddened serpents. Her sword fell from a nerveless hand.

Kat gaped in horror. Was it some trick of Hadîm's words? His tone? Something unseen? For the briefest moment, she thought she heard the chime of some sonorous, abyssal bell tolling through the wind.

She pushed away from the louvre. Even a rat could bite. Her straining fingers found the fallen shamshir and she flung herself at Hadîm's back.

This time the omen rot declined even to offer an itch as warning. Her left knee buckled, pitching her into the darkness behind her eyes, her left side numb and trembling.

Hadîm turned. The point of Kat's shamshir tugged at his robes, sending slivers of fine silk dancing away. His fingers closed around her weapon hand as she collapsed – a father relieving an errant child of a stolen possession – and twisted the sword away. The strike of his elbow emptied her lungs. She doubled over, sucking for breath that wouldn't come.

"Bold, but pitiful."

With a shake of his head, Hadîm planted a boot against her shoulder, and shoved. Still gasping for breath, Kat tumbled down the roof's gentle curve, fingers scrabbling vainly for purchase.

Tanith threw her weight against the decoupler. It scraped barely half an inch along its track. Across the coupling's linked hands, the troop wagon's door shook beneath the impact of angry fists.

"Come on," said Azra, her face flushed and damp with perspiration as she wrestled with the lever from the other side. "Where's that amashti strength?"

Tanith shot her a poisonous glare. Dealing with the vault ifrîti had taken more from her than she cared to admit. Her strength and speed – when it wasn't grounded in making its prey *feel* weaker – wasn't a matter of muscle and sinew, but spirit. Hers was flagging. Enough so that it was increasingly tempting to let Azra's soul restore the difference. It wasn't as though she didn't have it coming, and she *had* already resolved herself to its necessity, for Kat's sake, if not hers.

Yes, *definitely* for Kat's sake.

But that would mean giving in to her daemon-half, which had been entirely too forthright the whole time she'd been on the railrunner.

She tightened her grip on the lever and loosed the brew of fear, annoyance and frustration swirling about her cursed soul. "I don't ... have *anything* ... to prove ... to ... YOU."

200

The lever sprang free. The coupling's hands snapped apart.

Laughing with delight, Tanith grabbed at it to steady herself. "I did it!"

"You really did," said Azra.

She shoved Tanith across the gap between the two carriages.

With a shriek of alarm, Tanith grabbed frantically at the edge of the opposite stoop. Her fingers closed fast about the railing. Her right boot skittered along the track bed, jarring every bone between ankle and hip. Gasping, she pulled herself sidelong onto the stoop and stared daggers at Azra, already a dozen feet away and receding with every stinging, ragged breath.

"Why did you do that?" she shouted, already knowing the answer. Kat couldn't be expected to tolerate two monsters in her life. Reaching the same conclusion, Azra had acted first.

It wasn't *fair*.

Azra gazed back in mock concern, a hand cupped to her ear. "Sorry! Can't hear you!"

Tanith shrieked until her throat was raw and collapsed on the troop wagon's stoop.

Behind her, the door slammed open.

Kat kicked out instinctively as her feet shot over the edge. The desperate fingers of her right hand, raw from scrabbling, latched onto a ridge in the pitch-blackened planking.

Knuckles creaking, she hung on for dear life as her muscles acceded to her wishes and her diaphragm at last remembered how to breathe. The dull red roar of her pulse faded. Her lungs filled anew. Her left hand, numbness in retreat and tingling with sensation, found purchase alongside her right. Shoulders shaking, she dragged herself high enough for her knees to touch the roof edge.

Hadîm stood with his back to her once more, his swords sheathed and his attention given over to whatever glamour he'd woven about Rîma. He didn't so much as glance behind.

Kat's cheeks burned. Doubly humiliating that he couldn't be bothered to finish the job of killing her. Bad enough that she was no threat. Worse was that she'd lost the only weapon of any use – if she couldn't give Hadîm pause with a sword, her tiny dagger wouldn't achieve anything.

But that didn't mean she couldn't try.

As her boots found purchase on the rooftop, she reached for the dagger. Halfway there, her fingers brushed a small, hard weight in her pocket, forgotten after she'd left Fadiya's carriage.

She indulged a vicious smile. Why not? Fighting fair wasn't getting her anywhere.

Begging her omen rot not to sabotage her a second time, she flung herself at Hadîm's back.

He turned, one hand closing around her throat and the other bunching the tunic at her shoulder. "You're testing my patience, glint. My business is with the principessa, not you."

"Then your business *is* with me."

Kat twisted in his grip. The snap-flint flared warmly beneath her thumb in the moment before Hadîm flung her away. She rode the momentum, angling towards the front of the carriage where Rîma stood, shoulders slumped, lost in her waking dream. Kat bore them both to the rooftop, and glanced behind just as Hadîm's scowl vanished in a thunderclap of brilliant flame.

If the blasting prism's detonation left anything worthy of note beyond a greasy black smear, it had vanished in the carriage's wake long before the smoke cleared.

Rîma braced her palms against the roof and twisted to a sitting position, her voice shaking as she spoke. "Thank you."

"Who *was* that?" asked Kat.

Rîma reclaimed her fallen sword. "What's important is that he won't be back for a while."

"For a *while*? Crows will be picking pieces of him out of trees for a week."

Rîma flicked a strand of hair from her eyes and tucked it behind her ear. "I said it would be a while. We'd better get inside. There's no way anyone missed that."

Kat scowled, unhappy at the evasion, but knew there was no point pressing the matter. Not now. And besides, Rîma was right. By her count there were two more redcloak officers still in the front carriages. "Have it your way. For now."

Rîma twitched one of her small, almost imperceptible smiles, her eyes far afield. "Sometimes now is all we have."

Between sudden acceleration and explosion, the carriages were in uproar. However, those passengers and crew not dissuaded by Kat's expression – owing equal parts to weariness, failure and frustration – readily retreated from Rîma's bloody sword.

They found the two missing redcloak officers among the coals of the tiny tender built into the engine's rear. One lay huddled in a pool of blood. The other was so absorbed in trying to break down the locked door to the engine that he never saw Rîma's sword hilt strike his wits away.

Kat hammered on the door with a lump of coal. "Tatterlain! That had better be you in there! Tatterlain!"

The door creaked open, revealing Tatterlain's pale, strained features. He leaned heavily against the doorway, one hand clasped to a dark, spreading bloodstain over his ribs.

"Stars Below," breathed Kat. "What happened?"

"There was ... something of a disagreement," he replied breathily, barely the ghost of badinage in his manner. "You should have seen the other fellow."

"We did. Briefly."

Tatterlain wasn't listening. Eyes closed, he sank to his knees beside the doorway, upright only by dint of his shoulder resting against the jamb.

Kat's throat tightened. "Tatterlain?"

203

"I'll see to him," said Rîma. "You check on the engine."

Tearing her eyes away, Kat stepped into the engine cab proper. The steel walls were barely half her height, the better to dissipate heat to the outside air. A forest of levers and needle-gauges flourished between the pyrasti's crackling firebox and the high steel and glass windshield, all mysterious in form and function. She cast her mind back to the only other railrunner engine she'd seen, but that had been a superannuated hulk fit only for the scrapper's yard. The two were nothing alike.

More worrying were the two five-sided glass pyramids on a ledge behind the levers. Heraldic prisms, one of them still gleaming with the pale indigo of its messenger ifrît, the other cold and dark, its spirit gone.

She glanced back. Tatterlain sat with his back against the cab's rear wall while a kneeling Rîma tore strips from his steward's robes for makeshift bandages.

"The driver got a message away, didn't he?" asked Kat.

"Took ... offence at the stabbed redcloak," breathed Tatterlain. "No class, some people."

Which meant a new kind of trouble. Heraldic communication was almost instantaneous. The only consolation was that Osios lay far to the west – even the fastest dhow would be hours in arriving. Time enough to raid the vault, get clear of the railrunner and hopefully vanish into the Kemmuz Plains. It wasn't ideal, especially not carrying a wounded Tatterlain with them.

"How do I slow us down?"

Tatterlain's eyes fluttered. "Red lever ... closes off the drive valve. Brake ... below it."

Kat stared anew at the red lever, fully perpendicular to the floor as one might expect if someone had fallen heavily against it. She gave it an experimental tug and at once met the resistance of a motic bolt.

"Spiteful fellow," murmured Tatterlain.

The "spiteful fellow" in question was doubtless the driver, who'd locked off the levers before the struggle had borne him overboard.

"How is he?" Kat asked Rîma.

"I'm dying," Tatterlain murmured. "A great hero taken before his time."

Rîma pressed two fingers to his lips. "He needs more help than I can give. Last breath too. And quickly."

A numbing void opened up in Kat's heart. What little last breath they'd brought with them she'd already used to keep her failing body in line. "I'm sorry."

"Not your fault," Tatterlain murmured. "Sometimes . . . these things go wrong."

Kat swallowed a failing attempt to hold panic at bay. Sometimes things went more than wrong. Tanith, the redcloaks . . . whatever Hadîm had wanted. Between them they'd stretched fortune to breaking point. Tatterlain was paying the price. Of all of Vallant's band, he'd been good to her from the first. Now he was dying in her place, and all because she'd been too stubborn to ask for help.

Azra appeared in the doorway to the tender, face flushed and filthy. "You can forget the redcloaks. They're gone." She frowned at Tatterlain. "What happened to you?"

He closed his eyes. "Destiny."

Azra arched an eyebrow. "She could use some manners."

"Could be."

Knuckles whitening around the drive lever, Kat clawed back her composure. "Tell Tanith we need her up here, then if there's any last breath aboard this wretched railrunner you and I are going to find it." She started towards the tender door, only to stop short when she realised Azra wasn't moving. "What?"

"Kat . . ." Azra scowled and glanced away. "Tanith's gone."

"Gone? What do you mean, gone?"

"Redcloaks."

"What? How?"

"It all happened so fast. She'll . . . she'll be fine. She's a survivor."

Kat closed her eyes. She couldn't afford to fall apart. She'd got them

205

all into this. She had to get them out. "One of the stewards must have the glyphs to unlock these motics."

"I don't think it's going to matter," said Rîma.

Kat followed her gaze to the southern skies and the pair of lateen-rigged silhouettes swooping down from the Cloudsea. Custodium dhows, answering the driver's panicked heraldic. Osios might have lain far to the west, but Icorum lay barely beyond the southern horizon. Another miscalculation.

Kiasta.

Kat licked her dry lips, unable to pull herself away from the approaching skyships. Try as she might, she couldn't move, couldn't think. The world began and ended with those ships, speeding closer with every breath. They were all going to die. Slain when the custodians boarded or executed for their crimes, it didn't matter. It was over.

No. It wasn't over for everyone.

"Azra? Find Yali and Fadiya. Help them blend in with the other passengers and get them home."

"What about you?"

"I'm staying with Tatterlain and Rîma. I got them into this." She knew better than to suggest that Rîma go too. "I'm trusting you to get the others out. Will you . . . will you do that for me?"

Azra's brow pinched, precursor to argument. Instead, she nodded. "If that's what you want." She hesitated in the doorway, but left without a word.

Kat stared at the oncoming dhows, still small, but growing larger with every moment.

"You can go too," said Rîma.

Kat shook her head. She'd no longer the energy to do anything but stare, and hope that Azra had time to get Yali and Fadiya to safety. She snorted. There was no safety. The dhows were already close enough that their lookouts would notice anyone making passage of the rail-runner's roof.

"I'm sorry. I—"

The sky rippled with flame. The lead dhow shuddered, already slewing to starboard as the screech of the cannon's discharge and the hollow roar of impact washed over the engine cab.

A second shot set the custodium vessel's sail ablaze. A third cracked its portside buoyancy tanks, a thin stream of vapour wisping skyward as the vessel plunged towards the trees. The second dhow, captained with rather more pragmatism than valour, banked frantically west, yards and stays blossoming with fresh canvas as its master sought to harness every last scrap of wind. Climbing hard for the Cloudsea, it vanished beyond from Kat's sight.

She'd no eyes to spare it any longer, the whole of her attention given over to the char-black skyship bearing down from the east, its three lateen-rigged masts swamped by an array of smaller sails and its gunports streaming smoke. The *Chainbreaker*, the second of her name, heir to a legacy whose forebear had died a glorious death in the skies above Athenoch.

Bashar Vallant, come unlooked-for out of nowhere to save Kat from herself, all over again.

"He's going to be unbearable," she breathed, torn between laughter and tears.

But glancing back at Tatterlain, his life ebbing away in Rîma's arms, she decided that, just this once, she didn't mind a bit.

Twenty-One

With a rattle of capstans and a bloom of sails, the *Chainbreaker* climbed for the Cloudsea. From the portside quarterdeck, Kat watched the thin column of steam creeping towards the western horizon and the safety of distant Osios, a nervous steward in command of the railrunner's engine and its passengers already exchanging hushed tales of crossing paths with the great Bashar Vallant and living to tell the tale.

Her unbound hair dancing in the wind, she lost herself in the soft, sad song wafting from the direction of the helm. Typical that she'd lost Tanith just after finding a reason to care. The joy in her sister's eyes after she'd learned to cajole the vault's ifrîti ... it hinted at the woman Kat had hoped existed beneath the daemon's malice. One she might even save, if Nyssa was with her.

Azra had the right of it. Tanith was still alive. She had to be.

A shadow-chased patchwork of rust-red outcrops, treetops and dirt roads rushed past far below. Not wanting to push her luck – and her vertigo's patience – the day already having had more of that than was healthy, she straightened as the first skeins of mist threaded the forests, the ever-hungry Veil swirling across the lowlands and hissing to nothing where it strayed too close to a torch house's flames.

Mistfall. All across the kingdom, folk would be hurrying indoors, piling blesswood into their hearth fires and praying to Nyssa that they'd come through the night unharmed. Hopefully Tanith, marooned in the wilderness, had made it to the safety of a torch house's light. Kat had no fear for herself – not aboard the *Chainbreaker*.

She glanced back to see Vallant climbing the companionway from the main deck to the quarterdeck. They'd barely exchanged a word since she'd come aboard. Not that she'd been avoiding him, not *exactly*. He'd known well enough to leave her be. But ignoring him risked ingratitude, and friendship was friendship, however complicated.

The helmswoman flashed a smile of greeting as Kat approached the ship's wheels, her lament falling away into silence. She was little more than mist herself, her bluish-white skin paler than the clouds and her windblown hair an inky stain shining with the light of captive stars. Her diaphanous dress – which was not really a dress at all, but a form she wore out of desire to blend in as best she was able – rippled and fluttered with every gasp of wind. Only the silver and red-gold brooch upon her black-ribboned choker seemed truly real.

Zephyr was a daughter of the Issnaîm – what much of Khalad named "veilkin" – her people hounded to extinction by the Eternity King's armies. Even at her most solid she drifted like a cloud tethered to the world rather than part of it, aethereal in the truest sense, more dream than mortal woman. At least until she spoke, her words ranging between mischievous and acerbic, depending on her mood.

"Finally thinking to say hello, are you? Poor manners, even for a *waholi*."

"I needed time to get my head together." As ever, Kat had the feeling she was playing a game whose rules escaped her.

Zephyr offered a sly smile, her glassy, pupil-less white eyes unreadable. "Best go back, says I. A long way yet to travel."

"It's nice to see you as well," said Kat. "I think."

Zephyr's smile broadened, conveying that the one-sided game was over. "Of course it is."

Kat couldn't help but return the smile. Frustrating as Zephyr could be – not that Kat's life was otherwise free of frustrating people – like Rîma, she offered a glimpse of a world deeper and richer than the one Kat had grown into.

"What do you think of my ship?" asked Vallant.

Kat raised a hand to dull the worst of the setting sun. If Zephyr was a barely tethered wind, Bashar Vallant's roots went deeper than the mountains, a man whose earnest pragmatism reshaped everyone in his orbit.

At first glance he looked a young man, rugged and clean-shaven, his every gesture notable for the restrained energy coiling beneath. Only upon closer examination did middle years grow apparent in the creases gathered about aquiline nose and olive brow, his thickening jowls and the slivers of silver-grey in his curled brown hair. Even with his time as a Bascari overseer two decades in the past, he still dressed the part, his simple black tunic as stark and practical as Zephyr's not-dress was soft and threaded through with whimsy. It was inevitable that the two, as opposite as it was possible for any to be, were fast friends.

Kat turned wearily about. "It's in better shape than your last one. It has cannons too, I see."

The first *Chainbreaker* had possessed no such luxuries. Not from absence of need – many of Vallant's battles had gone harder than they should for a lack of firepower – but because the shrieker ifrîti would never have survived in the Veil, and more than anything it had been the Veil that had kept Vallant alive. Guided by Zephyr's uncanny ability to navigate the mists, *Chainbreaker* had been a plague upon the Eternity King's outposts and supply lines, striking from behind the Veil and retreating there before reprisal could follow.

Vallant nodded. "Cannons, motics ... even a surly helmic, though it's worthless once the mists fall."

"How do you keep them together?"

"There's a sliver of astoricum behind every prism."

So that was it. The red-gold astoricum – or oreikhalkos, as some

210

scholars named it – was the other key to Vallant's survival, for the metal had the unique ability to stabilise a soul lost within the Veil. It was also vanishingly rare. Zephyr's brooch was a family heirloom. The only place Kat had seen the metal in any quantity had been in the black tower at Athenoch's heart, where a vast silver and astoricum sphere held the mists at bay. Even had it been advisable to risk Athenoch by salvaging that sphere, she doubted anyone could have done so. Just looking at it had turned her upside down and inside out faster than any attack of vertigo. "Expensive."

He nodded. "It took months to scrape even that much together."

"Sounds like the perfect vessel to find a way through the Veil ... or have you given up on that to go picking up strays in Khalad's heartlands?"

She already knew the answer. Moreover, she knew that *he* knew that she knew, but tiredness made old habits irresistible, and needling Vallant was amongst her most deep-rooted.

"You're mischaracterising my words. I said that if I couldn't offer people freedom, I could at least offer them a choice. At the time, Issnaîm legends about a realm beyond the Veil seemed our *only* choice. Things have ... gotten a lot more complicated since then." Vallant shook his head. "A year ago, five hundred souls looked to me for guidance. Now entire cities clamour for my attention. For the first time in Nyssa alone knows how many centuries, Khalad is crying out for revolution. I can't ignore that."

"Sounds like you gave up ... or got scared at the prospect that Tzal was waiting for you on the other side."

Tzal was the other half of the legend Zephyr had once recounted, a proud and tyrannical god whom the ancestors of the Issnaîm had sought to cage within a silver pearl woven from his own obsessions, only to become trapped themselves. To the Issnaîm way of thinking, Khalad was the inside of the pearl, and the Veil its skin. What lay beyond the Veil – if anything did – remained a mystery, as did the fate of Tzal himself.

A smile tugged at the corner of Vallant's lips. "You really think so little of me?"

"I didn't say that."

"Your eyes did." The smile grew wry. "You've always been quick to judge, and maybe I deserve it. But it might just be that I'll surprise you."

There it was: that earnest, forthright tone. One that made him impossible to argue with but almost irresistible to thump. "I've had my fill of surprises today."

"Yes, Rîma told me something of that."

"She did?" Kat hadn't seen Rîma since she'd carried Tatterlain aboard the tiny felucca that had ferried them aboard the *Chainbreaker* while Kat had busied herself with the vault. "She'd one or two of her own as well."

"Did you get what you wanted?"

"I hope so." There was no way to know until she made a proper examination of her haul, a handful of battered volumes dedicated to the kind of historical curiosities her father had loved. "I . . . I don't know what I'd have done if you hadn't shown up."

She'd expected to hate the confession, and was therefore surprised that a weight lifted as she gave it voice.

"You'd have found a way. You've a knack for that."

She shot him a sidelong glance. "Yali sent you a heraldic before we left, didn't she? She told you what we were doing and where we'd be."

"I'm quite sure I don't know what you mean."

Kat sighed. "I'm to believe you were just out for a pleasure jaunt and happened upon us?"

"Does it matter?" He shrugged. "We were here when you needed us, and I've been meaning to speak to you for some time now in any case. Sometimes Nyssa provides."

"I'm going to kill her."

"Not allowed. The captain wouldn't like it."

She scowled. "You do know it's not polite to speak of yourself in the third person?"

"Oh, I'm just a distinguished passenger." Vallant grunted. "And speaking of passengers, I'm told you brought a Bascari aboard."

Azra wasn't *just* a Bascari. As Yennika Bascari, she'd plotted to destroy Vallant and everything he held dear. "She's in my cabin."

And with instructions not to wander. Vallant wouldn't be the only person aboard harbouring ill wishes. Most of the *Chainbreaker*'s sail-riders had lost someone dear to Azra's scheming.

"Is she now," he said flatly.

"It's complicated."

"Isn't it always?" He stared towards the high stern and the stylised sunburst flag that had come to represent the breakaway east. "Don't worry, I'm not going to lecture, even though after all the lectures you've directed my way I probably should . . . but are you sure you know what you're doing? Yennika's a manipulator."

"She goes by 'Azra' now."

He brushed the correction aside. "It doesn't matter what she calls herself. She's killed too many."

"Not like us, then."

"We've only ever killed to survive, or for a cause."

Typical Vallant, framing his failings as necessity and everyone else's as malice. "And how many did you kill before you parted ways with the Bascari?"

The air between them suddenly colder than the wind, he stared tight-lipped out over the high balustrade, past the furled spars and gossamer folds of the skyship's aethersails nestled among the spread canvas.

"If you're to be quarrelling, I'll thank you to do it elsewhere." Zephyr's every word carried its own sigh. "Disturbing my mood, you are."

Kat made a vain attempt to twist her hair into some semblance of order and stifled a fresh rush of guilt. Vallant hadn't been looking for a fight, but she'd started one anyway. "I shouldn't have said that. But Azra's trying to be different. You of all people can understand that, surely?"

Vallant had lived a life twisted to serve the Bascari stranglehold on Tyzanta, manipulated both in and out of his overseer's uniform to act first as their enforcer and later as an unwitting figurehead for an easily controlled rebellion. Tythia, Azra's cousin and Vallant's long-dead wife, might have loved him as deeply as she'd claimed, or might equally have been another of his puppeteers. Only their daughter, Sadia, had remained untouched.

Vallant offered the horizon his flat, level stare, likely recalling beatings taken at Azra's orders. It hadn't been personal to her, just a means to an end, but malice and pragmatism were twins to those on the receiving end.

"She stays in your cabin," he growled. "Otherwise I'll personally heave her over the side. Agreed?"

"Agreed."

"Good," he replied, not quite mollified. "I'll leave you to convey the message. She won't want to hear it from me."

With a terse nod, he retreated towards the companionway.

A dull, distant part of Kat pointed out that she should have been every bit as angry at Azra as Vallant was. She felt certain she *had* been at some point in the past, but couldn't say for certain when things had changed. Perhaps she'd simply become so used to defending her against Yali that doing so to Vallant had become second nature. Or perhaps she'd made choices she'd not meant to and was only now realising it.

Yes, she really *did* need to talk to Azra.

"Wait," she called out as a stray thought struck. "You said you wanted to talk to me. Why?"

"It'll keep," he replied without turning. "Get some rest."

Abuzz with frustration, Kat stared after him. Not their first difficult conversation, but this held the dubious distinction of being one that had gone sour because of her attitude, not his.

"Too similar, you are." Zephyr's musical voice cut across her thoughts. "Driven so hard that you forget what's doing the driving, and why."

"I know," murmured Kat. "It's been a long day. Maybe I *should* get some rest."

"See the captain first, you should."

The mysterious captain, to whom Vallant was but a passenger. "And who is he, exactly?"

Twenty-Two

The captain's quarters aboard the *Chainbreaker* remained grand beyond the dreams of most travellers. The table set beneath the leaded windows was large enough to seat eight comfortably – though at that moment it needed to manage only five – and a cluster of armchairs rounded out the potential accommodation to an even dozen. Like the pair of modest dressers, the faded plates and the rogue's gallery of wine glasses, the chairs were hopelessly mismatched, spoils and salvage of days gone by. In furnishings as in fortune, Vallant's followers were nothing if not pragmatic. However, the wine was rich, the bread crusty and fresh-baked, and the platters of spiced, aromatic komestri sausage, pickled radish and fresh greens tastier than anything Kat had eaten in a long time.

Fadiya set her plate aside, her thin self-selected serving picked clean. ||"I must say, Katija, the company you keep never ceases to prove … interesting."||

Kat savoured a sliver of komestri, letting the garlic and paprika mellow on her tongue. ||"I've been fortunate in my friends."||

But even as she looked around the table, she wondered if she drew that circle wider than she should. Yali and Rîma, certainly – the latter bereft of plate or glass, for her deathless body had long since forgotten its need for mortal sustenance. She supposed her relationship with Fadiya was friendship if it was anything. As for the table's fifth and

216

final occupant? Even at her most generous, "ally" was the best she could conjure.

Sitting immediately opposite, Ihsan Damant – once castellan to House Bascari, once mentor to Bashar Vallant, now traitor to the Eternity King's rule and captain of the *Chainbreaker* – raised his glass, the glint in his one good eye suggesting that he'd read her thoughts far more closely than she'd have liked. ||"To interesting company."||

"To interesting company."

Three glasses rose in reply, three voices alongside. Rîma offered a nod in place of a glass, her voice subdued. She'd been so ever since boarding. Everything about her seemed smaller, even distant, as if whatever piece of her had retreated before the phantom bells had not yet returned. Yali, of course, left the toast unspoken but drained her glass immediately. Kat felt the empty chairs more keenly than those filled. Tatterlain, lying bandaged in a cot while last breath and rest did their miraculous work. Azra, as good as confined for crimes past and the fear of those yet to come. Tanith, missing and maybe worse.

Fadiya's hand found hers and squeezed. "She's survived worse, Katija."

"I know." It should have rankled to be read so easily.

Damant nodded, his thoughts lent sardonic possibility by the jagged scar framing his milky-white eye. Though twice Kat's age and more besides, his hair long ago turned steel-grey and rich olive features worn deep by responsibility and regret, she'd learned to underestimate neither his vigour nor his wits. He'd likely still have held a castellan's rank but for a singular failing: he was also an honourable man.

||"We'll be passing Hezerin come the dawn,"|| he said, his words still the precise, almost clipped, speech of his authoritarian past, his signing studious and workmanlike. ||"The custodium head's an old friend. She may know something."||

"Thank you, Captain." Fadiya set aside her glass to sign. ||"Elinor always spoke highly of you."||

||"I'm sure she did."|| Damant's tone grew darker. ||"I certainly earned it."||

217

Kat winced. Affairs had ended badly between the late Countess Bascari and her former castellan, but Fadiya – whose infrequent visits to Tyzanta lay long in the past – couldn't have known. ||"And what of you, *Mathami*?"|| she put in before past unhappiness derailed a pleasant enough hour. ||"I'm assuming you don't want to return to Zariqaz."||

||"That would seem unwise,"|| Fadiya replied wryly. ||"Hargo wanted rid of me, now he is. Let him be content with that. I intend to thrive ... assuming I can remember how."||

||"I was thinking Tyzanta,"|| said Kat, ||"or perhaps Athenoch. That's possible, isn't it?"||

||"I don't see why not,"|| said Rîma. ||"Vallant will certainly agree."||

||You'd like Athenoch.|| Yali stifled a yawn. She'd taken more wine than anyone else at the table, and her usually elegant signs stumbled. ||It's tranquil. Not a custodian in sight.||

||"Then Athenoch it is."|| Fadiya drained her glass. ||"But Katija? I shall expect to see you and Tanith there before long."||

||"You seem certain that I'll find her,"|| said Kat. ||"And that she'll listen to me."||

||"I know that look. I know *you*. You were such a quiet, tidy child. Your father always worried there was something wrong with you. But you were unstoppable once you'd an idea in your head."||

||"That sounds somewhat familiar,"|| said Rîma, a flicker of her old self broaching a troubled surface.

||"She's exaggerating,"|| Kat protested.

Fadiya smiled, lost in memory. ||"You once piled half the books in my library, one atop the other, until they were almost twice your height, all so you could reach one set on the top shelf."|| She twisted in her seat, no longer talking to Kat, but Rîma. ||"I walked in and caught her just as it all gave way."||

Yali grinned. Rîma managed a soft smile. Damant remained stony-faced.

||"You've always known what you've wanted, Katija,"|| said Fadiya. ||"Hold onto that certainty, otherwise you'll be a prisoner as surely as I

ever was. We cage ourselves long before anyone else troubles themselves to do so."||

"I'll try," Kat murmured. A fine sentiment, but if her father's manifold obsessions proved anything, it was that certainty and single-mindedness were the most mixed of blessings.

||"I think I've embarrassed her enough."|| Fadiya pushed back her chair. ||"Better I have the good grace to leave while she still thinks kindly of me."||

Her departure proved Rîma's also, laden with a tray of provisions for Tatterlain, should he be once more among the wakeful, and a bottle of wine to coax him there if he proved reluctant. By the time Kat had offered her farewells at the door, Yali was slumped back in her chair, nose aloft and snoring like an avalanche.

Damant rose to refill Kat's glass. "Quite a pair of lungs, that one."

"Try sharing a room with her." Fortunately, Yali had a cabin of her own, though the walls were thin enough aboard the *Chainbreaker* that it would matter little to her immediate neighbours.

He lowered himself into one of the armchairs and beckoned for Kat to sit opposite. "I take it you've already spoken with Vallant."

"We argued, if that's what you mean."

"Hah! You're in good company there. Let me guess. Azra."

Interesting that alone of everyone Damant had adopted her new/old name without prompting. "Are you fixing to throw her overboard as well?"

"If I wanted that, Arvish, she'd be gone already." He tapped the cheek below his milky eye. "I almost feel like I owe her a favour for showing me what her family really was. If she makes no trouble, let the past stay in the past."

"As simple as that?" It was a more generous concession than Azra had any right to expect.

"As simple as that." He shrugged. "You know how Khalad works. If it hadn't been her, it would have been someone else."

Azra's unlamented cousins, most likely. Kat hadn't met them

219

personally, but she'd heard plenty. "I don't think Vallant sees it that way."

"Vallant's an ass. Being right more often than he's wrong doesn't change that."

Kat smiled to herself, the soft creak of shifting timbers the only challenge to Yali's wet, rippling snores. To people who'd never met him, Vallant was a beacon of hope, bright as torch house flames. To new recruits, he was a hero. But those who'd known him longer saw every crack in the veneer. Damant had known him longer than most. "You're the captain."

He grunted. "Only when it suits him. He keeps finding reasons to take command."

So much for Vallant only being a distinguished passenger. "Such as when?"

"When the first heraldic arrived warning us that a crew of skelders was about to get themselves in hot water on the Zariqaz–Osios railrunner." He fixed her with a level stare. "I told him that you'd get yourself out of it, and our time would be better spent patrolling out at Naxos. House Zanarîq still hasn't accepted that they're not getting their shipyards back."

Kat conveniently forgot that she'd not wanted Vallant's help. "That's cold, even for you."

"I think you mean 'practical'."

"I know what I— Wait a minute, the *first* heraldic? How many did you receive?"

"One at Naxos, two more as we passed Tyzanta."

Kat glared at Yali, still oblivious. "She really didn't have any faith in me, did she?"

Damant stared down into his glass.

"What?" growled Kat.

He met her stare, his amusement palpable for all that it never showed in his face. "It's a simple enough calculation. Three heraldics and—"

"And three people who knew where to send them," finished Kat. It hadn't just been Yali, but Rîma and Tatterlain as well. Kat's mood,

220

greatly improved by substituting Vallant for food and drink, shelved into dark waters. "So *none* of them trusted me." Only Azra had, in fact, and wasn't that ironic?

"You're reading too much into it," Damant replied. "Confidence can steer you false. If you've good people around you, listen to them. Otherwise, if they *are* good people, they'll take matters into their own hands."

Kat frowned. There'd been something about the way he'd said that. "Are we still talking about me . . . or about you and Vallant?"

"I suppose that's the question, isn't it?"

"You're worried he doesn't trust you?"

"He trusts me. He just doesn't *listen* to me." He paused and glanced at Yali. "Don't you think you should do something about that? If we hit an air pocket, she'll be breathing in her leftovers."

"Let her," said Kat, still not over the triple betrayal. "And don't change the subject."

He grunted. "Vallant's trust isn't the issue. He's struggling to let go. Easier to lead a rebellion than a nation."

That, at least, Kat understood. Taking responsibility for Tatterlain, Rîma and Yali had pushed her to the limit. "So it's *not* about Vallant. It's about you."

"I think . . . I'm still looking for somewhere I belong."

"Regretting your choices?"

"I thought the skies would bring me freedom. A fresh start. Turns out I'm just a foolish old man. I was a functionary for the Bascari; I'm now one for Vallant." His brow creased, his good eye far away. "I want . . . Nyssa help me . . . I think I want an adventure. To see something truly wondrous, to make a difference no one else can. All the things I might have done when younger, if I hadn't bound myself to the Bascari."

"Ihsan Damant, the dreamer." Somewhere between inception and speech, the words softened from mockery to empathy. Impossible to torment someone who trusted you with a glimpse of their soul. "Who would have known?"

He scowled into his wine. "This is why I shouldn't drink."

"You should tell him."

"Vallant? He wouldn't understand."

"So I always say. I'm always wrong."

But there was a lesson for her in all of it, wasn't there? Both Fadiya and Damant had sought to deliver it, if in different ways. Life was too short not to follow your heart. Lately, she'd been as wrapped up in untangling her father's secrets as Damant had ever been with the Bascari, too busy pursuing the future to consider the here and now. Doubly foolish, given the shadow hanging over that future.

Damant nodded. "Perhaps you're right."

"I do like hearing that." Pushing free of the chair proved harder than it should, the deck swaying ever so slightly in a manner that had everything to do with the wine. "I'd better put that delicate creature to bed."

Getting Yali to the comfort of her cot was a labour in name only, deep sleep and rich wine having delivered her to a boneless and unresisting state. Duty done, Kat picked her way along the corridor to her cabin, not so lost to her own indulgences that she'd didn't note the presence of two lingering sailriders. Vallant's orders, no doubt, making sure his unwelcome guest stayed put. More proof that the *Chainbreaker* was only conditionally Damant's ship.

Azra was perched on the edge of one of the two cots, reading in the dull lumani-light. Her straight-backed and tucked-leg posture evoked the image of a woman riding side-saddle, lending a hint of proprietorial allure to an otherwise shabby ensemble of dust-streaked trousers and undershirt. Not exactly glamorous, but she still shone brighter than she'd any right to. She always did.

"You've been gone a long time." She set aside her book – one of the small pile recovered from the railrunner – and offered a smile that flirted with hurt. "Forget about me?"

Kat set the door to. "Unlike you, I've friends aboard this ship . . . some of whom needed convincing you should stay here."

"Ihsan among them, I assume?"

Kat propped a shoulder against the thin wall and savoured the moment. It wasn't often that Azra misread people. "Actually, he made the case that you were just a – what's the phrase? – yes, an accident of history. If it hadn't been you, it would have been someone else."

"Ah, but no one else would have done it with as much style." Azra flashed a smile. "Darling Ihsan really does know how to twist the knife, doesn't he?"

"You have a way of making people re-examine themselves."

Azra's smile broadened, a little too mocking – a little too self-assured – for comfort. "People like you, darling?"

Kat smothered a flash of irritation. Whatever else had changed in their six months apart, Azra still had a knack for saying precisely the wrong thing at the wrong moment, and for no better reason than she could. Resolve gathered in Damant's quarters crumbled away, then hardened anew.

"We should talk. About what happened on the railrunner."

Azra stiffened, the smile faded into a suddenly watchful face. "Ah."

Kat hesitated, torn between joy at having caught Azra wrong-footed and guilt at having done so. "You told Tanith you loved me. Did you mean it?"

Azra's shoulders drooped. The smile returned, lacking its former edge. "You think I'd lie about something like that?"

"Maybe. You lie easily enough."

"About everything else, but not that." Eyes downcast, the last of the mockery slipped away. "Whatever else you and I were, that part was always real."

Kat drew closer, uncertain whether the creaking was in her heart or the ice underfoot. "You once told me that our futures were entwined. That nothing could alter that fact unless I wanted it to."

"I did, and you did," Azra murmured. "You sent me away."

Kat sat on the cot, hand inches from Azra's crooked knee. Close enough to see the wariness in her eyes. Maybe even hope, if she wasn't herself deluded. She remembered her father recounting how the Qersali believed that eyes reflected the soul and intent of both the beholder and the beheld – the challenge therefore lying in untangling the two. No easy matter, for Kat felt like two people in that moment, one burgeoning with intent and confidence, and the other desperate that things should go no further, fearful of what it would ask of her, what it would *mean*.

All paled before the knowledge that, no matter the betrayals, no matter the pain – no matter Yali's lengthy remonstrations – a piece of her had been missing those past six months. Warmed by wine's liquid bravado and the lessons of her elders, she wanted it back. Wanted *her* back.

It felt good to admit it, even in the quiet of her own mind.

"Maybe I'm different. Maybe you are." Her eyes met Azra's, the beholder and the beheld no longer distinguishable from one another, united in hope and uncertainty. She reached out. Her fingertips brushed Azra's slender neck and cupped her jaw. "Either way, I want to find out."

The last apprehension slipped from Azra's expression. A smile returned. Not the brash, self-confident grin of her fireblood heritage, but the quieter, almost vulnerable curl of the lip that disarmed like nothing else. "So do I."

Pulse quickening, Kat leaned in. Though she'd never have admitted it to another living soul, she'd imagined this moment across long, lonely nights. Never in a cramped cabin, nor haunted by the twanged muscles and grazed skin she'd earned aboard the railrunner. But skelders couldn't be choosers, and perfection was what you made of it.

The soft sigh of Azra's breath brushed her cheek.

She closed her eyes.

"Oh damn it all," murmured Azra.

She pulled away and dropped down from the cot. Moving as far distant as the confines of the cabin allowed, she jerked about to face the opposite wall, too slow to conceal a thin-lipped scowl.

"What is it? What's wrong?" asked Kat, her throat tight.

"About Tanith. I told you the redcloaks took her. That's ... not entirely true."

Kat lurched. The way she'd said that ... "Is she ... ?"

"I'm sure she's fine. Like I said, she's a survivor."

Something cold slithered into Kat's heart. "Then what?"

"When we decoupled the carriages, Tanith was on the wrong side." Azra paused, her swallow audible. "Because I pushed her."

Kat blinked, torn between surprise and crushing inevitability. Hope wilting before a furnace blast of anger, she leapt to her feet, finger levelled accusingly. "Stars Below, what's wrong with you?" she shouted. "Are you pathologically incapable of *not* stabbing people in the back?"

Azra spun on her heel, her features pinched. "You don't know her like I do. She's unstable."

"Right now," said Kat, "I know how she feels."

"I was protecting you."

"I don't *need* protecting. Except, it seems, from you." She gritted her teeth, disappointed in herself as much as Azra. For trusting someone who'd proven her unworthiness time and again. For another failure to add to the day's roster. For thrusting her hand into the fire, even knowing she'd get burned.

"You're right. I screwed up." Azra sank onto the cot opposite, hands on her knees and eyes fixed on the floor. "I could have kept quiet, but after everything you just said ... there has to be truth between us, doesn't there?"

Another day, another world, and maybe that would have been a point in her favour. A sign that she really was a different woman. But it wasn't a different day, and lost in a fug of anger and disappointment, Kat didn't trust herself to reply.

So in place of words, she did the only thing that made sense.

She left the cabin, slamming the door behind her.

Twenty-Three

The Veil's greenish-white skeins flowed over the beakhead bulwark, coiling across a deck hushed with the quiet of men and women awash in superstition. But for the presence of Zephyr's brooch and the slivers of astoricum threaded through the ship, they'd all have faded away long before reaching clear skies.

Kat clung to the bulwark's raised edge, adrift as she ever was behind the mists. Neither time nor distance worked quite as they should once the mists came down. Even the most determined lost bearings almost at once, travelling in circles until body and soul came apart. Of all the souls aboard the *Chainbreaker*, only Zephyr was immune to dissipation, and even she would have unravelled without astoricum's protection, her vaporous form reborn as something sharp-toothed and blood-hungry.

Awash in the scent of old memories and fond days, Kat's frustrations ebbed. The Veil was no place for doubts and recriminations. Indeed, it was no place for anything at all, save to simply *be*, for however long one's soul could sustain itself.

Even with her soul sheltered by astoricum, she couldn't shake the sense of danger. But better the mists than the Deadwinds skies of the hour prior, the deck and rigging awash with bobbing, dancing motes of magenta and indigo soul stuff she could no longer touch as once she had. Better still to have had the good sense to retreat below – her thin labourer's coat was in no way equal to the chill of the Veil. But still she

226

stayed at the bulwark, shivering and sullen, convinced that she deserved the discomfort for choices lately made.

She didn't notice Vallant at her side until he spoke. "You're up late."

Kat scowled, the temptation to walk away overwhelming. "It was that or throttle Azra."

He leaned forward, elbows propped on the bulwark. "Ah."

"That's all you're going to say?"

"Would you like me to say something else?"

"No."

He shrugged. "There you go then."

"You're an insufferable bastard," she said, at last facing him.

"It's been said."

But insufferable as Vallant could sometimes be, she owed him an apology. "Thank you for pulling me out of the fire today."

"You'd do the same for me."

So he always said. Kat was never sure it was true. Half the trouble with Vallant – half the frustration – was that although he was pragmatic to the point of callousness, she could never quite shake the suspicion that he was a better person than she'd ever be. Having lost everything to fireblood scheming, he sought to help others, while she struggled to think of anyone but herself.

"I know it wasn't just Yali who contacted you."

"Zephyr?"

In hindsight, it was surprising Zephyr *hadn't* spilled the truth. "Damant."

"Ah." Vallant's eyes fixed on a point somewhere in the mist. "They had your best interests at heart."

"I know." Kat closed her eyes. Easier to reconcile that truth in the dark. Easier too to deny its second lesson: that she should at least come clean about her omen rot and trust them to trust *her*. "What did you want to talk to me about?"

Vallant leaned the base of his back against the bulwark with a nonchalance that set Kat's vertigo cackling. For a long moment he was silent, arms folded and chin tucked to his chest. "I want you to rule Tyzanta for me."

She blinked. "I beg your pardon?"

"All this . . ." He waved towards the prow, the gesture somehow managing to encompass the distant and unseen east. "It's too much for one man. It has been for a while."

"Even for the great Bashar Vallant?"

He shrugged a soft, self-effacing smile. "Running around playing at the reaver king of Athenoch was one thing. A third share in the governance of Tyzanta was something else. Now a dozen cities look to me for guidance, with more teetering on the brink. It's more responsibility than I ever expected. I can't shoulder it alone."

"You're not alone. You have your adoring masses."

"I don't need people who look at me as a hero. I need friends who see the man beneath, flaws and all. Friends who won't fail to hold me to task."

"Ah, at last I see my qualification. What about the Triad?"

The Triad was the closest thing that Vallant's separatist east had to a ruling council, formed of Vallant himself alongside the deathless Marida and Javar – a bombastic ex-templar – Tyzanta's foremost crime lords. Or *formerly* Tyzanta's foremost crime lords. The difference between gang boss and fireblood ruler was so often little more than a royal charter.

"I want Javar to oversee the shipyards at Naxos. If civil war's coming, then we'll need all the ships we can manage, and beneath his blustery exterior he understands logistics better than anyone I've ever known." Vallant shrugged. "As for Marida . . . she suggested you."

Stranger and stranger. Especially given that the ageless qalimîri knew of Kat's failing health. "Why?"

"Who can say? But she's had a long time to learn about reading people. Tyzanta was the first city to turn its back on Caradan Diar. It's symbolic. I need to know it's in good hands."

"Then let Damant do it."

228

"I considered that, but he's plainly restless, and more than a little set in his ways. Revolution's no game for old men."

Kat shook her head in a failed attempt to dispel unreality. "I've no military experience. *Kiasta*, I don't handle people well even when they're not carrying swords."

"And despite that, you saved everyone in Athenoch not so very long ago."

Without meaning to, Kat glanced down at her wrist. She'd saved everyone ... and damned herself. Given the choice a second time, would she make the same decision? She hoped so, but knew herself well enough to know that it wasn't that simple. *She* wasn't that noble. "That piece of me is gone. I may never get it back."

"The weapon is nothing to the woman who wielded it. In any case, leadership isn't about fighting battles. It's about standing firm for what's right even when the world screams that you're wrong."

As was so often the case, his reply didn't quite jibe with her objection. "I don't even know how cities *work*. Guilds, custodians, tithes ... they're just words."

"You think Caradan Diar has more idea than you?"

"He has advisors."

"So will you. Cities like Tyzanta largely run themselves. They have to, otherwise everything collapses when a different fireblood house seizes power."

True. Even in Kat's short lifetime, Tyzanta had changed hands between House Jovina, House Bascari and now Vallant's Triad. She'd remarked herself how little difference the last handover had made to everyday life.

"We'll keep a Triad in place, but they'll answer to you." Vallant's voice quickened with enthusiasm. "And you'll have my support, whenever I can spare it."

Her ears pricked up. "Oh, really? And what will you be doing?"

"Whatever I can, for whoever I can, for however long I can." He stared off over the bow, eyes on some distant, unseeable goal. "If

229

the Eternity King makes this a war, I'll fight it. Otherwise, I'll bend every effort to making sure that what we've started to build here outlasts us all."

"King Vallant the First, is that it?"

"Not that." His features softened as he realised how sharply he'd spoken. "No. If the last six months prove anything, it's that Khalad's had enough of kings. I'll advise, I'll offer guidance and I'll protect those who need it, but I won't rule. And when the time comes and I can catch my breath, maybe I'll go looking for that realm beyond the Veil." The beginnings of a smile tugged at the corner of his mouth. "I vaguely recall someone taking me to task for not having done that already. Someone I trust."

And there it was. Beyond all the fine words and rationalisation about her suitability to rule Tyzanta, it all came down to trust. It freed and smothered like nothing else.

She closed her eyes to blot out Vallant's earnest, cajoling gaze. Always so much easier to disagree when you couldn't see him. "I can't be responsible for that. Everything that happened today proves it."

"It's different, isn't it, when you've no one but yourself to blame. From what Rîma tells me, you slammed face-first into circumstances that no one could have predicted. And yet you achieved everything you meant to and got everyone out alive." He pulled a rueful face. "I've never been good at that last part."

"*You're* the only reason any of us are still alive. I had nothing to do with that. I did everything I could to avoid bringing you into this."

"But I'm here all the same," he replied, unfazed. "Why?"

Kat glowered at him. How many times did she have to repeat herself? "Because—"

"Because the people around you made the right choice, even when you made the wrong one. Half of leadership is learning who to trust and giving them the space to *break* that trust when they feel it necessary. Most firebloods live and die never learning that. They want control above all things, just as the Eternity King wants control above all things.

230

It's why their custodians are so ineffective against real resistance. It's why we can win."

Damant had said much the same thing, if in different words. Whether either man liked it or not, mentor and student had much in common. "What's the other half?"

"I already told you. It's about standing up for what's right, no matter the cost. Because no one else can."

Kat allowed that Vallant's words held at least a little truth. Enough that a small, treacherous piece of her wanted to accept his offer. If omen rot was to consume her, surely it was better to do something truly selfless first? Maybe that was why Marida had recommended her for the task? She certainly wouldn't had she known just how fast the disease was killing her. Stars Below, it had almost killed her that past day, during the fight with Hadîm. "I can't, I'm sorry. The reasons I came to Zariqaz still hold. Even if they didn't, I can't have people die because of me."

He gazed at her, perhaps searching for words to marshal to another assault. Then he looped his hands behind his back and nodded. "Believe it or not, I understand." For all that, disappointment was palpable in his voice. "If you change your mind, you've only to—"

The ragged chime of the quarterdeck watch bell drowned him out, the tumult rising as other bells and running feet joined the chorus.

Kat jerked upright. "What is it?"

"I don't know," said Vallant, already moving.

She hurried after him, imagination seething. Had the Eternity King's forces at last learned the secret of astoricum, or was it simply an abandoned hulk, adrift behind the Veil, its crew long since dissipated?

A sudden chill at the base of her spine warned that it was neither.

The quarterdeck was crowded by the time Kat reached the top of the companionway, Vallant, Zephyr and a bleary-eyed Damant already surrounded by aghast sailriders. Some clutched swords, boarding pikes and crossbows. Others pressed threaded fingers to their chests in the Sign of the Flame.

All felt useless against the vast, bird-like shadow boiling through the mists directly to the *Chainbreaker*'s, emerald light blazing where its eyes should have been. Kat knew for certain that it could have swallowed her up without recourse, and quite possibly the entirety of the *Chainbreaker* alongside. It didn't so much as traverse the Veil as bleed through it, the mists dappling from greenish-white to grey-black with each beat of those massive wings.

"Zephyr ..." Vallant stood at the stern rail, motionless, as the shadow dived towards the *Chainbreaker*'s swirling wake, his voice the measured, even tones of a man clinging to calm. "Do you want to tell me what I'm looking at?"

"Never seen it, have I," Zephyr bit out. She was as tightly reeled in as Kat had ever seen, her vaporous form almost tangible, as if by mimicking those around her, she hoped to go unnoticed. "Nothing of Issnaîm is this, neither legend nor truth."

"So it's not Tzal?" he asked tautly.

She laughed with humour. "*Ayin*, swat this ship to blazing ruins would Tzal."

"I've seen it before." Even as Kat spoke, she felt eyes on her. "Or something like it."

A beat of the shadow's wings propelled it closer, its croak the raw, rough outrage of a hundred lesser birds.

Vallant spun around. "Well, don't keep us in suspense!"

"I said I'd seen it before," Kat ground out. "I didn't say I knew what it was. Out past Zoyen. It was hunting something."

"Hunting what?" demanded a pale-faced sailrider to her left.

"If you want to ask it, be my guest!"

"I've heard of it." Alone of everyone on the quarterdeck, Damant was unfazed by the sight – or at least possessed of sufficient self-control for it not to show. "Mistfall stories, going back a couple of years. Half the miners in the Avidri Hills will spin you a tale. Pair of drunks got caught in the mists out near Bassios, scrambled out bleating about a shadowy roc prowling the Veil, looking for its mate."

232

"I guess they weren't as drunk as all that," said Kat.

"It's a safe bet," said Damant.

Vallant nodded, and gestured to Zephyr. "Bring us around to port, but gently. Let's not be obvious."

Damant closed the gap between them in three strides. "You can't mean to give it a broadside!"

"Not unless I have to," Vallant replied evenly. "I'm just keeping our options open."

Not much of an option, Kat decided. The closer the shadow grew, the larger it revealed itself to be. Would it feel the shrieker cannons' flame? Would they even fire? So far as she knew, no one had ever sought to fight a Cloudsea battle behind the Veil. There'd never been a need.

With another grinding, croaking screech, the shadow dived out of sight, mists swirling in its wake. It burst into view again almost at once, close enough to the stern rail to send a fresh wave of greenish-white mist rushing across the deck and Vallant stumbling towards the wheels. "Zephyr, bring us about! Crews to your guns! Move!"

Sailriders scrambled for the companionways. Zephyr hauled on the lateral wheel. The *Chainbreaker* creaked as the army of motics laboured to realigned rudder and pinion sails.

Beyond the stern, the shadow banked to match, the outer tip of its wing brushing the armoured hull enough to set the ship shuddering. Kat grabbed at the companionway rail to steady herself. Away to her left, a sailrider lunged for a handhold on the bulwark too slowly and vanished overboard with a thin scream.

"Zephyr!" shouted Vallant.

As the *Chainbreaker* at last swung about, Kat straightened in a blaze of emerald green, the shadow's eye fixing on her even as it mimicked the skyship's banking turn. Transfixed, she gazed back, heart in her throat, drowning in a bleak, smothering presence that reached far beyond the shadow's extent. A presence that was not only aware of the panic it had provoked, but was also somehow amused by it.

Then, with a last croaking cry and another glancing blow from its outstretched wing, it plunged into the mists once more and did not return.

That didn't stop Damant from doubling the watch until the Veil at last gave way to the Deadwind skies above the Silent Sea.

Twenty-Four

So close to Zariqaz, the steady clockwise churn of the Deadwinds vortex was at its tightest, and no one aboard wanted to draw unwelcome attention from the redcloak fleet moored about the Golden Citadel. Accordingly, Damant laid out a course that swung north-east over the Silent Sea, riding the vortex some miles out from Zariqaz's perimeter. He also took care to keep the *Chainbreaker* clear of encroaching mist banks, much to Kat's relief and, she suspected, to that of the rest of the crew.

Kat spent her time cloistered with Yali and Tatterlain, the latter in growing health and good spirits thanks to the miracle of last breath. Time and again he shrugged off her apologies, repeatedly averring that having spent years in Vallant's company, he'd already beaten the odds – the average recruit survived maybe ten months before misfortune or fireblood malice found them.

Apologies aside, Kat expended every hour with Terrion Arvish's thin library. She read every one, cover to cover. No difficult task by volume, as by strictest definition they were more pamphlet than tome. More challenging was the detail, as all but one were copies made out in her father's spidery handwriting.

Most frustrating of all were the attacks of cramp that knotted most of her left side and the pulsing headaches that the *Chainbreaker*'s stockpile of last breath, carefully purloined, barely touched. She endured the latter by retreating to darkened passageways to read and concealed the former by holding the books as tight as she dared until the spasms passed, all the while praying that no one would grow suspicious. Sharing her secret with Tanith – involuntary though the act had been – had only reminded her how dishonest she'd been with her friends. The untruth festered like a boil, but she lacked the strength to lance it.

She learned far more than she'd ever wanted to about the Issnaîm ruins at Zarnac, the theological rift that had torn apart Travicorum's Historica Guild, the various treatises arguing for and against the Obsidium Cult's claim that Nyssa was a goddess with three faces, her true countenance struck from record by Alabastran creed; to say nothing of many other obscure – and resoundingly useless – historical curiosities. Nothing about her tattoo or its origins. Nothing that lent clues to Tanith's rifted nature. Nothing that might cure the disease ravaging her, body and soul.

Yali helped as best as she was able, but the tutelage of the streets hadn't prepared her for dense academic language. She for the most part resigned herself to fetching steaming cast-iron pots of feldir tea from the galley, pungent with apple and honey.

For his part, Tatterlain sat up in his cot, thin pillow bolstered by a bundled coat, and pored over the copy he'd made of Yarvid's journal – the original remaining safely concealed in the Maraji theatre – a piece of foresight that further brought home to Kat that she couldn't think of everything.

Others stopped by from time to time, Fadiya most often of all. She seldom stayed long, as if even being in the same room as her dead lover's possessions was too painful to bear.

Rîma made two visits on the first day, ostensibly to correct Tatterlain's Adumaric transcriptions, but clearly to ensure that he was truly on the mend. The swordstress otherwise remained distant and assiduously avoided Kat's attempts to discuss Hadîm. Indeed, the only time she engaged with the topic at all was when Kat addressed her as "Principessa Eskamarîma".

236

"That's not who I am," Rîma had replied, as angry as Kat had ever seen her, and stalked away. Kat would have gone after her had not Tatterlain – who'd known Rîma far longer – suggested that the fire be permitted to burn itself out.

Of Vallant Kat saw almost nothing, and of Damant only fractionally more. He only stopped by to relay the news from Hezerin that Tanith was alive, but that her fate was otherwise shrouded in secrecy. Redcloaks didn't like to talk about their mistakes.

Kat made no attempt to see Azra, shunning their shared cabin and instead electing for the slung hammock and rippling snores of Yali's. Like Rîma, she'd a fire inside her that had yet to burn itself out. Adding to her frustration was the feeling that she'd mishandled the matter, the noxious brew of desire, betrayal and disappointment ruling her actions rather more than head or heart. Unless her father's books contained a miracle, she was fast running out of time to indulge prideful quarrels.

She distracted herself with the only means at hand, studying her father's books forwards, backwards, trying to identify patterns from the quirks in his handwriting or the scuff marks and notes in the margins. Before long she found herself nodding in the cabin's threadbare armchair, dreams haunted by sketches of Issnaîm cuneiform and scribbled handwriting.

"I'm an idiot!" shouted Tatterlain.

Kat jerked awake, scattering pamphlets and pages of notes across the cabin. That the tea pot struck by her flailing arm didn't follow suit was thanks solely to Yali's headlong lunge to grab it before it toppled off the dresser's edge.

"Hardly worth disturbing my sleep for that," said Kat groggily, holding onto the remains of her pride with both hands.

Still clutching the single spine-bound book from among the collection, Tatterlain waggled his eyebrows. "You're not at your best on waking, did anyone ever tell you?"

"Everyone." She swallowed to clear a claggy mouth, her stumbling fingers belatedly remembering to sign. ||"*Why* are you an idiot?"||

No cat ever looked so pleased with itself as Tatterlain at that moment. "It's a book code." He waved the fistful of pages. "They're not words at all, but numeric references. First the page, then the line, then the position on that line."

Yali's brow furrowed, the dim light in the cabin and Tatterlain's rapid-fire excitement proving too much for her lip-reading. Kat flashed a quick Simah translation.

||I thought they were letters,|| said Yali.

Tatterlain shot her an apologetic look. ||"They are, but by inverting the letter's position in the Adumaric alphabet, you get a number. Three numbers to a letter. Simplicity itself, which is why I'm an idiot."||

It didn't sound simple and he didn't sound like an idiot. Indeed, even with the explanation, Kat couldn't trace the leaps of logic that had led him to the discovery. ||"Which book?"||

He tapped the unassuming volume lying atop the cot. ||"Book codes only work if all communicating parties have identical copies. That means all those copies have to come from the same printing."|| He gestured at the rest of the railrunner haul, scattered around the cabin. ||"Hand-copied pamphlets don't cut it. Too much scope for error."||

Kat prised herself from her chair. Braced against the slope of the *Chainbreaker*'s gentle port bank, she crossed the cabin and picked up the book Tatterlain had indicated.

Meditations on the Ruins at Zarnac, whose dry interpretations of various tabula and sand-worn friezes had served as the foundation of the florid, adventurous tales Kat's father had offered up at bedtimes. While his stories had always centred around gallant heroes, doomed romances and wickedness brought to account, *Meditations* dwelled rather more on foibles of language and – as Kat now understood – bigoted appraisals of the thought-vanished Issnaîm. Had her father understood the truth better than the long-dead author, or had he simply employed poetic licence? The realisation that she'd never know brought a lump to her throat, old grief summoned to the present by unforeseen association as old grief so often was.

"He'd have adored Zephyr," she murmured. A wisp of the past living in the present? How could he not?

||She'd have liked that.|| Yali shared a raised eyebrow with Tatterlain. ||Who are we talking about now?||

||"My father. He always held that the Issnaîm had survived Caradan Diar's purges."|| Though of course he'd called them veilkin, rather than Issnaîm. Zephyr wouldn't have liked that quite so much. ||"What do the pages say?"||

Tatterlain dipped his head to his notes. ||"There's a lot of nonsense about the third face of Nyssa. You know, the usual ranter's charter. But this section, by which I mean the last section – the pages have fallen out of order – seems to hold a warning. *Malizin is dead. Caldior is missing. So much for Ossed's promises.* The rest will take time to decipher."||

Two of the names meant nothing to Kat, but the third struck a chord. ||"Ossed? As in *Zaran* Ossed, the hierarch?"||

While she didn't know the man personally – the idea that a cinder-blood of even her somewhat elevated fortunes might rub shoulders with a senior temple official was laughable – they had a shared history all the same . . . starting with the night she'd accidentally helped destroy a vault full of priceless – but volatile – antique tetrams and the upper floors of Tyzanta's Xanathros Alabastra. Or perhaps it hadn't started there, if Ossed was in some way connected with her father.

Tatterlain rolled his eyes. ||"I know you don't have much of an attention span, but remember when I said it would take time to decipher? That still applies. But—"||

Clang-clang. Clang-clang. Clang-clang.

The lazy muffled chimes of the *Chainbreaker*'s watch bell warned of the final approach. Kat crossed to the brass-rimmed porthole and saw the polished white flank of a torch house minaret pass away. For'ard, a squat, ramshackle spire gleamed against a sea of red-tiled roofs, its cluster of fireblood palaces flanked by giant bronze statues of a begowned and smiling Nyssa Benevolas, her flame-like curls falling to her waist, and an altogether sterner Nyssa Iudexas, her ripple-bladed flamberge held at guard. A cluster of grey-feathered speybirds took flight from the latter, startled skyward by the *Chainbreaker*'s approach.

||"Looks like we're coming into Salamdi."|| Half a day earlier than planned, but the skies had been calm and the Veil generous. ||"I guess you can work out the rest in Zariqaz."||

Zariqaz. Where her father had died. And where, short of a miracle, so would she. But maybe, just maybe, there was a chance to thwart fate.

Salamdi's air was lighter than Zariqaz's and even Tyzanta's, untroubled by the bitter smoke and hot dust of industry that plagued its elder cousins. Or perhaps the air wasn't lighter at all, Kat allowed as the *Chainbreaker*'s mooring ropes went taut at a sailrider's barked command, but her own mood. For the first time since things had gone sideways on the railrunner, she'd a sense of tangible progress. A name to follow, maybe even a trail. Small things, but they made for a large difference.

But she wouldn't allow herself to feel hope, not yet. She'd been caught that way before.

The dhow eased into the mid-spire dockside, a slight wobble in its trim suggesting that the battered buoyancy tanks were in need of another repair. The old *Chainbreaker* had been forever falling apart, its antique hull patched and coaxed by a crew well experienced in such things. To all appearances, this one was fixing to be no different. Hopefully Vallant was better at keeping a nation together than he was his ship.

"The dress suits you," said Fadiya.

Kat grimaced. Viewed objectively, the gold and scarlet gown – fetched from Fadiya's baggage – perfectly complemented her bronze skin and inky hair, which was once again tied back in a loose bun. If she stood just so, with chin raised and back straight, her cinderblood birth and years of skelderdom fell away, leaving the striking image of a fireblood heiress. It only reinforced the sense that she didn't belong

240

in such clothes, but she'd eventually accepted both the generous gift – whose worth was measured in tetrams rather than dinars – and its necessity. If word of the botched hijacking *had* reached Salamdi, the local custodians would be looking for the desperate skelder she no longer resembled. "It was generous of you to offer it, *Mathami*."

Fadiya regarded her closely, her sapphire eyes piercing in the bright sun. "I don't think one dress – even if it is a genuine Slarini – comes close to settling the debt." Perfect lips hooked a wry smile, the creases and concerns of years falling away into an echo of a carefree youth. "I suppose this is goodbye ... for now, at least."

With a gentle shudder, the *Chainbreaker* came to rest alongside the timber quay, its streamlined keel easily clearing the masts of a fireblood's pleasure barge moored directly below. Damant, now dressed in the deep blue robes of a House Marquan captain – which not coincidentally matched the owl-and-sun flag rippling and snapping above the crow's nest – set out onto the gangway before it was fully lowered, a sheaf of forged documents and a purse of dinars ready to soothe the concerns of the fussy-looking dockmaster who stood shivering in the chill westerly wind.

Kat nodded, the urge to confess her illness suddenly overwhelming. "I suppose so."

"You will be careful, won't you?"

"As careful as I can be." For all that it mattered.

"He'd be proud of you, Katija. He wasn't perfect, Nyssa knows none of us are that, but he did his best."

The shadow of grief returned, hastened by the missed opportunity for learning more of Terrion Arvish from the woman who'd known him better than anyone living. She'd never had the chance to outgrow his parental shadow, much less become his peer. They'd never spoken as equals, but as a father to a daughter he'd tried to protect from his own failings as much as those of the world. His death had forced her to grow up, and not always in ways that she liked.

"If— *When* I see you again," she said slowly, the urge to keep that uncertain, vulnerable piece of her hidden made worse by her growing fear that this would be their final parting, "I'd like to know more about the side of him you knew."

Even that small confession put a tremor in her voice. She blinked away a rogue tear before it summoned reinforcements.

Fadiya squeezed her hand. "Gladly." She glanced over her shoulder towards the companionway. "But for now, I think, someone else wants to talk to you. Nyssa walk with you, Katija."

"And you, *Mathami*."

Fadiya nodded politely as she passed Azra, just as firebloods did among equals. Azra, her short black hair parted and pinned back above and behind her ears, offered a brilliant smile in return. Exile and outcast though they were, some conventions still applied, and Kat wondered just how much of recent days the two had spent together. Easier to dwell on that than acknowledge the guilt at having ignored Azra that whole time. Anger now was but a memory. Too bad, as it placed her at a disadvantage.

Azra's smile faded to a subdued, but not woebegone, wariness. Her silver and black dress – also salvaged from Fadiya's belongings – wasn't half as expensive as Kat's own, but somehow she made it look twice as grand, the fireblood posture Kat mimicked as natural to her as breathing ... or lying.

"Am I coming with you, darling?" she asked in a small voice.

"Do you want to?"

She pursed her lips in hesitation. "I think ... I think I would like a fresh start. You and me, I mean. Do you suppose that's possible?"

Kat's heart leapt at the prospect, glad that she'd not damaged whatever their relationship had become, and yet she found she was frustrated by that gladness. "Another one? I don't know how many more you get."

Or that *she'd* get, for that matter. The prospect of finding a cure only heightened her dread at not doing so. What she'd lose ... No. What the omen rot would take from her.

Azra's lip twitched. "Then I'll be sure not to squander it."

"There are conditions," said Kat. "No more little accidents. No more people falling from bridges or onto departing railrunner carriages."

"But I—"

"However much you might think it's in my best interests."

"You do take all the fun out of life, darling."

Kat cocked her head and wondered if she really had the strength to do what was needed if Azra proved difficult. "Is that 'yes' or 'no'?"

Azra shook her head. "I accept. Of course I accept. So ... what can I do to help?"

Plenty, if Zaran Ossed *was* to be their next port of call. As Yennika, Azra had glided through the same social circles that the hierarch frequented. She'd be certain to have some idea of how he could be approached. But for now ... ? "Tatterlain and Yali could probably use a hand gathering everything aboard the railrunner we're taking back to Zariqaz."

That wasn't strictly true, as they'd arrived on the *Chainbreaker* with almost nothing, and even after being supplied with fresh clothes they'd little enough to take with them. But the point was to see how Azra would react to so menial a task.

She shrugged. "I've *two* hands, and neither is doing anything right now. How about I check in with them, grab your things and I'll see you aground?"

She walked lightly away, a woman burdened only by innocence and a desire to be helpful. It was a shame, therefore, that Kat wasn't entirely certain either was real. Still, it presented the opportunity to roam in search of other farewells, which she gladly took.

For a marvel, Zephyr offered no mockery, only a solemn curtsey of vaporous skirts and a musical, lilting utterance as much prayer as farewell. *May moonlight guide your steps wherever the wind blows.* Not being entirely sure what moonlight was – Zephyr had a habit of lacing her Daric speech with Issnaîm words she refused to translate – Kat offered a curtsey of her own and went in search of Vallant, who readily clasped her proffered hand, their disagreements forgiven, if not forgotten.

243

"You're certain you won't reconsider?" he asked, earnestness again in full, frustrating force.

"Tyzanta's better off without me, and me without it. You'll work that out sooner or later."

"We'll see," he replied. "But if you change your mind, or if you find yourself in a tight spot again, all you need do is call. I'll be there."

"I thought you had a not-kingdom to run."

He shrugged, as if that were the most trivial of matters. "Friends come first. Always. I'm still not sure you understand that."

"I'm trying to get better at believing it."

When Kat returned to the main deck, Azra, Tatterlain and Yali were already aground, haversacks resting on the timber pier as the *Chainbreaker*'s sailriders busied themselves hauling supplies aboard from a clatter wagon. Tatterlain sat perched against a bollard, arms folded, watching with obvious mirth as Yali forcibly moved Azra's hands through the spread-fingered Simah sign of greeting, then, with a despairing shake of the head, offered her own fluid performance of the same. As Kat threaded her way towards the gangway, she found Rîma waiting, coat and black linen wrappings so dark against the brilliant blue skies as to form a woman-shaped hole in the world, punched through from whatever lay beyond.

Rîma dipped her head, setting strands of white hair dancing. "I'm not coming with you."

Kat's throat tightened. They'd not spoken since her gaffe of using Rîma's full name and title. "About before. I wasn't thinking. I'm sorry."

"It's not about that. At least, not in the way you mean. In any case, it is I who should apologise. I have been less than myself since ..." Rîma stared out across the dockside crowds, but gave no indication that she actually *saw* them. "For all that changes with the centuries, surprises are both the greatest gift and the bleakest curse. I have made my discomfort yours. Can you possibly forgive me?"

Kat embraced her, as ever taken aback by her slightness. Beneath coat and bindings, Rîma was withered and gnarled with age, rendered more like tree bark than flesh and blood. That her face retained any measure of mortality – let alone youth – was due to ready imbibement of last breath. Everything else was held together by bolts and steel splints as much as the tissue of her body. Living for ever was nowhere near as romantic a notion as the poets pretended. "There's nothing to forgive."

Rîma stepped away. "But you would appreciate some answers?"

"Only if you're comfortable giving them."

"You would have to wait many more of your lifetimes for that." Rîma offered one of her almost-there smiles. "But discomfort is sometimes necessary."

Glancing up at a sailrider clinging to the rigging above their heads, she steered Kat towards the base of the mainmast and the illusion of privacy. "I once told you I was born into Tadamûr, greatest of the Hidden Cities."

Kat nodded. She had, although without mentioning its name. "You said it fell into decay and sealed itself off from the world." It was a kinder summation than Rîma's own, which had described buried streets become tombs for witless, shambling inhabitants little better than corpses. "You said you could never return."

"It may be that I no longer have any choice." Rîma reached up to her shoulder and touched the hilt of her sword. "This was my grandfather's, as it was his mother's before him, and on and on, stretching back through the generations. Tradition holds that Nyssa Iudexas forged it, a weapon sharp enough to sever a soul, and gifted it to Amakala, our first queen, so that divine justice might rule even the deathless. When the time came for the crown to pass, Amakala's son used this to help her reach Nyssa's judgement in the Stars Below. Nothing else had the power to do so. The day I fled, I was to grant the same gift to my grandsire, setting aside a principessa's freedoms for the trappings of a queen. I have spent centuries fleeing that duty."

She spoke with self-pity otherwise so unthinkable that for a long moment she even looked different, a shrunken woman in thrall to the sound of phantom bells.

"Is it really so bad to be a queen?" asked Kat.

"You do not understand. My people are not individuals as you are individual. We feel the pressure of one another's thoughts, each one a chime in a bright carillon. While we are together, we are never truly alone. In the old days, we grew wise together. What was learned by one was soon learned by all. And as the years lengthened to a burden, we lost our minds together." Rîma stared off into the mists, though what it was she saw, Kat couldn't guess. "Can you imagine what it's like to feel another's madness pressing against your thoughts? It was leave or lose myself for ever."

"And now your grandfather's grown tired of waiting?"

"I fear so. Hadîm is a qalimîri and not so easily dissuaded as I might wish. Even if he has not survived, others will come."

Kat scowled. Bad enough to be pursued by Alabastra's bailiffs and bounty-hunters as she herself had once been, but to be the quarry of some deathless assassin … ? "Then hide! Run far away, where he'll never find you."

"I can't. He's seen you. Most likely Tatterlain and Yali as well. He'll use you against me."

Kat shivered, as much at Rîma's matter-of-fact tone as at what she left unspoken. "Then we'll find him, kill him." She tried to forget the whirling shamshirs that had fought Rîma to a standstill. "As many times as it takes."

"You took him by surprise. You won't again. I brought this upon you. I'll end it."

"How?"

"By returning home. If I can deliver my grandfather to Nyssa, perhaps she will take mercy on us and set things right. It will certainly annul whatever contract exists between my grandfather and Hadîm." She laughed without humour. "In freeing my people, I free myself. It seems Nyssa wishes to teach me a lesson."

Kat shook her head, heart aching at the fatalistic note in Rîma's voice. "As simple as that?"

"I don't expect that it will be in the least bit simple, but it can be done."

"Then why do you sound as though you never expect to see me again?" What a hypocrite she was, chiding Rîma for dishonesty when she couldn't bring herself to speak of her own illness.

Her eyes on Kat's, Rîma took her hands in hers. "That will not happen. You and I are bonded, as Vallant and I are bonded. You are old souls, sent anew into the world by Nyssa's grace. You may have forgotten who you once were, but I claim you nonetheless – closer than friends, closer than family." She squeezed tight enough to drive the blood from Kat's fingers. "We *will* see another again, Katija. It may just take a little while, by your way of thinking."

The softly spoken understatement couldn't hide Rîma's true meaning – that she didn't expect that reunion to take place this side of Nyssa's Obsidium Palace and the hope of rebirth. A slender hope, in the first instance because Kat couldn't imagine that Nyssa Iudexas would soon forgive her sins, and in the second because she'd never really dared believe the archons' promises of reincarnation.

"Can I convince you to let me help?" she asked, a lump in her throat and her own troubles oddly distant. Easier to fear for a friend than for oneself.

"No." Rîma shook her head. "You have your path. Your sister needs saving from herself, to say nothing of the rest."

Those last words, weighted down by significance ... "You know, don't you?"

The corner of Rîma's mouth twitched. "I've seen how you've carried yourself in recent weeks. You told me in every way save words. It breaks my heart to abandon you now, when you need me most. But I can see no other way."

"Have you—"

As ever, Rîma was ahead of her. "I have respected your secret. In return, I ask that you respect mine. But if I may be permitted to offer some advice ... ?"

"I should tell them. I will, I promise." Kat scowled, unsure if her own words were true. "Does Vallant know what you intend?"

The almost-smile returned. "Not yet. If I give him too much warning, he'll try to stop me, never caring that he has no hope of success."

"And you think I won't?"

Rîma shrugged. "You have a better grasp of the inevitable."

That much at least was true. Vallant never allowed a lost cause to slip past unheralded and unembraced. For the first time in her life, Kat wished they were more alike, or rather that she was more like him. But she wasn't, and Rîma was right. She *did* have a better grasp of the inevitable. Particularly of late. Omen rot brought clarity until it took everything. "He'll not hear of it from me."

"Thank you." So saying, Rîma offered a long, formal bow. "Until we walk the same path again, Katija."

"Until then."

Kat wished she'd words equal to her feeling of loss. Rîma had the right of it. They *were* closer than friends, than family. Leaving felt like betrayal, but that same closeness warned her that nothing she could say or do would alter Rîma's resolve, so with a last unsteady smile and a clasp of hands, she walked to the gangplank.

Damant was waiting for her on the quayside, his expression that of one who'd recently spent entirely too much time suffering a fool with little in the way of gladness to offer solace.

"Arvish. That's a long face."

Kat stared back up at the *Chainbreaker*'s bulwark, but saw no sign of Rîma. "It'll pass."

He grunted. "Vallant playing his mind games again?"

"No. This is something else."

"Anything I can do?"

His scar ensured his expression remained as coldly sardonic as usual, but to her surprise, Kat heard only genuine concern.

What was it he had said to her that first night aboard? *If you've good people around you, listen to them. Otherwise, if they* are *good people, they'll take matters into their own hands.* How much had she come to rely on Rîma's advice, her presence? And Rîma would soon be alone,

248

marching headlong into a situation Kat barely understood. If ever there was a time for Kat to take matters into her own hands, it was at that moment ... assuming there was a way to do so without breaking promises scarcely gone cold.

But that wasn't all he'd said, was it? And in recalling the rest, Kat found the answer she needed. Or so she hoped. What happened next wasn't really up to her.

She tilted her chin and squared her shoulders, borrowing all the authority and resolve of the fireblood she wasn't. "Actually, I think there might be."

Twenty-Five

After a day in the clatter wagon's hot, stinking gloom, Tanith was ready to scream. The sunlight from the roof's slatted bars forced a perpetual, headache-inducing squint, and the clanking, shuddering rumble of broken-down gears and rusting suspension jarred her bones with every dip and pothole.

Worse were the hunger pangs. Though it would be days yet before her daemon-half grew too strong to be denied – or so she *supposed*, recent days having given her reason to doubt old assumptions – confinement chafed at self-control.

At least the shackles biting into her wrists and ankles were steel and not silver.

Though her gloves were largely intact, the left one still concealing the cold flames of her tattoo, her expensive sapphire gown was now rags the colour of rotting autumn leaves, a casualty of a day spent in a half-flooded custodium cell stinking of isshîm powder and broken dreams.

If only the nice young soldier who'd "rescued" her from the troop wagon stoop hadn't wilted in the face of his *sarhana* superior's suspicions. If only her glamour had been strong enough to melt the *sarhana*'s resistance as it had her smitten junior's. If only they'd believed her claims of being nothing more than an innocent passenger, swept up in a nefarious skelder plot.

If only Azra hadn't been a duplicitous, selfish bitch.

In what brief moments of honest self-reflection discomfort allowed, Tanith was surprised to find that she didn't hate Azra as much as she should for playing the same game better than she. She'd just have to be faster next time. And that there *would* be a next time, she hadn't doubted, even when sodden to the waist in the flooded cell, eye-to-eye with a shrieking sewer rat. Wasn't she Nyssa's herald, beloved of the goddess?

"*Abdon Nyssa ivohê*," she breathed, and took strength from the words.

"What was that?" her redcloak escort growled from the clatter wagon's far end.

"Just a prayer," Tanith replied, her voice trembling out of habit. A young woman stiff with pride and the fear of failure, the redcloak was about as safe from Tanith's glamour as it was possible to be. Still, in their long hours together, there *had* been moments when her gaze had lingered longer than was strictly necessary ... "We could pray together, if you'd like?"

"Shut it."

Tanith allowed that a muddy, bedraggled wretch didn't offer much in the way of beguilement. A pity, because she knew precisely which pouch held the key to her chains.

As for the motic sealing the wagon door? Kat had helped her unlock a piece of her being she'd always known was there but hadn't learned how to tame. It was the one bright spark in the railrunner misadventure. Save, of course, for her long-overdue reunion with her mother, which had offered brief happiness so unrepentant and pure that it should have embarrassed her down to her toes, but had not. For a moment only, but Tanith supposed it was all she was owed.

And what of Kat?

It wasn't so much what Tanith had seen when they'd both been in the spirit world, but Kat's reaction. Her sister expected to die. Hard not to feel resentful about that. Harder still to determine whether that resentment arose from the possibility of Kat's imminent death, or being robbed of the chance to be the cause.

She clung to the latter and told herself it was true.

With a particularly egregious jolt, the clatter wagon stumbled to a halt. A heavy hand flung open the rear door. Bright morning sunshine drove out the gloom, the stale wagon interior yielding to the dry salt tang of Zariqaz.

Shoulders stooped against the low ceiling, Tanith's captor unlocked the eyebolt binding her shackles to the wall.

"Out!" An unnecessary tug reinforced the message.

Stiff joints shrieking at every shuffling step, Tanith dropped into the sunlit courtyard. Her heart sank as she took in her surroundings. She'd anticipated being transferred to one of Zariqaz's many down-spire custodia, there to await judgement. Such a fate would have offered plenty of opportunities to escape, or at least wheedle herself free.

However, the sandstone buildings framing the courtyard weren't the mismatched and time-worn structures of the lower spire. Rather, they were a forest of straight lines and architectural deliberation, every archway, wall and fenestra set precisely in accordance with its maker's intent. Every arch concealed a rich honeycomb of muqarnas stalactites, every lintel bore an emblem of outspread wings and unbroken circle. Nor was the roadway the familiar mishmash of cobbles, potholes and broken flagstones, but slabs of black marble gleaming in the same sunlight that rendered the buildings in rich, lustrous gold, and set stained-glass windows glittering like gemstone.

Here and there, nature softened implacable majesty. Bright lilac and foxglove adorned wrought-iron window boxes. Softly rippling water flowed from culverted streams into the courtyard's low fountain. And everywhere, the scarlet pennants and wall-hung gonfalons bearing the wing and circlet, threaded in gold. The heraldry of the Eternity King.

She was in the Golden Citadel.

She was as good as dead.

She shouldered her escort aside and broke for the courtyard's lower archway.

"Stop her!" bellowed a deep voice.

Tanith kept running. Another redcloak tackled her to the flagstones. His weight crushed her against marble, a jagged whisper rippling along her ribs as her gown tore past recovery. The redcloak's triumphant expression turned to crimson horror as she rammed her forehead into his. He fell away howling and she rolled free.

Scarlet uniforms and grim faces barred her path, shriekers levelled. Tanith froze. Something cracked against the back of her skull. The world rushed red and black and fell away as phantom hands bore her away into the dark.

The bruising scrape of skin on cold tile dragged her back, the squeal of hinges and the *boom* of the cell door deafening. The pressure of the shackles slipped from her wrists and withdrew alongside the indistinct shadows that had borne her there.

Her throat thick with nausea, she dragged herself upright enough to collapse on the bare bedsprings.

The Golden Citadel. They knew what she was. They had to. You had to be something special to earn the privilege of execution on the Golden Stair. She'd offer a rare treat alongside the traitors and apostates, a daemon cast to the flame just in time for Saint Marindra's Descension.

Maybe Nyssa didn't love her after all.

Awash with misery, Tanith jerked to her feet, the scream building ever since Azra's betrayal echoing back at her from the bare walls.

The door swung open. Two redcloaks stood framed on the short stairway: a crag-faced woman with a jailer's disinterested leer, her short-sleeved tunic exposing the banded soul-glyph tattoo about her right elbow, and a *gansalar*, resplendent in a senior officer's robes more gold than scarlet, his features hidden behind the immobile, austere glare of an ember-saint's mask and a shrieker in his hand.

Survivor's instinct sent Tanith sagging onto the bed. "Please . . ."

The jailer glowered at the *gansalar*. "This is most irregular."

"On that much, we agree."

Radiating resentment, the jailer laid a ceramic bowl, a jug of water and a burlap-wrapped bundle at the foot of the bed.

The *gansalar* nodded. "That will be all."

With a disdainful leer, the jailer vanished from sight. Slowly, invisibly, Tanith shifted against the cold metal of the bed frame, muscles coiling. She'd never be an easier target, but she *might* survive a shrieker shot. Anyway, better a quick death than the lingering spectacle of the flames searing her flesh away before the baying crowds.

The shrieker twitched in the *gansalar*'s hand. "Clean yourself up. Get dressed."

Tanith glared. "I'm to look my best for the Golden Stair, is that it?"

"The Golden Stair?" he replied, his flat-vowelled pronunciation increasingly familiar. "For failing to stop the hijack? You're thinking like a skelder."

Tanith reached for the burlap bundle. Inside were a simple black tunic, trousers and a scarlet cloak. "I don't understand."

He lowered his shrieker. "Your uniform will still fit even after all this time undercover."

She stared at the redcloak uniform, the *gansalar*'s identity at last sifted from the mask's distortions. Qolda, arrayed in the finery of the Royal Guard, and bearing it with confidence that could be nothing other than genuine. She'd known that the Obsidium Cult's influence ran deep, but not that it penetrated so far into the Eternity King's palace. Not counting the *gansalar* she'd disposed of at Kanzîr Station, there could only have been a dozen other redcloaks in Zariqaz with authority equalling Qolda's, and perhaps half as many *ursalar* generals who outranked him.

"I'm sure it will be just the thing."

Qolda stepped outside and set the door to. Abuzz with relief, Tanith stripped off her ruined dress, scrubbed herself clean as best as the limited tools allowed, and pulled on the uniform. It fitted better than it had any right to. By the time she stepped out into the corridor, her hair wetted and scraped back across her skull, she fancied that she passed acceptable muster.

Qolda had other ideas. "Shoulders back, chin high. You're not trying to hide."

Cheeks warming, Tanith complied. Her usual roles of seductress and waif called for vulnerability, the better to evoke empathy, but empathy was useless to a redcloak. "Sorry, sir. It's been a long time."

He grunted. "Better. Leave the talking to me."

She eyed his shoulder-buckled scimitar. "Don't I get a weapon?"

"No. If you get into another fight, we're both dead."

Ugh. But she supposed he was right. And she wasn't exactly helpless now her hands were free. The prospect of the rest of her following suit had even soothed her daemon-half's hunger. That and the fact that Qolda, unexpected saviour though he was, hardly made for an enticing meal. She glanced up and down the corridor. They were alone, with only a veiled statue of Nyssa Iudexas for company.

"Why are you helping me?"

He twitched a shrug, breaking his own rules of posture. "*Abdon Nyssa ivohê.*"

"Nyssa wills it? That's no answer."

"But it is. We stand together or not at all."

How badly she'd misjudged the man, who by his actions had revealed himself to be more similar in character to Enna than she had supposed. "And if we're caught?"

"*Abdon Nyssa ivohê,*" he repeated, though this time with a note of humour. "This close to Saint Marindra's Descension, everything is risk."

The last words might have been homily, but for a sharpness even Qolda's heavy Undertown accent could not conceal. "What do you mean? What's happened?"

"Later." He started for the door. "Now remember what I told you."

Tanith fancied she had a redcloak's stiff-shouldered walk perfected. Certainly, she noted no suspicions as Qolda led the way through the crowded barrack rooms and corridors, eventually bringing them outside into a larger version of the courtyard by which she'd made reluctant entry. Downhill, a pair of lamellar-clad redcloaks, armed with

255

scimitars, shriekers and tall ceremonial spears, stood watch over an open portcullis. Beyond the archway, the Silent Sea glittered, beckoning Tanith through the outer bastions of the Golden Citadel and into the Overspire's seemly streets.

Under cover of his cloak, Qolda gripped her elbow. "Not yet."

"There's no reason to stay," she murmured, eyes unblinkingly ahead and posture rigid.

"But there is. If all goes our way, you may be here again come Descension. Maps reveal only so much."

Tanith swallowed a grimace most unbecoming of a redcloak and offered a crisp nod. If Ardoc still intended to send her against the Eternity King, better she was familiar with the hunting ground. With a last, longing glance towards the lower gateway, she strode off after Qolda.

In the hours that followed, Tanith followed Qolda up through the five ring-walls of the Golden Citadel, the frisson of walking unnoticed through streets she'd no right to tread compensating for the growing weariness of exercise taken on little sleep.

Redcloak sentries drew to attention at Qolda's passing, and marching columns gained snap to their step. Rich-robed firebloods seldom spared either of them a glance, their cinderblood servants – marked by their duller silks and furtive, downcast eyes – even less so. Nor did the white-robed Alabastran archons pay them any heed, too busy hurrying back and forth to whatever it was they did when not gulling the masses with sermons, or bleeding them dry with loans that bartered slivers of soul for a meagre sum of worldly coin.

Little by little, Tanith even lost her fear of the macabre koilos alcoves, their skeletal occupants blank-eyed, waiting for the command of hestic or redcloak that would rouse them to slaughter. Dormant they remained, lulled by the soul-glyphs inked into Qolda's skin, and Tanith took care to keep her own soul spooled within the living world, so as not to draw unwelcome attention.

Through it all, Qolda pointed out hidden watch points buried in the walls of otherwise unassuming houses, and described the secret symmetry of streets whose layout otherwise seemed as haphazard as any in Khalad. The Golden Citadel was a fortress in function as well as name, with crossways and parapeted gateways designed to divide any assault from the lower city.

At the perimeter rampart of the cloud-draped second ring-wall, massive torsion ballistae – each taller than Tanith and crafted to launch fletched bolts as thick as her waist – stood alongside squat, brass-muzzled shrieker cannons whose tapered barrels echoed the wing-and-circlet heraldry. Redcloak sentries lined the ramparts, eyes ever outward for the possibility of an unauthorised sky-ship approach.

They rose through the cloud-laden streets to clear air and arrived at the great triumphal arch governing passage from the third ring-wall to the fourth, guarded by *sarhana* veterans, its portcullis biting deep into the marble roadway. Its koilos waited beneath the arch, the rippling blades of their two-handed flamberges shining in the sun.

The *sarhana* sentries gave no sign of sweltering in their black and gold armour, though they surely were. Qolda dipped his head to the nearest, his murmur of *Abdon Nyssa ivohê* only audible because instinct had warned Tanith to listen for it. At once, the *sarhana* beckoned to others on the gateway crest and the portcullis rumbled into motion.

They climbed the steep road into the fourth-ring wall – the last, save for the uppermost level where the Golden Stair guarded the approach to the Eternity King's palace. Of course there was more to Ardoc's schemes than a single subverted *gansalar*. He'd even spoken of it at conclave. Qolda aside, at least three others held true to the Obsidium Cult. Nyssa alone knew how many lesser redcloaks held similar loyalty.

The Great Library in which Tanith's father had wasted so much of his life dominated the streets of the fourth ring-wall, and she noted several doors etched with the inverted chalk triangle and stark "L" in the shadow of its towering onion domes. In one alley, leather-robed physicians in their crooked-beak masks loaded shrouded bodies onto

257

a clatter wagon. Her thoughts touched on Kat, ebbing away from omen rot. She shook her head. No distractions. Not now.

"I thought the lethargia was confined to Qosm."

"If it began anywhere, it began here," Qolda replied. "Firebloods preach purity, but they share their pleasures readily enough. I'll wager that every so-called cinderblood taken by the lethargia marks a trail of shame leading to a noble's door."

Tanith shuddered, the morning suddenly grown cold. Even those firebloods ignorant of her daemonic nature had shunned her for her cinderblood parentage. "Are we done yet? I'm tired."

Qolda cocked his head as a clarion of bright trumpets split the air. "One last detail."

They strode away downhill into the nest of crowded quaysides clinging to the northern streets. From her vantage on a spur of perimeter wall, Tanith gazed down at the great timber jetties, the waters of the Silent Sea barely visible beneath the spire-clinging clouds. A dozen vast scarlet-hulled dhows waited patiently at anchor, redcloaks scurrying like ants at deck and gangway.

A glint of gold drew her eye to a diminutive figure on the quayside surrounded by a small army of black-clad *sarhana* and foreboding koilos ember-saints. A figure with jet-black beaded hair and glittering gilded robes. Isdihar Diar, granddaughter of the Eternity King, a thousand generations removed. A girl on the cusp of womanhood who spoke with the full deathless authority of her sire.

Even as Tanith took in the sight, the trumpeters of the Voice's escort offered up another brazen fanfare to the skies and the first dhow slipped its moorings. "Where are they going?"

"East," replied Qolda. "To hold the line against Vallant. Bad for him, good for us."

Tanith nodded. Every redcloak sent east was one less to defend the Eternity King when the time came. "Is he . . ." She cast about, wary of being overheard. "Has he heard Nyssa's will?"

"I doubt it. But now he serves her just the same."

Twenty-Six

Damant leaned into what little shelter the dockside's fence offered from the bitter factory-smoke-laced wind and stamped his feet, setting a scavenging nightjar to flight. He told himself it was all no worse than when he'd been a younger man, patrolling the streets of Tyzanta. Those patrols – and the lumps taken in their pursuit – had made him the man he was. A man who saw duty in every shadow, and debts of honour alongside.

At least he wasn't down in Salamdi's night-draped streets. The red roofs and whitewashed buildings looked well enough in the daylight, but custodian's instinct told Damant that someone somewhere was on the wrong end of a punishment beating, a knife, a thwarted desire. Not that the sounds would carry far over rumbling factories and the drunken carousing that marked shift's end. Undefinable urge insisted he march to the nearest custodium, deputise all within and strike out into the streets – give Salamdi a dose of order and stability, if only for a night.

He drew his coat tighter and chuckled humourlessly. He'd thrown away what authority he'd possessed when he'd turned on House Bascari. But a lifetime's service wasn't easily cast aside. Duty to others remained.

One hour creaked into two. Had Arvish read the situation wrong, or had she simply spun a convincing tale to teach him a lesson? That

Zephyr had concurred with her assessment meant little, for the daughter of the Issnaîm delighted in capriciousness.

Was he being played for a fool?

A shadow appeared at the *Chainbreaker*'s distant bulwark and leapt lightly down to the pier. It lingered in the lee of the ship, reluctance palpable in the cast of shoulders and tilt of head, then it swept past Damant's hiding place, coat tails and the trailing ends of a scarf rippling in the wind.

Damant fell into step. "An odd hour to take a stroll."

Rîma didn't break stride. "On that we are agreed."

"Going somewhere in particular?"

"Yes." She lengthened her stride.

He quickened his own. "Alone?"

"Most definitely."

"I don't think I can allow that."

She halted so suddenly that Damant travelled on another full pace. She didn't stumble, or lurch, but simply ... *stopped*, as if doing so had always been her plan. Her eyes met his for the first time. "I thought a captain's authority ended at the gangplank."

Damant set his back to the pair of bored custodians at the gate. While their *vahla* masks concealed their mood, he'd stood too many eventless vigils to know that any activity would draw their curiosity, idle or otherwise.

"Probably." He didn't know Rîma at all well, the swordstress having buried herself in Zariqaz for almost his entire tenure with Vallant, but he knew enough to be wary of her. Even without the black corpse-bindings showing beneath her coat, and gentle rose water concealing the cloying scent of embalming fluids, there was no mistaking her smooth, confident movements for those of a killer. But Arvish had advised bluntness, and he'd always possessed a talent for that. "But then I'm not the captain any longer."

She unbent enough to crook an eyebrow. "Does Vallant know?"

"He will in a few hours. Zephyr's relishing delivering the news."

An almost-smile flickered across Rîma's lips. Or perhaps it was noth-ing more than a confluence of star-shadow and Damant's own wishful thinking. "Then it would seem you have no authority at all."

"What about the authority of a friend?"

"We are not friends."

She stalked through the main gate. A custodian's gaze touched briefly on her sword, but it was scarcely unusual for someone to go armed in Salamdi. He didn't even give Damant's shoulder-buckled scimitar a second look.

Damant caught up with her as the dock road began its winding descent through the tight press of uneven gable-fronted warehouses. "I wasn't speaking of my own authority."

"Katija." She sighed. "She said she wouldn't tell anyone."

"As I understand it, she promised not to tell Vallant. She didn't. She's concerned that you might do something foolish."

"And it is your intent to prevent this 'foolishness' of mine?"

"I've a shrewd idea of what might happen to me should I try. No, it's my intent to come with you."

Rîma stared, her long white hair dancing in a sudden gust. "Why? You cannot possibly know what will follow."

"Arvish owes you and seems to believe that I owe her. Maybe she's right."

"That's it?"

"That's it," he lied. Friendship was noble, debt was duty, but personal desire was selfishness. This wasn't the time for airing selfishness.

"So you're not running away from Vallant?"

He winced away a flash of annoyance. By chance or design, Rîma had hit on a nerve. "I don't run from anyone. I haven't the knees for it. He doesn't need me. Arvish seems to think that you might."

She cut down a side street, its boundary wall swamped by the waxy leaves and bright black-and-white blooms of overgrown mandevilla plants from the adjoining remembrance gardens. "I trained with the sword longer than your kind have walked Khalad. What can you possibly offer me?"

"Companionship. Counsel other than your own, should things go astray. And I'm not entirely helpless."

"You are to me." She halted, her back to an alley, eyes boring into his. "My path leads into darkness and despair. It is no place for children."

"I'm not a child."

"You are to me." Another almost-smile graced the words. "Should I close my eyes and be too slow in opening them, you will be gone, dust on the wind. Go back to the ship, Ihsan." Damant bristled at the use of his given name, reserved for those few he considered friends. "Vallant needs your conscience far more than I need a protector, especially one servicing his debt to another."

A vast black shadow rose skywards from the dockside. Sails unfurling beneath the stars, it peeled away westward around Salamdi's modest spire.

Damant shrugged. "Returning is no longer an option."

"I suppose you consider this an act of cleverness."

"This was Zephyr's refinement. I quote, 'No less a stubborn *waholi* is she for being an old *waholi*.' There was more, but that's the gist."

Rîma's chin dipped. "Then it would appear I have no choice."

She vanished into the alley. Damant glanced left and right before following, old instincts watching for pursuit. His attention thus divided, he barely saw the bunched fist that struck his wits away.

Damant came to bound hand and foot on a narrow bed, the pre-dawn light from a high window offering little kindness to a splitting headache. Blinking furiously, he swung his feet to the floor. Worse than the soreness from what he suspected was a black eye was the knowledge that Rîma had outmanoeuvred him so completely.

Maybe she'd been right to call him a child.

But whatever else she'd done – wherever he was – she'd not left him entirely defenceless. His sword belt rested on the bedside table, scimitar still sheathed. Atop it balanced the custodium-issued shrieker he'd not been able to give up, despite the fact that the ifrît within was on the point of dissipation. On top of *that* rested the smaller, easily concealed

262

holdout shrieker favoured by nervous firebloods and skelders with excellent connections, and the short dagger previously strapped to the inside of his left wrist.

Getting the dagger out of its sheath meant doubling over, clamping the burnished tip of the scabbard between his insteps and tugging the weapon clear with both hands. Further contortions saw the blade reversed – without dropping it, thank Nyssa – and resting against the tattered cord with which Rîma had bound his wrists.

The rest was just a matter of time.

Awash with humiliation, Damant retrieved his weapons and glanced in the cracked bedside mirror. The skin about his good eye was only slightly darker than its usual olive tone and barely mottled, suggesting that a wisp of last breath had chased the injury away.

Considerate, after a fashion.

The narrow landing outside the room was empty. The run-down decor, row of numbered doors and worn carpet suggested a hostelry, if a less than salubrious one, a notion confirmed by the narrow hosteller's cubbyhole and grille at the base of the spiral stairs.

"Didn't expect to see you up and around," said the wrinkled, head-scarfed woman behind the grille. "Couldn't take your Calvasîr, that's what your sister said. You're lucky, having someone like that watching out for you. Generous tipper, too."

"Fortune had nothing to do with it. How long ago did she leave?"

The hosteller shrugged. "Gone as soon as you were settled."

"How long?" he growled, impatience and humiliation getting the better of him.

She drew back from the grille, eyes narrowing. "No need to take that attitude."

Damant swallowed a scowl. He'd never been personable, even without the twin spurs of failure and lost opportunity digging into his flanks. "Sorry. My head ... you know how it is."

He fished a couple of dinars from his pocket and slid them under the grille.

A wrinkled hand whisked the coins from sight. "Maybe half an hour."

Damant stalked out into the street. Half an hour! If Rîma had caught a railrunner or a skyship, she could be halfway to anywhere. And here was he, stranded in Salamdi with nothing but failure for company.

But he was a custodian, or he had been. Good custodians – thin on the ground though they were – never gave up a quarry. Time wasted on self-recrimination was time better spent tracking her down.

Fortunately, even without her hat Rîma cut a distinctive figure. A few pointed questions to stallholders – though his uniform had long since gone the way of his former allegiances, his custodian's manner had not – and a smattering of dinars later, Damant was set firmly on the trail. She had not, in fact, headed towards the railrunner station, nor had she doubled back towards the dockyard. Instead, she'd travelled, straight as an arrow – insofar as that was possible in Salamdi's crooked streets – for the western tollhouse.

Damant pursued at a brisk stroll – nothing invited the attention of custodians or gang enforcers quite so readily as haste. Before the tollhouse was even in sight, the street filled with people fleeing the way he'd come, wailing and screaming as they ran.

He grabbed one by the collar and levelled an authoritarian stare decades in the making. "What's happening? Answer me, man!"

The fellow's instinctive attempt to struggle faltered beneath Damant's flat, level stare. "They're tearing up the souk," he stammered. "Let me go. Please!"

Damant broke into a run. Threading his way through the fleeing citizenry, he arrived at the gaudy red and yellow wooden gateway marking the entrance to a closed courtyard containing a souk of a dozen stalls. A custodian lay dead just inside the gate, *vahla* mask staring sightlessly skyward. Citizens cowered in doorways and behind the remnants of partially assembled stalls. And in the centre, boots splashing the waters of a shallow fountain, two figures duelled, swords a blur.

264

Rîma's coat tails were soaked and her sleeve torn. Her opponent, clad in a slaughterman's filthy leathers, was half a head taller than she, heavily built and with a bald pate the colour and texture of old yew. His cleaver too belonged to the abattoir more than the battlefield – an ill-match for Rîma's longer sword in both reach and grace, or it should have been.

Even as Damant pushed his way through the half-open gate, the man's wild flurry sent Rîma splashing back around the fountain basin.

"Can you not hear the bells, Rîma?" His cultured tone lent the words poetic rhythm. Phantoms chimes swept the courtyard, more imagined than heard. "They're calling you home."

Steel screamed as the cleaver flank scraped along Rîma's blade. Pivoting on her left heel, she rammed a bony elbow into his upper arm. The cleaver clanged against the statue of Nyssa Benevolas at the fountain's heart.

"I was unprepared for your glamour before, Hadîm. It won't work now."

"Apparently so."

A wolfish smile on his lips, Hadîm hacked twice at Rîma's head. She somersaulted out of the fountain and landed, sword angled away behind, the fingertips of her left hand splayed against the cobbles for balance.

Hadîm dropped down from the fountain. "Then let's resolve this another way."

Turning on his heel, he reached behind the tangled canopy of a half-assembled stall. A small boy yelped as Hadîm grabbed the scruff of his neck. The boy's mother wailed and flung herself to the child's rescue. Hadîm clubbed her away with the cleaver's haft and crushed the child to his chest, head against his shoulder.

"The boy would like you to surrender your sword and give your word of honour to make no further trouble." Hadîm turned his attention to the child. "Wouldn't you like the principessa to do that?"

265

A bright bead of blood trickled from the mother's brow and soaked away into the dust.

As yet unremarked, Damant sidled closer, staying always to Hadîm's rear. ||Keep him talking,|| he signed, as ever cursing his clumsiness with the simple gestures.

Rîma straightened, the point of her sword brushing the cobbles. "He is no part of this."

"He's a weapon in my hand," Hadîm replied evenly. "A weapon that will bleed a great deal if it *doesn't stop squirming.*"

The boy went deathly still. Now fully behind Hadîm, Damant gauged the distance. A dozen feet. Close enough. Probably. Twenty years before, it wouldn't even have been a consideration, but he'd been younger then, with two working eyes.

"Let the boy go," said Rîma.

"You've heard my price. Is your pride really worth his life?"

"I wouldn't expect you to understand."

Hadîm squeezed the jaw of the now openly weeping child. "I suppose she means 'no'. I'm sorry, little one. Maybe your replacement will change her mind. We have plenty of volunteers."

Damant drew his shrieker. This close, even he couldn't miss. Warmth spread beneath his trigger finger as the ifrît acknowledged his tattoo and roused itself to fury. "You should hear my counter-offer first."

The challenge was unnecessary, even dangerous, but its bravado was irresistible.

Hadîm spun, weapon raised. Damant squeezed the trigger. The bolt of invisible flame seared across the courtyard and set Hadîm's left shoulder ablaze just as the cleaver left his hand. Damant jerked aside, the wind of the cleaver's passage cold on his cheek, the dull *thock* of the butcher's blade embedding itself in a door frame sounding a heartbeat later.

Hadîm writhed on the cobbles, shoulder still crackling with the flame. His erstwhile hostage scrambled away and tugged at his unconscious mother's arm.

266

"Relying ... on glints, Eskamarîma?" Hadîm gasped. "You grand-father would be—"

Damant levelled his shrieker once more.

"No!" snapped Rîma.

Damant pulled the trigger. Hadîm went limp as fresh flames overtook him.

"You're welcome," said Damant, in reply to Rîma's cold glare.

A hue and cry arose in the streets beyond the courtyard – Salamdi's custodians at last rousing themselves to duty. Damant rammed his wisping shrieker into its holster and took comfort in the sound ... until he remembered that these days he was as much a fugitive as the man he'd shot down.

"Come on," snapped Rîma, and grabbed his hand.

Like the rest of the street, the warehouse had been derelict for some time. The mill wheel was rusted solid, the loading yard's paving slabs cracked and uneven, their seams thick with brittle yellow grass and scurrying lizards. But the walls were intact, and what remained of the first-floor timbers were solid enough to take a fugitive's weight.

Damant watched the pair of custodians make their slow, lazy search of the weed-tangled lower floor and spared a relieved sigh when they at last made their way back out towards the street. "That was not the start to the day I was expecting."

Standing arms folded beyond the ragged hole in the middle of the floor, Rîma regarded him coolly. "I imagine not."

"Would you like to tell me what it is I've done to earn that glare?"

"I am *not* glaring."

"Would you rather I'd let him kill the boy?"

"No, but now Hadîm is dead, he knows *exactly* where to find me."

Damant frowned. "I beg your pardon."

"Hadîm ... is a special case even among qalimîri. His soul is splintered across many thralls. When one dies, that portion of his being is distributed across those that remain. They learn everything

267

it experienced. They know everything it knew. They can be anywhere, anyone. Until Hadîm exerts his influence and remoulds them into a copy of his own long-dead body. The man you killed offered me a nod of greeting when I entered the souk, and then . . . he simply wasn't there any longer, and Hadîm had his cleaver at my throat."

Damant grimaced. Qalimîri always set him on edge, but this was two steps more horrific than most. "That's unpleasant."

"If we'd kept his body alive, only that piece of Hadîm would have known I was here. Now it's dead, every other piece of him knows where to find me. If there is to be any hope at all, I must return to Tadamûr a free woman with my sword in hand. I must arrive as myself, not a prize offered up to my grandfather. Otherwise . . ." She scowled and shook her head. "Why are you here?"

He hesitated, thrown by the sudden change of topic. "I told you, because Arvish—"

"The *real* reason." Her scowl slipped away into an almost-smile. "I will not ask again."

Damant had been in the business of law long enough to know when only the truth would serve, no matter how awkward or selfish. "Because I'm an old man who has spent the last six months looking back on his life and liking little of what he sees. I have stayed silent when I should have questioned. I have hidden behind duty when I should have stood tall."

"I understand, but with Vallant you have the chance to atone for those failings."

"Vallant's work is the labour of a lifetime." He furrowed his brow, hating how petty the words sounded. "I know it's selfish, but I don't have it in me to embark on something that I may never see completed. I want to go to Nyssa knowing – not hoping – that I made a difference. Maybe even that I saw something remarkable along the way. I don't suppose an immortal can understand that."

To his surprise, Rîma laughed. "She understands it better than you can possibly know, but has learned the hard way that no gesture, however grand, can satisfy the feeling you describe." She shook her head. "Very well, *old man*. You will have your adventure – maybe even your chance to make a difference. Someone should bear witness. I only hope you have no cause to regret it."

Twenty-Seven

"And where, precisely, have you been?"

Tanith flinched. In the time she'd known Ardoc, he'd seldom allowed his temper off the leash, and never once directed it at her. He hadn't now, not quite, but the knotted brow and the flush of colour to his tanned cheeks warned of an eruption barely held in check. Stark contrast to her stepfather, who'd seldom troubled himself with restraint. But then she'd long ago forsaken any attempt to have Hargo Rashace think well of her. Ardoc's disappointment cut deep as a knife.

At least they were alone in his book-filled chambers, the only light that from the small circular window overlooking the empty conclave hall. She didn't know how she'd have borne it otherwise. She hated herself for that weakness, but a small part of her was proud. Genuine affection, both given and received, was a precious and insidious gift – even addictive.

But affection was nothing to pride. "So I'm a prisoner, then? A pet who comes and goes only at your convenience?"

"Of course not!" The smoulder of Ardoc's anger showed at the corner of his eyes before he reeled himself in, his tone once again measured and paternalistic. "Forgive me. The last few days have presented certain … challenges."

She'd picked up on the tension in the haven as soon as she'd set foot inside. There was a new watchfulness in the buried streets, a coldness in the air that had nothing to do with the subterranean clime. "I had personal business. *Family* business."

"Your sister?" Interest replaced frustration. She'd made no secret of her animosity since joining the Obsidium Cult.

"And my mother."

"Ah." The last of the tension smoothed from Ardoc's brow. "Resolved to your satisfaction?"

Tanith hesitated. A week ago, she'd been almost certain she'd wanted to kill Kat, or at least go to whatever lengths were needed to ensure that Kat *believed* she meant to kill her. Now? Even without her failing health, it turned out that her sister was far harder to hate up close than at a distance. Yes, they'd shared a mutual goal, but Kat had offered understanding and if not friendship, then at least parity.

Zariqaz was abuzz with word of Vallant's raid on the railrunner and the sad disappearance of Countess Fadiya Rashace, which Tanith felt sure her stepfather would milk for all it was worth, his crocodile tears flowing like rain. Could she have done that alone? She wasn't sure, but it hardly mattered, because she'd lacked the *will*. While she'd sulked and railed, Kat had instead conspired to a rescue.

She risked a small smile. "Ask me again next week."

"Ah." Ardoc looped his hands behind his back. "Family is always complicated, isn't it?"

She thought again of the rot consuming Kat's soul. Her ally? Her enemy? She still didn't know. "Apparently." But ex-friends were not. Azra was a dead woman walking.

Should she tell Ardoc of Kat's illness? No. He'd only take it as a sign of divided loyalties. Besides, what could he do but mouth platitudes? Sooner or later, omen rot killed.

Tanith wished she knew how she felt about that.

She realised Ardoc was still speaking. "And your ... appetite?"

She hesitated. Her desire to feed was worse than ever. Even with Ardoc on the other side of the room, the lavender of his soul set her own itching. But at least the hunger lacked urgency. Knowing it for a phantom was the only thing that made resistance possible. "It's not pleasant, but I'm surviving. I haven't fed since Kanzîr Station."

"But you've wanted to?"

"Yes."

He nodded. "I regret that the discomfort is necessary, but you can feel it, can't you? The control, I mean."

"I suppose." What Tanith mostly felt was a deep, dark void that left her feeling forever hollow. But she *was* in control, at least for now, and after having gone longer without feeding than any time since the Deadwinds had spat her out. "It's not the same as it used to be."

"Good. It means you're almost ready. You've come so far from that skittish, feral thing I found in the temple. You're growing into your birthright."

Ardoc had no idea of what "feral" truly looked like. Hopefully he never would. "Does that mean I'm forgiven?"

"I just . . ." He turned away and braced his hands on the lower frame of the circular window, its glass carrying the barest lumani-chased reflection of a man lost in thought. "I wish you'd spoken to me first, that's all. I feel a responsibility for you. Surely you can understand?"

"Because as Nyssa's herald, I'm vital to your plans?" The frisson of ridiculousness the title usually provoked never arrived.

Ardoc grunted, a wry cast of expression revealing that her point wasn't entirely without merit. "I'm sure that seems very selfish. Certainly, the part of me that serves Nyssa was troubled on her behalf . . . but that was as nothing to the remainder, which regards you not as an agent of prophecy, but as a daughter." He dropped his chin to his chest. "I'm sorry. That must seem very presumptuous."

Something cold and rigid melted away in the pit of Tanith's heart. It should have seemed presumptuous, it truly should. But how else to define their bond? "No. Not at all."

"I'm glad, because now more than ever I need your support." He turned from the window, the springs of his armchair creaking in protest as he lowered himself into the faded cushions. "How much did Qolda tell you?"

"Nothing."

"Serrîq is dead. Murdered."

She blinked. "Alabastra can't have been happy that a senior archon was one of us."

Ardoc narrowed his eyes. "How did you know he was an archon?"

She hadn't *known* until that moment, but the trail of hints Serrîq had left scattered across various conclave meetings – and Qolda's revelation as a *gansalar* – had invited the conclusion. "I'm not blind."

He sighed. "No, I suppose you'd be little use to me if you were. In any case, Serrîq died here, in the haven. To one of our own."

The room shrank inward, its shadows more invasive than before. "Has the culprit been found?"

"There were those who set the blame squarely on your shoulders. You must understand, it happened the first night we realised you were missing, and the timing ... Coincidence is the greatest myth of all. I have since convinced them otherwise."

Tanith thought back to the hooded stares directed her way since her return. "I'm not sure that's true."

"They're scared, and with good reason. Nothing like this has ever happened before ... As to the truth? Enna also vanished that night, though her disappearance was not readily remarked. I think we have to accept that she was not, in fact, moved by the goddess but by shallower loyalties."

"To who?"

"Alabastra, possibly. One of the fireblood houses. Perhaps the Voice herself." He shook his head. "The possibilities are broad and not terribly inviting. Indeed, they may prove disastrous."

Tanith mulled his words. She'd not much liked Serrîq, but he'd been popular enough with others. Enna had been at least as much of an outsider as Tanith herself, distant and vigilant. And she'd done little to hide her rivalry with Qolda. During the provisions yard raid she had spoken of small, necessary evils. Had Serrîq become one of hers? Had she betrayed the raid herself, tarnishing Qolda's reputation as the prelude to some deeper scheme? That there was more to Enna than first appeared, Tanith didn't doubt, given how readily the koilos had ignored her.

But Enna had saved her that night, if not from death, then at least from a brutal encounter with that same koilos. She'd offered empathy, too. Her wisdom concerning appetites had been at least as pivotal as Ardoc's avuncular chastisement. And, of course, that raid had only ever taken place out of Enna's desire to feed the starving. Could all of that have been a shield for some deeper motive? Yes. Yes, it could. Its misdirection was precisely what Tanith herself would have done. *Had* done at many times in the past, in spirit if not detail.

"Let me kill her for you."

She felt a flicker of unease at the frisson of excitement provoked by the prospect of learning what Enna's soul tasted like. How quickly an ally became an enemy and an enemy became prey.

"We don't know where she is. Qolda believes she's gone to ground in Qosm, certainly in Undertown. He has kathari standing vigil. I've also ordered the soul-glyphs for the hestics be altered and doubled the patrols in the Underways. Should she return, she'll find the door closed."

Tanith folded her arms to disguise a guilty twitch. Ardoc would almost certainly disapprove of what she'd done with the hestics guarding the entrance by which she and Qolda had entered. A father's pride covered only so many transgressions. "And if it's simple malice?"

"Then she's of no immediate threat. Nyssa will judge her if we do not." Ardoc smiled. "But I will ensure Qolda knows of your interest. Should the opportunity present itself, be assured that you will have my permission to ... indulge yourself."

"Thank you." The second frisson of anticipation was sharper than the first, and Tanith elected to savour it. "I misjudged Qolda, didn't I?"

"He understands that we are all family. He's just not always the best at showing it." Ardoc leaned forward in his chair and steepled his

274

fingers. "I understand he gave you a tour of the Golden Citadel. I wish he hadn't."

"Afraid it would scare me?"

"Perhaps a little. Did it?"

She grimaced, recalling her initial, panicked reaction. "I was dazzled by myth. Not any longer. The Golden Citadel is impressive, but it's still just walls and guards. They're not enough to keep me out, not if I don't want them to. I can do whatever you need."

Rising, Ardoc laid his hands upon Tanith's upper arms and held her steady, his eyes boring into hers. "I can't tell you how glad I am to hear that. I will be asking much of you in coming days, Tanith."

She breathed deep, her heart swelling with pride – not the selfish kind that had always led her astray, but something purer, almost noble.

As noble as she'd any right to feel, in any case. Enough to crowd out the irrepressible, soul-jangling restlessness of his proximity and the sweet, cloying waft of his soul.

"I'm ready ... Father." The familial term slipped out unbidden, and she was surprised to discover how well it fitted. "*Abdon Nyssa ivohê.*"

Ardoc nodded, his eyes bright with turbulent emotion. "*Abdon Nyssa ivohê.*"

Twenty-Eight

The refectory's gloried past was the product of imagination more than present reality. Sculpted scrollwork bearing passages of flowing Daric betrayed its beginnings as temple school, as did the modest statues of Nyssa Iudexas and Nyssa Benevolas guarding the entrance, one watchful and the other welcoming. Both wore the ages badly, the verdigrised bronze cracked and dented for all that the haven's artisans had sought to restore it. The sunken tiles of the peaked roof had seen repair only on the west slope, where water trickled ceaselessly from the stalactites to hiss away along makeshift gutters.

A white-robed kathari stood guard at the atrium, her black mask offering Tanith a baleful glare as she descended the uneven steps. Tanith replied with a small smile crafted for aggravation rather than friendliness. However much her opinions on Qolda had shifted, his kathari had yet to earn similar largesse.

The tables of the main hall were full of men and women, young and old, partaking of the afternoon's generous ration of bread and steaming paprika stew, the hubbub of conversation coming and going with the clacking of cutlery. The hot, rich aroma almost drowned out the muskier notes of so many tantalising, delectable souls crushed into so small a space. But here at least, temptation was easily suppressed. Just as Tanith's growing, gnawing desire was instinct, so too was survival. Her daemon-half understood that feeding in plain sight was as good a way as any to meet Nyssa before her time.

Exchanging a nod with one of Enna's disciples – Tanith couldn't remember her name, chiefly because she'd never troubled to learn it – she walked the refectory boundary.

There.

Esram sat alone, prodding listlessly at his bowl of stew and staring at a discoloured book. Lost in the wisdom of yesterday, he didn't even look up. Driven by a flash of mischief, Tanith shortened her stride, the better to deaden her footfalls.

A pair of newcomers cut across her path. One wore a kathari's white robes, her mask hanging from her belt by its straps. Her male companion wore simple black silks. Without sparing Tanith a glance, they slid onto the bench opposite Esram.

The woman spun the book around. "More poetry?"

"*The Life of Saint Marindra*," Esram replied stiffly, his expression that of cornered prey, looking for an escape that didn't exist. "It's very old and very rare. Please treat it with respect."

"I see." The woman snatched the book and riffled the pages.

"Give that back!"

"Leave him be, Iliya," said the woman's companion, his voice absent of sympathy. "He's a sensitive soul."

"Nyssa doesn't need sensitive souls, she needs warriors." Iliya's eyes never left Esram's face. "Tell you what. You come down to the barracks and go a few rounds of sparring with me, we *might* make you a soldier and maybe I'll let you have your book back."

"Oh, hello." Gathering her skirts, Tanith slipped onto the bench beside Iliya and offered her sweetest wide-eyed ingénue's smile. "I think you should let him have the book back right now, don't you?"

Esram blinked. "Tanith, I don't—"

Iliya sniffed. "Stay out of this, skirl."

Tanith laced her smile with more sugar. Safe to say that Iliya didn't know about her. But then, not everyone could know everyone.

Such a shame.

Iliya's companion, however, went rigid. "Leave it, Iliya. We should go."

Iliya glared at Esram and slammed the book shut. "The sparring hall." She jabbed the book's corner at him in emphasis. "Three o'clock. We'll start making you into something that Nyssa can use."

"Actually," Tanith flashed Esram a smile, "I like him just the way he is."

With her left hand, she plucked the book from Iliya's fingers. With her right, she grabbed a fistful of coiled black hair and slammed Iliya face-first into the table with a thud that set Esram's bowl rattling. The refectory went silent at Iliya's pained howl. Fingers still wound about the woman's hair, Tanith jerked her hand back and let go with a graceful flourish. Iliya toppled bonelessly over the back of the bench and sprawled on the tiles.

"Oh no," said Tanith, emotionless, deadpan. "She slipped."

Iliya, swaying heavily and muttering with the indistinct garble of the punch-drunk, made it halfway to her knees before collapsing. Tanith swept the refectory with a long, unblinking stare, the sensation of a hundred watchful eyes more invigorating than concerning.

A wicked smile creeping across her lips, she fluttered her eyelashes at Iliya's companion, and filled her voice with concern. "You should probably take her to a physician."

Nodding with the fervency of a man desperate to be anywhere else, he helped the unsteady Iliya towards the door. The entertainment done, clatter and murmur returned to the hall.

Tanith rounded the end of the table and slid along the bench beside Esram. She turned the book over in her hands and held it out. "Yours, I believe," she said brightly.

He regarded her, torn between gratitude and misery. "You didn't have to do that."

"No, but I *did* enjoy it." Mischief returning, she slid closer, her shoulder pressed against his. "That's how you say thank you?"

He winced. "It wasn't very gracious, was it?"

She offered him a smile of the rarest type. One that didn't belong to the ingénue, or the seductress, or the amashti. A piece of her as she truly was – or *hoped* she was. A moment of intimacy amid the crowd. "Would you like another chance?"

He leaned back, wary at the mismatch of words and intent. "What would you like me to say?"

She hitched round on the bench, one leg tucked beneath the other, and faced him full-on. "Maybe you shouldn't say anything at all."

Moments creaked past. True to her suggestion, Esram said nothing. But neither did he *do* anything other than watch her closely, the creak of cogs visible behind his eyes. Then at last, when Tanith was on the brink of giving up on him entirely, he kissed her. Hesitantly at first, his lips barely brushing hers for fear of violent reaction, but with growing enthusiasm.

Tanith's daemon-half howled with frustration, tormented by the sweet proximity of Esram's soul but unable to act for fear of what would follow. She looped her arms around his neck as encouragement to linger, ignored the itch scratching away at her inner being and lost herself in the sheer joy of cheating the curse that denied her such simple pleasures.

When he pulled away, a wary smile replaced woebegone confusion. "I don't seem to be dead."

"And you haven't left," said Tanith, flushed with triumph as much as anything else. She'd not planned for this – she'd just wanted to *see* him – but as at their first meeting, she'd surprised herself. Surprised them both. But better even than that was the knowledge that she hadn't taken that kiss, or stolen it, or prised it from him through glamour's deception. She'd *earned* it, and without even really meaning to.

"I . . . I don't understand what's different this time."

She squeezed his hand. "What's different is this time I wanted you to." A simple truth atop writhing complications. But Esram didn't need to know about those. Not yet. "What was all that about?"

He frowned, caught off balance by the change of topic, then stared down at the book. "It doesn't matter."

"It matters to me." Tanith let a little sweetness into her tone. "I could always ask Iliya."

He sighed. "You know about Serrîq?" When she nodded, he pressed on, eyes pinched shut. "He and I used to discuss history – this book was his. The night you left, I went to return it. I found him lying in a puddle of greenish vomit, back arched and fingernails bloody where he'd clawed at his own throat. The smell . . ."

Tanith's throat tightened. Blood, yes. Bodies? Naturally. But there was something about vomit . . . "It's all right," she said hurriedly. "You can stop now."

Esram gave a small, taut nod. "I fainted. Next I knew, Jallar was slapping me awake. Word spread. No one thought I'd done it, thank Nyssa, but I've never quite fitted in around here. This has only made it worse."

"So Enna poisoned him?" murmured Tanith.

"Rattlebreek venom. There's no way to mistake it for anything else. She wanted us to know it was murder." His cheek twitched. "And she wanted it to hurt."

Her entire life, Tanith had lived in the shadow of discovery, always striving to draw no more attention than strictly necessary. Something very unpleasant and more than a little reckless lurked beneath Enna's cold exterior. But it wasn't all bad. Reckless people got caught, and Tanith promised herself that she'd be on hand. Not for Serrîq, but for Ardoc's broken trust.

"Let me show you something," she said softly.

"What, here?" Esram offered a sly smile. "With all these people watching?"

She shot him a look of mock disdain. "One kiss and he falls straight in the gutter."

No one was paying them any attention, and with her back to the rest of the room there was little they'd see in any case, so she laid her left arm on the table and peeled her glove back from her forearm. The fires of her aetherios tattoo flickered gently along the tangled black lines, barely a glimmer in the refectory's lumani-light, a reminder that she'd only days before she risked descent into feraldom.

Esram caught his breath. "What is that?"

"My father's gift. I can touch ifrîti, even talk to them."

"Incredible ... I've never seen anything like it." Slowly, hesitantly, he brushed the lines, the pressure of his fingers soft and warm. "Does it ... hurt?"

"No. It's just ... there."

His fingers reached the heart-shaped starburst just inside her inner wrist. "What's this?"

She smiled. This, more than the tattoo itself, was what she'd wanted to show him. It was why she'd sought him out. Triumph was better when shared. "It's the soul-glyph for the hestics guarding the exits to the Underways."

"Ardoc trusts you that much?" he said, hushed with awe.

Tanith winced, triumph ebbing. "I copied it."

He shuffled closer along the bench, his voice conspiratorial. "What? How?"

"One of the ifrîti showed me the pattern." Pride smoothed away her shame at the tacit breach of Ardoc's trust. Taming the hestic had been easier than dealing with the motic in the railrunner's vault wagon. That or her increasing familiarity with her tattoo's potential had made it so. "I changed my tattoo to match it."

"I don't believe you."

"Watch."

Holding her breath, she bent her will upon the tattoo as Kat had taught her – not the sentry glyph itself, but a handful of incidental lines at the tattoo's edge. Little by little, they curled inwards, the bar-straight edges weaving anew to a chrysanthemum petal's gentle curve. She exhaled as the shape formed, the experience still novel enough to provoke a rush of giddiness.

Esram stared agape.

Tanith rolled her glove back into place. "Impressed?"

"I . . . I . . . Well, *yes*." He shook his head. "How did you . . . ?"

"My sister taught me."

"Is she as scary as you?"

"No. She's an idiot." A dying idiot. Why did that feel like it mattered? Why should it change anything?

He nodded, not really listening. "You can do this for any ifrît?"

"I think so."

He smiled, his eyes alive with possibility. "There's something I'd like to try."

The tsrûqi fought, the coils of its soulfire worming through Tanith's thoughts.

Even with her eyes closed, her perception of the world shifted. She clung to the lichen-crusted column as *up* and *down* veered a solid fifteen degrees from where her senses insisted they should be. Nausea crowded her throat, the urge to pitch to her knees and empty her stomach almost overwhelming. The soft, dank smells of the depths grew sharper.

Eyes pinched shut, she willed the last frond of her tattoo's thorn pattern into place just inside her elbow. With a thin hiss, the tsrûqi fell silent, its tendrils retreating deeper into the spirit world even as Tanith herself surfaced. Up and down realigned. The sharpness faded from the world.

"It's asleep," she gasped, the thrill of success driving out her nausea.

Esram edged closer, wary of trespassing the passageway the tsrûqi had so jealously guarded. Wary, because on the first approach he'd misjudged the distance and practically fallen on top of her when the tsrûqi had lashed out. They were barely a dozen paces from where they'd first met – from the graven stone that had granted her a vision of the goddess – with only the luminescence of lichen and Esram's tiny lumani lantern to drive shadows from the rough stone.

"I still don't believe it," he breathed, lost in wonder. "Can you do the same to the others?"

"I think so," Tanith replied with a confidence she didn't entirely feel, but too proud to show hesitance. "Let's just take it slowly, all right?"

He slipped an arm around her waist and leaned in to kiss her. "Of course, my lady Tanith."

"No!"

Heart in her throat and senses drowning in lavender, Tanith pulled away, a stumble on loose stone crushing her shoulder against the passage wall. She willed the need in the pit of her stomach to abate. Half a mile down in the dark from the haven's buried streets via elevator and stairway there was no threat of discovery. No one to see her glut herself on Esram's hopeless, helpless, adorable naïveté. Nothing to keep her daemon-half in check but her own imperfect will.

"Not here. It's not safe. *I'm* not safe."

A hurt frown set shadows rippling across his face. "If that's what you want."

On balance again, Tanith pushed clear of the wall. More than ever, it was clear that what this was – whatever *they* were – she couldn't sustain it. She was going to have to tell him the truth. But not here. Not now. The truth would change everything.

"Esram, I—" Her fingers touched something cold and smooth. Glass. "The lantern. Quickly."

Frown giving way to curiosity, he drew closer, lantern aloft. Tanith grabbed his wrist, twisting it and the lantern until greasy orange light pooled across a multifaceted black prism buried behind the eyes of Nyssa's beautiful stone face.

"It's a sentry crest," said Esram.

Sentry crests were commonly home to hestics. The paths between the Underways and the haven were dotted with them. Tanith stepped back into the spirit world just enough to confirm her suspicions. "It's the tsrûqi's prism."

"Then it's not a natural phenomenon?"

"No. Someone placed it here as a guard."

"How has it survived this long? It must be ancient."

Tanith traced the crest's coiling, flame-like curls. "I don't think so. Look at the joins in the stonework – they're at an angle to the base of the crest. There's neither a doorway nor a fenestra in sight. What self-respecting architect would build something this crooked with nothing to protect?"

"You're saying someone put it here after all this was buried?"

"I'm saying someone doesn't want people coming this way."

Esram shook his head. "That doesn't make sense. Why not use a hestic?"

"Hestics only exist because shriversmen split them from the dying. Tsrûqi occur naturally." She should know, she'd devoured enough of them. "They don't arouse suspicion."

Esram glanced back the way they'd come. "We should tell Ardoc."

Tanith shook her head. "You brought me down here because you wanted to explore, didn't you? Are you *really* going to turn back now? The truths of ages past trapped in stone, remember?"

"What if whoever set the tsrûqi is still down here?" he hissed. "What if we run into them?"

"Then we'll have something worth telling Ardoc." She smiled. "Don't worry. There's nothing more dangerous down here than me."

Twenty-Nine

Into the darkness they descended, the soft, dry smell of old decay and the lichen's dull glow their only companions. Tanith lost count of how many tsrûqi she soothed in that first quarter-mile, all of them in prisms whose dark, glittering eyes rendered Nyssa's beatific face in foreboding malice.

Here and there, the rough sandstone gave way to more of the grey-white limestone panels Esram had first shown her in the cavern above, their bas-reliefs worn and choked with lichen, their colour aching to be revealed by the brush of a gloved finger. The winged, armoured women were again in evidence, their red-gold armour still bright. On some panels, the sun dominated the skies. On others, the silver disc from the broken panel Tanith had first seen. In some, the women bore long spears and circular shields into battle against spindly, crooked foes. In others, they stood framed by stylised flames, or knelt in mourning beside a wide, dark river.

Esram pored over every detail, eyes agleam and muttering excitedly. Tanith, whose interest in the friezes faded when touching them offered no vision of the goddess, found her attention wandering. Not that there wasn't a joy to seeing Esram's face bright with wonder, but she'd never had much in the way of an eye for art.

As Esram lingered at the tenth such frieze, gloved hands sweeping away lichen to reveal a vast flock of birds swooping above a field of broken swords and lifeless corpses, she closed her eyes and breathed deep, enjoying being as physically apart from the world above as she was by nature and inclination.

There was a tranquillity to this buried, forgotten domain, a stillness that owed something to the dry, cool air and comforting gloom, but also to something else . . . something Tanith found difficult to identify, much less define. Was this what it was to relax? To have one's cares float away? Even her daemon-half's desire seemed distant, unfocused. As if it too were distracted.

But in the darkness, there was no escaping another, singular truth: part of the joy – part of the contentment – came from sharing the experience with Esram. It didn't matter that their delights ran parallel rather than together, his in the ancient bibelots of long forgotten artistry and hers in simply being apart from the world. There was a pleasure unlooked for in whiling away those moments, and it seemed only right to give the matter voice.

"Esram?" she said, eyes still closed. When no reply arrived, she tried again, this time her words a little louder and tinged with annoyance at having been ignored. "Esram?"

Still no reply. Tranquillity broken by irritation, Tanith blinked open her eyes.

And stared out across a dead city.

Beneath her feet, a stone stairway the width of a road swept down into ordered, empty streets. Austere, squared-off black buildings stretched away into the middle distance, in design and arrangement as orderly as the streets themselves. What towers she saw were not the graceful minarets and torch houses of the surface world, but stolid, forbidding watchers. Bronze braziers sat cold and dark at the junction corners, their basins empty of all save dust. The darkness above was not a sky but the shrouded gloom of a cavern roof so distant that all Tanith beheld of it were seams of glittering gemstones.

Perhaps half a mile from where she stood, a barren hill rose out of the streets, its broken strata angled skyward like the tines of a great black crown. And cradled within those tines, the outer wall of a temple's roofless hypostyle sat silhouetted against the column of magenta and indigo flame that was the only reason Tanith could see anything at all. The flame seething in the temple's black bones spiralled upwards towards, or possibly downwards *from* – the roiling currents dizzied the eye and made certainty impossible – the hidden cavern roof, scattered wisps swirling on invisible backdraught winds. Even when she tore her gaze from that flame, still its pull tugged at her gut.

"Esram . . . ?" she croaked.

As she stood breathless, captured by the city, it offered up more details. The even flagstoned streets, converging upon the temple mound like the spokes of a wheel. The slow, methodical wind of a black river that was the only curve in a cityscape founded upon the straightest of lines. It took a moment longer to realise what the city lacked – save for people, of which Tanith saw no sign. There were no statues of Nyssa, in aspect of either benevolence or judgement. There were no statues at all.

What manner of realm raised no statues to the goddess?

She turned her gaze skyward, to the gemstones glinting in the reflected light of the distant magenta flames. Flitterwings churning her stomach, she wondered if they might not be gemstones at all, but stars set in a buried sky.

Kiasta.

Boneless legs collapsed, dumping her against flagstones. Alabastran doctrine was thick with parable and metaphor, the truth of transformation and reborn souls couched in poetry. But even among such concepts, Tanith had always held the reality of the Stars Below as patently ridiculous.

Now, though . . . ?

Transfixed by the impossible, she remembered that she'd arrived there unwillingly, or at least without ready cognition . . . and not alone.

Rising on trembling legs, she gazed back the way she'd presumably arrived. The roadway ended in a tunnel mouth blocked by some long-ago rockfall. There *might* have been a viable path threading between the banded stalagmites off to the tunnel's right. Maybe the shadow of a cave mouth higher above. Nothing was certain.

Well, not quite nothing. Her gloves were free of lichen and rock spoil, the knees of her skirt similarly so. However she'd come to that place, she hadn't climbed. But how had she arrived here at all? Maybe her daemon-half had found a quieter, subtler way to influence her? That made for a new and unsettling possibility, it never having happened outside of those disorienting, sanity-rattling periods of feral hunger she longed to forget.

That explanation might even have convinced if not for the fact that, though she was awake and very much in control, the city called to her. That was reason aplenty to go back, to tell Ardoc what she'd seen -- or better still, forget the place entirely – but even though a piece of her screamed to follow that very course, she found herself taking a step closer to the distant flames.

"Esram?"

Her voice echoed back threefold, unanswered save by itself.

Where was he? Someone had set the tsrûqi as guards. Had that same someone found Esram? Her throat tightened with emotion so unfamiliar that she stepped outside herself and offered the stranger who wore her face an appraising stare.

Was this concern?

For someone *else*?

She found herself staring back towards the dead city. Had she read it all wrong? Had she passed through those streets already? In Esram's absence, the only way to be sure was to see for herself. Maybe he was there already, roaming the empty streets.

She ought to check.

Oughtn't she?

She gazed across the rooftops and wondered whether the notion had even been her own, or instead belonged to whatever had brought her there. Though not unused to not entirely being herself – or at least not always being the part of her that she liked to *consider* herself – the hole in her recent past sent something unpleasant skittering across her shoulders. Was she unconsciously closing off other options because a part of her *wanted* to walk those streets?

She blinked, and realised that she was no longer at the top of the stairs, but four steps down.

The skittering sensation returned, bringing a chill alongside.

"Esram!"

"Tanith?"

A trickle of stone from the tunnel mouth accompanied the reply. A lantern's backwash shaped a crevasse in what she'd assumed was a solid barrier, and spilled shadow across Esram's pinched, worried face as he hurried over.

"I looked up and you were gone. Don't do that to me."

"You worry too much." Though she could get used to someone worrying *about* her, rather than *because* of her.

"Too much?" He stared, boggle-eyed. "It's taken me an hour to find you. I'd almost given up until I found your footprints."

Footprints? Tanith glanced down and for the first time realised that her boots were wet almost to the collar, the trailing folds of her skirt completely sodden. She'd been so out of it that she'd walked through a pool without realising it.

"I was beside myself," said Esram.

Enough. You *could* take concern too far. "Over nothing. I'm fine."

He didn't reply. In fact, Tanith wasn't even sure he'd heard. He was instead staring slack-jawed out across the city.

Ah.

"What . . ." He blinked, waking from whatever nightmare or dream-scape had fogged his thoughts. "Where are we?"

"I think . . ." The fear of being thought foolish made her hesitant. "I think we might be in the Stars Below."

"No . . ." And yet his reply was more horrified than dismissive. "No no no no no. Living souls don't come to the Stars Below. Only—"

"Only the dead, I know." Torn between the need to comfort and chastise, she struck out for middle ground and thus sounded little of either. "Do you feel dead? I don't."

It would have been a more reassuring sentiment had the empty black streets held any sign of life.

Eyes still on the distant temple, he swallowed. "We should leave. We don't have any weapons."

He looked pale, his copper cheeks sunken, almost greyish. Whatever else he'd expected to find, it hadn't been a foothold on the shores of eternity. "Can you find your way back?"

He nodded. "Whoever tunnelled down here made a thorough job of propping everything up and bolting ladders in place. You know that, you saw what I saw."

She nodded, unwilling to confess just how little responsibility she bore for her recent travels. Esram's assertion was another reminder that this place, Stars Below or otherwise, was not their chance find, but someone's deliberate expedition.

"Wait … Can *I* find my way back?" Esram tore his attention from the distant flames. "What about you?"

She'd not really thought about it, which should have been unsettling all by itself. "I want to take a closer look."

He grabbed her arm. "You can't. It's not safe."

She closed her hand over his and twisted it free. "Nor am I." She grimaced, recognising that he was owed at least a little truth. "It's calling me. Can't you hear it?"

Esram gave a long, slow shake of the head. "No, and I don't want to."

"Are you sure? Think of what you could learn."

His throat bobbed. "I'm thinking that knowledge isn't any use to the dead." Peremptoriness haunted his words, but his heart wasn't really in it.

"So go back," Tanith replied, disappointed despite herself. "I can look after myself."

He glanced at the collapsed tunnel, temptation in his eyes, then back at her. He stood taller, colour returning to his cheeks. "I'll wait here. I can do that much."

Disappointment ebbed. True courage was rare, but everyone could try a little harder when they'd a reason. Odd to think that she might be that reason. "You keep the lantern."

"I was going to." He offered a wan smile. "Be careful. If something goes wrong, I don't know if I can follow you down there."

Failing to find a witty rejoinder, she settled for a quick peck on the cheek. For a mercy her daemon-half stayed quiet, though circumstances being what they were, it was impossible to say whether that was because she was in control, or because it was simply attempting a subtler influence. But like it or not, something was drawing her onward. Better to go willingly and come back the same way.

Hopefully.

She reached the foot of the stairway – numbering some forty-two steps by her count – with as perfect recollection as to how she'd arrived there as made no difference. Now on the same level as the ordered streets, it became clearer than ever that the buildings were built on a far grander scale than those to which she was accustomed. Only by standing on her tiptoes could she even peer over the basin rim of the roadside braziers.

She glanced back up at Esram, now just a dark shape edged by lanternlight. Had she done the right thing to come down here alone? If this *was* the Stars Below, living souls had no business being here. But then, life had made it plain that she belonged nowhere, which was as good as belonging wherever she damn well wished.

Setting her shoulders, Tanith strode towards the distant magenta flame. She heard no sounds but her own empty footfalls and the occasional scurry of thumb-sized orange beetles.

From what she could tell without benefit of a lantern, the buildings were as eerily alike within as without, all with empty doorways and rotted drapes shielding filthy glass. Whatever possessions remained lay covered beneath thick grey-black dust ... or perhaps ash. Of the bas-reliefs she'd seen in the upper passageways, there was no sign. If stone held truth, as Esram asserted, the verities of the lower level were greatly different from those above.

She drew nearer the stone embankment, comparable to the seaward quayside at Zariqaz but of immeasurably more accomplished craftsmanship – as with the buildings, the stone blocks showed barely a joiner's seam. The river offered little more of interest than the streets. Its waters captured neither the light of the distant flame nor the maybe-stars, maybe-gemstones of the cavern roof. Even kneeling on the embankment edge, her hair falling past her face to disturb the water, Tanith caught nothing of her own reflection.

She recoiled as something cold and slimy touched her hand, but it was only a frond of black river weed, drawn against the embankment by the current. Warned by a flicker of movement, she glimpsed a corpse floating down the middle of the river – an ageing black-haired man, grey at the temples, a heavy, frogged jacket that should have dragged him under the surface instead spread behind him like a bridal train and his neck livid with the marks of strangulation. When she blinked, he was gone, dragged under at last, or perhaps vanished back into the depths of her overactive imagination.

She clambered to her feet, her unease ratcheting up another notch. Real or otherwise, the body in the river had served as a reminder of what she *hadn't* seen. If this was the Stars Below – and she'd yet to find a reason to believe otherwise – where were the ember-saints who served as Nyssa's scribes and servants? Where were the *vahla* spirits guiding the guilty to judgement? Where was the Obsidium Palace, for that matter? Was this just another layer to Zariqaz's buried majesty? Or had the Eternity King, who Ardoc claimed had chained Nyssa, also laid waste to her godly court?

She stared towards the temple and its column of fire, more certain than ever of finding answers at its base, but far less sure that she wanted them. Even a glimpse was enough to set yearning building anew.

It wasn't long after she'd left the river behind that she encountered the strains of a lilting, mellifluous song whispering through the streets. Or perhaps it was a chant, for while she couldn't make out the words, repeated phrases soon made themselves apparent. It grew louder with her every step, the notes of its disjointed, unsettling harmony borne by voices identifiable as neither male nor female, its underlying melody oddly familiar. She was now close enough to the temple to see silhouettes moving against the flames, and clung to the line of buildings for concealment.

Three streets out from the foot of the temple mound, her ankle went slack. Too late to correct, her toes skittered against the flagstones. She grabbed at a window casement for support. Even through her gloves, the stone felt distant, the pressure still present but the chill of the stone barely registering.

She blinked through thoughts gone suddenly sluggish. Sight, sound and sensation felt increasingly distant, as if she was becoming an observer to her own life. She flexed a fist purely to see if it would respond. It did, but with aching reluctance. Was this how she'd come to the city? Intransigent muscles screaming, she set her back to the column of flame. The numbness worsened, her fingertips and toes like stone, her shifting clothes a whisper of silk against skin that felt nothing. Only the haunting, rolling song remained, ever louder in her ears as all other sensation retreated.

Dimming senses warned of the soft scrape of movement beyond the building's corner. Fighting treacly thoughts and resistant limbs, she stumbled her way along the wall and collapsed through the outer doorway.

The scraping, shuffling steps drew closer.

Tanith risked a glance into the street just as a hunched figure appeared at the corner. Man-like enough in proportions, its semi-translucent skin was the colour of a fish's belly where it had any colour at all and glistened like running wax, distorting the turgid indigo flames that pulsed and flickered where artery and vein should have been. Bulging, distended eyes – dark as the surrounding flesh was

293

pallid – stared out from beneath a sagging brow. Of its body, only long, cadaverous hands showed beneath voluminous ash-stained robes among whose ragged folds the gleam of gold and the purity of white were but memories. Ash-blackened too was the golden circlet about its wispy, thinning hair.

It paused at the corner, swaying gently to and fro, a melted, stubby nose scenting the air. Then it gathered itself in and oozed towards the doorway where Tanith sheltered, slug-like in the undulating flow of its robes, and the soft, lamenting notes of its song growing ever louder.

Tanith flattened herself against the doorway and held her breath, more terrified than she'd been since the Kaldosi lynch mob had cornered her in the remembrance garden six years before. Then, she'd been vital, overflowing with soulfire; her hunters had been mortal, easily isolated and overcome among the bright petals of the mandevilla flowers.

But this?

What even *was* this?

A pale, crooked hand grabbed her wrist.

She yelped and tried to pull away, but the waxy, vice-like grip drove out all sensation below the elbow. A second hand grabbed at the doorway, and the melted, glistening face, even more repulsive in heavy shadow, peered at hers from mere inches away.

Numbness crept up Tanith's shoulder. A scream boiled up inside her chest, but her tongue was too heavy to give it licence. It took all she had even to breathe.

Her eyelids drooped.

Fire blazed. Not the magenta and indigo of the temple, but the brilliant orange of mortal combustion. A shadow slipped between them. A gloved hand thrust a burning brand into the creature's face. It jerked away, a bubbling, mewling cry of panic and pain swallowing its song, bony fingers slipping from Tanith's wrist as it clasped both hands to its dark, streaming eyes.

Still reeling, it oozed from the doorway, wispy smoke curling where the frayed edges of its robes had caught brief light.

"What was that thing?" croaked Tanith, the numbness of the creature's presence retreating as fast as it had arrived.

"Others will come," said the shadow, her back to Tanith. "You should leave. Don't come back."

A flicker of movement in the doorway, and she was gone.

Too late, Tanith recognised Enna's voice. Shivering, she stumbled to the doorway, but there was only the lament lilting down from the temple mound, and the roiling column of indigo flame. As she stared up at the latter, she felt no trace of the yearning it had previously awoken ... only a lingering, gnawing fear that she'd never admit to another living soul.

Tanith returned to Esram as fast as her legs would carry her, reckoning that it was better to outpace anything else lurking in the darkness of the dead city than risk further confrontation.

He hurried over as she reached the top of the stairs. "What happened? What's down there?"

She smothered his question with a kiss hungry enough to invite disaster. "You were right. We should have left."

He led the way back to the tunnel, and up through ladders and tunnel shafts of which Tanith had no memory. Questions rushed through her tired thoughts. About the city, the creatures that dwelled within, and about Enna most of all. But every time she tried to unpick what she'd seen, much less recount it to Esram, the details slipped away. By the time they reached the tsrûqi-haunted passageway – where she'd at least presence of mind to reawaken them – she'd resolved to tell Ardoc everything she remembered. *If* she remembered any of it at all. So much now was sensation and shadow more than memory.

But it soon transpired that any discussion with Ardoc would have to wait. The haven's streets were in uproar, with lamellar-armoured kathari and dead-eyed, silent koilos mustering towards the Underways and the city above. Esram at her side, Tanith fought against the current of seething bodies until she arrived at the square before the guild master's hall to find Qolda barking orders.

Ardoc looked on from beneath the hall's helical staircase, arms folded tight across his chest and his normally avuncular face frozen in a bearded scowl.

"What is it?" asked Tanith. "What's happening?"

"The redcloaks are attacking our safe houses in Qosm," he growled. "They're killing everyone."

Thirty

The trader, a middle-aged woman whose complexion was as weather-worn as her shop's wind-blasted frontage, leaned across the counter, her cracked lips moving silently as she totted up the supplies. Sailrider's biscuits, boiled and salted meat, dried fruit and twice-baked bread made for practical meals rather more than appetising ones, but years serving on the Bascari frontier had taught Damant that practicality was all. Besides, appetite was hard come by in that particular store, with its pervasive odour of old wax and dry timber.

Tally completed, she sank back. "Thirty-four dinars."

Damant counted out a handful for brass coins and set them on the counter. A high price for little more than a week's worth of provisions. Then again, Kassos wasn't exactly on the beaten path, barely two score buildings nestled in the shadow of the austere half-collapsed torch house, surviving through the patronage of a dozen outlying farms and mining outposts. The shelves held everything from books to boots, seeds to nails, sawn timber and smithed tools, as well as catalogues promising more exotic items from far afield.

Khalad was full of such places, living and dying with the shifting trade routes. But it was unsettling that so obviously doomed a settlement clung to existence in sight of Zariqaz. On that cloudless, sun-bright day, the capital was clearly visible on the south-western horizon – a great notched sword of a silhouette towering above the trees,

297

the blade of its uneven spire thrust into bedrock and the Golden Citadel a shining pommel, gleaming against cerulean skies.

While Damant busied himself stuffing his new possessions into a haversack, the trader deftly hived off the dinars into two piles, the larger for her pocket and the smaller into a sturdy cast-iron box, contribution to the protection levy that ensured Kassos had at least the illusion of law. A pair of custodians were visible through the window, sheltering in the shadow of a spread-armed Nyssa Benevolas, her plinth and lower robes mottled with the ruddy dust that clung to everything in the village. Likely the village's *only* custodians. Just as well given that the bounty board in the village square bore acceptable likenesses not only of Vallant, Arvish and a handful of more parochial ne'er-do-wells, but also Damant himself.

"You heading south?" asked the trader.

Damant glanced over his shoulder to where Rîma was eying the closely packed shelves with naked disgust. "*Are* we heading south?"

She didn't look up. "I ... think so."

He felt a familiar twinge of concern. Since leaving Salamdi, Rîma had grown increasingly vague, first in the matter of directions and increasingly in the business of conversation. At first, he'd put it down to standoffishness and frustration at being lumbered with an unwanted travelling companion. However, as they'd trod the dusty road to Kassos, he'd grown steadily aware that she was, in part, not really *there*.

"Anything we should know?" he asked the trader.

She drew herself up to her full, unimpressive height, and struck a pose not unlike an archon in the throes of delivering a sermon. "Not the luckiest road to take right now, that's all. The railrunner line subsided a couple of months back, took half the hillside with it. Lost all our business from Tulloq Mine, we did. Good customers, paid in full. Sad to see them go. Of course, the area's always been trouble." She leaned closer, her voice growing conspiratorial. "You ever hear of Boscai?"

"Can't say I have."

"Right nest of heretics. Midnight cavorting, daemon worship, the lot, until Nyssa sent fire from below to mend their ways." She offered a thin smile, an ardent believer drawing satisfaction from divine retribution. "You might hear them wailing on the hillside if Mistfall comes. Plenty do."

Damant grunted. *Don't go over there. They're not Nyssa-fearing folk. You can't trust them. Not like us.* Half the villages in Khalad had similar stories. "We'll keep our eyes open."

The trader nodded, not noting that his tone was a shade drier than before. "Anything else? I've got a little last breath . . . isshîm powder in case the journey gets boring." She shot a sidelong glance at the oblivious Rîma, still lost in morbid examination of the shelves. Her voice, already low, dropped another notch. "Maybe a talent wisp? I've a vial of Yavi Parsca, ordered in special from Phoenissa. Voice like a lark. Just the thing to keep the lady entertained on a dark night. Nothing more romantic than the Aurora Eternis and a blesswood fire while out in the wilds."

Damant found it hard to imagine anyone attempting to woo Rîma, with music or otherwise. In fact – and it wasn't an admission he made lightly, even in the privacy of his own mind – he found her intimidating. Save for those moments when she wasn't entirely present, Rîma was unblinkingly, unshakeably confident in word and deed. For a man well used to keeping his underlings at a distance through manner and social stiffness, the sensation wasn't entirely pleasant, but nor was it without novelty.

"It's a pilgrimage to Zariqaz," he lied. "She's mourning her family."

"Taking the long way around, then."

"She has a lot to mourn."

The merchant narrowed her eyes. Mourning pilgrimages, in which the bereaved undertook to sway Nyssa's judgement by offering prayer in the grandest temple they could reach – the goddess' inclination to heed such pleas famously scaling with the size of the temple in which those prayers were offered – were the purview of the wealthy. Most folk, without the time or funds for such indulgence, simply buried their kin and set black-and-white remembrance pinwheels in a memorial garden so that they might hear the whispers of their loved ones in each gust of wind.

Judging by the number of such pinwheels in Kassos' memorial garden – whose mandevillas and yews were the only greenery in otherwise barren streets – Nyssa loved its inhabitants so dearly she called them to her side with great frequency. Most likely through the medium of brawls and starvation, if Damant was any judge.

Rîma slapped a small silver ring down on the counter, its band fashioned in the shape of two serpents entwined like woven wicker. "Where did you get this?" she demanded.

"Lovely workmanship, isn't it?" The trader's patter channelled absolute authority. "It's a charm ring. Dates back to the last Age of Fire. The serpents ward off daemons."

"It's a wedding ring." Rîma's words crackled with ice. "And it is far older than that."

The trader shrugged. "Worth more, then."

Rîma tilted her head, her whole being otherwise so still and collected that it offered no warning to her sudden lunge. Her fingers gripping a double fistful of apron, she hauled the trader bodily onto the countertop. "I asked you where you got it."

Damant glanced through the window at the custodians – who thankfully had their backs to the storefront – and lowered his mouth to Rîma's ear. "Easy. Let's not draw attention."

"One of the boys from Tulloq brought it in, months ago," gasped the trader. "Care to make an offer, seeing as you like it?"

Rîma opened her hands and stepped back, swaying ever so slightly. "Keep it."

She strode for the door in a whirl of white hair and travel-worn coat tails, barely slowing as the strike of her open palm flung it open.

"My apologies." Damant set a handful of coins on the counter and offered the spluttering trader his best approximation of a regretful smile. "Grief is a powerful force."

He found Rîma in the alley between the shop and the village temple's crumbling perimeter wall, hugging her sword – scabbard and all – as tight as any mother clung to a child. She'd done a lot of that since leaving Salamdi. Eyes far afield and head cocked as if listening to some distant sound, she didn't react until he was practically on top of her.

"Did I hurt her?"

Damant couldn't quite find any regret in her voice. "I don't believe so . . . but that wasn't exactly helpful. I take it the ring belonged to one of your people?"

"Yes. Our inheritors have mimicked the design, but never correctly."

He nodded. In her talkative moments, Rîma had spoken readily of the mark her people had left on Khalad. Fragments of forgotten architecture, language and culture had bedded down deep. The embalming and spirit-bonding process that saw criminals transformed into koilos owed much to the mystical and alchemical techniques that preserved Rîma's body. Custodians' silver *vahla* masks mimicked the gold coverings worn for vanity in the Hidden Cities. Even the regal title of principessa was still used in the east to mark the ruling zol'tayah's female heir. "You think the work crews of Tulloq have been trading with Tadamûr?"

"My people have no interest in trade," she said dully. "They've no interest in anything at all. I think it more likely the miners ransacked the upper levels. How many did they kill, thinking them already dead?"

"I thought you hated your people."

Rîma stared at him with the frustration of a woman bedevilled by another's stupidity. "I hate the defenceless, mindless drones my grandfather's madness has made of them. But even the least of them deserves better than to be picked over by carrion."

Swaying again, she laid the flat of one hand against the wall for support. The other never left the sword's hilt. Whatever was happening to her was getting worse. As to precisely *what* that was, Damant still wasn't sure. He knew only that the subject couldn't go unbroached for long.

A flicker of movement drew his eye to the alley mouth just in time

to see the trader stalking towards where he'd last seen the idling custodians. "We've worn out our welcome. I take it we're heading south?"

"We are," Rîma replied.

But she didn't seem to be listening. At least, she didn't seem to be
listening to *him*.

That night they camped in a clearing above the Kassos–Tulloq road,
the low fire augmented by a few priceless splinters of blesswood fetched
from the depths of Damant's haversack, granting brief flashes of indigo
amid the orange. The green shimmer of the Aurora Eternis ruled the
skies and the air held entirely too much of the Veil's musty nostalgia for
his liking. Kassos – and the safety of its torch house – lay miles behind
and Tulloq yet lay far ahead.

Rîma stood on the clearing edge while he ate, her back to the flames.
Her sword was belted across her shoulder once more, but time and again
she cocked her head, brow furrowed as one trying to identify a distant
snatch of familiar song.

Damant washed down the last of his meal with a mouthful of
watered-down wine – a rare indulgence of civilisation's comforts, but
rare indulgence meant more in the wilds – took a calming breath of
the juniper- and jasmine-laced air, and wondered how best to broach
his growing concerns.

"Any of this look familiar?" he asked.

Rîma remained a silent and unmoving shape on the edge of the light.

He raised his voice. "I said, does any of this look familiar?"

Slowly, achingly slowly, she turned around. "You know it doesn't."
Tireless during the negotiation of the rutted and overgrown roadway to
the point that Damant had several times feared being left behind, she
now sounded weary beyond words. "I haven't been here in millennia.
More than enough time for the weather and curious children to make
a muddle of the landscape."

"That's right," said Damant, forcing a lightness he didn't feel. "Blame
us cinderbloods. The landscape may change but nobility doesn't."

Rîma offered a brief almost-there smile. "Firebloods, cinderbloods, ashborn, scaldera. The enduring and the extinct. Does it matter which clutch of children did the deed? If you're not building atop your precursors, you're pulling down their empty homes for your own convenience."

Not for the first time in her presence, Damant felt the epochs of history crushing him to insignificance. In an unsettling way, she *was* that history. "Ashborn and scaldera? I don't know those names."

Gathering the tails of her coat, she sat on a wind-felled tree opposite with all the deliberation of a judicator taking the bench and folded her hands across her knees. The scent of rose water softened the bitterness of the smoke.

"They belonged to different ages. Nyssa sent fire from the Zaruan peaks and ushered them to the Stars Below when she judged their time done. The ashborn were so vibrant, so innocent. They cared nothing for war, not like your kind. They went unresisting into the flames."

Damant stifled a shiver, unable to resist a furtive glance westward to where the holy ash-choked Zaruan Mountains lay cloaked by distance and the star-flung night. History recorded little concerning Caradan Diar's ascension to the throne immortal, merely that he'd fought a war against daemons, and triumphed only because the Zaruan had birthed the first Age of Fire at Nyssa's will, consuming those who'd opposed him – the peaceable ashborn seemingly among them. It was easier to contemplate such ideas in dry scripture than from the lips of one who had beheld the flames.

That Khalad itself survived was something of a miracle, for it had endured many Ages of Fire since. But nothing lasted for ever. Even the Eternity King wasn't truly ageless, not as Rîma was. Other kingdoms had existed before, and others would do so again. Some folk took solace in that fact, gladdened their hearts with the knowledge that life would continue even as flame swept the kingdom clean. To Damant it felt like failure. Grim Nyssa Iudexas had little mercy to offer those burdened by sin, nor those who failed to root it out.

"Why does she do it?"

"The goddess and I, alas, do not speak. I don't know that we ever did." Rîma twitched a self-deprecating shrug. "When you've lived as long as I have, what is forgotten defines you as much as what is not."

"Such as where your home lies?"

Her brow tightened. "It's not my home. It's merely where I once lived."

"Then where *is* your home? Athenoch?"

"Home isn't a place. It's in the company of those I care for." The almost-smile returned. "You think I'm lost, don't you?"

He grimaced, unused to hearing his own directness spill from another's lips. "Well ... Yes."

"And I am, but not in the way you mean. Our every step brings us closer."

"How can you know that if you don't recognise anything?"

Rîma gazed at him, a wordless argument raging behind her eyes. Not knowing the stakes, much less how to influence the outcome, Damant left her to fight it – or herself – alone.

"Because the bells are getting louder," she said at last.

A memory clicked. Hadîm had said something about bells back in Salamdi. But Damant was no clearer about what it meant now than he had been then. "I don't follow."

"My people. We're not like you. I feel part of what they feel. Hear what they hear. I'd built walls to keep them out, but back on the railrunner, Hadîm shook them to pieces. I hear the bells of Tadamûr chiming, here and here." She spread a hand and touched it briefly to her bindings, first above her stomach and then above her heart. "They're calling me, beckoning me to join them in the waking sleep. To let the burden of years slip away and ... drift."

Damant shivered despite the fire's warmth, the sudden chill awoken by the yearning in Rîma's voice. "Is there anything I can do to help?"

"Just your presence. It keeps me grounded."

He nodded. "That's what you meant back in Salamdi, isn't it? About me bearing witness. It wasn't about your deeds. It was about *you*. If you can see that *I* can see that you're real, you're real to yourself as well."

304

"Yes, that's very much it." The almost-smile returned. "Please don't take offence, but I didn't expect you to understand."

"I was a custodian long enough to know that the law only works if people *believe* that it works. This is no different." Damant stared into the fire. "What happens when that belief is no longer enough?"

Rîma eased her sword from its scabbard and laid it across her knees. The sword that was the bequest of regicides, all of whom had later died upon the blade. "Then I shall trust to those who came before. So many have borne this sword. Though they are gone, reborn to new lives, new bodies, my ancestors' resonance remains within the steel. When I hold it close, their strength becomes mine; the bells of Tadamûr fall silent, and I am myself. With my ancestors' help, I *will* free my people."

"And after that?"

Eyes closed, she brushed the blade with the back of her hand, her smile turning sad. "After that, we will see."

Thirty-One

Morning brought clear skies, but the nostalgic scent of mist endured where the dew did not. They broke camp and followed the road south, Damant stripping off his heavy coat and travelling in shirtsleeves as the sun crawled higher, Rîma as ever untroubled by the morning heat. With every step, Zariqaz's irregular spire grew larger on the southwestern horizon, as inescapable as judgement in the Stars Below.

"No matter what I do, I always end up staring at that city," grumbled Damant, his boots thick with red dust from the ill-maintained road.

"Not for nothing do they call it the City of Lost Souls; where else would you expect to find such as we?" Rîma replied, not entirely without humour. "My grandfather once told me that there was a centre to this world, an axis upon which the skies and Deadwinds turn. Tadamûr was founded there, or as close to it as my ancestors could manage. Perhaps your Eternity King did the same?"

Damant mopped his brow – even in the shade of the black pines, the heat was unbearable. "The Deadwinds spiral about Zariqaz because the Eternity King is there, not the other way around."

She flashed an almost-smile. "Such certainty. And how came you by this knowledge?"

"Alabastran scripture. Nyssa reshaped the Deadwinds to flow through Zariqaz so that the Eternity King could harness their power in holding back the Veil."

"Really? Does scripture record why Caradan Diar founded Zariqaz where he did?"

Damant hesitated. "Not that I've ever heard."

"You see? A new legend carried on the back of the old. The Eternity King takes credit for the turning of the skies, the defence against the Veil. A truly wondrous man ... or so scripture records." A sly note infused her final words, though nothing of it showed in her face.

Damant bit back an instinctive retort. Though he didn't consider himself an overly religious man, the stories of Caradan Diar and his deathless rule had been baked into his being since childhood. They were truth, or as near to such as the world allowed.

However ... Khalad had degrees of truth. Not the distorting curation of myth and ceremony alone, but outright fabrications passed off as reality. Take Vallant. Until recently, what threat he'd posed to the Eternity King's order had been illusion, his successes sculpted and trumpeted by the very firebloods who'd supposedly lived in fear of his rebellion – a rebellion they clandestinely supported as a pressure valve for discontent. Damant had been part of it all and never suspected. And if he could be fooled so completely by something so close to hand, then what might Alabastra and their deathless monarch conceal beneath the golden gleam of fable?

The scent of the mist grew thicker with every step. Time and again, Damant pressed a hand to his haversack, and the slim bundle of blesswood shavings concealed within. The last resort of a traveller in the wilds, and one he dearly hoped he wouldn't need. When the mists came, there was no telling how long they'd linger.

He had his first glimpse of Tulloq Mine before midday, its austere headstocks rising out of a hollow in the hills, a forlorn sentry of steel scaffold and cable tethers. The rest came into sight as they rounded a bend in the road: a cluster of squat, unlovely buildings, three to the west of the headstocks, two to the east, all adobe to the first-floor level, then metal and timber frames above. They sat silent in the hill's long shadow, the only movement the rustle of breeze-blown branches on the surrounding slopes.

Damant drew his shrieker. "It wasn't subsidence that stopped them trading at Kassos."

Rîma rested the blade of her sword across her shoulder, a hitherto unremarked shadow vanishing from her eyes. "Let us see."

Alert for movement in the silent buildings and with the butt of his shrieker crooked to his elbow, Damant followed the sunken, rutted fork from the main road and through the line of cast-iron braziers that marked the mine's perimeter. A torch fence. Not as efficient as a torch house, but quicker to establish. Brief examination confirmed that the blesswood within was unblackened, having never borne a flame. If Tulloq was as deserted as it appeared, the Veil wasn't the cause … unless, of course, it had come down so quickly that the miners hadn't had time to set the fence alight.

Deeper in, dust-clogged rails ran to a narrow railrunner platform. A battered clatter wagon sat motionless in the lee of the headstocks, its copious rust older than the mine buildings and its impressive collection of spiderwebs somewhat newer. Its flatbed held half a dozen open crates of iron ore. A stack of three others sat beside the rear wheel. Yet another lay upturned, its contents spilled across the rutted roadway. More proof that whatever had overtaken the miners had done so suddenly.

In the headstocks building itself, there was nothing of note save a few shovels and mattocks propped against a wall. Of the elevator platform, Damant saw no sign. He cast briefly around for the motic prism before belatedly realising that the mechanism was a manual rope-and-pulley. Like the torch fence, it spoke to an operation run on the barest of funds.

He nodded at the westernmost buildings. "You want to check those? I'll try the other." He patted the headstocks' outer wall. "Meet back here, and don't be shy if you find trouble."

Rîma inclined her head in acknowledgement. "As you say."

The door to the eastern building hung off its hinges, the twin rows of bunk beds within filthy with the ever-present red dust of the hills, blown in through the broken door and a shattered window high on the north wall. Tangled blankets lay strewn across the floor, their folds thick with smeared boot prints. A traveller's trunk lay on its side, spine-broken books and clothes scattered across the flagstones.

Damant picked his way through the upheaval, instincts honed by years of investigation picking out details not immediately obvious. Rucks in the blankets and heel trails in the dust where a body might have been dragged. The blood on the broken window, its glass flung outside. The wreckage of an upturned table by the damaged door. The nicks and gouges in the wooden furniture. The dark patches that spoke to bloodstains long since dried. All told the tale of a building besieged, and settled once and for all the notion that the Veil had taken the miners.

The mists didn't barge open doors or swing swords, nor did they drag away bodies, living or dead. Reavers might have done so, or even rebels – Vallant wasn't the only dissident haunting Khalad. However, Damant had never heard of reavers or rebels so close to Zariqaz, which lay barely an afternoon's walk away to the south-west, weather and roads being equal.

This was someone else.

Rîma waited at the headstocks cabin, sword still across her shoulder. Her unfocused eyes were fixed on the hillside, her thoughts distant. She blinked as he approached, a shudder returning her to a semblance of composure. "Well?"

"They were attacked. Some of them tried to barricade the bunkhouse. The attackers broke down the door and dragged them away. It's possible someone escaped through the window, but I don't imagine they got far."

"No, I don't imagine they did. There are shallow graves behind the storehouse." She held out an upturned hand, revealing a fist-sized glasswork in the stylised likeness of a mandevilla blossom, its sail-like petals black at the edge, fading to white at the bloom's centre. "Each had one of these at the head."

Damant took it, marvelling at the deftness of the craftsmanship. Each petal was barely thicker than the blossom that had inspired it, the flower almost without weight. Exquisite beyond any glasswork he'd previously beheld. "What is it?"

"Blow on it."

Feeling slightly ridiculous, he did so and was rewarded by a whisper of sweet, brittle song, the notes little more than a sigh and as soon forgotten. "I don't understand."

"It's a mournflower. We set them on graves to sing laments for the dead," said Rîma. "Look again, and tell me you don't recognise it."

"Of course I recognise it. It's a rare remembrance garden that isn't overgrown with ..." Damant blew on it again, the almost-familiar notes maddening as they floated away. But the colours ... the sail-shaped petals, broad at the base and narrow at the tip. "I'll be damned."

The mournflower was a pinwheel. Or rather a pinwheel was an imitation of the mournflower, created by a people without the skill to shape glass, or to make it sing. But the tradition remained, distorted through the millennia.

"I thought your people never left the city."

"So did I."

Damant considered reminding her of the wedding ring that had found its way to Kassos, but held his tongue. The obvious never grew more welcome for being spoken aloud. "How are the bells?"

A flicker of surprise chased across Rîma's brow. "Loud as thunder."

The Tulloq miners had delved deep enough to breach Tadamûr's upper levels, had plundered what they believed to be a tomb and thus stirred the inhabitants to reprisals. But even in revenge, Rîma's people had shown compassion for the slain.

The first skeins of mist wound their way through the pines. Mistfall had come. "I'd better light the torch fence," said Damant. "See if you can get that elevator moving, maybe? Rappelling is no pastime for a man my age ... Rîma?"

She blinked, her fingers tightening on the grips of her sword. "Yes ... Yes, of course."

He eyed her closely, far from certain that she'd heard. "Don't go anywhere without me. I'm to bear witness, remember?"

"I have forgotten nothing," Rîma replied, her eyes again unfocused. "Remembrance is what we do best."

Fortunately, the mine hadn't been derelict so long that the blesswood oil had dried out. Nor had the first brazier's sharae ifrît – kin to the one that powered Damant's shriekers, but considerably less volatile – dissipated to worthlessness. A brief rap on the striking plate and the sharae sparked, its magenta flames rushing across the treated timber and waking the brazier to life. At once, the mists coiled away, a numbness of thought Damant hadn't previously noticed retreating alongside the scent of old memories.

One down, five to go.

Already the sun was but a memory, lost behind the seething greenish-white of the Veil.

Picking his way through the desiccated tussocks, Damant worked counterclockwise. The next three braziers lit readily enough, the fourth with a little coaxing. No amount of gentle handling could have woken the fifth, whose sharae had fled into the Deadwinds an unknowable span of time in the past. With neither time to waste nor the inclination to take chances with the Veil, he simply set his shrieker's muzzle against the brazier and squeezed the trigger. The weapon's whine barely registered in the mists, but the blesswood took light, completing the circle.

Damant set his back to the fence. Even with the Veil at bay, the mine buildings took on a macabre appearance, the sun-bleached adobe drinking in the magenta of the flames. Nor was the mist held wholly in abeyance. Torch fences traded raw mist-banishing heat for longevity. They were the resort of the desperate and of mystics who sought visions in the mist. Even close to the flames the air was hazy. Further out, skeins crept through the trees, tendrils probing the defences as if at the direction of some malign intelligence. Thick patches clung to the buildings' eaves and the canopy above the abandoned railrunner platform, drifting in the clutches of a wind Damant couldn't feel.

How long could the fence be trusted to hold? Three days was the theory – longer if there was more blesswood somewhere in the mining camp. The Veil's stubbornness was impossible to judge. It might linger for a few hours or a week. Praying it was the former, Damant set out for the headstocks.

A booming, cultured voice brought him up short. "'You should hear my counter-offer first.' I liked that." A chuckle laced the words. "It had a certain rough style."

Hadîm.

Damant spun around. He saw only the crackling flames, his own dark shadow and those of the trees.

"I didn't expect the trail to lead here." Hadîm's voice echoed, distorted by the Veil's embrace. "I'd barely arrived back in Salamdi when my informant in Kassos sent a heraldic. I've been walking nearly two days straight, but I suppose I shouldn't complain. You've saved me a difficult journey. Now all I need do is hand her over and collect my bounty. I expect the king will be *very* generous."

There. A shadow moving against greenish-white. Damant brought his shrieker to bear and pulled the trigger. A bolt of invisible flame parted the Veil and blasted a spray of bark from a tree trunk. The mists spiralled back in to swallow it up.

"No, not me. Sorry."

Dull footsteps sounded behind. Again Damant turned. This time he forbore from shooting. Judging a shrieker ifrît's remaining charge was a ticklish business and wasted shots served no one. "Show yourself and we'll settle this with honour."

Laughter rippled through the mists, closer this time. "Fine words from a man who meant to shoot me in the back."

There. No. Just another tree masquerading as a man. Where was he? Back in Salamdi, Rîma had accused Hadîm of wielding a glamour. That Floranz girl had done something similar, making people see what she

312

wished rather than what was actually there. How much of the mist was in his mind, not his eyes? "You'll forgive me for trying."

The laughter returned. "Let me make an offer of my own. Go, live your life."

"Generous." Damant closed his eyes, blotting out a sense he was increasingly sure could not be trusted. "Care to tell me why?"

"Why not?" *There.* Midway between the two braziers. "I don't hold grudges and no one's paying me to kill you. Honestly, you're not worth the effort."

"Good to know."

Murmuring a silent prayer to Nyssa, Damant sent a bolt of flame shrieking towards the voice.

A deep-throated bellow of pain shook the mists. What *might* have been a brief waft of burnt flesh. Damant strained his ears, hoping for the sound of a falling body.

"No deal . . . I take it?" rasped Hadîm, his voice ragged.

Damant turned on his heel and ran for the headstocks, expecting at every moment to feel a blade in his back. Happily, it seemed the shrieker shot had at least slowed Hadîm down, and he made it to the heavy wooden door unpunctured.

"He's here!" he gasped, a combination of age, exertion and rising fear lending a quavering edge to his words as he slammed the cabin door shut. "Can you fight?"

Rîma sat cross-legged in front of the empty elevator shaft, hands on her knees. Her sword lay on the bare ground before her as if in prayerful offering. Her unfamiliar muttered words echoed beneath the cabin's sloping roof, rhythmic as a temple carillon at prayer time.

Damant skidded to a knee beside her, his heart sinking as he took in her closed, unresponsive eyes. "Hadîm's right behind me." His always less than bountiful patience burned away as frustration flared to anger. "Snap out of it, woman!"

A frown touched Rîma's brow. One did not address a principessa in such tones. But her dull, breathy chant never faltered.

313

Damant grabbed her sword above the hilt, surprised by the weight of it, the coldness of the steel. With the other, he wrenched her right hand from her knee and folded her fingers around the grips.

"Principessa Eskamarîma of Tadamûr," he filled his voice with the authoritative snarl that had for so many years made him the terror of the Bascari custodium, "I asked if you could fight."

Rîma's eyes flickered open. "I didn't think it would be so difficult." Her slack expression tightened to weary chagrin. "But yes, I can fight."

The door crashed back.

Hadîm stalked into the cabin, mist clutching at the tails of his black custodian's robes and a regulation-issue scimitar in his hand.

Rîma rose in one smooth motion, her open palm a heavy shove in Damant's ribs. Boot heels scuffing the impacted soil of the cabin floor, he stumbled back to the mouth of the elevator shaft, treacherous balance already fled. Hadîm's sword flashed between them in a vicious downward slice.

Damant's tailbone jarred against the floor. The shrieker jolted from his hand. Rîma rode the momentum of her shove into a dancer's pirouette and hacked at Hadîm's head.

Even reeling from the speed at which events had gone to dust, Damant saw that she did so too slowly, her usually fluid grace impeded by the sound of chimes only she heard.

"No!" He pushed against the bare dirt, skinning his palms in his haste to rise.

Hadîm took a long step inside the flashing curve of Rîma's blade and, with a crackle like rotting boughs underfoot, severed her forearm halfway between wrist and elbow.

Her sword, fingers still tight about its grips, thumped to the ground.

Hadîm spiralled away, raising his own sword to high guard as he trod lightly along the elevator shaft's edge. His booted foot gave Rîma's fallen blade a soft, almost gentle nudge. Weapon and hand vanished into the blackness of the shaft, red dirt trailing behind.

Rîma collapsed with a parched, stuttering gasp, momentum driving her on a pace before her knees struck compacted dirt. Head hung, she clutched the ragged stump to her chest, greyish dust gushing from between mangled bones, paling her black linen wrappings and time-worn coat. But greater than the physical harm was the loss of her sword, for even as she fumbled, shaking, for a hand no longer there, her eyes lost their focus, the silent carillon squeezing out what little of her remained.

Damant drew his scimitar and charged headlong at Hadîm, his guttural growl of fury unrecognisable even to himself. He'd the brief satisfaction of seeing the qalimîri's eyes widen in surprise, the fleeting glimpse of a charred shrieker-burn high on Hadîm's left shoulder. Then Hadîm's sword flashed to a parry. Steel scraped between them and all was survival.

Certain that he couldn't hope to match Hadîm's deftness with the blade, Damant hammered at him with every ounce of rage-born strength, his scimitar no longer a weapon of tutored grace, but a dead metal weight with all the precision of a cudgel or skelder's prybar. His own sword bucking with impact, Hadîm pivoted on his left foot to put space between them, the shift of his sole spraying red dust into the mist.

Knowing that to hesitate was to lose, Damant pressed the attack, varying the angle of his overhead strikes just enough to keep Hadîm off balance, leveraging every inch of reach granted by his fractionally taller stature to whatever advantage it could offer.

For the briefest of moments, he even indulged the notion that he could win.

Then Hadîm's sword flashed an impossible arc. The scimitars' guards met and locked with a screech of unhappy steel. Lips twisting to a wolfish, victorious smile, Hadîm jerked his arm sideways, ripping Damant's weapon from his grasp. Even as the masterless blade struck the floor, the qalimîri rammed his head forward.

Damant heard the hollow *thud* of impact more than he felt it. His knees' jarring impact with the ground drove out both. His world swam in murky red-tinged black, tongue thick in a mouth that no longer felt his own.

"You should have accepted my offer." Hadîm was an indistinct shadow moving against a grey world. He almost sounded regretful.

Blinking furiously, Damant shook his head. "I thought I wasn't worth the effort." Was that his voice? It sounded so distant. Not part of him at all.

His fingers closed around a handful of dirt.

"*That* was before you shot me a second time." For all the petulance of Hadîm's words, his tone held none. "Generosity has its limits."

Steel lanced through the murk. Damant flung himself aside, his handful of dust cast at what he hoped was Hadîm's eyes. A hacking, frustrated grunt told him that his blind throw had been more on target than not, but jellied knees betrayed him as he strove to rise and pitched him to the ground.

A dull, hollow chime split the air.

Hadîm, cast from shadow into some semblance of living form as Damant's thoughts cleared, pitched face-first into the dirt and did not rise. Rîma, swaying fit to collapse, towered above him, a miner's shovel clutched tight. Then collapse she did, the shovel falling from her fingers.

"Sorry …" she muttered, her words retreating to whatever distant place had claimed her thoughts. "I'm sorry …"

Damant caught her, the scant weight the lightest of burdens against his shoulder.

Behind her, the elevator rattled into motion, its chains rushing through the wooden guides.

As he knelt in the one-sided embrace, a dim part of Damant's increasingly foggy mind urged him to rise, to drag Rîma from the head-stocks cabin and seek shelter beyond. The rest, weary beyond words and throbbing with the headbutt's aftermath, recognised that there was no shelter to be had, not with the mists lying heavy upon Tulloq's hills.

In the end, it hardly mattered, for the elevator platform shuddered to a stop long before he'd have made it to the doorway. Three tall, cadaverous figures stood motionless upon it, their androgynous golden masks half hidden by gauzy veils of black silk. Black too were their

316

robes, at the cuffs and collar of which showed patches of grey-bronze desiccated flesh.

The foremost of the trio, indistinguishable from her companions save for the small red gemstone on her mask's brow – the point where a custodium overseer's triangle would have sat – stepped from the platform, the sightless sweep of her mask setting Damant's flesh crawling as she took in the scene. Without turning, she crooked a lacquered black fingernail at her companions.

"Bring them," she intoned. "Bring them all."

Thirty-Two

The broad-shouldered redcloak hacked down, his confidence betrayed twice over by his wolfish smile and self-satisfied laugh. Tanith stepped aside, the dancer's twirl unnecessary save for dazzlement of her audience, and rammed her sword between his ribs. Laughter sputtered to a wet gasp, smile to a fading rictus.

Planting a boot against his chest, she ripped her sword free and let his body fall. "Go!"

Moaning their terror, a man, a woman and a small girl fled for the steep stairs. Tanith kicked the dead redcloak in the head and followed.

She found her rescuees huddled in the alley, staring out into the carnage of the street. A double row of redcloaks stood beneath the deepening dusk, phalanx spears braced and shields locked, shuddering beneath a patter of bricks and ordure hurled by a skelder rabble further along the cobbles. One redcloak collapsed, wits swept away by a half-brick's strike. The others ground on. Behind the scarlet line, black-robed House Ozdîr custodians stood watch over bloodied prisoners.

"Not that way!" Marvelling at the dearth of self-preservation instinct, Tanith gestured back along the alleyway. "Come on, move!"

In the street, a captive shoved her jailer aside and sprinted for the alley mouth. Shrieker fire cut her down, stray shots blasting rubble and dust from the brickwork above Tanith's head.

An overseer's silver *vahla* mask snapped round. "Strays! After them!"

"Go!" Tanith shoved her nearest charge along the alley.

The others took flight upon his heels. Tanith followed, fresh screams sounding behind as rioters died on redcloak spears.

"I see her!"

The custodian's shout and the whine of his shrieker sounded as one. Not from behind, but dead ahead where the alley broadened around a crumbling well. The foremost rescuee screamed and collapsed, his chest ablaze.

"Down!" Tanith bore the woman to the filthy cobbles as a second shot blazed overhead.

Rising to one knee, she drew a dagger from her belt and took it by the blade. It left her hand as the custodian lined up his second shot. He toppled backwards, clutching uselessly at his throat, and vanished into the well.

Tanith stifled a petulant shriek. She'd liked that dagger.

"Get up!" She turned a baleful eye on the girl, now wailing and tugging at her dead father's hand. "And keep her quiet."

The woman glared up at her, defiance burning through her tears and her voice cracking. "She's scared!"

Patience fraying after eleven other forays into Qosm's bloody streets, Tanith met her gaze. "She'll be dead."

The woman flinched and gathered up her child. "Hush, Jaia," she stuttered, smoothing her daughter's hair. "It's ... it's going to be all right. *Abdon Nyssa ivohê.*"

"Make for the temple on Feldi Street." Tanith shoved her deeper into the alley. "Move!"

They threaded left at the next crossway, cutting across a narrow souk littered with bodies, its stalls ablaze. Jaia's wails faded to choked sobs. Or perhaps it was simply that her mother muffled her cries against her chest as readily as she shielded her eyes from the carnage. What occurred in Qosm that afternoon was no battle, but a massacre.

Tanith took the lead, heading always towards the old temple in which

319

she'd first met Ardoc. Alleys wended away behind them, shouts and screams smothered by drifting smoke.

"How much further?" gasped Jaia's mother.

Tanith bit back an impatient reply. "Get across Hadivar Crescent and we're as good as there."

"Why are they doing this?"

Tanith shrugged. Let Ardoc worry over the enemy's goals. Down in the streets it was blood and survival. "Because they can."

Hadivar Crescent proved impassable. A squadron of redcloak riders idled beyond the alley mouth, tall spears held skyward as they waited for luckless fugitives to cross their path. Bloody smears on the flagstones warned that some already had.

"Back," murmured Tanith, gesturing to a crossway just passed. "We'll find another way."

A shrieker shot blazed out of the smoke, its passage a hot wind on her cheek. Redcloaks came roaring in its wake, scimitars gleaming.

Tanith met them at a run. She slashed one down, scraped a parry and sent another away, reeling and bloody. Her ribs turned to fire at a spear's raking thrust and then she was falling, bowled over and borne down by a redcloak. She howled as a boot stamped down on her fingers and kicked her sword away. Jaia's mother screamed. The alley shook to running feet.

"Real slash-cat, aren't you?" The redcloak astride Tanith leaned in and leered, his sweat stifling as he pinned her wrists. "Don't make this more painful than it needs to be, little qori."

"No," Tanith said flatly.

She jerked her head up and bit down on the redcloak's nose. He jackknifed away, bellowing, hands clasped to his face.

Tanith spat away the gobbet of flesh and rolled to her feet. Bruised fingers found the grips of her sword. Another redcloak lunged at her, spear jabbing. She hacked down, splitting the staff inches behind the steel head, then back cut to slice open his skull. Breathing hard, one hand pressed to the indigo flames rippling from the slowly closing

320

wound in her flank, she sank against the alley wall, alone save for the dead. Jaia's mother lay among the redcloaks, sightless eyes skyward.

A wail sounded. Tanith glimpsed tangled black hair and a face streaming with tears as a trio of redcloaks bore the girl away.

Ugh.

She'd already done enough – far more than her share. Eleven successful forays into the bloody streets. Fifty people saved. Wasn't her fault the twelfth had gone to corpse rot. She was tired, she ached, and she didn't know *any* of these people. She didn't owe them anything.

Who'd stood up for Tanith Floranz when she'd needed them? No one. In the long run, it had made her stronger. Jaia was in line for toughening up.

Ardoc wouldn't understand, but then Ardoc didn't need to know, did he?

Kiasta.

She set off at a limping run, picking up speed as the spear wound at her ribs closed. Warned by her uneven footsteps, the rearmost redcloak spun around and died with a cry of warning on his lips. The second managed to bring her sword to bear before Tanith cut her throat to the bone and sent her soul to the Deadwinds.

Eyes wide with horror, Jaia's captor dropped the girl into the alley's filth and lunged. Tanith struck his scimitar aside and slammed a heel into his knee. Bone cracked beneath her boot and the redcloak fell howling atop his comrades' bodies. Tanith stabbed down and rounded on his erstwhile captive.

"If you start wailing again, I'm eating you."

Jaia's red-rimmed eyes filled with fresh tears.

Sighing at her own enfeebled resolve, Tanith sheathed her scimitar and picked the girl up.

Hoofbeats sounded in the alley. She glanced back at a redcloak rider, drawn from Hadivar Crescent by the commotion, and ran for it.

"Yah!" Hooves quickened behind her.

Tanith ran on. An amashti, even a starving one, was faster than a mortal, yes. Swifter than a horse, no. But for the confines, she'd already have a spear in her back. Steering back towards the crescent was a death sentence. She needed another path, and quickly.

A memory stirred from her previous stay in Zariqaz. The old tunnel of the Rat Hollow, serving a maze of drinkers' dens and bawdy houses abandoned once the lethargia had stifled their custom. It ran under Hadivar Crescent. If she was lucky, it'd be empty of redcloaks. Even if it wasn't, a horseman couldn't follow her.

The wailing Jaia bouncing against her shoulder, Tanith took a left. Half running, half slipping in the dust, she barrelled down the uneven slope, through a crumbling archway and into the darkness.

Beyond the archway, what should have been a dark, dank tunnel was suffused with the gentle greenish-white glow of the encroaching Veil. The air stank, thick with the aroma of old memories and forgotten chances.

Kiasta.

Tanith skidded to a halt. Qosm had been a different beast ever since the torch houses had gone dark and the mists had swallowed part of the streets. She'd not realised the Veil had come so far.

She turned about. At the tunnel mouth, a redcloak rider swung down from his saddle. Two more were already inside, scimitars drawn. Others crowded the daylight beyond the archway. Too many to fight, even for her. That left precisely one insane option.

She pressed Jaia's head to hers. "Hold tight to me and don't let go."

With one last glance at the pursuing redcloaks, she plunged into the mist.

The world boiled away, certainty and solidity lost behind roiling greenish-white. Tanith stumbled, glad that there was *something* beneath her feet, something to anchor her in a world suddenly bereft of texture or direction.

She looked back the way she'd come and regretted it at once. Nothing showed through the mists. Not redcloaks, nor the archway by which she'd entered, nor daylight. In fact, the longer she stared, the less certain she was of her heading. Was she even looking back the way she'd come? Without landmarks, it was impossible to tell. The tunnel's closeness vanished into memory, the air akin to open sky more than confinement.

She took a deep breath, the dry sorrow of yesterday filling her lungs. At least Jaia had gone quiet. Memory insisted the Rat Hollow tunnel was arrow-straight, emerging beneath Feldi Street after nary a twist or turn. Cling to that. Don't think about those tales of folk coming apart in the mist. Kat had travelled them and survived. She could too.

After all, she was better than her sister.

Righting herself as best she could, Tanith set out in what she hoped was the right direction, one hand about Jaia and the other extended into the mist to forestall collision with the tunnel wall.

Her fingers wisped like smoke from spent candles. She flexed them and strove for . . . *something*, some feeling fit for the sight, but emotion lay far beyond reach.

She forged on, the soothing, cloying mist blurring the edges of her thoughts, numbing what she suspected should have been panic to something dull and distant. Even her daemon-half was no help, sullenly buried in the depths of her soul as it was, terrified for the first time she could recall.

All she knew was that she wasn't scared. People came apart in the mists, yes. But not her. She was different. She was a survivor. She was . . .

Kiasta. What was her name?

She swallowed hard, fighting her rising panic. Her heartbeat was definitely faster now, her disquiet all the worse for not quite knowing why it was so. She held tight to the bundle sobbing softly at her shoulder. The girl. What was *her* name?

The child went rigid in her arms. "What's that?" she asked in a small, terrified voice.

The nameless woman spun around, her heart sinking further to see that the girl's thin, pointing finger was as vaporous as her own – her pale bronze skin grey in the care of the mists. The fear faded, consumed by a deep primordial terror.

Somewhere behind – or what *had* been behind, or might be again – a vast, bird-like shadow bled through the mist, billowing ever closer. It soared like a hawk upon thermals, head flowing hither and yon, blazing emerald eyes scouring the endless white.

Even as the woman without a name stumbled away, the mists shook with a cacophony of corvine screams. The shadow surged. It swallowed her whole, drowning her in darkness.

Let her go!

The words shook the shadows to their fibrous roots, deafening, cajoling, demanding. The girl wailed and clung tighter to the nameless woman's neck, the pale wisps of her being streaming away into gossamer black.

"You can't have her!" yelled the nameless woman.

Green eyes shone in the darkness. *LET HER GO!*

"Leave us alone!"

She staggered away. The darkness followed, the greenish-white of the mists nothing more than a memory in that abiding shadow. She missed her footing and sprawled. The girl slipped from her grasp, whisked from sight.

"No!" The nameless woman howled. "Give her back!"

The eyes vanished and she was alone in the thinning darkness, unravelling faster than ever before, her body little more than vapour and her thoughts thick with failure for which she'd no longer a name.

Something grabbed her by what had once been an arm, and *pulled*.

Tanith's head chimed off the flagstones with enough force to set her vision blurring. Groggy with the aftermath of the half-forgotten nightmare, she stared up to see Ardoc standing over her, the stars shining in a darkened sky above him. Just how long had she been behind the Veil?

"My apologies," he rumbled, "but you take some moving."

Grasping his hand, she rose and stared into the mist bank on the edge of the temple's overgrown gardens, the crumbing boundary wall half in, half out of its embrace. "What happened?"

"I saw something moving in the mist and pulled it out. It turned out to be you."

Nausea swallowed what passed for her memories. Urgency overcame both. "Jaia! Where's the girl?"

"Calm yourself." Ardoc pointed up the temple steps, to where a masked kathari carried Jaia to join a ragged procession, survivors of the redcloaks' assault. "I grabbed her first."

Tanith gazed at him, recalling fragments of a shadow in the mist demanding the girl's surrender. Was that what her Veil-ravaged mind had made of Ardoc? "You dived into the mist for me?"

"A small enough risk given those borne elsewhere." Ardoc nodded at the refugees, his rough humour turning solemn.

"There was . . . something in there." Even now the details were failing. "It wanted Jaia."

Ardoc grunted. "The mists are a peculiar country, home to many things better left undisturbed. If you encountered such, you did doubly well."

Tanith scowled, fresh unease joining that born of a mist-wreathed journey she barely recalled. She'd not done well enough to save Jaia's parents. Worse, she'd come close to abandoning the girl to her fate. That she hadn't offered some small solace. "Someone needs to pay for this."

He nodded, avuncular manner turning cold. "They will. Qolda had no warning, which means this wasn't hatched by an ambitious redcloak *gansalar*. Likewise, we have ears in every custodium across the city." Shading his eyes, he stared skyward towards the gleaming pinnacle of the Golden Citadel. "The Voice has thrown down a gauntlet. She may yet wish she had not. But it seems we need no longer wonder for whom dear Enna was working."

Enna. Still groggy with the lingering mists, it took a moment for Tanith to remember that she knew something about the traitorous conclave member that Ardoc didn't. "I saw her. Earlier today."

Ardoc gripped her arm and dragged her into the undergrowth, away from prying eyes. "Really? Where?"

"In the depths. Beyond the tsrûqi."

"Is that so?" His tone turned thoughtful. "And how did you come to be there, I wonder."

She decided he didn't need to know that Esram had been there too. "I was curious. My sister taught me to soothe ifrîti. I tested myself on the tsrûqi . . . and kept walking."

"Ah." His eyes gleamed, disapproval banished. "And was your curiosity satisfied?"

Struck by the distinct notion that he was toying with her, Tanith met his stare measure for measure. Black stone and a column of coruscating fire danced across her thoughts. "Why don't you tell me? Better than that, why don't you tell me what I saw?"

He lowered his voice to a whisper. "Something it took me a lifetime to find. Nyssa's prison. When Hierarch Nazaric drove me into hiding, I set the tsrûqi there to keep that knowledge hidden. Why do you suppose I built the haven where I did?"

"And those . . . things?" Even in recollection she shied away from the clammy, waxy creatures of the Stars Below.

"Aethervores. Priestly leeches who siphon her power for the Eternity King." He exhaled slowly. "I wish you hadn't gone there alone. The consequences . . . But never mind. Did you hear her? Did you hear the goddess?"

"I think . . ." She swallowed, remembering how she'd arrived at the city without conscious choice. It felt better to know that it had been Nyssa's will that had drawn her there. "I think she called to me."

Ardoc took her hands and held them tight. "Good. Not long now and we will see her freed." He glanced up at Qosm's refugees. "And all of this will be a bleak dream."

"What about Enna?" If Ardoc didn't need to know about Esram, he certainly didn't need to know that Enna had saved her from one of the aethervores. Tanith didn't want him questioning her loyalty.

"I'll have Qolda set guards, but I don't think we need trouble ourselves. Let her languish. There is nothing in those ruins but death. And speaking of death ..." His expression hardened. "Tomorrow marks the anniversary of the day Nyssa called the Voice's mother. Each year since, our dear principessa has marked the occasion by journeying to the Hallow Caves and placing a pinwheel at Nyssa's feet. I'm told it's a secret, solemn ceremony, with no more than a handful of guards in attendance. Would you see to it, dear Tanith, that mother and daughter are reunited in Nyssa's care? For me. For those who died today."

Tanith suppressed a shiver, but whether it was of fear or anticipation she couldn't say. "Of course, Father."

Thirty-Three

Rough strata rushed past, the miners' elevator shuddering and bucking fit to tear itself loose. None of Damant's companions seemed to notice. Hadîm wore a self-satisfied smile, Rîma that distant, unfocused look Damant had come to loathe, her good hand clasping her wrist stump to her chest. As for their captors . . . ? The woman held position at the platform's leading edge, a corroded lantern held aloft to shape the darkness. Her two companions stood behind Damant, their long, curved swords held vertically in a two-handed grip, like bas-reliefs upon a tomb. Silk-veiled golden masks held their emotions close . . . assuming that they felt anything at all. Fine gauze behind the eyeholes denied even a glimpse of their expressions.

None of the trio had spoken a word. Not the happiest of omens, especially given that they'd roughly divested Damant of his weaponry. Hadîm too, though he at least could anticipate gratitude for his efforts. Damant had few expectations for his own status, all of them bad.

"Well, you wanted an adventure," he murmured sourly. "Try to enjoy it."

The woman turned, the motion stuttering and awkward, her mask's empty gaze setting a shiver in Damant's spine. Hadîm snorted a slow, sardonic chuckle.

The temperature plunged, the air growing musty and bitter. The brake shrieked as one of the guards wrestled it into place. The lift shuddered to a stop in line with a yawning pit-prop archway. Steel rails and uneven walls led off into the darkness, the gullet of some massive slumbering beast that at any moment could wake and swallow them whole.

The woman headed into the tunnel, the feeble light of her lantern bobbing like a gloami wisp over a grave. Hadîm followed, boots crunching on grit with every languid stride. When Rîma made no move, Damant put a hand at her waist and her good elbow to guide her.

"It seems we're moving out."

She gave no sign of having heard him.

Deeper into the tunnel, the woman turned sharply about, the swaying lantern skittering shapeless shadows across the stone. "Do not lay hands upon the principessa." As in the headstocks cabin far above, she spoke in low, flat tones, the words issuing from some long-buried tomb.

"I'm helping her," Damant replied acidly. "I don't know if you noticed, but she's not at her best."

A heavy hand fell upon his shoulder and squeezed. Damant gritted his teeth to stifle a pained hiss as his collarbone creaked.

"Do not lay hands upon the principessa." The guard's voice was deeper than the woman's, but his tone and manner were otherwise uncannily alike.

"It's all right, Ihsan," breathed Rîma, her eyes fixed sightlessly ahead. "I can manage."

Taking heart from the fact that she was sufficiently herself to use his given name, Damant nodded and withdrew his hands. The pressure on his shoulder vanished, leaving behind an ache that promised trouble in the morning, should he live that long.

"Protective, aren't they?" he muttered sourly.

But whatever part of Rîma had driven her to speak had drifted beneath the surface once more. Her feet dragging on the tunnel's rough stone, she joined the procession. With few other options to hand, Damant followed, the glowering presence of their guards at his back.

In time, they branched off from the main tunnel, the passageway narrowing so much that his shoulders scraped rock dust from the walls. More twists and turns followed, though the confines thankfully tightened no further, the rush of an underground river growing ever louder. Meaningful landmarks were few and far between with so little light to hand. Still, Damant kept careful count of the side tunnels in hopes that he'd have cause to come back that way.

Another turn and the passageway ended in a spill of greyish-white stone blocks, what might have been a natural collapse later broadened by mortal means. Dipping her head beneath the low makeshift lintel, the woman stepped through.

Avenues of crates and barrels implied the chamber's function as a storeroom. The broken, desiccated spars betrayed it was one looted in recent memory, most likely by the ill-fated Tulloq miners. It was otherwise like no storeroom Damant had ever seen. The high vaulted ceiling, thick with sculpted muqarnas honeycomb, would have been the pride of any fireblood's palace. Underfoot, white marble and runners of thick time-soiled carpet lurked below the dust. Marble too were the walls, and beneath the thick spiderweb tapestries gleamed stained-glass panels of myriad colours. Soft light glowed behind the glass, dappling the room in echoes of reds and oranges, greens and blues.

Ushered on, Damant descended a long, straight stair and thence into a series of winding corridors as broad as Undertown streets.

Here at least there were landmarks, for every junction was marked by statues, no two alike, save in the verdigris-crusted metal of their forging and their larger-than-life stature. A handful bore lanterns, the light of their cracked prisms long faded. Some were girded and garbed for war, their layered armour distant cousin to that of Khalad's redcloaks. Others wore long, sweeping robes and bore the palettes and brushes of artists, or else mason's tools or a writer's quill. The men were firm-browed and handsome, the women beautiful, all the better to impress unworthiness on an interloper and awaken pride in those who belonged. Even Damant, witness to his share of cultural propaganda during his service to House Bascari, felt an unhappy stirring when their sightless eyes met his.

330

Yet all the grandeur in the world could not disguise decay. Dust gathered thick at the edges of each enclosed thoroughfare, the centres swept clean only by the swish of robes and the tramp of feet. More often than not, the stained-glass panels were cracked and crazed, fractured by the pressure of sinking stone.

The light behind the panels shifted as Damant passed. Coronae rippled and flowed from colour to colour as they strove to keep pace, thwarted only when glass gave way to stone. The sensation of watchfulness was unshakeable, akin to the itchy feeling he sometimes experienced around hestic ifrîti but a hundred times stronger, just as the lights behind the glass were brighter than any sentry crest or prism.

This light offered opportunity for closer inspection of his captors. Their robes, which had before seemed austere, were now revealed as ragged and moth-eaten, save where bright scarlet threads shone at the hem of the woman's skirts and sleeves. Withered grey-bronze flesh showed at tear and seam. Their sword blades were dulled with rust beyond the idleness of the laxest custodium initiate. So too did the light rob grace from stumbling, uneven steps dogged by the stiffness of limbs infrequently pressed to service. Even Rîma, shuffling in her silent bell-struck stupor and rigid with pain from her ruined wrist, moved more cleanly.

As they strode deeper into the city, rusty portcullis gateways passed away behind, their guards stooped and unseeing, their corpses held aloft only by the staves of their long spears and their age-fused joints. Through an open doorway, he glimpsed a web-strewn library, its shelves thick with dust and inhabitants motionless at their tables, their gold masks staring blankly at the spread pages of books. Through another, a narrow chapel in which row after row of golden veiled faces stared blankly at what was plainly a tarnished statue of Nyssa Benevolas.

What had at first seemed a palace more and more revealed itself to be a tomb, the resting place not just of men and women, but of the civilisation from which they had sprung.

They passed through a grand gateway, guarded by no fewer than a dozen withered, robed cadavers and a pair of verdigrised statues. The road became a descending stairway of white stone and the muqarnas ceiling yielded to a distant cavern roof. Damant caught his breath, assumptions of Tadamûr's size and scale hastily discarded.

The building from which he'd emerged was but one of a dozen in ready sight, all clad in that same white stone and gleaming stained glass, their sloped flanks and intricate spiral towers scarred here and there by long-ago rockfalls from the yawning cavern roof. Magenta flame blazed from pools of dark, oily liquid, framing the sunless streets in rippling light and driving back skeins of mist creeping in from vine-hung crevasses amid the stalactites where winged shapes flittered – bats or birds he couldn't tell from that distance.

Below the gate the stairs levelled out into a plaza as broad as any custodium muster ground, dominated by withered black trees whose branches spilled over the low containment walls and whose roots buckled and cracked the flagstones to an undulating sea of cracked stone. At the plaza's far end, a majestic many-spired temple rose against the cavern wall. A second broad stairway continued down towards a palace, its golden roof gleaming dully with reflected flames.

Damant stumbled to a halt, overcome by the impossibility of such a city.

"Ah, the first sign of awareness," said Hadîm. "Tell me, does it hurt?"

Somewhere amid the towers, a bell tolled. Then another and another, the clamour building to a dark and majestic carillon. Rîma's head jerked up, her stricken eyes awash with confusion.

Careless of earning a second reprimand, Damant leaned closer – though this time he was careful not to touch her – and strove for words worth saying.

"I'm still here," he said, straining to be heard above the bells. "I'm still real. So are you."

She nodded, confusion yielding to gratitude.

Their female captor glowered but said nothing.

The sound of shuffling footfalls overtook the chimes, so many in number that Damant didn't recognise them for what they were until the first crowds spilled forth from the gateway he'd lately left. They came in their scores, their hundreds, from every door across the cavern, filing down the stairs to the temple. All moved with purpose exerted from without, a swirling, shambling eclipse of moths, their robes ragged wings of every conceivable colour and their veiled golden masks gleaming in the magenta firelight.

They swirled about Damant's group, thick with the scent of long-sealed rooms flung open. Hadîm watched them with a contempt he took no effort to hide.

"Dawn-host prayer," murmured Rîma, lost in in reverie. "Blessed be the light of a new day."

Sure enough, the crevasses of the cavern roof were filling with a red glow, the winged shadows flitting away to roost among the vines.

As the crowd's stragglers stumbled down the steps, Rîma moved to join them. Their female captor blocked her path, masked head bowed respectfully.

"You have higher duties than prayer, majesty." When Rîma hesitated, the woman set a palm against her shoulder – not laying hands on the principessa was clearly not a rule that bound everyone – and gestured to the palace. "You've kept your grandfather waiting long enough."

Rîma's brow furrowed as one seeking to remember something gone just beyond reach.

"Rîma . . ." Damant started forward.

"Do not lay hands—"

". . . on the principessa. Yes, you've made that clear."

The woman gazed up at him. "You are concerned and it does you honour." This time her voice held a shadow of approval. "But there is nothing to fear. Today is a great day, and the king is waiting."

She gestured towards the palace. Rîma nodded slowly and began her descent. With no better option to commend itself, Damant followed.

Thirty-Four

"By Nyssa's grace, Prytaxis Sumaramadîq of the Inner Court requests an audience with His Majesty Eskamarîand, King of Tadamûr and protector of its traditions."

The usher spoke in stentorian tones, but his proclamation struck Damant as passionless, a man recounting by rote words that were so ingrained he barely even noticed them any longer.

As he brought the heel of his staff down a third time, it slipped from his gloved grasp. It struck the marble floor with a clang and a clatter that said much for its warped state, as did the slow resignation with which the usher stooped to reclaim it, as if the error had been committed so many times it was no longer worthy of haste or embarrassment and had instead become part of the ritual.

Eskamarîand sat so motionless as for it to not be immediately apparent if he was awake, asleep or else had passed into Nyssa's care even without the assistance of Rîma's now-missing sword. His golden mask – alone of those Damant had yet seen, it was fashioned in a handsome, regal likeness akin to those of Tadamûr's many statues, rather than a blank, androgynous face – offered up nothing of the man behind. His shimmering robes of gold-chased violet and azure did not so much as twitch. His head remained level and steady, no small feat given that he bore a heavy gold circlet as well as his mask.

Nor were the king's six guards – three stationed beneath each of the high windows either side of the time-worn carpet of the throne's dais – given to undue motion. Damant found it easier to keep his eyes on the king than on the guards' unblinking silver death's-heads. They reminded him entirely too much of koilos, but then he supposed that they should. Khalad had borrowed so much from Tadamûr and the other Hidden Cities, whether knowingly but forgotten, or through coincidences too impossible to describe.

Only the court's scribe, hunched over a lectern set beside a cob-webbed tapestry, showed industry, his silver-fletched quill scritching back and forth across parchment as he made dutiful record of events. It took no great imagination to determine where that record would end up. The palace's outer rooms had been thick with shelves and alcoves burdened down with scrolls.

"Majesty." Sumaramadîq – the woman who'd led Damant and the others down from Tulloq – bowed low, the gesture so slow as to be excruciating. "A glad day. Principessa Eskamarîma has returned to us."

The gladness in her heart didn't make it as far as her voice. However reserved Rîma was in speech and motion, she was a riot of activity compared to her peers. Or she had been.

"Returned to you?" Hadîm snorted and spread his hands wide. "She's here because *I* brought her to you, as contracted."

"She brought herself," snapped Damant, too weary and frustrated to worry over courtly decorum he'd no way of knowing. "You're nothing but a cur lapping at a blood trail."

For her part, Rîma said nothing.

Hadîm sneered. "All prey who come to the trap too soon curse their fortune rather than the hunter's wiles." Bold words for a man surprised that Rîma had come to Tulloq under her own volition, but Damant supposed he'd not be the first bounty-hunter to embellish his deeds. "The principessa is here, as requested, and I—"

"Be silent." For all that Eskamarîand didn't move a muscle, his whole sense shifted, his attention fixed on Hadîm. "You have not been gone so long from this city that your braggartry has grown welcome, Arzahalhadîm."

The longer form of his name didn't go unnoticed by Damant, who'd already marked the similarity between Eskamarîma and Eskamarîand. A blending of family and given name, perhaps, distilled to Rîma and Rîand as Arzahalhadîm resolved to Hadîm? He recalled such conventions being common in Kaldos, where by meagre coincidence the rank of prytaxis denoted a trusted councillor, much as castellan did in more civilised climes.

Hadîm went rigid and recovered himself to a deep bow, arms stiff at his sides. "My apologies. Majesty."

"Does he speak truly, Prytaxis Sumaramadîq? asked Rîand.

Sumaramadîq – or simply Madîq if Damant had read the convention of names correctly – rose from her bow. "We took them from the Wasteland together. How they came to be there, and why, I have no knowledge."

The Wasteland. The words clearly did not merely encompass the hills around Tulloq, but the world the folk of Tadamûr had left behind. Insulting at the best of times, but especially so given the condition of their city.

"It matters not. The principessa has returned." Rîand rose from the throne, not in the creaking, shuddering manner his appearance suggested, but in that of a man of middle years. Whatever malaise assailed Tadamûr, it touched no heavier on its king than it did on Rîma. "How long has it been, Granddaughter? How long since you abandoned your people. Since you abandoned me?"

Rîma stared at the floor. "I . . . I'm sorry, majesty." Though the timbre of her voice was unchanged, she sounded a stranger: uncertain, almost diffident – the sharp edges of her personality smoothed away beneath the grindstone of her people's collective will. "A selfish whim."

Rîand set gloved fingers beneath her chin and raised her eyes to the regal, impassive stare of his mask. "And you return willingly to your duty?"

336

"With all my heart."

Damant's own heart sank deeper into murky waters. For all that Rîma had warned him that returning home might change her, the speed and ferocity of that transformation set him on edge.

"Let her go," he growled.

Madîq's vice-like grip clamped across his shoulder. "You will not address the king without leave."

Hadîm shook his head and chuckled softly.

Eyes watering, Damant offered a curt nod and was released. Rîand withdrew his hand from Rîma's chin. At once, she returned her gaze to the floor. The throne room's temperature, already less than warm, dropped another degree as the hollow sweep of the king's mask regarded Damant.

"This cinderblood is your pet, Granddaughter?"

"Damant is my friend. He is to bear witness."

Rîand nodded. "Then he shall, so long as he behaves." His gaze tracked to the ragged stump of Rîma's wrist. "Your injury. How did it happen?"

Hadîm's chuckle faded. "An accident, majesty."

"Oh yes," said Damant dourly. "His sword just happened to sever her hand. Very careless."

Red crowded his vision as Madîq gave his shoulder another warning squeeze. Hadîm's venomous glance made the pain entirely worthwhile.

"You know how she can be," said Hadîm. "The contract didn't specify unharmed, only alive. I didn't want to take chances. She bore Amakala's sword."

Rîand flinched, his shimmering robes scattering light across stone walls and stained-glass panels. "Where is the sword now?"

"I have ordered it to be recovered," said Madîq. "Her hand should be salvageable with the proper care."

Rîand took the stump of Rîma's right wrist in his hands. His eyes never left hers. "If not, my child, we will have the artisans fashion you another, worthy of your station."

"Thank you, Grandfather." Though her eyes were downcast, her voice held emotion for the first time. Not apprehension or resentment, but warmth. Whatever returning to Tadamûr had done to her, it was accelerating in Rîand's proximity. What if her creeping transformation wasn't the result of collective will at all, but that of a single, oppressive individual?

His eyes still on Rîma's, Rîand snapped his fingers. A guard jerked to wakefulness from beside the throne. "Arzahalhadîm worries over his reward. See that he receives it."

Hadîm offered a low bow. "A pleasure to serve, majesty." Falling into step behind the guard, he offered Damant a mocking smile. "Such a brief pleasure."

Damant glowered. "And all of it yours."

"Naturally." Hadîm followed the guard from the throne room.

Absorbed by whatever he saw in Rîma's expression, Rîand didn't so much as look up. "As for the rest, I see no reason for delay, do you, Granddaughter?"

She smiled. She actually *smiled*. Not her customarily barely-there curl of the lips, but a broad expression of pure joy that scoured away Damant's final hope that she was any longer the same woman. Decades slipped away from her ageless face, gladness restoring a measure of youth even last breath could not provide. "Of course not, Grandfather."

"Good."

Rîand spoke with such fervency that for the briefest of moments Damant *almost* felt sorry for the ancient king. How long had he been waiting to die, unable to do so because of Rîma's absence? But sympathy suffocated beneath the weight of his own failure. He'd been every inch as useless to Rîma as she'd predicted, and now the fate she'd feared had come to pass.

He clenched his teeth. No. He wouldn't accept that. That was his younger self talking, who'd borne witness to Tyzanta's injustices and done nothing. He wasn't that man any more. There was still a chance. All he had to do was find it.

Rîand stepped away from Rîma. Robes swirling about his feet, he halted before Damant and offered the very slightest of bows. "As my granddaughter's friend and witness, the hospitality of Tadamûr is open to you ... so long as I have your word that you will behave as a guest should. Will you give it?"

Damant straightened his back and squared his shoulders, summoning the spirit of parade grounds past to the unhappy present. "Of course, majesty," he lied.

Thirty-Five

"**B**lessed Nyssa, guide your servant. Soothe his troubled heart, so that his soul might serve you."

Even now, supposedly alone in the candlelit gloom of the Abidtzal chamber save for the golden statue of Nyssa Benevolas wreathed in a necklace of black-and-white mandevilla flowers, Zaran Ossed's tone was more performance than prayer. Each syllable wavered with such plummy vibrato that only the most cynical onlooker could have doubted he was a righteous man.

Three days of fasting and Abidtzal confession was traditional for those due to join the Qabirarchi Council, thereafter to spend the rest of their life singing worship to Nyssa and advising the Eternity King of her desires. Ossed had been there a full week. Clearly he felt himself in need of more purification than was the norm.

"Send me a sign, Oh Nyssa," he murmured, his pallid, fleshy hands clasped together and his eyes clamped tight. "I beg you."

Entrance lines didn't get much better than that. Kat brushed aside the velvet drape and stepped around the slatted wooden screen.

"Greetings, hierarch."

Ossed jolted, his lavish white and gold robes shimmering. There was a great deal of cloth *to* shimmer – a lifetime of service hadn't been without self-indulgence. Rising from his knees, he spun around, grey-brown beard bristling.

"How dare you interrupt my confession, novitiate?" His outrage echoed around the chamber's dressed-stone walls.

Kat folded her arms. "You came to confess, didn't you?" She slipped her dagger from the sleeve of her stolen robes. "I'm here to help."

"You dare threaten one of the Qabirarchi Council?"

Fortunately not, as neither the Supreme Qabirarch of the Alabastran Church nor her advisory council ever showed their faces. Not even Tatterlain had met anyone who'd made it deep enough inside their silvered palace to catch a glimpse. But it was still three days until the eve of Saint Marindra's Descension, and thus Ossed was three days away from investiture.

"But you're not among their hallowed ranks yet, are you, your eminence?" Kat crooked a sly smile, determined to enjoy the moment. "Having second thoughts?"

Moving with a speed unexpected from so sedentary a man, Ossed lunged for the chamber door and wrenched it open. Three custodians in the green-flecked black of House Yesabi blocked his path, one with the heavy braided collar of a templar in dedicated service to Alabastra. None wore masks. Secrecy was discouraged so deep in the spire, and thus close to Nyssa's Obsidium Palace in the Stars Below.

"Where are my guards?" hissed Ossed.

The cool gloom devoured the words. Seventy yards of stone tunnel separated the Abidtzal chamber from the vast central cavern, followed by fifty paces of a wooden bridge that was little more than two ropes and a run of creaking planks. Finally, another fifty yards of stone causeway to the double-helical spiral of the Penitent's Stair whereby pilgrims made shuffling descent to the Hallow Caves. A score of other bridges – each leading to its own Abidtzal chamber – projected from the semi-enclosed columns of the Penitent's Stair like spokes of a mangled, misshapen wheel, no two at the same level.

Even if Ossed's words *had* reached sympathetic ears, they'd likely have gone unheeded. Abidtzal supplicants had a tendency to vanish screaming into the darkness, babbling of voices on the edge of hearing.

341

More than anywhere else in Khalad, folk in the Abidtzal chambers tended to be selective about what they heard.

"Unscheduled shift change." Tatterlain tugged at his templar's collar, which was a hair too tight. "Poor things were dead on their feet. Is there a problem, eminence?"

Standing to Tatterlain's left and not needing to hear the words to enjoy Ossed's discomfort, Yali grinned. The real guards were bound and gagged in an otherwise empty Abidtzal chamber.

Ossed's eyes darted to Tatterlain's other companion. "Yennika? Yennika Bascari? What is this? You have to help me!"

Azra pressed a gloved finger to his lips. "Hush. Yennika's dead. My name's Azra." She patted the shrieker on her belt – inert without the necessary soul-glyph, but Ossed didn't know that. "I'd go back inside."

Yali's heavy-handed shove propelling him on his way, Ossed stumbled back into the chamber. Azra and Yali pressed close behind, forestalling another attempt to run.

Tatterlain grabbed the door handle. "For shame, eminence. Three beautiful women and you the sole subject of their attention?" He shook his head sadly. "You don't know how good you've got it. Don't do anything I wouldn't, ladies."

"That's not exactly a long list," said Kat as Tatterlain closed the door with him on the other side. "Now, eminence . . . about your confession."

Ossed came to an unhappy halt in the middle of the chamber, flanked by wooden lattice screens and Nyssa Benevolas a silent presence to his generous rear. "You'll die on the Golden Stair for this."

Kat shrugged. "You already tried that, remember?"

Ossed frowned.

Yali grinned. ‖I don't think he recognises you.‖

Reasonable enough, as they'd never met. But given that she and Azra had part-demolished Ossed's Xanathros Alabastra, Kat had thought he might have *some* inkling of what she looked like. "Tell me about your work with Terrion Arvish and the Obsidium Cult."

"How dare you!" Ossed spluttered with just the right mix of

confusion and defiance. "I am a hierarch of Alabastra! I do not consort with apostates."

Yali rolled her eyes. Reliant as she was on visual cues, there was no one better for recognising a lie. Confirmation that Kat didn't need in this particular case. With the bulk of Yarvid's journal now translated, she'd an embarrassment of information linking the hierarch to her father's clandestine researches. That same information had proven beyond doubt that her father had been neither dupe nor hostage to the cult's desires, but a willing participant.

She shoved Ossed up against the statue and set her dagger to his throat. "You provided funds and access to the Great Library. You warned them when official scrutiny drew too close. My father trusted you, and now he's dead." She forbore from clarifying that Hargo Rashace had almost certainly been responsible for that. Even fake anger was leverage. "I should think very carefully before lying to me again."

His eyes went wide. "Father? . . . You're Katija Arvish. You destroyed my Xanathros!"

"I had help."

Ossed stared frantically past her. "Yennika, I beg you—"

"I told you, Yennika's dead," said Azra. "And the only reason we're not playing a game called 'hide the dagger' is because Kat told me I'm not allowed."

"I am *not* part of the Obsidium Cult," moaned Ossed.

"Then why protect them?" Kat flexed sudden stiffness from the fingers of her left hand. "Or should I give you to Azra?"

Azra lowered her lips to Ossed's ear. "Don't tell her anything." Her voice dropped, huskier and sweeter than before. "Please?"

"Last chance," said Kat. "Why were you helping them?"

"B-b-because that's how the Voice wanted it!" He clamped his eyes shut. "She wanted to know about their research."

Kat exchanged a glance with Azra. "The Voice? Isdihar Diar is a child."

Ossed's cheeks gained a modicum of colour and his voice a dash of

343

propriety. "She speaks for the Eternity King. Her age is neither here nor there."

"She was sharp enough when I met her," said Azra. "It might not even have been her idea."

It was said that the Voice heard the Eternity King's will at all times. Any scheme of hers could have begun with her withered grandsire.

Ossed scowled. "I am not in the habit of lying."

Which was itself almost certainly a lie. "Say I believe you," said Kat. "Why was she so interested in what my father was up to?"

"The Voice is not in the habit of explaining herself to hierarchs."

The question didn't need an answer. Though she'd been slow to recognise it, Kat's aetherios tattoo had the potential to make her a demigod. Most of her life she'd squandered it on petty scores and games, silencing hestics and persuading motics to motion, but at Athenoch she'd seized control of a koilos army. Of course the Voice – and the Eternity King – would be interested in such power.

Yali snorted ‖Why not lock the cultists up and 'persuade' them to talk?‖

"Now that's a good question." Kat ignored the twin glares of consternation from Ossed and Azra, neither of whom had any Simah. "Alabastra doesn't usually worry over torturing troublemakers to get what they want. Nor does the Eternity King. Did they really think they couldn't get a bunch of old men to give up their secrets?"

Ossed glowered, but said nothing.

"You still don't get it, do you, darling?" said Azra. "The Obsidium Cult is a pressure valve, just like Vallant was. Drawing in malcontents and keeping them somewhere in plain sight."

Ossed still in her grip, Kat rounded on Azra. "You knew?"

"Of course not. But I know how Khalad works. One plus one can only ever equal two."

Kat slammed Ossed against the statue. Black-and-white mandevilla petals fell like rain from Nyssa's necklace. "You let my father rack up debt even while aiding him?"

344

"I didn't *let* him do anything," said Ossed. "Dinars flowed through his hands, he never said to where. He wasn't the trusting sort."

Of course Ossed wouldn't consider something so mundane as her father's gambling or her mother's dependency on last breath, both of them "little people" problems. "Did you discover what he was working towards?"

"No. And once he was gone, his fellow conspirators vanished."

"And have since turned up dead," said Kat. "The Voice's work?"

"The cult's."

"They're covering their tracks." Azra shrugged and drifted towards the chamber's edge. "It's what I'd do."

Kat's heart sank. "Then the trail's cold."

||Not necessarily,|| signed Yali. ||He knows more than he's telling.||

Kat noted nothing save the same mixture of self-preservation and outrage. But if Yali saw something more, there was something more to find. She met Ossed eye to eye. "Tell me the rest."

"I don't know what you mean."

A catch in his voice betrayed him. A flash of triumph warmed Kat's stomach. "Azra? I think his eminence wants to play 'hide the dagger'. Try to leave him capable of talking."

Azra sashayed closer, her poise transmuting the humble custodian's robes to the most glamorous of attire and her wicked smile portending nothing good. "No promises, darling." She unsheathed her dagger and kissed the blade with perfect lips "You know I get carried away."

Ossed blanched, doubtless recalling Yennika Bascari's ruthlessness. "No, wait! The cult killed them, but we impounded everything they missed. Papers. Books. Everything."

That explained the guard outside Yarvid's house. The Eternity King's seal upon the door.

"And?" Kat pressed her dagger against the fleshy folds beneath Ossed's beard. "Where is it kept?"

"I don't know. The Voice won't let anyone else see it." He tried to

345

back away, but Nyssa's statue left him nowhere to go. "That's all I know, I swear . . . Please!"

"I—"

A wave of spasms washed over Kat, clenching and squeezing at her arms and legs, her chest. The dagger slipped from her useless fingers. Her knees buckled.

"Kat!" shouted Azra – the last thing she heard before the darkness swallowed everything.

She came groggily to with a kneeling Yali's hand tight around hers and marble flagstones pressing against her spine, cold through the thin novitiate's robes.

Yali squeezed tighter, her face thick with worry. ||Try not to move.|| She signed with one hand, the gestures slower and more awkward than normal. ||Just breathe.||

Azra glanced up from Ossed, now kneeling before her with his arm twisted up between his shoulder blades and her dagger at his throat. "I'm all for surprises, darling, but maybe something less dramatic next time?" Aghast expression belied jovial tone.

Rebelling body once more under control, Kat forced a thin smile. ||"It'll pass. They always do."||

||What do you mean, 'they always do'?|| Yali's frown changed character. ||What haven't you been telling us?||

Kat's gut lurched. This was just about the worst possible time for this conversation. ||It doesn't matter.||

Yali fixed her with a no-nonsense stare. ||It *really* does, honest and true.||

Kat stumbled to her feet, coursing with shame. No choice but to come clean, not now.

Raised voices flared outside the chamber. The door burst open. A copper-skinned and brown-haired young man in shabby silk robes stumbled in at the point of Tatterlain's sword.

Kat scooped her dagger from the floor, regaining what composure she could along the way. "What's this?"

346

Tatterlain kicked his captive's knees away and back-heeled the door shut. "*This* is a little idiot who wouldn't take no for an answer. Demanded to see the hierarch. It was let him in or kill him."

Azra rolled her eyes. "So kill him. What's the matter, not—?"

"Esram!" Ossed's eyes widened. "I told you not to disturb my meditations!"

"They're going to kill her," Esram gasped. "The Voice."

"Impossible!"

"I've been telling you for months, they're better organised than you think. Their agents have reassigned half the duty custodians. Most of the rest are probably dead by now. Surely you noticed how quiet it is out there?"

"How could I? I've been in here for days."

But Kat hadn't. In hindsight, getting into the Abidtzal chambers had been just a bit too easy, even with Tatterlain and Azra's connections and a fortune in bribes.

"Who?" Azra jerked Ossed's forearm an inch higher, provoking a howl of pain. "*Who* are better organised than you think?"

"The Obsidium Cult," moaned Ossed. "Esram watches them for me."

Azra shook her head. "They'll need more than organisation. I've never known her go anywhere without hundreds of redcloaks."

"Half of Zariqaz is watching the Voice distribute coins in the grand plaza from behind a row of spears, but it's her double." Esram's words tumbled breathlessly. "Isdihar Diar is in the Hallow Caves, commemorating her mother's birthday. I already spoke to Templar Javitra. She's mustering reinforcements, but until they arrive the Voice has no more than a dozen guards with her. None of them will listen to me. I thought they'd listen to you, Uncle, or at least your custodians. But I expect they're already dead," he finished, his tone surprisingly acidic for someone held captive by their supposed murderers.

"A dozen bodyguards when mingling with pilgrims?" said Tatterlain. "Sounds like a good way to lose her."

"Would you know the Voice without her robes and make-up?"

said Esram.

"My dear fellow, even I don't move in those kinds of circles." Only Tatterlain could sound aggrieved about something like that.

"That's my point! And if she dies—"

"The Eternity King will need another voice," said Kat. "He'll survive."

"Please." Esram turned his hollow-cheeked stare on her. "You have to help her! She's the *Voice*."

"Against an army of religious fanatics? I don't think so."

"You don't need to worry about the kathari. Just Tanith."

Kat blinked, certain she'd misheard. "Tanith?"

"Yes, she's terrifying! I've seen her in action."

"Haven't we all." Through supreme effort, Kat kept uncertainty from her face. So Tanith was mixed up with the Obsidium Cult? *Kiasta*. The assassin Ossed had mentioned – it could only have been her. Like father, like daughter, apparently. "She was one of them all along, wasn't she?"

"Not when Yennika knew her," said Azra. "My life on it. This is new."

"You have to help the Voice," snarled Ossed. "You owe it to the Eternity King."

Kat rounded on him, glad to have an outlet for her frustrations. "I owe him nothing! I owe *you* nothing. If I'd known you'd been meddling in my family, I'd have done more than blow up your damn xanathros. I still might."

Ossed glowered, fear ebbing into anger as duty asserted itself over self-interest. "You want your father's research? The Voice is the only one who knows where it is."

Thirty-Six

T he musty air thickened with chanted prayer as pilgrims shuffled towards the statues of Nyssa. Her guises of Benevolas and Iudexas, matriarch and judge, stood tall as a temple roof, their brows scraping the stalactites of the Hallow Caves and their golden skin shining in the reflected light of a thousand lumani lanterns set upon rock ledges or borne by faithful hands. Those faithful came from all walks of life, betrayed by clothing and posture, the ragged and the rich shoulder to shoulder in the candlelight as the procession snaked across the plateaus and pathways of the cavern floor. Here they were equals in Nyssa's sight, humbled by their need to walk the chamber in which Caradan Diar had once received the goddess' commandment to bring order to lawless Khalad.

The press of bodies was nothing to the torment of so many delectable souls in close proximity. Tanith's senses swam on clouds of lavender and honeysuckle, her daemon-half keening its frustration. Need shuddered through the pit of her stomach with every footfall, held in check only by the knowledge that while there may have been quicker routes to the Deadwinds, there were none so certain as indulging herself in plain view of so many.

Her glamour sang beneath the stalactites as she advanced. Milling pilgrims receded from her path like a retreating tide. Some wore befuddled frowns as they strove to make sense of their own behaviour. Most gave no sign that they'd noticed anything amiss.

The thrill almost drowned out Tanith's hunger. Hundreds of souls, and she was touching them all, nudging, guiding . . . dominating. Her black skelder's garb and braided hair were a poor fit for such glory – better to have come gowned and golden, so that her beauty might have captivated as readily as her will. For the first time she truly understood why Ardoc had bade her pursue abstinence for so long. If there were only a way of living for ever in that rapturous space between hunger and satiation, who knew what she might achieve?

She stared up at the austere, kindly beauty of Nyssa Benevolas and the grim stare of Nyssa Iudexas. Was this what it was to be her herald? To instil love and fear and in so doing rise above the common masses? At Athenoch, she'd spoken to Kat of dwelling in a palace of silks, admired and courted by all. This promised something more, something better. A life filled with breathless adoration because she willed it to be so.

If only she weren't so damn *hungry*.

But . . . could she learn to ignore that? To subsist not on souls, but on the worship of the enthralled? She licked her lips, adrift once more in that silken palace, basking in helpless reverence. With an effort, she shook the vision away. Ardoc had sent her here for a reason.

She cast about the cavern, searching for those who didn't quite belong.

Three House Yesabi templars standing watch near the votive bowl at the base of the plinth's short, straight stair, tasked by their Alabastran sponsors to watch over the statues. Six more custodians, their robes betraying allegiance to various houses – including Rashace – stood dotted through the crowd, acting as indiscreet bodyguards for wealthy pilgrims. A dozen redcloaks, the honour guard of the Hallow Caves, their long spears held at attention. And then the subtler standouts. The guilty stumbles of those seeking forgiveness for transgression against goddess or kin. And of course the two dozen or so kathari scattered about, their white robes unremarkable with their masks not yet donned.

There.

350

An unassuming bronze-skinned girl knelt at the foot of Nyssa Benevolas, her unbound jet-black hair draped across the shoulders of a scarlet robe whose obvious inexpense sat ill with her prideful posture. Description alone wasn't enough. Tanith marked three others just like her, save in the detail of clothing. There was never a shortage of fire-bloods in the Hallow Caves – they'd more to confess than cinderbloods.

She turned her attention to those close by. Two men in skelder's garb. A woman wearing a banker's chain and layered ormesta robes. A lithe young woman in a brightly coloured Kaldosi dancer's shawl. A near-identical pair of heavyset toughs with the sun-bronzed skin of sailriders. All too alert to be what they appeared. All of them moving with the confidence of predators.

She glanced over her shoulder at the nearest kathari and offered the slightest nod. Careful to keep her tread measured, she struck out through the sea of pilgrims, angling towards the statues. The crowd parted, their subconscious minds unable to resist her daemon-half's influence.

The closer she came, the more Tanith marvelled at how different the Voice looked when freed of her finery. Beneath the trappings, she could have been anyone. Just how many times had Isdihar Diar walked the streets of her kingdom, unrecognised and unremarked?

That she *was* the Voice, Tanith no longer doubted. In fact, she grew more certain of it as she ascended the stairs, though she couldn't say why. More troubling was the canker of doubt. Bereft of her finery, Isdihar Diar looked so *young*. Younger than Tanith could remember being, save in the abstract. A waif well in need of her protectors, for all the power she wielded. One, if Ardoc's information was true – and it was seldom otherwise – who had come to the Hallow Caves to remember her mother.

Could she really murder such a girl, even for Ardoc?

Even monsters had lines they didn't cross, didn't they?

She shook away her doubts and slipped her hand beneath her coat's folds to a concealed dagger. None knew better than she that merely *looking* innocent did not make one so. Whether you believed that the Voice channelled the will of the Eternity King or made her own decisions, she was complicit in every death, every injustice and every act of cruelty. Even had her death not been Ardoc's will, it would have been recompense for Nyssa knew how many souls. Childhood was no excuse and certainly no shield.

Lulled by glamour, the faux-banker spared Tanith barely a glance as she passed, head bowed. One of the maybe-sailriders looked her up and down, more interested in her body than her intent; the other ignored her completely That left the dancer and the two skelder-garbs just beyond the statue, lingering in the short passageway leading back to the Penitent's Stair ... and of course Isdihar kneeling in between, her eyes closed and her lips moving in soft prayer as the other pilgrims filed past.

"Mother..." she murmured, her voice holding just a trace of a north-land burr as she laid a perfect black-and-white mandevilla blossom atop those already present. "Why did ye nae warn me? Did ye love me so little?"

Three steps lower than Isdihar, with no other save the second oblivious sailrider between them, Tanith hesitated. The words could have been her own. The sentiment doubly so.

No. Ardoc was relying on her.

She clung tight to her brief memory of Jaia's parents, killed when the redcloaks stormed Qosm. Her dagger, still concealed, slid readily from its sheath. She returned the second sailrider's oblivious nod, felt his will soften beneath hers and continued on.

Isdihar rose. With one last untranslatable glance up at the twin Nyssas, she turned around.

Tanith kept her head low as the Voice's gaze fell upon her, felt the first pressure as her glamour pitted itself against the girl's will.

Her head snapped back under an impact akin to running into a wall. Punch-drunk and swaying, she staggered to keep her balance, the hubbub and lights of the Hallow Caves blurring in a riot of light and sound before snapping back into focus.

352

And three steps up, Isdihar Diar, Voice of the Eternity King, extended a perfect fingernail in her direction and spoke a single word with the unconcernedness of a girl commenting on the weather.

"Daemon."

Tanith's world shot sideways. Her back crunched on marble, steel shining above as one of the ersatz sailriders landed atop her, brandishing a serrated blade in one hand and clamping the other about her throat.

Spluttering for breath, she rammed her dagger into his belly. Blood rushed over her fingers. As the sailrider howled, she locked an elbow about his neck, her knees about his waist and *heaved*. The world lurched once more as he pitched down a step, unwittingly dragging Tanith with him. Startled pilgrims scattered from their path. The sailrider's head cracked on stone, and then Tanith rose up, her own dagger in one hand, his in the other, and bloody from the waist down.

"*Abdon Nyssa ivohê!*" she shouted.

Kathari pulled on their masks and flung themselves at custodians and redcloaks with concealed blades, claiming spear and sword as their victims fell. The cavern filled with screams and rushing feet, panic spreading as lanterns smashed and bodies were trampled underfoot.

The surviving sailrider flung himself at Tanith and died beside his fellow, his twin's serrated dagger buried in his throat from a careful throw. The faux-banker scraped a wicked Kaldosi shamshir from beneath her layered robes and collapsed to her knees, weeping crimson tears as Tanith's backhanded slash took her eyes. And the Voice . . .

The Voice was nothing more than echoing footsteps on the stairs behind the statue, lost in a panicked crowd. Sighing, Tanith broke the banker's fingers with a stomp of her boot, claimed the now-mistressless shamshir, and ran in pursuit.

Thirty-Seven

Pandemonium broke out just as Kat's run brought her to the far side of the bridge, Azra on her heels. Battle raged across the Abidtzal spoke-bridges and on the Penitent's Stair, white-robed and black-masked cultists trading steel and flame with redcloaks and custodians. Shrieker flames burst to brief light on impact with bridge timbers or time-worn stone. Pilgrims stampeded for the Penitent's Stair, for cover, for sagging bridges barely wide enough for two to stand together, for the sturdy doors of the Abidtzal chambers beyond, for anything that could save them from the unfolding madness, their hollow footsteps adding to the deafening clamour.

"You sure we're on the right side?" asked Azra, her eyes gleaming and a smile tugging at her lips.

Kat scowled at another plan gone to cinders. What were the odds? "No chance we're getting out through all this, and if the redcloaks take us, you can bet we'll catch a piece of the blame. We save the Voice, maybe we save ourselves." Breathing hard, she leaned against the low stone wall whose ritual carving had long since worn away. "Where's Esram?"

||Stayed with his uncle.|| Yali signed stiffly, lips taut. ||I guess the Voice is only important enough for *us* to die for.||

Tatterlain shrugged. "If I were spying on the Obsidium Cult, I'd keep my head down right now as well. They're certainly making a mess."

354

Kat pointed to the ring-shaped landing where the Penitent's Stair met their bridge's causeway. ||"We split up. If you find the Voice, help keep—"|| She yelped and shied away as a stray shrieker shot blasted acrid stone splinters from the wall. ||"Help keep her alive. And don't get killed."||

Tatterlain started along the causeway, custodian scimitar drawn. "I find that last part especially appealing."

Yali hesitated and followed.

"Lot of bridges around here." Azra cocked her head. "You're not going to give me a hard time if someone – or several someones – falls off?"

"Leave them breathing," Kat replied. "We've got enough enemies, don't you think?"

Azra blinked. "You're serious? Now?"

"Are you saying you can't cope without killing?"

Azra shot her the most old-fashioned of old-fashioned looks. "You really think that will work, don't you?"

"Yes."

She sighed and shrugged. "The things we do for love."

Her eyes on the next causeway down, which through accident of the cavern's anarchic design ran parallel and almost directly below, Kat barely heard her. A scarlet-robed girl with jet-black hair scrambled along the bridge's bucking slats towards the maybe-safety of an Abidtzal chamber, a knot of redcloaks and skelder-garbs forming a wall of flesh and silk behind her. Shrieker shots flashed out. A redcloak fell, his chest ablaze. Other shots charred the bridge's ropes or sputtered against stone. Two other redcloaks dropped back, swords drawn, to challenge the golden-haired woman running towards them from the direction of the Penitent's Stair.

Tanith.

She pounced one of the redcloaks to the ground, left her dagger in his chest, and snatched up his sword to cast the other screaming over the causeway's edge. Without missing a beat, she sprang away after her prey.

Kat held out her hand to Azra. "Give me your sword."

"You've made your point, darling. You don't need to—" Kat wrested the scimitar from her grip. "Hey!"

She ran back along the bridge. A vertigo-dizzied glance picked out Tanith a dozen feet below. Trying not to think about the distant cavern floor or the speed with which she'd meet it if vertigo or omen rot roused themselves to spitefulness, she launched out over the edge, and plunged.

A heart-wrenching moment of freefall lasted long enough to re-examine recent choices and find them wanting. Her shins slammed into Tanith's shoulders. The world spun end over end and righted itself with a scraping thud that left Kat breathless and face down on the bridge's creaking slats, sword still in hand. Inch by painful inch, dizzied by every shift and sway in the timbers beneath her, she clambered to her feet between Tanith and the Abidtzal end of the rocking bridge.

Inevitably, Tanith had already reached hers. Equally inevitable was her furious scowl as she brushed a hand towards the cultists still on the stairward causeway, motioning them to stay back. "Out of my way, Kat."

Kat risked a glance over her shoulder. The Voice and her guards were already off the bridge and into the tunnel. "I need her alive."

"And I need her dead."

She held her ground, her knuckles whitening on her sword. Had she really thought she might sway Tanith with reason? Had she been thinking at all? "Without her, there's no hope of a cure. Not for either of us."

Tanith flinched. Her sapphire eyes turned icy. "Nyssa loves me just as I am. So do I."

She lunged, her sword faster than Kat's eye could follow. But long hours training with Rîma had taught her that she didn't *need* to see the sword, only the arm that guided it. Her parry was instinct, the scrape of steel almost as surprising to her as it plainly was to Tanith, whose scowl slackened as the blades parted.

"You're faster."

Was that a note of approval? "I'm trying to be better."

"Try harder."

Tanith's sword flashed out again, more ferocious than before.

Kat's pride wilted at the realisation that the first blow had been a test. She chained clumsy parry to clumsy parry, all the while giving ground up the gentle slope as the creaking bridge rose to meet the tunnel causeway.

Her foot skidded on a plank's outer edge, her boot sole connecting only with darkness. Leveraging what little purchase the other offered, she flung herself at Tanith. The point of her sword flashed past her sister's guard, slicing the flesh of her cheek to the bone. Magenta and indigo flame oozed from the wound and rippled away.

"Enough!" shouted Tanith, the word ragged with frustration, and buried a fist in Kat's gut.

Kat's lungs emptied. Whooping for breath, she doubled over and fell to one knee, sword slipping from nerveless fingers.

Tanith brushed absent-mindedly at the wound on her cheek. Flame hissed between her fingers "Just stop it. I don't want to hurt you." She blinked, surprised by her own words.

Still shuddering for breath, Kat reached up with trembling fingers. "Tanith ... please ..."

Tanith strode on without a backwards glance, breaking into a run as soon as her feet hit stone.

The centre of the left-hand guide rope, charred by a stray shrieker shot and tortured to breaking point by the impact of Kat's fall, frayed apart in a shower of blackened fibres.

Kat yelped and stumbled after Tanith, the planks twisting away beneath her feet.

She was still half a dozen paces from the bridge's end when the second rope snapped with a whipcrack report. Heart yammering, she grabbed at the slatted planks as gravity reached up to claim her.

Straining fingertips found purchase on a plank's rising edge. Her shoulders screamed as they took her weight. Her feet kicked at empty air. The remnants of the bridge swung out *under* the causeway, then reversed as equilibrium took hold, leaving her dangling from the world's most impractical rope ladder.

She glanced below, praying for another Abidtzal bridge close enough to risk the drop. The nearest was at least thirty feet below, and worse, fifteen to her left. The cavern floor was lost in the darkness.

Eyes directly ahead to cheat vertigo and shoulders afire, she took the strain on her left hand and reached up with her right. Fingertips found the top of the next plank.

They slipped free as she pulled herself up.

A thin whimper escaping her lips, she spun outward, pivoting on her left hand's tenuous grip until she was facing almost directly back towards the other half of the causeway. The pair of cultists on the stair-ward causeway had their backs to her, their shriekers trained on three figures running headlong towards them, Yali in the lead.

"Down!" Azra tackled Yali to the ground, a scream of agony parting her lips as the shot meant for the girl turned her shoulder to flame.

Tatterlain vaulted them both and shoulder-barged a cultist over the edge. The other abandoned his shrieker and reached for his sword. As the chime of steel rang out, Azra, her left shoulder charred and her face tight with pain, crawled to the causeway's end.

"Kat! Hold on!"

"Keep those great ideas coming!" Kat twisted back around, the fingers of her right hand finding desperate purchase beside those of her left.

Her left wrist gave a warning twitch.

Her heart, already racing, kicked up another notch.

No. Not now.

The muscles of her left arm convulsed as the spasm spread. Her fingers, already numb, slipped from the plank, her entire arm leaden and unresponsive, a weight dragging her down. She gasped as the spasms spread to her chest, hot needles prickling her lungs. The sensation raced across her spine to her right shoulder. The texture of the plank faded beneath her right fingertips.

358

"Kat!" Azra's desperate shout echoed across the lumani-lit darkness. "KAT!"

Azra's desperate shout drew Tanith's gaze back to the gaping void between the two causeways and the cluster of horrified faces.

She skidded to a halt, torn between the commotion at the broken bridge and the sight of the Voice running headlong along the tunnel to the Abidtzal chamber. She could catch her, but only if she kept running.

Ardoc had ordered the Voice's death.

He'd given Tanith a home. He loved her as her own father never had.

She didn't owe Kat anything. Kat had brought it on herself by interfering.

Kat was her sister.

Enna's words, offered in the darkness so many nights before, danced across her thoughts. *You'll not resent the men and women you didn't kill, but you* will *regret those you didn't save.*

She growled them away. Enna was a traitor. What did her opinions matter?

Kiasta.

Shrieking frustration at her own stupidity, Tanith ran headlong for the bridge. Halfway there, the Abidtzal chamber door boomed shut behind her.

Her eyelids too heavy to keep open, Kat pinched them shut and put everything she had into keeping her numbing fingers locked around the plank. Every breath was a shuddering, heaving labour. Nyssa help her, but all she wanted to do was *sleep*. To just let go. Let it all go.

Her fingers slipped away. At least, she thought they did. They no longer felt part of her.

Gravity took her in its majestic grasp, and pulled.

An arm wended around her waist, pinning her to the makeshift ladder.

"Don't you skrelling dare," hissed a guttural voice.

Gravity, wiser than Kat when it came to fighting hopeless battles, relinquished its claim.

The creaking remnants of the bridge bounced, and Kat was once more in motion, borne upwards by a series of jerking heaves. The spasms receded, taking with them the numbness in her limbs and the hot spikes from her lungs. Her eyelids, no longer heavy as tombstones, flickered open.

"Tanith?" she breathed.

"One more word," her sister replied, brow beaded with sweat, "and I'll drop you."

Planked rung by planked rung, they ascended, Kat pinned to the "ladder" by the arm about her waist, her chin against Tanith's shoulder in an affectionless embrace and the bridge's remains swaying alarmingly.

By the time Tanith dragged her up over the causeway's edge, Kat *almost* had enough control over her own body to rise, but only almost. Giving up, she rolled onto her back, catching a glimpse of a worried Tatterlain at the edge of the far causeway; Azra sitting with her back against the stone wall, pale and shivering, as Yali peeled the charred clothing from her burned shoulder.

The cavern was quieter than before, the panic and tumult faded almost to nothing. Or perhaps it only seemed that way in the face of something more important.

"Why?" It took three gasps for Kat to get the word out.

Breathing hard – amashti or not, carrying twice her own weight during such an ascent had to have been challenging – Tanith clambered to her feet and shot her a look of pure torment. "I don't know." Swaying to and fro, she pressed a hand to her brow. "I don't—"

"There!" Zaran Ossed, a vision of unshakeable authority in white and gold, stalked into sight on the causeway behind Yali and the others, a cluster of redcloaks at his back. "I want them in shackles! All of them!"

Kat's sinking heart took with it the last of her energy. So much for the gratitude of officialdom.

Tanith stared down the tunnel towards the sealed Abidtzal chamber, wearing an achingly woebegone expression.

"Thank you," said Kat.

Tanith rounded on her, face taut. "Don't! Just ..." She sagged. "Just don't."

Backing up as far as the causeway allowed, she launched herself over the wall and out into the darkness. Where she landed, Kat never saw, because in that moment, a darkness of a different kind gathered her to its embrace.

Thirty-Eight

The haven's stalactites spinning above her, Tanith collapsed against the wall and begged Nyssa Iudexas to deliver death.

Not upon her, of course. On the redcloak who'd slashed her thigh to the bone. The custodian whose wild shot had fused the skin across her belly to a wet, crackling mess. Driven to headlong flight from the Hallow Caves by the stream of reinforcements from the surface, she'd had the chance to thank neither for their gifts.

That affront was bad enough. What was worse was that those wounds weren't closing. Even an hour later, they and other harms seeped steadily, wreathing her in an almost-there halo of magenta flame. A sure sign that she needed to feed, and feed soon, if she were to keep her sanity. She could have done so before charming the haven's hestics and entering the haven. Pride hadn't let her. Pride, and fear of further disappointing Ardoc.

Pushing away from the rough brick, she staggered on across the cobbles, ignoring the hushed whispers and pointed fingers of the gathering crowd. The heady scent of their mingling souls thickened in the cool air, tantalising, intoxicating, demanding. The sweetest agony, as temptation forgone always was. In the Hallow Caves, the crowds had parted at the soft insistence of suggestion. Here, they did so with drawn faces.

Daemon.

Tanith didn't see who muttered the word. She couldn't be sure if she'd heard it at all, or had instead conjured it from the worried faces. Until that moment, she'd not understood how much the haven had become her home. No more. It couldn't be now they'd see her as she truly was.

Her toe clipped the edge of a cobblestone, shedding the last of her tenuous balance. Her knees and palms cracked against stone, her wrists jarring as she fought for dignity.

"Won't somebody help me?" she breathed, too weary to marshal the seductress or the ingénue. She was naked without their borrowed confidence. What she wouldn't have given for a friendly face ... but Esram was nowhere to be seen. "I ... thought we were ... family."

No one moved. Tanith snorted humourlessly. They understood, didn't they?

Family was nothing but trouble.

The great guild master's clock chimed for six, its hollow tolls echoing through the caves. Five robed kathari slipped through the crowd and into the small quarantine circle they'd created around Tanith. The foremost gestured at the others to hang back. Boots scuffing puffs of dust from the cobblestones, he strode to Tanith's side and swept his masked gaze across the crowd.

"Have you no shame?" Qolda's stern words echoed no less than the chimes that had preceded them. "She's one of us."

The men and women of the crowd averted their eyes.

He let his gaze linger a moment longer, then squatted beside Tanith, gloved hand reaching for hers. "Come. Ardoc's waiting."

Tanith's shoulder blades prickled. His voice held no more friendliness than when he'd addressed the crowd. But what else was she to do?

She took his hand, cold magenta flames flickering across their linked fingers. Her daemon-half howled its hunger, physical contact only making his soul-scent all the sweeter. She banished it with a grimace, and wondered how much longer she could do so.

"Thank you."

A non-committal grunt his only reply, Qolda hauled her upright.

Two kathari took up position behind them and two ahead. A prisoner's escort. Tanith had been outside the law all her life, more than long enough to recognise such a thing.

Why, when Ardoc already knew what she was? Did he really think she'd so little control as to attack her peers? For all its practicalities, the unspoken accusation hurt. Too weary for anger, she fell back on defiance.

Fine. She'd show him.

Thus as the tiny procession strode off towards the guild master's lodge, Tanith walked with her head held high. She was a Floranz, and Nyssa's herald into the bargain. Let the rest of the cult fear her, so long as Ardoc did not.

He waited alone on the far edge of the lodge's circle of light. Another man might have borne his isolation in his posture or the cast of his brow, but Ardoc had never looked more resolute, a granite statue rather than a man.

Qolda brought Tanith to a halt opposite. Then he and the other kathari melted away into the darkness, taking their sweet, intoxicating soul-scent with them. She didn't see them leave. From the moment she met Ardoc's gaze she found she couldn't look away.

"Ardoc, I—"

"Perhaps you would be so good as to tell me why you disobeyed my instructions?" His voice held none of its customary warmth.

"Disobeyed?" Tanith's own voice cracked. "I nearly died carrying them out."

"I asked for a simple death. A quiet mystery unfolding by candlelight. You turned it into a war. Do you know how many of the faithful died for your mistake?"

She'd seen enough of the bodies to know the tally reached into the dozens. "It wasn't my fault. One look and she knew why I was there."

She sucked down a deep breath. A mistake, for it thickened the rich, heady aroma of Ardoc's soul at the back of her throat, setting fraying nerves abuzz. Her daemon-half rippled beneath her skin with every lavender breath, drawing ever closer to the surface. She felt the light change and looked down. She'd stepped deeper into the circle. She hadn't meant to. Couldn't remember doing so.

She was losing control.

She had to get out of there. To clearer air. To smother her daemon-half.

And yet part of her wanted to stay. Screamed at her to stay.

She clamped her fists tight, no longer sure if she trembled from weariness or desire. Much less which of the two she favoured.

"So Qolda tells me. And you pursued." Ardoc pursed his lips and closed his eyes. "And somehow this slip of a girl, who lives in a life untroubled by effort or exertion, escaped you."

Tanith twitched, her daemon-half gaining ground as she indulged irritation. She'd cut her way through half a dozen of the Voice's protectors before reaching the Penitent's Stair. No one else in the haven could have done that so fast, or so cleanly. But Ardoc expected more of Nyssa's herald, and his disappointment cut deep.

Still, he didn't know that she'd abandoned the pursuit to save Kat. Maybe this was recoverable. Failure was one thing, *wilful* failure another. "As soon as the Voice saw me, it was over. I . . . I did everything I could to recover the situation."

Ardoc nodded, his brow furrowing.

Tanith stifled a soft sigh. He was wavering. He just needed another nudge. Something to give her glamour purchase. She could apologise later, once her failure was forgiven, once he'd given her permission to slake the hunger gnawing at her sanity.

"Father . . . please, you have to believe me."

He crumpled, his chin falling to his chest, the man of stone mortal once more. Tanith felt his will soften beneath her glamour. Hated herself for wielding it against a man who'd only shown her kindness. But it had to be so. She'd no choice.

"I did everything you asked," she murmured, the words catching at the back of her throat. "I'm hungry. I'm *starving*. I need to—"

"How did you return to the haven?" Steel gleamed beneath his soft words.

Tanith blinked. "I . . . Through the chantry gate."

"Which of the watchers let you in?"

Too late, the outline of a trap took shape. What little instinct she had left warned her not to lie. "None of them. I charmed the hestics myself."

"As your sister taught you."

She hesitated. "Yes."

Ardoc's voice hardened. "And just how long have you been coming and going as you please?"

"I thought I wasn't a prisoner!" The defiance was a mistake, she felt it even through the lavender haze, but it was too late now.

His sudden shout echoed across the chamber. "Answer me!"

She flinched. "Just this once, Father. There . . . there was no one at the gate, and . . ." Something deep within her groaned. "Please, I must have something. I can't keep her—"

"The chantry gate was unguarded because its watchers are dead, killed by the same person who betrayed us to Templar Javitra." Ardoc hammered out his words, unstoppable, inevitable. "You really thought that would be enough, didn't you? But the custodium reinforcements arrived too slowly, so you revealed your intent to the Voice and gave her the chance to flee. Very tidy. Very deniable. Or so you thought."

"No!" Tanith's heart and voice creaked. How could he think that? "I tell you she knew me at a glance! She—"

"Don't lie to me! Not now!" Ardoc swallowed, his fists clenching and unclenching as he strove to control his temper. "You turned your back on us. On me. I thought it odd when you spoke so lightly of Enna. Now I understand. You and she were in this together."

"No, I swear." But it was too late. Something had changed between them, she saw it in his eyes, which no longer held any trace of the avuncular paternalism she'd come to know – maybe even love, insofar as she was capable.

"You think I can't hear the lies in your voice?" He tapped at his temple with fore and middle fingers as he ground out the words. "That I can't feel you trying to stifle my doubts? I'm an old man, Tanith, filled with holy purpose. My will is not so easily worn away, even when my heart hangs heavy. I *trusted* you."

She'd done this to herself, she realised, sick to her core. Her half-truths and outright lies. Her attempt to win with glamour when she should have convinced with words.

He stepped into the circle of light. Tanith's head swam with his closeness. Gasping, she doubled over, her daemon-half scratching at her skin. She was so close to the surface now, cold and empty and nothing but desire. For the life of her, she wasn't sure how she was still in control. The benefits of abstinence, perhaps. Abstinence that Ardoc had taught her. Had he ever suspected those lessons would save his life, his immortal soul?

All for nothing if she didn't get away from him.

Now.

Awash in lavender, she stumbled from the circle.

Ardoc snapped his fingers. Something stirred in the darkness. A cold presence Tanith might have noticed before had she been fully herself. A koilos stalked from the shadows, its gilded death's-head gleaming in the reflected light of the circle. Another.

Marching with the inevitability of the deathless, they drew down from either side. One with its empty, linen-wrapped arms outstretched, reaching for her, the other bearing a chain and shackles, their sheen too bright for steel. Silver.

The sight shredded her last hope of reconciliation. *No one* used silver shackles, not just because of the expense, but because the metal was too soft for such things – unless, of course, one was dealing with an amashti, for whom silver was poison.

Ardoc had made them especially for her. For all he talked of her betrayal, he'd broken her trust from the very start.

Her skin rippled with flame as her daemon-half tore at its bonds. Broken and sobbing, she'd no longer the strength to resist.

Keening with heartache and hunger, she rounded on Ardoc. The flame within her singing with the sweetness of the coming feast, she gave the last of herself to the exhilaration she'd denied so long. He held his ground as she pounced, stern and unafraid.

At the last minute, he opened his hand and blew a stream of greyish-white dust into her face.

She barely tasted the bitterness of the powdered blackthorn blossom before it swept what remained of her wits to the Stars Below.

Consciousness returned with a taste like week-old bread. Shivering face-first against stone, her head pounding but clear of lavender, Tanith opened her eyes onto darkness and pushed upright.

Metal clinked as her shackles went taut, the chain's anchor point lost in the gloom. Silver pressed at the thin silk of her gloves and turned her blood to fire. She collapsed, a scream tearing free of her lips and fading as the chain slackened. Trembling, she rose once more, tucking her legs beneath herself to keep the chain loose, and sat shivering in the dark as she pulled pieces of herself back together.

Her hunger remained, but distant, belonging to someone else, some other Tanith. Her daemon-half, too, was there beneath her skin, seething with rage against her cheated feast but no longer able to command her, held at bay by the silver about her wrists. The absence of sensation was comforting, almost pleasant, but for the knowledge that beneath it all she was still starving. Just because she couldn't feel the hunger that was killing her didn't make it any less real. That she would die lucid was of little comfort.

At least her wounds had closed, sore though they remained – the sword stroke in her thigh especially so.

Her gorge thickened as she followed the trail of splintered memories to its conclusion, the urge to vomit almost too powerful to overcome. She'd attacked Ardoc. She'd been ready to tear him to pieces and glut herself on the remains.

Then she remembered *why*, and sickness turned to misery.

368

Heart brimming and hot tears prickling her cheeks, she wept for her lost home, her lost *life*. All of it swept away by her confused loyalties and misfortune. She'd invited suspicion, trapped herself, and now ... And now *what*? At least Esram hadn't witnessed her horrific truth. What would Ardoc tell him of her? Even now, that mattered. She'd been so careful to shield him from her daemon-half. A romantic dream gone to dust. Or not. She was still alive.

Insidious hope flared. *She was still alive.* Ardoc would surely have executed her had he meant to do so. He'd had second thoughts, and she an opportunity to convince him of the truth.

Buoyed, she clambered to her feet and realised that the darkness wasn't so complete as she'd assumed. Little by little her eyes adjusted to the soft magenta light ushered in by the tiny barred window, shaping her cell's black stone walls and low roof.

Shivering again and careful not to pull the chain entirely taut, she inched towards the window and rose on tiptoes to see over the sill.

In the middle distance, a column of indigo and magenta fire spiralled up from the silhouette of a ruined temple and its supplicants, the bright tongues reaching ever towards a bleak, glint-speckled sky.

The Stars Below. She was back in the Dead City.

Numb, she turned her back on the fire and sank against the wall.

Opposite, the metal door creaked open. Tanith glimpsed a koilos' gilded skull before the creature lurched aside and Ardoc, his eyes hooded and his expression solemn, entered the room.

She started towards him, hands as outstretched as the chain would allow, her voice imploring. "Father—"

He cut her off with a wave of his hand. "I think we're beyond that now, don't you? I suppose this moment was inevitable, but I did hope that you might ..." He sighed, a man so evidently confronted by the death of dreams that she ached to see it. "I had hoped that you would willingly embrace what is coming. Nyssa curse me for a foolish old man."

Tanith hung her head. Just that morning she'd still been the means

369

by which the goddess might change the world. To think that she'd once laughed at the notion. "I still can. Let me prove it, please."

He brushed the tears from her cheeks and regarded her with brooding eyes. "Oh, my poor, forsaken child. I wish I could, but I see now that you have gone too long in want of a father's guiding hand. Please understand that I love you, Tanith, but we have both of us lived a dream these past weeks, and dreams must fade. I have held you too tight and now must hold you tighter still or all will be lost." Throat bobbing, he turned away. "I'd hoped you would serve the goddess with a selfless heart. Take solace in the fact that you will serve her nonetheless."

"You can't leave me here!" Tanith started forward and drew up with a hiss as the shackles pressed against her wrists. "Those creatures—"

"The aethervores will not bother you so far from the palace. They have their duties, as do we all."

"No, Father! Please!" The door slammed behind him. "Ardoc! ARDOC!"

Footsteps tracked away. Careless of drawing the attention of the Dead City's inhabitants, and her daemon-half so close to her skin that every inch of her felt ablaze, Tanith screamed his name until her voice failed.

Thirty-Nine

The morning began, as had all recent mornings, with the clamour of deep-throated bells that shook every corner of Tadamûr. Having learned the hard way that there was no hope of recovering sleep after the chimes had faded, Damant clambered out from between the faded sheets.

The bedchamber's lights rose with him, the prism-crystals of the chandelier and the light flickering behind the walls' stained-glass panels rousing to a dull glow that offered a reasonable facsimile of daylight. Rîand seemed determined to treat him as an honoured guest now he was there – more likely out of respect for Rîma, Damant suspected, than for himself – and had assigned him a suite of three lavish rooms within the palace.

Those chambers retained echoes of opulence, although the marble walls bore their share of cracks, the graceful, wave-like curves of the lacquered wooden furniture were badly scuffed, and the once-bright scarlet carpets and wall-hangings had long since faded to a lustreless brown. The fireblood's ransom in gold ornaments and statuary had borne the millennia far better. Dust and cobwebs remained here and there, although in sufficiently small quantity to suggest that a heroic clean-up effort had taken place.

Even for a man who'd spent a good deal of his life in the Bascari palace in Tyzanta, the ostentatiousness of it all made Damant's skin itch, but not so much as the unshakeable sensation that his every move was being watched.

After performing the necessary ablutions, he pecked at the thin ration of salted beef and twice-baked bread he'd assigned for the meal. Unimpressive fare when set beside the golden goblet from which he drank the spring water piped into the washroom. His hosts had made no attempt to feed him since his arrival – likely because there was no food to be had – and he'd soon elected to make his supplies last. As he sorted what remained into meagre piles, he allowed that it probably wouldn't be enough.

As he returned his diminishing rations to his pack, a sharp knock sounded at the chamber door. Right on schedule, just like everything else in Tadamûr.

"Please enter."

Madîq swept into the room. She offered a formal bow, the seam of her mask's veil brushing the aged carpet. "You slept well?"

"I did," he lied. Fortunately Madîq had worn a mask too long to recognise untruth etched in another's expression. "I was hoping to see the principessa today."

"Alas, the principessa is meditating in preparation for her coronation."

"I see." Damant took care to prevent his frustration from showing. He'd already learned that there was no point asking what those preparations were. "You'll tell her I asked to see her?" he asked for the third time in as many days.

"Of course," Madîq replied for the third time.

He felt his cheek twitch, the mask of urbanity practised on fire-bloods cracking.

During Damant's years of custodium service, Count Raith Bascari had frequently remarked that tomorrow was his favourite day of the week for it never arrived. He'd elevated bureaucratic inertia to an art form, waving aside protests with airy claims that "now is not the proper time". All a distraction from schemes gathering momentum in the background until the proper time had – not accidentally – slipped into yesterday. He and Madîq would have gotten along famously.

Even after three days, Damant found that he otherwise had little in the way of a read on the woman behind the mask. So much of how she moved and spoke seemed almost ... well, *rehearsed*. As if she were forever moving through the steps of an intricate dance. Far from uncommon in lifelong functionaries, but his instincts told him that the shadow of Rîand's will fell across her every bit as heavily as it did Rîma.

"I appreciate that your time hangs heavy," Madîq continued smoothly. "Perhaps you'd like me to show you some more of the city?"

"Thank you." Damant had seen enough of Tadamûr to last him a lifetime. Swathed behind cobwebs or polished to a semblance of old glories, the buildings felt brittle, almost desiccated, as if too sudden a gust of wind would render them dust. Its air hung heavy in his lungs, adding years to his existence that he could scarcely afford. However, familiarity with enemy ground was one of the highest maxims, and he had no doubt that he *was* on enemy ground, regardless of the fineness of words shared and accommodation provided. "I do have another request."

"I will be glad to hear it."

And ignore it, most likely. "I'm running out of food. I wonder if I would be permitted to return to the surface and resupply?" Every attempt he'd made to access the Tulloq tunnels had been politely but firmly denied by the crossed swords of soldiers stationed at the gates. Doubly galling as Hadîm had been permitted to depart. But then, Hadîm had been Rîand's tool.

"Forgive us. Your needs are not our needs and I'm afraid the breach to the Wasteland has been sealed in any case." Madîq tilted her head. "How many days do you suppose your supplies will last?"

"Three. Maybe four," Damant lied. With strict economies, they would last nearly double that.

She straightened. "Then you need not concern yourself. The coronation begins at midnight-host tomorrow."

"After which I'll be permitted to leave?" Assuming there was any longer a way to do so.

"That will be a matter for the queen."

All well and good, but with every passing day, Damant had less and less confidence that he'd recognise the Rîma he knew in the queen-to-be, and vice versa. She'd had three whole days in her grandfather's baleful, oppressive company, isolated from anything that might give her reason to resist.

He stifled a growl. Some witness he was. But unless something changed, there was little he could do except play the game. Bureaucracy was an insidious tool, instilling tradition and seemliness so deeply into every action that to contest its influence was to label oneself an unmutual troublemaker. Challenging Rîand's hospitality would only see what privileges he had stripped away.

Better to work within the system if he could.

"Is there a problem?" asked Madîq.

Damant forced a smile. "A touch of indigestion, forgive me."

"Of course. Perhaps exercise will settle things?"

Nodding, he rose from the table. "Perhaps it will."

On the third day, the streets of Tadamûr were much as they'd been on those preceding. In fact, so far as Damant could tell, they were *exactly* the same, even down to the order in which the crowds retreated from the temple as the bells chimed for dawn-host's conclusion. It seemed everyone in the city answered the chimes, save for those in the faded hawk-and-flame livery of Tadamûr's soldiers, Madîq herself and – presumably, because Damant never saw them – Rîma and her grandfather.

The same handful of individuals acknowledged his existence with a glance or – rarely – a polite nod. Of course, precise identification was impossible with the veiled masks in place. Likewise, their black robes were cut in broadly uniform fashion. But like those Madîq wore, what remained of the frayed hems bore threads woven together in complex geometric patterns that shimmered in the glow of the stained-glass panels, bright and vibrant where all else was dark and faded.

Some – often those who walked with the most shambling of steps – trailed dust and spiderwebs from shoulder and skirt. Others proceeded stiffly when they advanced at all, making painful, jerk-kneed processions of the tree-lined stairways and struggling with every root-shattered flagstone. None of these latter sorts ever acknowledged Damant's existence. Indeed, they seemed barely aware of their surroundings, their unfocused manner reminiscent of Rîma's moments of distance, but somehow deeper, more encompassing.

"What does everyone do when not called to temple?" Damant had asked Madîq on the first day, memories of rooms full of dusty, immobile citizens foremost in his mind.

"Why, they pursue their duties to the city, of course," she'd replied, puzzlement framing her answer, "as the king decrees."

"And what of *your* duties?" he'd pressed. "Who attends to those while you're with me?"

"Your well-being *is* my duty to the city, as the king decrees."

"And before I arrived, what were your duties then?"

She'd offered no reply save a long, unsettling stare, then turned away to wax lyrical about the sculptor who'd fashioned the golden statue of the long-dead Queen Amakala, in whose grand colonnaded shrine they stood.

At the time, Damant had assumed it to be evasion, but the longer he spent in the beautiful, mournful ruin of Tadamûr, the more he wondered if Madîq even remembered what her life had been before she'd captured him at Tulloq Mine.

For that matter, did anyone in Tadamûr have a purpose except when pressed to it by Rîand's will? There was no trade, no artisanry, no conversation – let alone revelry. None of the activities, in fact, that he'd come to associate with life and living. Were they all simply *waiting*?

All cities had a rhythm, of course, a cycle granted by labour, longing and the physical needs of those who dwelled within. This felt different, *mechanical* – as if the inhabitants were nothing more than gears in a massive clock marking the passage of hours because they'd no function but to do so.

If Damant had ever beheld a more distasteful sight, he did not recall it. Even in the bleakest corner of Khalad, there was hope of escaping one's circumstances. Tadamûr's people had no such hope. They were simply vessels for tradition, called to the bells because they had *always* been called to the bells, and withdrawing to empty, dormant lives for the same reason. It was all too similar to reports he'd seen of the lethargia spreading through Zariqaz, save that in Tadamûr it was no disease, but duty imposed from on high. The Rîma that Damant had first met – whom Arvish had convinced him to help – would have shattered Tadamûr all the way down to its corrupt foundations. The one from whom he'd parted in the throne room was a different matter.

Here and there, streets ended in spills of vine-covered rubble. At first, Damant assumed these to be just another sign of the decay haunting Tadamûr. It was only when he noted that some of the tunnels were sealed by dressed stone – and moreover were guarded as though they were still gateways – that he looked deeper at the others. Sure enough, they too had been mortared shut, the square-hewn blocks half concealed behind the spoil.

"Betimes, the aethervores claw their way towards the surface," explained Madîq. "The king decreed it better to sacrifice a piece of the city than to lose the whole."

The fear in her voice set a shiver down Damant's spine, not least because it was the first emotion he recalled her drawing forth. "I'm not familiar with aethervores."

She touched her hands to her chest in what might have been some precursor to the Sign of the Flame. "I pray Nyssa that you remain so. There is nothing in the lower darkness save hunger and loss."

Damant eyed the creaking, dust-stained soldiers at the sealed gateway. "How long ago did this happen?"

"Not long enough," she replied, on balance once more. "Please do not concern yourself."

As they wended deeper into the city, Madîq spoke at great length about the history of particular buildings and the proclivities of the artists who'd wrought beauty in metal and stone. Did Damant know that the emeralds of this particular muqarnas had been mined in the west, and that their beauty had instigated a war between Tadamûr and jealous Zaldamar? Had he noticed the flame-curled motif on the hem of that particular statue, denoting the artist's secret allegiance to a heretic sect? Did the Wasteland have anything as finely wrought as this stained-glass waterfall enclosure?

Damant respectively allowed that he didn't, hadn't and that he imagined not, but his attention was given over to charting the route taken, realigning his perception of the city's layout with each new junction and stairway.

Through it all, he couldn't shake the feeling that he was being watched, even when the streets were empty. Paranoia? Possibly, but preferable to the alternative: that what he took as surveillance was in fact the first subtle ingress of Rîand's influence. For all that Rîma's people and Damant's own were plainly not the same, they were more the same than they were different.

How long before the tolling bells called to him as they did to Tadamûr's own? Were they already doing so? Three days he'd been there, three days in which the determination of arrival had faded to acceptance, even as his supplies failed and Rîma drifted further from his sight. Arvish wouldn't have fallen for it, nor Vallant, but then they'd both parted ways with protocol long ago. As much as Damant might wish otherwise, he realised the same was not true of him. Earlier that morning, he'd even reminded himself that it was better to work within Tadamûr's bureaucracy than fight against it. But working within protocol didn't set you free, it only bound you tighter until you lost all desire to fight. Years in fireblood service made him more susceptible than he cared to admit.

377

More paranoia? Possibly, but no custodian ever died an early death from being *too* suspicious. In the end, he supposed it didn't matter whether his own habits or Rîand's glamour was responsible. Inaction would see him dead of starvation and Rîma abandoned.

He stared back the way they'd come, mapping out the twists and turns that had carried them from the palace. "I need to see the principessa."

Madîq turned in a swish of moth-eaten robes and regarded him with the tilt of the head he'd come to recognise as a frown. "Alas, the principessa is busy—"

"... with preparations for her coming coronation, I know. I need to see her all the same."

"That is not the protocol."

Damant heard no resistance in her voice. Then again, he never did. Why trouble yourself to gainsay when simply ignoring the situation would arrive at the same result? During his service to Count Bascari, he'd learned that no amount of force would overcome such obstinacy. You had to find your way around it. "This protocol ... it's ancient, yes?"

"Indeed."

"And it applies the same to outsiders as to your own kind?"

"I ... believe so."

There. A chink of light. Belief was *not* the same as truth and Madîq knew it. She just needed another push. "How about we let the principessa decide for herself? As Nyssa is my witness, I will abide by her decision."

Madîq remained still, her veil twitching slightly in the subterranean breeze.

Perhaps another nudge was merited? "And you did say that the king decreed my well-being to be your duty."

The first lesson of bureaucracy: borrow all the authority you could, even if others might liken it to theft.

With the merest hint of reluctance, Madîq bowed. "Very well."

378

Forty

The palace chapel was the city of Tadamûr in perfect paradigm, its gold and marble walls rich enough to shame a dedicated adherent of avarice and yet sufficiently dilapidated to make him weep. At some point in the past, a section of roof had crumbled away, the point of ingress for thick, waxy vines that choked the flowing flame motifs on the silk-shrouded altar and flowed like a carpet across the water-stained red-and-black tiles.

Madîq, her reluctance to be part of this potential protocol breach almost as thick as the dust on the mahogany pews, hung back by the door as Damant made his way along the central aisle. Two scarlet-garbed handmaidens bobbed brief bows and peeled away. He read no hostility in their posture. Either they didn't share Madîq's concerns of impropriety, or – more likely – such things were far above their station.

The gold and alabaster figure kneeling before the altar, head bowed in the shaft of greying amber light, gave no sign of hearing his approach. A patina of dust on her pooled skirts spoke to days passed in meditation – perhaps the full three days since their parting. Her withered grey-brown hands – dark suture threads showing at her right wrist – rested palm-down on the altar cloth either side of a mildewed cushion bearing a silver circlet.

A pair of golden statues topped the altar: Nyssa Benevolas and Queen Amakala, the former gowned and glorious, and the latter robed and armoured for war as she knelt to accept the goddess' sword. Damant felt a twinge of unease at the similarity between Amakala and Nyssa Iudexas. They might even have been the same woman, save for the latter's obvious subservience. And the other details. In cut and colouring, Rîma's robes resembled those of a hierarch; her meditations echoed those undertaken by archons due to assume fresh rank and responsibilities. Had the first Alabastrans, sifting the ruins of civilisations past, mistaken the justice-bringing queen for a goddess? How much of Alabastran creed was based on a misreading of the past? Or was Amakala simply the fabled – and heretical – third face of Nyssa that the Obsidium Cult supposedly worshipped?

Damant shook the distraction away. The past was dead. Only the present mattered. "Majesty? Forgive the intrusion, but we must speak."

Rîma rose, dust spilling from her robes and her gossamer-white veil shimmering. The polished gold of her beatific mask – more detailed than those of her subjects-to-be but not, in Damant's mind, as remarkable as the king's – gleamed in the light of the chapel's stained-glass panels. His heart sank to see it. He knew from their conversations on the road that while Rîma had permitted most of her body to shrivel with age, she used last breath to keep her face young and vigorous as her one concession to vain individuality. Now Rîand had stolen that too.

She tilted her head, white hair brushing her shoulders. "Are we acquainted?"

His heart sank another notch. "Damant, majesty. We were companions on the road. You asked me to bear witness to your return home. You lost your hand saving my life, remember?"

Rîma dipped her head, her mask's empty gaze touching on her right hand's clenching and unclenching fingers. Remarkable that she could do so, for even last breath had its limits, but Arvish had implied that a great deal of Rîma's body was held together by splints and even bolts. An immortal swordstress – even one as skilled as Rîma – would face such adversities.

380

"Ihsan." Her eyes rose to meet his, "But you don't like to be called that, do you?"

"Only by my friends, majesty, but a queen may do as she wishes."

"A queen must do her duty to the city. To think that I fled it so long." She shook her head, voice awash with a rapture utterly unlike the restrained, centred woman Damant knew. "But I am forgiven. Is it not glorious?"

"It isn't what you wanted," said Damant, hoping that his words wouldn't carry to Madîq. Protocol stretched only so far, and exhorting a queen to rebellion surely breached those bounds. "You came home to free yourself, to put an end to things."

"Because I was blinded by selfishness. Now my eyes are open to what must be."

"No." He spoke harsher than he meant to, bitterly aware that he was edging out onto dangerous ground. "This was your grandfather's wish, not yours."

Rîma's voice turned cold. "My grandfather loves me. He—"

The rolling chimes of the dusk-host bells boomed through the chapel, swallowing her reply. The two handmaidens swept away down the aisle and out of sight. As Rîma stared up into the fading dusk light filtering through the fracture in the broken chapel ceiling, Damant racked his brain for some argument that might pierce Rîand's glamour. His eyes fell upon the silver circlet, Rîma's crown-to-be. If the ceremony *did* mirror those of the Alabastran priesthood, she would take nothing to the coronation that was not present during her meditation. So where was her sword? Amakala's sword – the one by which she would send her grandfather to Nyssa's judgement? The one through which the echoes of her ancestors flowed? If words couldn't pierce the glamour about her thoughts, maybe that could.

The chimes receded. The light of evening faded into darkness as the shadows of the surface world drew in. Rîma dipped her head, her gaze on Damant once again.

"Are we acquainted?" she asked, polite but puzzled.

Bitterness clogged the back of his throat. "My apologies, majesty. I didn't mean to disturb you."

"You did not. A queen must do her duty to the city."

He bowed, as much to conceal his own stricken expression as for any other reason. "And I must do my duty to its queen."

"And she is grateful," she replied softly. "Truly."

Was that a note of recognition – a sliver of the Rîma he knew fighting its way towards the surface – or just the reflection of his own hopes? Damant straightened, wishing that he could read the face behind the mask. By the time he reached Madîq, Rîma was kneeling before the altar once more, her head dipped in meditation and her palms on the altar.

Madîq bowed. "I trust your conversation was fruitful."

"Was Amakala's sword not recovered?" asked Damant. "I don't see it among the principessa's vestments."

"It was indeed recovered, but she will not need it."

He frowned. "But I thought the throne could only pass with the ruler's death."

"Ah. Indeed this was true in ages past, but only because the incumbents had grown selfish with age and refused to relinquish their duties to the city. The king yields his willingly. Nyssa has called him to make pilgrimage into the Wasteland, where he might learn all that has changed there since the gates of Tadamûr closed."

In other words, Rîand knew he was trapped but had no desire to find his freedom in death. Instead, he meant to offer up his granddaughter to tradition even as he took her place in the surface world. Damant's opinion of the king, already black as pitch, darkened further. "Then what became of the sword?"

"It was returned to Amakala's shrine, of course."

Never alive in any sense Damant understood, after midnight the city was more tomb-like than ever. All to the good, as the lit stained-glass wall panels left few shadows in which to hide. Still, he clung to those that lingered.

At least he'd no fear of discovery by Madîq. Come midnight-host, she'd joined the temple-bound throng for whatever aeons-old ritual occurred inside, what little personality she possessed during the day drawn out by the strike of bells. Nor did the sparse patrols present much in the way of obstacles, for the shuffling, stumbling footsteps of Tadamûr's soldiery were deathly loud in the quiet of the night-time streets.

As during the day, Amakala's shrine sat unguarded – save perhaps by the statue of the long-dead queen, who stood watch over the colonnade and its glittering muqarnas archway. Once inside, it took no great perspicacity on Damant's part to find where the elusive sword had been concealed – if concealed was even the word, for the three sets of footprints, inbound and outward, sat stark in the cobwebbed dust. The soft glow of the stained glass dappling his advance, he followed the trail into a low rotunda whose ceiling was more gaping stone than vaulting and picked his way down a long, looping spiral stair. At the bottom, he passed through a small antechamber and into a darkened room, all but bereft of the stained-glass glow.

Amakala stared out of the darkness, her likeness softer, less angular than the others he had seen, some interplay of the light from the antechamber door and the sculptor's design smoothing away the Iudexas-aspect to something sorrowful. She stood in a pool of black, glimmerless water inset into the flagstones, her robed arms outstretched and the scabbarded sword laid across her palms. Damant glimpsed echoes of Rîma's face in the dead queen's, and he wondered how many generations of her forebears she'd witnessed pass to Nyssa's judgement on the point of the sword.

Heart quickening with success, he stepped forward.

Metal clanged softly under his boot, the ground no longer solid stone but a wide swath of grillwork – the egress point for the water cascading from the shadow-swamped ceiling to fill Amakala's pool – the lattice barely narrow enough for his foot to bridge. The space beyond was pitch black, its depth impossible to judge.

As he took a long stride to clear the grillwork, gilded, jewel-set skulls loomed out of the darkness, the armoured silhouettes of koilos ember-saints unmistakable.

Heart in his throat, he reached for his shrieker, instinct overcoming the knowledge that Madîq had long since divested him of it. But as his fingers closed on empty air, he belatedly realised that the koilos hadn't moved. Statues only, arranged in alcoves to stand vigil over Nyssa's chosen queen. Imagery Alabastra had later co-opted for the ember-saints who served in the Obsidium Palace.

"You've enough to worry about without imagining things," he murmured.

"On this we can agree." Rîand emerged from the shadows at the chamber's far end, his midnight robes setting a field of shimmering stars in the darkness as he circled anticlockwise around the pool. "I know what is in your mind. I have done since you asked after the sword. I cannot permit it."

Throat tight, Damant mirrored Rîand's measured tread, careful to keep pool and statue between them. Could the king read his thoughts? No, more likely Madîq had reported his interest. Flowery speech, that was all, otherwise he'd have been in trouble long before now.

"I don't really care for your opinion."

"You forget, I sent my mother to Nyssa's judgement with that very sword. From the moment I touched it, my forebears whispered the truth of Tadamûr to me."

"The truth that everyone down here exists only as an extension of their ruler's will, is that what you mean?"

Rîand halted. Again Damant mirrored the motion, leaving them standing opposite one another across the pool, Amakala – and her sword – equidistant between them.

"Not I. The city." Rîand pressed a palm to the wall, the stained glass glowing brighter at his touch. "As our people dwindled, Amakala loathed the idea that our souls might be reborn into lesser forms, so she sought to make Tadamûr itself a vessel for the dead, so that

384

reincarnation would not diminish us. As more of us perished, the more aware the city became, the souls of our dead blurring together in its bones. We walked with our ancestors, their hands ever on our shoulders, but little by little there were fewer and fewer of us doing the walking. The pressure of the city's will dwarfed ours. It has smothered us ever since."

Damant looked upon the stained glass with fresh eyes. A prism. The entire city was an ifrîti prism of impossible size. No wonder he felt watched all the time. "Rîma never told me any of this."

Rîand gazed blankly at him, his confusion palpable.

"Your granddaughter," Damant clarified.

The king nodded. "She does not know. She will not know until the crown is hers. It is the shame of kings and queens alone."

"So why tell me?"

"Because it does not matter what you know."

There it was. He'd realised it was coming from the moment the king had first spoken.

But he wasn't dead yet.

"If the city holds you captive, destroy it. Free your people."

Rîand withdrew his hand. Shadow bled back into place as light faded from behind the glass. "Tadamûr *is* my people. What otherwise remains are empty vessels, moved from place to place in echoes of what we once were. Called to worship Amakala beneath the bells."

"Sumaramadîq doesn't strike me as an empty vessel," said Damant, careful to use the formal name.

"All you see and hear are the city's memories of how she once was. When its attention wanders, she's no better than the others."

Damant scowled. Both Rîma and Madîq had spoken of duty to the city in rote, reverent terms. He'd dwelled more on their mentions of Rîand, and thus deceived himself. "What of Hadîm?"

"He went into exile long ago, before the city truly awoke. He was never one for loyalty . . . or tradition."

Damant grunted. "And your granddaughter?"

"Her coronation at the temple will be the making of her. The people have a duty to the city. The city has a duty to its king . . . or its queen. They will be one. Perfect and eternal."

And all it would cost was everything Rîma was. "I'd say it's better to let the city die," Damant said bluntly.

"No!" snapped Rîand. "Without our city, what are we? What *were* we but a memory? Who will remember how our armies brought this land to heel? Who will look upon our works with reverence? Our artists with wonder? No, the city must continue. It may not be life, but it is all we have. It is our monument."

Damant shook his head. "And all it costs is your granddaughter's freedom."

"I am her king. It is her duty to serve me. With sacrifice, if need be. It isn't the burden you think. By her will, the city shall endure. It is the greatest honour."

Damant's last vestige of sympathy bled away. Could there be anything more monstrous than abandoning one's descendant to cold stone and haunted glass? Like so many firebloods he had known, Rîand was willing to sacrifice anything . . . so long as the cost was levied on other shoulders.

"Fine words, from a man desperate to set that honour aside."

He lunged for Amakala's sword, the icy water of the pool rushing up over his boots.

The darkness in the doorway shifted, four black-liveried guards rushing forward with a speed Damant had not yet witnessed in the Hidden City's dwellers.

An unyielding hand clamped around his collar and hauled him back just as his fingertips brushed the pommel of the sword. The remaining guards crowded in, their dry, desiccated stench thickening in his nostrils as they held him fast at arm and elbow. Growling, he braced his feet against the pool bed, tugging and twisting. They dragged him away, his heels splashing in the water.

Head bowed, Rîand pressed the index and middle finger of his left hand to his mask's golden lips and then to the blade of the sword. "You gave me your word that you would behave as a guest should."

Damant glared, the only freedom left to him. "Any word given to the likes of you is worth less than nothing."

"I don't expect you to understand. Your kind's history is as shallow as this pool. You have nothing worth preserving. Nothing for the world to mourn if it slides into decay. Tadamûr is eternal. It must go on."

"If you're going to kill me, kill me," growled Damant, mustering bravado to drown out his sense of utter failure. "I'll go to Nyssa without the lecture, if it's all the same."

Rîand shook his head mournfully. "If you perish here, your wayward soul might contaminate that of the city."

Damant shivered despite himself. To die was one thing, but for his soul to become imprisoned in Tadamûr, for ever denied reincarnation to live anew, was a horror beyond imagining. "You'll forgive me if I don't empathise?"

Rîand offered a sharp bow to Amakala's statue and faced Damant. "Long ago, we judged traitors in this place, others whose souls could not be permitted to become part of Tadamûr."

At his beckoning wave, two of the guards released their grip and moved forward to lever the grillwork up. Damant thrashed against the two that remained, all to no avail.

"A soul devoured is of no threat," said Rîand. "The aethervores who dwell in the Stars Below will maintain the sanctity of Tadamûr, as they have done before."

The grillwork clanged back on its hinges, leaving a bleak, ominous hole wide enough for a man, with room to spare.

"If it is any consolation, Rîma will not mourn you," said Rîand. "By the time she's crowned, she'll have forgotten you ever existed."

A heavy shove sent Damant plunging into the darkness.

Forty-One

Wakefulness arrived grudgingly, accompanied by deep-seated weariness and aching bones. Kat lay still as long as she dared, clutching tight the aftermath of scattered dreams and relishing the darkness. But if she'd learnt anything since her father's death had upended her life, it was that evasion was *not* the same as escape. Like it or not, consequences had to be faced.

Slowly, painfully – the light beyond her eyelids impossibly bright – she cracked her eyes open onto a small, simply furnished bedchamber with a high ceiling and pale cream walls decorated with swirling russet leaf patterns. The scent of rose petals tantalised, the veil of drawn curtains softened the bright midday sun to dappled ochres. Not the theatre, but not prison. Ossed had let them go after all. Uncharacteristically decent of a ranking hierarch.

"Decided to wake up, darling?"

Nausea thickened in Kat's throat as the room spun. Azra sat in a chair at her bedside, her familiar brilliant smile haunted by relief.

"How long have I . . ." She barely managed a whisper, her voice brittle and cracked.

Azra poured a mug of water from an earthenware jug at the bedside. "Here."

Kat took it with trembling hands and forced a little past her lips.

"Better?" asked Azra.

"Almost." She sounded a hair more like herself.

A plate hoved into view, held in Azra's hand. Buttered bread, dates and an apple. Kat snatched a piece of bread and bit deep. It was all she could do to keep the ashen mouthful down. Throat tight, she made no attempt to take another.

"How long have I been asleep?"

"Nearly two days. The physician gave you as much last breath as she dared, and still called it evens as to whether you'd ever wake." Azra's smile lost its brilliance, turning wan. "I'm glad you proved her wrong."

Kat dragged herself to a sitting position and forced cheer into her voice. Two days? Taken together with the nausea and aches, the physician's opinion drained the colour from the room. It would wait. It had to wait. And not just because she wasn't ready to face it. "What about Yali? Tatterlain?"

"Both fine. I practically had to drag Yali out of this room so she'd get some sleep."

"I'm surprised she let you."

Azra offered a shrug, a flicker of pain dancing across her lips. "Turns out if you save someone's life, they start looking at you differently."

Kat noted the bulk of a bandage beneath the shirt at Azra's left shoulder. That made two of them fortunate to be breathing. She fought back a flash of guilt at not having remembered. "How is it?"

Azra twitched her shoulder. "This? Last breath and shriekers don't mix well. I'm told it will heal, but it it doesn't? I never was much of a zither player anyway . . . and it's nice to have Yali look at me with something other than disgust. For the record, I didn't kill anyone, just like you asked." She spoke hurriedly, embarrassed at the words. "A couple of sore heads and at least one more career as a musician in ruins, but they're breathing."

Kat fought not to smile at Azra's discomfort and mostly succeeded. "Thank you. I'm sure it wasn't easy."

Azra grimaced. "I'd rather talk about your omen rot."

Kat closed her eyes. So they knew. At least she didn't need to confess. "I didn't want to worry anyone."

"Yes, darling. We'd worked that out." Azra sighed, the last of her smile fading. "I get why you didn't tell me, I do, but you should have said something to the others. Yali's been wandering around looking like a piece of her heart's been cut out."

A shadow haunted her eyes. Yali wasn't the only one struggling with the unhappy news. Kat swallowed a flash of irritation. She was the one dying, not them. But then she'd had more time to get used to the idea. Get used to the idea ... That was a joke, wasn't it? Just thinking on it scared her down to her marrow.

"I meant to tell them, I did." She shook her head, a mistake that set the room spinning all over again. "When I first suspected, I didn't have the words. And then later ... it just never seemed to be the right time. They'd have fussed over me so much that I'd never have got anything done. Does that make any sense at all?"

Azra offered a wry grin. "What? Being so desperately afraid that your confession will irrevocably change how your loved ones look at you that you keep lying over and over, pushing the truth ever further away?" She laughed softly. "Stars Below, I'd never do that, darling."

"I suppose not." Kat returned the smile. Azra's betrayal – Yennika's betrayal, she supposed – felt as though it belonged to another life, another person. The Azra of old would never have put her life on the line for someone who hated her. She'd loved that Azra regardless, so where did that leave her with the new one? All too late, of course. Two days asleep and not a hunger pang to show for it. Just like her mother's final days.

She pulled aside the sheets and swung out her feet. The thick carpet tickled her toes as she pushed herself upright, the black nightrobe – like the room, not hers – brushing at her shins. "Where are we?"

Eyeing her tottering movements with concern, Azra rose. "See for yourself."

Metal rings clattering against the pole, Kat pulled the curtain aside. Immaculate sandstone buildings adorned with floral window boxes stretched away down-spire along roads of black marble, the regal circlet-and-wing motif golden and sun-bright against pennant and gonfalon. The familiar drab morass of Undertown lay almost out of sight, the rash of mismatched roofs and railrunner tracks of Starji district and the Veil-claimed streets of Qosm and its darkened torch house far beneath. The Golden Citadel, and by all appearances in the highest of its five ring-walls – maybe in the Eternity King's palace itself, given that the broad, straight expanse of the Golden Stair shimmered beyond the nearest gateway, the silver roof of the Qabirarchi Palace just beyond. Overhead, sparse clouds crackled with the green light of the Aurora Eternis, warning of Mistfall.

Her heart sank. "So we *are* prisoners."

"Perhaps," said Azra. "The Voice insists that we're guests."

Maybe the Voice *was* capable of gratitude. "You believe her?"

Azra shrugged, her faux-hurt tone fading. "Ossed's unhappiness is convincing, if nothing else. He'd have us all hanging from our heels along the Golden Stair if he could, but the Voice is . . . not someone you argue with."

Of course. As Yennika, Azra had moved in such circles. "Do you know her well?"

"I only met her once, back before—" She winced. "About six months ago. Very young, but with confidence to shatter mountains."

Or skelders. Kat supposed confidence came easily enough when you'd thousands of redcloaks at your bidding. She'd never been so high in the Golden Citadel, her visits limited to the Great Library during her father's lifetime, and the Xanathros Alabastra in order to gain entry to the Hallow Caves just days before. She'd always imagined the Eternity King's palace would be thick with redcloaks, but there were hardly any to be seen in the streets below her window. Then again, reaching so far meant fighting through four other ring-walls and their attendants, so perhaps it wasn't considered necessary.

"I want to see the others."

Azra's lip twisted. "What's the matter? Don't trust me?"

"No!" Kat bit back chagrin. "I just . . . I need to know they're all right."

The smile returned, softer than was usual. "Darling, I understand. I do. I'm not offended." Azra pointed towards one of the bedroom's narrow doors. "There's a washroom through there, and clothes in the dresser ... unless you need help?"

In times past, the words might have concealed an invitation. Not now. How quickly one walked the road from object of desire to subject of concern. For all that Kat was grateful for that concern – itself out of character for the Azra who'd broken her heart six months before – it proved beyond doubt that she'd been correct to keep her illness hidden. It would only get worse for however long she had left. Selfish to think in such terms, but if she couldn't be selfish now, when could she?

"I'll manage."

Azra nodded, unconvinced. "I'll be in the corridor if you change your mind."

"I'll be fine ... and Azra? Thank you."

Offering one last brilliant, unguarded smile, Azra swept from the room.

Kat was relieved to find that washing and dressing herself remained within her increasingly narrowing limitations ... just about. A paroxysm of spasms left her leaning hard against the door frame, biting her lips to stifle a moan. Even after they passed, her extremities tingled, her fingers not quite responding as they should and her feet apt to stumbles even on flat carpet and tile. Her mother's waxy pallor stared back from the mirror.

Gathering herself as best she could, she met Azra in a colonnade overlooking a vast, well-tended stone garden ringed by bright fox-gloves. They trod the courtyard's outer edge unchallenged by the paired redcloak sentries stationed at the grander doors, and avoided by the scurrying servants. Throughout, Kat strove to walk like a woman merely thrice – rather than four times – her age. Azra mostly pretended that she was successful in her goal, sparing only occasional stricken glances, swiftly concealed.

Azra led her through a banner-hung gateway attended by no fewer than four redcloaks and a single, baleful koilos, and then to a modest doorway. A broad sitting room lay beyond, arrayed in the same dark panelling and leaf motifs as the other rooms Kat had seen, and dominated by a vast circular window at the far end.

||Kat!|| Yali sprang up from a sumptuous armchair, her expression alive with delight. ||How are you feeling?||

||"Like I've been sleeping for two days,"|| Kat replied.

Turning his back on the window and its cerulean skies, Tatterlain folded his arms. "I told her you were too stubborn to slip away without making a nuisance of yourself." Taut features belied jovial tone. For all that Yali was swept up in the moment, his thoughts were on a future not all of them shared. "How are you really?"

Kat forced a grin. ||"Well enough to break out of here whenever you're ready."||

Yali narrowed her eyes. ||How is she really?|| she asked Azra.

Azra shrugged by way of reply, leaving Kat unsure if her growing but limited Simah vocabulary was at a loss to understand Yali's question or whether tact prevented her from doing so.

Yali took the non-answer in her stride and flung herself about Kat with sufficient force to set ribs creaking. Kat returned the embrace, the now familiar mix of gratitude, loss and guilt sloshing around inside.

||No more secrets.|| Yali's brow furrowed as though she meant to say more, but she held her peace.

||"No more secrets,"|| Kat agreed. The way things were going, she'd likely not have time to accrue any more anyway. Making certain her back was to Tatterlain, she switched to signing. ||I hear you've changed your mind about Azra.||

Yali gave a brief shake of the head. ||I've changed nothing, honest and true. It's her who's different.||

||So you're friends now?||

||I didn't say that . . . At least, not yet.||

More than she'd hoped, and Kat knew better than to press the matter. Reassuring to know that Yali's instincts backed up her own. ||"Are they treating you well?"|| she asked, addressing the room once more.

"Incredibly so," Tatterlain replied. "My suspicious nature's getting something of a workout. There was a bit of, ahem, rough and tumble back in the Hallow Caves, but one word from the Voice put a stop to all that. She's a remarkable young woman."

He sounded far too impressed for Kat's liking. Then again, she was never entirely certain precisely where Tatterlain's past took root. "She's the figurehead of a regime you've been fighting for a decade."

"She's the reason we're all still alive. You'll forgive me if I permit her a little politeness in exchange?"

Kat nodded. Even before gratitude got a look-in, antagonising their host could only end badly. "So you'd say we're safe here?"

"Safe enough. For the moment."

"You forgot 'I think'," said Azra, sourly.

Tatterlain shrugged. "What can I say? You'll have seen the guards. I've studied the patrol patterns, night and day, as well as koilos locations and the sentry crests governing access to the streets. I even got a glimpse of an armoury before I was turned firmly away. Aether bombs, shriekers, heraldics – enough to fight a war . . . but everything suggests that the eyes are facing outwards, not in. We're guests."

I don't suppose you found a treasure vault, piled high with antique tetrams? said Yali.

"If I had, I'd have left it well alone. I don't want to be a fine red mist."

Overcome by a wave of exhaustion, Kat braced her hands against the chair's backrest. "It sounds like you've been busy."

"We can't all go sleeping our lives away, can we?" Tatterlain immediately shrivelled beneath twin desiccant stares levelled by Yali and Azra. "A singularly ill-chosen remark, my apologies."

Kat offered a wan smile. "Don't worry, I'm getting used to it." She wasn't, but getting angry at an honest mistake wouldn't help anyone.

"Still, I should have thought," he said, crestfallen. "I—"

He broke off as the door opened, admitting a bearded, teak-skinned man in a *gansalar*'s flowing gold and scarlet finery, all save the ember-saint's gilded mask. His gaze swept the room, the appraisal of potential threat from each inhabitant in turn subtle but unmistakable.

"Mistress Arvish. The Voice requests the pleasure of your company."

Better to play along rather than push, Kat decided. After all, she wasn't the only one at the mercy of the Voice's good graces.

She glanced at Azra and saw her own thoughts reflected. "Go, darling. We're not going anywhere."

Offering a silent prayer to Nyssa that her dizziness would remain distant and thus not spoil things, Kat took Azra's hand and kissed her on the lips, lingering long enough for the other's surprise to soften to reciprocation. Strange how something unthinkable became inevitable. But with moments fast flowing away, those that remained counted for more than old wounds and scarred pride.

She pulled away. "I'll see you soon."

Her expression still clouded by uncharacteristic confusion that made the memory of the kiss all the sweeter, Azra nodded. "You'd better."

Forty-Two

Like everything in the Golden Citadel, the conclave hall was crafted in splendour and scale unapproachable even by the wealthiest of firebloods. The raised dais was fashioned from polished mahogany and traced with the gilded leaf motif seen elsewhere in the palace. So too were the concentric tiers of seating about the perimeter. But more than that, the council chamber was *bright*, the scarlet ceiling-hung banners woken to glory by a swarm of lumani lanterns set in twin spirals around the circular walls and a grand segmented window overlooking the towering gateway to the Golden Stair.

The baker's dozen of men and women upon the dais – twelve standing around the periphery like numbers on a clock and one at the centre – seemed insignificant by comparison, though nothing could be further from the truth.

Beckoned by her *gansalar* escort, Kat took up station at the opening of a tunnel running beneath the concentric seating. No sooner had she done so when a wave of dizziness struck, bringing spasms with it. The dull drumbeat of her heart quickened, louder and louder. She collapsed against the smooth wooden panelling of the tunnel wall, her rebelling lungs heaving and shuddering and still failing to draw down a breath worthy of the name. The *gansalar* made no move to help, her plight falling outside the bounds of his instructions.

Serve him right if she asphyxiated on the spot. See how he fared with his precious Voice then.

The tremors faded. Kat's lungs remembered their duty. Whooping down a breath, she braced head and palms against the tunnel wall. Nyssa didn't want her yet.

But how long would it be? Days? Hours?

No one on the King's Council spared her a glance.

"Preparations for the Feast of Saint Marindra's Descension are almost complete," said one minister, her long white hair stark against heavy scarlet robes of office. "There won't be a soul in Zariqaz with an empty belly come midnight tomorrow."

Kat mentally ticked away the nights. Descension Eve *today*? That was the trouble with obsession. Life passed you by, even when you'd only a little of it left. This time tomorrow the streets of Zariqaz – of every city west of Naxos and south of Tyracha – would be thick with the inebriated and overfed. Probably not what the austere Saint Marindra, the first Qabirarch, would have wanted ... but then you seldom got to choose how you were remembered.

"House Rashace, House Ozdîr and House Yesabi have been most generous," the woman continued. "The former doubly so given Count Hargo's grief at his wife's disappearance."

"I'm certain he misses her scandals not at all," a grey-bearded minister said with a wry smile. "I trust their custodia are alerted to the possibility of, ah, disturbances."

She nodded. "High spirits are expected, though I'm assured that last week's raids bled the streets sufficiently that trouble will be limited. The cells are full of malcontents and the shriversmen are glutted with possibility."

Kat shuddered. Though the raids had barely touched the Marajî district, she'd seen the aftermath in neighbouring streets.

"That won't stop them," murmured Hierarch Ossed, notable both for being the only face in the circle that Kat knew, and the only one of their number clad in gold and white, not scarlet. "I tell you, the Obsidium

Cult is still out there. But for Nyssa's grace, the Voice would be dead at their hands."

The white-haired woman dismissed his words with a wave of her hand. "The last gasp of a dying cabal. You're worrying over nothing . . . but that seems to be your pattern of late."

Ossed's face darkened. "Now you listen to me—"

The gold-gowned figure in the centre of the dais cut him off, but her attention was on the white-haired woman. "You will forgive us if we take another view, minister? It was, of course, our future in the balance."

At barely fifteen years old, the new speaker was a fraction of the age of even the youngest member of the King's Council. Even for that brief span, she was slight and unassuming. However, one did not need the authority of years when one spoke for the Eternity King. What manner could not provide, presentation bestowed. The heavy powder that granted metallic lustre to her bronze skin. The tentacular black lines that swirled forth from darkened eye sockets. Jet-black hair oiled and weighted by glittering beads so that it fell straight against the small of her back. Impossible to reconcile with the fugitive briefly glimpsed in the Hallow Caves, unthinkable to mistake now. Isdihar Diar, the nine hundred and fifty-second Voice and last of the Eternity King's direct line, was without equal or peer. A tyrant's mouthpiece and thus, to Kat's way of thinking, no less a tyrant herself.

The white-haired woman bowed her head. "Of course, majesty. I meant no disrespect."

"We know you did not." The Voice's clipped, precise speech lacked even a hint of absolution. "You may atone by taking personal responsibility for public order during descension."

The white-haired woman's lips thinned, her hurried glance around the circle finding no help. "Of course, majesty."

"We are gratified by your diligence, Minister Sulayan." The Voice stepped a small circle, her dark eyes touching on each of the council in turn. "If Hierarch Ossed's fears prove true, we shall trust to our redcloaks to protect us. We expect our council to protect the citizenry. Are we understood?"

"Yes, majesty," the council intoned, some with more enthusiasm than others.

"Then we may call this session ended." The Voice glanced at Kat. "Other matters now require our attention."

One by one, the ministers departed the chamber, a procession of scarlet robes and averted gazes as they shuffled past Kat. The omen rot or her lowly status? Probably a little of both, she decided.

Only Ossed remained on the dais. "Majesty, I humbly request to remain."

The corner of the Voice's mouth twitched. "Ah, but you do everything humbly, good hierarch. We would not wish to disrupt your final preparations for your own descension. Midnight will come soon enough as it is."

Ossed shifted his prodigious bulk from foot to foot, plainly unhappy but at pains to pretend otherwise. "As you wish, majesty."

He at least acknowledged Kat's presence, shooting her an acidic glare, which she readily returned with a blown kiss and a wicked smile of which Azra would have been proud.

A nod from the Voice and the *gansalar*'s firm but oddly polite hand about Kat's upper arm ushered her to the dais, close enough to glimpse the girl beneath her make-up's shield. Still haughty, yes, but the eyes held uncertainty. Kat took strength from the sight, for standing alone before the Voice as she was – the *Voice* – she'd uncertainty of her own aplenty.

"You too may leave us, Nasari," said the Voice.

"With respect, majesty, she is a notorious skelder—"

"Are all to question our decisions today?" Her clipped diction fell away into a soft northland burr at odds with her gilded appearance. "This woman saved my life. Had she wished me harm, that would've been the time."

The *gansalar* gave a stiff bow and retreated from the chamber. What would Vallant have given for this opportunity? What would he have done in Kat's place? One thing was for certain: the Voice would have been wise to keep her guards to hand.

Or perhaps not. From her position on the dais, Kat noted the koilos alcoves concealed among the concentric seating, their dormant occupants just waiting for the call to defend their mistress. Was that where she'd have ended up had Vallant not rescued her from execution on the Golden Stair months before?

"Ye've been treated well?" asked the Voice.

"So I'm told." Still haunted by the possibilities of the past – better to let omen rot take her than be enslaved as a koilos – Kat strove for politeness. "The hierarch doesn't sound like he approves."

"Ye *did* threaten his life. Maybe ye noted the great store he sets by material existence."

Kat blinked, thrown by lèse-majesté more suited to the girl of tender years than the position she held. "It hadn't escaped me."

"He fears he'll no longer be free to indulge himself once he takes his place on the Qabirarchi Council. Sacrifice disnae come easily to proud men."

A pampered seat on the august body that steered venal Alabastra didn't sound much like sacrifice to Kat, but she supposed part of the appeal of power was in seeing the change it wrought. Secluded in the Qabirarchi Palace, as severed from the mortal world as it was possible to be save through death, Ossed would witness nothing of his will enacted.

"Why did you want to see me?"

"Why did ye save me?"

"It was the right thing to do." A terrible answer, but a simple one. How else to express the duty to stop Tanith, to save Tanith, to protect her friends from reprisals?

"Simple morality? If only we had that freedom," said the Voice, her clipped precision and the royal pronoun returning. "Alas, our duty must always come first."

"You never answered my question."

"Sorry." The Voice's accent softened once more. "Selective answers are a rare joy that have become habit. Most people dinnae have the nerve to question." She cocked her head, her weighted black locks tapping at the base of her spine and a wicked smile parting her lips. "And now ye're wondering if I'm evading your question again, and what terrible fate I'll unleash should ye press?"

"Perhaps a little," said Kat, her preconceptions dissolving in the face of the Voice's mischievous manner. The stateswoman of the recently ended conclave was a different proposition to the girl alone. It might have been an act, but Kat didn't think so. The transition was too smooth, too practised. But then, wasn't it said that Isdihar Diar not only heard the Eternity King's voice but spoke with it as well? Perhaps that was more than mere allegory.

"Very good," the Voice replied, formal once more. "We brought you here out of hope that we can help each other."

Help the Eternity King? Kat clenched her fist to still another spasm. Fortunately, it passed without spreading. "Haven't you heard?" she said bitterly. "Very soon now I'll be in no position to help anyone."

The Voice narrowed her eyes. "We are not Alabastra. We do not quibble about collateral. Debt is transitory. Come. We wish you to see something."

She descended from the dais and waited expectantly at a section of wall seemingly indistinguishable from the others, a koilos ember-saint standing silent in an alcove to either side. The baleful glare of their presence shivered Kat's blood as she approached, what she could sense of their ifrîti fiercely protective even now. The Voice had been right – she'd no need of redcloaks here. Not that Kat was in any condition to offer her harm. The short walk from the dais felt like ten miles, her joints aching and trembling.

The Voice raised her hands to the wall, then swept them down and outward. The section between the alcoves whispered open on oiled hinges, the half-heard voices of the hestics and motics guarding the threshold buzzing like a swarm of bees as they read the soul-glyphs that darkened the Voice's bronzed forearms between golden sleeve and black glove.

Beyond, the long, narrow stairway – a *downward* stair, thank Nyssa – was as poorly lit as the conclave hall had been bright. Painted bas-reliefs lined the grey-white stone walls, depicting winged women in red-gold armour and horizons crowded by spears and pennants. A stylised sun dominated some panels, a silver disc the remainder, and across them all – sometimes as mere grasping, writhing tongues, and at others a full-fledged blaze – a dark, coiling flame. In panel after panel, it dragged the winged women from the skies and smothered armies, while hunched beasts, all claws and fangs, gorged themselves on the corpses left behind.

Kat had seen elements of the designs before, on Athenoch's buildings, but never assembled thus to tell a story – a tale of some great wickedness overcome at great cost.

The Voice descended with the ease of someone retracing steps trod a thousand times, Kat with one hand braced against the wall and her rebellious legs fixing to fold up under her at any moment. More than that, there was ... something ... in the air. An invasive, suffocating presence a hundred times stronger than an ifrît. A thousand. Watchful and stern, even with the spirit world closed to her. Familiar in a way she couldn't quite describe. It thickened the air with ever step, driving the light from behind her eyes.

The Voice repeated her ritual gesture at the lower door and they passed into the chamber beyond.

The room was of a size with the conclave hall, but there all resemblance ended. There were no windows, no lumani. The only light sprang from a seething column of magenta and indigo flame at the chamber's heart, ten paces wide and its orbit thick with Deadwind motes. A column that didn't swirl skyward as flame should, but rushed down from a ceiling many storeys tall, burrowing endlessly through the stone floor leaving neither scorch nor sear to mark its passage. Nor was there any heat to prickle or blister her skin as an inferno of such scale should. There was only the coruscating column of light and its dancing motes. Not mortal flame, but soulfire, as once she'd conjured to command ifrîti, present in impossible quantity. A torrent that legend claimed existed in once place, and one place alone, its inrush drawing the Deadwinds ever towards Zariqaz.

Its light gleamed against geometric walls of polished black stone, fashioned without obvious join or blemish. A black and glittering honeycomb ceiling stretched away into the shadows. At its apex, a meshwork sphere rotated agonisingly slowly within the flame, seemingly without support, its strands of red-gold oreikhalkos and silver shining against the dark. Kat glanced away as vertigo thickened her throat, her perception distorting as it tried to make sense of the sphere's impossible dimensions, both distant and near all at once. Another echo of distant Athenoch, whose lone black tower contained such a sphere to hold the Veil at bay.

And beneath the sphere, at the heart of the flame, sat a blurred, distorted shadow. A shrunken cadaver with brittle skin drawn tight and splinting across yellowed bones, arrayed in heavy black robes and a golden circlet, sitting immobile on an imposing throne of that same abyssal stone that formed the sanctum, both rendered indistinct by the swirl of shielding flame.

Caradan Diar, the Eternity King, whom Kat might have thought a corpse but for his baleful, deathless will filling every corner of the chamber. Sick to the pit of her stomach, she at last realised why it was so familiar. It had assailed her in the skies above Athenoch, roared at her to relinquish the soulfire she'd stolen from the Deadwinds. Had drowned her in fire when she'd refused, searing the aetherios tattoo from her flesh.

The thief who would be a god, the shackled Nyssa had named him in that brief vision.

Terrified, Kat stumbled backwards, desperate to put distance between them.

The Voice, her young face cold and hard in the magenta light, blocked her path. "He says he understands your fear, but it is unnecessary."

"Out of my way!" Not that it would have mattered had she done so, for the door was closed.

The Voice held her ground. "He says no harm will come to you."

Her breathing swift and shallow to match her racing heart, Kat glanced back at the motionless corpse. "I don't believe you."

"He says that shows wisdom. Everything in Khalad is a lie, he says." The Voice smiled softly, more to herself than Kat. "He says that you can be sure he will not tell you anything he does not want you to know. But he also says that even the most wicked lie contains some truth."

Shaking uncontrollably, Kat breathed deep of the dusty, acrid air in hopes of bringing her terror under control. The room swam, then steadied, bringing with it a measure of calm. Had the Eternity King wanted her dead, she'd already be so. Not that he hadn't tried to kill her six months ago—

Stop it! Panic helped nothing, and it wasn't just her life on the line. Tatterlain, Yali and Azra all survived by the Eternity King's grace. She had to get it together, for their sake if not her own. And then there was the other thing. In long centuries, no one had spoken to the Eternity King save his Voices. No one had even *seen* him. Had they really brought her here just to kill her?

Another deep breath. Her pulse steadied.

Unless, of course, others had stood in the Eternity King's presence but hadn't lived to speak of it . . .

The Voice took her hands, silk gloves cold against her skin. "Katija." The northland burr was back. "Ye saved my life. I wouldnae place yours in danger."

An easy thing for a tyrant's heir to say, but the physical contact anchored Kat more than any words of reason. "He holds the goddess prisoner!"

The Voice tilted her head, her tone formal. "He asks how you came by this information."

"She appeared to me in a vision." Kat pulled free and bared her left forearm, drawing strength from the memory of her pain. "Just before he did this to me."

She spun on her heel and fixed the Eternity King with her best defiant glare. All front, for her strength was fast ebbing away.

"He says that many have claimed to see Nyssa across the millennia," said the Voice.

"You think I'd lie about that? Now?"

"He asks your forgiveness. He meant not that you were the deceiver, but that you were deceived. He says that older and deeper than you might think is Khalad."

"I ..." Zephyr had once used almost those exact words, chiding her for ignorance of Rîma's people and by implication Zephyr's own Issnaîm kin. What proof *did* she have that her vision had been sent by Nyssa? She'd been adrift on the Deadwinds, assailed by a thousand whispering voices. Had she mistaken a daemon for a goddess, like the heretic prophets of old? "He tried to kill me."

"What you stole from the Deadwinds threatened his great labour. He reacted in anger, he says, not in wisdom." The Voice frowned, her voice once more her own. "He offers his ... *apologies?*"

An apology from the tyrant king of Khalad? One that surprised his Voice? For the first time, Kat's curiosity overtook her fear. "This labour? You're talking about holding back the Veil?" She'd not stopped to consider the possibility at the time. Nyssa, or the daemon wearing her face – she wasn't yet convinced, but allowed it was all too possible – had urged her to embrace the Deadwinds' flames. Desperate to stop Yennika's rampaging koilos army, she'd done so without thinking. How much of Khalad had the Veil devoured as a result?

"He says the Veil is but one threat to the order he has established for Khalad."

"Let me guess: Vallant?"

"Something far older. Your father served it."

The Obsidium Cult, in other words. "My father might have been weak, but he was a good man."

"He says Terrion Arvish was neither of those things."

Kat's determination not to endanger herself, her friends, vanished in a flash of anger. "And what would you know of good men?" She stabbed her finger at the Eternity King. "Your soldiers kill hundreds, thousands every year. The fireblood custodia and Alabastra execute thousands more and grind the survivors into poverty. Nyssa weeps to see what your order has made of Khalad."

"He says he understands your anger. He also suggests that it is difficult to achieve perspective from beneath the boot. But sometimes the boot is necessary."

Kat's knees buckled under another wave of weariness. "Why did you bring me here?"

The Voice circled around her, the hem of her golden skirts trailing into the column of soulfire without ill-effect. "He says your father stumbled on a secret not his to find. Everything that is, within Khalad's bounds or beyond the Veil, is fashioned from the Dark of Creation. He says it courses through his veins. It is what allows him to bend the Deadwinds to his will." She cocked her head, listening to words only she could hear. "He says that your father made a weapon of it. He says that in his fear of that weapon, he drew out the Dark of Creation from your tattoo's ink. Without that to sustain it, your tattoo has feasted on your soul ever since."

Kat stared down at the remnants of her tattoo. Her omen rot. Tanith's daemonic nature. Both of them aspects of aetherios tattoos running out of control and feasting where they could.

Vallant too had called her tattoo a weapon. Had he been more right than he'd known? A weapon even the Eternity King feared, that he'd already implied could unmake his rule. No wonder the constraints of ifrîti and soul-glyphs held back the Eternity King's forces just as much as they did the rebels. Giving redcloaks and custodians the ability to command machinery, shriekers and koilos at will would for ever tip the balance of power.

"He says he has reconsidered," the Voice continued. "Khalad is built on ifrîti, the order he has created depends upon them, but their control is difficult and complex. Your father's work represents another way, but even with Hierarch Ossed privy to the conspiracy and its research recovered, the secret remains elusive."

"Then perhaps you shouldn't have destroyed it," said Kat.

"He says that what he destroyed, he can restore. It is his hope that you will prove the missing piece in a maddening puzzle."

"I doubt I know anything he doesn't already."

The Voice nodded. "Perhaps, but a sword is more than steel. To truly understand it, one must behold it in motion."

"Putting that weapon in your hand would mean the end of everything we've fought for!"

We? This was Vallant's fight, not hers.

The Voice cocked her head once more, for longer this time. When she spoke, she did so slowly, talking time to parse the words with care. "He says the Khalad you know is not the one he had hoped to build, but that habit ossified temporary measures to permanent ones. That the boot distorts perspective as much from above as it does from below."

"You expect me to believe that?"

"He would remind you that he could have moved to crush Vallant's secessionists at any time since Athenoch, but you know that he has not. He also says that even as we speak, Vallant himself is holding what he believes are secret meetings with the ruling council of Zyrassa. We have a dozen ships within strike range and have had since before his arrival." The Voice's expression softened. "It's true, I promise ye. I issued the orders myself. They're there to contain Vallant should he threaten the citizenry. If he disnae, they'll let him be."

Kat looked from one to the other, unsure how much truth the words contained. Zyrassa was less than a day from Zariqaz, mere hours if the currents of the Cloudsea were kind. Even by Vallant's standards, that was bold to the point of recklessness, but no one had ever accused him of lacking ambition. Securing an alliance with Zyrassa would shield cities further east and send a clear message that Khalad's monolithic rule was crumbling. Had the Eternity King stayed his hand because he was truly re-examining his choices, or out of fear that Kat was not the only one of Vallant's followers who wielded an aetherios tattoo?

Wait. Had she just described herself as one of Vallant's followers? Nyssa, but the man had his hooks deeper than she'd ever realised. That, or it was the omen rot talking.

Hopefully it was the omen rot talking.

"What happens if I say no?"

"Then the omen rot will run its course. You will be devoured."

"By my tattoo?"

"By your father's selfishness."

Kat was too weary to argue the point. Tanith's curse proved that their father's work was flawed, and yet even knowing that, he'd risked Kat's soul alongside that of her younger sister. "And if I say yes and vanish into the wilderness, never to be seen again?"

"He says that we already told you that we are not Alabastra. He hopes that you will come to understand the necessity of his labour. And that if you do not, the shriversmen may learn much after your passing."

Kat snorted. "Sooner or later it all comes down to threats, doesn't it?"

"He says that is not what he meant. Be it today or in a hundred years, you will pass into the Deadwinds. What you leave behind cannot help but prove educational."

"That's a gamble."

"We are not Alabastra."

"If it's so important, why do you care if I agree?" Kat asked. "The name of Caradan Diar isn't exactly synonymous with freedom of choice."

"Your soul is but a mote, his an inferno. Resist even a little, and he will destroy you without meaning to do so." The Voice shrugged. "He says it takes all of his concentration to perceive you at all."

So thick was the chamber with the pressure of the Eternity King's will that Kat believed that much. Was the Eternity King truly a thief who would be god, as her vision of Nyssa had claimed, or had she been deceived all along? He offered her life, but she noted that no mention had been made of freedom. He promised the possibility of change without proof, but at the same time had indeed held back from annihilating Vallant's nascent realm.

It was all too good to be true. The Eternity King had surely lied to her – he'd as good as told her that he would – but about what? Her breathing shallowed and the room swam as the omen rot's spasms returned. Gasping, she dropped to one knee, upright at all only because the Voice slipped one arm around her waist and another beneath her elbow.

Little by little, Kat brought her rebelling body under control. How many more attacks before her omen rot – her tattoo – killed her?

"Please agree," murmured the Voice. "Ye saved me, let us save you."

Forty-Three

Swallowed by darkness and deafened by the rushing wind of his descent, the first Damant knew of the river was when he struck the surface. The shock of impact drove the breath from his lungs. The distant, dim light of the shrine vanished in a rush of bubbles as the waters closed over his head. Sodden clothing dragged him down, wispy tendrils of weed caressing his arms and legs.

His lungs already burning, he kicked for the surface.

What he *hoped* was the surface. No light pierced the icy waters. No way for his disoriented senses to tell up from down.

The current gathered up his waterlogged robes, dragging him ever faster through the darkness. His last gasp dribbled away as a stream of bubbles. The darkness took on a parched, ruddy sheen, his thoughts slowing to treacle.

A woman's face shimmered through the water, her hair tightly curled and her distant expression shifting to a comforting smile as she reached for him. Frantic, Damant kicked against the current and swam towards her. His fingertips breached the surface and found not the woman's hand, but a ridge of cold, smooth stone. His head burst from the water, the dank air of that first miraculous breath the sweetest he'd ever tasted.

He clung there, nose to stone, hands above his head and his mouth barely clear of the surface. The river's current still tugged at him, but less insistently than before, a listless child whose game had been thwarted by happenstance.

Red receded further from his vision, his eyes adjusting to the dim pinkish light until he found himself nose to nose with the woman who'd reached out to rescue him. Or rather, the cold-eyed bas-relief sculpted into the embankment's edge that he'd taken for such, her body submerged below the neck and her saviour's motion conjured by the rush of water and delirium.

Half laughing, half gasping, he dragged himself up onto the embankment and rolled onto his back. His laughter faded as he took in the distant cavern roof, its fundament glittering with what might have been stars, or might equally have been gemstones. Away in the middle distance, a column of magenta and indigo flame swirled atop a dark hilltop ruin, pinpricks of lesser light dancing about it.

"Blessed Nyssa ..." Damant staggered to his feet, his disbelieving glance taking in austere, empty buildings clad in the same black stone as the embankment set along streets that ran towards the hilltop like the spokes of a gigantic wheel. "Where am I?"

The words were rote, summoned to dispel truth. He'd heard of this place ever since childhood, its imagery scribed deep into his soul by the preaching of Alabastran archons.

The Stars Below. He was in the Stars Below.

The realisation drove him back to his knees. Though he held himself to be too practical a man to be truly religious, it was one thing to do so in the sunlight; quite another with the stars glittering above. He stared back out across the river, which now betrayed no flicker of motion. It might have been a smooth black sheet of glass, save for the fact that it offered no reflection.

"'I think I want an adventure'," he muttered to himself. "Idiot."

Water pooling on the flagstones behind him, he peeled a twitching frond of river weed from his sleeve and took his first, stumbling steps towards the nearest building.

What now? Rîand had meant to send him to his death, that much

411

was clear, and but for gracious fortune the river would have given him all he'd wished. Had all the talk of aethervores been anything other than insincere packaging for a ritualistic drowning? After all, if he *was* in the Stars Below – clinging to the possibility that things were otherwise offered some small respite – then surely Nyssa would claim his soul before Tadamûr could snare it?

Nyssa. If this *was* the Stars Below, the goddess' Obsidium Palace was somewhere nearby. Could he reach it? Might he petition her to set matters right in Tadamûr? Imagine that, marching into the Hidden City to rescue Rîma with an army of ember-saints at his back . . . Only, everything he'd learned in Tadamûr suggested that Nyssa Iudexas was nothing more than an Alabastran subversion of the long-dead Amakala. What else was a lie?

Was Nyssa even real?

As Damant reached the street corner, he spied a pale figure in the distance. For the first time, he caught a snatch of song, a low harmony sung in minor key by voices neither male nor female, its notes beautiful and sad. Achingly familiar, though he couldn't place the whys and wherefores of that familiarity.

Turgid memory offered up caution. Rîand hadn't been the only one to speak of aethervores. Madîq had done so, unbidden, to explain the sealed routes beneath the city.

Better not to take chances.

And yet, despite his resolve, he didn't move. He *couldn't* move, the mental command dissipating somewhere between conception and action.

"What the . . . ?"

The words sounded distant, belonging to a stranger. His skin prickled with encroaching numbness, the sensation – or rather, its lack – all the more disturbing for how little it concerned him. Almost like drunkenness, but for the small voice at the back of his brain urging him to run.

The sorrowful, cloying song grew louder.

Screwing up eyes that no longer felt like his own, Damant forced one leg to motion, then the other, turning lopsidedly back towards the river.

The embankment was empty no more. A second waxy, pale-skinned figure shuffled across the black flagstones in a rippling, slug-like undulation, its long crook-jointed fingers reaching out from beneath the ash-soiled sleeves of a once white-and-gold robe that clung to semi-translucent, flame-blooded flesh.

The voice at the back of Damant's thoughts screamed louder as the aethervore's inky black eyes met his, but whatever effort had spurred him to motion before was long since spent. Golden circlet gleaming in the reflected magenta flames, the creature oozed closer.

A shadow moved in Damant's failing peripheral vision. The aethervore screamed as Hadîm thrust a burning brand into the heart of its ash-blackened robes. The tattered cloth caught light, the hungry orange flames crackling across blistering, charring skin. The aethervore staggered away, already collapsing, its song turning to bubbling liquid shrieks and then to nothing at all. The cool air filled with the stench of oil smoke and burned leather.

Hadîm looked Damant up and down, a self-satisfied sneer on his lips. "I'll bet you wished you'd taken my offer now."

"How..." Damant swallowed, his tongue thick and unresponsive but his joints finally beginning to behave as they should. "How long have you been watching me?"

"Don't flatter yourself." Hadîm shrugged. "You'll never make an assassin. The entrance is everything."

Massaging life into his hands, Damant stared at the smouldering remains. The keening, familiar song endured, the other singers distant enough to weaken its effects.

"So that's an aethervore?" It looked more revolting than dangerous now it was dead, but then so did most things ... Hadîm included, from past experience. Even with sword and shrieker, Damant hadn't been the assassin's equal. That Hadîm too bore no weaponry didn't improve those odds. He could only hope that common circumstances, rather

413

than retribution, had prompted the intervention. "I take it Rîand's reward was not everything he promised?"

"Shall we withdraw somewhere safer before you start on idiot questions?"

Damant stared back along the street to the first aethervore, now markedly closer, and the phantom song growing in volume. His hopes of finding divine aid in the Stars Below faded to nothing. After previous encounters of crossed swords both metaphorical and physical, Hadîm was about the last person he was ready to trust. But if recent months had taught him anything, it was that sometimes you took what allies Nyssa offered – especially if they'd just saved your life.

"Very well. My idiot questions will wait."

Hadîm's safer place transpired to be a first-storey room a quarter-mile towards the city's edge, a low wood fire burning at its heart. Its soft crackle couldn't wholly banish the distant, haunting melody, nor could the gentle yellow-orange flicker compete with the magenta inferno on the ruined hilltop, but it steadily drove the damp from Damant's clothes.

Before long, he was feeling more like himself, though an increasingly peckish version of that man. So Hadîm told it, he'd salvaged the firewood from among the shrivelled corpses of some long-dead explorers, and what little food they'd possessed had long since ceased being edible. And so he drank water from the river, sat as close to the fire as common sense permitted, and reminded himself of long days trapped on Tyzanta's frontier without supplies. At least on those occasions he'd been armed. Trapped underground with soul-sucking monstrosities, and a qalimîri assassin his only dubious ally, a weapon would have been handy.

Hadîm tossed a bundle of kindling onto the fire. "So, enlighten me. How did you rouse King Eskamarîand's famous wrath?"

"About how you'd think." Damant swigged from a goblet rescued from the explorers' camp. Even in the goblet, the water offered no reflection, but it smelled right, tasted of little and he'd already swallowed a bellyful during his "swim", so if it was befouled or poisoned, it was taking its sweet time making that fact known. "I tried to get Rîma back her sword."

Hadîm's dark, handsome face cracked a grin, his teeth gleaming in the firelight. "So you broke into the shrine and stormed the palace, blade in hand?"

"The first part only. Rîand was waiting."

"Still, I approve your audacity. You didn't *really* expect to change things."

"I hoped for it."

"Ah, hope. Without it we'd live quieter, duller lives, would we not?"

"I wouldn't know," Damant replied stiffly.

"So formal. And I thought we were becoming friends."

"You're a hired killer. A body-stealing qalimîri."

"Yes, I suppose that would preclude friendship." If Hadîm was offended, he hid it well.

Damant glowered at him across the flames. "You mean I have morals?"

Hadîm brushed his objection aside with a theatrical wave. "Morals are relative. And none of it matters anyway. If I killed you, Nyssa would grant you a new life sooner or later, so what's the harm?"

It was disappointing, somehow, that he so readily fell back on a conceit favoured by so many common murderers, one Damant had heard many times in his custodium days. "The harm is the harm."

"Oh, very pithy. I'll remember that one." Hadîm paused and stared into the flames. "It occurs to me that we can be of help to one another."

"What possible goal could we share?"

"Don't be a child, it doesn't suit someone with all that grey up top." He spread his hands. "We both want out, don't we? More than that, we both want to get back into Tadamûr."

"There are other ways out?"

"Of course." Hadîm pointed through the empty window towards the

415

ruined hilltop. "There's at least one route up to Zariqaz on the other side of all that, but the problem is that they're *on* the other side of all that. The inner streets are swarming with aethervores. You'd be a rotting, soulless corpse before you made it halfway."

Damant followed his gaze. Was that another prick of yellow-orange firelight on the city's far edge? A possible ally? Even under the circumstances, Hadîm barely qualified. "Nyssa will protect me."

"Nyssa?" Hadîm chuckled softly. "Who do you suppose the aethervores serve? But by all means, do stop by and say hello. It'll save them the trouble of sniffing you out."

Damant narrowed his eyes, an unhappy frisson in his spine as he looked anew at the jagged black ruin and its column of flame. "No ... The goddess lives in the Obsidium Palace, attended by servants ..."

"One man's ruin is another's palace. As for servants, what do you suppose the aethervores are? I'd say they're her guards and keepers, and that she keeps them plump and docile with fresh souls. They'll welcome you with open arms and hungry gullets."

The fresh souls from the Deadwinds. So much for the promise of reincarnation ... at least for those Nyssa judged to be wicked. Would she look favourably on him? Would the good done in Bascari service outweigh wickedness pursued in the name of their laws? On the other hand, Hadîm didn't make for a reliable source. Better to cling to that. "You seem to know a lot about this place."

"I've lived long enough to hear all kinds of stories, most of them with a grain of truth if you listen carefully." He fixed Damant with a defiant glare and suppressed a shudder. "The river carried me deeper in than it did you. It's taken me the better part of three days to get this far out without ending up drained dry."

"Why not simply kill yourself? Possess another of your thralls?" Damant narrowed his eyes. "I'll gladly help with the first part."

Hadîm arched an eyebrow. "So Rîma told you?" He jerked his head towards the Obsidium Palace. "I have to be aware for it to work. That song's a hundred times the soporific to a naked soul than to one shielded by flesh. I doubt I'd recover before the Deadwinds claimed me. I'll be for ever diminished. Worse, the rest of me will never know how Eskamarîand betrayed me. He'll have won. Better to work together until I'm well away from it."

"Perhaps I'm prepared to take my chances with Nyssa."

Hadîm wagged a chastening finger. "And who'll help Rîma? Why, it can't be long now until the coronation. Once that crown's on her head, she'll belong to the city for ever, body and soul."

Damant's stomach tensed. "You *knew* about that?"

"Why do you think I left in the first place?" Hadîm stared off into the middle distance, vulnerable for a fleeting moment. "Had I stayed, by now I'd be just like the rest."

"And still you took the commission to drag Rîma back?"

He shrugged, his black robes rippling in the firelight. "I told you, morality is relative, and Eskamarîand promised me her weight in gemstones. I've a palace out in Kaldos with something of a squatter problem. Between the Qersali and Vallant making trouble, mercenaries don't come cheap."

"Must be some palace."

"Oh, it is."

"Except Rîand didn't pay, did he?" sneered Damant. "How do you feel about relative morality now?"

Still staring into the flames, Hadîm shook his head. "Ah, such a shining wit. You're right, of course. He probably never meant to, but severing Rîma's hand didn't help me. An unacceptable breach of protocol. It's nothing to what *he* means to do, of course, but alas the argument didn't take. Nobody double-crosses me." He spoke the last words in a voice solid as stone. "Rîand denied me, I'll help you deny him."

Damant eyed him with suspicion. "As simple as that?"

"As simple as that."

Except it wasn't, was it? It meant trusting a duplicitous qalimîri who lived by no code beyond expediency. But Damant wasn't exactly overflowing with options. No food. No weapons. No allies of consequence.

417

And mere hours to save someone who'd made the mistake of placing her faith in him. He didn't have to trust Hadîm, just his desire for vengeance.

"Say I agree … What comes next?"

Sometime in the immemorable past, the arched gateway and the spiral stairway beyond had been loved. Even from a distance that much was clear. The long balustraded approach, flanked by bronze braziers. The bas-reliefs depicting rising flames and gathered crowds. The lone gowned figure of Nyssa Benevolas – or as Damant was beginning to think of her, the sole true Nyssa, as distinct from the stolen Amakala – above the keystone. Alas, those days of reverence lay long in the past, before the cavern rock face had half buried both gate and the broad flagged roadway.

"You're sure this is the place?" asked Damant, his makeshift wooden torch held high.

Hadîm snorted. "Certain. Nizarid wrote of the pre-Amakalan rituals in great detail."

"Oh, did he?" Damant replied sourly.

"Yes, *she* did. You think I didn't expect the possibility of betrayal? I *always* have a contingency plan."

"How's that working out for you?"

"I grant you that much remains to be seen."

Assuming the stairway led anywhere. "I thought everything was sealed."

"Once perhaps, but you've seen the state of the city." Hadîm shook his head. "It's the bells that keep the aethervores at bay – they can't abide the sound. I expect that's why Tadamûr maintains that particular tradition when it has let others go to rot. Imagine the feast its bloated city-soul represents."

Damant elected not to. Sanity was already hard enough to come by.

"Fine, but there's a problem."

He pointed to a motionless figure standing stooped two paces in front of the gateway. Familiar and yet not. Familiar, because his duties had brought him into contact with any number of koilos. Not, because those koilos invariably wore the glittering golden robes and black lamellar of ember-saints, or else nothing but grave bindings to disguise the horror of embalmed and fire-blackened flesh. This specimen wore simple black robes, even duller and more practical than custodian uniform, skelder's garb in all but name. A short scimitar drooped from its hand, the point propped against the flagstones. A second figure lay at its feet, huddled in the shape-lessness of death.

Hadîm considered. "The expedition I found? They were dressed the same."

"It doesn't look Alabastran," objected Damant, "but only Alabastra has koilos."

"Don't be naïve. Alabastra stole the preservation rituals from us. Someone else could steal from them. You can't trust anyone, these days or in any others." Hadîm offered a dry smile. "At least it's inert."

"It *looks* inert." More likely it was guarding the corpse of its former master. Damant racked his brains. How long could a koilos ifrît hold itself together? He'd no ready answer, Alabastra having taken great pains to shroud such details. In any case, without knowing how long the koilos had stood there, any answer was worthless. Even armed, he'd have thought twice about going up against a koilos. "Let's hope you're not wrong."

"You go left, I'll go right."

"No. You go left, *I'll* go right." A petty correction, but pettiness was easily come by in Hadîm's company.

Hadîm started for the gateway. "Suit yourself."

They advanced, Hadîm to the right and Damant to the left, his torch held high. The koilos remained motionless, its empty eyes downcast at the withered corpse. Closer now, Damant noted a black mask beside the body, similar in design to the one he himself had worn as a custodian, and resonant with old rumours of an Obsidium Cult lurking below

419

Zariqaz's civilised veneer. So many secrets crawling beneath the skin of a world he suddenly understood so little.

Careful to give both corpse and koilos a wide berth, he headed for the stairs.

As Hadîm drew level, the koilos jerked to life with a dry, ear-splitting screech. Once-dormant eyes blazing with magenta flame, it lurched about, a sweep of its rusted scimitar slicing a tatter of cloth from Hadîm's black skirts, its bony hand grasping for his arm.

Damant took his makeshift torch in both hands and brought it down on the koilos' gleaming golden skull. The timber haft split two-thirds of the way along, scattering dying flames and oil-soaked cloth across the lower steps.

Shrieking malice, the koilos spun around and hacked down. Damant threw himself aside. The scimitar sparked as it struck rubble and then Damant was past the koilos and scrambling up the stairs.

As his right foot found the fifth step, his left shot out from beneath him, seized in a vice-like grip. He lurched backwards, head and knee chiming on stone. Head ringing and half blinded by his own blood, he scrabbled at the stairs for purchase and came away with a handful of loose stone. He twisted around and let fly.

Driven by a vestige of mortal instinct, the koilos raised its sword arm to shield its eyes. Damant took the opening and slammed his free heel into its robed chest. A rib crunched. The koilos didn't even stagger.

He threw a desperate glance higher up the spiral stairs. "Hadîm!"

No answer came but the scuff of feet on stone.

Growling at his stupidity for ever trusting the man, Damant braced his elbows against the step and threw every ounce of his frustration into a second kick. The koilos brushed his boot aside with the back of its blackened skeletal sword hand and tugged hard on the other. Another step shot away beneath Damant's back, the crack of his spine against the rising edge a hammer against bone.

"Hadîm!"

The koilos tugged again and levelled its scimitar for the thrust.

Hadîm plunged from above, robes whipping around him and a head-sized chunk of rock clasped tight to his chest. He landed atop the koilos, toppling it backwards through the archway. It struck the cavern floor in a crackle of splintering bone, Hadîm's knees in its chest. Before the koilos could throw him clear, he brought the rock down on its golden skull, smashing it to fragments. At once, the koilos' limbs went slack.

Breathing hard, Damant staggered to his feet and wiped blood from his eyes. "Took your time, didn't you?"

Hadîm nodded vacantly, his eyes still on the remnants of the koilos' skull. "Told you ... you have to know how to make ... to make an entrance ..."

He slipped sideways off the koilos' remains and lay twitching on the ground, six inches of rusted steel and a battered scimitar hilt protruding from his ribs, his robes already slick with blood.

Disoriented from his head wound, Damant missed his footing, skinning his hitherto unwounded knee as he stumbled to Hadîm's side. A glance at the wound drew forth a grimace; the distant strains of the aethervores' song drew forth another. Surely too close, even now. When this sliver of Hadîm's soul passed, it would be gone for ever.

"I ... There's nothing I can do for you." He at last remembered where he'd heard the aethervores' song before. Zephyr's lament, sung so many times aboard the *Chainbreaker*. A coincidence that could be no coincidence at all, though its rationale escaped him.

Hadîm closed his eyes. Blood glistened on his lips. "Yes ... there is." He shuddered with the effort of speaking, each word a stuttering rasp. "When you free Rîma, make sure ... make sure Eskamarîand knows ... Make sure he knows that I helped you. Promise me. Promise ..."

"I promise," Damant murmured, though Hadîm's soul had already fled.

Heart heavy and his head throbbing, Damant stumbled to his feet, wincing at a panoply of aches that would only be worse come the morning. But he supposed his chances of seeing the morning were slender at best. As if to reinforce the point, a clamour of distant bells echoed down the stairway. Dusk-host. Mere hours remained until the coronation.

Scowling with distaste, he planted a foot against Hadîm's chest, twisted the scimitar free from its prison of dead flesh and started up the stairs.

Forty-Four

Kat had visited temples smaller than the vast stained-glass-windowed chapel, which could have accommodated easily fifty people between the fluted columns of its nave. For a city as cramped as Zariqaz, it was a wanton flaunting of space-as-wealth, made all the more ostentatious by the inevitable gilding and rich scarlet altar cloth. The spread-armed statue of Nyssa Benevolas looked to be cast of solid gold, rather than film over base metal.

All for nothing, for no amount of prayer garnered reply.

"Blessed Nyssa, hear me. Send me a sign, a word ... please."

Her murmured prayer, crowded by the thick floral fragrance of incense, went as unanswered as those that had preceded it. There was only the darkness behind her eyelids, the smooth stone of the altar beneath her fingertips and the soft pressure of the geometric Phoenissan carpet beneath her knees.

"Blessed Nyssa ... You urged me to harness the flame. You told me to seek Tanith in Zariqaz. Will you not hear me now?"

The words echoed away along the chapel. Kat strained in hope of seeing some flicker of flame in her self-imposed darkness. Some sign that the goddess heard ... that the vision about Athenoch had indeed been Nyssa, and not some malevolent daemon of the Deadwinds.

Nothing.

She released her grip on the altar, sinking lower into a fresh wave of dizziness. She gasped, her lungs shaking and spasming, her thoughts drowning in a dull, ruddy flood. She heard a distant, stuttering moan, not realising it was hers until she pitched fully forward, her limbs cramped tight.

Unable to move, barely able to breathe, she lay in darkness no longer hers to end, for her eyelids were as recalcitrant as the rest of her.

Was this it? Was there nothing left for her to do but slip away into the Deadwinds? At least it spared her the burden of her choice ... or would have, were inaction not a choice all its own. Had she accepted the Eternity King's offer, she might have avoided this. Had she gone back to her friends, she might at least have had the chance to say goodbye. They deserved that from her at least.

By and by, she became aware of a shuffling presence elsewhere in the darkness, the sound of a large man walking with unaccustomed care. Her skin prickled as he knelt, his breathing laboured.

"Should I send for a physician, Arvish?"

The warmth of his hand on her brow gave Kat something to anchor herself to. Inch by inch, she pulled herself out of the darkness. Fingers twitched, then obeyed. Eyelids followed, the dim light of the chapel giving shape to Ossed's bearded face, his expression frozen halfway between concern and discomfort.

Joints screaming, Kat inched her way to a sitting position against the altar, head on her knees. "I just ... need to catch ... my breath."

Ossed stood, his attention on the golden statue of Nyssa Benevolas now that slender mercies had been performed. Still, that he'd troubled himself at all struck Kat as far at odds with his nature.

"If you wanted the chapel," she murmured, flexing the last stiffness from her fingers, "I was just leaving."

He nodded distantly. "Did Nyssa hear you?"

"If she did, she didn't answer."

"Indeed," he said softly, his eyes still on the statue. "Prayer is slim solace when it goes unanswered."

Kat drew down a deep breath, letting it drive the last of the numbness from her extremities. She'd expected a chiding for her bitterness, not . . . whatever she'd received. "Not a sentiment I'd expect from one destined to take a qabirarchi throne in a few hours."

He shot her a look of pure poison. It softened, leaving him more haggard than a man of his generous avoirdupois had any right to expect. He pinched his lips tight, his bearded chins falling to his chest. "I dreamed of this my entire life. To serve Alabastra and the goddess as only a few can, and yet . . . so why is my heart so heavy?"

"Change is always hard." Kat rose haltingly and wondered why he was telling her all this, or why she felt moved to solicitude. She supposed the answer to both questions was the same: because they were there. Strangers grew less so when certainty faltered. "If Nyssa won't offer comfort, perhaps you should seek it with your family . . . your nephew?"

"Esram's work monitoring the Obsidium Cult makes him difficult to reach, now more than ever. His mother and I . . . have not spoken in some time. I can't expect her to understand this." He stared again at Nyssa. "I wish she'd offer a sign. Have I not been faithful? Have I not done my duty?"

Now feeling as hale as she was likely to, Kat flirted with the temptation to point out that far from following Nyssa's precepts of generosity and forgiveness, he'd earned his lavish robes and gilded throne-to-be by indulging Alabastra's rather more self-serving doctrines. How many families had he bled dry? How many souls had he shackled in payment of unsettleable debts? But something about his pathetic, shrunken posture held her back. Or perhaps it was her sudden certainty that Nyssa had sent her a sign after all, if in unexpected form. Ossed had no one but the goddess to offer counsel, but Kat did.

Leaving him kneeling before the altar, she stole away to seek it.

"I say you take his offer, darling," said Azra as Tatterlain signed a translation for Yali.

The three of them sat in the drawing room where they'd first reunited, the purpled dusk beyond its glorious window now thickening with the greenish-white of the descending Veil. They'd listened to Kat's stumbling account of her audience with the Eternity King with what under other circumstances might have been a comical ebb and flow of expression. Disbelief, horror and confusion had ruled each of them at various points. The lion's share of the former still belonged to Yali, who'd no experience with fireblood dealings to cushion Kat's tidings.

Tatterlain, engulfed in a lushly upholstered armchair, broke his thoughtful silence. ||"Of course you do."||

Azra glared. "And what's that supposed to mean?"

||"That this is an opportunity and that you're an opportunist."|| He shrugged. ||"I'm not judging, I'm one myself. But there are other considerations."||

"Kat's dying. That's all I care about."

Yali nodded. ||And me, honest and true.||

Kat, exhausted from having spoken at length and glad for the chance to simply sit and recuperate, caught Yali's frown as the girl realised how readily she and Azra had fallen into alignment.

||"Please understand,"|| said Tatterlain, his eyes beseeching Kat, ||"I want nothing more than a good many more years of enduring dear Katija's disapproving stare—"||

||"I do *not* have a disapproving stare,"|| interrupted Kat, too weary to be angry.

Azra shrugged. "You really do, darling."

Even Yali nodded.

||"My point, if I may be permitted,"|| said Tatterlain, his voice thick with strained patience, ||"is that it's not just *her* life at risk."||

"I wasn't thinking about mine," Azra murmured. "Not at all."

||"Actually, I was thinking about Vallant—"||

Yali snorted. ||He'd like that.||

Tatterlain shot her a long-suffering look. ||"About Vallant, Zephyr, Vathi, Damant, Rîma . . . Everyone on the sharp end of redcloak spears if the balance of power shifts towards the Eternity King. Kat's tattoo

426

saved Athenoch and everyone in it. I can't help but worry what even a dozen redcloaks might do with that power."||

Rima. More than ever, Kat wished she were with them. She could have used the perspective of ages. She stirred in her chair. ||"Assuming I even survive his 'cure'."||

||"Assuming that, yes."||

||"You don't believe that the Eternity King has regrets?"||

||"One opportunist knows another. And let's face it, seizing a throne is all about opportunity. Seeing it slip away might rouse a body to all kinds of unpleasantness."||

Azra gave a slow, reluctant nod. "And even if he is genuine, what about the hierarchs, the counts and countesses? Will they really follow his lead? Especially Alabastra."

||Are they even doing so at the moment?|| signed Yali.

||"She makes a good point,"|| said Tatterlain. ||"We blame the Eternity King for what's done in his name, but how much of it is really *him*?"||

"True. I know better than anyone that authority is usurped more than it's given," said Azra.

||"So I should pass quietly into the Deadwinds?"|| asked Kat. How strange to say those words and not feel anything at all, as if the matter barely touched her.

||"Not at all."|| Tatterlain brushed away what might have been a tear. ||"I told you, I look forward to enduring your disapproval for years to come. But you asked for counsel. I'm trying to be responsible."||

||"Does it hurt?"||

He smiled, but his heart wasn't in it. ||"Like you wouldn't believe."||

"Perhaps we're looking at this the wrong way," said Azra. "Who's to say you can't learn to reconstruct your father's work yourself, now you know the secret of the ink?"

||"The Dark of Creation isn't exactly a secret revealed. It's just more mysticism hiding fact,"|| Kat replied.

"Not to the Eternity King, it would seem," said Azra. "It might just be that he's given you enough of an answer to work with."

||Assuming he didn't lie about that,|| put in Yali.

Azra squinted, her lips moving silently as she parsed the signs. "If that, yes. But who says the balance has to shift in the Eternity King's favour? I'd like to see the koilos keep their fearsome reputation when anyone can set them sleeping."

||"There's also Tanith,"|| said Tatterlain. ||"It may be the Eternity King can help her the way he claims he can heal you."||

||"Maybe,"|| said Kat. ||"I didn't ask. Better he doesn't know about her unless we're sure this isn't a terrible mistake."||

"If she even wants to be helped," said Azra sourly. "One decision at a time, darling. You saved everyone in Vallant's rebellion once. You're allowed to risk them to save yourself now."

Yali gaped. ||That's horrible.||

"She says—" Tatterlain began.

"I got the message, thank you, and I've been called worse." Eyes tight, Azra glowered at Yali and Tatterlain in turn, each word louder and thicker with emotion than the ones that had come before. "You want to play at impartial philosophers, that's up to you. Kat's all I care about. You, Vallant, little Azarian the one-eyed orphan boy who wants nothing more than to have a real family? It can all burn." She gritted her teeth and pinched her eyes shut, her voice barely more than a whisper. "So can I."

Fighting a wave of dizziness, Kat struggled to rise from her chair. To her surprise, Yali got there first, looping an arm about Azra's shoulders in a one-sided embrace, a small smile acknowledging the other's grateful glance.

Tatterlain cleared his throat. ||"There is, of course, nothing to say that the Eternity King won't discover how to replicate the tattoo without you."||

Kat nodded, frustration thickening in her chest as she realised this conversation was doomed to follow the same hopeless spiral as her own deliberations. But that wasn't the point, was it? They were her friends. Rîma excepted, her closest friends in the world. They deserved to be part of this decision, despite the pain.

"What would Vallant tell you to do?" asked Azra, extricating herself from Yali.

Kat frowned her surprise. ||"Do you really care?"||

Azra snorted. "Of course not, darling, but I thought you might."

||"He'd tell me that he trusts me to make the right decision."|| She didn't even have to think about it. ||"He's an idiot."||

Tatterlain grinned. ||"No argument from me ... but maybe he's not wrong."|| He leaned forward in his chair. ||"Put the rest of it aside. What do *you* want?"||

Kat sagged. ||"I know it's selfish, but I want to live."||

||"Then live. You're not Khalad's keeper."||

||"It's that simple?"||

He shrugged. ||"Everything else is ifs, buts and maybes. When the time comes – if the time comes – we'll face them together. All in favour?"|| He raised a hand. Without a flicker of hesitation, Azra and Yali raised theirs. ||"That's settled then. You called this conclave, you have to abide by its decision. Nyssa wouldn't like it otherwise."||

Kat smiled wanly, grateful for his attempt to lighten the mood. ||"I'll sleep on it."|| Rising from the chair on legs that felt steadier than they had in hours, she embraced each of them in turn. "Azra, you couldn't walk me back? I keep getting turned around in this place."

"Always, darling."

Glancing over Azra's shoulder, Kat glimpsed Yali's questioning frown, readily dismissed by Tatterlain's surreptitious wave. So much for subtlety, but there was no shame in being read by a master dissembler.

They passed the brief walk in silence, untroubled as before by the palace sentries, arriving at the bedroom door before Kat's weary legs had a chance to tire. She set her back to it, nervous uncertainty returning to a decision taken long before.

"Where's your room?"

Azra nodded further along the cloister. "In the next courtyard, overlooking the main gate."

"Wrong answer," Kat replied firmly. "This is your room. *Our* room.

Even if only for tonight ... or a piece of it. At least, if that's still what you want," she finished, her limited stocks of assertiveness fading into the cool dusk.

Azra's smile twisted to wryness. "You're not going to sleep on it at all, are you?"

"I ..." Kat swallowed. "I don't know that I have that kind of time. But I can wait a little while. Whatever happens next, I want things to be right between us, because we may not get another chance. Does that make any sense to you?"

With that small, vulnerable smile she shared with no one else, Azra took her hand. "All the sense in the world, darling."

"Good."

Her soul lighter than for weeks, Kat eased open the door and led Azra inside.

Kat left Azra sleeping, taking with her nothing but the clothes on her back and the warmth of embraces ended too soon. The stone garden was shrouded in darkness, the soft trill of nightjars and the throaty buzz of cicadas deafening in the otherwise quiet night. Walking as swiftly as unsteady limbs allowed, she retraced her steps through the palace, eyes dead ahead for fear that distraction would further erode resolve she could already feel slipping away, and arrived at the now-darkened conclave hall.

The Voice waited upon the dais, alone save for the koilos slumbering at the chamber's edge. "Ye've made your choice?" The soft burr betrayed that – at least for the moment – her words were her own. Isdihar the girl, rather than the majestic Voice.

"I have."

"I'm glad. Ye seem too kind to die."

What basis she had for such an opinion, Kat couldn't guess. Perhaps she was simply trying to be kind herself. She much preferred Isdihar to her imperious alter ego, though wasn't so foolish as to pretend she understood which was real. "I wouldn't know."

She nodded, Isdihar at once in retreat and the Voice pre-eminent once more. "Come. He says he is ready for you."

The spasms returned halfway down the stairway to the throne immortal, so debilitating that Kat managed the journey only because the Voice set a shoulder beneath hers to share the burden of her weight. With every step, she wondered bleakly if even the few hours stolen in Azra's company had been too much, had rendered the agonising choice redundant. But at last, the Voice half led, half carried her into the Eternity King's presence.

Kat slumped to her knees before the column of flame, her legs twisted beneath her, and stared through the downward spiral of magenta flame to the half-seen corpse within.

"What . . . now?" she gasped.

"He says you are to enter the fire," said the Voice. "He warns you that you will see things not to your liking, but that you must not resist, or else—"

"I'll die." With the last of her strength, Kat tottered to her feet. "So it goes."

Before she could change her mind, she stumbled into the flames.

Forty-Five

Tanith's world had long since lost all meaning save hunger.

Her daemon-half raged in the pit of her soul, screaming, begging, cajoling; tearing her inside out, searing her gut with need she was powerless to fulfil. Waking moments teetered between self-pity and unbridled rage, wordless screams and unbidden spasms of limb that only set the silver shackles biting deeper into her wrists.

Sleep passed fleetingly, soon banished by the cold, hard stone of the floor and the endless, maddening gnawing that shivered her soul to its foundations. Her brief dreams sang with jumbled, flame-wreathed imagery of a shackled goddess reaching for her hand, cold, beautiful features running like molten wax to reveal another half-seen beneath. In those dreams, Tanith felt her own skin sloughing off beneath her fingertips, the exposed flesh alive with flame as the something inside her fought its way to the surface.

She awoke to her own scream as she had countless times before, her skin three sizes too small and marred by small scratches where she'd clawed at it to dull the itch.

As she lay on the filthy black stone floor, cheek mashed in a puddle of drool, whimpering with the effort of lying still, a key rattled in the lock.

Ardoc loomed in the doorway, silhouetted against the magenta light of the Stars Below. "I wish you hadn't forced my hand in this,

432

I truly do." He crouched and stroked her cheek with a tender hand. "My poor dear daughter."

"Please ..." mewled Tanith, something within her growling as the lavender of his soul thickened in her nostrils. She felt her glamour building, clawing at Ardoc's perceptions, only to dissipate in the presence of her shackles. It took all she had not to launch herself at him. "I'm starving ..."

Ardoc stepped away. "From the first I promised to see that you were fed. I have broken my word." He beckoned at the empty doorway. "Permit me to make restitution, offered freely."

Her eyes half lidded, Tanith made out the black-robed koilos as it stomped into the cell, a trussed and burlap-hooded bundle over its shoulder. Fires dancing in its eye sockets, it laid the body in the corner, just beyond reach of her shackles, and lurched to stand motionless at Ardoc's side. For its part, the body made no move. The sweet scent of a living soul betrayed that it was unconscious, not a corpse, though just barely.

Her elbows trembling with exhaustion and need, Tanith pushed up into a sitting position, wisps of her golden hair glinting as they caught shafts of light from her cell's tiny barred window. Her daemon-half, ordinarily dismissive of an unconscious meal, clawed harder at her failing defences, slavering all the while.

Ardoc looped his arms behind his back, his tone belonging to the avuncular man of the recent past. "I regret that this will not be an especially delectable meal, but neither of us would wish for you to slake yourself on an innocent, now would we?"

A part of Tanith supposed she should have cared about that, but starvation and isolation had weathered almost to invisibility the line between the woman she wished she were and the monster she was.

"Who was he?" Even in her torment, her instinctive use of the past tense called out to her. She'd already accepted his death.

"Another who abused my trust and was observed in his treachery. This seemed fitting. Chastisement with the hope of redemption. *Nyssa Abdon ivohê.*"

433

"Let me go," she murmured. "Please."

Ardoc's bearded cheek twitched. "Your choices led you here, not mine. Midnight approaches. Already the stars align. The bonds of Nyssa's cage tremble. By this time tomorrow, she will be free and you her herald. These things I promise you. Rejoice in them."

He spread his hand before her and the air filled with the bitter, dizzying fragrance of blackthorn blossom. Tanith spluttered and shrank away, her eyes streaming and the room spinning as her senses upended. By the time they rallied, Ardoc and the koilos were gone, the door was locked fast . . . and her shackles were open.

The world sank into lavender clouds and the piece of Tanith that she thought of as herself bled away. No longer chastened by silver, her daemon-half's need – *her* need – smothered what passed for conscious thought, misgivings and doubts rendered ashen by the flames of hunger.

More beast than woman, she pounced, landing astride her unconscious prey. The outer flame of his soul parted at her caress, sweet and succulent, its vigour reknitting her wounds in an exhilarating rush. Delirious with the pleasure of the feast after so long denied, she plunged deeper into the faltering soul, uncaring that in her haste, precious slivers slipped free of her grasp, the dissipating scraps straining instinctively towards the Deadwinds they would never reach. Growling and trembling with exhilaration she glutted herself on what remained, awash in her victim's fading fire.

"Tanith . . ."

His voice, so familiar, so weak, parted lavender clouds already dissipating with his fading soul.

Tanith froze, the warmth of the feeding become an ice-cold fist squeezing tight about her heart. A keening hiss already parting her lips, she tore at the burlap hood and hurled it away. The face beneath had never been handsome, even before unknown hands had levied the beating that had left it bloodied and bruised. But it had smiled at her in a way no other had ever done and had offered hope that maybe – just maybe – a piece of her was worthy of being loved.

434

"Esram?" She cradled his head with shaking hands, her throat already so raw as to reduce the words to a thin moan. "No! ... I'm ..." She swallowed, unable to continue.

"Tanith?" He spoke in the thinnest whisper, soft as a breath, his eyes unfocused and glassy. "Tanith, you ..."

And then he was gone, lost to the Deadwinds, leaving Tanith alone with her tears.

Forty-Six

As Hadîm had predicted, the masonry sealing away the spiral stairway had crumbled with age, leaving it no barrier to a determined man – if one soon filthy, sore and weary beyond words. Reaching Tadamûr's empty streets, Damant had forced his way into a nearby house and helped himself to a spare mask and robe from a moth-haunted wardrobe, ignored the whole time by the vacant, dead-eyed couple whose home it was. Fortunately the city-soul's attention – if indeed it was sentient enough to *have* attention – clearly lay elsewhere.

Alas, even a determined, fortunate man could be undone by the passage of time, and Damant – now masked and with the rusted sword that had slain Hadîm concealed beneath his borrowed robes – had barely reached the open gateway to Amakala's shrine when the first midnight-host chime rang out.

Leaving the increasingly crowded streets behind, he descended into the shrine, retracing his fateful steps of the day before. As on that occasion, he encountered no guardians save the proto-koilos statues arrayed around the buried sanctum's pool. Clearly, when Rîand banished someone to the Stars Below, he expected them to remain there.

He barely felt the water's chill as he crossed the pool. Amakala's sculpted likeness gazed down, her scabbarded sword – Rîma's sword – outstretched upon her upturned palms. She was never more alike to

Nyssa Iudexas than at that moment. Would she approve? Would she despise what he intended for Tadamûr and the last daughter of its royal bloodline?

Shaking the thought away, Damant seized the sword by its hilt and slid it clear.

No godly voice rang out in protest, no divine fire seared his bones. Amakala's sword was simply a sword, if one colder and heavier than he'd expected. The weight of old souls, perhaps, the fragments of Rîma's ancestors borne within the blade. He hoped they were ready for a fight.

Moved by an impulse he couldn't explain, he set the rusted scimitar across Amakala's palms. A decaying sword for a decaying city, held by a goddess who never was.

A second midnight-host chime echoed down from the streets. Pausing only to hitch his belt higher to conceal his new scabbard beneath his tattered robes, Damant joined the crowds flocking to the temple.

His body screaming impatience at every step, he matched the shuffling, uneven gait of those around him, jostled and buffeted as one of them. His own clothes, worn beneath the borrowed robes, grew musty with sweat; the golden mask hot and stale with his expended breath. They became a second skin, sealing him away from a world more distant with every step. Soon Damant, who'd never known claustrophobia his entire life, was fighting for every breath, his stumbles no longer entirely for show.

After a seeming eternity he passed beneath the temple gateway. By now, he was no longer surprised to see how the interior so closely matched an Alabastran xanathros, down to the swirling pungency of incense. Here too the ages had taken their toll. What had once been polished wood was blackened with rot and thick with the same dust that robbed gilding of lustre. Black roots showed through rucked and broken floor tiles, and the entire left transept lay buried beneath rubble, the remnants of statues protruding from beneath the sea of stones. No pews remained, eternity having long since taken its toll, the congregation of thousands forming serried rows in the space between the cobwebbed pillars. Black-liveried guards stood to attention along the stained-glass walls, their rusted swords clasped vertically against their chests.

Only at the altar dais did glory remain. A thirty-foot-tall statue of Nyssa Benevolas, gowned and graceful, stood with her arms wide in welcome beneath a glittering muqarnas ceiling too reminiscent of the Stars Below to be coincidence. And before the altar – a slab of black marble, unadorned save for a shabby velvet cushion and a simple silver circlet – barely visible through the incense clouds, a throne inset with sapphires and opals, flanked by two scarlet-robed handmaidens and Madîq standing close attendance, a woman in white and gold robes sitting rigid and unseeing against its backrest.

Rîma.

Rîand stood to Rîma's front, his handsome golden mask contriving to wear a gloating expression in the dappled stained-glass glow, his violet and azure robes glittering like a fish's scales as the light shifted.

The bells chimed once more and fell silent.

"Citizens of Tadamûr," the acoustics gathered up Rîand's sombre words and sent them booming across the nave, "I welcome you to Nyssa's sight on this day of days, and call upon you to bear witness to the descension of your queen-to-be."

Throat tight, Damant picked up his pace, no longer caring who he jostled. Tadamûr's citizens, who had no life save that which the city gave them, were in no position to bear witness to anything. The ceremony was a farce, an inverted puppet show where the audience jerked about on strings and only the performer had free will. Did Rîand even recognise the vainglorious nonsense of it all, or was he so lost in his precious traditions that he didn't care?

Or maybe – just maybe – he was no freer than anyone else in the temple, and only believed himself so because the city willed it. A fate Rîma would soon share.

Rîand held his arms aloft. "In her capable hands, the glories of our city will endure through the ages to come, a beacon to those who followed us into Nyssa's light."

Hastened by concern and his mind gummed by long hours without sleep, Damant's next jostle became an outright shove. The target of his impatience staggered into two others, sending a ripple through the congregation.

"As the throne passed to Amakala, and from Amakala to her son, so do I willingly relinquish it to my granddaughter. So do I—"

Damant let his posture sag as the king's gaze swept towards him. The sinking feeling in his heart told him it was already too late.

"One of us is not what they appear." Rîand extended a gloved finger in his direction. "Bring him."

Guards strode into the crowd. With nothing left to lose, Damant shoved and elbowed his way through the unresisting morass. A guard lurched into view directly ahead, the congregation parting willingly before his advance.

Concealment and evasion having run their course, he abandoned both. He ripped away mask and veil and reached beneath his outer robes.

A gloved hand closed about his wrist and twisted it aside.

Damant braced his feet against the cracked tiles. The guard jerked on his hand, reeling him in without obvious effort. The impassive mask gazed down at him.

"Don't let's be rash," the guard said softly.

Damant gaped. Despite the mask's muffling effect, the voice was unmistakably Hadîm's. "So even the Deadwinds didn't want you," he murmured as the other two guards closed, one to either side.

"I said they'd take me before I reached my thralls. Happily, I had another option."

"Which was?" asked Damant, relief ebbing away beneath irritation.

"You're a canny fellow, you'll work it out." Hadîm dipped his head. "Meanwhile, a lesson in memorable entrances."

So saying, he whirled to Damant's right, corroded sword whistling.

The other guard was still moving to the parry when Hadîm's blade hit home with the sound of an axe striking a rotten log. The guard's body went one way, his head the other.

Hadîm was already in motion, his victim's sword now in his left hand. A vicious flurry battered the second guard's sword aside and half severed his weapon arm. The guard staggered back. Hadîm kicked his leg away and, as the man dropped groaning to one knee, crossed his swords against his throat, the flats resting on the fellow's shoulders. He brought the blades together with a savage jerk, and the second guard too fell headless. A needlessly theatrical *coup de grâce* to Damant's mind until he saw the first body thrashing and scrabbling at the ground in an attempt to rise. The citizens of Tadamûr hadn't been alive for long centuries. With the city-soul guiding their bodies, only the showiest of injuries would even slow them.

Ripping away his mask to reveal a familiar face and black, glimmerless eyes unhidden by glass lenses, Hadîm whirled about in the widening circle of citizens – who either at the city-soul's urging or some long-dormant instinct had wisely opted for self-preservation – and raised a sword towards the altar in mocking salute.

"Old debts come due, your majesty," he bellowed. "You betrayed me."

"The throne owes a renegade no debts," Rîand bit out, his body quivering with rage.

The remaining guards plunged into the crowd. Hadîm turned his back on the altar, his dark eyes finding Damant's. "I'll keep them occupied."

Damant ran for the altar. A guard emerged from the silent crowd, sword drawn. Damant slid Rîma's sword from its scabbard, the weapon still cold to the touch but no longer heavy, as if it understood his need. His lunge cheated the guard's parry, the blade puncturing lamellar and withered flesh to find the heart in one clean motion. Too late, he remembered that the soulless vessel was immune to such mortal wounds. He twisted the sword, desperate to free it of the guard's body before the counterblow fell.

The guard toppled to his knees, the sword sliding free of his ribs.

With a thin, stale hiss he collapsed sideways and lay still. Damant squeezed the grips tighter as realisation dawned, bringing with it a surge of vicious hope. Rîma's sword. Amakala's sword. The gift of a goddess, granted to usher even an immortal to oblivion. No finer blade for the task at hand.

A ragged scream dragged his attention back across the nave. Hadîm vanished beneath a tide of black lamellar, withered grey-brown hands clutching at his arms, his legs, his chest. A trio of guards raised their swords high and rammed them down, silencing the scream.

"Long overdue," sneered Rîand. "Now the other."

As one, Hadîm's slayers lurched about and started towards Damant, two headless comrades crawling in their wake. Others made stumbling approach, threading through the silent citizenry. Damant glanced at Rîma, still unmoving upon the throne. They'd be on him before he reached her.

The rightmost of the advancing guard trio lurched, halted and pulled away his veiled mask, the face beneath already flowing from a desiccated sunken rictus to Hadîm's self-satisfied smirk. His sword flashed out, severing his erstwhile companion's leg above the knee.

One of the headless crawlers grabbed at Hadîm's ankle, holding him in place while the surviving guard ran him through. This time, he sank without a sound. He'd barely vanished into the sea of silent citizens when a guard on the far side of the congregation flung his mask towards the altar dais, a familiar mocking laugh echoing beneath the glittering ceiling.

"You can't stop me, majesty. You can only kill your own subjects one by one." Hadîm glared impatiently at Damant. "And you should be running."

The pieces of the puzzle snapped into place. Hadîm was a qalimîri, a daemon that survived by suppressing vulnerable souls and stealing their bodies. And in that temple – in the whole of Tadamûr – there were considerably more bodies than souls to go around. He would never have easier prey.

441

Damant bolted for the altar dais.

The scarlet handmaidens moved to block his path. He cut them down without a flicker, their puppet strings sliced through by the goddess-given sword. He hesitated with Madîq, but reminded himself that she was only a memory enshrined in embalmed flesh. Empathy was wasted on the citizens of Tadamûr. All save one.

As Madîq's body fell, Damant knelt before Rîma's throne. Ignoring the scrape of vying steel from elsewhere, he held out the sword, mimicking the stance of the statue from the shrine. Formality seemed important somehow. "This is yours."

Slowly, agonisingly slowly, Rîma dipped her head, the blank eyes of her mask settling on him. "I do not know you."

"Take it." Heart creaking with loss, Damant grabbed her wrist. Formality be damned. He forced her fingers around the grips. "You don't belong to this city any longer. Only to yourself!"

Heavy hands seized his shoulders and hauled him backwards, breaking his grip. The sword clanged from Rîma's nerveless fingers and onto the altar dais.

Rîand's handsome golden mask pressed close. "Enough." Snarling, he shoved Damant from the dais and into the congregation. "Hold him!"

Damant gasped as a dozen clawing, grasping hands fastened around his arms and legs, pinning him fast. Bodies pressed in, their dry, rank stench stifling, smothering.

"No more delays." Rîand plucked the silver circlet from its altar cushion. "Tadamûr awaits its queen."

"Rîma, you wanted me here to bear witness." Damant thrashed against his captors as Rîand made solemn procession across the dais, twisting, kneeing, kicking. For every grip he broke, another hand took its place. "You are not Queen Eskamarîma of Tadamûr. You've spent a thousand lifetimes fighting everything this city has become!"

Reaching the throne, Rîand raised the circlet high. "Willingly do I pass the duties of monarch to you, Granddaughter. Rule wisely and well, in Nyssa's sight and Amakala's memory."

442

Bowing low, he set the crown atop Rîma's head. The stained-glass walls blazed bright. Damant narrowed his eyes to slits, with Rîand and Rîma little more than hazy black shapes against a storm of searing colour.

When the light dimmed, Rîand stood at the front of the dais, Rîma a pace behind him. The congregation, all save those holding Damant – and now, he saw, Hadîm – were kneeling in reverence.

"It's done. You've failed." Rîand pointed a lazy finger first at Damant, then at Hadîm. "Cast them into the Stars Below . . . but this time break their legs so that they cannot crawl back."

The congregation made no move to obey.

"You forget," said Damant, determined to extract even the smallest nugget of triumph, "they're not your subjects any longer."

And then he looked again upon the dais' tableau, and caught a detail that offered the possibility of still greater triumph.

Rîand snorted. "Then I suppose it falls to the queen to choose what is done with you." He turned about. "The command is yours to give, majesty."

The point of the sword pierced his chest with the dry whisper of a knife slicing parchment.

A thin wheeze of laughter parted his lips. "So be it . . . " He sank to his knees. "The old king dies as the new queen is crowned. My last . . . duty to the city."

"Farewell, Grandfather." Compassion rippled beneath Rîma's words, which she offered not in the hollow, listless voice that had haunted Damant's recent memory, but the measured, deliberate tones he had thought never to hear again.

She slid the sword free of Rîand's ribs and struck his head from his shoulders in a single smooth motion. Only when his corpse hit the dais did she tug her golden mask free, long white hair spilling across the shoulders of her glittering queenly robes. The mask fell face up, empty eyes meeting her own. Each expression as immobile as the other as her sword point touched the dais' stone.

443

Damant pulled free as his captors' hands lost their force. When he'd seen that the sword had gone, he'd hoped Rîma had claimed it, that the brief clasp of hand on steel had given her back to herself. Now he wasn't sure. She wore the circlet. She was the queen she'd striven never to be. The death of the old ruler had sealed coronations in times past. Granted, that death usually came first, but tradition never held sway as tightly as people like Rîand believed. Was this victory or defeat?

"Welcome back." He reached the dais, eyes straining for some glimmer of recognition that would make his words true. Finding none, he drew down a deep breath. Evasion no longer served any purpose. "You *are* back?"

Rîma offered no response, the silence between them fertile ground for growing doubts. Damant stared out across the hushed temple, and what he might have considered an expectant atmosphere ... had any within been capable of such emotion.

The crowd parted before Hadîm, his host body's armour bereft of plates about his right shoulder and his robes torn. "Well?"

Damant eyed Rîma again. "I don't know."

"I can feel it, Ihsan," she whispered. "The emptiness of every street. The longing of every stone. The loneliness. The river flows through my heart. I feel the wind in my hair. Amakala sought to forge a legacy to outlast the ages. Instead, she destroyed us."

She drew up to her full height, her deportment regal for the first time. When she spoke again, it was with certainty fit to shatter mountains; with disappointment, and a loss that made Damant's heart ache. "I always wondered what set our decline in motion. Why those of us who escaped these halls were reborn among the younger races and not our own. They fled us. They fled *you*."

The congregation offered no reply, but Damant realised with a start that her words weren't for them. *They will be one*, Rîand had said. Damant had thought it metaphor, another facet of the dead king's beloved tradition, but it was plain that Rîma heard the city's thoughts as clearly as she felt its sensations.

444

The stained-glass panels pulsed with angry light, scattering shards of colour through the incense smoke. Rîma flinched, but steadied at once. "Scream at me all you wish. I will not hear you." Her brow softened as she glanced at Damant. "My friend was wrong, but he is also right. I *am* your queen, but I do not belong to you. You took everything from the people you were made to serve. I do not blame you for that, but I cannot permit it to continue. This ends now."

Closing her eyes, she planted the point of her sword between her feet with enough force to drive sparks from the stone. The stained glass flickered and strobed the city-soul's voiceless scream of dismay.

"What's happening?" asked Hadîm, his eyes wary.

"You're asking the wrong man," Damant replied.

It began slowly, a groaning, distant yawn. So too did the tremors start so small that Damant dismissed them as imagination. But in the space of a breath, the yawn became a rumble, the censers swaying on their brackets as the ground shook. Citizens staggered to and fro on the temple's shuddering tiles.

Damant stumbled for balance as the dais bucked beneath his feet. "She's bringing down the city."

Hadîm gazed at him agog. "She can do that?"

The notion had been so apposite that Damant had voiced it without thinking, but on further examination, he found no fault. "'By her will, the city shall endure'," he shouted above the thunderous cacophony. "Looks like the reverse is also true."

With a tortured shriek, a chunk of glittering muqarnas broke away from the ceiling and shattered to rubble. The citizens caught beneath made no attempt to save themselves and vanished beneath the spill of stone as their neighbours looked blankly on. Cracks crazed to columns and archways. A jagged tiled expanse rose up like the prow of a sinking ship holed beneath the waterline, scattering robed bodies.

Rîma stood impassive as stone shattered around her, eyes pinched shut and lips moving in time with the mad pulse of the stained glass.

Fighting for balance, Hadîm stared through the rubble deluge to the temple gateway. "I'd be more impressed if we were some-where else!"

"No one's asking you to stay," snapped Damant. "Besides, Madîq told me they'd sealed the Tulloq entrance."

"There's always the Stars Below."

Damant shuddered, the choice between being crushed by the collapsing city or straying into the territory of the aethervores too close to call.

Every stained-glass panel in the temple burst apart into glittering shards with an ear-splitting screech. A blizzard of magenta and indigo motes streamed free of the remnants, swirling towards the widening fissures in the temple roof, Tadamûr's captive souls straining instinc-tively for the distant Deadwinds.

Rîma's eyes snapped open. "It's done. May Nyssa forgive me." She offered one of her almost-smiles. "We'd do well to leave, I think."

Ever after, Damant struggled to recall the details of what followed, the memories swallowed up by the grinding roar of collapsing stone, the stark terror of roadways yawning open beneath his feet and rock faces flowing like water as he and his companions fled for the relative safety of the Stars Below. Glimpses remained of the mote-wreathed city, its towers toppling and its buildings devoured by hungry chasms, the puppet citizens of Tadamûr, strings cut, staring blankly as hungry stone consumed everything.

His only clear memory, which lingered to his dying day, was of Rîma standing on the threshold of the spiral stair leading to the Stars Below, her eyes bright with tears as she took one last opportunity to behold the glorious doom she'd wrought.

"It was a beautiful city once."

Forty-Seven

Esram's blank stare haunted the darkness of Tanith's cell, his cooling body already collapsing in sweet decay as corpses did when the soul was ripped from them. She huddled in the opposite corner, shunned by sleep, her face red raw from weeping, the euphoria of feeding washed away by the deluge of its cost. It was her fault Esram was dead, tainted by association after her failure to kill the Voice. Worse, his death had dispelled the last illusion.

She didn't have a daemon-half. She *was* a daemon, body and soul.

But she'd learned too that the world held worse than daemons and men crueller than monsters. Ardoc had known what Esram had meant to her. He'd wanted to hurt her – and he had, worse than she'd ever known. However, Ardoc was but a man, and men should fear daemons. In his arrogance, he'd forgotten that. And in the darkness of the Stars Below, her only true light the flickering flames from her aetherios tattoo, a corpse her only company, Tanith squeezed her grief so tight it became determination. Even with the shackles gone, she was a prisoner – the window too narrow and the door's bolt too heavy to allow escape.

But Ardoc would return, and she'd be ready.

For all the expectation of catharsis to come, grief ruled her as the hours ticked by. Why hadn't she removed his hood before feeding? Why hadn't she demanded answers from Ardoc? Why hadn't she recognised

447

the scent of his soul? She wasn't even sated. Esram should have left her fit to burst. Instead, the gnawing precursor to hunger's onset scuffed the corners of her psyche.

Round and round the questions swirled, the answers always the same and never offering a crumb of comfort: mad with hunger, she'd not been lucid enough to think, let alone question. In a sense, Esram's hood had been a mercy, leaving her free to pretend – to hope – that ignorance had fuelled her rapacity. But more than anything, she wondered what he had tried to say with his last breath. Accusation, forgiveness? Surely the former. Who could forgive a creature like her?

Certainly, no one should expect forgiveness in return.

Footsteps beyond the door dragged Tanith back to the present. The scrape of someone making heavy weather of a key in the lock. Careful to keep clear of the discarded shackles, she gathered herself to her haunches in preparation for the pounce. She'd only get one chance. Even a second's delay would fetch another lungful of blackthorn blossom.

The door creaked open. A black-robed figure took its place, a koilos standing sentry just behind, its back to the doorway.

Tanith sprang. Black silks swirled as she bore Ardoc to the ground, bones jarring with the impact. Lock charmer's tools skittered away. The door slammed shut. Kneeling atop him, hands about his throat, she unfurled her daemon-half, her glamour urging him to silence even as she clawed at his rotten soul.

Neither found purchase.

Not resistance – the absence of anything at all.

As if there were no soul to find.

Nor, Tanith realised belatedly, was it Ardoc. Her captive was willowy, whereas he tended towards the rubicund. Even the cell's gloom couldn't disguise her pallor, nor the cold blue eyes that gazed up with impatient disappointment. For the first time in their brief association, Tanith considered the possibility that it wasn't the stare alone that was unsettling, but whatever lay behind it.

448

"Are you done?" hissed Enna. "Because we'd both rather that koilos doesn't get curious at the noise."

A koilos that had let her walk right up to the door and charm its lock without tearing her limb from limb. A different koilos had ignored her completely the night of the provisions yard raid ... *and* she'd made her way through the depths without being troubled by Ardoc's tsrûqi. Tanith's daemon-self couldn't touch her. Ifrîti couldn't see her.

Tanith blinked. "What *are* you?" she said softly. "You can't be real."

Enna snorted. "I'm the realest person you're ever likely to meet. And if you don't stop kneeling on my hip, I'm likely to become the angriest. You wouldn't like that."

Tanith backed away and let her stand. "I thought you were Ardoc."

Enna made a play of dusting herself down and tugged her short sword's curved scabbard back into place. In the darkness of the cell she seemed more insubstantial than ever, as if a piece of her wasn't there at all. "Understandable. We're practically twins." Her eyes touched on Esram's body. "Ah. I suppose that explains the smell. So he found out after all."

"That Esram was working with you?" Tanith made no attempt to conceal her bitterness.

Enna shook her head, the white streak in her ink-black hair gleaming in the wan light. "That he was spying for Alabastra," she corrected gently. "Serrîq suspected, and we all know what happened to Serrîq, don't we?"

"No, he's dead because of me. He ..."

At the foundry, Esram had distracted her from keeping watch and downplayed the possibility of the attack when it finally came. He'd flattered her into charming the tsrûqi, opening a path through the depths that Ardoc had long kept secret. He'd pried into her private conversations with Ardoc.

Tanith stared at his corpse, her guilt ebbing. She hadn't tainted Esram through association. He'd used her.

Just how much of what she remembered had been real? How much

449

had been a glamour spun of words and smiles? She'd never know, would she?

Her heart broke for the second time, this time the worse for the knowledge that she deserved it for what she'd done to countless others.

But she could choose to believe that Esram had intended his unspoken last words neither as accusation nor forgiveness, but apology. Who was to say otherwise?

None of which forgave Ardoc *his* deeds.

Enna leaned against the door. "I liked him too, right up until the point he started rumours that I'd poisoned Serrîq." She sighed. "I am sorry. I don't think anything hurts more than discovering the man you loved wasn't who you thought he was."

"I didn't love him," snapped Tanith, and sounded a liar even to herself.

"Why did dear Ardoc turn on you?"

"He sent me to kill the Voice. I failed." Better not to tell Enna it was her fault she'd failed. She'd be unbearable. "He keeps saying that I'll be Nyssa's herald. I'm starting to think it's not something I'm supposed to enjoy."

"I'd say so."

"Your turn," Tanith murmured, mindful of the koilos beyond the door. "If you're not with Alabastra, who *are* you working for?"

"Nobody. I only joined the Obsidium Cult because I thought I could help people while I looked for a way home. But Ardoc doesn't help. He promises the moon but does nothing save for himself." Enna shrugged and glanced around the cell. "But I imagine you've worked that out."

Tanith frowned. "He promises the what?"

Enna twitched a smile. "All these years and I still forget. Where I'm from, the moon rules the night as the sun does the day. She bestows truth, which is probably why you don't have her here. There's precious little truth in Khalad."

"What's that supposed to mean?"

"It's hard to explain. There's something terribly wrong with this

450

realm, but none of you can see it because you're part of it." She drew back the sleeve of her robe, revealing the undertunic beneath. "What colour is this?"

Tanith eyed both Enna and her sleeve warily. "Red."

"Not to me," Enna replied, her voice oddly sad. "Everything here is shades of violet and magenta, like I'm watching through coloured glass."

"Are they all as strange as you in . . ." Tanith paused, trying to think of somewhere sufficiently distant that its people could keep secret their absence of souls. " . . . Phoenissa?"

"Oh, I'm definitely a one-off. And I'm from much further away than Phoenissa. My travelling companion – my guide, of sorts – warned me against taking this particular path. But stubbornness is something of a family trait. The mists closed up behind me and I've been trapped here ever since."

"And he just left you here?"

"He doesn't always appreciate my . . . forthrightness. More likely he doesn't want to get trapped as well." She shrugged. "Maybe he's looking for me even as we speak. Probably he's sitting with his feet up on the other side of the mists, sipping wine and laughing at his good fortune at being rid of me."

"You expect me to believe that you're from the other side of the Veil?"

"I don't expect anything, and I don't particularly care what you believe."

"Then why are you here?"

"Because I want to know what Ardoc's really up to. For a man obsessed with a benevolent goddess, he's really not so benevolent himself. It makes me doubt the shape of this new era of his. And why bring you here? In a few hours the entire cult embarks on an uprising that will shake Zariqaz to its foundations and their leader's scrabbling around in the dark? I thought I'd find answers down here. Instead I've spent the whole time avoiding his koilos and hiding from those pale horrors."

So the aethervores could see Enna? "I once asked Ardoc if he wanted me to kill the Eternity King. He told me that I would help him free Nyssa, and that she would do the rest."

"I suppose that *is* a herald's role." Enna offered an almost-smile. "I assume it's no longer one you want?"

Tanith thought back to the vision she'd had upon touching the stone in the depths. The goddess had loved her, cherished her ... hadn't she? Or had it been another of Esram's deceptions? Some intoxicant smeared on the stone?

Could she follow through with Ardoc's plans but on her own terms? If Nyssa truly did love her, surely she'd side with her against Ardoc when his sins were revealed? Killing him would settle things for Esram, but better to take from him that which he'd longed and schemed for. Wouldn't that be the sweetest revenge? "I don't know."

Enna stooped and reclaimed her lock charmer's tools. "I suppose that's a start. The answer lies in the ruin at the heart of the city, I'm certain of it." Her lips twisted in another almost-smile. "How about we take a look?"

Right into the thick of the aethervores? Tanith shuddered. "I thought you said you'd tried that."

"I didn't have someone to watch my back before."

"You'd really trust me to do that?"

Enna shrugged. "Why not?"

Tanith's gaze touched on Esram's corpse. "Because I'm a monster."

"Only if you want to be." Enna's expression lost its archness. "We all do monstrous things from time to time, Tanith. Sometimes in error, sometimes we tell ourselves we had no choice. What matters is how we atone ... if we choose to."

Tanith sagged. "It's not that simple."

"I never said it was. Welcome to life."

Despite everything, Tanith found a morsel of solace in the sentiment, but she couldn't bear to admit it for fear of looking weak. "You're only saying that because you want me to come with you."

"You're welcome to stay. Ardoc will be back for you soon, I'm sure."

Ardoc and his blackthorn and his silver and his koilos. Advantages that even a glutted amashti would be unwise to face head-on. "Fine. I'll come."

"Good." Enna reached for the door. "Make sure I'm between you and the koilos until we're out of its sight."

The cell left behind, they passed deeper into the abandoned city, their path lit by oil-soaked brands recovered from Enna's makeshift refuge. So too did the aethervores' eerie song billow to ever greater height, every note and murmur a numbing caress on Tanith's thoughts.

"Does the song do that to you?" she asked, as they left the river embankment behind.

"Do what?" asked Enna.

"It's ... it's like a lullaby, urging me to sleep."

"Then no. But I hate the tune."

They pressed deeper in, what aethervores they glimpsed always at a distance, either unaware of the intruders or held at bay by the smoky orange flames of their torches. Tanith watched the road behind almost as much as the one ahead, skin prickling with foreboding.

"Is it me, or are there fewer of them than last time I was here?" she murmured as the last of the streets fell away, leaving only the broad circular sweep of the central boulevard before the ruin-crested hill and the coruscating flame held within.

"They'll be here somewhere." Enna gestured to a three-storey building within the boulevard's inner curve, its roof served by a wide stone stairway. "We'll see more from up there."

And so it proved. Standing on the far side of the building from the stairway's head, their vantage laid fully half the city bare, the neat spokes of its streets stretching away into the distant shadows of the Stars Below, no longer merely organised, but arrayed in perfect symmetry.

"What if they're not streets at all," said Tanith. "Or not *just* streets."

"What do you mean?"

"In Kaldos, there are those who follow older ways than Alabastra.

453

This looks a lot like the mandalas they use to focus their meditations. All the better to commune with the goddess, so they say." She shrugged. "Probably nonsense."

"Maybe." Enna dipped her torch, indicating individual aethervores across the city. "But it's not just the buildings that follow the pattern, is it? Maybe it's designed to channel something? Draw it inward, perhaps?"

"The Deadwinds," murmured Tanith. "It focuses the Deadwinds."

"Could be."

Tanith stared at the spiral of flame at the city's heart, at the silhouettes of aethervores clustered about its base. The fire seemed patchier than before, what had previously been a sheet of uninterrupted magenta flame now stuttering, darker at the edges than at the core ...

The next she knew, she was on her hands and knees, her thoughts muddied and her cheek throbbing. Enna peered down at her, flexing her fingers as she wafted her hand back and forth.

Tanith blinked and worked her jaw. "You *hit* me?"

"You tried to push past me," Enna replied, unrepentant. "Completely unresponsive and your eyes blank as mist. It seemed warranted."

Tanith clambered to her feet, the pain already fading. "It's that fire. I don't know why."

"Then my suggestion is not to look at it."

"Such wisdom," Tanith said sourly. "Got anything else?"

"Only that it's definitely dimmer. The conjunction is almost here."

"What *is* the conjunction?" she asked, eyes lidded against the flames' influence. "Ardoc goes on about it all the time, but he's never explained."

"A reordering of the realms beyond the Veil."

"Realms? I thought you were talking about stars."

Enna shrugged. "The shifting pressure alters certain ... mystical alignments. We're right under Zariqaz. If these streets really are why the Deadwinds are focused here, disrupting the flame at the conjunction's height will shake the bars of Nyssa's cage in the Golden Citadel."

You need only open the way. "It's why he wanted me down here, isn't

454

it? He wants *me* to do it." Which meant the goddess would owe her, and not Ardoc. What favours might that command?

"That's one interpretation."

Enna was watching her, Tanith realised, curious to see how she reacted. Nor was it the first time. "When you asked for my help in the provisions yard – all that insistence on not killing people – that was a test, wasn't it?"

"I already knew what you were. I wanted to see who you wanted to be."

Good luck with that. She still didn't know herself. "Why do you care?"

"You're not the first person I've known who's grappling with a side of herself she can't control. I look at you and I wonder how different their life might have been had someone offered kindness before their fears hardened to a cage."

Was she talking about herself, or someone else? As ever, she had offered just enough information to remain unclear. "What happened?"

Enna grunted. "I think we'll have to know one another *much* better for that story. That, or I'll have to be just the right level of drunk ... Oh, hello."

Careful not to find herself enraptured by the flames, Tanith followed her to the rooftop's inner edge and her gaze to an arched causeway running from the ruined crest to a distant gateway beyond which the telltale steel cage of an elevator gleamed dully. A dozen redcloaks advanced in sombre procession, their masked helms blinkered with leather patches that prevented them from seeing anything but that which lay directly ahead. The foremost and hindmost pair bore tall staves topped with clusters of altar bells. Their chimes were lost beneath the ever-present song, but not their effect. Aethervores scurried from their path like shadows from the light, oozing into alleyways and the crevasses between the sundered stone, and beneath the causeway's arches, thereafter flowing into place behind the marchers, always careful to stay out of sight.

At the centre of the procession walked a lone bearded figure arrayed in a hierarch's finery, a gold circlet about his greying hair. He walked with stumbling steps, even at that distance his expression the unfocused stare of a man lost in the hallucinogenic clouds of isshîm powder, insensate to his surroundings.

"Who is that?" murmured Tanith.

"Hierarch Ossed," Enna replied. "But he's supposed to be taking his seat on the Qabirarchi Council. Not . . . whatever this is."

The procession reached the nearer side of the causeway and a single, lopsided wooden throne set upon a dizzying swirl of concentric tiles. Two redcloaks seated the sightless Ossed upon it. The bell-bearers stomped their staves twice against the tiles, then the redcloaks turned on their heels and marched back along the causeway, leaving him alone.

As they passed, the aethervores swarmed back into sight, converging on the unseeing hierarch like vultures on carrion. One moment he was alone in a circle of waxy, oozing bodies. In the next, he was gone, lost beneath the glistening swarm.

Tanith gagged and looked away. "The Eternity King feeds those things?"

"No," said Enna. "I don't think so."

The undulating mass of bodies parted, offering no sign of Ossed. At least, no sign of the man he'd once been. In his place sat another hunched, waxy aethervore, indistinguishable from the rest save for the fact that its robes were still bright and hale, where theirs were blackened and ragged from untold years far from the light. As Tanith watched, the creature that had been Ossed slunk from its throne and followed the others into the ruins, indigo fire pulsing beneath its sickly, translucent skin and its pallid lips moving in time to the mournful, cloying song.

"I think that *is* the Qabirarchi Council," said Enna, drily.

The vortex of fire flickered and went darker still, brief tongues of magenta flaring at its circumference. Forgetting that she wasn't supposed to stare, Tanith shaded her eyes and gazed deeper.

A second, indigo flame arose within the fading magenta. It sprang from a multifaceted black prism set among the ruins and leapt taller than the encompassing stones, its tongues thrashing and writhing in opposition to all principles of convection. For all that it lacked identifiable form, Tanith knew at once that it was not only alive, but aware, the sudden pressure of its will suffocating, smothering . . . not malignant, but *hungry*. It tugged at her with invisible strings. She felt a piece of herself drift towards it. Another.

She felt herself take a step, her legs moving by a command not her own.

"No!" Enna stepped in front of her, blotting out the indigo flame.

It took all Tanith had to look away, to drop to hands and knees beneath the parapet where she could no longer see it. Where *it* could no longer see *her*.

Her stomach lurched, emptying its thin contents across black stone.

"What is that thing?" she gasped.

"That *thing*?" Ardoc stepped from the shadows, a cluster of white-robed and golden-masked kathari at his back. "It is our goddess . . . and your future, Qori Arvish."

Forty-Eight

Damant's second journey into the Stars Below was little more to his liking than the first. Arriving on its darkened shores by foot had plenty to recommend it over being washed up like a drowned rat, but an improved journey added scant appeal to the grim destination. Growing hunger pangs, the aethervores' ever-present song and his dearth of confidence that Hadîm knew where to find another exit to the surface steadily eroded patience already in short supply. But he kept trudging along the arrow-straight street, the magenta flames of the Obsidium Palace growing ever closer.

"No more adventure for me," he muttered, sending a stray stone skittering across the roadway. "A quiet life, with everything in its place."

A pace ahead of him, Rîma turned and regarded him with an unreadable expression. "Be careful what you wish for. You've seen how that can end."

Damant offered a rueful smile, glad that she'd found her voice. It was the first time she'd spoken since they'd left the remnants of Tadamûr behind. Her regal finery long abandoned, she wore only the black linen grave wrappings that swathed all save head and hands, a rangy, skeletal shadow in the dark. Further ahead, Hadîm's torch bobbed onwards into the streets. If their last visit was anything to go by, they'd soon be in aethervore territory. Better to tighten their ranks before that happened, especially as Rîma had the only weapon worthy of the name – he and

Hadîm could only count on decaying Tadamûr steel – but until then distance was appreciated.

"And how are you?" he asked.

"Feeling like I cut my own throat but keep on walking around. I have a hundred phantom limbs, and they itch terribly." Rîma shook her head. "I suspect I will be carrying pieces of Tadamûr for a long, long time."

Damant reached for something to say, all the while knowing he'd never truly understand how she felt. "You did the right thing."

She reached up to brush the hilt of her sword, once again scabbarded at her shoulder. "That's what they say, too. They thank me for having possessed the strength to do what they could not. That isn't the consolation I might have hoped."

"No, I suppose not."

Hadîm's impatient basso sigh echoed along the street. "Can you please stop bleating?"

"No one's stopping you from striking out on your own," growled Damant.

"And leave you poor lambs alone when the pack comes hunting? I have my pride."

Damant caught a wisp of fear beneath the bravado. For all that Hadîm had spoken glibly enough of his life continuing without this particular piece of his soul, it didn't alter the fact that this particular piece would still be gone if his host body died before he got clear of the aethervores' song. Which was assuming the rest of it was true. His pursuit of Rîma had cost him several thralls. Did he even have any left?

Rîma shrugged and tilted her head towards Hadîm, indicating that they should catch him up. "Pride. Where would we be without it?"

Damant considered. "In Tyzanta, running the custodium."

"Do you miss it?"

"More than I should. I guess I'm too old to change my habits."

Head bowed, Rîma laughed under her breath. "And what do you know of being old, or habits burned into the bone?" She flashed her first

459

almost-smile since she'd awoken from Tadamûr's glamour. "Thank you, Ihsan. I owe you a debt I cannot repay."

He glanced away, embarrassed. "A dozen others might have done the same."

"They might, but they didn't. And I am a queen without a court, without a people. I have nothing to offer you save my thanks." Her voice hardened. "If you do not accept them with grace, I am likely to become offended."

For all that offence glinted in her tone, her grey eyes sparkled and a smile tugged at the corner of her mouth. Damant returned it with one of his own, the gloom of the Stars Below a fraction less oppressive than before. "I wouldn't want that."

An other-worldly gurgling shriek tore through the aethervores' song, the voice as discordant and mellifluous as that of the singers and reverberating with an agony that set every nerve in Damant's body screaming.

"What was that?" he gasped as the sound faded, his eyes darting hither and yon for possible threats.

A second shriek arrived hard on the heels of the first. A third. Within a ten-count, the air was more full of agony than song, the notes of the aethervores' lament fading as the voices fell into silence.

"Here!" Hadîm had already climbed a stairway to the roof of a nearby building and was staring out across the Dead City's concentric streets.

Breathless from the climb, Damant joined him, Rîma with the measured, untroubled tread of a woman out for an afternoon stroll, and both of them with an unparalleled view of a massacre.

Figures in white robes, black masks and lamellar armour stalked the geometric streets, hunting the aethervores without quarter or hesitation. They converged in ones and twos, sometimes alone, sometimes with a koilos trailing balefully behind, the thrust and sweep of burning brands goading the pallid, oozing creatures onto spearpoint and sword. They died hard, distended fingers locked around attackers' throats as the spears stabbed home, but with the weight of number in the attackers' favour, the outcome was never in doubt. The song faded further with each one that perished, the magenta flames of the hilltop ruins overtaken by a dark indigo stain.

"What is this?" asked Damant, unable to entirely quash his sympathy for the massacred aethervores.

Hadîm shrugged. "Who cares? Revolting creatures."

More of his relative morality at work, no doubt. "Rîma?"

She stood on the adjoining edge of the roof, staring not down at the streets but across them. "That's Tanith."

Damant followed her gaze to a procession marching towards the central causeway, led by a dark-robed figure trailing thick greyish smoke from a censer chained to a long black staff. Behind him came two women also in dark clothes, urged on at swordpoint by more of the masked figures, one of them with brilliant golden hair that could have belonged to no one else. Two more censer-bearers brought up the rear. "What's your point?"

"She's Katija's sister."

"And destined for a sticky end, it looks like. Khalad's better off without her."

Rîma's shoulders shifted, her head dipping in disapproval. "Katija doesn't think so."

"She's not here."

"No, but we are."

Hadîm snorted. "Yes, and I'm wondering why. Whatever all this is, it's nothing to do with us." He extended a finger out and away beneath the stars, at a shadow-drenched patch of wall in which Damant's straining eyes just about made out a tunnel mouth. "Our way out's over there. Assuming it's not collapsed, it'll bring us up in the heart of Qosm district. It'll never be easier than with this lot knocking seven bells out of each other. I say we leave them to it."

Damant nodded. Tanith Floranz. Murderess and manipulator, to name but two of the crimes laid at her door. Not someone worth dying

461

for, even if he wasn't bone-weary. Nyssa Iudexas or not, maybe there was some justice to be found in the Stars Below. "Much as I hate agreeing with our tame assassin, he's not wrong."

Rîma folded her arms. "You didn't abandon me. I will not abandon her."

Hadîm exhaled with disgust. "Fine. We'll vote on it."

Kat's world shook with flame. She *was* the flame, suspended within it, around it, formless but aware in the spirit world's lavender-scented darkness. The whispers of the Deadwinds billowed around her, beseeching, cajoling, demanding. What did she desire? Who was she? On and on, over and over, by turns playful and threatening.

She couldn't answer for she couldn't remember. Freed from the tyranny of flesh, of mortal existence, for the first time she realised just how heavily omen rot had dogged her thoughts, had tainted even her smallest deed. Distracted by the morsels of soul hissing around her, it had no power over her.

But something else *did*.

Even bodiless, she felt its grip tight about her, squeezing, stifling, probing. Aware where the flames were not, a shadow cast against the spirit world's gloom.

DO NOT RESIST.

The void shook to the dry, withered roar, each word vaster that her entire existence. The pressure about her formless self intensified. Panicked, she strove to pull free, to lose herself elsewhere in the flame. The stifling presence shifted, distracted by something beyond her sight. She seized upon that moment, diving down through the billowing torrent as the presence bellowed and raged above.

The flames – her flames – re-formed about a hollow in the Deadwinds, a cavitation sheathed in the starlight gloom and reverberating with mournful, discordant harmony. Nyssa knelt at the hollow's heart, the coiling indigo spill of her hair boiling into the black. Somehow she-who-had-been-Kat knew the goddess even when she did not know herself and felt a frisson of indescribable delight as Nyssa offered a welcoming smile.

I knew you'd find me.

She-who-had-been-Kat recognised the goddess' voice just as she'd recognised the goddess herself. Transfixed, she soared closer and closer. For the first time in a life she scarcely recalled, she felt complete. Desired. *Necessary.*

Indigo tongues flickered into the darkness from Nyssa's empty eyes. Her pleated dress shimmered with heat haze. Shackles ran like molten glass about her wrists. Her pale skin charred and peeled as a deeper, darker flame roared beneath.

And in the depth of that flame something howled for freedom.

Strands of indigo fire uncurled from within the facade of flesh, wending into the Deadwinds like river weeds in rapids, rippling towards she-who-had-been Kat.

Too late, she recognised her mistake and clawed upwards, but now the current of the Deadwinds was against her, dragging her down towards the grasping tendrils. One bound itself about her, colder than ice. A piece of she-who-had-been Kat went numb.

Another tendril coiled around her. Another. She fell faster and faster, and with each tendril snared about her being, less of her did the falling.

Above her, the Deadwinds darkened. An angry black wind bellowed from on high and gathered her up.

Awash in blackthorn incense, it took all Tanith had to set one foot in front of the other. Figures washed in and out of view, their like-nesses distorted by the intoxicating, debilitating smoke. Fixing her swaying sights on the darkening flames above the ruins helped, even if with every step she grew more certain it was the one place she least wanted to be.

Her goddess, Ardoc had named those fires. A hungry goddess, for Tanith felt that same desire resonating in her bones, growing stronger with every step. A piece of her yearned to reach the flames. To consume them and be devoured in return.

On the last step up onto the causeway, she stumbled, upright only because Enna steadied her.

"She needs to rest!" Enna's words phased and distorted through the clouds of blackthorn, drowning out the fading aethervore song.

At the procession's head, Ardoc turned about, a shadow spread against the hilltop's flame. "She's stronger that you might think. She's proved so many times." His shadow rippled in the smoke. "But I suppose we cannot begin until the last of the aethervores is silenced."

His staff chimed against stone and the column halted. Tanith clung to Enna and let the older woman take her weight, hating her weakness but this once grateful to have it acknowledged.

"Try breathing through your sleeve," Enna murmured. "It should filter the worst out."

Spluttering, Tanith tugged her left sleeve low and stuffed the trailed end across her mouth and nose. For a wonder, it worked – far from perfect, but enough to settle her vision and bring a measure of peace to heaving lungs. She cast about, trying for the third time to get a count on her kathari escort. She reached a dozen before she could keep her watering eyes open no longer.

"What are these creatures to you?" she heard Enna ask.

Ardoc grunted. "They are apostates, seduced by Alabastra's greed, consumed by their festering faith until nothing but appetite remains."

"And Hierarch Ossed?"

"Like all corruption, their wickedness spreads readily, if presented with a suitable vessel. One does not reach high office in Alabastra without a soul cankered by ambition and venality. This is where such paths end: singing to lull the goddess in her cage, smothering her virtue with their wickedness while the Eternity King steals her power." He chuckled. "No tears for any of them. In life, they destroyed more innocents than you can imagine. Now they're not even truly aware. Death is a mercy, believe me."

Sourness that had nothing to do with the blackthorn gathered at the back of Tanith's throat. Eyes screwed shut, she let her sleeve drop. "I should save my tears for myself, is that it?"

"Not at all. I said from the first that you would be Nyssa's herald, and you shall. She has been apart from the world too long. To walk it again she needs a soul strong enough to contain her. You are the perfect conduit. Your father made you so. And to think he rejected you as imperfect."

Tanith gagged as he drew closer, the clouds of blackthorn billowing stronger with every step. He propped a knuckle beneath her chin and tilted her head so that her watering eyes met his.

"You've come so far since the goddess sent you back to me. That wretched, burned soul that awoke in the temple could never have contained her magnificence, but see how strong you've grown. How glorious you've become. I had my shriversmen examine Esram's body. Not a trace of soul remained, and I imagine you're hungry already, aren't you?"

Tanith's throat thickened. All that talk of abstinence, of controlling herself ... he'd been flexing her hunger like a muscle, hollowing her out in readiness for his moment. No wonder she'd felt less and less like herself. There'd been less and less of her to go around.

"And what happens to me?"

"You will be her and she will be you. My offering to you both. My masterpiece. *Abdon Nyssa ivohê.*"

A final ululating scream brought the aethervores' song to silence. A deafening shriek arose in its place: older, resonant, the voice neither male nor female, but thick with triumph. Above the ruin, the indigo flames swallowed the last of the magenta, drenching all in darkness save the stars glinting above. Tanith clapped her hands to her ears – all worthless, for she heard it with her soul, not her mortal senses. Enna and her escort staggered and reeled. Only Ardoc stood tall until the shriek faded, jaw set and eyes agleam.

He spread his arms in reverence. "After millennia of slumber, she is awake."

*

Kat clung to the throne room's tiles for dear life, gasping and spluttering like a shipwrecked woman as the Deadwinds' flames seeped away, leaving her skin unburned. The Eternity King had lied. She *had* seen the goddess in the skies above Athenoch. But the goddess ... was not the warm, beneficent Nyssa that Kat had worshipped her whole life, nor the being whose noble likeness stared down from statue and sentry crest.

"He says he warned you that you would see things not to your liking." The Voice's calm speech stood stark against her taut expression. She heard her sire's will, didn't she? Just how much had she beheld? "He says he hopes now that you understand."

Shuddering, Kat twisted around and stared at the column of flame. Its fires were weaker than before, the magenta torrent sputtering about the corpse of the Eternity King and his throne immortal. "What did I just see? Was that really Nyssa?"

The Eternity King offered only an empty, malignant stare.

The Voice answered for him, her face drawn. "He says that Nyssa is merely a name given to something worshipped out of fear, bestowed by those who came before you. It has lain dreaming beneath the world for millennia, touching its people with dreams and visions. If it wakes, it will dominate everything that is. And that will be just the start. He says he created Alabastra to redirect that worship to more productive efforts. The Cold Flame cares for nothing save itself, he says. It desires nothing save escape."

Kat wanted to argue, if only to dispel her creeping dread, but there was no gainsaying the lingering, skin-crawling malice she'd felt. "Escape from where?"

"Khalad. It wishes to return beyond the Veil, to realms once dominated. To bend them to its will anew. He says it has been his great labour to keep it contained here in the prison created to hold it. He says he has done so since before Khalad's first cities rose against the plains. He will do so until the last fire goes out."

Kat's gut went rigid, her throat crowded with nausea. She'd never heard of the Cold Flame, but she *had* heard this tale before, though told in different words. A malevolent god that the Issnaîm had sought to seal away within a silver pearl. Zephyr had claimed that the striving had failed, that she and her kin had become trapped instead. But that wasn't so, was it?

"Tzal," she breathed. "But Tzal was a man."

"The Cold Flame is whatever it wishes to be, especially here."

Kat pinched her eyes shut, her thoughts awash in nausea. The world as she knew it lay in ruins, redefined for ever. No promise of equitable judgement beyond the grave. No loving matriarch to balance retribution with grace. Just a hungry god cast out from a distant realm, feasting on the souls of the departed. What hope then of reincarnation? Of a life after death? What to cling to in the face of nothingness?

And this sanctum, twin to Athenoch's foreboding black tower, was therefore likely the pinnacle of another tower itself, one impossibly taller than its twin for it to stand so high above Zariqaz. If the Eternity King had truly been here since the beginning, this tower too must have existed from the start, long before Rîma's people retreated beneath its surface. But Rîma's people pre-dated Caradan Diar's rule, or so the histories said. Ages of Fire had come and gone. Unless all of it – *all of it* – was a lie.

The Eternity King wasn't a fireblood, wasn't of Rîma's kind, or of anything that had come between.

What *was* he?

"Why are you telling me all this?"

The Voice cocked her head, her translation slowing as the Eternity King struck out on a new course. "He wishes to know . . . how you feel."

Kat had no ready answer.

How did she feel? She chuckled without humour. She wasn't sure she'd feel anything ever again.

Head drooping, she stared down at her hands and realised she'd misunderstood the question. Somewhere in the horror and revelation, she'd forgotten why she'd entered the flames at all. Her aetherios tattoo, pale and faded for so long, was dark as night once more, the geometric

467

swirl of the koilos-commanding glyph she'd forged at Athenoch black and strident beneath gentle flickers of magenta soulfire.

Elation crowded out nausea as she bent her thoughts upon the design, the lines twisting and reflowing at her slightest touch. Breathless, she reached out across the throne room, slipping into the spirit world as she had so many times before, the glints of the chamber ifrîti bright in the lavender dark. It was only then that she realised how clear her thoughts had become, how distant were the myriad aches and tremors she'd come to accept as normal as the omen rot had gained ground.

She clenched her left fist. Soulfire flickered up from her tattoo, wreathing her knuckles, a match for the laughter welling up inside.

How did she feel?

Even with her faith in ruins, she felt more like herself than she ever had. "Whole."

"He says that is good. He says—"

A terrible, soul-wrenching shriek shook the air, driving Kat to her knees. She clapped her hands to her ears in a worthless attempt to blot out the sound resonating in her soul. Even after the scream faded, its memory lingered, dizzying her senses worse than any vertigo.

When her vision cleared, the magenta flames swirling about the Eternity King had darkened to indigo, their presence somehow colder than before. The throne room shuddered in tune with a distant rumble. Dust spilled from the ceiling, hissing through the column of soulfire.

The Voice blinked, her young face suddenly haggard with years not yet lived. "He says . . . He says that he has made a terrible mistake. And that he must request a change to your agreement."

Kat eyed them both, her unease souring further. "Of course he does."

"He says the Cold Flame has awoken. It needs only a body. Once it has one, it will dominate all in its path. Whatever it cannot bend to its bidding, it will destroy." The Voice stumbled through the words. "He says arrogance blinded him. He says— No! That cannae be right . . ."

Withered skin scattered across black stone as the Eternity King's corpse jerked to life and reached through the flames. Kat yelped as his bony, desiccated hand closed about her wrist. Dust spilled from his creaking jaw.

The cage is broken and the Cold Flame comes for me. Like the shriek before it, the Eternity King's words whispered across Kat's soul without troubling her ears. *Protect her. If she dies, the Cold Flame will take you all.*

His fingers sprang open as the column of flame shrank inwards. Isdihar, bronze skin pale beneath her make-up, stared blankly as her world fell apart. The Eternity King slumped back against his throne, robes and shrivelled skin crackling in the dying flames.

Go.

Not knowing what else to do, Kat ran for the door, dragging the unseeing Isdihar Diar with her.

Forty-Nine

The spiralling indigo flame pulsed and the Stars Below shimmered with its reflected light. A piece of Tanith pulled away as she righted herself, desperate to join the flame. Still leaning on Enna, she clung tight to the rest as best she could. She longed to kill him then and there, to drain his soul and patch the pieces of her own. But in the blackthorn smoke it was all she could do not to fall asleep. Despite Ardoc's fervent promise, she'd a horrible gnawing feeling that if she did, it wouldn't be her who did the waking.

"So she's the main course." Disdain dripped from Enna's tongue, but her eyes never left the distant indigo flame. "I take it I'm the appetiser?"

Ardoc let Tanith's head drop. "You conspired to thwart Nyssa's will. I expect she'll want to thank you personally."

Enna sighed. "For the last time. I'm not part of any conspiracy." Her eyes met his with an intensity that should have withered him on the spot. "I just don't like you, that's all."

"It is the fate of many a great man to be misunderstood by petty minds," he sneered.

"I've known great men, Ardoc. I don't see the resemblance."

Snarling, he stepped closer, eyes ablaze and hand raised to strike her. With a deep breath, he let his hand fall. "You would have Khalad continue as it always has? Thousands ground down by the tyranny of

470

Nyssa's usurper? Do you know what I've sacrificed to stand here now? The others that will come before this is done?"

"I know that people like you sacrifice others, never themselves."

He struck her a vicious backhand across the face. "The song is done. The goddess stirs. She will forgive me a small indulgence." He seized Tanith's wrist and pulled her away. "Hack this traitor apart!" he bellowed.

Dark shapes moved through the smoke on the edges of Tanith's vision, their swords drawn.

They halted, priorities shifting as another silhouette bled into being three paces behind Ardoc, her weathered black bindings almost invisible in the indigo murk and a long, slender sword resting across her shoulder.

"Tanith, dear, you're out past curfew. Your sister is surely beside herself."

The maddeningly familiar voice resolved itself to a name, learned a seeming lifetime ago, thought it was barely weeks.

"Are you sure you wish to—" Rîma tilted her head, her white hair spilling across the blade, and looked Ardoc up and down. "No. On reflection, I have the feeling you're not worth it."

The causeway erupted in uproar. Kathari rushed past, their bellowed challenges turning to screams as they belatedly recognised the terrible depth of their mistake. Ardoc stumbled out of sight, trailing blackthorn smoke behind.

Released, Tanith dropped spluttering to the ground and stuffed her sleeve across her mouth, willing her swimming senses to clarity. Fresh screams rang out, this time from *behind*. Enna, hair in disarray and looking ever more insubstantial in the smoke-wreathed darkness, hauled her upright and dragged her back towards the causeway stair.

Still groggy, Tanith grabbed at the brazier at the head of the stairway. Twisting in Enna's grip, she stared back through the thinning smoke at the blur of white robes and bloody steel. "No . . . I need to help her."

471

She blinked, her ears catching up with her tongue. Had she *really* said that?

It was the blackthorn poisoning, wasn't it? Still, it provoked a flush of pride. Maybe Enna was right. Maybe she didn't have to be a monster. Not all the time, at least.

A shame then that her knees buckled and a paroxysm of coughing racked her lungs as soon as she started forward.

Enna caught her and pushed her back against the brazier's stone pedestal. "You can't help anyone in that state." She glanced along the causeway in the other direction, the one from which Ossed had taken his final steps. A kathari stumbled out of the darkness, mask gone and blood streaming from his face. Shadow whirled away through the smoke towards another, twin swords hacking down with graceless efficiency. "Besides, I think she's already got as much as she needs. Friends of yours?"

"I don't—" Tanith broke off in another fit of coughing. "I don't ... have any friends."

"Cultivate them."

"*Abdon Nyssa ivohê!*" A maskless kathari stepped out of the darkness and lunged at Enna.

She sidestepped, the sword flashing past her ribs, then rammed her forehead down. The kathari yelped and dropped like a stone. A vicious grin on her lips, Enna gave a brief drunken sway, flicked a smear of the other woman's blood from her forehead and dipped to claim her sword.

All without seeing a second hulking kathari bearing down on her from the other side.

"Enna!"

Warned by Tanith's choked shout, she spun around. Roaring, the kathari hacked down at her shoulder with a blow fit to cleave her in two. A wet rip sounded. The roar faded to a choked, spluttering gasp. His white robes already rushing red, the kathari lurched and toppled sideways, propelled down the causeway steps by the strike of a boot.

Tanith found herself face to face with Enna's rescuer, whose milky eye and scarred cheek did nothing to soften his glare.

472

"Ihsan Damant ..." she gasped, the words coming easier with the thinning smoke. "I suppose my sister's behind this?"

"Only by the most roundabout of means." He snorted. "You're welcome, by the way."

Judging by his tone, he'd have gladly run her through. And to think that six months before, lost in her ingénue's glamour, he'd have died for her. It hadn't lasted because it hadn't been real ... and the odd murder along the way couldn't have helped. As the last scream faded to a whimper, Tanith pondered on what it might take to earn his true regard, and wondered why it suddenly mattered to her.

Blackthorn poisoning. Had to be.

She pushed away from the brazier's plinth and stood tall, revelling in her first painless breath.

Rîma stalked out of the darkness with the manner of a woman well satisfied with herself, sword bloody to the hilt.

"Did you get the leader?" asked Damant.

"He is faster on his feet than he seems." She cocked her head as a chorus of angry shouts and running feet echoed up from the darkened streets. "I believe he's very angry with us."

A bald man with dark brown skin joined them, his lips twisted to an abiding scowl. "I am so very, *very* surprised. And it sounds like most of them are between us and our way out of here." He half lidded his left eye and glared at Damant. "Thanks for that."

Damant shrugged with an insouciance alien to the man Tanith had known months before. "We voted, you lost." He peered at the indigo flame, which to Tanith's increasingly leery eye seemed darker and angrier than before. "Do I even want to know what that is?"

Enna grimaced. "If Ardoc's right, that's your goddess."

The skin tightened around Damant's eyes. "Then I hope you ladies know a way back to civilisation."

Mist crowded the conclave hall's high windows, blotting out the midday sun and muffling the sounds of the world beyond. The air stank of old

473

memories, embittered by smoke. A clock chimed midday, forcing Kat to reappraise how long she'd lingered in the Deadwinds' grip. Twelve hours, maybe more. Twelve hours and the world had changed beyond recognition. Her omen rot was gone, or was at least in remission. Nyssa wasn't Nyssa. The Eternity King was dead.

What more could fate throw at her?

Isdihar stumbled on past the koilos alcoves, never more a child than at that moment, trembling like a reed, her arms wrapped tight about her thin body as she muttered fitfully.

"I cannae hear ye . . . I cannae hear ye . . ."

As she crossed the dais, Gansalar Nasari marched to intercept her, three redcloaks at his back, all in full lamellar and armed with shriekers and scimitars.

"Majesty," he said, relief as thick in his voice as was worry in Isdihar's. "Thank Nyssa you're safe."

The once-comforting oath curdled Kat's blood, another reminder of how she now stood apart from the world.

"Safe?" Even standing a pace behind her, Kat barely heard the Voice's whispered reply. "None of us are safe."

"The city is burning." For all Nasari's level tone, his cheeks were taut and his eyes frantic. "Riots are breaking out everywhere. The streets have been at war since dawn."

"The Obsidium Cult." It wasn't a question.

"I fear so, majesty."

The Voice's gaze tracked across the dais to where Ossed had stood the day before. "He was right. We should hae listened. We . . ." With visible effort, she straightened and regathered her poise. "Send our legions to help the custodia maintain order."

Nasari gritted his teeth. "Majesty, it *began* with your legions. They're tearing themselves apart. There's fighting in the ring-walls – even in the palace! We've no hope of reinforcements until the mist rises."

"Where are my ministers?"

"We've had no word. Likely they're dead."

Kat scarcely believed her ears. Zariqaz in open revolt against the Eternity King? Vallant's dream, and he was leagues away, negotiating with Zyrassa's ruling council. Perhaps it was for the best. For all Vallant's pragmatism, he'd never have aligned himself with the Obsidium Cult and their dogma of Nyssa's third, true face, hidden by years of Alabastran preachings.

The three-faced goddess. She'd seen that third face. It wasn't the equal of Benevolas and Iudexas as her father's books had preached, but their foundation – a hungry, all-consuming flame. Had her father known just what he was worshipping?

Nasari gestured at Kat. "Take this skelder to the cells."

Two redcloaks stepped forward. Both halted at Isdihar's upraised hand. "No."

"But majesty—"

"I ... *We* grow tired of repeating ourselves." She fixed him with a stare, a measure of confidence returning to her words. "Are we to assume that her companions are already detained?"

Nasari hesitated, then nodded.

"If what you say is true, we cannot spare loyal swords as guards. Have them brought here."

Nasari scowled, but gestured to one of the redcloaks, who marched away.

Isdihar swept past him and up the stairs to the grand window. Preferring her company to Nasari's evil eye, Kat followed, leaving the *gansalar* and his remaining redcloaks on the dais.

Beyond the window, Zariqaz burned. Angry orange-red flames rose to challenge the magenta of the city's few functioning torch houses, swallowing up palaces, warehouses and temples and thickening the mist with coiling black smoke. What little wind existed beneath the shrouding Veil carried screams and bellows, the wail of shriekers and the heavier *crump* of blasting prisms. Even as Kat reached the Voice's side, the room shook, the window glass cracking as an explosion blossomed at the base of the torch house adjoining the silver-roofed

Qabirarchi Palace. Wreathed in smoke, it crumpled sideways in an avalanche of stone, the mist rushing in as the magenta blesswood flames sputtered out.

"This is the anarchy we feared," said Isdihar. "And it will only spread now that the glamour's broken."

Kat understood all too well. Order – especially one enforced by threat of violence – thrived on the uncertainty of individual survival and the inevitability of reprisal. For centuries, the Eternity King had squeezed Khalad tight, bleeding off resistance through carefully managed outlets, such as Vallant and the Obsidium Cult, their fleeting freedoms and thin successes underscoring the kingdom's singular truth: that those who opposed Caradan Diar might prosper for a brief time, but ultimately paid with everything they held dear. With Kat's help, Vallant had thrown off his shackles, breaking the illusion. It now seemed that the Obsidium Cult had achieved something similar – the timing was too perfect for it to be otherwise. Perhaps the Eternity King had only ever thought them under his control, while all along the truth was very different.

Among his final words, the Eternity King had spoken of arrogance. In the end, he'd known.

How many folk believed in the Obsidium Cult's cause? Not all – probably not even a majority – but all would carry grievances. All had lost too much to stand idle.

But it wasn't anarchy alone. Destroying torch houses wasn't the mania of a mob, but strategy. The Veil played no favourites and would claim all it touched, body and soul – the perfect weapon with which the few could battle the many, as Kat knew from her own conflicted experience. One way or another, the Obsidium Cult meant to purge the Golden Citadel of loyalist forces.

Walking slowly, trapped in a nightmare, Isdihar descended to the dais and the waiting *Nasari*.

"Majesty, tell me," said Nasari, a man holding onto his courage with both hands. "What is the Eternity King's will?"

Isdihar stared up at him, her eyes wide. "The Eternity King . . ."

Standing behind the *gansalar*, Kat went rigid and shook her head in warning. Now was not the time to test how much authority of her own the Voice possessed. If it became known that the Eternity King was dead, there was every chance that what little order remained in the city would disintegrate.

Nasari frowned. "Majesty?"

Four redcloaks hurried into the conclave hall by the far door, the sounds of distant battle flooding in behind them until it swung shut once more. Nasari moved to intercept them, his two companions falling into step behind him. Kat regarded the newcomers with unease perfected around unfriendly redcloaks. Isdihar, still lost in a nightmare, barely acknowledged their arrival.

More surprising was the reserve in Nasari's expression as he drew up before them, the two lines of redcloaks facing each other beneath an iron lumani chandelier. "Sarhana Gasar. I ordered you to hold the north courtyard."

"Apologies, Gansalar." The lead newcomer bowed. "*Abdon Nyssa ivohê.*"

Nasari frowned. "What did you—"

The redcloak immediately to his left – one of those who had accompanied him to the conclave hall – snatched her shrieker from its holster and shot him down.

"Traitor!" As Nasari fell, his other companion drew his own shrieker and loosed a shot that set the *gansalar*'s killer ablaze. One of the newcomers ran him through and kicked the body clear.

The others advanced on the aghast Voice.

The nearest levelled his own shrieker. "*Abdon Nyssa ivohê.*"

Reacting without thinking, Kat reached into the spirit world, searching for the bright angry spark of the shrieker's ifrît.

There.

With no time to attempt anything fancy, she fed the shrieker all the soulfire it could take. Then she clenched her fist and fed it more.

The dull clap of the explosion and the redcloak's scream wrenched her back into the mortal world. The Voice's would-be killer fell to his knees, clutching a ragged stump of blood and bone.

Another redcloak started towards her, scimitar in hand. "The skelder's mine."

The Voice stumbled away. Kat cast about for a weapon and found nothing worthy of the name within reach. "Run!"

A crestfallen Isdihar stared at her, still lost in a fog of disbelief at the unfolding treachery.

Her throat tight, Kat retreated before the scimitar's point. No repeating the trick with this redcloak, who didn't have a shrieker to detonate. But there had to be *something*.

There was. Giving ground before the redcloak, she stepped as deep into the spirit world as she dared and reached out for the nearest koilos ember-saint, slumbering in its alcove.

Both times she'd tried this before, she'd tempted disaster. The first time, she hadn't even meant to, had lashed out in grief and the koilos had responded to her pain. The second, she'd almost lost herself in the malice of the tormented ifrît. Not this time. The koilos was already ill at ease, torn by the threat to the Voice but lulled by the glyphs borne by her attackers burning bright in its thoughts.

Wreathed in soulfire, Kat reached into the glowering scraps of the koilos' consciousness. Growling her satisfaction, she wiped the redcloak's soul-glyph from its tortured mind.

With a desiccated scream that set broken glass rattling in the windows' remnants, the koilos lurched down from its alcove.

The one-armed redcloak scrambled away. "It's awake! The skrelling—"

The flamberge flashed out and cut him almost in half. He dropped, a sodden crimson mess. Shriekers blazed as the two redcloaks bearing down on the Voice found more urgent priorities. Screeching like the damned soul it was, the koilos stormed into the fire, its ember-saint's robes already alight.

Seeing her own opponent gape at the horrific sight, Kat flung herself past the point of his scimitar and kicked him in the groin. He doubled over, sword clattering away. She rammed her knee into his face, felt something crunch and let him drop.

She claimed his scimitar and turned around in time to see the charred, blazing ruin of the koilos pitch forward onto the tiles, pinning one of the two remaining redcloaks beneath it.

The survivor, bleeding heavily from livid gashes in his forehead and thigh, rounded on Kat. His sword bucking in an unsteady hand, he spat a crimson gobbet to the floor and lunged. "You are damned, skelder!"

"Probably."

Kat practically felt Rîma's hand upon hers as she parried, the redcloak's blade scraping harmlessly away along her own. The slash that took his throat was barely an afterthought.

She took a moment to admire her handiwork. From death's door to four redcloaks without a scratch. Granted, the koilos had helped, but still . . . "Not bad."

She flexed the fingers of her left hand, revelling in the sight of the flames rippling up from her wrist. Six months, and it was as though no time had passed at all. For all their differences, Vallant and the Eternity King had been right. Her tattoo *was* a weapon.

"Majesty?" Receiving no response, Kat turned to find the Voice still standing in the middle of the hall, her eyes wide. "Isdihar," she said softly. "Are you hurt?"

"I . . . Ye . . ." The Voice blinked. "Forgive me. I'm nae used tae this."

Kat glanced around the charnel house the hall had become. "You learn fast, trust me." She thought back. "You managed in the Hallow Caves."

"That was just a place," Isdihar replied in a small voice. Even in her golden finery, she looked less the tyrant than ever. In fact, she reminded Kat of herself at an earlier age, cast by fate from the shelter of the Rashace estate into a city she'd barely known. "This is my home."

Protect her. If she dies, the Cold Flame will take you all. "The Eternity King said you were the only one who could stop Tzal." Easier to think

479

of the Cold Flame that way. Easier to pretend her faith hadn't been for nothing. "What was that about?"

"I don't know."

Great. "Then I guess we'd better keep you alive until we figure that out. Are there any redcloaks you can personally trust?"

Isdihar shook her head.

Stooping, Kat tugged Nasari's shrieker free of his corpse and dipped into the spirit world long enough to coax out the ifrît's soul-glyph. It took but a thought to reflow her tattoo to the shrieker's liking, the lines reknitting to an inverted cruciform. What now? The palace wasn't safe, and there'd be no escape along the Golden Stair. "If we can send a heraldic, is there a dhow close enough to get here before we're overrun?" However long that was.

Isdihar shook her head. "Even if there was, it couldn't reach us until the mists rise."

"It was a thought."

But even rejected, that thought became the germ of another. Pride hated it, but this once, pride didn't get a say. Besides, Kat took consolation in knowing that she'd not be the only conflicted soul. Assuming any of it worked out. The Veil made things damn difficult, but hours before, she'd been dying. This was a day for the impossible.

A door swung open, admitting a redcloak, Azra, Yali and Tatterlain. Kat sighed and let her shrieker dip, only to regret it when the redcloak took a long step clear of Azra and levelled his own.

"Stand away!"

"Lower your weapon!" snapped Isdihar, her voice regaining a little of its confidence.

"But majesty . . ."

"Of the two of us, which is the Voice? Which of us is to be obeyed without question?" The redcloak lowered his shrieker. "There has been another assassination attempt. Gansalar Nasari died thwarting it. This woman saved our life – for the second time, we would add. Find Gansalar Qolda. Tell him we will speak to him at the main gate. Go!"

All resistance gone, the redcloak left the hall at a run.

"Can you trust this Qolda?" asked Kat.

"I may never trust anyone ever again," Isdihar replied. "But Qolda's responsible for the second ring-wall. It'll take time to reach him, if he ever gets there at all."

Kat glanced around the conclave hall, her nascent plan gathering shape. Only one door, not counting that to the Eternity King's sanctum, both of them guarded by hestics. The grand window was four storeys above the ground level outside, making it no use for a speculative ingress. It wasn't a fortress, but it was likely the best they were going to get. "Then we hold here."

"Darling?" Azra picked her way across the dead redcloaks. "Not that I'm not pleased to see you up and around, but what in Nyssa's name is going on?"

Kat flinched. Her first of many, she suspected, when the goddess' name was mentioned. ||"Zariqaz is burning, the Obsidium Cult have suborned half the redcloaks in the city and we'll be lucky to live to see tomorrow."|| Nyssa, Tzal and the Eternity King could wait. She didn't know how to touch *that*.

Tatterlain shrugged.

||Oh, is that all?|| asked Yali, her eyes shining as she recovered a fallen redcloak's scimitar and gave it an experimental swish.

Azra narrowed her eyes. "But you're all right?"

Kat kissed her. ||"Better than ever, I promise. You and Yali hold here. Keep the Voice safe. Tatterlain and I will join you soon."||

||"Oh will he?"|| said Tatterlain airily. ||"And why's that?"||

||"I need to borrow your brain."||

||"As long as the rest of me can come too."||

Azra scowled. "I thought you trusted me, but here you go again, leaving me behind."

||"Because I *do* trust you. If anyone comes after the Voice, they die. Understand me?"||

The scowl bled into that wonderful, arrogant, self-satisfied smile – a chink of sunlight on a day drowning in mist and terror. "Like nobody else can, darling." She hesitated. "Are you sure about this? I saw the city. If we were down in all that, whose side would we be on?"

Tatterlain cleared his throat. ‖"Speaking for myself, I think I'd be on the side of keeping my head down."‖

Yali rolled her eyes and elbowed him in the ribs.

Kat glanced at the Voice and received a small nod in return. In the end, she supposed it hardly mattered. ‖"There's more to this than you know."‖

Taking a deep breath, she told them everything. By the time she'd finished, Yali was gazing at her with an empty, punch-drunk expression. Tatterlain was pale beneath his tan.

Azra folded her arms and levelled an appraising stare, her rakish smile still in place. "Do you at least have a plan?"

‖"I've better than that. I'm surrounded by good people. The best."‖ Kat glanced back at Isdihar, a girl who mere hours before had been the power of life and death over not only Zariqaz but Khalad itself, and was now more alone than anyone Kat had ever known. "So keep her safe for me?"

Azra glanced at Isdihar and nodded. "For you, darling, yes."

Tatterlain at her side and her stolen shrieker at the ready, Kat ghosted through the palace, shrieker fire and screams echoing all around. Even with Tatterlain's mental map of the layout at her disposal, it took fifteen minutes to find what she was looking for and the better part of an hour to return to the conclave hall, the delays necessitated by the course of running battles between redcloaks whose loyalties she'd no way of knowing or trusting.

Every moment of delay screamed disaster at her, for it was another moment in which the cult's redcloaks might find their way to the hall. But certain that haste would get them all killed, she clung to the shadows or doubled back as the dying ebb and flow of battle shifted their way. At least it meant ample opportunity to scavenge supplies:

food swiped from the wreckage of the kitchens, shriekers recovered from dead redcloaks. There were servants too among the dead, and she wondered how many – if any – had made it to safety.

By the time they at last reached the conclave hall, the fighting elsewhere in the palace had grown sporadic, though the growing preponderance of white-robed and black-masked newcomers in the corridors told Kat all she needed of which side had gained the upper hand.

Thus it was with no small relief that she set the door closed behind her and saw Azra, Yali and the Voice rise from concealment among the uppermost pews.

"Did ye get what ye wanted?" asked Isdihar, still pale but no longer terrified.

"Better than that," said Tatterlain, brandishing a haversack. "We have vittles and plunder to raise the spirits . . . and set bad men on fire."

He shot Kat a subtle wink. They'd already agreed not to rouse false hopes.

"Well, what now?" asked Azra.

||"We hole up here, seal the doors and wait for the loyal reinforcements to get things back under control,"|| said Kat. ||"Or until things calm down enough that we can make a break for it."||

Yali gazed around the chamber, unimpressed. ||We can't keep the redcloaks out if they come. They have all the glyphs they need to bypass the motics and the hestics.||

||"About that . . ."||

Kat closed her eyes and let her soul soar into the spirit world, the position of every hestic, motic, pyrasti and half a dozen other minor ifrîti singing out to her. The conclave hall's koilos she ignored, knowing a mistake there would set a deathless killer loose in their midst. The others she embraced one at a time and, as she'd done for the koilos, wiped their commanding soul-glyphs.

She opened her eyes as the last faded. She forced sunlight into her smile, her doubts returning. ||"Now *nobody* has the right soul-glyphs to get in here."||

Fifty

The elevator shuddered, the shriek of unhappy gears and the rattle of its steel cage doing little to dispel the tense atmosphere of its weary passengers. Clinging to the bars, Tanith peered down into the darkness of the shaft. Far below, the firefly bob of lumani lanterns revealed white robes climbing ever higher on the narrow adjoining stair.

"Do they never give up?"

Across the elevator, arms folded, sword sheathed and looking more like a woman at meditation rather than one spurred to flight, Rîma twitched the smallest shrug. "Driven souls seldom do."

Ardoc's driven souls certainly hadn't, their drive carrying them through a two-hour pursuit, always following the line of the causeway but keeping to the lower ground in the hope of losing the cultists in the Dead City's streets. A vain hope, for the only ones they'd left behind were those who'd strayed too close and paid the price on one sword or another.

The elevator jolted, inconveniencing Rîma not a hair but setting the ceiling's lumani lamp swaying madly and sending Hadîm and Enna grabbing at the cage.

Damant, sitting on the floor, his face drawn with weariness, splayed a hand against the oxblood tiles to steady himself. "Speaking for myself, I'm grateful to be spared the climb. Your sister teach you to do that?"

Tanith nodded, annoyed that Kat would now take the credit for her convincing the elevator's motics to behave. "Only right she's good for something."

Irritated by the disappointed look Rîma shot her, she turned her attention to Hadîm, who'd taken up position in the corner as far from the others as he could contrive. From the bitter cast to his expression, it was plain that he didn't much like Rîma or Damant, which struck her as odd given how smoothly they'd worked together during her rescue.

The lift's counterpart, driven by the same ropes and pulleys as their own, rattled past in the darkness beyond the cage, making rickety descent into the Stars Below in mirror of their ascension. Halfway. What would they find waiting for them? The Golden Citadel's redcloaks with spears levelled? The city tight in the Obsidium Cult's grip? Either way, not a good time to be alone, even if loneliness was all you knew.

"I'm not very good at saying thank you, but that doesn't mean I'm not grateful." The words came easier the more Tanith spoke. "To her . . . and to the rest of you."

Rîma offered Damant a knowing glance, returned by the expression of a man on the losing end of a bet. Hadîm had the grace to give a curt nod, Enna a rather prouder one.

"He's not finished yet," said Enna. "It'll be nightfall before the outer realms recede and the conjunction passes. Nyssa's bonds will only grow weaker until then."

"What happens if she doesn't get our golden skirl?" asked Damant.

Tanith grimaced and tried to ignore the tiny, rebellious part of her that longed for the fire's embrace. Ardoc's promises of some kind of dual existence – her as part of Nyssa and vice versa – didn't much appeal.

Enna shrugged. "I've no idea. Ardoc kept his secrets close. It may be that even he doesn't know. He's forever claiming that the goddess speaks to him. Perhaps she keeps her secrets close too. But this isn't the first conjunction on record, not if you know where to look. I'd say there's a reason the cult put so much effort into creating the perfect host. It may be that an imperfect vessel carries risk."

The perfect host. Tanith stared down at the flickering flames of her tattoo and grimaced. It was a perfection she could well do without. And it hadn't just been Ardoc who'd made her that way – he'd merely completed a project her father had abandoned, first through neglect and then through death.

She closed her eyes, only to be greeted by an image of Nyssa, the goddess' austere face peeling away to reveal her own. Gagging, she blinked them open. The goddess had plucked her from the Deadwinds not to save her, but to save herself. Just days before, she'd wondered what it would be like to be venerated by the enthralled masses. If this was the price then she wanted nothing to do with it. Perhaps she never had, and that desire was just another manifestation of her childish need to seize by force the love she hadn't earned.

Put that way, she *was* the perfect host, wasn't she? She *deserved* it. The shame went so deep as to even keep her hunger in check. That and the knowledge of why Ardoc had roused it so.

"I don't want her to take me," she said, not realising she'd spoken until she saw the others watching her. Her glamour rose with the surge of misery, the doe-eyed ingénue reaching forth to tug at her protectors' heartstrings. She reeled her back in. Whatever came next, they deserved honesty. So did she.

Light from above trickled into the darkened shaft. The elevator settled into its lobby cage with a soft but none too gentle *thunk*. The landing outside was empty save the cold, expressionless marble gazes of Qabirarchs long dead.

Damant clambered to his feet. "The moment of truth."

"You don't think someone might question what we're doing here?" asked Hadîm, acidly. "No offence, but you're not exactly Qabirarch material."

"Good to know."

Enna jerked her head down the elevator shaft, towards the echoing footsteps and strained breaths coming ever closer. "You're welcome to go back."

Hadîm offered a silent sneer, but left it at that.

Damant reached for the door. "If we're not attacked on sight, let me do the talking."

No one attacked them on sight in the corridor because there was no one to do the attacking. Though the floor tiles gleamed with fresh polish and not a scrap of dust clung to ornaments or portrait frames, there was no sign anyone had passed that way in a long time.

Tanith tried an adjoining door. The hinges gave with a deafening creak, earning her an unhappy glance from Damant. The room beyond the threshold was in darkness, drapes drawn and its only illumination that which spilled in from the corridor. What had once been expensive furniture lay beneath a thick carpet of dust and cobwebs.

"It's abandoned." Tanith's nose wrinkled at the sour smell of burnt isshîm powder. Ossed's guards had drugged him long before he'd reached the elevator.

"This one's the same," Rîma replied, pulling shut the next door along. "Just like Tadamûr."

Damant grunted. "Why maintain a palace no one uses? All you need is a nice corridor so as not to frighten the fish-to-be."

Tanith grimaced. With their cold, dead eyes and waxy, pallid skin there *had* been something distinctly piscine about the aethervores.

"Tanith, are there any ifrîti we should worry about?" asked Rîma.

Tanith shook away the memories of aethervores and stepped into the spirit world, not with the brash unconcern she'd practised all her life, but the gentler stride Kat had taught her. Bright hestic motes gleamed against the lavender dark, curious and attentive, all of them facing outward against intrusion from the city. Reaching out a tongue of soulfire, she soothed the nearest, which had grown too interested in her for her liking, and searched for the darker, malevolent flames of slumbering koilos. She found none, though the trails of several lingered at the corridor's far end.

Taking a deep breath, she reeled herself back to the mortal world. "We're in the clear as long as we keep moving forward. There were koilos here, but they've gone."

487

"I wonder why," said Rîma.

"I don't," said Enna darkly. "Ardoc had plans for the city as well as the Stars Below."

The view of the city from the atrium steps was the finest anyone could have wished for, and Damant would have given anything to unsee it.

Up-spire, the mists of the Veil swamped the northern extent of the Qabirarchi Palace, clinging to the blasted, skeletal remains of the torch house that should have held them at bay. Below, smoke hung low over Zariqaz, dirtying the mist where convection carried it beyond the torch houses' influence. Fires still raged across the palaces and temples of the Overspire, feeding the toxic brume, filling their air with the bitter stench of hot stone and charred meat.

Walking like a man in a dream, Damant stumbled out into the Golden Citadel's sandstone streets. They were thick with bodies, shattered koilos and broken barricades, the redcloaks joined in sightless death by the firebloods who'd sought shelter behind their spears. Screams rising over the ring-walls told of a battle still under way.

No. Not a battle. That implied order. Maybe even honour.

Enna stared at the carnage stony-faced. "This is the Age of Fire Ardoc promised. It's only the beginning."

Hadîm prodded a redcloak's corpse with his foot. "I think this is where we part ways."

"You really think you can survive alone?" snapped Damant.

"Better alone than with you trampling my heels."

Rîma glowered at him. "Don't you care what's happening here?"

Hadîm shrugged. "Kingdoms rise and fall."

"And morality is relative?" asked Damant.

"More than that, it's expensive ... and I don't imagine any of you can foot the bill." Hadîm sauntered away backwards past a ruined clatter wagon. "The Stars Below are behind us. My advice is to consider all debts settled. I do. Enjoy your revolution."

Damant watched him until the curve of the ring-wall's street carried him from sight, all without really seeing him, transfixed by the horror of the smoke. Perhaps the assassin had it right. Perhaps he was just a stubborn old man.

Rîma joined him among the dead. "You're troubled."

He laughed without humour. "What gave it away? I'm hungry, exhausted and getting too old for all this running around."

"I see. And the truth?"

How did she do that? Look at him and right through him at the same time? A dozen like Rîma and there'd have been no crime in Tyzanta. For one reason or another.

He hesitated. "This was more than a city. It was proof that order could prevail, that there was at least some justice – even if it was imperfect. And less than a year after I help Vallant take Tyzanta, this happens." He stared at her, stricken. "We proved that the Eternity King's unassailable will was a lie. We did this."

Tanith shook her head. "I'm as old as Vallant's rebellion. All this started before I was born, when my father or his predecessors first conceived of this tattoo. Maybe even before that. It isn't your fault." She shrugged and offered a wan smile. "*Abdon Nyssa ivohê.* It's Nyssa's will."

Nyssa's will. The first haven of the faithful and a scoundrel's last resort. It offered no solace and did nothing to assuage Damant's guilt.

"They can't be far behind us," said Enna. "What's it to be? Upspire or down?

"Down," said Damant. "Those railrunner stations not ablaze will be locked up tight, but we might find a skyship. The further we get from Zariqaz, the better I'll sleep."

He set out just as a column of twenty battle-worn redcloaks marched around the corner, a golden-armoured *gansalar* at their head.

Damant frowned. Far from ideal, but he'd spent years talking fire-bloods into and out of things. Pitch this right, and he could pass them off as survivors, maybe even wangle an escort down to the city proper.

Taking care that his hand was nowhere near his sword, he glanced back at the others. "No sudden moves. I can handle this."

489

"It won't work," said Enna, her crestfallen expression a close match for Tanith's. "That's Qolda."

Qolda's eyes met Tanith's, his cadaverous features tightening. She abandoned at once any hope of her glamour softening his suspicions. There wasn't another like her in the entire city, just as there wasn't another quite like Enna, whom Qolda hated like nothing else under the sun.

Twenty redcloaks, and who knew just how many more within range of a hue and cry.

Qolda's features tightened to a familiar scowl as realisation struck. "After them! Be wary of the girl, but take her alive!"

"Run!" shouted Rîma. "Make for the Golden Stair!"

Tanith bolted uphill past a torsion ballista turret thick with the corpses of its crew, Enna on her heels, Damant and Rîma bringing up the rear. The air wailed with shrieker shots, the flames from near misses setting corpses ablaze and shattering sandstone facades.

Clearly some of Qolda's troops had a broad definition of "alive".

As Tanith passed the Qabirarchi Palace, she glimpsed kathari on the atrium steps and others mustering from the darkened inner chambers. No sign of Ardoc, but she could scarcely imagine a man of his bulk or years lumbering up the stairs from the Stars Below. Likely these hadn't either, she realised, but had instead clambered aboard her elevator's twin as soon as it had reached the lower lobby.

Not that such details mattered, only numbers. And the numbers were getting worse all the time. She glanced behind.

Enna ran past, skirts whipping as she continued up the spiral street. Tanith's gaze settled on Rîma and Damant, who she at last realised weren't bringing up the rear out of caution or nobility, but because the latter was making heavy, red-faced weather of the slope. Even with Rîma practically dragging him, Qolda's headlong pursuit gained ground with every moment.

She eyed the buildings to either side. The window boxes, balconies and banner poles that had survived the fighting offered an embarrassment of handholds. Maybe Hadîm's had been the right idea. She could leave the others to take their chances, lose Qolda's redcloaks on the rooftops and in the streets. Be far away from all this before Ardoc even knew she'd fled.

The idea tempted like a cool drink on a hot day, or a welcoming smile from someone who deserved every last thing a hungry amashti might do to him.

But that wasn't her, not any more, even if she couldn't rightly say when that had changed.

Boots skidding on the blood-slicked cobbles, she ran back. Nose wrinkling at his hot, sweaty closeness, she propped her shoulder beneath Damant's and took the bulk of his weight.

"Friend of yours?" gasped Damant.

"Friend of Ardoc's. Move your feet, old man."

His laboured breaths a gale in her ears, they forged uphill, rounded the corner and came face to face with a roiling wall of mist, the pillars of the Golden Stair's gateway rising above them like a ship's masts from a fog bank, its shrieker cannons abandoned by crews dead or fled. Beyond, the Eternity King's palace reached untouched into the magenta glow of its encircling torch houses.

Breath rasping in his throat, Damant reached for his sword. "That's it then."

Rîma's was already drawn, laid flat across her shoulder as she stared at the oncoming cultists.

"No!" said Tanith. "Just keep going!"

A shrieker shot wailed overhead and crackled into the mist.

"That's ... the *Veil*," said Damant. "It'll ... eat us alive. I'd rather ... die with a sword in my hand."

He didn't much look like he could even hold a sword.

"It's just a barrier," said Enna. "Barriers can be crossed."

He shook his head, a man playing a losing hand and finding no help from the dealer. "There's something terrible in there. I saw it when we ... crossed the Silent Sea."

491

"I saw it too," said Tanith. "In Qosm, just days ago."

Enna frowned, a peculiar look in her eyes. "What did it look like, this terrible thing?"

"It didn't look like much of anything, just a shadow in the mists. Green eyes and wings."

"It ... attacked the *Chainbreaker*," said Damant. "Arvish thought it was ... looking for something."

"Did she now?" Enna straightened and levelled a determined stare at the Veil. "Inside, now. While there's still any hope at all."

Tanith nodded, wondering at the silent debate that had resolved in the other woman's thoughts. "I made it through, down in the city. It's a straight stair. Just keep moving."

Enna had already vanished, absorbed by the billowing greenish-white. Damant and Rîma shared an unhappy glance and followed. Tanith took a deep breath and plunged after them.

She felt herself coming apart as soon as the mists closed around her, pieces for which she'd no name wisping away into the roiling white. Her fingertips streamed like smoke from guttering candles, translucency creeping down her hands, her wrists, her forearms as solidity became a memory. Setting her shoulders against an imaginary current, she forged on, the steps of the Veil-drenched Golden Stair falling away behind her, holding her name close, determined not to forget it as she had before. Still she felt her perception creaking as the moments stretched and slowed, at times stumbling past and at others hissing away like a mill race.

In the middle distance, where the white became an impenetrable wall, Enna stood tall, head cocked as if listening for something, the coiling mist clutching at her hair, her skirts, but never finding purchase. In that unreal place she was somehow realer than ever.

The same couldn't be said for Damant, who even with Rîma's help was stumbling slower.

As Tanith drew level with him, a distorted shout rang out through the mists. A backward glance confirmed that the cultist redcloaks too had broached the Veil. Their garb pinkish where it wisped away into greenish-white, they charged on, Qolda at their head.

"Don't they know ... nothing survives the mists?" gasped Damant.

"We'll have to make a stand after all," said Rîma. "At least they don't have shriekers now." The ifrîti would have faded almost at once.

Tanith bit back the sour taste of defeat. Damant was fading worse than she was. If he didn't get clear of the mists soon, he never would. They'd all put themselves on the line for her. If there was ever a time to prove to them – to herself – that she was more than a monster, it was now.

"No," she said softly. "They're here for me. Give me your sword, I'll hold them back. You know I can."

Whether she could hold herself together and make her escape was another matter. But the knowledge didn't bring fear, only clarity. She might even have called it peace but for Nyssa's insistent pull at the back of her mind.

Enna swept back towards them, a stark, solid presence in a world bereft of the same. "You're the one person we can't let them have. This one's on me."

Tanith moved to block her path. "I can't let you do this."

Enna laid a hand on her shoulder. "Don't worry for me. This isn't what it seems."

She stalked away towards the approaching cultists, the falling stairs and swirling skeins giving her the appearance of one walking on clouds.

Tanith started after her. Rîma grabbed her arm. "It's her choice. Don't waste it."

Tanith grimaced, but nodded. "Come on, old man."

Between them they dragged the exhausted Damant in what Tanith hoped was the right direction. She turned back when a shout rang out through the mists.

"All right." Enna stood in what Tanith guessed was the middle of the Golden Stair's causeway, her arms spread wide. "Let's get this over with. I know you've been looking for me."

493

"Arrogant to the last," bellowed Qolda, his nasal voice somehow deeper in that unreal place.

"I wasn't talking to you." She folded her arms and tapped her foot. "Well, what are you waiting for? Do you want an apology? Fine! I'm *sorry*. I promise to listen in future."

She didn't sound in the least apologetic. She sounded unhinged, broken by the burden of the Veil.

"Keep going," Tanith told Rîma. "I can't leave her."

But it was too late. Qolda, less a man in the swirling mist than a vengeful blood-red spectre, bore down on the weaponless Enna, scimitar drawn. "Any last words?"

"Yes." Enna cocked her head. "It's about time."

A sudden suffocating pressure wave squeezed at Tanith's skin, her eyes, her thoughts. She clapped her hands to her ears just before they popped, deafened by the death cries of a hundred malevolent birds, screeching vengeance with one voice. Darkness bled through the Veil's uncertain skies as a vast shadow plunged, formless wings trailing like smoke behind and emerald eyes gleaming with liquid fire.

Qolda staggered backwards, expression stricken, his coiling Veil self swirling and eddying in his wake. His redcloaks cried out with dismay, scattering in all directions in a desperate attempt to flee. Only Enna held her ground, arms wide in welcome and laughing with a child's carefree abandon.

The diving shadow swallowed them all, then burst apart where it hit the hidden roadway, a black bloodstain spreading through the Veil's greenish-white. It faded away as soon as it had come, leaving no sign of those it had taken.

Tanith found herself laughing, Enna's claims of being a wanderer from beyond the Veil no longer as ridiculous as they'd seemed in the Stars Below. She really hadn't belonged in Khalad. *LET HER GO!* the shadow had demanded the last time Tanith had walked the mists, saving the wailing Jaia from the redcloaks. She'd thought it had meant to claim the girl. Instead, it had been seeking Enna, thinking her a prisoner. In a way, she had been. The captive of a realm not her own. "She was right. He *was* looking for her all this time."

"What just skrelling happened?" breathed Damant, his mouth agape.

Tanith shrugged, too heartsick and elated to put all Enna had told her into words. "She's gone home."

Fifty-One

The conclave hall's western doors shuddered beneath booming, rhythmic strikes. Not the sporadic pounding of fists so familiar across previous hours, but driving hollow impacts with the metre of a marcher's drum. That made it a battering ram, Kat decided, and with the hestics long since spent from turning previous besiegers to flame, it was only a matter of time before hinges or lock gave way.

So much for help arriving. It was always going to have been a race, the passage of time increasing the odds of salvation and disaster. In the end, disaster had the upper hand. In the moment before the final hestic had died, it had given her a glimpse of white robes and black masks, stifling the last hope. Redcloaks might have proven loyal to the Voice.

From her perch on the dais, Azra scowled at the door. "They don't give up, do they?"

Tatterlain shrugged. ||"Not exactly a shortage of stubbornness on this side either."||

||That's different,|| signed Yali.

Was it? Kat glanced back at Isdihar, doubled over on a chair in the lowest of the concentric tiers, elbows on her knees and eyes downcast. Hand her over to the cult and the rest of them would maybe walk free. They owed her no kindness, much less their lives. In fact, as the Eternity King's heir – his sole heir, so far as Kat knew – her hands were dripping with blood. But even if the cult could be trusted, even if the girl's death

496

wouldn't have haunted her – that they meant to kill her she didn't doubt – there were still the Eternity King's final words to consider.

Protect her. If she dies, the Cold Flame will take you all.

Kat was no more inclined to trust the Eternity King than she was the cult, but Khalad's strata of lies were peeling back too fast for her to make sense of them. Until she could – assuming she ever did – it made all the sense in the world to keep her alive.

She stared down at her tattoo. And the Eternity King *had* kept his word. She'd experienced neither spasm nor numbness since emerging from the flame. Whether the omen rot was gone for ever or he had merely granted a stay of execution, whatever she now achieved was possible only because of him.

Boom!

The doors creaked, the lock housing splintering the polished timber.

"Take cover." Kat offered a smile she didn't feel. "And try not to shoot each other."

She, Azra, Yali and Tatterlain carried shriekers recovered from the dead, their glyphs wiped so that anyone could wield them. More than that, Kat had passed the quiet moments between previous assaults in the spirit world, reshaping her tattoo to match the soul-glyphs of the remaining koilos slumbering away in their alcoves. She'd no guarantee that her command would override those of others, but at least it was *something*.

As the others took shelter amid the upper levels of seating, she crossed to Isdihar. The girl alone had refused a shrieker, had refused even to speak, for all that Yali had tried to coax her into conversation. "You should return to the sanctum. You'll be safer there."

Isdihar's bleak gaze flickered to the golden door. "I cannae go down there. I cannae look at him. I'd rather stay."

Kat felt a twinge of sympathy. Its fires faded to nothing, the Eternity King's sanctum was little more than a cold, lonely tomb. Just how empty was Isdihar's world without his voice in her head? Kat knew she'd never understand. "Then stay down. We're none of us good shots." An understatement, for she herself was nothing short of abysmal. "I'd hate to do the cult's work for them."

She climbed up to the middle seating tier and crouched low behind the backrest of the row in front. A glance out of the grand window confirmed that the Veil's grip remained tight around Zariqaz, though its purchase on the Golden Stair was thinning. Her palm was already clammy on the shrieker's grips. She squeezed the weapon tight and levelled the brass sights on the shuddering door.

Boom!

The doors leapt, the lock all but tearing free of the timbers.

Kat held her breath, counting down the seconds to the final blow.

Instead, muffled screams rang out from beyond the door. A shrieker's wail.

The doors crashed open, tortured hinges finally pulling free of the wall under a cultist's weight. As he collapsed atop the timbers in a sodden bloodstained heap, a slender black-clad figure stalked through the gap, sword across her shoulder, eyes surveying the room for threats.

Kat blinked, her jaw hanging open in surprise. "Don't shoot!" she shouted, the words choked by relieved laughter as she took the steps three at a time. "Don't shoot!"

"I don't know," called Tatterlain. "Looks like trouble to me."

Rîma swept her sword point down to the floor. "I am certainly that."

Yali and Azra emerged from concealment, their expressions as baffled as Kat knew her own to be.

"This was your plan?" said Azra.

"No. I'm as surprised as you are." Kat embraced Rîma. "I didn't think I'd see you again."

Rîma shook her head in mock dismay. "And yet I told you otherwise."

"Your grandfather . . . is it settled?"

Her cheeks tightened. "For whatever it's worth. A story for another time."

Kat nodded. "If that's what you want. How did you know we were here?"

Damant entered the conclave hall, the very image of a man ready to drop from exhaustion. "We didn't. The city's a battleground. We were hoping the King's Council might give us sanctuary, but the gatehouse was empty and every damn room's full of cultists. Figured that anyone they wanted dead were folk we wanted to meet. You're about the last people I expected." He propped an arm against the wall for support and jerked his head back towards the door. "You lost this, I think."

Kat cast her eyes to the doorway and the grubby golden-haired figure standing apprehensively on the threshold, more her amashti self than ever, for stories insisted that they had to be invited in ... or perhaps simply nervous. "Tanith?"

She nodded and slunk warily into the chamber, her eyes darting to each of Kat's companions in turn. Isdihar watched her transfixed, torn between outrage and the urge to bolt.

Tanith's eyes briefly met Kat's and glanced away. "I'm not going to apologise."

Kat closed the distance between them, her emotions a tangled brew. "For what? Saving my life?"

Tanith scowled. "You know what I mean."

Kat didn't, not in the detail, but supposed there were plenty of unhappy deeds from which to choose. But with the world upside down, none of them seemed important any longer. Her sister was there, alive and carrying herself with unaccustomed maturity. More than that, she wasn't *actively* trying to kill someone. You had to start somewhere. "Then don't. Let the past be the past."

Tanith shot her a suspicious look. "You sound like Enna."

"Who?" Kat was fairly sure she'd stolen the sentiment from Rîma.

Tanith's eyes shifted, no longer looking at Kat, but through her. "All my life, people told me that I was a monster." Her brow creased in sorrow. "She's the only one who said I could be something else if I wanted."

"And do you?"

"Yes. I didn't think so before, but ..." She straightened and grimaced, on balance once more. "We can't stay here. He'll be coming. He won't give up."

"Who won't give up?" asked Tatterlain, signing a translation for Yali.

"Ardoc. He . . ." Tanith winced. "He wants to give me to Nyssa."

Isdihar paled. "The Cold Flame has awoken," she said, repeating part of the Eternity King's final warning. "It needs only a body."

Damant blinked, noticing her for the first time. "Wait . . . the Voice is here too? You're keeping strange company, Arvish." He winced and offered Isdihar a weary bow. "My apologies, majesty. I trust the Eternity King is safe?"

Azra folded her arms. "As safe as only the dead can be."

Damant sagged, his cheeks hollow. "That's not funny."

"It's not meant to be," she replied tautly.

To Kat's way of thinking, it was the first time in months that the two had had something in common. Neither of them had turned outcast gladly. Little wonder the Eternity King's death had hit them as it had. That said, she was still trying not to think about it herself.

"The goddess killed him, didn't she?" murmured Tanith. "Ardoc said she would."

"Tzal killed him." Kat eyed the doorway's wreckage. "Azra, watch the corridor?"

Azra hefted her shrieker. "With pleasure, darling."

"No heroics. Just warn us."

"Heroics?" She brushed the suggestion away. "Look at who you're talking to."

Once she was gone, Kat launched into a hurried explanation of everything that had transpired since Tanith's failed attempt to murder the Voice in the Hallow Caves. Isdihar remained silent throughout, her eyes never leaving Tanith, though Yali – always a mistress of siding with lesser evils over those she deemed greater – made sure to stand between the two, the muzzle of her shrieker not quite aimed in Tanith's direction. When Kat had finished, Tanith laid out her half of the tale, the details about the Dead City and the Stars Below not as shocking to

Kat as she supposed they should be, but then she'd already seen them that day, if through the fires of the Deadwinds.

"Why you?" she asked when Tanith's story petered out. "What makes you so special?"

"What do you think?" said Tanith sourly, raising her left wrist. "The same thing that always has."

Kat grimaced, another piece of the puzzle falling into place. Ever since the Eternity King had challenged her assertion that Nyssa had spoken to her in the Deadwinds over Athenoch – no matter that her assertion had since been proven true, if flawed – she'd wondered why Tzal had directed her to Zariqaz. Now she knew. She'd been the Cold Flame's backup plan.

||What now?|| asked Yali.

That was the question, wasn't it? The same question they'd faced since the Eternity King's death: stay or go? The city wasn't safe, but even if they barricaded the open doorway, they couldn't hold it against a second attack – from Tanith's pursuers, or anyone else. Everything now was a tangled equation of time, distance and trust, all of them imprecisely known.

||"We need to find somewhere more defensible."||

||"We passed a guardroom on the floor below. It'll be cosy, but these kathari…"|| Damant finished wolfing down a hunk of bread taken from their scavenged supplies and kicked the white-robed corpse lying atop the wreckage of the doors, ||"had already stripped it bare. It'll do."||

A shrieker's wail echoed along the corridor, two more close behind. Azra.

"I'll go." Rîma set off towards the doorway at a brisk stalk. "Get the others ready to move."

As she passed the last koilos alcove before the door, its occupant jerked to macabre life.

"Look out!" bellowed Tatterlain.

A skeletal hand ripped Rîma's sword from her grasp and cast it away. The other grabbed her by the throat. The koilos slammed her against the wall, dust trickling across her shoulders.

Bleak malice flooded Kat's senses as the remainder of the conclave hall's koilos lurched into motion. Tatterlain managed a shot before a bony forearm clubbed him down. Yali loosed a panicked salvo that left a koilos a smouldering ruin, only to be gathered up in a bear hug, her shrieker clattering to the floor as unfeeling bones squeezed tight. Tanith shoved Damant clear of a flamberge's sweep and hacked down to sever his attacker's wrist. At once, two more shifted course to intercept her.

Kat plunged frantically into the spirit world and ordered the koilos to sleep. They ignored her, their deathless wills in thrall to another presence, lurking just beyond her sight.

Changing tactics, she focused on the nearest koilos and poured soulfire into its ifrît.

Its bleak spirit was orders of magnitude stronger and hungrier than the hestics and shriekers she was used to confronting. But almost everyone she cared for was in that room. The outcome was never in doubt.

With a thin cry, the tortured ifrît burst apart, its remnants rushing to the Deadwinds.

Kat subsided breathless as the koilos collapsed to the dais in a pile of masterless bones, cast back to the mortal world by the effort. But her aetherios tattoo still sang with soulfire. She gritted her teeth. What she could do once, she could do again.

"Enough!" called a woman's voice.

White-robed kathari flooded into the hall through the ruined doorway, shriekers levelled and swords drawn. Azra came with them, a dagger at her throat and her arms held fast by two kathari.

"Weapons down," said the woman, her voice rendered metallic by her stylised black mask, "or everyone dies."

Growling, Damant let his half-drawn scimitar slide back into its scabbard. Tanith gathered herself to pounce.

One of Azra's captors howled as she bit down on his hand. The other grabbed a handful of hair and dragged her head back, exposing her throat to the dagger's blade. Yali gave a thin cry as her captor squeezed tighter.

"Tanith, please," hissed Kat.

Tanith threw down her sword.

"Ah, there you are, Tanith," the newcomer rumbled as he stepped through the doorway, the long censer-staff he used as a walking stick trailing smoke. "I apologise for our lateness, but it took time to clear the mists from the Golden Stair and I've laboured too long to take risks on such things."

Unlike the other cultists, he moved with a measured, considered gait, not a foot out of place and no urgency to be seen. That confidence betrayed him more than his features, for his thickening jowls were concealed beneath a full beard and his hair was thinner than when Kat had seen him last. Though that separation could barely be counted in years, it felt like a lifetime, for they'd been hard years, full of grief and desperation.

His voice – basso, avuncular and deeply pleased with itself – became thoughtful as he turned his attention to Kat. "Well ... this is most unexpected."

She felt no joy when her eyes met his, no relief – not an echo of the sorrow that had nearly destroyed her. There wasn't even surprise. It felt somehow inevitable that she could be left without a single truth in a life running out of her control. There was only a childhood in tatters and a dull, distant anger she'd no words to describe.

"That's certainly one way to put it ... Father."

Fifty-Two

Tanith stared blankly at Ardoc as the kathari bound her with rope, the blackthorn incense only partially to blame for her fogged thoughts.

Ardoc was her *father*?

For the dozenth time, she strove to reconcile childhood memories of ready smiles and doting affection with the man who now watched with naked satisfaction as the last knots pulled tight, leaving her as trussed as any banquet fowl ready for the spit.

For the dozenth time, she failed. It was all too long ago, the memories painted in brighter colours than they'd truly been, something to cling to in the misery of later years spent on the run. A life to which he'd abandoned her before her eighth birthday. And these last six months he'd known who she was, and who he was to her. Known, and said nothing. Known, and had all the while conspired and tormented, moulding her for sacrifice.

She wanted to weep, to scream ... but lost in blackthorn haze, emotion came hard.

And so she drifted, senses wandering on bitter clouds, and barely felt the heave as the koilos hauled her over its shoulder.

Ardoc's censer-staff in one hand and Tanith bundled over its shoulder, the koilos stooped through the ruined doorway and into the passageway. Propped in a sitting position against the edge of a now-empty koilos alcove, her ankles tied and her wrists bound behind her back, Kat ignored the threat of the kathari shriekers and strained at her bonds.

Nothing. Not a scrap of give.

His breathing laboured, Ardoc – it was easier to think of him thus, and not as her father – squatted before her and steepled his fingers. His right sleeve fell back, revealing an intricate soul-glyph tattoo. Not an aetherios tattoo, but ordinary ink, yet one that shared designs with those Kat had seen when studying the koilos.

She brightened, sensing opportunity. Once Ardoc was gone – and hushed conversations between him and the kathari, to say nothing of Tanith's kidnap, suggested he would be leaving – she'd have a chance to turn the tables. Rîma, Tatterlain, Damant, Yali and Azra – the latter with a heavy bruise weltering the left side of her face – were scattered around the conclave hall, each with a pair of kathari guards. Discounting the now-absent Tanith, that left only Isdihar unaccounted for. Kat had no idea where she was, or even when she'd slipped away. The main thing was to keep Ardoc from suspecting he'd missed someone. The main thing, not the easy thing. All she wanted to do was scream at him.

He caught her interest, offered a knowing nod and pushed his sleeve back into place. "I confess, I'm impressed that you destroyed that koilos. Please don't get any ideas. I'll be taking the rest with me, and Iliya has very clear instructions should you prove . . . intractable."

Kat met him eye to eye and wondered what had become of the man she'd loved so dearly. "She'll shoot me, I suppose."

"Of course not." He shook his head. "If your sister proves . . . unsuitable, shall we say, it may yet be that the goddess will find you otherwise. Until that eventuality, I have a momentous duty to perform, and I fear you'll prove a distraction. Better you're up here. But make trouble, and Iliya will shoot one of your friends. Then another, then another. Hopefully your stubbornness won't outlive them all."

"And I thought Tanith was the monster in the family." An illusion rapidly in retreat. "If you love Nyssa so much, why don't you offer yourself as a host?"

Ardoc grunted. "Would that I could. I'm sure she'd prefer someone truly willing, but without the tattoo to bridge the mortal and the divine, I wouldn't last as long as she deserves." He narrowed his eyes. "You mustn't take it personally. This is destiny."

"How can I not take it personally? You're my *father*." The rising scream crackled beneath Kat's words, desperate to escape. "I thought you were dead."

He twitched a one-shouldered shrug. "Everyone was meant to. Alabastra's munificents, Hargo Rashace – one or two other associates I shan't sully your ears with. They were all growing a little too ... *insistent*. Terrion Arvish had served his purpose."

"I suppose that wasn't even your real name."

"I was him and he was me. He died so I could continue."

Despite herself, Kat took some comfort in the fact that her inherited family name held truth. But not nearly enough to ease the tightness in her chest. He hadn't escaped Alabastra. He'd slunk off into the night and left her to face his debts. Debts, it was increasingly apparent, he'd incurred not through gambling, nor even through easing her mother's omen-rot-driven decline, but to fund his cause. "Do I even want to know whose corpse I wept for?"

No wonder the shriversmen had never let her see it.

Ardoc grunted. "I couldn't tell you his name even if I wanted to. I paid and a service was provided. It's not healthy to dwell on the minutiae of such things."

Another piece of the tapestry of Kat's life, so carefully preserved through flight and hardship, rotted away. "I spoke to Fadiya a little while ago. She still loves you, even now. At least, she loves the man she thought you were."

"Ah." A faraway look came into Ardoc's eyes, a flicker of the wistful, contemplative man Kat remembered. "To think I nearly gave this up for her. She begged me to leave Zariqaz, leave all this behind. But in the end . . . I understood that Nyssa was testing me. I have no regrets."

Kat closed her eyes, unable to look upon him any longer. It didn't help. Fadiya lurked in the darkness, staring out across the estate that had become her prison, her only comfort the love she'd shared with a man who'd abandoned her. "Was any of it true?"

"Only one truth matters, a higher truth. I have been in service to it since long before you were born."

"To the third face of a goddess who isn't really a goddess at all?"

Ardoc stood and shook his head in disappointment. "Propaganda, parroted by veilkin and other apostates, though even those words hold a few useful truths. The goddess speaks to me. She visits me in my dreams. Whispers to me of what must be done to free her. She has done so ever since I first stumbled into the Stars Below. I don't expect you to understand."

"What if it's all a lie?"

"It isn't. It can't be." Ardoc's voice hardened, driving out even the possibility of doubt. "It has been the work of a lifetime. Now the Eternity King is dead and the new Age of Fire calls. We will finally be free. It will be glorious."

"And all it will cost is your daughter, is that it?" Maybe both daughters, if Tanith proved difficult. Kat doubted she'd make it easy for either the goddess or her self-appointed high priest.

"You're wasting your breath, Arvish," growled Damant. "You can't reason with fanatics."

"Tanith will be reborn!" said Ardoc, his voice trembling with reverence. "Not entirely as herself, perhaps, but she is to be the vessel by which the goddess will walk this world. Can there be any greater fulfilment?"

Across the room, Tatterlain cleared his throat. "I hate to say it, Kat, but your father clearly needed to get out more. I tell you, there's a little establishment down in the Starji district where—"

A kathari thumped him into unconsciousness with the butt of his shrieker. Tatterlain slumped forward, head lolling. Eyes afire, Yali tugged frantically at her bonds and went rigid as Iliya pressed her shrieker's muzzle against the back of her head.

"You don't want to pull that trigger," said Rîma, in tones that could have blackened the sun. "You're not ready for what it will cost you."

"That's enough," said Ardoc. "*Abdon Nyssa ivohê.*"

Iliya nodded and stepped away.

Kat bit back her mounting concerns. Was there anything left of her father to reason with, or had decades of Tzal's visions eroded his sanity to nothing? *I don't know how much you remember, but he was less and less lucid towards the end. Almost like a man possessed.* Fadiya had seen it; why hadn't Kat? The answer was simple enough. Love had blinded her to his eccentricities and foibles. It had coaxed her into thinking that there was nothing strange, much less abhorrent, about a man who experimented on his daughters.

"And all I am to you is Tanith's understudy, is that it?"

Stepping behind her, Ardoc knelt and twisted the inside of her left wrist to face the ceiling. "I felt sure that the third attempt would be a success," he said, his breath warm on the back of her neck, "but you never showed even half Tanith's ability. The tattoo brought her closer to the goddess, as it was meant to. All it gave you were parlour tricks." He leaned in closer, his eyes hard. "What are you to me? You were only ever a disappointment, shallow and weak, too easily distracted by material things and mortal pleasures, chasing after firebloods for approval you could never earn. Why do you think I left you behind?"

Kat's throat thickened as her battered, abused heart finally broke apart, the shrapnel driving ice-hot spikes into her lungs. There was nothing to reason with in what remained of her father, nothing worth trying to save. Maybe there never had been.

"Ardoc, Terrion ... whatever your name is." Azra's voice was as flat and murderous as Kat had ever heard it. "Would you come over here?"

"Why should I do that?" he asked without turning.

"Because I'd really, *really* like to kick your face in."

Kat drew down a deep breath and with it found a sudden, horrible clarity. Third attempt, Ardoc had said. Tanith had been the first, Kat herself the second ... or so she'd always believed. But now ... ? That was the trouble with truth. Once it sang to you, it couldn't be unheard. Omen rot had taken her mother. But for the Eternity King, it would have taken Kat too. The first time her father had set a needle to her skin, he'd explained that the process required a young, malleable body. She'd never thought to ask how he'd known.

"How did my mother die?" she asked, her voice trembling.

Releasing her, Ardoc stood. "I did everything I could for her, you know that. But she knew the risks. She *believed*. And Nyssa will reward her, in the end."

For the first time, he spoke with obvious affection, proof perhaps that he had truly loved Siette Arvish, even if he'd cared for no one else. It might have stirred sympathy, had Kat any longer a heart with which to offer it. When she looked on him, she no longer saw her father. She barely saw a man. Just a monster whose obsession had broken everyone who'd ever loved him, or might have done so.

"I'm going to kill you," she said softly.

The corner of Ardoc's mouth twitched. "No. No, I don't think so, and I must deliver the goddess her vessel before the conjunction fades." He strode away towards the door, sparing no glance for his other prisoners. "Iliya, I leave her in your care. *Abdon Nyssa ivohê.*"

With one last, empty gaze at Kat, he left the conclave hall behind, the procession of koilos marching unevenly in his wake. The kathari took up positions around the chamber, half watching either door or captives while others made slow, deliberate circuits of the dais, somehow unwithered by the glares sent their way.

Kat stared sightlessly at the mists beyond the grand window, fear and loss congealing to cold, hard anger. At Salamdi she'd told Fadiya that she wished she'd known more about her father's hidden life. If only she could take it back. The more she peered into the past, the thicker with lies it became. The father she remembered was no more real than Nyssa.

He and Tzal deserved one another. And Tanith, despite everything she'd done, deserved neither.

The only question was what to do about it. With Ardoc's departure, the equation of time, distance and trust was shifting. Time had become a resource Tanith could no longer afford, nor could Khalad if half of what the Eternity King had said was true. Call it Nyssa or Tzal, the Cold Flame was a god that had humbled the Issnaîm. She didn't know how to even start fighting something like that. Tanith, though? There was still time to save her. Maybe.

But how? Twelve kathari, including Iliya, was a steep obstacle for half a dozen bound, weary prisoners. There was no help in the spirit world, not now Ardoc had gone. Kat could only detonate their shriekers one at a time, and the first would begin the executions – scimitars would be enough for that.

She saw it as the nearest pair of circling kathari passed her by, continuing around the circle to where Rîma – who rated three permanently stationed guards of her own – sat trussed: a pallor beyond the window, drifting across the mist-draped sky, moving against what little breeze stirred the pennants of neighbouring buildings. A shape that imagination might have read as belonging to a woman, save that it was four storeys up with neither ledge nor handhold for support.

A slow smile crept across Kat's face. Maybe time wasn't against them after all.

She felt a gentle breeze at her back. A tug on her bound wrists. Another. The ropes shifted beneath a sawing motion.

"Dinnae move," whispered a small voice, filled with fragile bravado. "I have a dagger."

Isdihar? Kat re-examined her mental map of the conclave hall and realised her back was to the hidden sanctum door. She twisted her head just enough for her peripheral vision to confirm that the door was ajar. No wonder Ardoc hadn't seen Isdihar – she'd fled into the sanctum. If only she'd stayed there a little longer. Though the edge of the alcove and the positioning of Kat's own body shielded the girl for the moment, they wouldn't once the second pair of kathari drew closer.

"They'll see you," she murmured, careful not to move her lips more than she had to. "Go back. Trust me."

"No," Isdihar replied flatly, a little of the Voice's assertiveness resonating beneath. "I owe ye."

Recognising the uselessness of argument that would only draw the attention she hoped to avoid, Kat glanced up at the grand window. The pallor – assuming she'd not imagined it in the first place – had gone. Not so the approaching kathari, who'd passed a glaring Yali. Twenty paces and what passed for Isdihar's cover would be worthless.

"Please go back," hissed Kat.

The sawing motion intensified. "I'm almost through."

Twelve paces.

A small sob of frustration brushed the back of Kat's neck as Isdihar realised too late she wasn't going to win the race.

Six paces.

"What is this?"

Kat jumped at Iliya's barked demand, in her mind's eye the shriekers already aimed at the girl sheltering behind her. It took her a moment to realise that the question hadn't been levelled at her or Isdihar, but at eight masked kathari marching in through the outer door. All wore robes bloodied from recent battles, and scimitars sheathed at their shoulders – all save the leader, who carried a short, stubby mace barely worthy of the name.

"Reinforcements," snapped the leader, crisp parade-ground delivery and the mask's metallic echo not quite disguising his voice. "There are notorious troublemakers among this lot. Better not to take chances."

Across the dais, Damant caught Kat's eye, the scowl he'd worn ever since the kathari had stormed the conclave hall curling to a grim, wolfish leer.

Iliya squared her shoulders, her sudden petulance leading Kat to reappraise her age downwards by a full decade. "I told Ardoc I could handle it."

The leader shrugged. *"Abdon Nyssa ivohê."*

Iliya hesitated, then nodded. *"Abdon Nyssa ivohê."*

"I'm glad you agree." At the leader's signal, the newcomers spread out through the hall. Kat felt Isdihar shrink back as the blank mask of his gaze tracked across each prisoner in turn before falling on Kat. "It's good to have friends, isn't it?"

Turning on his heel, he brought his mace down in a vicious arc. Iliya's mask crumpled and she dropped like a stone.

Screams rang out as the other newcomers drew their swords and turned on their erstwhile peers. A shrieker shot punched clean through a chair backrest, flung off course when Damant's jackknifing legs swept a kathari's feet away. Yali, her hands free and ropes dangling from her wrists, hurled herself sideways and clung madly to a guard's trailing ankle, dragging him back while a newcomer ran him through. Another kathari trained his shrieker on the newcomers' leader, his sudden howl drowned out by the explosion as Kat goaded the shrieker's ifrît to detonation.

And just like that, it was over. The ropes around Kat's wrists snapped free as Isdihar's dagger at last did its work. The guards were all dead or moaning in their own blood and the newcomers set about slicing the prisoners free of their bonds. Their leader stood in the centre of the dais and tugged away his mask and bloody robes to reveal a severely cut black tunic.

||"So this is the conclave hall of the King's Council?"|| said Vallant. ||"I thought it would be larger."||

For all that Kat had hoped – had *known* – it was him, ever since she'd glimpsed Zephyr performing reconnaissance at the grand window, her spirits lifted to finally see him face to face, to tolerate that self-effacing earnestness that wasn't self-effacing at all.

Yali grinned. Tatterlain, still groggy and his face slippery with blood, clambered to his feet. ||"Took your sweet time, didn't you?"||

||"Everyone's a critic."|| Vallant cast about the room, his stern tone undermined by a self-satisfied grin, and settled on one of the

now-maskless newcomers, all of whom Kat recognised as sailriders from the *Chainbreaker*. The bloodstains on the discarded robes took on fresh significance. ||"Vathi? I saw a storeroom back there with a nice heavy door. Perhaps you'd lock the survivors in?"||

Vathi, his dark-featured face adding gloom to an already woebegone expression, nodded morosely. "Guard duty, is it? Typical."

"Try not to enjoy it too much."

Vathi grunted and, with help from a pair of sailriders, goaded the bleeding, muddled Iliya and the two remaining kathari from the room. Rîma retrieved her sword and went with them, her expression alone a discouragement against making trouble. She passed Zephyr in the doorway, and surrendered gladly to the daughter of the Issnaîm's vaporous embrace.

Azra rubbed her wrists. "Just kill them."

"It doesn't come as easily to me as to others." Vallant turned about to greet Damant rather more warmly. "Ihsan ... So you prefer Kat's company to mine, is that it?"

"It's a long story."

Vallant clapped him on the back. "They always are."

Kat, Isdihar's dagger in hand, sliced away the last of her bonds and accepted Yali's helping hand. ||You never told me you were good with knots.||

Yali waved an airy hand. ||After locks, everything's easy. You didn't tell me Vallant was coming for us, so I reckon we're even, honest and true.||

||So much could have gone wrong, I didn't want to get your hopes up.||

Yali's expression turned wry. ||I suppose that makes a twisted sort of sense ... for you.|| Her face settled, subdued. ||Your father makes mine look like a hero. I'm sorry.||

Kat grimaced. ||At least I know the truth.||

She turned to Vallant, fighting a feeling of awkwardness now the moment was upon her. She'd hated asking for his help – putting herself

513

in his debt *again* – and silently begged him not to make a mountain out of it. ||"We always meet under the nicest circumstances."||

||" I almost didn't believe your heraldic. Zephyr convinced me."||

||"Sorry. I didn't have time to go into it all."|| Heraldics had notoriously fickle memories if asked to carry too much information. In the end, Kat had focused on the important things: where they were, the pass-phrase *Abdon Nyssa ivohê*, the Eternity King's death . . . and that what remained of the Golden Citadel's defenders were in anarchy, all eyes inward. ||"Can you get everyone out of here?"||

||"Nothing easier. The *Chainbreaker* took a bit of a knock from a torsion ballista whose crew weren't as distracted as you thought, but she's had worse. We're moored off the north tower."|| His gaze shifted to Isdihar, a mute, wary presence at Kat's shoulder. ||"First you bring a Bascari aboard my ship, now I'm rescuing the Voice, is that it?"||

Kat examined Vallant's expression, searching for a clue to his mood. Even travelling at their father's less than impressive turn of speed, Tanith was getting further away with every passing second. There wasn't time to explain everything, just enough to keep him happy. ||"A lot's happened this past day."||

||"I'm not blind. I've seen the fires in the city."||

"I suppose this is what ye wanted," said Isdihar, striving for aristocratic hauteur and not quite finding it.

Vallant fixed her with an earnest stare. ||"Not in the least. I want freedom. This is madness."||

Azra shook her head. "Madness lacks purpose. Kat's father has nothing *but* purpose." She aimed at a smile and missed by degrees. "Yennika would have been jealous."

Vallant stared at Kat as if she'd grown a second head. "Your father's dead."

Kat might have enjoyed seeing him so wrong-footed that he forgot to sign for Yali, who was watching their exchange with rapt attention, but they were wasting time. ||"If only that were true. Instead, he's fixing to free Tzal from the Stars Below. He's giving it my sister to wear as its body. Only we don't call it Tzal. We call it Nyssa."||

For the first time, she realised that she had everyone's attention. Not just her friends, but the sailriders who'd joined Vallant's rescue attempt.

"Tzal?" Zephyr drifted closer, her skirts billowing behind and her expression aghast. "*Ayin*, not a name to joke with is that."

||"I'm not. Your ancestors caged him after all and we're trapped here alongside."||

||"I believe it,"|| said Damant. ||"I've seen some of it. However bad you think this is, it's worse."||

||"We made a goddess of your great enemy and now it's awake."|| Kat recalled the formless, numbing presence in the Deadwinds. ||"I don't think it's going to be grateful."||

Zephyr's whole being flickered, the captive vapour of her body turning almost translucent with shock. She pressed a spread hand to her chest. "Sun and moon preserve us. Make slaves of us all, will Tzal."

Vallant's brow tightened, Zephyr's horror convincing where Kat and Damant's words had not. Kat didn't blame him for that. She didn't want to believe it herself. ||"Well ... you wanted me here. I'm here. What do you need?"||

She frowned, her turn to be wrong-footed. "As simple as that?"

"I trust you, Kat. One day you'll believe me." He made no attempt to sign his reply, making it as intimate as a crowd permitted. "Tell me what you need."

And there it was again, the earnestness that made her want to thump him. But for once, she was glad to see it. She could always thump him later.

||"Get everyone aboard the *Chainbreaker* and wait as long as you can. I'll be back."|| She took a deep breath. "If I'm not, I need you to keep Isdihar safe."

||"Isdihar?"||

||"The Voice."||

515

Vallant scowled. ||"I know who she is. It's the 'why' I don't understand."||

The Eternity King's last words again chimed through Kat's thoughts. *Protect her. If she dies, the Cold Flame will take you all.* ||"I don't know. Nor does she."|| She glanced at Isdihar, a pensive mass of apprehension in smeared make-up and filthy golden silks. ||"Keep her alive long enough and I guess you'll find out."||

||"Why? Where are you going."||

||"She's going after her sister."|| Rîma stood by the doorway, arms folded and head tilted.||"She thinks she's going alone."||

||"She is—" Kat began. "I mean, *I am* going alone."||

Vallant shook his head. ||"Absolutely not."||

||"You asked me what I needed. This is it."||

||"And you'll have it. The Voice goes to the *Chainbreaker*. Then to Tyzanta, Athenoch … one of the other cities, if that's what she wants. But your father has an army. You'll not get anywhere near your sister without help."||

Azra levelled a deathly serious stare. "And if you think I'm letting you out of my sight after all we've been through, darling, you've another think coming."

||What she said.|| Yali folded her arms.

Tatterlain cleared his throat. "I've always wanted to see the Stars Below while I was still alive enough to enjoy them."

Kat rounded on him, riven between frustration and gratitude. "Every time you follow me somewhere I almost get you killed."

"But *only* almost." Tatterlain grinned, only to wince almost at once and touch a hand to his purpling bruise. "Vallant's much better at this leadership business. He gets people killed all the time. It's only fair you have some practice."

Vallant shot him an unimpressed glance. "Thanks."

Tatterlain shrugged. "I said you were *better*."

Damant offered a rare, sardonic smile. "Give it up, Arvish. We've got the numbers. All arguing's doing is wasting time."

"What if numbers aren't enough?"

Damant's good eye fixed on Zephyr, who, while still pale even by her standards, looked a lot more solid than she had a few minutes before. "Actually, I have a thought about that ..."

Fifty-Three

Tanith drifted on clouds of lavender-scented darkness, the mortal world barely a patch of shadow. The flame coursed through her, part of her, soothing and caressing, smoothing away the echoes of loss and fear. It was a belonging so complete she nearly wept. Sensation was distant, almost forgotten. Just one facet of herself among so many others that she needed no longer.

Nyssa's face formed among the flames; regal, welcoming, loving.

Hush, child. We will be together soon.

A piece of Tanith drowned in indigo. She let it go, glad if she was anything at all. She perceived now how her every step had brought her closer to the flame. To Nyssa. To apotheosis – a gift offered by the goddess and received by the same.

Do not think of it as death, child. You lived only because I willed it. All that you are, you owe to me.

Death? Tanith clung to her sudden concern. The flame darkened, displeased, its embrace closer and colder than ever. Her concerns melted away into the fire, dark streamers of smoke amid indigo, soon swallowed up and forgotten.

Her eyes clouded. She felt Nyssa's hand on her brow. Her breath on her cheek.

Yes. You're close now. Embrace me. Live through me.

An atonal wail split the dark. Another. A third. Each closer than the last.

Nyssa's hand withdrew. The darkness ebbed, bordered again by flame. Sensation bled back into Tanith's limbs as the goddess' attention wandered. Voices burbled on the liminal edge between mortal gloom and writhing fire. Shouts. Screams. The cries of the dying.

For the first time in a lavender eternity, the past unfurled across Tanith's thoughts. The blackthorn haze. The glittering skies of the Stars Below. Her father's triumphant grin as swords goaded her into the column of fire.

Determination kindled warmth in the cold flame.

A new sound joined the shriekers' staccato wail and the battle's roar. The song danced between the flames, haunting and sorrowful, a tale of loss woven from forlorn aspirations, its meaning borne by every lingering, mellifluous note.

Nyssa's face melted like running wax, revealing something darker, older and formless. As the song grew louder, that formless thing *screamed*.

Kat felt it from the moment she entered the Stars Below – a presence, vaster than her own, unfolding across the spirit world. She'd encountered it before, adrift on the Deadwinds above Athenoch, only there it had comforted and cajoled. Now it burned with frustration.

She flinched as the presence screamed its rage, the hot flash behind her eyes distracting her from the kathari to her front.

"*Abdon Nyssa ivohê!*" He struck her scimitar aside and sliced at her throat.

Adrenaline drove the bleak pressure from Kat's thoughts. She ducked the kathari's hissing blade and shoved him in the chest. He stumbled, boot heel finding nothing but darkness beyond the causeway's edge. He vanished with a thin cry, the dull triple impact of his body bouncing off the hillside swallowed by the clamour of battle elsewhere.

Kat spun around, warned of the koilos ember-saint's approach by the malevolent shadow its ifrît cast in the spirit world. Golden armour betrayed it as one Ardoc had stolen from the conclave hall; blood spatters on its robes and a smeared flamberge blade that it had already killed. It ground towards her, dust rising from its footfalls.

A shrieker wailed. Robes ablaze, the koilos took another faltering step before a second shot blew apart its gilded skull.

Breathless with exhilaration, Azra ran to Kat's side, brandishing her shrieker. "You should have kept this."

The koilos collapsed, scattering charred bone fragments across the flagstones.

Kat peered along the causeway to where a knot of Vallant's sailriders hurled themselves at a band of kathari twice their number. Rîma led the charge, ever at the front despite never picking up her pace. Yali was there too, her slashes more enthusiastic than skilled. Kat's heart leapt as a kathari's parry left her wide open, then she exhaled in relief as Damant shoved Yali aside and all but severed the kathari's arm.

She'd tried convincing Yali to wait with the *Chainbreaker*, but she'd burned all that capital persuading Tatterlain. She trusted Vallant's crew in the ordinary run of things – but not with Isdihar Diar, the Voice whose words had brought ruin to so many and whose youthful vulnerability might tempt all manner of reprisals. Tatterlain's popularity gave him an authority second only to Vallant himself. Which wasn't to say he hadn't argued against it.

Still, it was strange not having him there.

She looked again at Azra's shrieker and shook her head. "I never could aim worth a damn."

And there were few enough shriekers to go around. Most of those they'd recovered from slain redcloaks and kathari along the way to the Qabirarchi Palace had exhausted their ifrîti to nothing, testament to the savagery of the day's fighting. Using the last of the soulfire she'd stolen from the Eternity King's sanctum, Kat had wiped the soul-glyphs of those that remained. Of the three-score sailriders Vallant had brought down from the *Chainbreaker*, perhaps one in three carried a shrieker. The rest made do with swords, handspikes and crossbows.

And make do they had, brushing aside the thin line of kathari who'd guarded the lower elevator landing, momentum carrying them deep onto the causeway before the cultists' battle-cries had risen out of the streets to challenge Zephyr's lament.

Azra stared past Kat to the jagged ruins of the Obsidium Palace and its vortex of indigo flame. "How can we fight something like that?"

Zephyr's song billowed, sweeping deeper into the Dead City. Magenta flickered alongside indigo in the Deadwinds vortex anchored in the Obsidium Palace's broken crown. Damant had been right: Zephyr's lament wasn't really a lament at all, but ritual wielded by the Issnaîm of old, its purpose forgotten save among the aethervores of the Stars Below – a song to cage an ancient enemy.

"We don't have to fight it," Kat replied, hoping beyond hope that it was true. "If Tzal doesn't have Tanith, it doesn't have a body. It can't leave."

"What if your father's right?" said Azra. "What if Tanith *is* the key to a new age? A goddess, like he says?"

"If he believed that, he'd give himself to Tzal, not her."

"Yes, but to be a goddess . . ." murmured Azra.

Kat's attention wandered back along the causeway to the shrinking knot of sailriders, Vallant and Zephyr among them, fighting like daemons to hold the causeway stair against the counter-attack rising out of the Dead City. Buying time so she could do what had to be done.

They'd followed her lead before at Athenoch, but there they'd been fighting for their own survival. None of them had anything at stake in this. Some fought and died for friendship, others because they trusted Vallant and because Vallant trusted her.

How did he live with that pressure?

How could she?

Weary, sore and with the pressure of Tzal's malice ever-present in her thoughts, Kat seized upon the only answer worth having. How could she live with it? Because she had to. Because it wasn't just Tanith's life at stake. Her faith in Nyssa shattered beyond repair, she believed one thing still: that the Issnaîm had caged the Cold Flame for a reason.

521

"You still with me?"

Azra grinned. "Until the end, darling."

On they forged, across the lifeless bodies and cooling copper blood of friend and foe, the shriek of steel and triumphant cries echoing out beneath the distant glittering stars. Kat lost track of how many times she almost died, saved from a cultist's blade by a bellowed warning or a shrieker's discharge. How many times she stumbled to a skinned knee and rose again, Azra's hand in hers.

With every step, the ruins coalesced in the darkness, the walls tumbled from within by some long-ago explosion, the pillars spearing skyward to give the hill its crown. The outer wall passed away, a spill of rubble thick with the cold-eyed corpses of aethervore and mortal. Then Damant's hand was at her shoulder, pushing her onwards to the summit and the palace's inner wall.

Breathless, Kat reached level ground, Yali to her left and a stranger to her right. Ahead lay the remnant of the inner wall. The Deadwinds vortex pulsed, setting motes of soul-stuff dancing, the poisonous indigo once again consuming the magenta. And glimpsed through an archway, a lone dark figure suspended in the coruscation's heart, a motionless puppet hanging on invisible strings. Arrayed between them, a wall of malice-driven bone and deluded hearts, the cult's last defence.

Kat glanced back at her companions, now no more than a dozen facing three times that in kathari alone, not considering the koilos.

Damant pushed his way to her side. "We'll go hard for the centre, make you an opening. Let us worry about the rest." He raised his sword high and his voice to the roar of a parade ground. "Now send them to the Deadwinds!"

Screaming with the fury of men and women drowning their fear, the sailriders surged. A koilos blazed, struck as one by twin bolts of shrieker fire. Rîma cut down a hulking kathari and pirouetted away to slice open the arm of another as part of the same swing. Kat parried a kathari's slice, Yali darting in to finish him with a thrust.

And then there was nothing between her and Tanith but the ruins of the inner wall.

||Go! Go!|| Yali signed one-handed, her face alive with the grim joy of battle.

Lungs burning, Kat ran headlong for the flames. Petrified, charred corpses marked the circle's perimeter. Some stood, propped upright by long staves and recognisable in silhouette as the men and women – the Issnaîm – they'd once been. Others knelt, hands outstretched in prayer or pleading. The ember-saints of old, set not to serve Nyssa but to cage Tzal.

She forged on through the palace's cracked and toppled remains. The Deadwinds vortex, vast from afar, seemed even larger close to – broad enough to swallow the Rashace palace and everything in it. Tzal's presence grew more suffocating with every step.

Tanith was close enough that Kat saw that her eyes were clamped shut and her lips peeled back in a rictus of pain. The crude Adumaric characters daubed across her cheeks and brow dribbled away as the ink mingled with sweat.

"Fight him!" shouted Kat. "I won't let him take you!"

She rounded the last pillar. A heavyset shadow lumbered between her and the fire, his staff swinging. Stars burst behind Kat's eyes. She sprawled, jarring her shoulder against stone.

She rolled to her elbow, blinking away the ruddy drumbeat pounding at her thoughts. Ardoc loomed above her, his staff tight in both hands.

"Arrogant child!" he roared. "Her fate is not yours to choose!"

Fifty-Four

Even gasping for breath and his ears ringing with the din of battle, Damant heard Zephyr's song falter, the notes momentarily losing their force before rising anew. In that brief cessation, the small, insistent voice that whispered without words grew louder still. He swayed, fighting for balance as the world lost focus.

Fingers clamped around his arm, dragging him back to the present. The blurred, indigo gloom resolved itself to Rîma's frown. "You feel it too, don't you?"

Damant shook his head to loosen the cobwebs. They scattered readily, not so the whispers he couldn't quite hear. He'd strayed to the edge of the fight. Rîma aside, everyone else was merely a shadow in the gathering dark. "Ever since we came back here."

A kathari came screaming out of the darkness. Her back turned and her eyes still on Damant's, Rîma cut the cultist's legs away and stabbed down. "It's like Tadamûr. A soul vast enough to smother all."

Damant stared across the thinning battle and up at the vortex, the magenta now in full retreat before indigo. "Does it call to you as Tadamûr did?"

"No," Rîma replied, her face tight. "But that doesn't mean it will not call to others."

He nodded, images of the shuffling citizens of the Hidden City rising unbidden to greet him. "Azra, Yali ... have you seen them?"

The Deadwinds take Yennika Bascari, whatever she called herself, but Yali was still as close to an innocent as was possible. Worth an old man's life, if it came to it.

"No." Rîma stared past the ruined inner wall to the deepening flame. "But I'm sure I know where to find them."

Ardoc thrust his staff down. Blinking to clear red shadows from behind her eyes, Kat rolled clear. The staff's brass heel raised brief sparks as it cracked against stone.

"You will not stop my life's work! My legacy!"

Kat ducked back towards the flames and misjudged the distance. She cried out as the blow that should have whistled past her chest struck her left shoulder with numbing force.

"Most people think their children are their legacy," she gasped.

The staff whirled again. Kat parried, the impact all but ripping the blade from her hand.

"You used to call me your masterpiece, remember?"

Ardoc bore down, his face stony. "We all make mistakes."

He struck again, his heaviness of gait nowhere to be found. Or perhaps his speed wasn't his alone, but Tzal weighting the scales in his favour.

Kat lurched back, the suddenness setting the drumbeat pounding even louder behind her eyes. Rîma's lessons howled at her to get in closer, inside the reach of that lethal staff.

She lunged, but the staff was already in motion. Her knee cracked against stone as Ardoc swept her leg away.

Above her head, the Deadwinds vortex deepened to wrathful indigo as the last slivers of magenta sputtered out. The pressure of Tzal's will howled at the back of her mind, driving her to both knees. The staff blurred, striking her sword from her stinging hand.

Ardoc stalked closer, his tan skin mottled and purpled in the back-wash of the flames.

Kat gazed up at him through watery eyes, one shadow among many in the flickering dark, and dredged up the energy to laugh. "You were right after all, Father. I'm not going to kill you."

"No." He stared up at the vortex in grim satisfaction. "She will not allow it. *Nyssa Abdon—*"

The shadows flowed apart. Glinting steel ran red. Ardoc crumpled sideways, his face frozen in consternation and his robes already slick from the dagger's kiss Azra had set upon his throat.

"Darling, I'm sorry. But he was a dreadful man. You're better off without him."

Rising on aching legs, Kat flung her arms around Azra, who held her tight enough to crumble the world to dust. "And you know dreadful men better than anyone."

"Charmer." Azra considered. "One less, now."

Kat stared at the twitching corpse and wondered if death might offer some semblance, reconciling it with the man who dominated her memories – the only family she'd ever truly known, and yet hadn't known at all. But in death as he'd proven himself to be in life, Terrion Arvish, whom some knew as Ardoc, was merely a stranger.

But she'd family yet, by blood and by choice.

As Zephyr's song faltered a second time, Kat disentangled herself from Azra's embrace and stepped into the spirit world.

The woman who'd called herself Tanith drifted like ash, the pieces of her being so dissolute that they no longer recognised themselves as parts of the same whole. And yet they held tight to what slender identity remained, the urge to resist though the reason for that resistance had faded.

But even then, little by little, those scraps of soulfire felt the call of something grander. The same, and yet not. A completeness for which they'd forever yearned and never found, though they'd sought it in a hundred devoured and desiccated souls. A greater formless flame to which they were but sparks.

You're mine, breathed that greater flame. *And I am yours.*

Another flame flickered into being in the darkness, a mere glimmering to the one already there, but brighter by far.

Tanith. I'm here. Take my hand.

The glimmer spilled across the threshold of the greater flame, its radiance reshaping old memories. No longer alone, the scraps of soul recalled a time when they'd been one, and in that recollection became so again. Made whole, she remembered what it was to fight and why she had done so. She remembered her name.

Come home, breathed the glimmer. *Please.*

But alongside her name, Tanith found old memories. Of being cast out, thrown aside, banished, hunted, discarded and tortured. A sea of snarling faces and harsh words fit to drown an ocean.

You came back for me? she murmured without words. *Why?*

Because you're my sister ... and I'm not ready to lose you.

The greater flame shone darkly, angrier, more alluring. *You belong here. To me.*

Tanith looked from one to the other. Maybe the glimmer was lying. People always lied to her. But all her life, no one had come back for her.

Perhaps it was worth the risk, this once.

She took Kat's hand.

The greater flame howled with rage.

Kat tore free of the spirit world too swiftly for her mortal senses to adjust. Eyes hot with tears, she struck stone with hands and knees, the jarring pain nothing alongside the after-image of Tzal's wrath. She rose, trembling. No ifrît had ever come close to casting her from the spirit world. Tzal had done so with the simplest shrug.

"What's wrong?" Azra crowded close, eyes tight. "Kat ... you're bleeding."

Kat wiped her eyes. The back of her hand came away dark and smeared. Another unhappy first. "He won't let her go." She swallowed, despair fogging her thoughts. "He's too strong ... I can't fight him."

Azra grimaced. "Then it's over."

527

"No! It can't be!"

But the thought of contesting Tzal's will a second time turned her knees to jelly. She glanced at the petrified Issnaîm on the circle's perimeter. All those and more had perished caging Tzal. How was she to do so alone? More than at any other time in her life, Kat longed for a goddess to take pity on her. But Nyssa was the only goddess she'd ever known, and Nyssa was a lie.

Azra grabbed her arm. "You've done everything you can."

Kat gazed at her, misery overcome by a sudden serenity she couldn't quite identify. There was only purpose, and the knowledge that would see that purpose fulfilled.

"I haven't, not yet ... I'm sorry."

Azra blinked. "What do you mean, you're sorry?"

Kat stared up at the Deadwinds vortex. Even now, she didn't really know if it was part of Tzal's cage or the god himself. Whether she could survive crossing the threshold or it would burn her to cinders. "Tanith's fighting him. My father said Tzal preferred a willing host. I'm going to give him one."

Azra stared at her in horror. "Part of why we came here was to stop him getting a body, remember?"

"The only choice left is whose body he gets. Tanith saved my life. She deserves one of her own." She swallowed. "Maybe my father was right. Maybe I will be a goddess."

"A goddess ..." Azra said dully, her eyes on the flame.

Kat kissed her, stealing one last memory of warmth to hold close in whatever came next. "Just as we'd worked things out. It doesn't seem fair."

"Life isn't fair," murmured Azra, her perfect eyes bright with tears. "Never is, never was. You find your place, or someone finds it for you."

Kat released her and started towards the flame. "Tell Yali this was my choice."

"No."

Still turning, Kat barely saw the punch that set her world spinning.

"I'm sorry, darling," said a distant voice as the darkness took her. "This isn't meant for you."

Zephyr's song fell silent as Rîma and Damant reached the inner wall.

Wrestling with the rising pressure behind his eyes, Damant glanced back at the causeway and glimpsed Zephyr amongst the sailriders of Vallant's band, a sword in each hand. What had started as a rearguard had become a fighting retreat, the causeway ceded to the cultists' superior numbers. Even as he watched, the survivors of his own band, Yali among them, ran to reinforce Vallant.

"Ihsan!" Rîma vaulted a crumbling section of wall and ran into the circle. Halfway to the Deadwinds vortex, a golden-haired figure knelt beside a crumpled body, magenta fire flickering from a grazed cheek and through rents in the torn clothing along her left side. Damant picked up his weary legs and set out after Rîma, somehow arriving only a three-count behind.

"What happened?"

Tanith stared up at him with uncertain eyes. "I don't know. I was coming apart . . . and then I was here. I don't know what she did."

Rîma knelt beside them and set her sword aside. "Katija, this is no place to die."

Arvish groaned and dragged herself to a sitting position, nursing a swollen jaw. "Where's Azra?" Her gaze met Tanith's, suddenly stricken. "Oh no."

With Rîma's help, she made it all the way to her feet.

"I have to get her."

Tanith shook her head. "It's too late. She's gone."

The Deadwinds vortex pulsed one final, triumphant time. Damant clapped his hands to his ears as the pressure in his thoughts rose to a sonorous roar.

The world slid away behind glass.

*

529

Kat shielded her eyes as the Deadwinds vortex birthed a pulse of searing darkness. A woman stepped from the fire, indigo flames trailing not *from* her but *to* her, drawn forth from the vortex to feed the shimmering halo encompassing her body. She still moved like Azra, her stride that collected, self-assured arrogance that Kat loved and hated in equal measure. She still looked like her, down to the sweat, grime and blood earned in their battle to reach the Obsidium Palace. It was only the eyes that gave her away. In jest or anger, Azra's had never failed to sparkle with light. Though this woman's were the same rich brown Kat knew so well, something about them was cold and dark.

The halo faded until the woman might have passed for mortal.

"Hello, Katija." The knowing smile was Azra's too, as was the voice . . . though the resonance beneath was not. It rippled in time to the pressure at the back of Kat's thoughts, playful, almost teasing.

Her throat and gut knotted tight, Kat forced herself to breathe. "Give her back."

Tzal shook her head in mock dismay. "Why should I reject a gift given freely? She chose this." Her tongue flickered across her lower lip. "Her anticipation really is quite something. Whether she knew it or not, this is what she always wanted."

"And what's that?" bit out Tanith, her face still weeping flame.

"To never be afraid of anyone, ever again."

Kat closed her eyes, hoping to find solace. The darkness was as empty as Azra's gaze. As the yawning hole in her heart.

Stooping, she picked up Rîma's sword. "Give. Her. Back."

She started forward. Tzal gave a small, almost imperceptible nod.

Damant stepped into Kat's path, shoulders set. "I can't let you do this, Arvish."

"Out of my way," snapped Kat. "I know what I'm doing."

He drew his sword and set its tip against her breastbone. For the first time, Kat saw that his good eye was as dead as Azra's – as Tzal's – some undefinable piece of the aggravating, intolerable but above all *honourable* man lost from sight.

530

Tanith tensed in a clear precursor to violence.

Rîma grabbed her arm, the sudden tightening of Tanith's brow indicating that she'd done so none too gently. "Ihsan, no ..." She spoke softly, sorrow roiling beneath still waters.

"You've seen the city," Damant replied, his voice brisk and steely. "The Eternity King is dead. Khalad needs order. The Eternity Queen will provide it."

"This isn't you." Rîma's voice shook. "She's in your head."

Tanith pulled free of her grasp. "She's in all our heads. Or looking for a way in."

Rîma drew level with Kat. "Ihsan, please. You brought me back to myself in Tadamûr. Come back to me now."

"You won't get through to him like that," said Tanith. "It's a glamour. He no longer sees what we see, only what she wants."

Tzal tilted her head, her smile approving. "Clever girl. You'll never know what you missed. We could have been ... remarkable."

Kat looked from Tzal to Damant, the pressure in her thoughts now revealed as not merely presence, but intent. So easy to see how Tzal had worn Damant away. Castellan. Custodian. Servant. He'd worn the mantle of rebel poorly, his course chosen by guilt and perceived debts to strangers and friends alike. In the march down from the Golden Citadel she'd seen for herself just how much he despised the anarchy brought to Zariqaz. The responsibility borne for actions not his own. Penance made slaves of honest men. "He's still just one man."

"You believe you can kill a god?" Tzal's eyes dipped to the gentl curve of Rîma's sword, bright in the backwash of the vortex's magent light. Was that the tiniest flicker of uncertainty in her voice? A shive of recognition as she looked upon the sword that in legend she-a Nyssa had granted Amakala to ensure that justice would find even th immortal? "And what of Azra?"

What *of* Azra? Was she the willing participant Tzal had implied, h "sacrifice" merely another selfish play in a roster stretching back year Could it be both? Too late, Kat recalled how Azra had lingered on t

notion that Tzal's vessel would become divine. Had she been planning this even then? With heavy heart, she realised she'd never be sure. Azra had been two different women as long as she'd known her. She could search a lifetime for the truth of things and never find it. Much as she wished otherwise, love and truth were not the same.

She glanced at Rîma and Tanith and saw her intent mirrored in both. "One way or another, I owe her this."

Tzal smirked. "And one man isn't enough to stop you? How about ten? Twenty?"

The darkness of the inner wall filled with shadows, a handful driven onwards by swordpoint, most doing the driving. Cultists formed the majority of the latter group, but sailriders too – the lurching, shambling silhouette of a koilos at the very rear – all with that same lightless gaze as Damant. Their dozen captives were familiar faces. Vallant cradled a blood-soaked sleeve; Zephyr wore an expression of abject terror. Kat recognised others of Vallant's crew, though their names escaped her, but the face she most wanted to see couldn't be found amongst them.

"Ah . . ." breathed Tzal, her eyes alighting on Zephyr. "So some of you survived. I should have guessed."

Zephyr – who Kat had only ever seen return belligerence with more of the same – shrank against Vallant, eyes downcast.

Tzal snapped her fingers, somehow conspiring to add languor even to that brisk action. Fully half of her thralls broke off from guarding the prisoners. They formed a wall of bodies in front of her . . . And Kat at last found the face she'd sought, and screamed inside.

||You too?|| she asked one-handed, her signs heavier for the burden of her heart.

||This is what we wanted, Kat,|| Yali replied, her eyes bright. ||A new Khalad.||

Tzal watched their exchange in polite confusion, Azra's usurper as confounded by the Simah signs as the woman whose body she'd stolen.

Wounded arm cradled to his chest, Vallant lurched towards her, only to be brought up short by a thicket of swords. "Release my people!"

Tzal offered a predatory leer. "But they're not your people any longer. They're mine. Khalad's mine . . . As for the rest of you? You should leave. You're boring me."

At her sweeping wave, the thralls to the rear of Vallant's group sheathed their swords.

Kat blinked. "You're letting us go?"

The arrogance slipped from Tzal's face, and she was briefly the Azra of quiet shared moments – uncertain, almost vulnerable. "Of course. Azra made it a condition, and a bargain with the divine binds all parties." Her expression darkened with hauteur. "Easily agreed, because it's what I want as well. Not everyone's as tractable as dear Ihsan. They need a cause to rally around, an enemy to fight. Who better than Bashar Vallant and his band of cut-throat rebels? After all, it's worked before."

"I won't do it," growled Vallant.

"You will. You won't be able to help yourself." Tzal's gaze touched on each of the captives in turn, perhaps lingering a hair longer on Zephyr than on any other. "So take your mongrel Ithna'jîm and the followers I've graciously spared and leave my city. Run if you like. Fight me if you wish. Either way, it's only a matter of time."

Though it clearly pained him terribly, Vallant drew himself up to his full height. Gone was the man who remained earnest and amiable even when the hour was darkest. In his place stood the overseer he'd once been, but whom Kat had never met – as cold and unflinching as death itself. "And if I prefer to die here and now, my hands at your throat?"

Kat recognised the madness in his voice. It had ruled her minutes before. But in her it had faded to weariness. She might have countenanced killing Tzal, believing it a mercy to Azra, but could she cut her way through Damant to do so, much less Yali?

Even as the thought formed, Yali's eyes met hers. Her hands moved at waist level, the signs so surreptitious and half formed that Kat barely read them as signs at all. With Tzal the centre of attention, she felt certain no other had done so.

||I'm still with you, honest and true. Don't be angry.||

533

A ghost of a wink, a twitch of her lip, and Yali's hands fell still.

"You won't do it," Kat heard herself tell Vallant.

Vallant glowered at her. "What makes you so certain?"

"Because I've already killed my father today. You won't make me kill my friends."

"She's right, Bashar," said Rîma, her eyes never leaving Damant. "You know she is."

Vallant nodded, his face still hard but the madness gone from his eyes. "This isn't over."

Tzal's eyes gleamed. "I'm counting on it." Her lips parted in a liquid, languid smile. "*Abdon Nyssa ivohê.*"

Fifty-Five

Whatever authority the Eternity King had possessed in whatever had passed for his life, in death he was nothing more than charred bones draped in rags and wreathed in the magenta flames of the Deadwinds vortex. A lesson there, Damant supposed, for those who failed their people so completely.

He scowled, discomfited, though he couldn't quite conjure the reason why. It wasn't the first time in recent days, but it aggravated like an itch just beyond reach. Zariqaz had come to order with an efficiency he still couldn't believe. True, some cultists had scurried away into Undertown's shadows, but most had embraced the new, wondrous truth and thrown themselves on the mercy of their queen. A mercy of which Damant privately considered them undeserving, not that it was his place to do so. As Nyssa reborn, the Eternity Queen *was* forgiveness. No one else could have redeemed so flawed a vessel as Yennika Bascari.

"You look troubled, Ihsan." Lit by the magenta flames of the Deadwinds vortex, the Eternity Queen's bare-shouldered gown of white and gold all but shone, as radiant as the divine spirit it clothed.

||"Not at all, majesty."|| A little of the stiffness left Damant's shoulders, his doubts dissolving beneath her stare. ||"It's not a pleasant sight."||

The third occupant of the sanctum – saving the corpse atop the throne immortal – nodded her thanks for his lacklustre signing. The

535

Eternity Queen had not yet seen fit to grant Yali a title. That hadn't stopped her plundering the fugitive Voice's wardrobe for a golden dress that shimmered in the Deadwinds' reflected light. But then it was only natural for a queen to have a handmaiden to tend her burdens. A castellan could only do so much.

"No," said Yennika. "I suppose it's not."

Hand on hip, she reached through the flames and set the other to the corpse's charred shoulder. Slowly at first, then all at once, it creaked sideways and toppled to the floor. Ashen fragments scattered across the black stone and hissed to dust, entropy at last concluding what fire had begun.

||That's better,|| signed Yali, her smile wide enough to bridge any gap in translation.

The Eternity Queen grinned. "So much for eternity."

She stumbled, eyes pinched shut in private pain and a hand pressed to her brow.

"Majesty?" Damant reached her a hair before Yali, concern outweighing his awkwardness about touching her. Sumptuous though the gown was, it revealed rather more of the woman beneath than he considered seemly. She sank shivering into him, her shoulders pimpling with gooseflesh, some trick of light and shadow making it appear as though indigo flame shimmered across – *beneath* – her bronze skin.

"The throne . . ." she murmured. "I must have the throne . . ."

With Yali's help, Damant carried the Eternity Queen through the cold magenta flames and set her upon the throne immortal. The vortex guttered as she gripped the armrests.

||What's wrong with her?|| signed Yali.

Damant shook his head, uncertain.

The vortex roared back to fulminescence. Her tremors subsiding, the Eternity Queen sat tall in her throne, her skin smooth and unblemished once more, her weakness banished.

She curled and uncurled a fist, examining every curve and wrinkle.

"Not quite a prisoner, but not quite free," she murmured. "But you'll serve for now, dear Azra."

Damant frowned, knowing he'd heard her speak but finding no trace of the words in his memory. The itch in his thoughts was back, just out of reach. "Majesty . . . ?"

He glanced at Yali, who shook her head.

The Eternity Queen sank back in her throne and shot him a dazzling smile. "It doesn't matter, darling. It doesn't matter at all."

Bathed in the lazy red rays of the setting sun, Tyzanta was almost beautiful. Even Undertown's ramshackle tangle of overbuilt streets, stretching away far below the balcony on which Tanith stood, seemed unusually calm in the lengthening shadows. Seemed, but were not, for the rumble and roar of heavy industry ruled the dusk as readily as the day, filling the air with smoke's bitter fragrance. Rather, what calm Tanith knew was in her own mind. For the first time in years – perhaps her entire life – she felt safe . . . until she stared out past the setting sun to where Zariqaz lay hidden beneath the horizon.

She let the gentle creak of the apartment door go unanswered, but the soft knock on the balcony door frame that followed – offered in politeness only, as both doors were open to the evening air – required acknowledgement.

"Hello, Kat."

The burnt lavender of Kat's soul preceded her to the balustrade. "How are you finding the rooms?" Her tone held just a sliver of mockery. "It's not exactly a palace of silks."

"I'm accustomed to better," Tanith lied. By the standards of most mid-spires apartments, hers was spacious, its walls free of the cracked plaster and spreading damp that were the trademarks of unscrupulous landlords the realm over. And it was a palace compared to her cramped quarters in the haven. "But it's only for tonight. Tatterlain's taking the *Chainbreaker* to Athenoch at dawn."

"And you want to see Fadiya?"

She nodded reluctantly. Even that small confession felt like she was giving a piece of herself away. Trust, it seemed, took longer to embrace than safety. "She'd like to see you too, I'm sure."

Kat's lip twitched. "Are you asking me to come with you?"

"No," Tanith replied, more defensive than she intended. "I was just talking, that's all."

Kat propped her elbows on the balcony and stared at the murmurating swallows spiralling over the Mestiz aqueduct. "And after Athenoch, then where will you go?"

Tanith shrugged. "Further east, perhaps." She stared again towards the horizon. "As far from Zariqaz as I can get."

"If that's what you want."

Tanith rounded on her. "You're not even going to try to convince me to stay, are you?"

"If you're anything like me, you have to make that decision for yourself, otherwise you'll always resent it."

She glared at Kat, annoyed at having been seen so clearly. "You might at least say that you want me to."

"I only want you to if you want to."

She threw up her hands. "Stars Below, you're annoying!"

Kat grinned. "I'm your sister. I'm meant to be."

Tanith sighed, the storm of her anger blowing itself out. Tzal's rising had swept away everything she knew about Khalad, maybe even about herself. Bickering with Kat seemed petty in the grander scheme.

For a time, they shared a companionable silence, lost in the setting sun.

"How's the hunger?" asked Kat.

Tanith winced. "Still there."

"Should I be worried?"

She shook her head. "On the voyage here I skimmed enough from the Deadwinds to keep it quiet. I can handle the rest . . . at least I think so. Ardoc taught me that, even if he didn't mean it for my benefit."

Kat grimaced. "I really thought I could save you."

538

"You *did* save me, you and . . . you and Azra."

"That's not what I meant."

"I know, but there's no saving me from who I am, Kat. I'm not possessed or cursed. I *am* an amashti. I don't get to pretend that I'm not." It was the first time she'd said the words aloud. Against all expectations they felt good. Made her feel like just maybe she *was* in control. "But Enna was right. I get to choose whether I'm a woman or a monster."

At least, she hoped that was true. And even if it wasn't, some people deserved the monster, didn't they? Not everything needed to be black and white. And it was no one's business but hers where she drew that line.

"She must have been remarkable," said Kat.

Tanith stifled a flash of guilt. "I still don't understand why she bothered." Had Enna made it home in the end? Had anything about her story been real? She suspected she'd never know.

"Maybe she saw something in you worth the trouble."

"Maybe." Tanith didn't want to think about that. It felt oddly pressuring, as if the debt might need to be paid forward. "I'm sorry about Azra."

"You don't need to be. She made her choice."

"Do you really believe that?"

"I have to." Kat sighed. "I keep telling myself that this is exactly the same as when I lost her before. There's something walking around out there that looks like the woman I loved, even sounds like her, but it's not *her.*"

"Is it working?"

She offered a wan smile. "Ask me again tomorrow . . . if you're still here." She straightened as chimes echoed out across the city below. "I'm late. For whatever it's worth, I *do* want you to stay. The world's different now and the choices we make count more than ever. Maybe it's enough that we're sisters and that we're not actively trying to kill each other. But I'd like us to try being friends."

The simple words melted Tanith's resolve. She might have hugged

539

Kat then and there but for the certainty that there'd be no recrossing that bridge. She wasn't ready for that, not yet.

But she flashed a small smile. Kat had earned that much. "I'll think about it. What about you? What comes next for you?"

"I haven't decided yet."

Tanith heard the lie but decided against challenging it, just in case Kat decided to challenge some of hers. Instead she turned her eyes to the setting sun and dreamed of a new future.

Kat closed the door to Tanith's apartment and breathed deep. For all that what she'd said of Azra was true, shaped and rationalised for ready consumption by those who enquired, it was still just words. The heart cared little for what was spoken, only what was felt.

Composure regained, or nearly so, she made her way downstairs. Rîma waited at the building's crooked gate, her new hat and coat somehow conspiring to look as battered as the old. "What did she say?"

"That she'd think about it. That's more than I'd hoped."

"Stubbornness is in the blood."

"Thanks."

Rîma inclined her head. "Any time. In recent weeks, I've gained a new appreciation for the value of obstinacy."

"I've never done well with change. I'm not sure it's a strength."

"Nor I, but it seems destiny cares little for our choices." She offered a distant smile. "Now neither of us is exactly who once we were. Tadamûr may be gone, but its queen I remain, bound to those who would have been my subjects in ways I do not truly understand and perhaps never will."

She still hadn't spoken much of her time in Tadamûr, though the memories clearly lay thick with sorrow and tangled up with the loss of Damant to Tzal's glamour. That she needed to air them, Kat was certain. A job for Tatterlain, perhaps?

Or maybe, she conceded, it was better the task fell to her – for Rîma's sake and her own. After all, in the matter of tangled lives, she herself was increasingly an expert. Tanith. Their father. Her relationships with Azra and with Fadiya Rashace. The wasting grip of omen rot. What she'd once held as Khalad's fundamental truths. The last few weeks had upended everything. Making sense of all that was surely impossible, but she had to try, if only to shake the sense of existential unease that had followed her from Zariqaz.

Yes, perhaps they both needed an evening of good wine and loose tongues.

They walked in silence through the streets, heading up-spire through the evening crowds. Again and again Kat felt a maskless custodian's gaze linger. After so long in Zariqaz, it felt strange not to shy away or cover her face, but then in Zariqaz she'd been a fugitive, if only in her own mind. In Tyzanta . . . she was something else.

As she approached the conclave hall – once the Bascari custodium, but repurposed in line with Vallant's desire that Tyzanta's triad should be seen to take their deliberations not from on high, but from the heart of the city they ruled – the roadway drowned beneath a skyship's graceful shadow. Crew labouring to furl the sails, the dhow slowed towards the piers of Kazzar's Quay, the hawk-and-tower flag of Naxos joining the emblems of Sumarand, Azzarin and a host of smaller cities, as well as the rampant horse of Qersal. Strange to see so many in one place. Stranger still to see scarlet flags streaming alongside the *Chainbreaker*'s stylised sunburst, the Eternity King's wing and circlet now flown for his Voice alone.

The custodians standing sentry at the conclave hall let them pass without challenge. A knee-wearying ascent later, Zephyr and Vallant met them at the head of the spiral stair, she a diaphanous presence barely troubling herself to touch vaporous foot to flagstone, he in a pressed black uniform, his right arm bound in a sling.

Zephyr sniffed. "*Waholi* never learn their manners. Late are you."

"I know," Kat replied, glad that Zephyr had recovered something of her waspishness.

"Is everyone else here?" asked Rîma.

541

"Everyone who'd come," said Vallant. "Some lost heart after the redcloaks moved against Zyrassa."

Kat winced. They'd been in Tyzanta barely a week before the news had broken that the Eternity Queen had brought the city under siege. "I didn't think it would start so quickly."

Zephyr's white eyes tightened, her terror controlled more than banished. "Trapped a long time was Tzal and never a patient soul was he."

"So now it's war."

Vallant grunted. "It was always a war, Kat. The enemy changes, but the struggle never ends."

"So speaks the royal protector." She smiled, knowing her words would irritate him. "The Voice's voice."

"Don't. I'm still getting used to that."

For all Vallant's distaste, it had been a pragmatic decision. Cities that had refused a rebel's leadership now embraced it to restore the Eternity King's heir to his throne. All an illusion, readily condoned by Isdihar herself. She'd passed the days since Tzal's awakening distraught almost to the point of catatonia. Let Khalad's firebloods think they were fighting to restore the old order, so long as they fought.

"Perhaps that's why the Eternity King told you to save the Voice," said Rîma. "She's a useful figurehead."

If she dies, the Cold Flame will take you all.

"No ... I don't think so." But Kat sensed the answer was out there in the darkness of her thoughts and fears. Always tantalising, always out of reach. But that was a problem that would wait.

"At least Zyrassa proves that Tzal can't control everyone," said Vallant. "You don't fight to capture a city you can take by other means."

"Unless she wants Zyrassa as an example," said Rîma.

"Maybe, but every contact I have in Zariqaz insists that everything's as close to normal as can be." Vallant shook his head. "That I even *have* contacts there any longer tells us that there's a limit to Tzal's influence."

"*Ayin*, for now," said Zephyr.

542

"Yes, for now." Vallant shook away his grimace. "Have you heard anything from Yali?"

The ache in Kat's heart returned. Azra's fate was one thing, Yali's another. "Nothing."

"You're sure she's still with us?"

"She's with us." She had to be. If only because it offered hope that Tzal didn't know for certain who her glamour touched. If only because it meant that Kat hadn't regained one sister only to lose another.

"Then why did she stay?"

"To watch Azra. She's always read people better than I have. I think – I hope – she saw something I missed. Something that means maybe Azra's still in there."

Zephyr shook her head, the light of captive stars shimmering in the breeze-blown ink stain of her hair. "Didn't think she cared for the trallock, did I."

"She did it for me," Kat replied firmly, the chain of her assumptions creaking. "Because she knows I need to know if there's anything of Azra left worth saving."

"And if there isn't?" asked Rîma.

Kat drew herself up, claiming a certainty she didn't feel. "Then I need to know that too."

Vallant nodded, his voice thick with compassion. "I hope you're right, Kat, I really do." Above his head, the conclave hall bell chimed. He offered a wry smile he surely wasn't feeling. "I have to get in there. But first . . . Once before, I asked you if you'd rule Tyzanta for me. I'm asking again." He held her gaze throughout; earnest, imploring.

Kat met his stare and took a deep breath. No turning back now, but as she'd told Tanith, the world was different. Time to make better choices.

"No."

A scowl flowed across Zephyr's face. Rîma narrowed her eyes. Vallant, who'd more reason to be affronted than either of them, simply raised an eyebrow. "And I can say nothing to change your mind?"

"Nothing. It's not what I want."

543

"I see." His brow tightened. "And what *do* you want?"

"I want in. All the way in." Unfamiliar passion filled Kat's words as they gathered pace. "I can't sit in a conclave hall or a palace settling squabbles and worrying over taxes. I need to be part of this fight. I *want* to be part of it. For Azra, for Yali ... even for Damant. I don't know if Tzal can be stopped, but I know I have to try."

"And why's that?"

He didn't believe her. Typical of the man to finally get his way and now reject it because it hadn't come how he'd wanted it, when he'd wanted it. Kat cast about for something – anything – to convince him and settled on words he'd spoken months before. "Because I don't have it in me to close my eyes and do nothing."

He held her gaze a heartbeat longer, and nodded. "Then you'd better come with us."

Shaking with emotion she couldn't name, Kat fell into step behind the others and into the conclave hall proper, barely noticing the custodians snapping to attention as they passed. Another gateway beckoned. Vallant in the lead, they passed inside to a conclave dais more crowded than any Kat had ever seen.

Silk-clad firebloods from the eastern cities filled the semicircle opposite the door. Clockwise, at as discreet a distance as could be allowed, the zol'tayah of Qersal shimmered in a silver sari, her hair bound by gemstoned chains. Nearer too, Marida cut a slight, willowy figure in a blood-red gown, the ageless black-eyed qalimîri spirit gazing out from her teenage host's pale, beautiful face. Opposite her, the brooding, hulking figure of fellow crime lord Ardin Javar looked as out of place in such company as it was possible to be.

Rîma and Zephyr, representatives of forgotten peoples, took their respective places beside Marida and Javar. Two spaces remained. One where the statue of Nyssa might once have stood, now reserved for the man whose word and reputation had brought the conclave together. The other lay to its immediate right, the station traditionally reserved for a fireblood's heir ... or failing that, their most trusted councillor.

Kat gaped, drowning beneath the inevitable. The ordering of the conclave had been established days before, a necessary precaution against fragile egos and bruised pride. A full day, in fact, before she'd finished agonising over what she wanted from the future and found the confidence to demand it. That whole time Vallant had known – or had at least assumed – what she'd say. Had he ever even wanted her to rule Tyzanta? The arrangement of the circle suggested something far greater.

Vallant halted at the top of the dais steps and offered her his good hand. "Shall we?"

She stared at him, moved – not for the first time – by an overwhelming urge to thump that earnest expression clean off his face. "You really are an insufferable bastard."

"So you keep saying." He grinned. "Welcome to the war council."

In the End

Kat stumbled home beneath a starry sky through streets as quiet as Tyzanta's ever were, the chill of the early hours barely noticed. Her thoughts buzzed with names and titles, of hardships recounted and the seeds of strategies sown. But weariness couldn't stifle the sense of place, of belonging. Surrounded by the war council's great and good – or at least by the self-important and infamous – she should have felt like an imposter ... and yet she never had. She belonged there, among them. A realisation as strange as it was exhilarating.

Rîma had been right: destiny cared little for the choices of the living, but this once, Kat found she didn't resent its presumptions.

Weary beyond words, she all but dragged herself up the final steps to her modest apartment and passed through the imposing curlicued door. The waning lumani prism in the plaster ceiling rose did little to dispel the long shadows. The rooms felt emptier than they should without Azra to share them, without the prospect of Yali's mischievous, irrepressible cheer. For the first time, Kat realised just how long it had been since she'd been truly alone – not that she felt so now, though she couldn't say exactly *why*.

Discarding her boots in the middle of the hall – living alone had some small perks in the matter of not having one's slovenly habits chastised – she goaded leaden legs to carry her into the tiny washroom. A twist of the tap filled the basin from the building's pyrasti-fuelled boiler and ghosted the mirror with steam. She splashed the weariness from her eyes and towelled the worst of the steam from the mirror. She barely recognised her reflection, which looked older that she recalled. Not in the flesh, but in how that flesh mirrored the soul within. Purpose. Certainty. Determination. For the best, perhaps. She'd need them in the days and weeks to come.

So intent was she on the stranger she'd become that it was a long moment before she noticed the second reflection standing at her shoulder. A shrunken cadaver with brittle skin drawn tight and splinting across yellowed bones, arrayed in heavy black robes and a golden circlet. Its empty gaze met hers.

Heart in her throat, Kat yelped and spun around, half falling against the washbasin as she scrabbled to arrest her fall.

Nothing. Just an empty doorway and the shadows of the corridor beyond.

"Stars Below," she muttered, shock giving way to chagrin. "I really need to get some sleep."

And that might have been the end of it, had she not looked in the mirror once again to find the skeletal figure waiting for her.

Indeed, that does seem wise, the Eternity King breathed through her thoughts. *But first, we should talk.*

The story continues in...

Book Three of the Soulfire Saga

Glossary

Note that the Daric language of Khalad commonly employs a circumflex to lengthen and lend emphasis to vowels. Thus "î" is pronounced "ee" and "û" is pronounced "oo".

Cinderblood	One born to the lower class
Fireblood	One born to the upper class
Ifrît(i)	Fragment(s) of soul, shackled to service
Lock charmer	One accomplished in opening locks without benefit of a key
Skelder	Broad-ranging term for criminals and the societally undesirable
The Deadwinds	Vortex of soul-laden winds, centred on the city of Zariqaz
The Veil	The ever-hungry mists at Khalad's border
Adobe	A brick made of sun-dried straw and clay (also buildings constructed thereof)

Alabastra	State religion of Khalad
Amashti	Soul-sucking daemon
Archon	Member of the Alabastran priesthood
Ashanaiq	Curative elixir
Astoricum	Mythical metal, also known as oreikhalkos
Aurora Eternis	Sky-borne portent of a coming Mistfall
Ayin	Issnaîm expression of dismay
Azasouk	A grand marketplace
Blesswood	Sanctified timber burned in torch houses
Custodian	Keeper of the law
Custodium	Body tasked with enforcement of the law
Daric	Primary language of Khalad
Dhow	Large, lateen-rigged military skyship
Felucca	Small lateen-rigged skyboat
Gansalar	Redcloak commander
The Golden Stair	Approach to the Eternity King's palace
Helmic	Ifrît that governs guidance
Hestic	Protector ifrît
Hierarch	Senior Alabastran priest
Ilfri	Kleptomaniac daemon
Isshîm	Illicit narcotic

Issnaîm	Race better known to the people of Khalad as 'veilkin'
Kathari	Soldiers of the Obsidium Cult
Kiasta	A mild Daric curse word
King's Council	Governing body of Khalad, subordinate to the Voice
Koilos	Preserved indentured servant
Last breath	A restorative harvested from the recently dead
Lumani	Ifrît that provides illumination
Mistfall	The descent of unnatural mist
Mistrali	Seasonal rainstorm
Motic	Ifrît that governs simple mechanisms
The Obsidium Cult	Supposedly mythical (and secret) society
Oreikhalkos	Mythical metal, also known as astoricum
Overspire	A city's more well-to-do streets (generally the highest)
Pyrasti	Flame ifrît
Qabirarch	Supreme head of the Alabastran temples
Qabirarchi Council	Assemblage of hierarchs
Qalimîri	A deathless, parasitic soul
Qori	Term of affection in Daric, roughly equivalent to "daughter"

Railrunner	Steam engine governed by ifrîti
Redcloak	Soldier of the Royal Guard
Sailrider	Crew member on a skyship
Sarhana	Redcloak veteran
Shrieker	Flame-based weapon, powered by an ifrît
Shriversman	Craftsman responsible for the dissection of souls
Skirl	Slang term for an annoying youth
Simah	Widespread sign language
Talent wisp	Distilled essence of deceased talent
Tessence	Distilled soul
Torch house	Beacon that burns back the mists of the Veil
Trallock	A shiftless and unreliable individual, too focused on their own pleasures
Tsrûqi	Disorienting ifrîti
Undertown	A city's lowest (and most insalubrious) levels
Vahla	Spirits who escort the guilty to judgement
Veilkin	What the people of Khalad call the Issnaîm
Waholi	(impolite) Issnaîm word for outsiders
Xanathros	A high temple
Zol'tayah	Ruler of the Qersali people

Acknowledgements

Well, here we are at the end, and everything is different.

As has become customary to say on pages such as this (but no less in need of airing), I shall be forever indebted to my wife Lisa and my agent John Jarrold. Without their unflagging support and encouragement these stories would never see the light of day. My thanks also to my editor, James Long, who occasionally lets me get away with murder (most recently at a point roughly 90 per cent of the way through this very book, though the seeds were sown much earlier).

Where will the next instalment take Kat, Vallant and the others? That remains to be seen, but hopefully you'll all return with me to Khalad to find out. There's a way yet to go until the story's done, and in Khalad nothing is ever quite as it seems . . .

extras

orbit

meet the author

Photo Nottingham

MATTHEW WARD has frequently been accused of living in worlds of his own imagination, though really he lives near Nottingham with his extremely patient wife and several attention-seeking cats.

Find out more about Matthew Ward and other Orbit authors by registering for the free monthly newsletter at orbitbooks.net.

if you enjoyed
THE FIRE WITHIN THEM
look out for

BETWEEN DRAGONS AND THEIR WRATH
The Shattered Kingdom

by

Devin Madson

The Celes Basin has been split into city-states, but there are those who seek to reunite the shattered realm—by force if necessary. Amid the turmoil there are three who will find their destinies inextricably tangled.

Tesha is a glassblower's apprentice who becomes a tribute bride when her city is conquered by the south. In the enemy's court, she's perfectly placed to sabotage them, but her heart has other plans.

Naili is a laundress in the house of an eccentric alchemist who is awakening to strange new powers. When radicals approach her, she faces a choice between keeping her magic to herself and using it to change the world.

And in the desolate Shield Mountains, dragon rider Ash protects the cities from the monsters in the Sands beyond. But soon he'll have to learn how to protect his dragon when hunters unlock the secret to killing them.

As war sweeps across the land, Tesha, Naili, and Ash must fight for survival against political enemies, dragon hunters, and monsters both within and without.

1. TESHA

Afternoon Bulletin

To all criers for announcement throughout the city of Learshapa

Grievous blow for the city as a second critical scale shipment fails to arrive from Therinfrou Mine. Attacks by Lummazzt soldiers to blame.

Emergency council meeting called to discuss rising border tensions with Lummazza, despite initial plans not to meet again until after next week's vote. "We would be stronger together," says Reacher Sormei.

Nine ritual carvings have gone missing from Lord Sactasque's public gallery. It is the second such incident this month. Information is sought regarding this assault on Celessi history.

212:34

The shatter of warm glass hitting stone has a particular tenor, a sound that reaches deep, more feeling than noise. It touches every memory of broken glasswork and shattered dreams, of beauty lost and time torn away. Even when it's Assistant Jul's ugly carafe that looks better as a pile of shards.

"Sweep it up!" Master Hoye called over the roaring furnace. "Life is glass!"

"Life is glass," the boy mumbled back, the lesson too sharp to fit into the ugly-carafe-shaped hole in his heart. Likely it would be a few more years before he realised what our master's favourite phrase really meant. Not that glasswork was all we lived for, but that life *was* glass. Like life, glass is infinitely malleable when warm and well-tended, yet fragile enough to shatter at a single wrong move. It can be moulded by any hands into any shape, but the more skilled and prepared the hands the better the outcome. Even the addition of scale for strength was akin to the way people gathered wealth and resources about themselves and called it resilience.

I'd been staring out the back window, lost in thought, but as broken glass tinkled into the scrap bucket I shoved the last bite of honey-crusted bread into my mouth. Outside, the slice of Learshapa that had been my lunch-break companion went on unchanged. Overhead, sunlight reflected off whitewashed walls beneath an endless blue sky, yet little light reached the courtyard of faded tiles on the other side of the window. Once it had been a fine atrium, but now it was full of dusty, cobwebbed pots owning lethargic plants more grey than green.

I licked my fingers and wiped the sticky residue down my apron as Master Hoye called, "The gather won't shape itself!"

To Master Hoye, everything was about glass. He likened his desire not to rush out of bed in the morning to glass being stronger when cooled slowly in vermiculite, and the suffering of stress to the drawing of thin canes. Even wrong words spoken at the wrong time earned a hiss from him, like hot glass being dunked in a quenching barrel.

Back at my workbench, I gathered materials for the next job. *Cobalt. A pinch of scale. Sand bed. Two moulds.* Even with the scale shortage, there was a lot to do. The upcoming vote to decide Learshapa's place in the Celes Basin seemed to have energised the city, sending everyone bustling about with renewed purpose and a determination to finish long-neglected projects. That afternoon, my list contained a dozen replacement armour scales, two matching brandy glasses, a trio of scaleglass blades to fit carved handles, and twenty unification badges I would rather have smashed on the floor. *Unification.* I sneered as I laid everything out ready. It was a fine word for conquest.

As I prepared to gather molten glass from the furnace, an arrival sent our bead curtain tinkling. "Good afternoon," a young man said, unclipping his veil and casting his gaze around the large, smoky space.

"Good afternoon." Assistant Borro hurried forward, wiping his hands on his apron as Master Hoye always did. "What can we do for you?"

"I'm hoping to leave a small pile of flyers on your counter in support of the vote." As he spoke, the man handed Borro a paper-wrapped sugar curl from a basket he carried. "Is there perhaps someone more senior I could speak to?"

A glance back found Master Hoye in the middle of shaping a vase and shouting at Assistant Jul, both dripping sweat, and poor Borro rolled his gaze my way.

I strode over, but before I could speak, the young man thrust one of his sugar curls into my hand—a traditional Memento curl of skulls and suns. "A Memento Festival token for next week's Memento Eve vote," he said, all bright cheerfulness. "Might I leave a small pile of flyers here for your customers?"

I glanced down at the flyers, able to make out only two words at the top of the page: *Stronger Together.* "I take it you're supporting the 'conquer us, please, we can't take care of ourselves' vote then," I said, utterly failing at what Master Hoye called civil indifference.

Likely the man had a ready response for most arguments, just not one so blunt. For a long moment he stared at me and I stared back, sugar curl growing sticky in my warm hand.

Behind him, the glass-bead curtain tinkled again, heralding the arrival of two women, arm-in-arm as they let down their veils.

"Good afternoon," I said, grateful for the distraction. "Can I help you?"

"We're looking for scaleglass wedding bands," the younger said, a shy glance thrown at her companion. "I know scale is in short supply, but, well, we're asking around anyway."

"Wedding bands?" I scoffed, the disgusted words escaping before I could swallow them. The women froze—a startled tableau of horror.

With a hiss mimicking hot glass hitting water, Master Hoye stepped forward. "That's not Apprentice Tesha's field of expertise," he said, patting my arm with one hand while wiping his damp brow with the other. "Best to speak to me about that. I'm Master Hoye, and you're right, scale is..." His words trailed off as he guided them to the other side of the entry space, away from the ever-present roar of the furnaces. Neither young woman glanced back to see my heated cheeks.

"Oh, so you're that kind of Learshapan, are you?" the man said, finding his voice again. "Traditional. Against all change."

"You say that like change is a neutral term," I snapped back. "Like taking up a new fashion is the same as giving up our ability to decide our own future, because that's what this is. A vote for unification is a vote for assimilation into the Emoran empire."

"And a vote for separation is a vote to stay weak and risk further Lummazzt attacks!"

"Bullshit!"

Master Hoye and the two women broke off their low-voiced conversation, all three turning to stare at us. Cheeks reddening for the second time, I leaned over the counter, bringing my fury face-to-face with the flyer man's. "Lummazza has never attacked us and has no reason to now. But if you give Emora the power to make us in their image there will be no Learshapa. And certainly no Memento Festival." I crushed the softening sugar curl in my fist, snapping its artistry like tiny bones. "The answer is no, you can't leave your flyers here."

"And you think I'm the fear monger," the man scoffed, and in a flurry of skirts, he spun away, pushing through the glass-bead curtain and out into the bright heat before he'd even clipped his veil into place.

"That went well."

I turned to find Master Hoye watching, the two women having departed, leaving our entry empty.

"I'm sorry," I said, anger chilling to regret in a heartbeat. "I ought not to have lost my temper with him. It's not good for business."

"No, but neither is complete Emoran rule, so you're forgiven." There was nothing more to be said, yet he remained watching me.

"What is it?" I said, instantly breathless with worry.

"You need to be more respectful when people come in looking for wedding bands, but I think you know that already, don't you?"

I closed my eyes and gave a solemn nod. "It's just so ridiculous. Especially in a scale shortage."

"Times have been rough." His voice sank to a quiet murmur. "Who am I to judge what people choose to make them happy?"

"Marriage? Family?" I all but spat the words. "You know as well as I do how dangerous those customs are to our communes and care groups."

Master Hoye dropped his hand on my shoulder. "These are concerns for the meeting house, not my workshop. And yes, I know you haven't been attending meetings, like I know you're a fool who can't find her place in the world, but I'd say it's been long enough, huh?"

I nodded slowly, shame at my outbursts weighing me down. "I'm sorry, Master. I will take more care."

"I know you will."

Again, he patted my shoulder, and would have turned back about his work had not a question burst from my lips. "What did you mean when you said I was 'a fool who can't find her place'?"

"I meant exactly what I said."

"I'm happy here. And in my care group."

"For now, yes. But happy has never been what you're looking for, has it?"

With a wink, he turned away, already calling for Assistant Borro to ready his punty. It was his way of ending conversations that had run out of usefulness, a sure sign that asking what he had meant a second time would earn no better answer.

As I returned to my work, hoping no one else would step through the door, a registered crier passed by in the street shouting the afternoon bulletin. "...scale shipment fails to arrive from Therinfrou Mine. Attacks by Lummazzt soldiers to blame," she called, her voice carrying well in the narrow street. "Emergency council meeting called to discuss rising border tensions with Lummazza, despite initial plans not to meet again until after next week's vote. 'We would be stronger together,' says Reacher Sormei..."

Her voice faded away on the reacher's name, leaving me with the bitter taste of it in my mouth. Reacher Sormei, leader of Emora and the rest of the Celes Basin. At that very moment he was somewhere in Learshapa campaigning for the unification vote so he could rule us too, and people like that idiot with his flyers wanted to help him do it.

A long time ago the Celes Basin had been home only to roaming Apaian tribes, who had done nothing more with the basin's vast scale deposits than carve death mementos into the stone. The discovery it could be mixed into glass to create a substance stronger than any metal had changed everything. With scaleglass, the Apaians had built permanent settlements, water catchments, and roads that crossed the basin's empty stones, even made an early form of blasting powder that dug the pits of our great cities—Bakii, Orsu, and Learshapa. Perhaps it would have stayed that way had the Emorans not been forced from their own lands into the basin, or perhaps they would have attacked anyway, coveting the scale and all it could do. Either way, as the Lummazzt conquered Emora, Emorans had conquered the basin and built their own city—Emora—from which to govern. The war had been brutal, but so long ago now it hardly seemed real. Only Learshapa had kept any form of democracy when the Emorans finally took over, a concession earned through bloodshed that some were now ready to vote away.

Returning to my abandoned tasks, I couldn't extricate myself from the fear that grew daily. What if the unification vote won? What if my home was about to change forever no matter how tightly I clung? What would become of me then?

I might have relaxed had the day continued like any other, but in the middle of the afternoon it became even less like any other when Sorscha sauntered in, all at ease. His visits to the forge weren't rare enough to herald trouble, but I hadn't seen him for weeks. Not since I'd stopped volunteering at the west quarter meeting house. Not since I'd walked out on Uvao.

"Tesha. Master Hoye," he said, shaking out the dark hair he loosed from his veil. "A fine afternoon to you both."

He leaned on the counter, possessing none of the nervousness I felt at his arrival. As though I'd forgotten how to stand or smile or what to do with my arms. The urge to ask after Uvao was strong.

"Afternoon, yes. Fine, I'm not so sure," Master Hoye said, handing his work to the boys and striding over. "What can we do for you, Sorscha?"

"Always business with you, Master Hoye." Sorscha's smile held a mocking edge, and his single-slit brows hovered low and sleepy. "I'm well, thank you for asking. Though the heat out there is quite something. Almost as bad as the heat in here."

Despite his complaint, he looked cool and at ease, his dark hair ruffled in a careless style and his blackened leather tunic laced tight—as tight as the three brass bands constricting one arm. His glance flicked my way, his mocking smile unmoving, and I could only hope I looked untroubled lest he report my embarrassment to Uvao.

When Master Hoye didn't answer in kind, Sorscha sighed and pulled a folded paper square from his skirt pocket. "Here then," he said, unfolding it with painstaking diligence. "Something to keep you busy for the rest of the afternoon."

"This afternoon? I'm full up."

"Then give this one to Tesha."

"No."

Master Hoye's sharp refusal was entirely expected and yet utterly disappointing in a way that should have made me feel ashamed. The jobs Sorscha sometimes brought in were not only illegal but flouted Learshapan ways. Learshapa had always sustained itself by being a collective political community in which decisions were made together, but with that on the verge of change there was much allure in being able to just...*do* something about it. Quickly. Quietly. Changing the world.

With a silky hush, Sorscha slid the paper across the counter. Before Master Hoye snatched it up, I caught the words *identical wine glasses, fast-acting poison,* and *illness.* "And you need it tonight?"

"The client will accept tomorrow morning."

"Then tomorrow morning it is. Come at opening, not before."

"Naturally. Before would mean being up far too early."

Master Hoye grunted and walked away, taking the paper and leaving me facing Sorscha, still leaning against the front bench. "Long time, no see, Tesh," he said in his lazy way. "Arguments at the meeting house haven't been as fiery without you. Will you be attending tonight?"

A shrug was all I could manage. Mere weeks ago, I would have been there every night helping out, but accidentally uncovering Uvao's identity had changed everything. No matter how often I might wish, as I lay awake at night, that I'd never found out at all.

"This second scale shipment failing to arrive has everyone on edge," Sorscha went on, thankfully unaware of my thoughts. "Even more on edge than the coming vote and the presence of Reacher Sormei walking the streets shaking everyone's hand, that is."

For people who didn't know him, it was unnerving witnessing Sorscha's shift from charming insouciance to serious political discussion. I'd spent too long in his company to be shocked, but it sent a thrill up my spine every time. "I think we'd all be better off if someone killed Reacher Sormei and let us get on with our lives," he added. "And no, before you ask, that's not the job I just gave Master

Hoye. Unfortunately. At least we get to vote, huh? Imagine living in Bakii and having no say over anything at all."

We both grimaced, momentarily in accord as he readied his veil to depart. "Catch you around, Tesh."

"Wait, before you go. Tell me...how do you think the vote will go?"

"Are you asking me as me, or asking me as someone whose friend turned out to be an Emoran lord who knows more of what's going on than we do?"

"Both."

A soft laugh brushed his veil as he drew it up, pinning it to his hair. "It's the same answer anyway. I don't know, so I find myself grateful that I'll be at least somewhat protected from the worst of the fallout by said friend turning out to be an Emoran lord. Same place you would be in if you hadn't made such a pointless moral stand when you found out who Uvao was."

"Pointless?"

"You asked," Sorscha said, and with a little wave, he headed for the door, skirt swishing. "Goodbye, Tesh."

He was gone on the words, leaving me stunned and flustered with an increasing urge to run after him and argue. An urge quashed only by Master Hoye dropping half a dozen jobs on my bench.

"No time for daydreaming, Tesha, we're swamped," he said, before retiring to the back of the workshop alone. There, the box he always used for such jobs already sat out. It was flat and rectangular, little bigger than a book, but with wooden panels so finely decorated it would have been worth a fortune even without the secretive contents. Master Hoye had never told me what was inside, but over the years I'd come to believe it was all poisons—poisons over which his hands danced with ease, each vial touched with the gentleness of old friends.

Having chosen vials from the box, he turned to make a fresh gather, and I spun away. Nothing was as sure to incite his ire as curiosity about his box of poisons and the glassware he sometimes put them in for money.

Despite my worries, there was so much work to do that for the rest of the day I lost myself in glass and heat and sweat. For a time, the mysterious box was forgotten, as was the vote, Uvao, Sorscha, and the political plays of Reacher Sormei, each melting away beneath the singular focus of practising my craft and practising it well.

By the end of the day, I was worn out but satisfied and had started tidying the workshop when a registered crier passed, calling the evening news. As always, we all paused in our work to listen.

"—to the scale shortage, yet another shipment of sand has failed to arrive as scheduled due to ongoing blockades between Orsu and the northern mines. Learshapans advised to ration their glass needs," the crier shouted, slowly passing the open portico. "After this afternoon's emergency council meeting, Lord Councillor Angue is expected to address crowds in the chamber square at sundown, while Reacher Sormei..."

Her voice faded as she moved on, once more taking with her the Reacher's dreaded name and much of the air left in our stifling workshop.

"Sand too," Master Hoye grumbled. "I'll have to go through the orders and see what can be put off."

What more was there to say? With a huff of breath, he waved a hand at the assistants, both elbow-deep in the washing tub and looking miserable. "Go on, run along home, boys. I'll wash up tonight. You too, Tesha. I need to think."

Waved away with a preoccupied scowl, there was nothing to do but swap apron for veil and head out into the street, leaving him to his thoughts.

Although the sun was setting, the air outside still held the day's heat, drying everything it touched. Learshapa could get as hot as our forge, but the city never smelled of burning paper and coal and wax and scale; rather the street held tangs of life, of cooking food and warm earth and sweat, of water and flowers and spilled date brandy. It was all so very *Learshapa* that I breathed deep.

At the end of the street, the public house was already full of noise, all chatter and laughter and the squeak of worn sandals on the glass-tiled floor. A tangle of vines shaded the outdoor plaza, where cooler air gathered around the spill of a central fountain.

It took a few moments to find an empty table near the netting edge, but I soon had a tall glass of brandy laced with benki flowers and my very own sticky cake I utterly deserved. Overhead, the sky was turning pink with the setting sun, which meant Lord Councillor Angue would be speaking soon in the chamber square. I tried not to think about what he might have to say, tried not to think about the vote and its consequences, not to think about war with Lummazza or Reacher Sormei or scale and sand shortages, and ended up thinking about them all. Around me, people chattered and laughed and shared drinks, but not everyone was cheerful. Little knots of argument broke out here and there, each akin to the conversation I'd had with Flyer Man earlier that day. The sense that whatever the vote's outcome, Learshapa was fracturing couldn't but worry at me, and though I drank my brandy and ate my cake, I tasted neither.

Perhaps I ought to go to that evening's meeting after all.

While I weighed my desire for political debate against what I told myself was an aversion to seeing Uvao again, a scuffle broke out near the entrance of the public house. An argument over who was next in line for a table perhaps, fierce enough that someone was shoved against the netting, causing a wave to flow across the sheer roof—a sheer roof beyond which the sun had set. In the upper city, Lord Councillor Angue would already have spoken.

A knot of apprehension tightened in my gut as people at nearby tables rose to stare at the spreading disagreement in the entryway. Whispers hissed around me like a buzz of insects, abruptly cut off as someone cheered. Another screamed. Shouting broke out and patrons turned on one another, fingers jabbing into faces and spit flying, and for a moment all I could do was sit, frozen in place, holding tight to my terror.

At the next table, an old man who'd been drinking with a friend rose to his feet looking as confused as I felt. "What in dragon's breath is going on?" he demanded of no one in particular, but he needn't have.

Rising above the noise came the clear tone of a crier. "Due to the imminent war with Lummazza, the council have used their executive power to accept Reacher Sormei's treaty," she called. "There will be no vote. Learshapa is to unite with the rest of the Celes Basin."

The words rolled over me, a tide of shouts and cheers and cries I knew couldn't be real. The Learshapan people had a vote because we'd always had a vote; that was how the city worked. Yet someone threw a punch, others cried, a group danced on the tables and drinks were thrown at them. And amid the noise I found my gaze meeting that of the old man, his horror what made it all too real.

They'd sold us out.

Chest tight, I was up before I had a plan, pushing my way through the chaotic crowd. The crowd pushed back, all manic energy, but I needed to get out, needed answers, so I turned my shoulder and cut my way through, brandy splashing my skirt and fingers catching in my hair.

Outside was little better. Learshapa had erupted, equal parts joy and anguish and hissing with rage wherever the two met, but I had mind only for my destination, and for the question burning my tongue. A question only one person I knew could answer.

I hardly saw the city, hardly felt my own steps, time seeming to freeze and yet speed ahead like it had become untethered from the world, spooling away into nothing. One moment I was pushing through the crowd, the next I was at the back door of the meeting house—the door out which I'd walked when I'd cut Uvao from my life. Now I dared not think what I would do if he wasn't inside.

The moment I pushed it open, a sweet-scented bundle crashed into me, slowing the world to its natural pace. "Tesh! You came back!"

"Jiiala!" I returned her tight embrace, grateful for the moment of comfort. We were alone in the narrow back room, a tiny air pocket in a world of noise that thrummed through the surrounding walls. "I heard the news. Is . . . is Uvao here?"

Still holding my arms, she looked up, lips parted upon words she couldn't utter—words lost as the door into the main meeting hall opened and closed upon a short burst of noise, spilling Sorscha free. He'd been bright and full of charm earlier, but this was a Sorscha buckling under unexpected weight.

"It's bad out there," he said, ruffling his hair and dropping onto the bench. "I guess it was always going to be if this happened, but not getting any warning..." He trailed off and blew out a heavy breath. "If you're here to shout at Uvao, Tesh, pick a better time."

"No, I—"

With another short burst of noise, the meeting hall door opened and closed again, wafting the scent of dusky panawood into the room. My chest constricted an instant before Uvao appeared in the corner of my vision—a memory at which I dared not stare. Seemingly as intent on ignoring me, he sighed. "What a fucking nightmare."

"Ought I go back out there?" Sorscha lacked all enthusiasm for his own suggestion.

"Maybe later, if the crowds stick around. I have to go, but I should be back in—"

"Go?" I blurted, forgetting the question that had brought me. "Something is more important than the council surrendering Learshapa?"

Uvao didn't turn, but his dark, tired eyes glanced my way in the barest acknowledgement. "Of course there is," he said. "You don't think my hair stays this nice without constant appointments with a pommadeur, do you?"

Jiiala gave a hearty sniff. "Don't listen to him, Tesh. He's just being silly."

"I would never dare be silly, Jii," Uvao said, grabbing his veil from its hook. "Such a thing is, of course, entirely beneath my exalted position."

Ignoring this jibe my way, I unlatched myself from Jiiala. "And what are you planning to do about all this, given that exalted position of yours?"

He turned then, anger simmering in his bright eyes. "Why, I'm going to wave a magic wand and fix it to my liking because that's what lords do. Strange I didn't think of that when you walked out on me. Now, if you'll excuse me, I really do need to go."

"Where?"

Uvao didn't look up from tying his veil. "To a meeting, if you must know. About *all this* that you want me to fix."

"A meeting of the council?"

Uvao barked a humourless laugh. "Hardly. Now I've let you throw your darts, Tesh, so goodbye."

"No!" I cried, desperation throwing me between him and the door. "No, please. I'm not trying to throw darts. I need to know what we can do. What...what *I* can do. This wasn't supposed to happen, not like this."

Caught there between him and his way out, it was all I could do to hold the fiery heat of his gaze as it raked my features, all anger but for a tiny hint of need that sent my thoughts wheeling back to a better time, when I'd been crushed to the wall by his passion, breathless and ecstatic. That heat boiled all air from the small room, silencing even Sorscha, and though I knew myself a fool for having come, I would have made the same choice given it again. Somehow in this moment, he was the only one I trusted to give me answers.

At last, he gave a careless shrug. "Come then, if you must. Behind the old playhouse on Fourth. Twenty minutes. You make your own way."

"That's it?"

"That's it, Tesh, take it or leave it, just get out of my way."

I stepped aside, heart and mind racing with possibilities as he pulled open the door. A nod to Jiiala, a word to Sorscha, and he was gone, leaving me unsure if I still remembered how to breathe.

A clink startled me as Sorscha poured himself a drink. "Better you than me," he said, and raised the glass. "But I guess we all get what we deserve one way or another."

"Shush," Jiiala snapped at him. "Don't be more of a shit than comes naturally, Sorscha. And don't pour a drink without pouring one for me too." Two steps brought her to my side, and she squeezed my arm. "You'd better hurry if you're going, Tesh."

"Yes. Thank you, Jii. I'll…" I gestured to the door. "I guess I'll be going then. Yes."

Sorscha snorted. "Yes, do. Goodbye, Tesh."

Once again out in the warm evening air, the streets through which I hurried were packed with people and a breathless unease. Fear of imminent war sat on the tip of every tongue, and even those grateful for unification decried our lack of choice. The city itself hadn't changed, yet I couldn't shake the feeling I wouldn't recognise it come morning. Somewhere in the upper city, Reacher Sormei would be smiling at the chaos he had wrought—and at the expansion of his empire.